Roger Taylor was born in Heywood, Lancashire, and qualified as a civil and structural engineer. He lives with his wife and two daughters in Wirral, Merseyside, and is a pistol shooter and student of traditional aikido. He is the author of the four Chronicles of Hawklan, *The Call of the Sword*, *The Fall of Fyorlund*, *The Waking of Orthlund* and *Into Narsindal*.

Dream Finder

Roger Taylor

HEADLINE
FEATURE

First published in 1991
by HEADLINE BOOK PUBLISHING PLC

First published in paperback in 1992
by HEADLINE BOOK PUBLISHING PLC

A HEADLINE FEATURE paperback

10 9 8 7 6 5 4 3 2 1

ISBN 0 7472 3726 3

Typeset by Medcalf Type Ltd, Bicester, Oxon

Printed and bound in Great Britain by
Collins, Glasgow

HEADLINE BOOK PUBLISHING PLC
Headline House
79 Great Titchfield Street
London W1P 7FN

To my wife and daughters

Morloy

Calarn

Paran

Irman

Voldra

Miduc

Morbeth

Bethlar

Hyndrak

Stor

Flechr

Whendrak

Tellar

Naith
W. E.

Meck

Veldan

Herion

Imaith

Nestar

Mellathry

Jonil

Breiss

Lingren

Haile

Rollans

Vazie

Crowhell
(independent)

Glovr

Lorris

Prologue

In the dark times, in the great movements of peoples, many looked upon the shores of the land and knew joy, thinking their long wanderings ended. But the darkness had spread even unto the people of the land, and they fell upon the newcomers and slew them, men and women and children, and rejoiced in the cruelty of the deed.

Then, in their long boats, came fugitives tempered by the heat of the many battles they had fought against the darkness. And though they sought only peace, still the peoples of the land slew them, and there was great conflict.

And, through the years, others came, and alliances were made, and the peoples of the land declined and were driven to the north and into the mountains. But in their final struggles, some among them, consumed with hatred and steeped in evil, sank yet deeper into the ways of darkness and drew upon the power which was in all things, and, using it corruptly, as a terrible magic, were themselves corrupted.

And for a while, they prevailed, bringing yet more horror to the land. But as the sword begat the shield, so did their wickedness show the way to their downfall, for others learned the way of the power and, learning it more truly, were not corrupted.

And in the end they prevailed, and peace came to the land.

And the victors turned to the future.

And the memory of the great conflicts that had brought them to the land, and even the battles they had fought there, faded into legend and myth, as too did the knowledge of the use of the power.

Yet it is ever there . . .

Ivaroth Ungwyl reined his horse to a halt and stared around balefully. In every direction the view was the same; a flat, bleak plain spreading to a vague winter-misted horizon. It was covered with the harsh and stunted vegetation that alone could stand the bitter cold and the dry biting wind that blew there for most of the year and was blowing now.

In spring and summer he knew that the dun monotony would be transformed into greens and yellows and a myriad other bright and subtle colours, as grasses and flowers appeared at the touch of the warmer sun and the light rains. Stags and bulls would fight for supremacy of their herds, old giving way to young, and birds and insects and countless small animals would emerge and hunt and mate and live their lives as if the cold, relentless touch of winter was gone never to return.

Ivaroth's lip curled into a vicious sneer at this sunlit image and he looked west towards the grey disc of the sun hovering indifferently there. He spat towards it, as if in challenge, then wiped his chapped mouth roughly with his fur-gloved hand. It was a thoughtless act and both the pain and the realization of his carelessness made him start and swear angrily.

His horse reared slightly in response and he jerked it back to stillness none too gently. Then, having at once assuaged his brief anger and demonstrated his dominion, he urged it forward again.

Sullenly, the horse turned north, the direction it had been travelling in since Ivaroth had captured it many days earlier.

To the south lay gentler terrain but, even without the dangers that lay there for him, Ivaroth's mood was more in harmony with the surrounding bleakness and the impending winter.

'Go,' had been the decision of the elders. 'Only respect for the spirit of your father and the testimony of your brother's wife have saved you from immediate execution.'

Opposing ties of fear and anger had held Ivaroth in lowering stillness more effectively than any guards as this sentence had been passed on him. Part of him had wanted to sweep his captors aside and fall upon these dotards who saw fit to stand in judgement over him – *him*, the son of Ivaroth Dargwyl and true heir to his mantle as chieftain. But there were too many hostile eyes in the watching crowd that had encircled him. Too many hands waiting for the opportunity to launch spear or arrow at him and clear their own way, or the way of their kin, more effectively to the leadership of the tribe. And those that were his friends were too stunned and uncertain; rendered impotent by the sudden slaying of his older brother, albeit apparently in self-defence.

'You are banished from the tribe. From dawn tomorrow your life is forfeit.'

Ivaroth hunched his shoulders against the wind as he recalled the words. Anger welled up inside him again, black

2

and overwhelming. He would return. He would punish those who had brought this upon him as surely as he had always destroyed those who stood in his way. And he would rule as none had ruled before. He would be the greatest chieftain the tribe had ever known. It was his destiny. And he would lead not only his own tribe, but all the others. United into a great army they would set aside their own petty feudings and follow him down through the mountains to the rich fertile land to the south, razing its vaunted cities and putting its hated peoples to the sword.

It was the song that had filled his every waking dream for as long as he could recall and the long-rehearsed vision possessed him and carried him for a moment beyond the grim and perilous reality of his present position.

His destiny would not be gainsaid.

Banished without food and weapons, had it not, after all, been this destiny that had brought young Ketsath his way; returning triumphant from his lone ordeal of manhood in the wilderness in anticipation of being greeted a warrior and fit to join the society of men? Returning, well clad, mounted, and armed, and with food and water at his saddle. Returning to an early death at the hands of Ivaroth Ungwyl, like a god-sent sacrifice to serve a greater need.

Ivaroth smiled at the memory. He could have hidden the boy's body but he had left it for the carrion. Let the tribe know that while he was beyond their reach, they were not beyond his. Let their hunters watch for the spear and the arrow from the shadows, until he would emerge once more to claim his true inheritance.

Yet, in truth, they were far from his reach now. A native caution had quietly prevailed over his wilder thoughts and brought him to this desolate region where any pursuing avengers would be reluctant to follow and in any event, would be easily seen. And he was no callow youth. He had skills enough to survive here until . . . until what?

As always, Ivaroth's euphoria faded and a bitter desperation began to seep into his thoughts. How could he fulfil his destiny here? What great deeds could he do? What great armies raise? Were all his dreams no more than some jest by the gods to taunt him into madness as he finished his days as a wandering hermit, ranting at the howling wind?

A sudden stinging gust of wind struck him as if in confirmation of this conclusion, bringing him back sharply to the present and making him bow his head and crouch low over the horse's neck. As he did so, something caught his eye.

It was a figure in the distance; a small, but stark and ominous pillar in the bleak loneliness.

For a moment, fear tightened across Ivaroth's stomach. Had he been pursued and found? Was this the vanguard of Ketsath's kin seeking revenge? Or his brother's followers? Surely he couldn't have been so careless as to let them come so close unseen?

His mouth dried and his eyes flicked rapidly from side to side, seeking for signs of ambush. But nothing else was to be seen. Just the solitary figure walking towards him.

Yet there was an oddness about it. It moved strangely and seemed in some way to have a presence that was greater than that of a single man. Ivaroth scowled. As fear of avenging men faded he found a more primitive fear waiting. The ancient fear of the unknown; the ancient fear of strangers.

But, though treacherous, Ivaroth was no coward. And he had met no man yet who had defied him and not died or yielded for his pains. Involuntarily he shrugged his shoulders loose, eased his sword in its scabbard and checked his spear and his several knives; belt, sleeves, and, with a twitch of his calves, those in his boots. Then he turned the horse towards the distant figure and gently urged it forward.

For a while, it seemed that he came no nearer to the figure. Indeed, it was almost as if it were in some other place that must remain ever beyond reach. Ivaroth felt the unease of a strange dream rising within him.

He shook his head vigorously. You should've eaten before, he rationalized. You're just lightheaded through lack of food and too much travelling today.

Then the unease was gone and the figure was just a man walking hesitantly over the hard ground.

Ivaroth admitted to a twinge of both disappointment and distaste as he neared the man. The stranger was wearing a dirty and unkempt robe, the large cowl of which was pulled over his bowed head. Briefly he seemed to Ivaroth to be the personification of his own dark thoughts of a moment ago; a wandering hermit ranting at the howling wind.

Ivaroth, however, was not given to idle musing; his thoughts being invariably pragmatic. It was a pity the man didn't have a horse, but he looked old and feeble, and he might have food or drink about him even though he carried no pack. Ivaroth soon concluded that a little effort now might well save him a day's hunting. All that remained to be done was to check that the man had no companions nearby.

A friendly smile lit up Ivaroth's face. To those who knew him closely, it was an indication that it was time to make a discreet leave-taking.

'Greetings, traveller,' he said jovially, halting his horse some way in front of the still-approaching figure.

The man stopped immediately and, without looking up, twisted his head slowly from side to side as if he had just heard some faint but familiar sound. There was a birdlike, almost serpentine, quality to the movement that set Ivaroth's teeth on edge. Casually, he rested his hand on his sword hilt.

'Greetings, traveller,' he repeated, more loudly. 'This is a harsh place to be wandering on foot. Where are you bound? Have you lost your camp?'

The head twisted again, and the whole body craned forward slightly. Then an arm reached out and swept slowly from side to side as if seeking something in darkness. A long bony hand emerged from the ragged sleeve and, clawlike, groped at the air. But there was no reply.

Ivaroth's eyes narrowed at this seeming defiance and he eased his horse forward until he was by the man.

'I said, "Have you lost your camp?"' There was an unexpected harshness in his voice which surprised him. Had he heard it in someone else's he would have called it fear.

His smile faded and was replaced by a scowl. He reached down to seize the cowl and expose the face of this impertinent stranger, but as he did so, the bony hand swung round and gripped his wrist.

Ivaroth's fighting instincts registered several things simultaneously: the hand was the hand of an old man, and the stranger's posture was that of an old man, but the movement had been effortless, swift and accurate, and the grip was full of the green strength of youth.

He did not, however, dwell on these contradictions, but instinctively tightened his knees about his horse for support so that he could tear his arm free. Even as he did so, however, he felt the grip controlling his balance.

With his free hand he drew a knife from his belt, twisting it so that he could slash the extended arm.

A sigh rose up from the stranger. Not a sigh of sorrow or despair, but one of . . . satisfaction . . . recognition even.

5

The sound made Ivaroth hesitate and he peered down at the cowled head, his face betraying both anger and curiosity. The head turned upwards to meet his inquiry and the cowl slipped back to reveal the face of the stranger.

It was the face of an old man, lean and haggard and with an unhealthy whiteness about it. But what made Ivaroth start was the sight of the ragged bandage bound about the man's eyes.

Blind!

Thoughts flooded into Ivaroth's mind. A blind man, here? So far from the normal range of any of the tribes. How? Most of the tribes either dispatched the blind or treated them as holy men. None that he knew would simply abandon them.

And the man did not have the look of a tribesman, nor for that matter one of the southern city people.

He felt a brief touch of fear. It was said that across the great plains, far to the west, were other lands, strange mysterious lands full of great wonders, and peopled by tribes that were both beautiful and terrible.

Could this old man be . . .

The grip about his wrist tightened and he found himself being pulled down.

'I have been asleep. Lost in my torment. And now I am found again.' The old man's mouth moved, but it seemed to Ivaroth that there was one sound in his head and another in his ears.

And there was a monstrous, insane delight in the voice. Ivaroth tightened his grip on his knife.

'I am not forgotten after all. I am guided yet. Guided to this place . . . To this man.'

The old man turned his head away from Ivaroth and took in a deep breath. He was like some predatory animal catching the scent of its prey and knowing that only patience was needed now before he would feed.

'Guided to this place so rich in the ancient power.' The bandaged eyes turned back to Ivaroth. 'And to you.'

A primitive terror filled Ivaroth at the recognition alive in the old man's face. His knife hand would not move.

'I don't know you, blind man,' he blustered, his voice shaking. 'But I'll give you your length of this rich place for all eternity if you don't release my hand.'

The old man chuckled. A disgusting, bubbling sound, full of great confidence and certainty. Then, with his free hand, he reached up slowly and pulled the bandage from his eyes.

Ivaroth tried to look away, but his black-irised eyes were held by the stranger's sightless gaze as if it were a blazing spear, passing right through him and impaling his very soul. The orbs were white and cloudy as if the sight had been bleached from them by too great a light, though, Ivaroth suddenly knew, it was because they had seen too terrible a truth.

'There is blindness and blindness,' said the stranger's voice. 'I see more than you will ever know, yet you will be my eyes and I shall be yours . . . Ivaroth Ungwyl . . . fratricide, murderer of the young, and . . . chieftain to be . . . chieftain of all the tribes.'

Chapter 1

The light from the doorway sent Antyr's shadow leaping ahead into the swirling gloom of the dense fog that greeted him as he emerged from the inn.

He paused, an unsteady silhouette, at the top of the short flight of stone steps. Then he grimaced. He had lived in the Serenstad contentedly enough all his life, but these appalling fogs always reminded him of childhood holidays in the country. There, for all their cold dampness, the wintry mists had been grey and soft, but the fogs here were always tainted yellow with grime and smoke from the city's innumerable forges and workshops. They made the roads and footways slimy and treacherous, they clung to clothes, making them damp and sulphurous, and they made every breath a chest-burning ordeal.

His dark reverie was interrupted by mounting cries of abuse from the noisy inn parlour at his back.

'Go, if you're going, man. You're chilling us all,' was their gist.

Without turning, Antyr waved a scornful dismissal to his erstwhile companions, then, seizing the heavy wrought-iron latch, he yanked the door shut. It was a heavy door, notorious for its stiffness, and its frequent noisy closing through the nights was the constant bane of the neighbouring sleepers. Now, however, its window-shaking slam was muffled by the clinging fog, and the image of a closing tomb came into Antyr's mind as an eerie reverberation echoed back at him out of the gloom.

The darkness of this unexpected image was deepened by the sudden ceasing of the clatter from the inn, and the equally sudden vanishing of the warm yellow light that had thrown his long shadow so boldly out into the fog. For a moment he felt disorientated, as if he had only been in someone's dream about the inn and his raucous friends and had wakened suddenly to find he had been sleep-walking.

It was an unsettling thought for a Dream Finder and involuntarily he reached back and briefly touched the familiar rough wooden door for reassurance. Then, more relieved than he cared to admit, he growled into the fog, and wrapped his cloak tight about himself.

'Too much ale,' he muttered. 'I'll have less tomorrow.'

It was a ritual nightly utterance that, like most rituals, had long lost its true meaning.

He glanced up and down the street. In both directions the only things visible were the flames of the pitch torches, flickering, despite the stillness, and issuing coils of their own black smoke to add to the murk. The fog's clammy touch might have swept the people from the streets as effectively as any blustering winter storm, but the Guild of Torchlighters knew their duty. Antyr curled his lip unpleasantly.

Sanctimonious lot, he thought, as he tried without success to bring the shimmering corona around one of the wobbling lights into focus. He couldn't stand these pompous Sened-appointed Guild men with their unctuous self-satisfaction.

If it wasn't for them doing their jobs, *you'd* be staggering around lost all this night, wouldn't you? said a quieter, kinder, part of his mind.

He declined the offer of a debate and carefully made his way down the slippery steps. The iron handrail was cold and unpleasantly damp and he wiped his hand on his cloak as he reached the street.

Unhooking a torch from a nearby rack he offered it, a little unsteadily, to one of the street torches. It spluttered into life almost immediately and its warmth and light were welcoming. Its hefty weight comforted him too; he had stayed longer at the inn than he had intended and, even without the fog, the streets would have been deserted and uncertain at this time of night.

Not that he was likely to be attacked around here, he thought hopefully, but the brief spark of optimism faded as soon as it appeared. He knew that despite the vigilance of the Watch, there was always a risk at night; carousing young bloods from one of the Sened Lords' Houses, conscripts from the barracks, malcontents out of the Moras district. Certainly it would be no great feat for anyone so inclined to avoid the Watch and lie in wait for lone walkers such as himself.

Puffing out his cheeks, Antyr tightened his grip on the torch, loosed his weighted club in his belt, then strode out boldly, if a little erratically.

His footsteps echoed dully behind him in the torchlit gloom.

As various landmarks loomed out of the fog, identified themselves and passed on, Antyr's uneasiness faded a little. For all its unpleasantness, the fog held some comfort. After all, any lone street thief would be as unsighted as his victims. Besides, he was hardly a defenceless old woman, he concluded as the evening's ale clouded his judgement further.

Dutifully, the street torches continued to light his way, each smoky flame seeming to hover in the air at some unfocusable distance. Occasionally some other late wanderer would hurry past him, head craning forward into the darkness. Sometimes, alarmingly, footsteps came and went nearby without their creator appearing.

The hasty purposefulness of such passers-by increased Antyr's feeling of isolation rather than eased it and his thoughts darkened again.

All of us fleeing, he thought. But from what? He gave himself no answer.

Eventually, he reached a street that ran alongside the high wall which surrounded the city. He looked up and saw its rough lichened stones disappearing damply into the torchlit canopy of fog. Built to keep out the city's enemies, the wall seemed to him now to be more like that of a prison; herding together the people like rats in an overcrowded lair.

Too much ale, he thought again to excuse the gloomy vision, though licking his lips he found them damp and greasy from the fog, and the acrid taste of soot on his tongue effortlessly displaced that left by his evening's drinking. He spat.

'Ho there!'

The voice made him start, and he groped awkwardly for his club. As it tangled incongruously in his belt and cloak, firefly lights appeared, floating some way ahead of him. They were followed by the muffled clatter of arms and before Antyr could decide what to do, a dark shadow formed beneath the lights. As he watched, it shifted and then broke into a group of individuals. One of them strode forward, holding a torch high. It was an old man, though he carried himself straight and tall.

'Oh, it's you, Antyr,' he said, peering forward earnestly. 'I might have known you'd be the only one around here wandering the streets on a night like this.'

There was a familiar reproach in the voice that irritated Antyr, but his relief at finding that he had been stopped by the local Watch, and not by the Liktors or some more sinister group, took the edge off his reply. Besides, under the older man's gaze, he could not argue against the truth.

'You wouldn't begrudge a man his evening's tipple with friends, would you, Avran?' he managed to reply, with a noisy heartiness that failed to hide his sense of inadequacy.

Avran looked at him stonily. 'Yes, I would,' he said unequivocally. 'When the man's the son of an old friend and is destroying himself and his gift with his antics.'

Antyr opened his mouth to speak, but no protest came, only a slow steaming breath which hovered yellow in the gloom like some listening spirit. Part of Antyr, blustering, uncaring, wanted to tell Avran that he was in no mood for one of his lectures, but the look in the old man's eye told him that he would just as soon lock him up in the Watch Pen for the night as restart an old debate in this fog-shrouded street.

Wiser counsels thus prevailed and Antyr held his peace, even managing a look of contrition.

Meeting no resistance, Avran's gaze softened. 'The streets are quiet tonight, Antyr,' he said. 'But don't linger more than you have to, and . . .' He hesitated. '. . . take more care of yourself. You're travelling down a road that's darker and more dangerous than this one by far, and one you may not be able to return along. I've seen it too often before. It's . . .'

A brief fit of coughing finished the sentence prematurely, and Avran made no attempt to restart it when he had recovered. Instead, striking his chest ruefully, he dismissed Antyr with an irritated flick of his head and rejoined his waiting companions.

Antyr spat again as the Watch disappeared into the swirling gloom. The taste of the fog still dominated, and the cold dampness now seemed to have entered into his very bones. His stomach felt leaden and ominously mobile.

As he walked on, he found that Avran's words had resurrected the memory of his father and with it the turmoil and the deep sense of failure that had pervaded him in the practice of his art since his father's death.

He paused for a moment, and gazed around at the torchlit sphere of moving brown and yellow fog that he centred. His inability to see what he knew lay beyond seemed to mirror the blindness he had felt on so many occasions as he had searched through the dreams of his diminishing number of clients . . .

Damn the old buzzard, came a defensive thought, to save him from the grim voices of self-recrimination that were gathering in the outer darkness to bellow out his weakness and folly.

'Why doesn't he mind his own business?'

The spoken words, flat and strange in the soft silence, completed the rescue and goaded Antyr forward again.

He finished the rest of his journey in a mood as dark and formless as the fog itself and with the headiness he had brought from the inn mocking him where before it had seemed to uplift and sustain him.

Rapt in thought he found himself at his door almost without realizing how he had come there and, unthinkingly, he doused the torch in the pointed hood that hung by the door.

Plunged abruptly into darkness, Antyr swore and threw down the hood angrily. It bounced at the end of its chain with a clatter and then grated sullenly against the wall as it swung from side to side a few times before coming to rest.

While his eyes adjusted to the dim light offered by the street torches, Antyr groped irritably through the clutter in his pockets in search of his key. Then, eventually finding it, he groped, equally irritably, to find and open the lock. It took much earnest squinting and several unsuccessful attempts before he succeeded.

Slowly he pushed the door open and stepped inside. Despite his caution, however, the door gave its familiar screech to remind him that he neglected other things than his calling. Then, despite further caution, it repeated the complaint as he closed it.

With a small, but weary sigh, Antyr drove home the large bolts then reached up in the darkness to a familiar shelf and took down a flint box and a cracked earthenware candle-holder. The flint box flared up boisterously as he struck it and the darkness in the hallway was suddenly fragmented into dancing and jostling shadows.

Antyr ignored the silent throng, however, and concentrated on lighting the bent and reluctant candle. Then, gently extinguishing the flint box, he hung his damp cloak on a well-worn wooden peg and walked softly, if unsteadily, along the hallway towards a room at the back of the house.

'You needn't bother creeping in.'

A familiar voice filled his head. 'I felt you coming three streets away. It's a wonder Avran didn't throw you into the Watch Pen as soon as he saw you, the state you're in.'

Antyr scowled. 'I wish you wouldn't do that,' he said angrily. 'You wouldn't have pried into my father's thoughts like that.'

As he spoke, he reached the room and stood swaying in the doorway for a moment. The shadows from the hallway flooded past him to line the walls like waiting jurors, nodding purposefully to one another at the behest of the dancing candle flame. The remains of a fire glowed dimly in the grate.

Antyr entered and placed the solitary candle on a small shelf. The jury gradually became still and watchful.

As Antyr flopped down on to a nearby chair, the voice came again. 'I don't pry, Antyr, you're perfectly well aware of that,' it said, crossly. 'You *shout*. I can't help but hear you. I've told you before. I don't expect you to have your father's control, but—'

'No, not now, Tarrian,' Antyr intoned wearily, leaning back. 'I'm in no mood . . .' He released the comment he had prepared for Avran. '. . . for another of your lectures.'

There was a more purposeful movement among the swaying shadows as the candle flickered. In the far corner of the room a dark shape stirred and began to move across the floor towards the Dream Finder.

'Don't speak to me like that.' Tarrian's voice was angry and the sound of it in Antyr's head mingled with a menacing growl from the approaching shadow. '*I* can't avoid your confusion, and it washes over me like a foul stench. You seem to forget that.'

'I'm sorry,' Antyr said hastily, sitting up. 'It's been a bad night. I—'

'It's been a bad decade,' Tarrian replied pitilessly.

Antyr winced. He had had many quarrels with Tarrian, but they had been growing increasingly more unpleasant of late and there was a tone in his friend's voice that he had not heard before.

Briefly the eyes of the approaching shadow shone a brilliant green as if lit from some unfathomable depth. It was only a trick of the candlelight, but it chilled Antyr, reminding him not only of the true nature of his companion but also of the dark strangeness of his own calling.

14

Tarrian emerged relentlessly into the candlelight. The luminous green eyes were now their normal cold grey, though they were only marginally less menacing for that: Tarrian was a wolf. Old, but wild and full of the muscular vigour of youth.

'Ah,' he said, catching Antyr's momentary fear. 'You still have some perception left, I see. You should remember more often what I am and how we are bound to one another.'

Antyr turned away. He opened his mouth to speak, but no sound came. Almost plaintively he reached out and stroked the wolf's sleek head.

Tarrian's voice filled his head again, though now full of compassion and concern. 'Avran was right. More even than he understood himself. The path you're following will destroy you more terribly than it would an ordinary man. You *must* turn again to the disciplines of your calling or you'll doom us both.'

There was another note in the wolf's voice that Antyr had not heard before: fear.

'Yes, I am afraid,' Tarrian said, even before Antyr could clearly form the thought. Then, impulsively, 'Here's how afraid I am.'

'No!' Antyr cried, pushing himself back in the chair as if to escape. But the wolf's powerful personality held him firm and suddenly his mind was filled with swirling terrors and the dark, flitting shapes of nightmare. He struggled to set them aside, but in vain, Tarrian's anger was too great. Then he felt the presence of an unseen menace seeking him out. Its power swept hither and thither, like a flailing arm. Despite himself, Antyr urged his legs to run but, as is the way in dreams, they would not respond to his desperation, they were beyond his control.

Abruptly he was free; and angry.

'Damn you, dog,' he shouted. 'Don't do your party tricks on me.'

Tarrian's mouth curled into a snarl and a deep growl rumbled in his throat. His voice burst into Antyr's head. 'You're only fit for party tricks, Petran's son,' it said, scornfully. Do you think you could face my *true* fears? I, who stood by perhaps the edge of the Threshold to the Great Dream itself, and felt your father slip away from me? Do you want me to show you that?'

Antyr stood up clumsily and pushed past the wolf, his eyes

wide. He snatched up an oil lamp and lifted it towards the candle.

'Enough,' he said breathlessly. 'Let's have some light.' His hands, however, were trembling so violently that after several unsuccessful attempts to light it, he had to put the lamp down on the shelf for fear it would slip from his grasp. The waiting shadows danced and jigged expectantly.

Tarrian watched him, his grey eyes unblinking.

For a moment, Antyr leaned forward against the wall until he had recovered some composure. Then carefully, but still breathing heavily, he lit the lamp.

As the shadows dwindled and the familiar commonplace of the room asserted itself, Antyr sat down again, holding out a pleading hand to the wolf.

'No more, please, Tarrian,' he said, withdrawing the hand and using it to support his head. 'I need no demonstrations of your superior skill, nor reminders of my own failings.' Then, angrily again, in spite of himself, 'And I need no reminders of my father, nor your ramblings about his death.'

The wolf turned away from him and padded back to its corner of the room without replying. It flopped down heavily and, resting its head over its extended forelegs, stared at Antyr patiently.

A faint echo of the fog outside hovered yellow in the air between the two antagonists.

'My father's heart failed him,' Antyr said defensively into the silence after a moment, returning the wolf's gaze. 'It troubled him constantly after his fever.'

Tarrian still did not reply, but his denial filled Antyr's mind.

'No,' Antyr protested. 'I'll have none of it. The dream of a dying man is notoriously dangerous . . .' His voice broke. 'My father should never have attempted to search for it . . . And you . . . his Companion . . . his Earth Holder . . . You shouldn't have let him go.'

The reproach was unjust and Antyr knew it: Tarrian could not have defied the will of the Dream Finder in such a matter and Antyr found Tarrian's own reproach rising in reply. He raised his hand in apology.

'I'm sorry,' he said. 'I shouldn't have said that.'

He massaged his forehead as if the deed would erase his casual and cruel remark. 'But I won't accept your . . .

beliefs,' he continued, after a moment. 'I wouldn't accept them from my father and I won't accept them from you . . . They're foolishness . . .'

Tarrian's eyes closed. 'Your acceptance or otherwise will have no effect on the reality, Dream Finder,' he said. His tone was one of resigned indifference: it was an old argument, now far beyond any passion. 'You may choose not to believe in falling masonry if the notion offends you, but when a piece falls on your head, it'll kill you just the same.'

Antyr rebelled at Tarrian's cavalier presumption of rightness. 'That's different and you know it. We're not . . . masons . . . working with the solid and the real. We . . . we . . . we're just . . . guides . . . helpers,' he spluttered, gesticulating irrelevantly to the unwatching wolf. 'We have a gift to comfort people, that's all. The bewildered, the tormented . . .'

'But you don't even believe that any more, do you?' Although Tarrian was apparently asleep, his voice brutally swept aside Antyr's ramblings. 'You think we're all just charlatans, using our "party tricks" to gull pennies and crowns from anyone foolish enough to pay for our services, don't you?'

Antyr reeled under this quiet but savage onslaught. 'No . . . Yes . . . I—'

'You don't know,' Tarrian finished his sentence for him viciously. 'You're so addled with ale and self-indulgence that you're forgetting your own puling excuses. You're beginning to scrabble round like a rat in a wheel. Going faster and faster to nowhere. Go to sleep you sot, you sicken me. We'll talk in the morning when you're sober.'

The sudden, blistering contempt in Tarrian's voice struck Antyr like a blow and choked his reply in his throat. He struggled unsteadily to his feet, and snatched up the candle.

'Go to hell, dog,' he tried to shout, but the curse degenerated into a strained squeak as his voice, marred by fog and drink, declined to respond.

Leaving the room, Antyr lost the small remains of his dignity by colliding with the door jamb.

He had intended to go upstairs to his bed, but his sudden rising and his collision with the door released the forces he had set in train earlier that evening. His stomach took urgent and explosive charge of events.

Somehow, Antyr reached the kitchen and an empty bucket

just in time, and a few retching minutes later he was sitting on the cold floor leaning miserably against the wall with his arm draped around the stinking bucket like a grotesque parody of a repleted lover and his chosen.

His head felt a little clearer, though that merely served to accentuate his distress.

'You have a rare gift, Antyr,' his father had said. 'Greater by far than mine. But it will bring you nothing but pain if you do not embrace and cherish it. We are Dream Finders. In some matters we have no choice. Some dreams seek us, not we them.'

'You'll doom us both.' Tarrian's words returned to him in the wake of the memory of his father's anxious words. Antyr tried to curse the wolf again, but the oath died unborn as he gazed up at the kitchen window, etched a dim yellow in the darkness by the fog-strained torchlight outside. He knew that Tarrian was right and that even now the wolf would be silently prowling the dark edges of his addled mind to protect him from unseen dangers, just as its wilder fellows would prowl the woods in search of prey. No matter what Antyr did or thought, Tarrian would do what he knew to be his duty, waiting for that moment when his charge would accept the burden of his calling.

Antyr wiped his mouth with the back of his hand and stood up. His head ached with it all. He walked to the stone sink and took a ladle full of water from a bucket. After noisily rinsing his mouth he drank a little. Its coldness mapped out the route down to his rebelling stomach where it landed like retribution.

Then he dashed a handful into his face by way of penance.

'Tomorrow, we *will* talk, Tarrian,' he said, to the yellow window.

A faint whiff of doubt and regret seeped reluctantly into his mind that he knew came from the watching wolf.

'No, I mean it this time,' Antyr said earnestly, well conscious of the fact that his protestation of good intentions was by no means new. 'I mean it,' he repeated, pointlessly.

'Someone's coming.' Tarrian's voice was suddenly awake and alert. Antyr started. It never failed to amaze him that the wolf could come from the deepest sleep to the fullest wakefulness in the blink of an eye.

'No,' Antyr said, shaking his head slowly. 'The streets outside are as dark as any dream likely to be dreamt tonight.'

'There's several of them,' Tarrian said, ignoring the denial. 'I can smell no danger, but . . .'

Antyr felt Tarrian rising up and walking inquisitively into the hallway, but before he could speak again, someone beat a purposeful tattoo on the door.

'Ye gods,' Antyr muttered, frowning. 'I don't care who it is, I'm not turning out tonight for anyone.' Then, as Tarrian's comment registered, the concerns of the daily round impinged on him. 'Several of them! It's not the Exactors is it, Tarrian?' he hissed, lowering his voice.

Tarrian's voice was scornful. 'Since when did you earn enough to warrant the midnight attention of the Exactors, Antyr? Just answer the door quickly, this is intriguing.'

Reinforcing Tarrian's advice, the tattoo sounded again, echoing through the darkened house. Antyr picked up the lamp.

'Are you sure it's not the Exactors?' he whispered again to Tarrian.

The wolf's sigh filled his head. 'Don't be *ridiculous*,' came the irritable reply, then, with an unexpected touch of humour, 'besides, the Exactors are predators, they wear soft-soled boots so that you can't hear them coming – and they don't knock.'

'Very droll, Tarrian,' Antyr replied, as he cautiously opened the small sentry flap in the door. He was relieved that these unexpected visitors had set the mood of acrimony aside, at least for the time being, but he was a little concerned by the excitement he sensed surrounding the wolf's thoughts. Tarrian had probably smelt an 'interesting' client and he really was in no mood for working tonight.

'Who is it?' he shouted as he peered through the small opening. 'Don't you know what time it is?'

By way of reply, a clenched fist appeared immediately in front of his face so that he had to withdraw a little to focus on it. On the middle finger of the fist was a signet ring. It was the seal of the Sened Watch.

'Open the door,' came a commanding voice.

Hastily Antyr drew back the bolts and opened the door. He twitched an apologetic smile as it screeched its usual protest, then he stepped forward and peered, bleary-eyed, at the unexpected visitors.

The man who had offered him the seal of the Watch stepped deferentially to one side and raised a torch high to

19

reveal another figure standing about a pace behind. Despite the large cloak wrapped about him and the hood hiding his face, this second figure radiated authority, and behind him again, merging into the fog, as Tarrian had said, were several others. Some were carrying torches. The others were carrying – Antyr peered further into the gloom, then his eyes widened in alarm – the others were carrying the lethal-bladed short pikes of the palace guard.

The Sened Watch? Palace guards? What . . .?

'You are Antyr the Dream Finder, the son of Petran,' said the man. His voice confirmed his posture, and cut through Antyr's mounting confusion.

Antyr swallowed nervously. 'Er, yes,' he managed after a moment. 'Who are . . .'

'Come with us. You are needed,' the man continued, disregarding the half-formed question.

'But . . .'

'We will escort you,' said the figure, half turning away and indicating the men behind him. 'Bring your Companion.'

Antyr was about to repeat his question when the man's cloak fell open to reveal the insignia on his tunic. It was an eagle with a lamb in its talons: Duke Ibris's insignia. And the only people who wore that were—

'The Duke's personal bodyguard.' Tarrian finished the thought for him.

Chapter 2

Aaken Uhr Candessa, once humble Aaken Candes, sheep-herder, mercenary, shield-bearer and successful conspirator, now chancellor to the Duke Ibris, stood fretfully by as his erstwhile co-conspirator and now master paced to and fro.

The room was lit by only three lamps, and though they were bright they reflected the Duke's mood and cast more darkness than they did light: the lavish paintings around the walls had become like black night-watching windows, and the faces of the many carved figures that graced the room were prematurely aged in their motionless vigils by shadow-etched lines.

Only the armour and the weapons responded to the lamps, glittering watchfully as if lit by the light of some blazing enemy camp.

'Sire . . .' Aaken ventured.

The Duke waved him silent and continued his pacing. Aaken surreptitiously shifted his weight from one foot to another and resigned himself to not returning to his bed for some considerable time that night – if at all.

The Duke might be four years his senior but in his many appetites and strengths he could have been ten years his junior, and he was more than capable of pacing the floor all night in pursuit of some unspoken problem without saying a word until the palace began to rouse itself the next day. Aaken began to fidget with his sparse grey beard.

Abruptly the Duke stopped in front of a small statuette. It was a warrior crouching forward behind his shield and preparing to thrust with his spear. As was the current fashion, his eyes had neither iris nor pupil, giving him a cold and deathly gaze, yet the work was alive with the desperate and immediate passions of the fighting man.

Duke Ibris was a ruthless and cruel man when the needs of his office required, but he was also a man of fine discernment who cherished all manner of beautiful and finely crafted things. Thus, despite his fearful reputation among his enemies, many artists and craftsmen flourished under his patronage, and in turn, both his palace and his city flourished under their many talents.

'I will make Serenstad a city so dazzling, that the whole universe will be drawn to it,' he had once said, at the same time resting his hand on his sword hilt.

He reached up and touched the statuette. 'Buonardi's work is magnificent,' he said, without turning. 'So vivid. He trained with the Mantynnai, didn't he?'

Aaken nodded. 'Yes, sire. He left them just before the siege of Viernce, I believe. It seems he's as fine a judge of events as he is a sculptor.'

The Duke turned to look at him. 'Or lucky,' he retorted, recommencing his pacing.

Aaken shrugged a little and risked a smile. 'An essential attribute in a soldier,' he said.

The remark, however, did not seem to impinge on the Duke who was once more engrossed in the concern that had brought him from his bed.

'How long is it since Feranc left?' he said, stopping and looking at his chancellor again.

Aaken retrieved an ungainly timepiece from his robe and manoeuvred it until some of the room's light fell on it.

'Almost an hour, sire,' he said. 'But the city's choked with fog and we've no guarantee that this . . . Antyr . . . will be at his home, or even indeed if he still lives in that district.'

The Duke scowled.

'Feranc will find him if he's in the city,' Aaken added reassuringly. 'You know that. But it may take some time. Is this matter truly urgent?'

The Duke did not answer immediately but scratched his stubbled chin pensively. 'I don't know,' he said hesitantly after a moment. 'But I fear so.'

Involuntarily, Aaken's eyes flicked quickly from side to side, to see if any servants might have witnessed this uncharacteristic uncertainty in their lord. All this nocturnal activity was enough in itself to fuel a dozen rumours which could swirl into as many plots and conspiracies, or cause alarm, even panic, among the city's merchants. If such rumours were to be laced with some sign of weakness on the Duke's part then who knew what consequences might come to pass?

But even as he peered into the shadows, Aaken knew that his action was merely one of habit. He knew that the room was empty save for himself and Ibris. The Duke above all was aware of the need to guard against ill-considered utterances.

'You fear so?' Aaken echoed. He risked a battlefield familiarity on the strength of the confidence that this remark implied. 'Ibris, what's happened?' he said. 'There've been no messengers tonight have there? I've not seen you so agitated for years. Even in wartime . . .' He paused, becoming agitated himself at the direction of his own remarks. 'You haven't caught wind of a Bethlarii attack have you? Or one of our border cities seceding?'

The Duke shook his head absently. No, Aaken thought, Serenstad had never been stronger, both militarily and economically. In any event, had news come of an unexpected defection of one of their subject cities then it would have been a foolish servant who disturbed the Duke's sleep to tell him. And as for a Bethlarii attack after all this time, the Duke would have been mobilizing the army, not pacing anxiously to and fro.

Receiving no rebuff, Aaken pressed on to the point that most concerned him. 'And why a Dream Finder, sire?' he asked, lowering his voice. 'They were much respected when we were young, but this is a different age. Superstitions wane in the light of reason and civilization . . .'

The Duke held up his hand to end the questions. 'Sit down, Aaken, you look tired,' he said as if only now aware of his chancellor's presence.

Aaken bowed and lowered himself stiffly into a nearby chair. The Duke watched him and smiled slightly. 'You look older than me, old friend,' he said. 'I always said you were too anxious to get out of the saddle and into a chair. Now see what it's done for you. You creak like a galleon in a wind.'

Then his smile faded, unable to sustain itself against his darker thoughts. 'And you were ever without faith,' he concluded softly, his manner preoccupied again.

Aaken almost started at the word, faith. Ye gods, it's something religious, he thought. His mind raced and he bowed his head. He must keep his feelings hidden and be more circumspect than ever in his questioning if that were the case.

Ibris's remark was quite true. Aaken had no faith, least of all in the preposterous and vast pantheon of gods that were called upon from time to time by the peoples of the cities.

23

Like most practical, rational men of this age, he believed that chance and the wit to respond to its vagaries shaped his destiny, and certainly he feared his fellows far more than he feared any deity. But religion was a potent and dangerous force; one which had brought chaos to the streets, and dreadful, savage armies to the field within his own memory. And one which the Duke never ignored or treated lightly, although he never hesitated to use it for his own highly secular ends.

Yet, despite his own seeming cynicism, Ibris would brook neither mockery nor intolerance of religion, and indeed he carried within him some belief of his own, some strange, deep silence which over the years Aaken had learned to avoid as he might avoid the lair of a dangerous animal.

He had seen many leaders of men in his time and had truly understood none of them. Suffice it that he knew that the Duke was the man to rule Serenstad. What inner forces made him so were of no concern . . . at least while they remained hidden and thus unassailable, he had concluded.

As Aaken gradually recovered from the initial alarm that the Duke's remark had caused, his curiosity and concern rose to dominate again. There had been no recent unrest, religious or otherwise, in the city, not even in the Moras district. Nor had there been news or even rumours of some new 'Messenger of God' causing problems elsewhere in the land. He risked his question again.

'Sire, what's happened?' he asked. 'And what's my faith, or lack of it, got to do with it? Dukes pace the floor at night and call their creaking chancellors from their beds to solve urgent political problems, not to debate philosophy. And Dream Finders . . .' He allowed himself a modest sneer. '. . . Are for quietening the overheated imaginations of rich and idle women.'

Ibris raised his eyebrows and a faint smile appeared again, albeit briefly. 'I'd forgotten how petulant you could be when your sleep was disturbed, Aaken,' he said. 'But bear with me in this and stay silent for the moment. Help me wait. Soon you'll know all that I know.'

Help me wait! A warrior's plea; it could not be denied. Aaken blew out a short breath of surrender and acquiescence and sank back into his chair. The Duke seemed to consider his own request for a moment, and then he too sat down. Choosing a long, winged couch, he threw one leg along it casually, draped his arms along the back and one side and leaned his head back so that he was staring up at the dimly lit ceiling high above.

The two men became as motionless as the watching statues and the night's silence slowly returned to the room. The soft hiss of the lamps served only to deepen it.

Antyr drew his cloak about him and pulled his hood forward. From its confines he cast a surreptitious glance at the leader of his escort. On two occasions, as was the duty of all the male citizens of Serenstad, Antyr had served with the army in defending the city's increasingly widespread domain, and although he was no expert in military hierarchies, he had the foot-soldier's pride that he could smell a senior officer at fifty paces: and this was indisputably one. His latest examination, however, yielded no more than his previous attempts. The man was half a head taller than he was, though he seemed more, holding himself very straight as he walked, yet without the rigidity that Antyr associated with the officers of the palace guard.

'You're slouching, as well.' Tarrian's acid comment entered his head, and he straightened up in an involuntary response.

An indignant reply began to form in his mind, but he dismissed it. Tarrian was preparing himself and Antyr knew better than to try verbal knocks with his Companion as the wolf's ancient hunting instinct rose up to join his incisive intellect in readiness for the search.

Then Tarrian was ready and for a moment, Antyr found himself looking through the wolf's eyes and rebelling at the assault of the smoke-laden fog on the wolf's keen sense of smell. More pleasantly he felt also the strange, deeply balanced movement of his four-legged gait. Despite the disturbing implications of the fact that he was being escorted through the city in the middle of the night by palace guards and someone from the Duke's own bodyguard, he was amused by Tarrian's underlying vexation at the slowness of the pace of these ungainly long-legged creatures towering around him.

Antyr stumbled slightly as Tarrian returned his mind to its own body, and a powerful hand caught his arm. 'Sorry,' came the thought from Tarrian. 'Never could manage the way you walk.'

25

'Are you all right?' the officer's voice seemed loud and raucous in Antyr's ear after the subtle nuances of his thought conversation with Tarrian. But though it was authoritative, it was leavened with some genuine concern. It was the first time the man had spoken since they had left the Dream Finder's house apart from answering Antyr's initial surge of questions with a polite, 'In due course.'

Antyr nodded. 'Just cold and a little tired, thank you . . . sir,' Antyr replied. The man nodded and released his arm, but did not speak again. The pressure of the man's grip seemed to linger for a little while and Antyr felt a small but uneasy swirl of emotions eddy through him. The hand had sustained and, for whatever reason, cared for him. It was a long time since anyone had touched him thus. Yet that same hand, with that same purposefulness, would surely have killed men in the past as its owner had made his way through the wars and through the sometimes bloody labyrinth of city and palace politics to serve with the Duke's bodyguard.

Antyr felt an unexpected surge of approval from Tarrian at this insight.

Tentatively, Antyr tried again to reach this hooded guardian. 'I hadn't expected to be out in this filth again tonight,' he began. 'I haven't seen it so bad since . . .' But the attempt faded into nothingness as he felt it rebound off the man's indifference.

This time it was dark amusement from Tarrian. 'I told you before, you weasel,' he said. 'He's a pack leader. He won't deal with the runts of the litter except to tell them what to do.'

From the shade of his hood Antyr gave his Companion a malevolent look.

'Forgive me if I don't share your levity about this, Tarrian,' he said. 'But these are palace guards escorting us, and this "pack leader" *is* one of Ibris's personal bodyguard.' Fear churned inside him again, 'We could be heading for one of the palace dungeons for all we know.'

Tarrian replied as if to an exasperating child. 'What for?' he said wearily. 'Personally *I'd* lock you up for the crimes you've committed against yourself, but you've certainly not committed any against city law. And since when do Ibris's personal officers do the Watch's work? This is business, that's all, I can feel it in my fur. It'll be some important courtier's wife . . .' His tone became ironic. '. . . seeing "great horrors ahead" for the . . . city . . . the land . . . the whole world. A routine nightmare, nothing more.' He paused. 'But there should be a good fee in it – and good contacts if you shape yourself.'

Antyr frowned. 'Minutes ago you were reproaching me for thinking like that,' he said.

There was no immediate rejoinder. Instead there was an untypical and awkward silence, then, 'We've still got to eat, Antyr.'

But behind the words was something else. Some fear – some *great* fear.

'You're hiding something.' So vivid was the alarm that had suddenly slipped from the wolf's control and bubbled up into his mind, that Antyr almost spoke the words aloud, and again his step faltered. He felt the officer's gaze turning towards him. 'We're just preparing ourselves,' he said with a dismissive wave of his hand. Both voice and gesture were harsher than he had intended and he winced inwardly at his folly in behaving thus to such a man, but the officer simply turned away without seeming to take offence.

Silence hung in the minds of the Dream Finder and his Companion, while around them the rhythmic tread of the marching guards and the fluttering hiss of their torches echoed flatly through the fog.

Antyr felt Tarrian wilfully recover himself and the fear was taken from him. 'What was that?' he demanded urgently.

Silence.

'Tarrian!' He shouted into the wolf's mind.

'Nothing!' Tarrian snapped back angrily. 'At least nothing that concerns us here.'

'That's not good enough, for pity's sake,' Antyr said. 'You said yourself we're probably going on a search—'

'I know where we're going, and there's nothing that concerns us here. Trust me.' Despite the last words however, Tarrian's interruption was almost ferocious and, echoing his inner speech, his lip curled back and a deep menacing growl came from his throat.

The officer looked down at him sharply and then at Antyr, his hand moving discreetly but ominously into his cloak. Antyr returned the unseen gaze and tried to repair any damage his earlier hastiness might have done. 'It's all right, sir,' he said, raising his hand reassuringly this time. 'He means no harm. He just doesn't like the fog. The scents upset him.'

At the same time he replied to Tarrian, 'All right, all right. Calm down. You forget how nervous you can make people. I'll trust you – not that I've any alternative at the moment. But I didn't like the feel of that and I want to know what it is you're keeping to yourself. I don't—'

Tarrian interrupted him again, though now his voice was calm and controlled. 'I'm sorry, Antyr,' he said. 'It was a slip on my part. We'll talk later . . . I promise.'

'But—' Antyr began.

An order from one of the guards cut across his doubts and made him look up. Preoccupied with his inner debate with Tarrian, and content to be swept along by his escort, he had not paid any attention to where they were walking. Gazing around, he saw that there were now many more street torches. Some were isolated and brilliant, others formed ordered lines that curved away from him in all directions. There was something familiar in the pattern, but seeing the lights hovering seemingly unsupported in the fog disorientated him for a moment.

'It's the palace square,' Tarrian said.

'I know, I know,' Antyr lied irritably. 'I'm not that addled.'

A scornful silence rose up from the wolf.

As the group strode purposefully across the square, the torches that decorated the surrounding buildings with their balconies and high, winding walkways faded into sullen dots, while overhead, several lines of torches began to converge.

They would meet, Antyr knew, at the top of the spectacular Ibrian Monument, a legacy from an earlier Duke Ibris who had had it built following a great victory by a then much frailer Serenstad over a numerically far superior alliance of other cities, if cities they could have been called in those distant days. Now, however, the horrors surrounding its origins had long been softened by time, and the monument was regarded with amused affection by those citizens of Serenstad who ever gave it a moment's thought. Current critical opinion – though not that of artists and craftsmen – patronized it witheringly.

Sure enough, as the converging lines of torches faded into the gloom overhead, there appeared ahead of the advancing group those torches that decorated the monument itself. By their light, Antyr could just make out the lower tiers of the monument; close-packed ranks of ferocious infantrymen brandishing their heavy-bladed pikes. It should have been a familiar sight, but looming out of the swirling, ill-lit fog, the motionless stone figures looked like some grim ambush and Antyr felt a brief shiver of alarm. Worse, he realized abruptly the alarm was not his, but Tarrian's. He glanced down at the wolf, but the moment was gone and Tarrian's resolute control forbade any questioning.

Then they were at the palace, its great double-leaved gate emerging from the fog to greet them. The massive close-timbered body of the gate was secure behind an ornate iron facing, brutally decorated with great spikes and bolt heads. At the centre of each leaf, lit by large, flickering torches, was a carved relief of the Duke's insignia, the lamb in the talons of an eagle. The carving was traditional and cruelly realistic, but *no one* commented on the merits of *this* particular piece of work.

In the unsteady torchlight, the insignia seemed more alive than ever, and Antyr looked at the terrified lamb nervously. Abruptly, however, his concern vanished and, for an instant, he found himself looking up at the lamb through Tarrian's eyes and savouring the warm taste of freshly hunted quarry.

'Sorry,' came Tarrian's hasty and sincere apology before Antyr could rebel against this unexpected and unwelcome intrusion.

Returned to his own mind again, Antyr looked up at the gates expecting them to swing open. Instead a small wicket door opened anti-climactically and the officer, with Antyr and Tarrian following, strode through without even pausing. Behind them, the escort broke formation and lowered their pikes to follow in their turn. Glancing over his shoulder to watch them as they came into the brightly lit courtyard, it seemed to Antyr for a moment that the ancient stone figures from the monument were pursuing him.

The officer paused while the escort reformed itself into two straight lines and came to attention. Antyr gazed about him, momentarily a forgotten spectator. Never in his life had he been on this side of those great gates, though from the square outside he had many times glimpsed the courtyard. Now, however, even this was as he had never seen it, for it was so ablaze with torches that their very heat seemed to be dispersing the fog.

'Come with me.'

Antyr started out of his reverie. It was the officer again; his voice still quiet but, like his entire demeanour, radiating unopposable authority. Antyr turned away from the silent ranks of the escort and followed the cloaked figure as it strode up a wide flight of stairs.

As they neared the top, a door opened and, as at the wicket gate, the man passed through without even having to break his step. Antyr noted a servant behind the door as he followed the man, but this did nothing to assuage the feeling he had that the door would have opened at the inexorable approach of this figure without any human aid.

After the brightness of the courtyard, the interior of the palace seemed quite dark and Antyr hesitated until his eyes adjusted. The warmth of the place, however, washed over him luxuriously, and with some relief he threw back his hood. The officer did the same, then he swung off his cloak and threw it over his arm. The quality of his livery alone confirmed Antyr's guess about the man's status as an officer in the Duke's bodyguard, though he had no idea what the various symbols of rank meant. As he took in the man's appearance, Antyr's eyes were drawn to his sword and dagger. The hilts of both were finely decorated, but worn with use.

Then the man looked at him. Antyr judged him to be a few years his junior, though his striking angular face was pale and drawn from the cold. Beads of moisture in his short black hair sparkled in the lamplight like inappropriate ornaments.

Brown eyes that in a woman Antyr would have been glad to gaze into, scanned him coldly, critically, and without faltering. That too told him much about the man, for few could look easily into the eyes of a Dream Finder who was one with his Companion. Antyr felt his stomach go cold and he remembered his earlier thought about this man's probable history. 'Be afraid,' said the man's gaze.

'Don't be afraid,' said his voice in contradiction. 'The Duke asked me to bring you to him . . .'

The *Duke*? The word thundered in Antyr's ears and he did not hear the end of the sentence. His eyes widened and, despite himself, he drew in a sharp breath and held it. His mouth began to go dry.

'Duke Ibris?' he managed shakily after a moment.

A faint hint of amusement lit the searching brown eyes and

the set mouth pursed a little. 'How many dukes do we have in Serenstad, Dream Finder?' he said, running a hand over his damp hair.

Antyr replied with some vague, silent mouthings. 'The *Duke*!' he gasped inwardly to Tarrian. The wolf made no reply, but Antyr felt him alert and watching.

'I'm going to take you to him now,' the officer continued, his voice commanding attention through Antyr's confusion. 'Just bow when you meet him, then stand up straight, speak when you're spoken to and answer quickly, honestly and straightforwardly. The Duke's hard on fools and ditherers.'

'But . . .?' Antyr began.

The officer waved him to silence and motioned him to follow.

'I really should . . . clean myself up,' Antyr stammered as he trotted after the retreating figure.

There was no reply, however, and it came to Antyr, as vividly as if it had been bellowed out loud, that had his appearance been important it would have been corrected by now. As it hadn't then it was not important and no answer was warranted. The man's manner told him this, without a word being spoken.

From his past came long-forgotten memories of men he had met on occasions during his army service. Men who seemed to see through to a truer, more basic reality in whatever they looked at. Men who acted without hesitation but with a strange economy of effort and totality of purpose. Men who were perhaps not always comfortable to be with, but with whom he was profoundly relieved to lock shields when the arrows and spears were flying. This man was one such, beyond a doubt.

And the wolf had called him a pack leader, he remembered.

Then he noticed that Tarrian was trotting by the side of the officer and a small spur of pride goaded him forward to join them.

As he followed the man's easy stride, he tried to make a note of the route they were travelling, but after some three changes of direction, he gave up. In any event his impending meeting with the Duke, and whatever that might imply, was looming across his future like a dark and unclimbable rock-face and he could no more think beyond it than fly.

Despite this, however, and despite the low night-time lamplight illuminating the tall vaulted corridors through which they were passing, Antyr found himself gazing around in some awe. Apart from the architecture itself, the walls were lined with pictures and carvings of extraordinary quality. He knew that the Duke was a patron of many artists and craftsmen, but had never before thought about the extent of this patronage.

'This is overwhelming,' he said softly, largely to himself.

Again the man did not reply, but he inclined his head slightly in acknowledgement of the remark.

The corridors were largely deserted, but the occasional servant they passed would stop and bow to the officer, and sentries stiffened at their posts.

Eventually the pace slowed a little and the elaborate tiled floor gave way to a soft, patterned carpeting. Apart from other, more subtle changes in the decoration, the muffling of their marching footsteps in itself made the atmosphere more intimate, and Antyr's stomach began to churn painfully as he realized he must be in or near the Duke's private quarters. He licked his lips uneasily, but his mouth was dry.

No more ale in future, he thought piteously, wincing a little as the word 'future' seemed to mock him.

'Be calm,' Tarrian offered gently, but to little avail.

Then they stopped. Outside an imposing double door set inside a deep archway, Antyr noted that the sentries who stood either side of it wore a livery similar to that of his guide.

'Excuse me,' the man said to him, unexpectedly polite. 'Stand still.'

Before Antyr could protest, the man was running his hands over him; expert searching hands. Around his neck, down his arms, his back, front, sides . . . There was a pause.

'Empty your pockets,' came the soft command.

Antyr obeyed without thinking, emptying his keys, coins, scraps of paper, a small knife, bottle opener, and various other oddments on to a small, immaculately polished table nearby. A small flicker of irritation . . . or was it distaste? . . . passed over the man's face as the untidy little heap grew.

'I've no weapons on me,' Antyr said reassuringly but with an indrawn breath as the man completed his search with an examination of his legs that left the Dream Finder balancing gingerly on his toes.

The man nodded curtly.

'Do you want to search my Companion?' said Antyr,

scarcely believing the note of injured dignity that had crept into his voice.

This time, however, he saw the man wilfully suppress a smile.

'No, no,' he said. 'The wolf might be fiercer than you but treachery's the danger here, not ferocity, eh wolf?' And he reached down as if to stroke Tarrian's head. Without thinking, Antyr reached out quickly and stopped him. As the Dream Finder's hand closed about his arm, the man looked up sharply. This time, however, although he held Antyr's gaze, he flinched a little.

'My mistake,' he said softly as Antyr shook his head in mute appeal.

Then one of the sentries opened the door and the officer walked through, signalling Antyr to follow.

'Feranc,' came a voice as the man stepped inside. 'At last. Have you found him?'

Feranc! Antyr thought. Ye gods! Ciarll Feranc; variously Feranc the shield and Feranc the slayer, and bearer of many other, harsher names in the mouths of those who had opposed the Duke with force. Not one of the Duke's bodyguard, but their *commander*. A man whose name alone had sent shivers through the armies of the city's enemies and stiffened the resolve of its allies more than the arrival of an entire division on the battlefield.

And I tried to talk to him about the weather . . . twitted him about searching Tarrian. *And grabbed his arm!* The last residue of moisture in Antyr's mouth dried up.

'I have, sire,' Antyr just heard Feranc reply through the noise of his pounding heart. 'This is he.'

Then the shield had stepped to one side and Antyr found himself staring open-mouthed at a figure stretched out casually on a long couch, his face largely hidden in the shadows thrown by the three lamps that strove to illuminate the room.

'You're gawping!' came Tarrian's furious thought abruptly. 'Bow smartly and then stand up.'

Somehow, Antyr managed to obey his Companion's instruction. Then the lounging figure reached out and beckoned the Dream Finder and his Companion forward.

Chapter 3

Menedrion, eldest son to Duke Ibris, started upright, suddenly wide awake. His heart was pounding with terror, and he was bathed in sweat.

For a moment he flailed his arms about wildly as if fending off a multitude of closing enemies. Then quite suddenly he stopped as awareness joined his wakefulness and familiar surroundings began to take shape around him in the faint glow of the small night-lamp.

Pulling up his knees he wrapped his arms around them and dropped his head forward. He stayed thus for some time until both his breathing and his heartbeat had quietened. Wilfully he kept his mind from returning to contemplate the nightmare which had just wakened him. He would think about it in a moment – when time had interposed a little more safety.

Eventually, still resting his head on his knees, he turned and looked at the night-lamp. It stood on a nearby table, and a soft yellow halo surrounded its flame to tell him that not even the guarded depths of the palace were proof against the assault of such an intangible enemy as the fog. But he was oblivious to such a conclusion. For a moment he was a child again, seeking the comfort of the light in the darkness.

Yet that very comfort angered him. Menedrion frightened in the dark! Frightened by a dream! Almost guiltily he glanced quickly from side to side as if fearful that this lapse might have been observed. Then his mouth curled viciously. It wasn't possible. It couldn't have happened. He would not be unmanned by the unbridled ramblings of his own imaginings.

But it was not in Menedrion's nature to accept blame or any form of self-reproach and, clenching his fist, he lashed out angrily at the body next to him.

It landed with a satisfying thud and was followed almost immediately by a desperate cry of pain and terror. The sound rose like a spectre to mock him with the fear he was trying to excise and in a fury he struck again.

'No, please, Irfan,' came a fearful, trembling voice out of the darkness. In the gloom a figure was struggling to evade this unprovoked onslaught. 'Please, I—'

Menedrion lashed out again, ending the plaint by inadvertently catching the speaker in the mouth. Teeth grazed his hand painfully, and with a snarl he brought his other hand round, open-palmed, to deliver a merciless slap to the face of his victim.

The body crashed down on to the pillow and, swinging round, Menedrion straddled it and seized it by the throat.

'Enough!' he roared, tightening his grip. 'You sicken me!' Hands – pleading hands – reached up and covered his face.

Then, as suddenly as before, he was awake again. But though he knew he was awake, there were hands still clawing at his face.

'No!' he cried out, before realizing incongruously that the hands were his own.

In a mixture of anger, humiliation and relief, he brought his hands down savagely on the embroidered sheets that covered him.

There was a grunt from beside him. 'What's the matter, Arwain?' it articulated eventually.

'Nothing,' Arwain replied hastily, laying a now gentle hand on his wife's arm. 'Just a dream. I thought I was—' He stopped. 'I'm sorry I disturbed you. Go back to sleep.'

The instruction, however, was superfluous, as the lady Yanys was already breathing steadily and peacefully. Arwain patted her arm again affectionately.

Just a dream, he thought. But not a dream. A nightmare. And a nightmare within a nightmare at that. He shuddered at the horror of his first awakening. To awaken as *someone else*! And Menedrion of all people!

He could not have imagined such a thing, yet, beyond doubt, he had been utterly and completely his half-brother, full of his hates and fears – his darkness. He shuddered at the memory.

Tentatively he ran his hand over his chest . . . he was dry and warm. As Menedrion he had been soaking wet with terror.

And that fearful assault on his bedmate . . .?

He looked at the sleeping form of his wife. What if he had been truly awake? What if, in the demented mind of Menedrion, he had . . .

36

The thought was unbearable and with a grimace he turned his face sharply away as if just seeing his wife there might in some way bring back his half-brother to possess him.

Carefully he got up and pulled his night-robe about him. Part of his mind told him he was too wide awake to return to sleep, but another part told him he was too afraid. Too afraid to sleep lest he waken as Menedrion again.

'No,' he muttered angrily into the soft darkness. That way lay madness. It was a bad dream, nothing more. Probably something he'd eaten; or this damned, smoke-laden fog; certainly that would bring Menedrion to mind. It was his forges and mills that turned the grey winter mists into yellow, choking fogs.

Arwain shook his head. Just a dream, he thought again. Insubstantial, and powerless to do anything other than frighten. No person, no thing, least of all an image of that lout Menedrion could make him harm his wife.

Yet it had been extraordinarily vivid.

Arwain stared at the low flame of the night-lamp. Somewhere in the palace a muffled bell struck the hour and brought him back to the present. Four o'clock. A long way from the daylight in both directions, but not too long before the palace would begin to stir. Arwain knew that, whatever the reason, he would not sleep again that night and, turning up the night-lamp a little, he began to dress himself quietly.

He would go into his room and read a little; think a little. He smiled to himself. Perhaps his dream had been no more than his wiser self shaking him from his natural lethargy and giving him this opportunity to consider quietly some of the many problems that, as usual, were besetting him.

His face became grimmer. Problems was an inadequate word to describe the confusion of plotting and counter-plotting that always seemed to be swirling through the palace, as members of the court and the Sened and the Gythrin-Dy struggled endlessly for power and advantage. Plotting that at times he would willingly walk away from were it not for the fact that to do so would turn him into a ready victim. Almost certainly it would see Menedrion falsely accusing him again of some treachery against his father, or perhaps even making some attempt against his life. He scowled. Walking away; that was a dream. All his life he had known intriguing and he was as good a player as most of the others . . . yet now, since his marriage to Yanys, it seemed to be both so

37

much worse and so much more important. Now, it was no longer a game. Should he fall, she would fall with him. And perhaps her family . . .

He set the thoughts aside. He knew from past experience that he could do only so much planning; not least in dealing with Menedrion. More important to his survival were his continuing vigilance, his good standing in the city and its institutions, and the protection his father's affection gave him.

He struggled with a stiff belt buckle. No, instead, he would pause and reflect on the dream – the dreams – that had woken him to give him this strange unsought interlude at the stillest time of the night when amid the soft-breathing silence the dreams of a myriad sleepers roamed unfettered and unchallenged through the dark by-ways of the world.

For a moment he paused and looked up, as if he might suddenly be able to hear this silent pandemonium.

Then he realized that the dream – the *first* dream, from which he, as Menedrion, had awakened, terrified and drenched with sweat – was gone.

No, it can't be, he thought. Not such a nightmare. And, briefly, there was a sliver of a sensation – a swirling distant darkness? – then like a snowflake that had drifted into the warmth through an open door, it was gone. Not a vestige remained. He was no longer Menedrion and the dream was no longer his.

He puffed out his cheeks in self-mockery, and shook his head. It would seem that dreams had the power to irritate and torment as well as frighten, he decided.

And he let it go. If the dream had meant anything then it would reveal itself in due course. If not, then why waste time fretting about it?

He finished fastening his tunic and walked over to the heavy curtains that covered almost half the length of one wall. They were decorated with scenes from the mythology of the founding of Serenstad and were not really to either his or his wife's taste. But they were thick and he was grateful for the warmth they kept in the room during the city's cold winters.

Indeed, as he stepped through the curtains into the wide windowed alcove beyond, the difference in temperature was immediately noticeable, and he closed them behind himself quickly to prevent the room becoming chilled.

The alcove overlooked a courtyard lit by a great many bright torches. Despite their smoking efforts, however, they seemed only to emphasize the yellow opacity of the fog, and the far side of the courtyard was barely visible.

Arwain leaned forward against a stout timber mullion and gazed out at the sight. Then he looked up above the choked brightness for some indication that this was only some shallow emanation of nature, but neither stars nor moon were to be seen; the fog would be as deep as it was wide. It was as if it wanted to smother the city forever.

Strange thoughts, he mused. Born out of strange dreams, doubtless.

His breath clouded the glass and he reached up idly to wipe it clear. As he did so, a movement caught his eye in the courtyard below; it was a figure.

All Arwain's musings and concerns evaporated immediately and he stepped behind the mullion so that he could observe without himself being seen. It was an unnecessary action in such light but it was an inevitable one for anyone who lived in the palace and it was done before he even thought about it.

Peering intently through the yellow gloom he made out not one, but three figures. They were walking rapidly across the courtyard, but they were not guards, and there was a stealthiness in their behaviour. And at least one of them appeared to be armed.

Arwain scowled. Something was wrong. There was no curfew, but no one wandered the palace grounds so late without ensuring that one of the guards was with him. He did not wait to see anything further, but stepped back through the curtains and, snatching up his sword and dagger, slipped quietly from the bedroom.

Leaving his personal quarters, he ran silently along a short, dimly lit corridor, then down a wide, curving stairway that brought him to the spacious entrance hall which opened on to the courtyard.

'Be quiet,' he hissed as he saw the two door guards moving forward to intercept and challenge him.

As ordered, the men remained silent, but their pikes came down ready to destroy the unexpected arrival well before he came within a sword's length if need arose. Only when Arwain moved into the light did they raise them again.

He acknowledged them with a nod but, without pausing, pushed open a nearby door. Of the four men inside the room, two were half dozing in their chairs, and two were sitting at a table playing a board game.

Standing in the doorway, Arwain made no preamble as they began rising hastily to their feet. 'There are three men in the courtyard, at least one of them armed,' he said with an unflustered urgency. 'Two of you stay at this door. Sterne . . .' He met the gaze of one of the men at the table, and raised a significant finger. 'Guard my rooms.' Then with a glance at the others, 'The rest of you follow me.'

He added no injunctions to haste but simply turned and strode across the entrance hall towards the outer door. One of the duty guards opened it for him and, without even breaking step, Arwain stepped out into the torchlit fog.

Sterne, the officer in charge of the guard, allocated the duties with a few silent gestures as he left the room and then ran softly towards the staircase. The others were less ordered in their departure, but Arwain had barely gone ten paces through the gloom before they were running alongside him, pulling on helmets and fastening straps and buckles.

At a corner, Arwain hesitated a little, momentarily confused by the fog.

'This way,' he said, almost to himself. And then he was running, with the three guards following anxiously. Briefly, Arwain cast a glance up towards the window of his bedroom. Whatever was happening, it was moving away from him this time, but it reassured him to know that Sterne would be quietly guarding Yanys.

It occurred to him for a moment that perhaps he was being foolish. Perhaps the figures he had seen were no more than lingering figments of his strange dreaming? But he dismissed the thought. He had been awake, and the figures had been real, and armed. And just as they were not apparently moving against him in his isolated wing of the palace, so they were moving into the main body of the palace, and that might bode anything.

Reaching the far side of the courtyard, Arwain peered into the glowing fog for some sign of the three figures, his head craning forward anxiously as though, like a hound, he might catch some elusive scent. But nothing was to be seen.

'Sir.' One of the guards took his arm. He was pointing towards a small door at the bottom of a short flight of stone steps. It was an entrance to part of the palace's labyrinthine cellars and it should have been bolted from the inside. Now it stood ajar.

Arwain nodded towards a nearby torch rack and then ran

40

down the steps. They were damp and treacherous due to the fog and he slipped as he reached the bottom. Reaching out to recover his balance, he bumped into the door and it swung wide open, striking the wall with an echoing thud.

He cursed to himself. Little chance of a discreet pursuit if they're still nearby, he thought. But no sounds of alarm or sudden haste reached him and, taking a torch from one of the guards, he stepped inside. The guards followed.

The door opened into a cavernous cellar with a low vaulted ceiling supported on rows of squat, square columns. Each was scrolled about with ornate carved patterns and capped with a wide flaring stone, from which peered carvings of strange, watching faces, all of them different.

A vanguard of the fog had preceded them into the cellar, as if searching for its natural home, and a faint yellow haze hovered like a miasma among the barrels and kegs, and anonymous piles of materials too precious to be discarded but for which no other place could be found. Through it the flickering torches cut great swathes of dancing black shadow, bringing the stillness abruptly alive.

Arwain's gaze, however, was drawn almost immediately to the damp footprints which moved down one of the wider aisles. He set off in the same direction.

'Should we sound the alarm, sir?' one of the guards asked.

Arwain shook his head. 'No. Their coming down here shows that they know the palace and that they're on some ill errand. If we sound the alarm it'll be easier for them to move around in the confusion. We must find them quickly.' And, his actions following his words, he began to run.

The damp footprints soon disappeared, but not before they had clearly confirmed which aisle their creators had taken and, for a while, the four men ran on as silently as they could past the host of carved, watching faces.

Arwain hesitated as they passed under an arch at the end of the long chamber to find themselves at a junction of four aisles. The head of some kind of demon had been carved on the keystone of the arch and in the torchlight its gaping mouth seemed to laugh silently and malevolently at Arwain's doubt.

'Hood the torches, and be quiet,' one of the guards whispered urgently.

Blackness and silence closed round the group, then, as the dull glow of the hooded torches began to appear, 'There.'

Arwain felt rather than saw the pointing arm come past him to draw his gaze to a faint light in the distance.

'Quietly,' he whispered, fearing that one of the guards might suddenly shout out a challenge. 'They don't seem to have heard us. Unhood one of the torches a little so that we can see where we're walking.'

Cautiously he drew his sword and started forward, keeping the light ahead only in the side of his vision so that he could still see the floor faintly in front of him.

As he drew nearer he felt his heart begin to pound. So far, the heat of the chase had protected him from more sober considerations, but now he was closing, sword in hand, with a possibly armed group about whom he knew nothing, except that they were sufficiently desperate to wander the palace grounds at the darkest time of the night, and knew their way through the palace cellars.

'Mistake,' part of him said. 'Starting a battle without proper intelligence.' But his reason just managed to hold the reproach at bay. It was no mistake. He had three palace guards with him and he himself had faced men in combat before now. To have sounded the alarm might indeed have enabled these . . . conspirators? . . . to escape, or worse, to fulfil their mission quietly amid the confusion. He had had no alternative.

Abruptly he found he was angry at having to justify himself to himself. He found too that he was baring his teeth and loosening his sword arm.

The light was coming from around a corner ahead, throwing the faces on the column heads into silhouette. And, as if the faces themselves were talking to one another in the gloom, there came the sound of lowered voices. Arwain turned to the guards and whispered a brief order, then, suddenly, the torches were unhooded and with the guards at his back Arwain stepped around the corner with his sword levelled.

'Stand, in the Duke's name,' he shouted authoritatively.

There was a gasp and a scream, then someone dropped a torch. Finally came the sound of a sword being drawn as a figure pushed to the front of the surprised group. The three guards brought their pikes down alongside Arwain's sword.

'No, wait, Dirkel,' came a stern voice from the group.

Arwain took in his quarry at a glance. There were five in

42

all, but they were not what he had expected. True, the man who had stepped forward looked sinister, with the hood of his cloak hiding his face, but from the guard he was presenting with his sword it was clear that he was no swordsman; and he was faltering, either at the sudden command or the sight of Arwain's grim face and the three pikemen with him. Behind him stood two others, an old palace manservant who looked as if he had been running and who had obviously thrown on his livery in great haste, and another man with his cowl pulled forward. Between these two and leaning heavily on the hooded man was a young woman. Her head was bowed and her long brown hair had fallen forward hiding most of her face, but Arwain could see blood on her gown and her hands. At the rear of the group was an old woman, wringing her hands; another servant, Arwain guessed, probably from the laundry or the kitchens.

With an irritable gesture, the man supporting the young woman threw back his hood to identify himself.

Arwain stared in disbelief. He had thought the voice was familiar.

'Drayner?' he exclaimed. Then, after an awkward pause, 'What's my father's personal physician doing prowling the courtyards and the cellars in the middle of the night?'

'Nearly suffering an early demise thanks to young men leaping out of the darkness and waving swords at me,' the old man replied acidly. Arwain winced a little at the characteristic tone, but having delivered his barb, Drayner turned fussily to practical matters.

'Dirkel, put your sword down,' he said. 'You're only going to cut yourself and I'm going to have enough to do tonight without sewing you up as well. And someone pick up that torch for mercy's sake, there's enough fog outside without making more in here.'

The old woman's hands disentangled themselves and fluttered nervously for a moment until with a noisy effort, she bent down and picked up the spluttering torch. Drayner's defender somewhat sulkily sheathed his sword, as did Arwain, and the three guards raised their pikes. Eron Drayner was not only Duke Ibris's personal physician, he was highly respected both in Serenstad and beyond, and was one of the few men in public life who could stand contemptuously aloof from the perpetual bickering and scheming that marred it.

He also had a tongue 'worth ten pikemen' according to those who had cause to know, and pointing a weapon at him was a decidedly unwise act.

Drayner's face puckered up indecisively for a moment, as if he had lost his train of thought, then the woman he was supporting gave a low moan and with a brief grimace of self-reproach he took abrupt charge of the proceedings.

'Anyway, now you're here, you can help me get this young lady to my surgery,' he declared. He turned to the servants. 'You two can go back now, lord Arwain will escort us from here.'

The manservant bowed and turned to leave, but the old woman laid a hand on his arm to restrain him. She cast an anxious look first at the young woman and then at Drayner. 'Go, go,' Drayner said urgently, but gently. 'She'll be all right.' Adding significantly, 'Look to yourselves.' The old woman hesitated a little longer then, at another nod from Drayner, she made a brief curtsy and left.

Without being asked, Arwain stepped forward and put his arm round the young woman, but she started violently at his touch and shook it off, taking hold of Drayner's arm tightly. 'I can manage, now,' she said, her voice muffled and distressed.

Arwain looked at Drayner, puzzled.

'Let the lord support you. He's stronger than I am,' the physician said, patting her arm reassuringly. 'And he's not like—' He stopped in mid-sentence and turned away from Arwain sharply.

'Dirkel, run ahead with one of the guards and make the surgery ready,' he said briskly to cover the apparent slip. Arwain nodded his confirmation to the guards and then hesitantly reached out to support the young woman again. This time she accepted his arm.

'What's happened?' Arwain asked as they walked slowly back. 'And why were you trailing through the cellars?'

'The young lady's had a nasty fall,' Drayner said. 'And we came this way because it's the quickest way and because the fog will chill this poor girl into a fever in her present condition.' His voice, however, was a little too loud, as if he were anxious not to elaborate on the incident. For a moment, Arwain considered pressing him, but the woman was obviously in need of attention and if Drayner was choosing to lie about what had happened then it was not a matter to be aired in front of the guards: Drayner might be above politics but he was not oblivious to them.

Arwain nodded slightly and remained silent until they eventually arrived at Drayner's surgery and he dismissed the guards.

'Thank you, lord Arwain,' Drayner said as they entered the surgery. 'I apologize for disturbing your sleep, but your help was most timely. If you'll excuse me I'll have to look to my patient now. I'll let you get back to your bed.'

He was leading the woman into a nearby room while he was speaking and he concluded his comments over his shoulder, almost offhandedly. Arwain made no reply, but instead of leaving, sat down on a long wooden bench.

The surgery was warm and bright after the journey through the cold cellars and the even colder fog, but welcome though the warmth was, Arwain felt uneasy.

Apart from the effects of his strange early rising, and his curiosity about the events that had brought no less a person than Drayner from his bed, the room held old childhood memories for him, most of which were not particularly pleasant. Drayner had been the court physician for many years before he had risen to become the Duke's, and Arwain had been his reluctant patient on more than one occasion.

As he sat waiting Drayner's pleasure, he did as he had done as a child; he stared around at the shelves that lined the room. A battle array of ancient mysteries defied his adult gaze: tall bottles, green and bulbous; short ones, brown and squat; dull ones, red and menacing. Dusty bottles with peeling, faded labels, strangely stained; shiny, freshly labelled bottles; bottles with strange fluted spouts and twisted necks. Then there were the flank guards: ranks of small boxes and solid commonplace clear glass jars full of pills and powders and . . . other things.

Arwain's gaze yielded the field and drifted to the cupboards. Some were glass-fronted, dimly revealing the fearsome weapons of Drayner's art; others, mercifully, were blank-faced with polished wooden doors and polished brass hinges and handles.

Briefly, he took in the rest of the room: the large cabinet with its ridiculous little legs and its row upon row of tiny drawers; the pictures and charts; the occasional mournful bone; that damned skull with its hollow eyes, and finally, *the table*. Then the vividly evocative smell of the room reached through his fog-stifled senses and he puffed out his cheeks unhappily.

Straight from his childhood came the urge in his legs to flee and, urgently, and rather self-consciously, he brought his hands to his knees to still them. Then, sitting up stiffly, he dragged his attention back to the matter in hand.

There was some coming and going in the adjacent room, and the occasional muffled comment which Arwain could not distinguish. Once or twice, Dirkel, a round-faced, earnest-looking youth, came out to retrieve a bottle or a jar, but he avoided the gaze of his erstwhile adversary.

Finally, partly out of curiosity and partly to assert his authority over his legs, Arwain stood up and walked over to the door of the room. As he did so, Drayner emerged, looking both pleased and angry. He started slightly when he saw Arwain.

'Go back to bed, Dirkel,' he said back into the room hastily. 'She'll be all right now, and I don't want you yawning all day, we'll be busy after this fog.' Then, fatherly, he took Arwain's arm.

'There's nothing you can do, lord,' he said understandingly, endeavouring to shepherd Arwain away from the door.

Arwain, however, did not move, leaving the physician heaving awkwardly on his arm for a moment.

'Some goblin saw fit to wake me at this ungodly hour and draw me to the window just as you were passing,' Arwain said. 'I'll see this matter through to its end.'

Drayner bridled briefly but he was unable to meet Arwain's gaze and, reluctantly, he stepped to one side to allow him past.

The room was small and simply decorated, and a soft lamplight gave it a restful quality. Along one wall was a bed in which lay the young woman.

'She's asleep,' Drayner said. 'And will be for several hours. I've given her a draught. There *is* nothing you can do.'

Arwain ignored this last effort to deflect him and walked over to the bed.

As he looked down at the sleeping figure his frown deepened. The young woman was probably very pretty, and really little more than a girl; Arwain doubted she was twenty years old. But it was difficult to judge, for though her features were relaxed in sleep, they were swollen and discoloured by bruising; her lip was badly split and there was a gash over one eye. He had seen similar injuries often enough – on men.

'This was no fall,' he said quietly, turning to Drayner. 'She's been beaten. And savagely at that. Who did this? And why does it warrant the attention of my father's personal physician in the middle of the night?'

This time Drayner held his gaze, but he did not reply.

Arwain was about to press him when the memory returned of teeth accidentally gouging his hand as he lashed out in his fury. Gently he reached down and parted the swollen lips; a bloody cavity squired a milk-white partner. Arwain grimaced, then he looked at the side of the woman's face; four great weals scarred it such as would result from a powerful blow with an open palm. He knew that if he pulled back the sheet a little, he would see bruising on her throat.

His hand started to shake and he felt the blood draining from his face. For a moment the room began to spin, but he stilled it with a long, deep breath. He turned to Drayner. The old physician's face was quietly resolute. Arwain knew that he would not discuss what had happened, and there was little point in pressing him.

Arwain looked at him thoughtfully. He could walk away now with a shrug, and the incident would be servants' gossip for a while, then it would be forgotten. But the vividness of his first awakening was still with him, unsettling him for reasons he could not understand. He had had similar feelings walking into an ambush once.

He had to go forward.

'Tell me about the dream that made Menedrion do this,' he said.

Chapter 4

Antyr stepped forward nervously, trying to bear in mind Feranc's instructions and supported by Tarrian's resolve.

'Sire,' he managed, mustering what professional authority he could.

It quailed, however, in the face of the presence that rose from the couch to meet him. Antyr had seen many portraits of the Duke and had actually seen him several times in the flesh. But the portraits, he realized now, though accurate, missed the reality of the man, as did the previous glimpses he had had of him; a distant figure on horseback during a battle, or trotting past surrounded by his entourage on some grand civic occasion. This man was unequivocally a 'pack leader'.

Ibris was about the same height as his bodyguard, Feranc, but much heavier, although, despite his age, he gave the impression of muscular solidity rather than fat. But where Feranc had an eerie, disturbing aloofness about him, the Duke radiated power like a great rock-throwing siege machine. Antyr's confidence fled him utterly.

'Stand up straight,' Tarrian's angry voice rang in his head.

Antyr had too few wits left to make a reply, but somehow he managed to obey the injunction. As he did so he became vaguely aware of another presence in the room, then his attention was absorbed totally by the Duke again, now stood barely a pace in front of him.

And he was speaking!

'He's apologizing for disturbing us so late and in such weather,' Tarrian rasped as Antyr nearly panicked again. 'It's a routine courtesy to put you at your ease. *Will you get a hold of yourself!*'

'You look a little jaded,' came the Duke's voice through the terror. 'Would you like some refreshment?'

'The truth!' Tarrian demanded.

'Thank you, no, sire,' Antyr said hesitantly. 'To be honest, with the fog being so bad, I was not expecting to be called out tonight and I celebrated perhaps a little too well with some friends earlier in the evening. My stomach is a little . . . fragile.'

The Duke pursed his lips and frowned a little. 'An unwise thing, Dream Finder,' he said. 'You above all should know the dangers of such behaviour.' His voice became regretful. 'I remember your father saying he thought you didn't know the true worth of your gift.'

Despite himself, Antyr gaped, taken aback not by the reproach, which was a familiar one, but by the unexpected reference to his father. The Duke, however, ignored the discourtesy and, taking his arm, led him across to the couch and sat him down.

'Still, forgive me,' he continued, sitting down by him. 'You're no child, and you can attend to your affairs without my advice, I'm sure. It's just that I value great talent, and waste distresses me. We seem to have such an endless capacity for it, and—'

He cut himself short with a gruff snort and tapped his hands thoughtfully on his knees. For a moment he looked at Tarrian, then he nodded his head appreciatively.

'To business then, Petran's son,' he said. 'You and your Companion have my trust. Seek through my dreams.'

The brusqueness of the command took Antyr aback. Most clients usually dithered on for a while, explaining what it was they wanted before making the traditional request.

Antyr, still overawed, had been about to declare his unworthiness to help such a man as the Duke; there were, after all, more successful and prosperous Dream Finders in the city; but the Duke's manner swept the excuse away.

Ah well, a job's a job, he thought resignedly. And there should be a good fee in it at least.

'A chair, please,' he said, glancing towards Feranc, standing in the shade by the door. The bodyguard did not move, but a chair appeared by Antyr's side. He looked up to see a lean-faced old man with a sparse grey beard and a pronounced stoop. Bright searching eyes however gave the lie to his body's age. This person Antyr *did* recognize.

Aaken Uhr Candessa. The Chancellor carrying a chair for me!

But, buoyed up by the Duke's confidence and set upon the start of his search as he was, the presence of this third illustrious person had little effect on him and he simply took the chair and placed it by the couch with a nod of thanks.

As he looked up at the chancellor, however, the old man turned away sharply.

Antyr glanced down at Tarrian for final confirmation of the cause of this apparent rudeness. The wolf returned his gaze, opening his eyes wide. Antyr nodded, satisfied. Where the wolf's eyes had been grey they were now yellow, and bright, like sunlight, but penetrating and feral, the eyes of a Companion who would be his guide and defender in both worlds. Then, briefly, Antyr was Tarrian again, looking up at himself staring down with eyes whose black irises had spread to fill their entire sockets so that they were like deep, fearful caves of night.

All was well.

Antyr moved on to the chair while Tarrian turned two spiralling circles and flopped down beside him.

As the wolf's baleful eyes slowly closed, Antyr turned to the Duke. 'Would you lie down and close your eyes, sire,' he said softly.

Without speaking, the Duke did as he was bidden, and held out his hand. Antyr felt a momentary spasm of grief as he noted the Duke's behaviour: it bore the marks of his father's influence. Questions rose inside him again, but he laid them aside.

Gently his right hand took the Duke's, and his left moved over the Duke's closed eyes. 'Sleep easy,' he said, his voice dwindling. 'Whatever befalls, nothing can harm. Dreams are but shadows and you are guarded in all places by a great and ancient strength.'

Antyr nodded as he felt the Duke drifting almost immediately into sleep. Then he felt the room slip away from him and the darkness that shone through his eyes seemed to flood through his entire spirit until there was *only* darkness and silence; though at its heart, hard as a diamond yet insubstantial as an idle summer breeze, lay his awareness.

Gradually, into the darkness, but with no apparent beginning, came faint wisps of light. Slowly they brightened and began to move about him. A myriad of colours, some darting to and fro like sparrows flitting between hedgerows, others circling and twisting, and yet others hovering watchfully: all shifted and changed, grew and shrank. All eluded examination.

With them came strange disjointed sounds like many distant conversations carried on a silent but blustering wind.

51

Then, seemingly without any change, the Dream Finder was whole again; conscious, purposeful, and as solid as the figure that sat holding the Duke's hand. By him was his Companion; present, but not visible.

Antyr gazed around. Here was the Dream Nexus of the Duke of Serenstad; the strange, crowded jostling of images and sounds which were the portals to the countless dreams, forgotten and remembered, sleeping and waking, that the Duke had created through his long and turbulent life.

Here, Antyr was lost, utterly.

Here, only the Companion could guide.

Antyr felt Tarrian reaching out and seeking the way, just as his waking form would raise his head and search the air for scents beyond human perception. And, as always, he felt the wolf resisting its desire to wander at will through the rich byways that it could sense. He reached down and stroked the soft fur that was not there to remind the wolf, unnecessarily, that he was not alone.

A low whimper reached him, then, 'This way. This way,' said Tarrian.

Antyr felt himself moved forward by the wolf's will.

The shifting sights and sounds passed around and through him until, again without any seeming change, Companion and Dream Finder were the Duke.

'We are here, sire,' Antyr said. 'All will be as it was. As you see and feel, so shall we.'

But there was no reply. In this dream, the Duke had been struck dumb. Struggle as he might, he would make no sound, he knew. Yet the warrior leader in him accepted this and set aside the fear that would have had a lesser man waken, gasping for breath.

He was in his receiving chamber.

Matters of the day, Antyr thought. On this frame would be built the dream.

Figures came and went, with noiseless queries; a floating mixture of the known and the elusively familiar. Their roles and liveries were confused and mixed irrelevantly, and some were long dead, though this caused the Duke no surprise.

Despite his silence, he somehow held a series of brief, disjointed conversations which set easily to rights the many problems of business and state that had been brought to him for his special attention. Something, however, was troubling him and, finding that he was now in a strange banqueting hall, he brought his hand down loudly on the table. The hall, which dwindled into a far distant darkness, fell silent, and all eyes turned to him.

Slightly embarrassed, he looked down at the table. In front of him was an elaborately decorated silver goblet. The engraving seemed to be finer than anything he had ever seen and it glittered temptingly in the light of the innumerable and huge candelabras that strove unsuccessfully to light the vast hall. He reached out to pick it up but, as he tried to lift it, he found it would not move.

Puzzled, he bent forward to examine it closely. Great round-headed rivets secured it to the table. Their heads were carved with sneering faces. From somewhere he heard a snigger. He was the butt of some joke.

Angry at this affront, Ibris placed his large hand over the top of the goblet and twisted it violently. Those who would mock him so lightly must learn why it was he was the Duke of Serenstad.

The goblet did not yield.

There was a strange timeless moment in which the goblet and his powerful hand filled Ibris's vision to the exclusion of all else, though he knew that he was being watched and that the resistance of the goblet was a threat to his entire power.

Contempt for his weakness rose around him.

'I need no help.' The words formed in Ibris's mind, and though he could not speak them, their import reached his unseen watchers, who wavered before his will. Then the contempt changed to an inarticulate but vivid menace.

In the Duke's chamber, Tarrian's yellow eyes opened suddenly and a low growl began in his throat. Both Aaken and Feranc knew that there would be no danger to them unless the Dream Finder was threatened in some way, but the wolf's actions were frightening and, involuntarily, the chancellor stepped back a pace, while the commander of the Duke's bodyguard focused narrow and alert eyes on the animal.

With a black anger, Ibris heaved on the goblet, his entire body tense with effort.

'Something's amiss.' Tarrian's voice, hesitant and uncertain, came into Antyr's head and echoed his own thoughts.

Then the goblet yielded and with a silent roar of victory

the Duke pulled it towards him. But it was not the goblet that had yielded. The whole table was being pulled over. Indeed, as he continued to pull, it seemed that the Duke's endeavours were moving the very floor he was standing on, for the air was suddenly filled with a terrible rumbling and, though he stood firm and solid, all else moved around him.

Triumphantly he held on to the goblet, though it was no longer a goblet and the table was no longer a table. Instead it was a great door decorated with a strange mobile design, and he was clasping a carved metal handle shaped like the head of some mythological horned animal of consummate ugliness.

Silence.

Ibris waited.

Antyr and Tarrian waited, their uneasiness growing. Something *was* amiss. For the first time since he had been an apprentice, Antyr wanted to flee the dream.

Aaken swallowed nervously as the hairs on Tarrian's back rose ominously, and his top lip wrinkled upwards to reveal flesh-rending teeth.

From behind the door came a . . . command? . . . a plea?

Ibris felt a powerful will setting his own aside and moving him to pull open the door. He hesitated. 'Only your great strength can do this,' came some courtier's allurement that both attracted and repelled him, but, as he scowled at this remark, the will had become his own and, tightening his grip on the glittering handle, he began to pull.

He felt rather than saw the door begin to open, and a sighing like a great rush of wind swirled around him; it was a mixture of relief and triumph. The shifting design became frenetic. A dark line appeared at the edge of the door as it moved but Ibris found himself struggling against some unseen resistance. Briefly he felt himself to be the pawn between two great forces, but it was of no import; he was committed.

With unbearable slowness the door opened, and the dark line at its edge deepened and spread, as if some great blackness were beginning to seep around it.

A spasm of panic – no, terror – suddenly seized him, tearing the breath from him.

Then a hand seized his wrist and pushed the door forward irresistibly.

The door slammed shut with an echoing boom, and the blackness vanished.

Ibris sat up sharply, wide awake. Antyr wrenched his hand away from the Duke's tightening trip, and Tarrian let out a soft, eerie howl.

As his cry died away into a distant whimper, a deep silence filled the room and the three figures became very still. Eventually Antyr said awkwardly, 'This was the dream you sought, sire?'

The Duke started a little at Antyr's voice, then he swung his legs round and stood up a little shakily, only to sit down again almost immediately. 'Yes, yes,' he said, his left hand rubbing his right wrist as if it had been injured in some way. 'You have your father's deftness. With time and discipline I suspect you could be even better than he.'

The remark was offhand, as though the Duke were saying something while his mind was on other, more important matters. Antyr, however, bowed his head slightly in acknowledgement; offhand or not, it was a rare compliment.

But the Duke's dream had unsettled him profoundly. Something had been dreadfully wrong about it and he wanted to be away from here. Duty held him for the moment however. 'Did you find what you were seeking, sire?' he asked.

The Duke turned and met the Dream Finder's still, night-eyed gaze unflinchingly. 'I'm not sure,' he said. 'Whose was the hand that closed the door?'

'Your own, sire,' Antyr answered simply.

Ibris nodded as if this answered some other question, then he lifted up his two hands and looked at them. 'My left defied my right?' he muttered.

An image of doubt, sire, Antyr was about to say, glibly. Nothing more. Merely a reflection of the difficult balancing of interests which must constantly beset you.

But though in many a lord it would have been so, here it was not, he knew. He had walked through countless nightmares, faced, and smiled at, all the demons and ogres that the human mind could invent, but the Duke's dream had had a . . . strangeness . . . in it that he had never known before. It had been as if the will that had sought the opening of the door had truly been from beyond the Duke. Not simply some 'mysterious presence' which was no more than a creation of the dreamer's guilt, but some separate, distinct entity. And seeking some unknowable end.

Suddenly he felt very afraid.

He needed a drink.

Tarrian's dismay and anger flooded through him but the Duke cut across the impending silent argument.

'Who else was there, Antyr?' he asked.

Antyr's throat dried. The Duke had ruled the city and its dominions for over forty years. Years full of battles, riots, plagues, factional quarrelling and plotting, civil and military upheavals of every form. Yet too they had been years full of achievement, with magnificent buildings rising above the city's walls, great works of scholarship, poetry, music, and paintings and sculptures, and . . .

Antyr looked down. Ibris had both survived and brought about these times. He was too complete and perceptive a man to have sought out a Dream Finder on some foolish whim.

At one with his Companion, a Dream Finder could not lie, but Antyr wished profoundly that the question had not been asked.

'I don't know, sire,' he said eventually.

'But you're afraid?' the Duke continued.

Antyr did not reply.

'You needn't answer,' the Duke said. 'I can smell your fear. Feel no shame about it. I . . .'

He stopped and lowered his eyes.

For a long moment he sat motionless, then he laid his hand briefly on Antyr's and stood up. 'Thank you, Petran's son,' he said. 'And you, Tarrian. You've done me good service tonight.' He gestured to Aaken and Feranc. 'See that he's duly paid and safely escorted home before you both retire.'

Then he was striding towards a nearby door, leaving Antyr scrambling to his feet and bowing awkwardly while trying to prevent his chair from falling over.

As he reached the door, Ibris turned. 'I may need you again,' he said curtly. 'Don't leave the city. And speak to no one of this visit.'

Antyr seemed to feel the walls and ceiling of the room closing about him like a prison. Shakily he bowed again.

When the Duke had left, Antyr turned round. Feranc had moved from the door and was close behind him.

Antyr jumped. 'I . . . I don't leave the city much anyway,' he stammered hastily, but the bodyguard's face showed no expression other than a flick of the eyes towards the approaching chancellor.

'Go with Lord Aaken for your fee,' he said flatly. 'Then

I'll have you escorted back home, unless you'd rather spend the rest of the night here.'

Antyr's every instinct was to flee. To get back to his own home, away from the lingering, persistent strangeness of the Duke's dream and the cold hardness of Feranc's presence.

'And to get back to that bottle,' came a scornful blast from Tarrian, though it was edged by doubt and uncertainty.

Antyr gathered up an angry denial, but it faded almost before he could form it. The sense of menace from outside that had touched the Duke's dream had been like that which, only a little while earlier, Tarrian had brought to him from his memory of the death of Petran.

'Yes . . . No . . . I . . .' Antyr faltered. 'I don't want anything to do with this. It's . . .'

His reply faded away. He had no choice. Independent of his feelings, if the Duke wanted him again then that was the end of the matter; he was not a man who could safely be gainsaid by a mere Dream Finder. Antyr's stomach turned over and for a moment he thought he was going to be sick again.

'I think perhaps you'd better stay here,' Aaken said, his voice concerned. 'You've had an even more disturbed night than the rest of us and you don't look very well at all.' Antyr hesitated. 'We'll find somewhere for you and some food and drink. It's a long way back to your empty house through this fog,' Aaken concluded.

Antyr nodded. He had the feeling that he was being manipulated, but Aaken was right. He was tired, and being marched through the gloomy streets had little appeal.

'Thank you, sir, I will stay, if I may,' he replied. 'And if it's no imposition, a little food would be appreciated, and perhaps a little ale . . . or wine . . .?'

A hand fell on his shoulder. 'Food, yes, but ale and wine, no, Dream Finder.' The voice was Feranc's and it too offered Antyr no choices. 'I know little about your strange . . . craft . . . Dream Finder, but I know enough to know that ale and wine will impair your skills severely and I have my duty to the Duke to ensure that he is served only by the most able.'

Briefly it occurred to Antyr to protest against this arbitrary prohibition; to stand on his rights as a free Guildsman. But even if Feranc's presence alone had not indicated the futility of such an attempt, he knew that the words 'Needs of the State', with their subtle combination of an appeal to his

57

loyalty and a threat of force if he did not respond appropriately, would end his rebellion with a single stroke.

He affected an indifference. 'Water will be excellent,' he said, with a weak smile, allowing Feranc to guide him to the door. Tarrian chuckled malevolently.

A little later, after a confusing trip through winding corridors and stairways, and a promise from Aaken that he would pay him, 'Tomorrow, without fail', Antyr found himself sitting alone on the edge of a bed, in a small, simply decorated room. On a small table in front of him was a bowl of hot, thick stew, a plate liberally covered with slices of meat and large chunks of bread, and a plain glass jug of water.

A dish of food had been brought for Tarrian also and, after a brief and noisy chase, he had successfully nosed it into a corner and was greedily devouring the contents.

Feranc had left them there with a cursory 'Good night', and the meal had appeared shortly afterwards, carried on a wooden tray by a bleary-eyed servant whose surly face clearly said, 'This is the Duke's palace, not an inn, you know!'

Any thought the man might have had about voicing such a comment however, vanished when Antyr and Tarrian, their eyes dark as night and cruel as a desert sun turned towards him.

For a while Antyr sat motionless, staring darkly at the jug, and toying uncertainly with a spoon, then the sound of Tarrian's furious eating stopped and a snout edged towards Antyr's bowl.

'I'll have that if you don't want it,' Tarrian said.

Antyr wanted to ask him why he had never told him that his father had been Dream Finder to the Duke, but he knew it would be to no avail.

'Does *nothing* stop you eating?' he asked instead.

'Nature of the beast,' Tarrian replied. 'We don't survive out there by dallying delicately over our prey. Every meal's our last. Have you finished?'

'No, damn it, I haven't started yet,' Antyr said crossly, picking up a piece of meat and throwing it over the wolf's head. Tarrian twisted round and caught the piece before it reached the floor. He swallowed it with a single gulp as he turned back in anticipation of more. His unbridled pleasure at this unexpected meal was infectious and, though not without some effort, Antyr made a start on the stew.

Despite the sour face of the servant who had brought it,

the stew was excellent, and after the first few hesitant mouthfuls, Antyr began to eat with some relish.

Gradually his dark mood gave way to a quiet litany of self-reproach, and a train of well-worn thoughts started to parade through his mind. He really should do something with himself; get some order into his life; stop his drinking, get more clients, start studying his craft again – his father *had* been highly regarded by his colleagues, and the skill was hereditary.

But now he seemed to be viewing the thoughts from a different vantage. Something had changed. It was as if the Duke's disturbing dream had shifted a great weight inside him which he had thought to be unmovable and now it was beginning to move like some slow avalanche.

His own words came back to him – it was a Dream Finder's duty – privilege, his father would say – to help and comfort people – the bewildered, the tormented. But the craft, in Serenstad at least, had been severely assailed by an unwitting alliance of medical practitioners, scientists and philosophers, all of whom had prospered and progressed under Ibris's tutelage. Antyr's father had been the mainstay of the Guild of Dream Finders, and his dignity and experience had done much to sustain the craft. But when he died, his successors proved to be timid and futile, and they had stood by, wringing their hands as their ancient craft had fallen in public esteem and degenerated towards charlatanism.

Young, grief-stricken and only partly trained, Antyr could not begin to fill the vacuum left by his father in the Guild and he found himself standing by, a bewildered and increasingly bitter spectator.

For a while after his father's death he had tended to the needs of his father's old clients. But these had gradually diminished in number; some had thoughtlessly died, but the majority had turned away from him, alienated by his increasingly unpleasant and disparaging manner. This same trait had also made it difficult for him to acquire new clients.

Now, sitting in this simple room in the Duke's palace, Antyr's view of his life changed. He saw now that he had *chosen* the path of bitterness and recrimination; he had *chosen* to watch the deterioration of his craft and to do nothing to stop it, while freely laying the blame on others.

His father would not have done that. He would have spoken

out as need arose and pitted his integrity against all mockery and scorn.

True, he was not his father, but the word, chosen, disturbed him. He realized, chillingly, that he was what he was through his *own* endeavours. He had not had the wit, the cynicism, to become rich by pandering to the whims and fancies of the wives of merchants and aristocrats, yet he had not had the courage to offer them his skills honestly and without fear.

Idly he picked up a piece of meat and held it out to Tarrian, but the wolf ignored it. Instead he sat down beside him and leaned heavily against his leg. Antyr felt the ancient, silent companionship of the pack close about him. He put his arm around the wolf in reply.

'Don't be too severe on yourself, few could have followed in your father's footsteps, and wiser than you have done worse with their lives,' Tarrian said, unexpectedly sympathetic.

Antyr nodded and patted the wolf. 'Is this just a late night and good food talking, dog?' he said.

'No,' Tarrian replied after a long pause. 'It's the Duke's dream. I think the masonry's starting to fall about you at last.'

His tone was both grim and regretful, and Antyr shivered. A final item entered his revelation: fear.

Even now he was reluctant to face it. But it was coming, he knew, with the inexorability of a flood tide. It would make itself felt regardless of his wishes or his actions. That distant alarm that he had always felt, even as an apprentice. That elusive sense of the deep mystery of the dreams that he so casually wandered through.

'We don't know what we are doing, how we do it, or what true end it serves,' he said softly to himself. 'We have too little humility, too little awe.' He looked down at Tarrian. 'We're children playing in the armoury, hedged about by points and edges we know nothing of. We don't even know how we came to be, do we, dog?' he continued stroking the wolf's head. 'You're not truly of your kind, nor am I of mine. We call the finding a skill, a craft, but it can only be learnt by those whose fathers possessed it.'

Tarrian did not reply.

Then slowly, Antyr concluded, '*Such ignorance can be nothing other than dangerous.*'

'Our lives are but dreams in the Great Dream,' the ancients of legend had said. But they had not been called Dream

Finders, they had been called the Dream Warriors, Adepts of the White Way, men of great power and wisdom, who guarded the spirits of men from . . .

From what? And from where?

Superstition, Antyr thought, out of habit. Tales for children, like tales of wizards and elves and dragons . . .

But . . .?

Fear burst inside him suddenly, and for a moment he lost control completely. His entire body trembled and shook violently. He had never known such fear; not even when he'd stood shield to shield with his fellows, facing the Bethlarii's cavalry charge at Herion. And there he had truly expected to die!

The sudden recollection was like cold water dashed in his face. Those pounding horses and screaming men turning only at the last moment in front of the hedge of spears. Then he had seen friends and strangers alike die all around him in the hail of arrows and spears from the Bethlarii infantry. People alive, talking, shouting but seconds before, suddenly, starkly, no more; their bodies like empty mansions; like things that had never been. Yet he had not been so frightened as he was now.

Why? he asked himself. What is more fearful than death?

No answer came, but in the silence, he realized that he was no longer trembling; that his fear was waning. Somehow, just as Tarrian would shake off the rain from his coat in a great flurrying cloud of spray, so his own convulsion seemed to have scattered his terror.

Just a bad night, he rationalized briefly. Too many things happening, too quickly.

Almost immediately, however, he denied this explanation with a rueful smile. Tarrian turned to look at him.

Masonry, Antyr thought. Inevitability.

'What's happened, Tarrian?' he asked, gently pushing the table to one side and laying back on the bed. 'What's frightening you that you won't tell me? What do you know?'

There was a long pause.

'I know that you're a finer Dream Finder than even your father,' came the reply eventually. 'I'm sorry I frightened you earlier, but it seemed to be the right thing to do.'

Antyr frowned, he had never heard Tarrian so uncertain, and the wolf's self-reproach was quite uncharacteristic.

'I probably asked for it,' he said. 'But don't avoid my

61

question. The Duke's dream was bland and ordinary yet it was full of threat and doom beyond any nightmare we've ever found. What . . .?'

'Go to sleep,' Tarrian said before Antyr could finish his question.

'What?' Antyr exclaimed in some irritation.

'Go to sleep,' Tarrian repeated. 'I'll keep watch. This day's been too long. We'll see what we think about all this tomorrow.'

Antyr opened his mouth to argue, but Tarrian shut him out. For a moment he considered opposing his Companion, but he knew it would be futile. Besides, Tarrian was right. Whatever was stirring within him it could not be dealt with while he was so tired.

He reached up and extinguished the single lamp that was illuminating the room, then lay back and closed his eyes. As he drifted into sleep, however, he was aware of Tarrian's presence, unusually alert and vigilant, prowling the fringes of his mind.

It seemed that he had scarcely drifted off, when he was awakened suddenly. A moving lamp came into focus in front of him, then its holder, a tall, hooded shadow, towering ominously over him.

Chapter 5

Antyr opened his mouth to cry out at the apparition, a mixture of nightmarish fantasies and wild fears of palace conspiracies flooding into his mind.

At the same time, his mind involuntarily cried out to his Companion. 'Tarrian!'

There was no reply.

He tried to sit up, but some force restrained him. More thoughts of palace conspiracies swirled around him. The food had been drugged. He had been taken silently to some lord's torture chamber to have the secrets of the Duke's dream torn from him . . .

No. This couldn't be true. There was the law. He was a Guildsman. He couldn't be arrested without warrant like some ruffian from the Moras, but . . .?

His thoughts faded away. The law of Serenstad was strong, but power and wealth were power and wealth.

Antyr tried to calm the turmoil in his mind by turning his attention to the dark figure above him.

The lamp swung to and fro as if it were being shaken by an unsteady breeze, but it did not illuminate its holder. Indeed it seemed to obscure the figure, almost to make it darker in some way.

And were there other shadows at its back?

Antyr felt a hand reaching out towards him.

He tried to cry out again, to demand of this strange visitor, 'Who are you? What do you want?' But no sound came.

Though his voice was bound, however, his mind remained free. 'Tarrian, Tarrian,' he cried out desperately. The figure hesitated and inclined its head to one side as if catching some unexpected sound. But still there was only silence.

Then Antyr became aware of a strange quality in the silence. It was absolute. That the figure made no sound was frightening in itself, but worse than that was the silence in his mind. There was nothing except his own increasingly frantic thoughts. Nothing. No sign of those faint stirrings that had marked the constant presence of Tarrian for as long as Antyr could remember, even when they had been far apart.

A chill struck at him. Such a silence could only mean that Tarrian was dead.

But how? Despite his long life among humans, Tarrian retained fully all his natural faculties; he was wild and cautious to his very heart. It couldn't be that he would be killed without at least a desperate cry. Was it perhaps some subtle poison in the food? A swift, unexpected sword stroke? Antyr recalled Ciarll Feranc reaching readily for his knife. And the City was not short of men and women skilled in killing.

The feeling of loneliness was fearful and appalling, and Antyr felt a terrible cry of fear and grief forming inside him.

But the cry could find no release, and Antyr began to tremble as it grew and grew.

The swaying lamp began to shake as if in sympathy, and the watching figure seemed to merge hesitantly into the shadows behind.

Antyr felt the unseen hand withdraw and in some way he knew he was no longer the focus of attention. The shadows shifted uneasily. Then deep inside him, in answer to his silent cry, he heard a faint sound like the frantic scrabbling of a tiny insect. And for the briefest instant he saw, somewhere, a tiny distant light, motionless and calm like the evening star, yet also moving and flickering, like bright sunshine on distant armour.

The image was gone almost before he could register it, but like some alchemist's trickery, its brief appearance irresistibly transformed the whole in the instant, and Antyr's grief and fear was suddenly transmuted into a boiling anger while his trembling body began to tear him free from whatever power held him.

The figure seemed to make a final effort to reach him, lurching forward sharply like a striking snake, but the shadows were drawing it away and the strange scrabbling was growing louder and more frenzied.

Then it seemed to him that for a moment he was at the heart of a great battlefield, one hand clutching a torn and bloodstained standard, the other a hacked and battered sword.

'*To me! To me!*'

His voice filled the universe, echoing and echoing, and with a final exhalation of loathing and hatred, the shadows were gone.

'Where were you? Where were you?' Tarrian's voice crashed over him, frantic and desperate. 'Where did you go?'

Antyr found himself still on the bed but staring now into the wolf's eyes, bright yellow and feral as if he had been dream-searching.

'What . . .?' he muttered, bewildered.

'Where did you go? What happened?' Tarrian repeated the questions, seizing Antyr's shirt in his mouth and shaking him violently. 'Are you all right . . .?'

Antyr reached out and put his arms about the wolf's neck both to stop him and for needed solace. He could feel the animal trembling, as he himself had trembled. And, he realized, he had never known his Companion so distraught, so out of control.

'I don't know,' he managed to say as slowly he recognized the palace room and remembered the events of the evening.

'Don't know? Don't know? Ye gods, man . . .' Tarrian's voice showed his relief, but was still full of a barely controlled hysteria.

'Please, Tarrian. I'm all right. I don't know what happened. Just give me a moment to gather my wits,' Antyr said, tightening his hold on his friend. 'Just a moment.'

Tarrian lay still briefly, then wriggled free and jumped down on to the floor.

Antyr struggled upright until he was sitting on the edge of the bed. A rectangle of dim grey light indicated a window he had not noticed when he first entered the room, and indicated also that it was dawn, or later. He sat motionless for several minutes with his head resting in his hands, then he looked up and stared into the watching wolf's eyes.

'I need a drink,' he said.

Tarrian's anger overwhelmed him. 'It's probably the drink that did this, you jackass,' he thundered. 'Eroded such enfeebled discipline as you have and left you defenceless against—' He stopped for a moment, unable to finish the sentence. 'In all the time I was with your father I never met anything like this – never! And your father ventured into regions where many others wouldn't go, I can tell you.'

Despite himself, Antyr responded in kind. 'I don't want to know,' he shouted out loud. 'All this is madness. What am I doing wandering about other people's dreams? Scrutinizing their fantasies like some quack priest peering into entrails. Hell knows what phantoms I've let into my own mind. I've had enough. I wash my hands of it all before I lose my mind. I'm—'

'Going into the country. Get myself a simple job on a farm somewhere, tending vines, cutting corn.' Tarrian completed his plaint for him with blistering scorn. 'Somewhere where there's peace and calm. Somewhere where I can get my throat cut by bandits—'

'Damn you, dog,' Antyr said through clenched teeth. 'Go back to your pack.'

A silence came between the two protagonists, such as can only exist between two old friends; sour and bitterly unpleasant.

Tarrian lay down and rested his head on his front paws. His eyes were still brilliant, and fixed resolutely on the Dream Finder. Antyr swung his legs back up on to the bed and lay down again to avoid the gaze.

'Tell me what happened,' Tarrian said simply, after a moment.

Antyr shook his head. He was about to swear at the wolf, but the brief explosion had been cathartic. 'I don't know,' he said resignedly. A spasm shook him and he wrapped his arms about himself. 'I don't know. But it was terrifying. We were apart. Truly apart. As if you'd been . . . killed. And there was someone here. A figure . . . with a lamp . . . and shadows at his back. Watching, waiting . . . trying to reach me . . . I . . .'

His voice faded and the silence descended again. Gradually the sounds of the awakening palace began to seep softly into the room.

He looked up and met Tarrian's gaze. 'It was like a dream,' he said, his voice flat, but fearful.

Tarrian did not reply, but his concern and denial flooded into Antyr's mind. Dream Finders did not dream; *could* not dream. Yet despite this response there was doubt also.

'You were gone . . . somewhere,' he said eventually. 'Your body was here, but your Dreamself was gone. Gone as if it had never existed. And all ways were closed to me. Like when your father died.'

The wolf's very quietness brought chills of fear to Antyr again.

'Do you really think I've brought this on myself?' he said, almost plaintively.

This time there was confusion in Tarrian's response: the

66

habitual anger that inevitably arose when Antyr's indiscipline was discussed, and a newer, deeper anxiety; a sense of the need to set old matters aside and to both give and receive companionship in the face of some unknown threat.

'I don't know,' Tarrian concluded soberly. 'Let the daylight in and then tell me *exactly* what happened . . . what you saw and felt.'

Antyr was surprised how unsteady he felt as he walked to the window to draw back the curtain. Nevertheless he was mildly expectant. He had a vague impression that behind it would lie some splendid view of the city, the palace being a high and dominating building. Instead, however, he found himself overlooking a small, enclosed chasm of walls, gloomy and lichen-streaked in the grey morning light that filtered down from a ragged skyline high above. Looking down, he saw a paved yard littered with random and ill-repaired outbuildings, their roofs shiny with the morning's dampness.

A small piece of the Moras district in the very heart of Ibris's palace, he thought wryly. The light, however, brought with it some optimism.

'Well, at least the fog's gone,' he said as he turned away from the window. 'And we've survived to greet another day.'

It was a phrase he had not used since he was last in the army. Tarrian, however, was indifferent. 'Tell,' he demanded.

It took Antyr only a few minutes to relate the events he had experienced but he found that the daylight did little to mitigate the deep alarm which he had felt and which was on the fringe of returning even as he recounted the tale.

'Well?' he asked when he had finished.

Tarrian had been silent during the telling, and now he offered no observations.

'Let's leave,' he said, standing up and stretching luxuriously. 'Let's get out into the country for a while. We both need to think.'

Antyr hesitated. 'Do you think we should?' he said. 'The Duke said we shouldn't leave the city.'

Tarrian was dismissive. 'He meant travelling abroad,' he said. 'As if we ever did. He won't mind us wandering the countryside for an hour or so.'

Antyr was unconvinced. 'I don't know,' he said. 'Perhaps we should tell someone.'

'Open the door, for pity's sake,' Tarrian said testily. 'After what's happened – whatever it was – I need room to move, and air to breathe. And you need . . . something . . . I don't know what. Exercise probably. Come on, no one's going to be bothered about us and we'll be back before noon.'

Antyr bowed to his friend's insistence and cautiously opened the door. He had half expected to find a guard standing there and was uncertain whether to feel relieved or disappointed to find the corridor deserted.

'I told you no one would be bothered,' Tarrian declared in offhand triumph. 'Come on.'

Antyr, however, had no idea where he was or how to go about finding his way out.

'You should pay more attention,' Tarrian said impatiently. 'It's this way. Just follow your nose.'

They had no difficulty in leaving the palace. Tarrian guided them unerringly through a bewildering maze of corridors, hallways and staircases, and such people as they met paid them little heed, seeming intent on tasks of their own. Indeed, as they passed through the palace gate, some of the guards acknowledged them. Their escort from the previous night, Antyr presumed.

The weather was cold and damp, with a residual taint of the night's fog still lingering, making the grey sunless sky yellowish. The streets too bore the glistening signs of the fog and were virtually deserted except for the Torchlighters' apprentices dutifully extinguishing the public torches. A forest of ragged black pillars of smoke rose up like slender supports to the greyness above.

Tarrian trotted on relentlessly through the waking city, occasionally stopping to wait for Antyr, but making his impatience quite clear.

Eventually they reached the great Norstseren Gate. As it was still early in the day, the main gate was closed except for a wicket just large enough to admit a horse. This had been opened to allow in those travellers who had been benighted outside. Later in the day there would be carts and caravans and innumerable travellers arriving and leaving, and both leaves of the gate would be thrown wide in welcome.

'Tarrian taking you for some exercise,' guffawed one of the guards, echoing the wolf's own comment, as they passed through the wicket into the shelter of the broad arch of the gate. Antyr gave a self-conscious shrug, disoriented for the moment by the surge of disapproval that came up from Tarrian.

'One of your drinking cronies, I suppose,' he said scornfully.

The guard came over to them and gave Antyr a look of knowing confidentiality. 'Make sure you see the Exactor,' he said softly through barely moving lips. 'He's new and a real son of a whore. He'd Gate Tax his mother for the mud she brought back on her shoes.' He terminated the advice with a broad wink.

Antyr nodded his thanks, at the same time throwing a small jibe at Tarrian. 'You see. My cronies sometimes prove useful. You'd be less than pleased if I'd to spend half the day proving you were mine when we came back, wouldn't you?'

'Yours?' Tarrian replied with withering disdain. 'You people are unbelievable.' Then, despite his preoccupation, a small flood of righteous, very human, anger burst out. 'And you're as stupid as you're barbarous. Exactors! Who in their right mind would pay taxes to pay for wars to make more money to pay more taxes. . .?' The brief diatribe ended in an incoherent snarl.

Antyr grunted. 'Yes, yes,' he said dismissively, walking across to the small enclosure that housed the Gate Exactor. 'You're right. You've said it all before and your logic's impeccable. I know exactly where we fit into your scheme of things. In the meantime, a little less philosophy and a little more pragmatism, please. Just make sure this one remembers you for when we come back if you want to get home before sunset.'

Their brief, familiar skirmish ended, the two became trusted conspirators again and Tarrian bounded into the enclosure.

Antyr, several paces behind, heard the startled cry from within and as he stepped through the door he beamed his friendliest smile.

Tarrian had his feet on the collecting table and was leaning forward and panting dubiously into the face of a wide-eyed official who was sitting motionless, his red cap of office incongruously askew.

'We'll be back before sunset,' Antyr said heartily. 'No goods in or out.' The Exactor's eyes flicked an appeal for rescue which Antyr wilfully misconstrued as an acknowledgement and, with a friendly wave, he turned and left. Tarrian stopped panting and, craning forward a little further, abruptly licked the Exactor's face wetly, before dropping back on to the floor and following Antyr.

Outside the Norstseren Gate, Antyr and Tarrian made their way through the tents and temporary dwellings that were always clustered there. Known as 'The Village' by the residents of Serenstad, this strange, ever-changing community consisted of all manner of people drawn from all manner of distant places by the fame and splendour of Ibris's city. Merchants, scholars, entertainers, travellers, seekers after fame and fortune, seekers after anonymity; all were there from time to time.

It was often a colourful and exciting place, but today the cold dampness of the morning following on the night's dank fog gave the place a sodden, down-at-heel appearance and such gaudy signs as there were looked glumly futile while streams of pennants and buntings hung listless and unmoving like some weary fisherman's unsold catch.

For a little while, Antyr and Tarrian walked on in the self-satisfied glow of the small mischief they had wrought on the Gate Exactor, but the only signs of life they encountered were four dour-faced riders, and as the mournful atmosphere of the Village gradually weighed in upon them, the strange events of the night soon rose to dominate their thoughts again.

'Where are we going, Tarrian?' Antyr asked eventually, some time after they had left the Village.

Tarrian started from some silent reverie. 'Er . . . west,' he said absently, as if he had only just thought about it.

'West,' Antyr echoed neutrally. 'To the cliffs, I suppose?'

There was another pause before Tarrian replied vaguely, 'Yes . . . yes.'

Serenstad was built by the river Seren in a lush and fertile valley, but the practical difficulties of building in the soft valley soil and the incessant need to maintain defences against many enemies had led successive rulers to expand the city up the side of the valley until, in the west, it had reached a ridge which dropped away sharply in precipitous cliffs and afforded the city at least one boundary that needed little or no defence.

Antyr offered no comment. There was little point. Tarrian needed to walk, needed to think, needed to do whatever it was a wolf did when it was burdened with human follies and happenings that ran contrary to everything it had ever known.

It would be a long walk, and steep at the end where the city's walls began to dwindle as they merged into the rising rocks.

Antyr felt reluctance dragging at his feet like soft dune sand as his long-held doubts about his calling surfaced again. What was he doing searching the Duke's dreams? Keeping the company of the likes of Aaken Uhr Candessa and Ciarll Feranc? And what was he doing, following Tarrian on some chilly and pointless ramble around the city? He knew that Tarrian was not listening to his thoughts but, fearing the wolf's acid responses, he tried to dismiss his fears and the longings he had for some other, less . . . bizarre, calling.

But even as the familiar thoughts emerged again, they changed. He did not long for some other calling. He longed for *any* other calling. Deeply and profoundly. He longed to be free of the burden of his gift, his talent.

The intensity of the feeling made him stop.

'How are you burdened?'

Tarrian's voice made Antyr start. 'I . . . I . . . didn't know you were—' he began awkwardly.

'Listening?' Tarrian finished the sentence. 'I wasn't. I was elsewhere. But you called me back.'

'I don't understand,' Antyr said.

'Nor I,' Tarrian replied simply, then he began walking again, keeping his usual station several paces ahead of Antyr as is the way with pack leaders.

Antyr's thoughts reached out to question him, but there was no response; Tarrian was 'elsewhere' again.

They continued their walk, each preoccupied with his own thoughts and largely oblivious to both the terrain and the dismal weather. When Antyr finally looked about him he was surprised. He had not realized that they had walked so far or so high, though, almost immediately, his legs began to ache.

From where they were, the view could be breathtaking. To the east, the sweep of the city walls down into the rich greens of the valley, and the silver thread of the river Seren winding south through the undulating countryside on its way down to the port of Farlan and the wide ocean. While, to the west, stood the dark, imposing rock-face of the neighbouring valley, a fitting partner to that which formed the western boundary of Serenstad.

Today, however, the winter mist hid not only the horizon but most of the valley. Antyr looked up at the dark bulk of

71

the city's outer wall rising above him in response to the steepening slope of the rocks. It was solid and grim in the greyness. Last night he had thought it a prison, but now it seemed to assume once more the mantle of protector, standing steadfast and immovable, taking upon itself the anger and hatred of the enemies of the city.

The anger and hatred of enemies. The words resonated around Antyr's mind.

Enemies. Whose enemies? What enemies?

The questions came unbidden, and had an insistence about them that made Antyr frown. He had no interest whatsoever in the complex and convoluted politics of Serenstad and its subject domains, except in so far as he had been obliged to serve in the army when younger to defend its interests or to punish some upstart town or city that was getting above itself.

But the questions hung in his mind, almost defiantly. Antyr looked up at the wall again. It glowered back at him, like a stern matriarch, allowing him no relief.

Why should he be asking himself such questions here, now? It was not as if it were a matter that needed any subtle debate. There was always opposition to Ibris's rule from one faction or another, but, in its more violent forms, it almost always stemmed from the agitations of the Bethlarii, the citizens of Bethlar, several days' ride to the north-west.

A severe, warlike people, they had once dominated almost the whole of the land south of the northern mountains and even now they held sway over most of the cities to the north and west.

The problem with the Bethlarii was that they still claimed dominion over the whole land, declaring, perhaps rightly, that they were the direct descendants of the original settlers, the sea peoples who had arrived to drive out the barbarian tribes that had then occupied it.

The Serens, they said, were usurping newcomers, mere merchants and artisans, who should bow the knee before the warrior founders of the land.

But, as every Serens knew, the true hatred of the Bethlarii stemmed from their black, misanthropic bigotry and was in reality for what they saw as the Serens' easy, hedonistic ways and the fact that the despised merchants and artisans had brought such wealth and power to Serenstad, both from their efforts at home and their trading abroad, that one by one Bethlar's subject cities had changed their allegiance.

Whatever the truth of the matter, there had always been animosity between the two cities and their allies, sometimes culminating in savage and bitter fighting. The Bethlarii, however, had found that the effete and degenerate Serens could make war well enough when need arose and could also afford to buy a leavening of mercenary soldiers to stiffen their lines and train their people.

It was a point of some dark amusement to the Serens that while the Bethlarii scorned such a practice, they were obliged eventually to resort to it themselves.

Now, however, since Ibris had negotiated the Treaty following the siege of Viernce, an uneasy stability existed in the land. The Serens continued to despise the Bethlarii for their grim military ways, their dismal communal houses, their stone-faced mindless discipline, and their ghastly priesthood with its worship of the warrior god, Ar-Hyrdyn, to the exclusion of all others. And the Bethlarii continued to despise the Serens, ostensibly for what they considered to be their corruption and decadence, but in reality for their continuing and growing economic success and the power that it brought.

The stability, however, was dynamic, and within the loose framework of the Treaty, there was a constant swirl of plotting and counter-plotting, jostling for this advantage or that, bribing, coercing; individuals, factions, whole cities; both sides manoeuvring to gain more power and influence to protect themselves from the other.

Antyr understood enough of the political realities of the land to know that such matters were beyond rational analysis, and that though he might despair at the folly of it all at times, he had neither the wealth nor the power to change it.

True, like any other Guildsman, he could run for office in the Gythrin-Dy which, with the Sened, advised the Duke, but that seemed to be but the same folly writ small, with dozens of factions shifting and changing allegiances, and treachery and mistrust being the stock in trade.

It was true also that his position of disdain for the political institutions of the city could equally not stand rational analysis while he chose to avoid participating in them, but that was something he avoided considering, along with the majority of the Serens. It was sufficient for him that he pursued his calling, paid his taxes, where unavoidable, and generally conducted himself within the law of the city.

Why then should he find himself wandering the western

edge of the city, on a damp and dismal day, pondering about its enemies? Yet he was; for the word, enemies, not only persisted in his thoughts but seemed to carry a different meaning, a meaning that hovered at the edges of his awareness like some mysterious shadow which disappeared when stared at directly.

Further reverie, however, was prevented by their arrival at the end of their journey; the western cliffs, the Aphron Dennai, Aphron's stairway, named after the tyrannical Duke Aphron whose favourite pastime was to have people hurled over them on to the shattered pinnacles below, until one day the people rebelled and allowed him a closer view of the spectacle.

Possibly climbable by the foolhardy, but not quickly and certainly not by many, the Aphron Dennai formed the city's most secure boundary.

Tarrian jumped up on to an overhanging rock and peered over the edge. Antyr contented himself with staying a comfortable distance back from the edge.

The two stood silent for some time, the only intrusion being the faint sounds of distant streams flowing down to the valley below. Then, from above, a throaty croak reached them. Tarrian looked up. Two ravens were circling high above.

'I knew a raven once,' he said distantly.

'What?' Antyr exclaimed irritably at this seeming irrelevance.

'Never mind,' Tarrian replied softly. 'It was a long time ago.'

Antyr let out an exasperated sigh. 'What are we doing here, Tarrian?' he said. 'My feet are soaking, and I'm frozen half to death. I need hardly remind you that this was your idea. I'd have been quite happy to stay in the palace.' He paused, brought to earth briefly. 'Which reminds me, Aaken never paid us for last night's work.'

He looked out across the great open cauldron of space that the cliffs bounded, and then up at the sky.

'And it's going to start raining soon, I'll swear. We're going to get soaked. And it wouldn't surprise me to find the palace guards waiting for us when we get back. The Duke *did* say—'

'For pity's sake, be quiet,' Tarrian's voice was like an axe blow. Antyr was used to stern words from his Companion, but there was a quality in the rebuke that he had never heard

74

before and it left him too stunned to muster an immediate reply.

'We've got worse problems than your footling discomfort and an unpaid fee to contend with,' Tarrian went on. 'Or for that matter, even Duke Ibris's displeasure.'

Under other circumstances, Antyr would have begged to differ on this last point, but Tarrian, alone on the jutting rock, silhouetted against the grey sky, was a creature in complete harmony with his element and he spoke with such command that it might have been the mountain itself speaking.

Antyr opened his mouth to reply, but no sound came.

'Something's amiss,' Tarrian said, using again the words he had used in Ibris's dream. 'There was a wrongness in the Duke's dream. A profound wrongness.' He paused, then, as if he were speaking something that he had already repeated countless times, 'There *were* others there.'

Antyr began to shake his head as if the act would scatter Tarrian's words before they reached him. 'I don't want to discuss it,' he said petulantly. 'I don't want to discuss it. There was nothing wrong. It was just our imagination. I was tired and shaken and not at my best – being marched through the streets at that time – and under escort. And don't forget, we . . . I . . . have never seen the dreams of a man like that. He's a great leader, a warlord, a statesman. His dreams are bound to be unusual. We misunderstood, that's all. How *could* there be anyone else in a dream? Let's get back home . . . get warm . . . perhaps go to the palace . . . get our fee . . . and . . .'

Tarrian ignored him, as if he were just another babbling stream.

'There were others there,' he said again, more surely. 'Others with . . . skills . . . that I can't begin to understand. Skills that brought them looking for you and that snatched you away from my protection . . .'

His voice tailed off into bewilderment.

'Tarrian, stop this,' Antyr's mind was beginning to reel. 'I've told you, I don't want to discuss *any* of this. It was a long, strange day and . . .' He waved his hands in submissive concession. 'Perhaps you're right . . . in fact you *are* right . . . I've been drinking too much, not attending to my affairs properly. It's just caught up with us, that's all. I'll really get to grips with things when we get back this time. Honestly.

Start looking after myself better . . . getting us some steady clients . . .'

'Antyr!' Again Tarrian's voice abruptly stopped the Dream Finder's increasingly frantic rambling. 'Stop it. Stop it, for pity's sake. I'm trying to think. Trying to make some sense of what's happened . . . what's happening. I'm frightened. I need your help, I don't need a recital of your well-worn promises to improve yourself.'

Suddenly, the all-too-human reproaches with which Tarrian was filling Antyr's mind were gone, and the wolf threw back his head and howled.

Antyr listened, wide-eyed and fearful. The song rose and fell and though Antyr understood none of it, he felt its poignant intensity.

When it was finished, Tarrian was silent for a long time, his head bowed. From out of the greyness before them came no reply.

'You see,' he said eventually. 'My pack is gone. Gone to other hills, to other valleys. My mates have other sires. My cubs too are grown and gone. Do you think you're alone in your desire to be other than you are? Do you think I'd tolerate this life, this appalling stench of humanity, if I had a choice?'

Antyr winced at the bitterness and anger in Tarrian's voice.

The words, I'm sorry, formed in his mind but he did not speak them. They would have seemed like a wilful insult in the face of Tarrian's distress.

Instead he walked out on to the overhanging rock and sat down beside him.

'No one binds you, old friend,' he said gently.

'You bind me, Dream Finder,' the wolf replied. 'You bind me. As did your father before you. Through none of our own choosing, we bind each other. It's the nature of our calling, and it's beyond our changing. I understand your pain. I really do, your pain is mine. But it comes only from your struggle to avoid the truth and will stop only when you accept it.'

'I don't understand,' Antyr said after a long silence.

'Yes, you do,' Tarrian replied. 'You understand more than you realize.' His voice softened. 'Perhaps your pain is partly my fault. Perhaps I tried to make you into the Dream Finder that your father was when I should have stood and watched you more carefully. Guided you more subtly. Not tried to force you into the ancient ways of our craft just because that was the way it had always been done. Perhaps I stood in the light that I was supposed to show you.'

Antyr shook his head. The spirit of Tarrian's song still seemed to possess him. He reached out to console the animal in some way. 'No. You did as my father bid you, and you did it well. I'm what I made myself, not what you made. If it's me that binds you, then I release you. Go back to your own kind where you'll be happy. I'm no true Dream Finder nor have I any wish to be.'

Even as he tried to speak the words sincerely, he heard their falseness.

Tarrian turned and looked at him.

'You have no choice,' he said. 'You *are* a Dream Finder. What I've never told you is that you have an ability far beyond any that I've ever known. Even your father would have been dwarfed by you.'

Antyr turned away from the compassion and pain that filled the wolf's thoughts.

Tarrian continued. 'I think that's why I get so angry with you. I doubt my ability to guide you as I should. I'm frightened I might be either a spectator, impotently watching you destroy yourself, or your inadvertent destroyer.'

Antyr shook his head slowly, but Tarrian's will would allow him no denial.

'Why are you saying these things?' he managed eventually.

'Because I don't know what else to do,' Tarrian replied unexpectedly. 'Something's wrong. You know it as well as I do. Something . . . someone . . . assailed the Duke last night, and then assailed you. You must begin to accept what you are and stop trying to be something else or . . .'

'Or what?'

'Or we will be doomed, destroyed, and others with us. They will come again. You stand between them and the Duke.'

'They? Who . . .?' Antyr made a last attempt to escape. 'How can you know this?' Antyr asked angrily.

'I know it the way you know it, but you won't listen to yourself,' Tarrian replied softly, then he stood up and began walking back down the rocks. 'Antyr, you didn't stand solid in that pike wall against the Bethlarii cavalry, shield to shield with your fellows, by pretending you were somewhere else. You saw your enemy for who they were and you faced them squarely. This is no different. An enemy you won't face will outflank and encircle you, and then crush you utterly.'

'But . . .?'

'I need to run,' Tarrian said, his voice still quiet, but almost desperate. 'Go home. Wait for me. I'll be back later.'

And then he was gone, his dark bobbing form soon lost amid the scattered rocks.

As he began to run, his voice sounded distantly in Antyr's mind. 'You have two enemies, Antyr. Yourself and whoever is trying to destroy the Duke. Take up your spear and shield against both. Defend yourself. I'll be with you.'

Antyr stood up and stared after him. Tarrian's words had carried him back to that fearful battlefield; the stomach-wrenching waiting, as the enemy marched to and fro, manoeuvring and feinting, then the screaming terror when the thundering charge came, when only each instant existed and all you had to do was hold; hold at any cost; for yourself, for all the others around you.

'Hold your ground and you're safe,' had been the constant cry in training. 'Ever see a horse daft enough to run on to a pike?' Uncertain laughter. 'And after that, it's just men. Ugly, I'll admit, but I can see uglier standing here. Remember your drills, keep together. And be angry not frightened. They started this. They're the enemy.'

Antyr shivered violently, though whether from fear or cold he could not have said. He had been frightened – and angry. And he had held. And survived. Faced the enemy, steel for steel, arrow for arrow. Faced them and prevailed.

Face the enemy.

He shivered again, then folding his damp cloak about him he set off down the rocks towards the pathway that would take him back to the Norstseren Gate.

Chapter 6

Nefron examined herself thoughtfully in the mirror. Her long black hair was as full as ever, and pulled back just enough to display the elegant bone structure of her face. Her complexion was unblemished and, though pale, was not pallid. A lingering touch from her long hands confirmed that her skin was as soft as it looked. She nodded in approval. Though she affected to despise such vanities, Nefron was well pleased with her appearance. It would serve her well as a weapon for some time to come yet.

In fact, she decided, her narrow, finely drawn face was in many ways more handsome than it had been those – what was it? – thirty-six years ago, when she had married Ibris.

Sixteen years old she had been then. And beautiful. But with a blandness about her, a naivety. She was a foolish consort for a powerful, worldly man almost twice her age. A wiser man would have passed her by. Now both she and her face were far more interesting.

The memory of her early self made her lip curl into a withering sneer. What Nefron never truly saw in her mirror was that sneer and the fine lines about her eyes that highlighted their searching, scheming gaze.

Turning from her inspection she looked again at the letter lying on the table. The arrival of a letter was an unusual event for Nefron as she gained most of her information by word of mouth. It was a necessary discipline for her, developed over many years. Written messages could be lost, forged, copied, held in evidence against her. They had little to commend them. There were, however, one or two of her most trusted 'allies', as she called her spies, who could not safely seek her ear at any time and for whom the coded letter was the only way. This was one such. Her sneer became a mildly triumphant smile. It was always a source of satisfaction to her when one of her eyes and ears in Ibris's palace brought her something that the Duke wished to be kept secret.

The contents of the letter, however, were puzzling and, for a little while, she thought she had misinterpreted it. Ibris consulting a Dream Finder? She shook her head pensively.

Somewhere in her memory lay a faint recollection that Ibris had used Dream Finders in his youth, but he had certainly not done so in all the time they had been together. Nor since, as far as she was aware. And she was aware of most of the things in the palace that Ibris did.

And who was it he had consulted? Antyr. She mouthed the name silently, testing it. It was quite unfamiliar. Whoever he was he wasn't one of the popular, successful Dream Finders. What was Ibris up to? Whether it was something or nothing, she must know about it. It would inevitably come in useful eventually. She would have someone inquire of the Guild who this unexpected adviser to her Lord and erstwhile husband might be.

A soft knock on the door ended her consideration.

'Come in,' she said, laying the letter down and tapping it thoughtfully with her long fingers.

It was her maid with another letter. Nefron frowned. Two letters in one day. Was this a scheme by Ibris to incriminate her in some way? To lay a false plot and then threaten to expose her to the Sened? Had one of her spies been discovered and turned against her? It wouldn't be the first time, and Ibris was always seeking opportunities to restrict her freedom even further. Her eyes narrowed as she took the letter from the maid.

It bore the seal of the Guild of Physicians. Nefron could not forbear raising an eyebrow in surprise.

'Who delivered this, Maara?' she asked as she scrutinized the seal carefully.

'It was Dirkel, lady, physician Drayner's servant,' the woman replied. 'I wouldn't have taken it otherwise.'

Nefron nodded approvingly and dismissed her. Maara was loyal to her beyond doubt and almost as vigilant as she herself in guarding her interests.

Drayner! Nefron's lips parted to show her teeth as she broke open the letter and unfolded it. What could Ibris's incorruptible leech want with her?

The letter, however, was unequivocal to the point of bluntness about that.

'My lady,' it began. 'You must speak with your son, the Lord Menedrion.' Must! Nefron registered darkly.

Last night he almost killed a young girl – one of the servants' daughters. This is not his way, as you know.

80

He will not see me, and his servants say that though he seems well in his body, he is in some way distracted. From what I hear in their words I am deeply concerned and I ask you to intervene because I sense the need for your particular affection to calm him. Should the incident reach the Gythrin-Dy, as well it might, and the Lord appear in a distressed condition, then great harm may ensue. I remain your respected servant, Eron Drayner.

Nefron hissed an oath of disbelief under her breath. She turned the letter over as if looking for some sign that it was false, but the seal was indisputably that of the Physicians' Guild, and in any case the writing and style were unmistakably Drayner's.

What in thunder had Menedrion done? She read the letter again: 'almost killed a young girl . . . not his way . . .'

Not his way, she echoed to herself. No it wasn't, she agreed. Menedrion was a physically dangerous man who had killed willingly and often both in battles and in brawls, and, when he was drunk, it was a commonplace for him to beat servants and even innocent citizens who might inadvertently cross him. He was also a lecher and utterly unscrupulous in his use of women. But the two cruelties had never come together before. Despite his callousness, his women returned to him and pronounced him a gentle and thoughtful lover.

Nefron scowled. She had her elder son clearly marked as a brute and she always found the idea of his being gentle and thoughtful extraordinarily amusing in its incongruity. His father certainly hadn't been, but then, neither had she. Now, however, the humour rose unwanted, to mingle with serious concerns, and the disturbance angered her.

'. . . distracted . . .' the letter said. Did he mean mad? No, had Drayner meant mad he would have said mad.

With an effort Nefron sat down on a long settle by the window and forced herself to read the letter again, slowly and carefully. The grey morning light fell coldly on the paper and quietened her. She could see no subtle plot beneath it all, nor did she sense any danger. There was nothing in the letter that could not be brought before the Duke himself. Only a concern for a patient and for the harm to the city that Menedrion's strange behaviour might cause should it become too public.

Drayner knew well enough that though bitter differences

lay between the Duke and his wife, these were concerned predominantly with the succession to the rule of Serenstad and its dominions and no benefit lay to anyone, except perhaps the Bethlarii, if some scandal involving the Duke's eldest son were to undermine confidence in the future. And he would not have written had it not been a truly serious matter.

For a moment, it occurred to Nefron that if there were more like Drayner in public affairs, then much of the factional and family quarrelling that bedevilled them would stop. The thought barely received an acknowledgement, however. Drayner could afford to be above it all. All he had to do was mend cracked heads and gashes. Greedy merchants, scheming, envious relatives, malcontented citizens, power-hungry lords and Guild Leaders were a different matter by far.

Then a genuine spark of motherly concern rose within her. Her little boy was ill. Abruptly she was by his cot again, next to her concerned Duke, bathing a fevered brow, and hanging on to Drayner's confident reassurances. 'Just a childish illness, there's nothing to fear. He's a strong boy, he'll be well again in a day or two. Don't worry.'

The memory and its attendant emotions caught her unawares and she raised her hand to her throat as had been her way in those days when she was anxious. Then, catching sight of herself in the mirror she straightened up and, slightly embarrassed, called to her maid.

'Have the Lord Menedrion come to me straight away,' she said imperiously as the woman entered. Maara's mouth opened as if to question the order, but seeing her mistress's demeanour she remained silent. 'I must see him now, no matter what he's doing, do you understand? Make sure that the message is clear.'

Maara bowed and left rapidly.

Since Ibris had confined Nefron to her old family palace, the Erin-Mal, he had allowed no one to visit her without his express permission except their sons, Menedrion and Goran. It had been a risk, but he had had little alternative. The effective imprisonment of his wife, the daughter of one of the city's most powerful Senedwr, some thirteen years previously had caused a great deal of political unrest, which assurances that 'The Lady Nefron has been advised by her physicians to retire from public life' did little to allay. To have denied her 'the comfort and solace of her children', as her supporters pleaded on her behalf, would have been to court disaster.

Ibris conceded all such matters at that time with a splendid public grace and a very ill private one.

'The bitch is lucky I haven't had her hanged,' he declaimed to his immediate advisers on more than one occasion. 'She can thank her father for that. I need him too much.'

On their last meeting, however, he had been unequivocal. 'Father or no, Nefron. If I catch one whisper of you or your followers plotting against Arwain again, you can look to a pillow over your face one night.'

Nefron had blanched at the sight of her husband's rage, as many a fighting man would have done, but she had held his gaze and her demeanour. 'I don't deny that I'd have rejoiced if those assassins had been successful,' she replied viciously. 'But if you think it was I who hired them to kill my sister's precious bastard, then you're wrong, and you know it. If you'd an ounce of proof you'd drag me through the courts regardless of my father and family just to have done with me, wouldn't you, great Duke?' Then she looked at him enigmatically. 'What a pity all the assassins were killed,' she added.

Ibris's eyes blazed. 'Cling to your solitary thread of good fortune, Nefron,' he said. 'One day . . . One day . . .' The sentence faded impotently.

Nefron picked it up. 'One day, *our* son will be the Duke of Serenstad. Duke Menedrion will rule in your wake. You'll have no choice but to decree it sooner or later. And should anything befall him before then, whatever the cause, I'll see the spawn of your adultery in hell, though you throw me from the Aphron Dennai.'

'Don't tempt me, woman,' Ibris retorted furiously.

Nefron laughed. The cruel taunting laughter that only a lover can inflict.

'Tempt you, my love?' she said in mock allurement. 'Didn't you know that *none* of my insatiable sister's *innumerable* lovers was worth tempting.'

Ibris strode forward, his hand raised. Nefron's face twitched involuntarily in anticipation of the blow, but apart from that she did not flinch.

For a long moment, they had looked into one another's eyes, then Ibris had lowered his hand and, without speaking again, turned and left.

83

The quiet closing of the door behind him had unexpectedly struck Nefron to her heart and, despite herself, she had sent a silent oath after him as she wiped tears from her eyes.

Now she had few tears left.

Menedrion was in a foul mood when he eventually arrived, bursting into his mother's room virtually unannounced.

'Mother! What the devil . . .?'

Nefron casually raised a hand to still his thunderous approach and, looking past him, she smiled at the indignant and flustered Maara who had attempted to escort him into the room with due decorum and who had been swept aside for her pains.

'You may leave us, Maara,' she said. 'I apologize for my son's hastiness. He's unused to the company of ladies of refinement. Oh, and please thank whoever carried my message for their speed.'

Mollified, Maara bowed and left, and Nefron turned her attention to her son.

'I'll thank you to have a little more regard for my servants, Irfan,' she said in mild reproach as she offered her cheek for a kiss. 'Heaven knows, I've few enough that I can trust these days.'

Menedrion bent forward and, unclenching his teeth, just managed to kiss his mother without growling.

'Mother—' he began again, purposefully.

Nefron waved a silencing finger in front of him. 'Let me look at you,' she said, reaching up and brushing a maternal hand over his tunic. 'I haven't seen you for weeks and weeks.'

'You said, ''Don't come so often,'' the last time we met,' Menedrion protested immediately in mitigation.

'There, there,' Nefron said, irrelevantly, at the same time taking his arm. 'Sit down, you're too big for my little room.'

Menedrion cast a brief, ironic glance at the large, ornate receiving room, then followed the prompting of his mother's hand like a convalescing invalid.

Nefron sat down in front of him and looked at him earnestly.

'Tell me exactly what happened last night,' she said briskly, just as he opened his mouth to speak again.

The question left him gaping as he looked into his mother's wide, inquiring eyes.

There was a flicker of something in his face that startled

84

Nefron, but she showed no outward sign other than intensifying her penetrating gaze.

Menedrion seemed to chew around the possibility of a denial for a moment, then bluntly said, 'Why?'

'Because I need to know,' Nefron said in a tone that would brook no debate. 'I know that you nearly killed one of your women. What I want to know is, why?'

Again Menedrion seemed briefly to consider denying the charge, but suddenly his face distorted with anger and, pushing his chair back, he stood up. 'Who told you this?' he shouted. 'If it was that—'

'Sit down,' Nefron demanded before Menedrion could outline his vengeance. He hesitated.

'Sit down!' his mother repeated forcefully, looking up at him but speaking directly to the knees of the child she had reared. They bent in compliance.

Seated again, and momentarily quelled, Menedrion leaned forward and affected to be examining his boots. 'Never mind who told me,' Nefron continued, addressing the top of his head. 'Suffice it that I know. And if I know, then others will. And if others know then it might well come to the ears of the Gythrin-Dy . . .'

Menedrion echoed the name with a dismissive snarl.

A brief look of angry frustration passed over Nefron's face. 'I despair of you sometimes, Irfan. The Gythrin-Dy is not the Sened. They're jumped-up traders and Guildsmen full of their own importance. Always anxious to chip away at the authority of the great merchant houses and the lords. Even your father has difficulties getting things quietly set aside there. If they catch wind of this there are those who'll gladly call for your father to punish you in some way, and some who'd speak to have you prosecuted.'

Menedrion looked up, his face a mixture of alarm and disbelief. 'They don't have the authority,' he said uncertainly.

'No,' Nefron confirmed. 'They don't. But they're free to speak and they have money and the public ear. And if this blows into a scandal then you'll soon find the mob who acclaimed your battle successes will be howling for your head, and there's precious little anyone can do if that happens.'

She paused. Even Menedrion knew the power of the mob, but he did not seem to be listening.

'Don't you understand?' Nefron ploughed on, her eyes narrowing and her tone sharpening. 'You could end up being banished to one of the islands for a year or more and the succession denied you forever. Arwain would rule in your stead.' She could see that no response would be forthcoming so she drove her final words in like a lance. 'Now *what* happened?'

Physically, Menedrion was his father's son. Slightly shorter but equally powerfully built, he was a brave man and had a commanding presence. There, however, the resemblance ended, for Menedrion did not have his father's innate and subtle understanding of people, placing his faith instead in his ability to use force and bluster to deal with most problems. He had many staunch and loyal allies, but on the whole, his wild behaviour had made his popularity brittle and uncertain.

A phrase that Aaken Uhr Candessa had once used about Menedrion came to Nefron now as she waited for some response. 'The Duke could hang a thousand and be cheered by their friends and relatives as he did it. Menedrion could get himself hanged for kicking a cat.'

It was not a statement that Nefron could wholeheartedly deny as much as she would have liked to. She was thus prepared for a robust, blustering rebuttal, either denying the incident or proudly and defiantly proclaiming it. Instead, however, Menedrion put his hands to his head, and, for one heart-stopping moment, Nefron thought he was about to burst into tears.

But the expression on his face was one she had never seen before. The faint flicker, that she had glimpsed earlier, bloomed to full light as she watched. Her son's face was haunted.

Her own face reflected his expression and, uncharacteristically, her hands dithered uncertainly, involuntarily drawn to reach out to him, but also repelled. 'What is it?' she said in soft alarm.

Menedrion looked at her, then his eyes began gazing about the room like some trapped creature looking for an escape. And, indeed, Nefron's hands were not unlike striking predators as they suddenly shot out and grasped his oscillating head to hold it firm.

'What is it?' she said again in a voice calculated to drive out *any* phantom.

Strong though he was, Menedrion could not pull himself free from his mother's grasp. 'I did hit her, Mother,' he said hesitantly, as though unable to believe his own words. His eyes met hers and Nefron released him. 'In fact . . . I . . . beat her.' He held out his powerful hands and stared down at them. 'I half strangled her. But it wasn't me. I . . .' His voice faded.

'What do you mean, it wasn't you?' Nefron asked severely, ill-disposed towards any pleading.

Menedrion pulled away from her again. 'I don't want to talk about it,' he said brusquely, preparing to stand. 'I'll deal with the girl and her parents. They're the only ones involved. There'll be no problem, no scandal. I'm not so foolish, mother. I've sorted out worse than this before now.'

But his heartiness rang hollow.

'*Drayner* told me about you, Irfan,' Nefron said starkly. 'He said that you needed my help in some way. And Drayner is considerably less foolish even than you, isn't he?'

'He had no right.' Menedrion began, goaded by his mother's acid tone. 'What game's he playing?'

'He had *every* right,' Nefron said, sweeping his protest aside. 'Drayner plays no games, you know that. He sides with no one, but he's more political wits in his finger than many a Senedwr has in his entire body. And if he's concerned enough to bring your affairs to my attention then the matter's serious. Now, stop this nonsense. I want to know *everything* that happened. Do you understand?'

For a moment Menedrion held his mother's gaze, then he conceded defeat with a scowl. 'It was just a bad dream, that's all,' he said with airy self-consciousness. 'I was fighting. Fighting in a battle . . . unhorsed . . . surrounded . . . I wasn't awake properly . . . I didn't realize . . .'

Nefron shook her head slowly as he spoke and his voice tailed off. 'No dream about a battle put the look on your face that I just saw,' she said, leaning forward and bringing her own face very close to his. Menedrion swallowed and she went on. 'Because you're half-berserk when you fight, Irfan Menedrion, and no battle odds would frighten you. And while you might wake up thrashing and flailing, you wake like a warrior; wide awake and well aware of where you are. You know dream from reality well enough. And no dream of a battle would make you go pale at the memory hours later.'

Menedrion looked away from her slightly and stared across the room, but he did not see what his eyes focused on. There was a long silence. Nefron watched and waited. The grey daylight from the window cut cold shadows in Menedrion's face.

'It *was* a battle, mother,' he said eventually, reluctantly turning towards her again. 'But I'm not sure it was a dream.'

Nefron frowned in genuine concern. For an instant all her ambitions for her son began to teeter as images of insanity formed before her. There was no history of it in either family, but . . .?

'It was . . . real . . .' Menedrion continued. 'I was . . . somewhere else. Somewhere bleak. And dark, like an unnatural night. And cold.' He began to rub his arm with his hand. 'Bitterly cold. And all around were shadows. Blacker than the darkness. In the distance at first, but moving, searching. Searching for me.'

His breathing became shallower. 'I looked round, but I couldn't see anything but this expanse of dark emptiness. Nowhere to run, nowhere to hide. They knew I was here because they'd brought me here and now they were just looking for me.'

Nefron watched in mounting horror as the blood drained from Menedrion's ruddy face and the haunted gaze returned. 'Then, as if they'd heard my thoughts, they saw me . . . sensed me. They began to close in . . . like hunters. Slowly at first, then quicker and quicker. I couldn't run, because that was what they wanted and I knew they'd take the power of my running for themselves and pursue me the faster.' Menedrion's hands rose up as if to protect himself. 'As they closed. I struck out, but . . . they weren't there . . . yet they were.' He looked at his mother intently, explaining now. 'When I struck, I passed right through them . . . and they through me . . . like a coldness . . . a deathly coldness. Possessing me, mother. Wanting me. "Yes," they kept saying. "Yes, yes, this one too." They were drawing me away . . . drawing me . . . I couldn't stop them . . . I didn't want to . . . I . . .'

He let out a massive gasping breath and seemed unable to continue for a moment. 'And then someone else was with me, inside me . . . no . . . I was someone else . . . someone who didn't belong there . . . and they couldn't reach me any more . . . except one . . . more silent, more terrible than the others. He, it, touched me just as I . . . woke . . . came back.'

Menedrion ran his hand over his chest as if to assure himself of something. 'But some of it was still with me . . . tiny, but real . . . dancing deep inside me like a black candle flame. And I was still someone else. Someone else being me. Someone else who didn't feel the flame. Who didn't hear it say, "Strike. Let me be fed." But who struck anyway.'

Suddenly he let out an anguished cry and dropped his head into his hands. Nefron looked at him, wide-eyed and, for the first time in her life, speechless with shock.

'I'm not mad, mother,' Menedrion said unexpectedly, without looking up. 'I'm not mad.'

Nefron opened her mouth to speak some reassurance, but she knew her voice would betray her. Instead she laid a hand on his head as the cold, reasoning part of her mind struggled to dominate the powerful emotions that had swept through her in response to her son's pain.

Menedrion looked up. 'I'm not mad,' he said viciously into her silence. 'I know that. I thought I might be, but telling you about it has told me I'm not. It could have been a madman's dream, but it wasn't. But I *am* frightened.'

Nefron had never heard such an admission from her son in all his life, but still she could not trust her voice. Menedrion had many flaws in his character, but he had both faced and dealt out death in combat and his judgement in the heat of action was to be trusted utterly. Beset by enemies, Menedrion knew where every part of his mind and body were to an extent that would be the envy of a meditative sage. It was his wholeness that made him so formidable, often robbing his opponents of their will even as they attacked him.

It came to Nefron gradually that she must do as others had done in the past. She must shelter behind his shield while she sought a few moments' respite. She must trust his battle-tested judgement.

Yet she knew she could not be seen to be doing this for that in itself might mar this judgement.

'You're right,' she said firmly, standing up and hoping that the flow of her words would lead her correctly. 'There's no question of madness here. Your feet are far too well planted on the ground and besides . . .' She allowed herself a knowing smile. 'You haven't the imagination to go mad.'

It was a gentle taunt, but an old familiar one, and Menedrion's grim face lightened a little.

'We have two problems,' Nefron continued, taking command again. 'One is the girl.' She turned to her son. 'You must see to that. Go and see her, see her parents. Make what amends you can. Say . . .' She shrugged. 'Say it *was* a nightmare . . . probably something you ate . . . something noxious in the fog . . . it kills enough people, after all. Be contrite. I don't have to tell you, do I? A judicious combination of money and that grotesque charm of yours should do it.' She paused pensively for a moment. 'Attend to that as soon as you leave here, don't delay.'

'What about Drayner?' Menedrion asked, glad himself to be shielding behind his mother's will.

Nefron was dismissive. 'Drayner doesn't gossip,' she said. 'And if anyone else knows about it, it won't matter if there's no complaint from the family.'

She nodded to herself, satisfied. Then, as she had expected, the answer to the second problem came to her. She smiled to herself at its elegance. It would deal with this matter and help with another one also.

She sat down opposite Menedrion again. 'This other business is more serious, though,' she said, concerned, but purposeful. 'We need to know what happened to you last night, but we can't find out on our own.' Then, as if the thought had just occurred, she laid a hand on his knee. 'You must consult a Dream Finder,' she said in mild triumph.

Menedrion looked at her uncertainly. 'A Dream Finder?' he echoed.

Nefron nodded by way of a reply.

'No one uses Dream Finders these days,' Menedrion said, dismayed. 'They're quacks. Like . . .' He searched for a word. '. . . fortune-tellers. Reading the future from the dregs of a wine cup. They're for merchants' wives with too much time and money on their hands . . .'

Nefron smiled broadly at the outburst and shook a silencing hand at him. 'No, no,' she said. 'There are some charlatans about, but they're still a respected Guild and they were much used once. I heard of one recently. Not a famous one, but very good. Used by some important people . . .' She snapped her fingers softly. 'What was his name now?'

Her face lit up. Menedrion bathed in its certainty.

'Antyr,' she proclaimed. 'That was it. When you've made your peace with the girl and her family, Irfan, go and find the Dream Finder, Antyr.'

Chapter 7

Arwain scowled as he jumped down from his horse and handed the reins to the waiting groom.

'Is something wrong, sir?' said an officer stepping forward to greet him.

Arwain returned his salute and, with an effort, smiled. 'No, no, Ryllans,' he said. 'Just the dampness after the fog. It seeps into the bones.'

Ryllans raised his eyebrows. 'I heard there was some disturbance at the palace last night,' he said straightforwardly.

Arwain shook his head and chuckled. 'One of the servant girls had a bad fall and needed help, that's all,' he said. 'Is there anything you don't hear about, Ryllans?'

'Not too much, I hope, sir,' the officer replied. 'Your safety . . . and the Lady Yanys's . . . are my responsibility and I need eyes and ears everywhere for that.' Arwain nodded appreciatively.

'Doubtless you'll tell me why this servant girl warranted the attention of the Duke's personal physician when you're ready, sir,' Ryllans went on softly, his slight foreign accent betraying his true anxiety.

'Doubtless,' Arwain replied, laughing. 'If you don't tell me first.'

But Arwain's laughter did not invoke the same in Ryllans. Instead, the older man held Arwain's gaze in silent, but relentless, inquiry. His charge and his guards wandering the cellars at night had to be explained to his satisfaction sooner or later. That they found a physician and his patient instead of secret plotters was irrelevant. Clandestine movement through the palace was always a matter for concern. And there *was* the matter of the Duke's physician being called out in the middle of the night to attend to a mere servant.

'It's all right,' Arwain said, more soberly, and also lowering his voice. 'There was no danger, and there's no plot brewing. It was just an . . . excess . . . by my beloved half-brother. I'll tell you what happened later, have no fear, there's no urgency, trust me. Let's proceed with the task in hand.'

Ryllans nodded and turned on his heel.

Arwain looked at the back of the Commander of his bodyguard as he followed him. A little shorter than himself, balding and clean-shaven, Ryllans walked with a slight roll which made him look heavy and clumsy. He was neither. Arwain knew that he would already have quietly wrung all that happened from the guards who had accompanied him through the cellar and that he would probably be well on his way to identifying the girl and the servants.

He knew, too, that the fact that Drayner and the others had been spotted purely by chance would be concerning him greatly, for the security of Arwain and his house came second only to his ultimate loyalty to the Duke, and dominated his thinking.

Arwain liked and respected Ryllans, yet he was always aware of a distance in the man. Not that he was cold or aloof – indeed he was invariably good company – but somewhere inside, there was a part that Arwain knew he could not reach. Not that he was alone in that, however, he consoled himself, for Ryllans was the most senior of the Mantynnai; the men who had defended the city of Viernce during the Bethlarri-inspired rebellion and siege some ten years ago. To a man, they were, at bottom, unreadable.

A small group of foreign mercenaries in the employ of Duke Ibris, and garrisoned at Viernce, the Mantynnai had put down the rebelling faction after the local militia had thrown down their arms. Outnumbered, that in itself had been no easy task, but they had then found the city besieged by the Bethlarii army and had taken appalling losses holding it until the Bethlarii, not expecting and not equipped for a long siege, were put to flight by the unexpected arrival of the Serenstad army with the Duke at their head, soiled and raging, after a prodigious forced march over the snowbound countryside.

As a reward for their exceptional courage and loyalty, Ibris had immediately appointed the survivors to his own palace guard, an elite regiment, entry to which hitherto had been exclusively restricted to the citizens of Serenstad only.

It was a decision that had caused some controversy at the time, prompting angry and anxious debates in the Sened and the Gythrin-Dy. 'They're not Serens,' was the cry. 'They're not even from this land. A raggle-taggle bunch of foreigners. Warriors for money. We know nothing of them. Not even where they come from, or how they came here.'

The comments were accurate, but the Duke had rounded furiously on the carpers, at one stage throwing a handful of gold on to the floor of the Sened House, and standing over it, sword drawn, shouting, 'Warriors for money! That's a half year's pay for a Mantynnai infantryman. Which of you here would die for it, or for ten times that amount?'

Then into the silence he had said, 'They stood, fought and died, where our own kind surrendered or fled. Had they not done so then Viernce would now be a subject city of Bethlar. Do you think we'd be sitting here debating so calmly with the Bethlarii holding all our northern territories?'

'Nevertheless, they are foreigners and we don't understand them truly. They should not be brought so close to the seat of power,' had come a quieter voice from an older Senedwr.

The Duke had answered him in like vein. 'Power goes to those who are most fitted for it,' he said sadly, sheathing his sword. 'And, believe me, such men could have taken power at any time had they so wished. If they take it now, then it will be by stealth and silence and it'll be a gentler bargain than that which our ancestors, as foreigners, offered the original inhabitants of this land.' It was the definitive statement of a man who understood the true value of force in governing a people.

The opposition had eventually faded in the face of his determination and as the full truth of the events at Viernce became more widely known. Subsequently, the Mantynnai survivors had taken up their new roles in the palace guard as quietly and inconspicuously as they did most things.

'One of my better decisions,' Ibris later remarked as he watched this 'raggle-taggle bunch of foreigners' gradually improving the weapons and tactics of his guards, and thence the whole army.

More subtly, they also began to develop in the army a sense of discipline and independent loyalty to him as Head of State which did much to lessen the more bloody partisan excesses that stained the politics of the cities.

Now all the Mantynnai held high-ranking posts in the palace guard, and were regarded in many ways as its heart.

'We've made them more Serens than the Serens,' someone said to the Duke, but he shook his head and replied, 'No. They've made us more Mantynnai, and we're better for it.'

And I have their finest in my bodyguard, Arwain constantly reminded himself.

It was a source of some irritation to Ibris's other sons that 'the bastard' had such a bodyguard, but Ibris was straightforward.

'As you know, certain factions are particularly ill-disposed to him,' he said to them. Menedrion looked at him darkly, but Ibris carefully avoided mentioning Nefron's name. Her imprisonment was still a topic which they both avoided if possible.

In earlier days, Menedrion, ever headstrong, had quarrelled violently with his father, naively protesting Nefron's innocence. For a while it seemed that nothing would restrain him, but eventually he became quieter. This Ibris attributed to his own quite specific threats, but ironically it was Nefron herself who bade her offspring keep silent for fear that his wildness would permanently estrange him from his father, and see him banished and barred the succession.

Not that she was alone in her concern about that matter. It taxed Ibris also. In the past, internecine fighting between the great families over the succession had done fearful damage to Serenstad and, gradually, the tradition of hereditary succession coupled with the approval of the Sened had evolved. But the problem was still fraught with hazard, and violence was always near the surface.

Like many rulers before him, Ibris found himself facing a dilemma. While he did not name an heir there was the risk of fighting among his sons, and of sudden coups by other families either before or after his death. If he did name an heir, however, the situation would be little improved, as the chosen son would then be a particular target for other aspirants, and he himself perhaps a target for his heir.

In an attempt to minimize this possible mayhem, Ibris had gradually devolved more responsibility for government to the Sened and the Gythrin-Dy. But, as the Mantynnai had equally gradually consolidated the loyalty of the army to him, he decided on balance that there would be more chance of stability if his family knew his mind while he was alive and strong. He fulfilled Nefron's prophecy.

'Menedrion, I name you as my heir. You're the eldest and you've shown yourself a capable leader in battle if little else. Arwain, you in turn shall be his heir until he settles down and breeds one of his own. Goran . . . Goran! . . . Don't mutter. And stop sulking! Arwain's bastardy *doesn't* preclude him as you know full well! You'll be third in line, though the gods protect us if it ever comes to that.'

Then he had wilfully dominated them all. 'You can choose to fight among yourselves if you wish, but if I get one whiff of it, I'll disown you utterly and banish you to the farthest island I can find. And you've got plenty of cousins waiting to step into your shoes. Menedrion, you will swear the Ducal oath of protection over your brothers, here and now. Arwain and Goran, you will swear your allegiance to Menedrion in turn.'

The oaths were duly sworn and Ibris then gave them his final, quieter benison. 'Look at our city,' he said. 'Rich, powerful, a fine place and one that will become even finer given peace and thoughtful guidance. Wealth and prosperity are what we must seek. Men won't leave comfortable hearths for the warring streets, believe me. Honour your oaths all of you, not because they're oaths but because they're in everyone's best interests. No one will benefit from a succession war except the Bethlarii. Menedrion, settle down, get married, breed. Listen to your brothers when you're Duke. Arwain, if I've judged aright, you've little desire for leadership, but help Menedrion for my sake and for the people's. Goran . . . Goran! Pay attention! You're a fine artist. You above all will make Serenstad the city that will draw the universe to it. Be what you are and be well pleased with it. I envy you.'

It was the best he could do, he reasoned. Menedrion lacked much that was needed in a good duke but he might well grow into one with help from the others. And he did covet the role, which was no small consideration. Naming him might also diminish the influence of his scheming mother. Arwain, on the other hand, was probably ideally suited for the task. But he seemed to have neither ambition nor expectation and, it had to be admitted, to have named him ahead of Menedrion would have been to sentence him to death. As it was, there was little love lost between him and Menedrion.

And yet, of the three sons, Arwain was the most like his father, and Ibris knew he could not read him fully. That caused him some concern, but he consoled himself with the thought that if Arwain secretly intended to oust Menedrion, then he'd have the wit to at least attempt to do it both efficiently and quietly. Yes, Ibris's darker side mused, it had been right to place his most loyal guards around Arwain. They might well also be protecting all of us.

Arwain followed Ryllans along the familiar corridor and through the familiar double door. 'You'll enjoy this today, sir,' Ryllans said, turning and smiling at him as he stepped through the door. 'At least it'll get the damp out of your bones.'

Arwain looked around the enclosed courtyard and returned the smile. 'I had a feeling that was a foolish remark when I made it,' he said.

The palace was an ancient building and had been altered and extended many times at the whims and wishes of its successive occupants. As a result, apart from innumerable towers and spires joined by high arching bridges and walkways, there were many isolated alleyways and courtyards such as the one Arwain now stood in. This particular one, however, was unique in that all the windows and doors that opened on to it, save the one the two men had just used, had been sealed.

This courtyard was used by the Mantynnai as a training ground. It had a further uniqueness in that it was the only area used exclusively thus, it being the Mantynnai's general practice to train anywhere that suited the needs of the moment; fields, mountains, rivers, corridors, stairways, rooftops and cellars, and, on occasions, even the rambling, cavernous sewers.

Arwain looked up at the now blind windows with their panels of wood and masonry, each carefully chosen to harmonize with the room or the corridor they had opened from.

Though the surrounding buildings were high, the courtyard was large and spacious, yet to Arwain it always felt claustrophobic. Somehow, he felt, it was the almost obsessive care that had been taken in sealing the windows that affected him. It was like a secret within a secret. And yet the courtyard and its function were not secret. Many knew of its existence, many used it, and any could walk into it should they be so inclined. But only the one way.

It was like the Mantynnai themselves, he thought suddenly. At once secretive and open, approachable and distant.

Ryllans watched Arwain's customary inspection of the courtyard then he pushed him, not violently, but unexpectedly and enough to send him staggering backwards against the wall.

Arwain opened his mouth to protest, but Ryllans pointed an admonishing finger at him before he could speak. '*You* tell *me* why,' he demanded.

Arwain knew what was expected of him; an explanation of the lesson he had just been taught. Ryllans' lessons were always simple but their very simplicity usually obscured them.

Arwain's mind raced for some clue but nothing was apparent. From experience he knew that he had missed the moment and that any amount of searching would not reveal it now.

'I don't understand,' he said apologetically.

'Go out and come in again,' Ryllans said, indicating the door. Arwain frowned a little but did as he was bidden.

This time he watched Ryllans carefully as he stepped through the doorway. There was nothing unusual in his behaviour. No indication of a threat. Then his eyes flickered upwards to the sealed windows and Ryllans' hand came out and struck him lightly on the face.

'Every time you come in here, your actions are identical,' Ryllans said simply, laying emphasis on the last word.

Arwain nodded. Sometimes Ryllans taught by talking, long and expansively. At others, as now, his actions were enigmatic and his words brief to the point of terseness.

'And therefore predictable,' Arwain finished the small lesson.

Ryllans acknowledged the reply with a slightly mocking smile.

'How many times will I have to learn that lesson?' Arwain asked self-consciously.

'As many times as I will,' Ryllans replied, taking him by the arm and motioning him towards a group of men at the far side of the courtyard. It was Ryllans' willingness to admit himself as much a pupil as a master that particularly endeared him to Arwain.

Like all male Serens, Arwain had undergone the basic military training that was both necessary for the security of the city and its dominions and traditionally marked the passage of young men through into manhood. As the Duke's son and as a future officer, his training, like Menedrion's and Goran's, had been more severe than average and he had encountered enough instructors who used brutality and humiliation as their stock in trade to value Ryllans at something like his true worth.

And indeed, as yet another measure of this, Arwain realized that he was alert now. Not tense or anxious, fearful of some impending but unknowable event, but . . . wide-awake, for want of any more profound phrase . . . more aware of everything that was going on around him. It was as if Ryllans' brief lesson had released some inner resource just as a strike on a flint box would make it burst into crackling brightness with the flame that could go on to banish *any* darkness.

Body and mind, both to be trusted, both to be trained, both to know their strengths and weaknesses. That was the essence of all Ryllans' teaching. And an unthinking habit was a weakness beyond doubt.

As he walked silently by his mentor, Arwain searched for the deeper lessons that must lie beneath this last one.

Why did he always look up at the walls of this man-made pit? Was he, as he would like to have imagined, quickly and shrewdly examining the terrain for any subtle signs of change that might perhaps mean danger? Ryllans certainly would have approved of that. Or was his action simply a childish retreat into the comforting familiarity of ritual in an attempt to avoid the challenge of newness that must inevitably occur in this place?

Or was there yet some deeper unease that disturbed him?

'This place is alien,' he said, stopping suddenly, his breath steaming in the chilly air. Ryllans stopped also and half turned his head towards him, inviting an explanation. 'It's a Mantynnai place, wherever you come from,' Arwain went on.

Ryllans did not reply, but looked up at the walls as if he had not done so for a long time and gave a slight, pensive nod.

'Or perhaps not,' Arwain went on. 'Perhaps it's just a Serens place, made alien and sightless by your Mantynnai touch.'

'Blinded, eh?' Ryllans said.

'Blindfolded,' Arwain added, more compassionately.

Ryllans chuckled, intrigued. 'Interesting,' he said. 'I'll think about that.'

'Or perhaps it's that lonely place that each of us carries inside, even in the middle of the crowd,' Arwain said, warming to his thoughts, but adding, almost inadvertently, 'especially in battle.'

'Ah,' Ryllans said significantly. 'You *are* in good fettle

today. I'll think about that too. In the meantime, let's continue your training.' He nodded towards the waiting men. 'I've asked Hadryn to work on your close-quarter fighting with you.'

Apart from his formal military training, Arwain had received training in the arts of war throughout his youth in the course of his normal education. He was familiar with the principles involved in the use of cavalry and infantry in many terrains, ranging from large set-piece battles across open plains, to close-quarter skirmishing in the mountains. He had been taught about the logistical problems involved in raising, maintaining and moving, armies, and he had learned about siege warfare and the use of artillery and blockades and sapping.

As a classroom discipline, this had been interesting, exciting even, but subsequently he had also had much of this theory complemented by some grim practical experience as the constant political manoeuvring of the many cities and towns of the land gave rise at times to outbreaks of armed violence.

What he learned from Ryllans and the other Mantynnai in his bodyguard, however, was different.

Initially, when Ryllans had suggested that he train and practise with his bodyguard, Arwain had declined; time had lent no charm to the memories of his basic training.

Ryllans, however, knew when to charge and when to infiltrate.

'Your father has given me charge of your protection, sir,' he said. 'This is a relatively simple matter on the battlefield, but here . . .' He waved an airy hand around the busy palace grounds they were walking. 'It's much harder, perhaps even impossible, given the will and power of the lady Nefron even though she is confined to the Erin-Mal. And there are others with little love for the house of Ibris. Only you can truly protect yourself and protection is more than skill at arms. It's here.' And he had patted his stomach and then tapped his temple with an extended finger. The latter in particular was to become a familiar gesture to Arwain.

At this further assault, Arwain had weakened a little, but still he held. 'I've every faith in you and your men, Ryllans,' he said, airily. 'I'm sure that we'll be able to work out arrangements that will satisfy your concerns.'

Ryllans had bowed and then made his frontal attack. Fixing his lord with a polite but unflinching gaze, he said, 'All defences can be overcome, given time, knowledge and resolution, sir. This you know from your studies. And anyone seeking your life will have these resources and also the benefit of surprise. Surround you as we may, there will always be that one moment of inattention. That opening in the shield wall for a stray arrow.' His voice had dropped. 'And, sir, we each of us have our price. Something, somewhere. Those who stand closest to you, armed, will be your enemies' first choice as weapons. It was ever thus. You know this too from your studies, I'm sure.'

The clarity of vision in this remark had truly shocked and frightened Arwain, such was the reputation of the Mantynnai for loyalty and such was the faith placed in them by his father. He wavered visibly and Ryllans moved in and quietly finished him off. 'And then there is the protection of your intended, sir. The Lady Yanys . . .'

Ryllans' instruction had, however, been as far from Arwain's basic training as he could possibly have imagined. Indeed, it proved to be a continuing revelation and Arwain found a new quality developing within himself that seemed to affect almost his every action.

Not that many of the things he learned seemed, at first glance, to be very different from what he already knew. The slight changes that the Mantynnai showed him however, made them vastly different, at once easier to execute and more powerful in their effect.

'Where did you learn these things from?' he asked once in the early days. 'From some secret warrior sect?'

Ryllans had laughed outright. 'No, no. What we know is far too simple to be kept secret. That's why it's so difficult for people to see it.'

'I don't understand,' Arwain had replied, oscillating between plaintiveness and irritation.

'Just practise,' was all that Ryllans would offer him. 'And think. And feel.'

What won Arwain over eventually, however, was the spirit of learning and humble inquiry that permeated his new training, so utterly different was it from the brutal savagery inherent in much of his previous training.

Now, Arwain relished his practice sessions with the Mantynnai, finding them both relaxing and stimulating if, occasionally, shattering. He sensed too that he was also being surreptitiously forged and strengthened to become part of the team that was his bodyguard.

'Better the shell, than the shrimp within,' Ryllans had said once, casually, but with some amusement.

Arwain was greeted by the men as he approached. They were laughing at the double entrance he had had to make. Here he was not their lord, he was one of them . . . or nearly so. For though they were seemingly no more than men, relaxed and humorous, they were also Mantynnai. A dark bonding stillness lay at their heart.

'Having to practise door opening now?' came one voice, with a despairing, motherly sigh.

'Don't worry, it's harder than it looks, but you'll pick it up eventually,' came another.

Arwain turned to Ryllans in mock appeal against this welcome.

'Just practise,' was the dismissive reply. 'Hadryn, as we discussed, help the lord with his close-quarter work, one against many. He's still showing too much inclination to lose his awareness when he's dealt with one.' Hadryn was a tall, black-bearded man, loose-limbed and powerful. He nodded. 'For the moment, unarmed,' Ryllans continued.

He turned back to Arwain. 'Work hard on this.' He tapped his head with his finger. 'You turn your mind away too easily and it'll get your throat cut. You still think in terms of victory and defeat, and while you do that you will always be defeated.'

Arwain had seen this form of training and even participated in it to some extent as an attacker, but it was a form that was liable to be more frightening for the attackers than the single 'victim' and he had ended with an acute sense of his own inadequacy.

As Ryllans walked away towards another group of guards, he clapped his hands loudly. Arwain's assailants moved purposefully towards him.

For an instant, all Arwain's training seemed to leave him, but he retained sufficient wit to realize that someone might be behind him, and he turned round quickly as he retreated.

Then one of the attackers charged at him suddenly, levelling a powerful blow at his head. Arwain knew that the blow would be pulled if he faltered and failed to take action, but that did little to reassure the response of his body to the onslaught, and he ducked wildly, just remembering to step to one side as he did.

Then came another and another. Most he avoided

101

successfully, though gracelessly. Others he managed to avoid and deflect, but eventually, fortuitously finding himself on balance, he stepped deeply into one, swept the striking arm downward and threw the attacker towards two of the others who were just approaching. It prompted an ironic round of applause, then, as he paused to watch his assailant roll back up on to his feet, a powerful pair of arms encircled him and two of his attackers gleefully moved forward to seize his legs.

Ryllans, practising swordwork nearby, favoured him with a knowingly raised eyebrow as he was dumped ignominiously on the hard stone flagging. It was a customary end to such exercises. Or was it?

Arwain rolled suddenly into the nearest pair of legs, causing their owner to lose balance, then he struggled to his feet as quickly as he could, turning to face his attackers as he did so.

A white smile parted Hadryn's black beard.

Then there was some explanation, some debate, a few brief demonstrations, and the exercise was repeated – several times.

Gradually the sweating figures made a mist of their own in the sealed courtyard as Arwain struggled to be calm and yet alert amid the plethora of attackers.

He knew that he was making progress but, as he practised, he knew too that he could never be as these men were. They absorbed his wilder punches with such ease, either by solid and painful blocks or by gentle deflections that took his balance utterly. And when thrown they simply rolled back up on to their feet as if they had been training on soft spring turf. True, he could do that himself, but two small bones at the bottom of his back told him he did not do it so well, and usually told him for several days afterwards.

Then there was an unexpected voice close behind him.

'Lord.'

He spun round, seized the speaker by the throat with one powerful hand, and thrust him against the wall, only to let him go immediately amid some laughter from his companions.

The man was one of the Duke's messengers.

'Tut tut,' someone whispered in his ear ironically. 'Assault on a Ducal messenger. That's a summary flogging if the Liktors get to hear of it, I fear. Shall I call one?'

Arwain dismissed his tormentor with a push.

'I'm sorry,' he said to the messenger, helping him vainly

102

to straighten his rumpled collar. 'I'm afraid you picked an inopportune moment to approach me. What is it you want?'

The messenger cleared his throat in a slightly injured manner, though directing his reproach at the smirking guards rather than his Duke's son.

'Your father wishes to see you, lord, immediately,' he said.

Arwain could not forbear a brief scowl of impatience. But his father's word was not to be disputed.

He held out his hands in a plea. 'Immediately?' he asked.

The messenger, still struggling with his collar, looked at the soiled and sweating figure in front of him, momentarily bewildered. Lords did not ask advice of messengers.

'Immediately,' he echoed dutifully.

Chapter 8

Antyr threw his wringing cloak on to the floor, dropped into his chair and let out a pitiful groan. His back was aching, his legs were aching, his feet were burning, and he was soaked to the skin and chilled to the marrow.

He sat motionless, gazing blankly up at a familiar smoke stain on the ceiling immediately above a lamp. Acute self-pity at his physical plight had long since driven all other concerns from his mind and it was some time before coherent thoughts began to seep back again. When they did, they were rudimentary and primitive and he was moved to speak them out loud.

'I'm dying,' he said to the smoke stain. 'If not dead. Tarrian, wherever you are, don't come back, there'll only be my exhausted corpse waiting for you. You faithless hound, leaving me to die of exposure.'

'Stop moaning, and open this door.' The unexpected reply rang sharply in his head, making him start.

Despite this, however, and his previous complaint, Antyr felt a sense of relief stirring somewhere underneath his fatigue. Then, closing his eyes, he pushed himself up out of his chair with a monumental effort. His sluggishness was greeted by an impatient scratching on the front door.

'Stop that,' he shouted. 'That door's damaged enough with your impatience.'

A short but eloquent string of abuse from Tarrian entered his mind, embellishing the information that he was not the only one who was cold and weary. From its tone Antyr deemed it wiser not to reply. Instead, he stepped well back and lifted the latch of the door. It was a routine precaution based on previous experience and its value was confirmed as Tarrian crashed the door open even more violently than usual on his way towards the kitchen.

Antyr cast a brief, irritated, glance at the well-scratched door then, wincing at its screech, slowly closed it and walked down the passageway after the wolf. He felt much easier now that Tarrian was back; there was always the risk of his being killed by hunters or farmers outside the city.

The thought was pushed aside by a spasm of disgust from his Companion. 'I'd rather take my chance with the farmers and hunters,' Tarrian declaimed. 'At least they wouldn't either try to starve or poison me.'

'What do you mean?' Antyr said in some indignation, recognizing the complaint.

'You know perfectly well what I mean,' Tarrian replied. 'When was the last time you ate dried-up, two-day-old food?'

'You ate well enough last night,' Antyr replied unsympathetically. 'And I've no doubt you found something fresher outside.' The image of a desperately fleeing rabbit flashed suddenly through Antyr's mind but was cut off sharply.

'Ah-hah,' he said significantly.

'Shut up,' came the swift reply. 'You can get me some fresh water at least. And give me a brush, I'm a mess. And do something about the stink in here, it's appalling.'

On that point, Antyr had to agree. 'I'm sorry,' he said, picking up the bucket he had vomited into the previous night and carrying it to the door.

'It seems a long time ago,' he said, wrinkling his nose as he threw the evil-smelling contents down the drain and vigorously worked the pump handle to send a cold, glittering spray of water after them.

There was a short silence, then Tarrian spoke again, 'Come back in and brush me, Antyr.' His voice was unexpectedly gentle. Antyr looked up in surprise. Tarrian was standing at the open door, gazing at him earnestly. Antyr stroked his damp head as he stepped inside, and Tarrian leaned against him briefly.

They did not speak for some time after that. Antyr found a dry cloth and wiped Tarrian down before rekindling the fire. Then he dried and changed himself and set about brushing his Companion.

Grooming the wolf was a strange, satisfying experience. Antyr knew he was touching on some quality that came from deep within the wolf's being, somewhere far below where Tarrian could take him, or indeed where he would wish to go.

'A pack thing,' Tarrian would say when he chose to speak of such matters at all. It was sufficient and they both understood. Tarrian knew himself for a wolf, just as Antyr knew himself for a man, and though they also knew themselves to be strange, they were still just that, wolf and man. Where they touched and talked to one another more or less as equals was little more than an uncertain tideswept causeway that joined two great and alien lands.

After a while, Antyr felt Tarrian's mind rising to the surface again, relaxed and quiet.

'I told them at the Norstseren Gate that you'd be back on your own,' Antyr said casually as the spell dispersed.

'Yes. Thank you,' Tarrian replied lazily. 'I caught the thought as I came in, but I sneaked through out of habit.'

There was an element of amusement in the answer, but Antyr did not ask.

'I came in with a flock of sheep,' Tarrian volunteered, chuckling and rolling over to have his stomach brushed. 'What a dozy shepherd. And as for those dogs. They've no idea. I'm surprised you're not up to your ears in my kin, the living must be so easy out there.'

'Dozy or not, the poor beggar's probably had to pay Gate Tax on you, you know,' Antyr said, trying to sound reproachful, but laughing in spite of himself.

Tarrian pondered. 'Yes,' he concluded. 'Now I think about it, the shepherd was arguing quite heatedly with the Exactor when I left.'

He rolled over again and, clambering to his feet, shook himself massively. 'Very pleasant,' he said. 'I enjoyed that.'

'But . . .?' Antyr said, catching the doubt in the thought as he hoisted himself on to his chair.

'But we must talk,' Tarrian said soberly.

Antyr found himself looking into the wolf's grey eyes. 'Do you want to go out for a drink?' Tarrian asked.

The question was unexpected, indeed unique in their relationship.

'I don't know,' Antyr said after a long hesitation. 'The day's been . . . so long . . . so full of change. Being marched through the fog by the Duke's guards, Ciarll Feranc, Aaken Uhr Candessa, searching the Duke of Serenstad's dreams . . .' He paused as the unease about the Duke's dream returned to him, followed on the instant by the memory of the sinister dark figure that he had woken to find examining him, and, worst of all, the terrifying absence of his Companion, his Earth Holder. Tarrian let out a slight whine.

'Then walking mile after weary mile through the rain and

the cold greyness, something changed,' Antyr went on. 'Something in me is different. A part of me is crying out to run away, to run while I can. Run anywhere, into a bottle, down to Farlan and on to some foreign boat, anywhere, just get away. But it's a distant wailing infant. I can't pay it any real heed. The rest of me is saying, remember your drills, keep your pike held firm, hold your ground for everyone's sake. Ever seen a horse run on to a pike? Ever seen what cavalry does to fleeing infantry?' He fell silent.

'Fleeing infantry,' he muttered softly after a long silence. 'Easier than a rabbit to a wolf. And they keep on coming . . . no matter how fast you run . . . hacking people down . . . spear and sword. Don't break whatever you do.'

'Do you want to go out for a drink?' Tarrian repeated his question softly, penetratingly, as a lull came into this almost whispered catalogue of memories.

Antyr's eyes widened and he shook his head slowly. 'I don't know,' he said. 'I'm frightened. I don't know what I want. Except for the fear to go away.'

He looked at Tarrian. The wolf was lying very low on the floor, his ears flattened back along his head. 'You too?' he asked.

'Me too,' Tarrian admitted. 'But by your battle memories not by what's happened today. At least that might be understandable if we think about it. Humans never will be.'

'I'm sorry,' Antyr said.

'Don't be, it's my fault,' Tarrian replied, his manner easing. 'I should be used to people by now.'

There was a brief silence and Antyr felt Tarrian trying to clear his mind of the alien horror of the battlefield in order to return to the fears of the moment.

'Come away, Tarrian,' Antyr said, offering his Companion the words like a small signpost to a sanity. 'It's not your world. And in answer to your question, no, I don't want a drink, I think. And anyway I'm too weary to go to the inn.'

Antyr made the remark as if it were an intellectual decision, but to his surprise, he felt a wave of disgust pass through him as the memory of the sounds and smells of the inn came to him. Yet even as he noted this unexpected response, the urge to be away . . . anywhere . . . returned to him. He frowned uneasily, then somehow turned and faced the darkness.

'What's happening, Tarrian?' he said. 'Is it me? Has my neglect of my craft, myself, unleashed something?'

'No,' Tarrian replied simply. '*That* I'm sure of now. Neglect makes it harder to reach the nexus and dims the perception of the dream being searched. It just makes you less of a Dream Finder. You certainly deserve to be totally incompetent by now, but your natural ability has protected you from your best efforts.'

There was a familiar element of reproach in Tarrian's voice, but he himself set it aside quickly and apologetically before the two of them locked into the futility of one of their old quarrels.

Antyr noted the gesture with thanks, but he frowned. 'I don't understand,' he said. 'What's all this about my natural ability you're suddenly talking about. My father used to say I'd be far better than he was if I worked, but . . . I thought that was just father's talk . . . something to encourage me. Then he died . . . and my training ended . . .'

His voice tailed off as the emptiness that his father's death had left came back to him.

Tarrian's voice intruded gently. 'Antyr, in so far as it ever really began, your training was ended before your father died.'

Antyr looked at him, his frown becoming pained.

'You had skills from the outset that your father didn't understand,' Tarrian went on. 'That I didn't understand – still don't. He couldn't teach you, Antyr. He could only learn from you. And his pain, like mine for a long time, was that he didn't truly see that. He felt constantly that he was failing you.'

The eerie certainty that Tarrian had shown as they stood at the edge of the Aphron Dennai returned. 'You're no ordinary Dream Finder, Antyr. You move to the nexus as if you were walking from one room to another and you release me utterly. I've known none who moved with such ease, nor gave me such freedom. You let me soar through all places as though I were some great bird. And yet you're flawed.' He paused. 'I don't know what you are, Antyr, but you're different. And whatever, whoever, we felt in the Duke's dream, knew . . . or sensed . . . it too. That's why it came looking for you afterwards.'

Antyr's eyes widened in horror at the implications that reverberated in Tarrian's word. He glimpsed again the image of the hapless, fleeing rabbit.

'This is nonsense,' he said, but hearing the futility in his own voice. 'How can anyone from the outside enter a dream?'

'We do.'

Tarrian's simple statement of the obvious struck Antyr like a hammerblow and he fell silent. The reply formed in his mind, 'That's different, we're there with the dreamer, we have the contact, we have the consent, the trust.' But it had a hollow ring and he could not speak it.

'Even the Duke sensed the presence of another will in his dream, that's why he opposed it,' Tarrian said. 'Then we felt it with him. And it felt us.'

Antyr sought solace in an irrelevance. 'He must be a sensitive, then,' he said.

'Dream Finding's an ancient skill,' Tarrian said brusquely. 'And its practitioners hardly constitute a celibate order, do they? He's probably got a damn sight more than one Dream Finder back in his ancestry somewhere.'

Tarrian's curt dismissal of this diversion left Antyr nowhere to go but forward again.

'What shall we do then?' he said reluctantly and with a feeling of unreality. 'If someone can invade the Duke's dream, then find me when I'm asleep, for whatever purpose . . .' The memory of the shadow's parting hiss of hatred passed over him and he shivered. '. . . What can I do? Am I to stay awake forever? And if they can reach out and snatch me from your protection in some way, what can *you* do?'

Tarrian was silent. Both stared into the black pit of ignorance, helpless.

'What about the Guild?' Antyr offered, after a moment. 'There must be someone there who can help us.'

'Name one,' Tarrian said tersely.

Antyr looked at him pleadingly. 'Come on, think, Tarrian. You pay more heed to Guild affairs than I do. They're not all concerned with wringing tax concessions from the Exactors and arguing about fees, surely. There's got to be someone left who's still interested in the craft.'

Antyr sensed Tarrian about to make the same reply and he held up a warning finger. Even when Petran had been alive, Tarrian had been ill disposed towards what he called the futility of this particular manifestation of the human pack instinct. Since his death, however, it had grown to cynical and growling disdain.

Tarrian made the effort. 'I can't think of anyone at the moment,' he said apologetically. 'I'm out of touch myself.'

Antyr put his head in his hands. 'We should go to the Guild House, all the same,' he said. 'We could inquire. Someone else might have run into this problem. We might be fretting about something that's already well known.'

Tarrian stood up. 'Yes, of course,' he said, suddenly enthusiastic. 'You're right. I'd forgotten about that.'

'Forgotten about what?' Antyr asked.

'The Guild House,' Tarrian replied. 'The library. There could well be something there. Come on, stir yourself.'

Like some predatory but short-sighted bird, the old porter looked narrowly over his eye lenses as Antyr pushed open the stately door of the Guild House. It was covered with elaborate carvings and richly tinted glass panels showing past dignitaries posing solemnly in their formal robes of office. Tarrian padded in behind him and as Antyr closed the door the grey winter light passed through the glass panels to throw a brief kingfisher flash of summer colour across the patterned floor.

The porter adjusted his tunic with a hint of annoyance at this interruption to his meditations. 'Yes, sir?' he inquired authoritatively, of this potential trespasser. 'What can I do for you?'

'Nothing, thank you,' Antyr replied. 'We've just come to use the library.'

'I'm sorry. The library's for Guild members only,' the porter said in an injured tone, hobbling out from behind his counter and placing his ancient frame unflinchingly between Antyr and further intrusion into the building. 'And we don't allow dogs, sir,' he added, eyeing Tarrian.

'Tell him,' Tarrian said menacingly. 'Quickly.'

'I am a member,' Antyr replied politely, pointing to his black-irised eyes and producing a battered card after a brief struggle with his cloak. 'I don't come here very often.'

The porter scrutinized the soiled card with some distaste, and then hobbled back behind his counter with a 'Just a moment, sir', which obviously meant, 'We'll see about that, sir.'

With an audible effort he unearthed a large book from a shelf somewhere underneath the counter. 'Now sir,' he said, opening the book with great dignity, but quite at random.

'Brilliant,' Tarrian said acidly. 'Opened it right at M for Antyr.'

Antyr shushed him discreetly. 'He might be able to hear you,' he said.

Tarrian snorted. 'So might that door,' he said. Then, in a thunderous bellow, 'Hurry up, you dozy old sod!'

Antyr cringed as the shout echoed around his head, but, gritting his teeth, he managed to maintain an uneasy smile. The porter, however, showed no sign of responding as he continued painstakingly turning the pages of the book.

Eventually he reached a page where, after much glancing from margin to margin, he decided that his search could be continued by means of a solitary forefinger.

'Ah,' he said finally after a further long study of Antyr's card. 'Here we are, sir. Antyr, Andor Endryth.' His tone reluctantly mellowed. 'And this will be your Companion, I presume. Tarrian, is it?' He closed the book and peered beadily down at Tarrian. 'Not common, wolves, not common at all,' he said absently, then turning back to Antyr, 'I'm sorry I didn't recognize you, sir, but one has to be so careful these days, there are so many ruffians about and your robe . . .' He cleared his throat and changed direction quickly. 'I presume you don't come to many of the meetings, sir. Otherwise I'm sure I'd have known you straight away. I know most of the regulars and—'

'Yes, thank you.' Antyr interrupted the lecture and, taking his card back, set off after Tarrian who was already walking across the wide, circular entrance hall towards the staircase that led down to the library.

It occurred to Antyr as he strode after him that he had not been in the Guild House almost since his father died, and, despite the contempt which he shared with Tarrian for much of the Guild's work these days, he felt an unexpected twinge of nostalgia as he looked up at the splendidly decorated entrance hall with its high-domed ceiling and stone-balustraded balconies.

The place, indeed the Guild, had meant a great deal to his father and he had always played an active part in its affairs, fighting diligently to maintain the integrity of the craft against an increasing tide of commercialism and downright quackery that was even then beginning to overwhelm it.

A pack thing, I suppose, he thought ironically as the memories fluttered in the pit of his stomach.

'Come on.' Tarrian's voice interrupted his reverie. The wolf had reached the central well and was clattering busily down the wide stairway somewhat to the consternation of two dignified souls in formal regalia who were coming up it. Both were carrying large cats which they embraced protectively as Tarrian passed.

Antyr uttered a brief prayer of thanks that Tarrian had not given the two men the benefit of his normal opinion of such 'flatulent peacocks' as he passed by them, and a much longer prayer that he had not started on their Companions. It was merely a postponement however.

'Those two must have been lost,' Tarrian said sarcastically, as he reached the library door, and stood waiting for Antyr to open it. 'I doubt either of them could read anything except their fee notes. And did you see those disgusting moggies? Imagine having one of those crawling about your dreams. Peeing everywhere and coughing up fur balls.' He concluded with a retching sound.

Antyr glanced round quickly, mortified by this unwarranted onslaught yet trying not to laugh. 'Just remember where you are and keep your thoughts to yourself, dog, or one of those . . . moggies . . . will be calling you before the council for unbecoming conduct.' He managed some sternness, with an effort, but Tarrian just chuckled malevolently to himself.

'Get in,' Antyr said fiercely, pushing open the door to the library.

As if in confirmation of Tarrian's brutal comments, however, the library was silent and deserted and it had a stale, neglected air about it. Faint haloes wavered about the few lamps that were lit as if the previous night's fog had returned here to recover itself.

Both Antyr and Tarrian wrinkled their noses in dismay. 'Your father used to spend hours here,' Tarrian said, sober now. 'Looking for things that might help his clients. Looking for things that might help him understand you. Looking for anything that would make him a better Dream Finder. And there was always someone else here as well. And it was bright. Not like this. It's . . .'

'. . . like a catacomb.' Antyr finished Tarrian's eulogy.

They stared round in silence.

The library was a large, annular room, radiating out from the central stairwell and occupying much of the basement

113

of the Guild House. Circular rows of shelves stood tall, silent and burdened in the gloaming, marking out shadowy circular pathways which were cut at intervals by equally shadowy radial paths to form a rudimentary maze of dark high-walled alleyways. Here and there, small clusters of tables and chairs stood huddled together under solitary lamps as if gathered there for protection against the weight of darkness that surrounded them.

Antyr chewed his lip uncertainly, feeling suddenly helpless as he stared at the rows of books and scrolls vanishing into the gloomy distance. It was said that the library contained every known written work on the art and craft of Dream Finding and certainly it needed no keen perception to realize that a lifetime could be spent in study here.

Yet would there be an answer here anyway? Despite Tarrian's positive denial, Antyr could not yet be certain that what had happened was not in some way his own doing.

He pulled a wry face. 'I don't know that this is going to help,' he said, his anxiety surfacing again. 'We don't even know what we're looking for. Or for that matter, why.' He waved his arms around the waiting ranks of shelves. 'And as for where we start . . .' He shrugged in some despair.

Tarrian's tone was unexpectedly sympathetic. 'Your father used to say, "If you don't know where to start. Start!" It's a very sound principle. Come on; don't let this place intimidate you. Myths and Legends are over there if my memory serves me correctly.'

'Myths and Legends?' Antyr queried in some surprise.

'Myths and Legends,' Tarrian confirmed confidently. 'Where else would we look? There's precious little in the standard texts that we don't already know and we'll get less than nothing from some of these modern learned papers.' He placed a withering emphasis on the word 'learned'. 'What's happening has got to be something that's either never happened before or happened so long ago that everyone's forgotten about it, and my instincts are for the latter. Come on. Into the past.'

Antyr picked up a nearby lamp and struck it into life, then dutifully followed his Companion down the gloomy canyons formed by the lower shelves.

Tarrian's memory did serve him correctly and soon he was running along the aisles, enthusiastically dragging books from the lower shelves and issuing instructions to Antyr to collect those that he could not reach.

'That's enough, that's enough,' Antyr cried, as he struggled with the lamp and the ninth volume that Tarrian had just pulled to the floor. 'It'll take us a week just to read through these.'

'Have you never heard of skimming, for pity's sake?' Tarrian replied heatedly. 'Come on, don't . . .' Further comment, however, was forestalled by an uncontrollable spasm that seized his snout and, after two of three tentative and grimacing starts, he let out a ferocious sneeze that sent a vibration running from his head to the very tip of his tail. Then another, and another. Then came a stream of abuse.

'It shouldn't be beyond the bounds of even this Guild to employ someone to dust this place occasionally.' He blasted out another sneeze. 'I've been in barns that were less dusty.'

'If you weren't so impatient, you wouldn't stir it up so much,' Antyr offered unsympathetically.

'That's hardly the point, is it?' Tarrian retorted crossly. 'They should never have let this place get into such a mess. This isn't what we pay our Guild fees for—'

'Yes, yes,' Antyr said indifferently, turning away and heading towards the nearest table with his burden.

Still muttering and emitting the occasional small but explosive splutter, Tarrian followed him. 'There's a lot more, you know,' he said.

Antyr dropped the books on to the table, and picked up the largest. 'I'm well aware of that,' he said. 'But what are we doing with these, Tarrian? Just look at this.' He brought the book close to the lamp and peered at the title intently. '*The Saga of Mara Vestriss, Weaver of the Great Dream.*' He thrust the book at Tarrian, thumbing through it quickly to reveal pages black with densely packed print. 'Or these.' He waved at the others. '*The Lore of the White Guardians. An Anthology of the Tales of the Knights of the Light – Defenders of the Golden Nexus. The History of Andrasdaran, the Fortress of the Gateway.* What on earth can we find in these? We need logic and reason not superstition or the ramblings of ancient storytellers.'

He picked up another and read the title. '*Marastrumel, the Evil Weaver and the Making of the Dark Mynedarion.*' But even as he read out the name, his voice faltered and he cast a hasty glance into the shadows beyond the lamplight, muttering, 'May the Blessed protect us.'

No sooner had he uttered the words, than his hand started towards his mouth and his face began to redden. He prepared himself for a mocking onslaught from Tarrian.

There was a long silence, then Tarrian said, 'Well, well,' very softly, as if he had just seen something profoundly surprising.

Antyr braced himself, but Tarrian simply said, 'If that's the way things are then I think we'd better start with that one.'

Antyr could not restrain himself. 'All right. All right. Spare me the sarcasm. It's not my fault. It's just a foolish leftover from my childhood.' He glowered at Tarrian defensively, still expecting to receive the full benefit of his acid humour. But it was not forthcoming. Instead Tarrian just repeated his previous comment. 'We'll start with that one, definitely.'

Antyr's expression turned to one of uncertainly, but Tarrian simply stood on his hind legs and, with his front legs on the table, flicked opened the book awkwardly with his nose.

'You turn the pages, I'll read,' he said. 'You're too slow.'

'What are you up to?' Antyr said, still embarrassed at his brief display of superstition and still suspecting that Tarrian was laying an ambush for him.

'Nothing,' Tarrian said, his manner serious. 'Truly.'

Antyr shuffled self-consciously. 'It's just a childhood thing,' he repeated, still attempting to defend himself against a non-existent attack. 'My father used to read me—'

'It's a pack thing,' Tarrian said before he could finish, then he turned and looked at Antyr. 'We perceive with more than our eyes and our ears and our noses, and our deeper selves guide us in ways we can't begin to appreciate. Good as you are, you don't even know how you can take me to a dream nexus and I don't know how I guide you to the dreams. But we do it and we do it well because we trust these strange resources of ours. Now you've led me to some strange nexus and I'm hunting. Trust yourself, Antyr. Trust me.'

Antyr looked pained and a hint of impatience began to creep into Tarrian's voice.

'Just reflect a moment, Antyr,' he said. 'It's fair to say that *nothing* would have possessed you to speak the invocation in my hearing, would it?'

He returned to his study of the book while Antyr sought for a reply to this harsh question.

'Indeed, you do your best to not even think it whenever the word Mynedarion is mentioned, don't you?' Tarrian went on. 'Turn over.'

'Well, you can be quite caustic,' Antyr managed after a moment. 'Not to say downright unpleasant if you're in the mood.'

'Quite true,' Tarrian conceded. 'And rightly so, I would have said up to a moment ago. And yet you said it – turn over – said it out loud – walked into my den at feeding time, as it were. In the very same breath as a plea for reason and logic, you invoke the Blessed Mynedarion at the mention of the Dark like some frightened apprentice or some demented priest.'

Antyr stared at him in silence.

'Whatever guided you to that indiscretion, Dream Finder, I intend to follow it – turn over.'

'But—' Still discomfited by his slip, Antyr was unbalanced further by Tarrian's uncharacteristic response.

'Turn over,' Tarrian repeated.

'I don't understand you,' Antyr said, shaking his head.

'Of course you do,' Tarrian retorted. 'I told you. Your wiser self made you point the way. Pushed aside our petty foolishness and pointed. Now I'm following. Turn over!'

Antyr sat down and put his hand on Tarrian's powerful shoulders affectionately. Reason and logic he had asked for, and now his Companion had pinned him to unreason with it. Part of him still wanted to bluster away from his childish utterance. But why? he asked himself abruptly. Tarrian's analysis had been right. Their faith in one another was total yet neither understood the true mystery of Dream Finding. Perhaps the inner self that guided him to the nexus had indeed prompted him thus. He relaxed. If Tarrian thought it worthy of attention then so should he. In any event, what harm could come of it? When you don't know where to start: start.

'Turn over.' Tarrian's voice interrupted his reverie. Idly fingering the page, Antyr glanced down at the book. The paper was thin and, in common with the first book he had opened, the print was small and dense, making reading difficult in the poor light. Gently he raised the page vertical and then let it fall with a light tap of his fingers.

The page floated down to reveal an illustration.

Antyr felt, rather than heard, a choking breath being drawn in noisily through his throat as he looked down at the picture, and from somewhere deep inside him came a black spiral of terror. He stood up suddenly, knocking over his chair.

The lamplight wavered, making the figure in the picture seem to move. It was the silhouette of a tall, hooded figure set against a background of ominous, live shadows. The figure held a lamp and was leaning forward.

Chapter 9

Antyr reeled under the unreasoning terror that, with the suddenness of a night ambush, had suddenly surged up within him. He felt panic beginning to overwhelm him.

Tarrian dropped down on to the floor and backed away slightly, his lip curling into an uncertain snarl. His powerful voice, however, smashed through the swirling confusion in Antyr's mind like a battle cry.

'Antyr! Nothing's happening! It's in your head! There's nothing here! Look at me! Look at me, damn you!'

Antyr clutched at the sound in desperation, then, briefly, as he turned towards Tarrian, he was the wolf, looking up to see himself swaying unsteadily in the lamplight, eyes wide in horror, mouth gaping. Yet almost before he could feel the wolf's purposeful, confident body about him, he was himself again, but now he was trembling less and breathing a little more easily. Tarrian, free of the inner terror that was unmanning Antyr, had used his brief tenancy to calm at least the body's frenzy leaving Antyr the task of stilling his mind.

Antyr nodded a grateful thanks to his Companion and reached out to steady himself against the table. He leaned forward heavily on his hands for some time until his breathing eased still further.

The open book with its menacing picture lay undisturbed by his violent reaction. With an effort, he forced himself to look at it again.

The figure in the foreground was beyond doubt that to which he had woken in the palace. His pulse started to race again as he looked at it, but this time he mastered it without Tarrian's aid.

He ran a hand over his face, and found it damp, then, almost angrily, he reached up to the lamp above the table and brightened it. It hissed with the effort, but the library became a little smaller and the book became more obviously a book.

'What was all that about?' Tarrian asked, his voice alarmed. 'I've never seen you in such a state.'

Antyr, still breathing a little unsteadily, nodded towards the book. 'The figure,' he said. 'The shadows, the lamp, everything.' He jabbed at the book with his finger. 'There. Just like last night. And before you ask, I've never seen this picture before, or even the book.'

Tarrian jumped up and put his front legs on the table again. After peering intently at the picture, he began to read. ' "Marastrumel, the Evil Weaver. The spirit of darkness seeks for the Mynedarion, the Shapers who span the worlds, in his eternal search for possession of the Great Dream—" '

Antyr felt the fear returning. 'Stop it,' he shouted, though his voice fell dead among the countless watching tomes. Seeking some escape in simple acts, he bent down and picked up his chair, then he sat down and, resting his elbows on the table, sank his head into his hands.

'It's only a story, a legend,' Tarrian said, his voice a mixture of concern and embarrassment. 'Marastrumel's just a symbol from a primitive age, a personification of the destructive side of human nature. It's—'

Antyr looked up, his face grim, and Tarrian's voice faded.

'My head knows that, Tarrian,' Antyr said softly. 'Just like yours does. But something inside both of us is less certain, isn't it? Something strange is happening. Something bad. Something that's reached out to the Duke, that's reached out to me, and also to you, Earth Holder.'

A protest formed in Tarrian's mind but Antyr rejected it. 'You followed the promptings of your instincts, and they led us to this,' he said quietly, waving a hand at the book. 'And from out of nowhere comes a terror the like of which I've not known even on the battlefield.' Tarrian's ears flattened along his head, and he turned his face away from Antyr sharply. 'It's left me feeling raw and exposed as if I've been pared free of all unnecessary thoughts and habits. Seeing clearly. Seeing the charging horses and facing death and making myself not run because I saw that that would have drawn death after me as surely as water is drawn to a breach in a river bank. Stand by me, Tarrian, shield to shield, while we move forward.'

Tarrian did not reply and when Antyr continued, his voice was very steady. 'You've seen *my* fear, but last night, as we marched through the fog, you let slip some fear of your own. You said it wasn't relevant to the business in hand. "Trust me, we'll talk later," were your words if I remember correctly. I think it's later, now, and I want to know about that fear. I want to know what you know and what you've seen fit to keep to yourself.'

There was a brief silence, then Tarrian replied, 'It's not that simple.'

Antyr nodded. 'Maybe,' he said. 'But tell me what you can, while I can hear you calmly.'

Unexpectedly, Tarrian let out a high lingering whine. Antyr heard the sound and felt the distress, but he could grasp no meaning. Some part of him, however, recognized it as the depths of the wolf striving to reach out to him and knowing that it could not.

He put his arm around his Companion.

'I'm sorry,' Tarrian said. 'This is difficult and I'm as bewildered as you are. So many strange things happening, as you say. Coming out of the darkness unheralded, shaking the very foundations of our reason.'

'Describe your fear,' Antyr said.

Again, Tarrian did not reply immediately, and when he did his voice was hesitant. 'No figures appeared to me, Antyr,' he said. 'No malevolent presences . . .' He shook his head. 'There are no words to describe it.'

'There are no words while you choose not to seek them,' Antyr said, unexpectedly stern.

Tarrian bridled angrily at the comment, but some deeper need set the response aside.

'It's a fear without cause,' he said, thoughtfully. 'So strange . . . so complex . . . so primitive. It's as if there were something there. Silent and unmoving. And invisible. And yet . . . it's as if it's always been there, waiting, ready to emerge. And when I sense it, fear bubbles out. But no knowledge. No knowledge, Antyr, truly.' He paused. 'I don't know whether it's old age, my imagination, something good, something bad, or what.'

'If it frightens you then it can hardly be something for your good,' Antyr suggested.

Tarrian disagreed. 'No,' he said. 'The fear's just a flag, a signal, to tell me I don't understand something. When I have the understanding, then perhaps I can decide how good it is, and how bad. Because it *will* be both.'

Unexpectedly his voice brightened. 'When I was a pup I had a fear like that. Nameless and vague. Lurking in the shadows like your figure in the picture.'

Antyr frowned at the digression, but Tarrian ignored him.

'And when the cause emerged, it was more terrifying than anything my ignorance could have conjured up,' he said. 'And yet, too, it wasn't.'

Antyr's scowl deepened and he made to interrupt.

'Oh yes. Far more terrifying,' Tarrian said, reflectively, as if talking to himself. 'It's a terrifying thing when you're a pup to learn that you're not only what you are, but also partly one of them.' A faint hint of bitterness came into his voice. 'Partly human. Partly one of those who slew your mother and gave you to the sing—'

He stopped abruptly as if recollecting himself. 'No. I'm sorry. I'm rambling. That's a long time ago and a tale for another time, if ever. No gift is without burden and theirs was more blessed than it was cursed.' Tarrian's voice had become distant again, but, briefly, it was almost ecstatic, and Antyr realized he was listening to a paean of praise to life itself.

His frown faded as he felt Tarrian's mood briefly uplifting him. We are both of us stripped raw, he thought.

Tarrian went on. 'I'm sorry,' he said again. 'All manner of old memories are being shaken loose. But I'm no nearer to telling you about what's been fretting at me these . . . past weeks . . . or however long it's been. It's been like walking over a frozen pond covered in snow without knowing it. Nothing is different, but there are mysterious noises, and subtle movements under your feet that could perhaps just be your imagination. And yet you can feel the cold darkness below. But you don't know what it is. Only that it's there and it's waiting to engulf you when you suddenly tumble through.'

Tarrian paused for a moment and when he began again, his voice was almost matter-of-fact. 'I thought perhaps I was sick, but there was nothing else wrong with me. Then I thought, perhaps it's pain for Antyr. Destroying himself and his gift with his indifference, his indiscipline. Then I don't know what I thought and in the end I ignored it. Limped along, made the best of things. But every now and then, the fear, the unease, bubbled out – the sound of the cracking ice – and I could do nothing. Nothing but wait and hope. Hope that something, sometime, would come clear, and that I could deal with it then.'

'And has it?' Antyr asked.

Tarrian tilted his head on one side. 'Maybe,' he said. 'We're here, aren't we? Talking, searching. Instead of you pickling your brains in the inn and me fretting in a corner, and the future looking blacker and blacker for both of us.'

Antyr let out a noisy breath. 'I'd have appreciated something clearer,' he said. 'Something that might have given us a clue about what's happening before I go to sleep tonight.'

'Look at the book again then,' Tarrian offered.

Antyr hesitated. Despite the increased light from the hissing lamp the picture still disturbed him.

'Is one man with a lamp worse than the Bethlarii cavalry?' Tarrian said, sensing his concern. 'And are you going to stand in terror of a mere picture?'

Antyr looked down at the book and forced his mind to accept the logic of Tarrian's words, though it proved to be no easy task. The image in the illustration was almost identical to his vision of the previous night and he could feel some primitive terror teetering at the edges of his mind.

'A book,' he said to himself deliberately. 'Just a book. Paper, ink, men's words.'

Men's ancient memories, came the thought, but he brushed it aside.

Then he reached out and idly flicked over a few pages. There were other illustrations scattered through the book, many of which had obviously been drawn by the same hand. But none of them produced any reaction and finally he returned to the figure with the lamp.

Marastrumel, the Evil Weaver, he mused as he read the text. Throughout most of the land, Marastrumel was the traditional personification of all things evil; the balancing force, some would say, of MaraVestriss the Creator of all Things, or in Dream Finding legend, the Weaver of the Great Dream.

The old tale was still vivid within him, from the many tellings he had made his father recite when a child.

MaraVestriss, it was said, came from the timeless time beyond all beginnings and, knowing himself to be, filled the universe with his searing greatness and then wove his joy into the Great Dream. And such was the greater joy that he found in this labour that he created Marastrumel to be his companion and helpmate and to share in his joy. But Marastrumel was flawed, or, as some would have it, he was the finest creation of MaraVestriss's art, and was more perfect

123

even than his creator. Whatever the truth, and it is beyond the gift of mere men to judge such matters, Marastrumel grew to despise MaraVestriss. And, too, he began to be consumed by a desire to possess the Great Dream for his own.

But he was cunning and kept his true intent well hidden from MaraVestriss, dutifully working as he was bidden yet endeavouring constantly to fathom the mystery of MaraVestriss's subtle weave so that he might secretly change the design for his own ends.

Then MaraVestriss declared that the Great Dream was complete and he stood back and took joy in the totality of his creation.

But Marastrumel, fearful that the Great Dream would be withheld from him forever, came to him and said, 'Look, the work is yet incomplete. See, here is imperfection, and here, and here. Surely only the merest touch will draw tight these blemishes and render perfect your design.'

But MaraVestriss shook his head and laid a hand on Marastrumel's arm. 'These blemishes are the least that can be,' he said. 'Only in the timeless time was there perfection, when none was there to see it. Then I became, and saw, and knew that I had become. But in my becoming and seeing and knowing there was separateness, and separateness is imperfection. The Great Dream is completed and can be made no better.'

And Marastrumel, fearful of MaraVestriss's sternness, fell silent, and pretended to take joy in wandering through the Great Dream. But his lust to possess and change it grew as he wandered through its many wonders, and, eventually, in great secrecy, he laid his hand to the weave and drew out one of the offending blemishes.

But the Great Dream was woven from a single thread, and to touch one part was to touch all others, and on the instant, MaraVestriss knew of the deed, and with a wave of his hand, he spanned the Dream and stood before the errant Marastrumel.

'Look,' he cried, in dismay. 'See the harm your folly has wrought. That which you have removed from here has been multiplied tenfold across the Dream. Why did you do this thing?'

But Marastrumel looked upon his creator with scorn. 'I did this because you would not, because your eyes are too dim, your mind too slow and your will inadequate.

I shall achieve the perfection that you deny the Dream.'

'No!' said MaraVestriss angrily. 'It cannot be. You would unravel all into chaos in your arrogance and your ignorance. You are banished from the Dream. Go now lest I unmake you as easily as I made you.'

And though Marastrumel was wroth, he feared MaraVestriss, knowing that in truth his eye and his mind were sound and true, and his will was not to be defied.

And he set forth immediately for the edge of the Dream.

But as he neared it, he turned. And seeing his creator distracted by the damage that had been wrought and by the deep sorrow and pain of their parting, he seized a part of the Dream and driving his powerful hands into the fabric, strove to tear it asunder.

But the fabric of the Great Dream could not be torn, for the one thread was of the nature of the timeless time and was indivisible. But so great was Marastrumel's strength in his anger that he split the weave and plunged his hands between and beyond and a strange new pattern was formed, the like of which was not to be found throughout the whole of the Great Dream, so pained and tortured was it.

And in this pattern could be seen the world of men, each of whom bore within him the shadow of his two creators.

And fearful of MaraVestriss's anger at this deed, Marastrumel wrenched free his hands recklessly, injuring them sorely. And, in great pain, he fled the Great Dream, departing into the outer silence.

But MaraVestriss had no true anger for his child and he looked upon the fleeing figure only with sadness. For he had seen that Marastrumel had so harmed his hands that he would weave no more. Then he turned his gaze to the strange new pattern that had been made, and he pondered.

For though the damage had been done to but the tiniest portion of the Great Dream, yet also it was great, and he saw that in its repair there would lie yet greater harm to the Dream. And, too, he saw that this strange new pattern was one beyond his imagining and that it held many great wonders, such as the world of men, and other worlds, and the rich layered world of dreams within the Dream.

And he asked himself, 'How could this, which is beyond my imagining, have come about?'

But he could find no answer.

Then, for the first time, he asked, 'How was it that out of the timeless time, I became?'

And still there was no answer.

And the strangeness of the pattern haunted him, so deliberate and purposeful did it seem; so well wrought despite the manner of its making. So MaraVestriss knew that he too was ignorant and he turned from the Great Dream and resolved to seek an answer to his question elsewhere before he could turn his hand to mending this strange, chance, pattern.

But before he departed, he looked again at the world of men newly formed within the weave of the Dream. And he saw pain from the manner of its making and in its separateness from the Great Dream. So, in response to some unspoken voice, he touched the pattern gently, giving to certain of mankind the skill to weave the fabric of the Great Dream themselves.

And these were the Mynedarion, though in his wisdom MaraVestriss left them unaware of his touch.

And he gave to others the skill to walk amid the world of dreams within the Dream.

And these were the Dream Finders.

And MaraVestriss departed to seek an answer to his question.

But from the silence beyond, Marastrumel, still lusting for possession of the Great Dream, had seen his final touch. And when MaraVestriss had departed, he returned stealthily and sought among mankind to find the Mynedarion, hoping through them to reshape the Great Dream in accordance with his own will.

But they were few, and mankind was many. And their gift was hidden in the finest of the fine weaves of the pattern, and save for the occasional chance, he could not find them.

'But he searches still,' Antyr said into the library gloom, finishing the remembered tale and recalling how he would dive under the bed covers when his father reached this traditional end with mock menace. It was a warm, comforting memory.

There was a long silence, during which only the hissing of the lamp could be heard. Antyr could feel Tarrian wanting to say, 'A creation myth, nothing more. There are many such,' but he could also feel uncertainty restraining him.

'It *is* a creation myth,' he admitted, sparing Tarrian his

debate. 'But even as that it must be the shadow of some dark reality. And that reality seems to be alive and happening to us now, doesn't it?'

Tarrian made no reply.

'What shall we do?' Antyr asked.

Tarrian shook his head. 'I don't know,' he said. 'All I can think of is that we keep searching through the legends for some kind of a clue.

Antyr looked at the picture again. At worst, his finding it was a remarkable coincidence. On the other hand . . .

Tarrian interrupted. 'Doesn't the legend tell about some of the Dream Finders arming themselves to protect the Mynedarion and oppose the will of Marastrumel?'

Antyr recalled his thoughts as he and Tarrian had talked together after leaving the Duke the previous night.

'Yes. They were the Dream Warriors. Adepts of the White Way.'

Antyr and Tarrian stared at one another. Neither had spoken. Then a shadowy figure emerged silently from a gap between the shelves nearby. It stopped, and turned towards them. Then it emitted a blood-curdling shriek of rage.

Chapter 10

Antyr jumped to his feet in terror, and Tarrian, tail well between his legs, scuttled behind him, crouching low.

'I'm so sorry. I'm so sorry,' the figure said hastily, stepping forward and waving a reassuring hand. 'I'm afraid it's Kany, my Companion, he's just realized that your Companion's a wolf.' There was a pause as the figure craned forward, obviously listening to something intently. Antyr caught part of a high-pitched and earnest babble. 'And that he's just eaten a rabbit,' the figure concluded, his voice fading into nothingness as the sentence proceeded, so that the word 'rabbit' was mouthed significantly rather than spoken.

Antyr's wits cleared sufficiently for him to see that he was being addressed by an old man, grey-bearded, hunched and frail.

'You frightened us half to death,' he said, both more loudly and more aggressively than he had really intended. 'Coming out of the shadows like that . . .'

'I'm so sorry,' the figure apologized again. 'I can see I've upset you.' He held out his hand. 'My name's Pandra, Indares Pandra. I'm afraid we dropped off when we were reading and when we woke we accidentally overheard your conversation.' He cleared his throat awkwardly.

'You mean you were eavesdropping,' Tarrian said, erect now, and mildly indignant as he stepped out from behind Antyr.

The old man began a long and pensive 'Er . . .' which was obviously rising to buttress a strong denial, but which concluded in a staccato 'Yes', as the speaker opted for the truth at the last moment.

'Forgive me . . . us,' he added.

The sudden slide into abject contrition released Antyr's tension and made him smile. He sat down again and indicated a nearby chair for the new arrival.

The old man hesitated for a moment.

'It's all right,' Tarrian said, his voice echoing slightly so that Antyr knew he was speaking so that both Pandra and his Companion could hear. 'Don't be afraid. I won't hurt you.'

'I'm not afraid, you savage,' came the high-pitched voice that Antyr had heard briefly before. 'I'll have your snout off if you give me any trouble.'

Somewhat to Antyr's surprise, Tarrian sat down looking rather sheepish and made no attempt to answer this seemingly unwarranted abuse. Then, as Pandra sat down, he pulled from the pocket of his gown a black rabbit. It was quite small, but its ears were well chewed and its face was scarred, giving it a distinctly bad-tempered, not to say ruffianly, appearance. After a pause for a brief and rather laboured scratch it scuttled lopsidedly to the edge of the table and peered over at Tarrian.

Antyr caught a whiff of some swift animal exchange between the two, during which Tarrian spent most of the time with his ears drawn back while Kany chattered his teeth fiercely at him. Then, after some hesitation, Tarrian craned forward slowly, and rabbit and wolf touched noses briefly.

Antyr knew better than to inquire into the details of the debate. Companions were necessarily wild and free, and their animal affairs were very much their own, as most Dream Finders usually discovered quite early in their careers.

Satisfied, however, that the two Companions had made some kind of a professional peace – albeit, he suspected, based on a mutual dislike of 'moggies' – Antyr turned again to the old man.

'Perhaps it's we who should apologize for waking you with our noise,' he said. 'We thought we were alone.'

Pandra shook his head. 'No, it's fortunate you came,' he said. 'We could have slept till Dreamsend if you hadn't. I doubt anyone is likely to be down here before then.'

'Yes,' Antyr agreed regretfully, though smiling again at the old man's manner. 'I was surprised to see the place so deserted. It used to be so busy once.'

'Before *your* time, though, I suspect,' Pandra replied, then he looked at Antyr intently. 'What's your name, young man?' he asked. 'You've got the look of someone.'

Antyr introduced himself.

Pandra's eyes narrowed. 'Antyr,' he said, testing the name for a moment before realization dawned. 'You're not Petran's lad, are you?' he asked.

Antyr nodded. 'Yes, I am,' he said. 'Did you know him?'

'Well, well. Fancy that,' Pandra exclaimed, ignoring the

question but sitting up and smiling broadly. 'Kany, it's Petran's lad.'

'I heard,' said the rabbit irritably.

Pandra continued, unabashed by his Companion's manner. 'Well, well,' he repeated. 'I should have known from the wolf, I suppose. They're not common these days. Now what's your name, Antyr's Companion? Don't tell me.' He turned his face up towards the gloomy darkness of the ceiling for inspiration. 'Tra . . . Tra . . . Tranian . . . no . . . Tarrian, that was it. Tarrian. Well, well. Don't you remember him, sitting alongside Petran, Kany?'

'All carnivores look the same to me,' Kany replied testily, muttering as an afterthought, 'all teeth, curled lips, and slobber.'

'I'm sorry,' Pandra mouthed softly to Antyr. 'Neither his memory nor his manners are what they were once.'

'I heard that,' Kany said. Pandra stroked him gently and made a clicking noise with his tongue.

He looked at Antyr and shook his head proprietorially. 'It's good to see you, Antyr,' he said. 'I can just about remember you as a little thing by your father's side. I didn't know him well, you understand. I don't think anyone really did. He was a bit stiff in his ways. But he was a fine man. Great integrity. Knew his craft, and always willing to help. He was highly regarded by those who mattered. I was shocked when he died so suddenly.'

He pursed his lips reflectively.

'Let's leave,' Tarrian said privately to Antyr. 'We've things to do and we're going to get his life story in a minute.'

Antyr flicked him with his foot discreetly.

'He used to worry about you, as I remember,' Pandra went on. 'Used to say you were something special, but he didn't know what. Still, that's parents for you, isn't it. Fuss and fret. Think their kids are going to be great artists, or Senedwrs, or somesuch, but you go your own way in the end, don't you? End up like the rest of us. Getting by. Earning a crust. Fussing and fretting over your own children in your turn.'

'Antyr . . .' Tarrian murmured significantly.

'Do you remember anything particular that my father said about me?' Antyr said, on an impulse. Tarrian let out an audible sigh and flopped down on the floor.

Pandra shook his head. 'To be honest, I can't say that I

do, Antyr,' he replied. 'It was just fathers' talk, and as I say, I didn't know him all that well. He was always a bit distant.' His eyes met Antyr's. 'Why do you ask?'

Antyr was about to shrug off his enquiry casually, but something in Pandra's gaze drew him forward. 'I've a problem,' he said somewhat to his own surprise. 'Something strange has happened – to both of us.' He indicated Tarrian. 'And I, we, just don't know what to make of it or where to turn for advice.'

'Oh dear,' Pandra said sympathetically, but not particularly hopefully. 'If I can help you I will, of course, but I'm very slow these days, virtually retired now. Very much out of touch with modern developments.'

'I don't think it's a modern problem,' Antyr said. 'I think it might be a very old one.'

'Ah. I wondered what you were doing thinking about the MaraVestriss legend.' Kany's high-pitched voice interrupted the conversation. 'What were you looking for?'

Though the rabbit looked old, the curiosity in its voice was that of inquiring and vigorous youth, and both Antyr and Tarrian started.

Pandra lifted a restraining hand. 'I'm sorry,' he said. 'I'm afraid Kany's very nosy. Not to say rude.'

'Well?' asked Kany ignoring the comment.

'I don't know what we were looking for, but this is what we found,' Antyr said, indicating the illustration.

Kany sidled over to the book and peered at it, his nose twitching. 'And?' he asked.

'Master of the monosyllable, this one,' Tarrian muttered, prompting another prod from Antyr's foot.

'I was visited by such an apparition last night,' Antyr said bluntly. 'And separated from the protection of my Companion.'

Pandra's eyes widened in disbelief and then alarm, and he drew in a noisy, shocked breath. Kany made a strange, high, whistling sound.

'Separated? What do you mean? What happened?' the old man managed, after a moment, his face full of concern.

Briefly, Antyr told him, aware that Kany and Tarrian were communicating between themselves as he did.

When he had finished, the dusty silence of the library seemed to close around the group. Pandra shook his head in dismay. 'I've never heard the like,' he said, eventually.

132

'Never. How could such a thing be? If you weren't a Dream Finder I'd say you'd been dreaming.'

'I don't know,' Antyr said. 'That's why we're here. Floundering around. Searching for anything that might tell us what's happening or what to do.'

'It should be a matter for the Guild Council, I suppose,' Pandra said, without conviction. 'But it's not what it was.' He pursed his lips and rubbed his thumb and forefinger together. 'Fees seem to be the only thing that they're interested in these days. And anyway, I wouldn't trust some of them to find the Duke's palace on Viernce Liberation Day, let alone a dream. And as for dealing with this . . .' He shook his head. 'Kany, what do you think?'

'I think I'm too old for this,' the rabbit replied. 'And so are you. I've heard Tarrian's side, and it's bad. Beyond anything we can help with. Take me home.' There was a brief private communication between the two which ended with Pandra picking the rabbit up and placing him back in his pocket. He threw an appeal for understanding to Antyr.

Antyr nodded. 'I'm sorry,' he said. 'It was thoughtless of me to burden you with such a problem. Maybe I will take it to the Council, after all. They should know about it even if they don't know what to do about it.'

'They'll either form a committee to look into it, or strike you off the roll for intemperance,' Kany said unexpectedly.

Antyr's mouth dropped open.

'I'm sorry, I had to do a little burrowing into you,' Kany said sincerely, but in a tone of regretting the need rather than the deed. 'But if it's any consolation, the wolf's right. What happened was none of your doing.'

Antyr shot an angry glance at Tarrian who must have conspired in this intrusion, but his reproach was met with the same attitude. 'Companion's need,' Tarrian said, almost tersely. 'Who knows what danger we're in. And we need all the help we can get.' Adding privately, 'He might be a bad-tempered old rabbit, but he's sharp, believe me.'

Antyr heard the justice in Tarrian's words but he still felt humiliated by this clandestine observation of his inner thoughts. 'Damn you both,' he said turning away. 'You could have asked.'

Kany chuckled darkly in the warm comfort of Pandra's pocket. 'Since when does a hunter tell the prey?' he said.

'He means you'd have shut him out, Antyr,' Tarrian

interjected hastily, seeing Antyr's jawline tighten. 'It's very difficult not to. Especially when you're afraid.'

Pandra reached across and laid a hand on his arm. 'Don't be angry,' he said. 'You know he's right. Kany's confirmed the reality of what happened. Something like that *could* have been an accidental coincidence of thoughts between you and Tarrian. A sort of unknowing mutual deception. I've heard of such things happening. Never actually met anyone to whom it's happened, mind you, but . . .'

Antyr put his hands to his head and closed his eyes. He had not even been aware of the faint, flickering hope that he now felt dying out, but its passing left him feeling starkly alone.

And frightened.

He stared into the shapeless colours that flitted behind his eyelids, and wished himself far away.

'I need a drink,' he said bitterly, only just overcoming an urge to sweep all the books off the table.

'Have as many as you like,' Kany said brutally. 'Drink yourself into a stupor if you want, but you're the focus of this problem and it won't go away.'

'How the hell do you know anything?' Antyr said angrily.

'I know because I'm old, like the wolf here,' Kany snapped back, in like vein. 'A damn sight older than you, I might add. And because I know most of my strengths and weaknesses.'

'I know my weaknesses well enough,' Antyr replied acidly. 'As does everyone else in Serenstad judging from the amount of advice I'm given about them.'

'I really am too old for you humans and your endless foolishness,' Kany said wearily. His voice was suddenly quieter, but there was such restrained fury in his reply that Antyr quailed before it. 'It's your strengths you don't know, not your weaknesses.'

The rabbit's words seemed to burn into Antyr's head.

'Strengths, Antyr,' Kany repeated, more gently, and speaking privately to him. 'Pandra here is a fine Dream Finder. One of the old school. Cares about his craft, cares about his clients, and me. I couldn't wish for better. But you're different. You're far beyond him. I can tell that even without working with you. And Tarrian is beyond me. He keeps it from me but he must have been touched by humans of rare skill in his growing.' He paused, puzzled. 'And by something, someone, else . . . strange . . . subtle . . . but . . .'

His voice drifted into silence.

Antyr, still shaken by the unexpected power radiating from such an incongruous source, picked up his last word. 'But what?' he said in some despair. 'I'm not aware of any strengths in myself. And if I were, what use is this strength if I can't know how to use it?'

Kany was silent and Antyr could feel his sense of impotence.

'There's old Nyriall, of course, perhaps he can help,' said Pandra.

Antyr felt Kany's mood fill with self-reproach and then brighten. 'Ah,' he exclaimed. 'I'm a useless old doe. I'm getting so forgetful. Of course, Nyriall. And he's got a wolf for a Companion too. Or he used to have.' He became ecstatic. 'Yes, yes, that's it. Go now. Go quickly. See Nyriall.'

Antyr found himself standing up under the urgency of Kany's appeal.

'Where does he live?' he asked in some bewilderment.

'I've no idea,' Kany said brusquely. 'See that old fool of a porter. He'll have it somewhere in one of his precious books. Go along. Hurry up.'

Bustled out of the library by Kany's urging, Antyr turned to Tarrian as they trotted up the stairs. 'What are we doing, running about like this at the behest of a *rabbit*?'

'I really can't comment about a fellow Companion,' Tarrian said, with dignity.

'Yes. Unless they happen to be feline,' Antyr replied with some amusement, finding an unexpected release in the simple physical activity of walking. 'I noticed he had you jumping as well.'

Tarrian glowered at him. 'Not at all,' he said. 'I just deferred to an older colleague as is fitting.'

Antyr was still chuckling at Tarrian's discomfiture as they crossed the wide hallway with a purposeful clatter.

Reaching the main door, they found they had to wait through another of the porter's small rituals after Antyr made his request for the address of Nyriall. First came the look over the eye lenses and then the scowl at this interruption to his duties. Next came an inquiry. 'And what is the reason for wanting this address?'

'Don't take that,' Tarrian said indignantly. 'It's none of his business, cheeky old devil.'

'A Dream Finding matter,' Antyr said diplomatically but firmly, returning to the porter a portion of his scowl.

Then came another search through the book, even more leisurely than before, and finally there was a painstaking search for paper, pen and ink and a writing down of the address. Throughout this Antyr managed to maintain a fixed smile, but as the porter finally began to wave the paper with exaggerated slowness in order to dry the ink, Tarrian put his forelegs on the counter and, craning forward, fixed him with a grim grey-eyed gaze.

The porter thrust the paper into Antyr's hand quickly and gave him a surly nod of dismissal.

Antyr looked at the smudged writing as he moved to the door and his heart sank.

'What's the matter?' Tarrian asked.

'Dream Finder Nyriall might find favour with our bumptious rabbit, but seemingly not with anyone else,' Antyr replied. 'He lives in the Moras district.'

Before Tarrian could voice his opinion on this revelation, however, the main door opened and two soldiers entered. Antyr recognized the livery of the Duke's bodyguard again and he stepped back to let them enter. As they passed him, he saw they wore the insignia of the eagle without the lamb. They were the guards seconded to Lord Menedrion.

'Wait a minute,' Tarrian said as Antyr made to leave. 'Let's see how happiness there treats the Duke's men. I doubt they'll be as patient as we were.'

Tarrian's prognostication was correct.

'You,' said the first man authoritatively, slapping his hand smartly on the counter.

Antyr and Tarrian chuckled privately at the alacrity with which the porter stood up and, smiling sycophantically, began rubbing his hands together.

The soldier eyed him coldly. 'We're looking for the Dream Finder Antyr. Where can we find him?'

The porter's eyes gleamed knowingly.

Chapter 11

Arwain was still soiled and sweating as he dismissed the messenger and walked towards the large stateroom that he had indicated.

Already puzzled by the sudden summons from his father, Arwain's curiosity was further heightened by being directed towards this particular room. It was not the one which the Duke normally used for day-to-day business matters, but one of several small halls which were generally used for private entertaining and minor state occasions, such as the presenting of an honour or the receiving of some petition or a work of art. Yet no such occasion had been planned for today as far as he knew.

Two servants opened the double doors to admit him, at the same time releasing the considerable hubbub that was filling the room. Taken aback by the unexpected noise, Arwain hesitated, then stepped inside quickly.

The room was very full. Looking around, he saw his father was at the far end, sitting in a large wooden chair richly inlaid with gold and decorated with engraved marble panels. From the top of it stared the glittering, watchful eyes of a great eagle. Indeed, so skilfully had the bird been carved and painted, that no matter where an observer stood in the room, its eyes would always seem to be staring at him. Significantly, its wings were raised slightly so that it might be either landing or just about to take flight after some prey. The detail that Arwain always appreciated, however, was in the carving of the talons, which had been done in such a way that they appeared to be crushing the wide, carved, top rail of the chair.

Seated either side of the Duke were Ciarll Feranc and Aaken Uhr Candessa, the one very still, the other fidgeting restlessly. In front of them was a semicircle of empty floor while behind them stood various other of the Duke's close advisers. Behind the whole arced a semicircle of the Duke's bodyguard.

The rest of the hall was filled with a random assortment of senior court officials, both civilian and military; high-ranking Senedwr and Gythrinwr, standing conspicuously apart;

various lords and their advisers; some senior Guild officials; several of the city's major merchants; and a leavening of scholars and artists. As usual too there were petitioners from Serenstad's allied towns and cities, distinctive in their local dress and brighter eyed than the normal courtiers.

Arwain raised his eyebrows in surprise. This was a far larger gathering than normally surrounded his father. Had he indeed forgotten some formal event that required his presence? He could remember nothing and, moreover, there was a feeling of tension in the air which had an uncharacteristically sharp edge to it.

As he made his way towards his father, Arwain also saw that several of the Duke's bodyguard were wearing their normal court clothes and mingling casually with the crowd.

With a little gentle pushing and apologizing he managed eventually to reach the empty space in front of his father.

'Father,' he said, stepping forward a few paces.

The Duke, who had been talking quietly to Aaken, turned to him and beckoned him forward.

'Ye gods, Arwain, you look like an ostler's rag,' he said, then, wrinkling his nose, 'and you smell like one, too. What have you been doing?'

'Just training with Ryllans and the others,' Arwain replied.

Ibris gave a shrug eloquent with both approval and regret. 'Ah well, I did tell you to come immediately so I suppose it's my own fault.' He took Arwain's arm and pulled him forward so that he could talk more quietly. 'Anyway, you're here,' he said. 'Menedrion's nowhere to be found, as usual, and Goran's down at Farlan looking at some new marble that one of our merchants has managed to import from somewhere . . .' He furrowed his brow and waved his hand to bring his conversation from the desirable to the necessary. 'It's perhaps as well you look so rough. We've a Bethlarii envoy coming. Ciarll's men are bringing him and his escort from the Norstseren Gate right now.'

Arwain's face darkened. 'An envoy?' he said. 'And escort? Here? Now?' He put his hand to his head and shook it as if to waken himself. 'Without a formal request; notice to the Sened and the Gythrin-Dy? To-ing and fro-ing of heralds etcetera? Endless debates about location and precedence? Have they forgotten we've a treaty with them which deals with these procedures? What are they up to?'

Ibris acknowledged Arwain's bluster with an offhand shrug,

and, taking a letter from Aaken, held it out to his son. Arwain wiped his hands on his tunic, then took the letter and unfolded it carefully. It was written in the harsh, angular script typical of the Bethlarii scribes.

'To our vassal, Ibris of Serenstad. You will receive our envoy and discuss with him a matter of great mutual concern. His person and escort of three are inviolate. Harm to them will constitute an act of war.'

Underneath this brief missive was an illegible signature and the seal of the Handira, the council of five that governed Bethlar.

Arwain looked up from the sheet and stared at his father open-mouthed. 'This is unbelievable,' he said. 'Coming unannounced is a breach of the treaty, as is bringing their own escort, but . . .' He gaped as he struggled for words, waving the paper about vaguely. Ibris took it from him gently and returned it to Aaken. '. . . the tone. It's arrogant by even their standards. *Their vassal!* It's a . . . wilful provocation . . . How did it get here?'

'It arrived barely an hour ago,' Ibris said, watching his son carefully. 'Brought by a Bethlarii Ghaler disguised as a messenger from Hyndrak, and—'

Arwain interrupted before Ibris could continue. 'In disguise? A Ghaler?' he exclaimed. 'A Bethlarii foot soldier?' He shook his head. 'Never. Their colours are sacred. A Ghaler wouldn't go into enemy territory with them covered under any circumstances. It would be sacrilege. Whatever the man is, he's no Ghaler. He's probably one of their officer corps. And probably an assassin. Has he been questioned? Searched? Don't let him near you—'

Arwain stopped as he caught a small admonitory gesture from Ciarll Feranc and looked up to see the irritation on his father's face.

'Arwain, I need thoughtful counsel, not lectures on Bethlarii religion, and elementary personal security,' Ibris said coldly. 'Besides you should know by now that priests of any colour don't hesitate to excuse the gullible the trappings of their creeds when political necessity demands. The man could be a Ghaler or anything, though I incline to your view that he's likely to be an officer. Probably tasked with noting our initial response to that letter. Anyway, what he is is irrelevant. To question him would have been in breach of the treaty, and at the moment all the breaches lie with them. He's been offered food, drink and rest – all of which he's declined, I understand – and he's being quietly, but very well guarded by Ciarll's men.'

Arwain lowered his eyes. 'I'm sorry, father,' he said. 'I should have thought before I spoke. I'm still heated with the training and rushing over here.' He risked a smile. 'Perhaps I should take a leaf from the Bethlarii way and wait for your permission before I speak.'

Ibris leaned back in his chair and some of the coldness left his voice. 'Perhaps you should,' he said. 'The Bethlarii are not without some worthwhile ideas.'

Then he tapped his temple with his forefinger, looking significantly at Arwain. There was a father's need in his eyes. 'Diplomacy or battle, Arwain, always the head first,' he said. 'Always. It'll tell you when to use your instincts. I'm sure that Ryllans has told you that, I know I have often enough.'

Arwain nodded and looked down again. It was true that he had come from the training yard too heated and flustered, but it was also irrelevant. There was never an excuse for not thinking. He must calm himself before he spoke again. His father would be more troubled by this unexpected and bizarre visit from Bethlar than he would allow anyone to see and he should not have to take pause to instruct his children. He should be able to look to them for support.

Arwain looked across the crowded stateroom with its broad cross-section of Serenstad's ruling and commercial classes and the sprinkling of travellers from its dominion cities and towns. It was, he realized, a testimony to Ibris's own advice. His father's initial response to the letter must have been something to behold yet the messenger was not hanging from the battlements. Arwain knew that it would have taken but seconds for his father to channel his doubtless monumental rage into cold calculation.

After a moment, Arwain risked a cautious irony. 'I sit at your feet, father,' he said. 'Allow me to redeem myself.'

Ibris looked at him and slowly raised one eyebrow.

Arwain, in reply, raised a confidential finger. 'Since Viernce, the Bethlarii have been much less inclined to do any extensive political or military adventuring.' He cast a glance at Feranc. 'I'm assuming that there's been no unusual military activity very recently. Just the usual, eternal war games and minor raiding between border villages.' Feranc nodded a confirmation.

'I need no history lesson either, Arwain,' Ibris said, glancing over the room impatiently.

Arwain continued. 'They've been too long without war. The futility of their endless training saps their spirit. Indeed, peace gnaws at the very roots of the reason for the existence of their whole society. And it grieves them bitterly too that *we* thrive and prosper in peacetime.' He paused briefly, gathering his thoughts. 'They could, of course, send their army against us without pretext, but that would almost certainly turn their less enthusiastic allies on the borders against them. I don't think it's beyond imagining that some clique in the Hanestra has sent this envoy, with his . . . appalling . . . letter, to be sacrificed to your anger so that his death can be used as a justification for abandoning the treaty and beginning the old round of armed campaigning again.'

'No man goes lightly to his death, Arwain,' Ibris said. 'Not even a Bethlarii. Don't *you* confuse reality with myth. They like fighting and killing, not dying.'

Arwain pointed to the letter in Aaken's hand. 'Maybe,' he said. 'But I can't imagine that and their secret journey here being just diplomatic carelessness. An inadvertent forgetting of the details of the treaty. They're too fussy about the niceties of form when it suits them. Given that, what are we left with? I think this . . . envoy . . . and his escort, have been sent to die.' A new thought occurred to him abruptly. 'I'll wager that there's some fanatical new sect of their grotesque religion beginning to seize power.'

Ibris's face became impassive. 'And my response?' he asked.

Arwain waved his hand across the crowd. 'Exactly what you're doing,' he said. 'You've scraped this civic greeting together and you're going to welcome their envoy formally and courteously, in public audience as befits a representative of a . . . friendly . . . neighbouring state.' He looked at his father intently. 'Your reasoning's like mine,' he went on. 'You've even placed a large number of your bodyguard inconspicuously throughout the crowd not only to protect yourself should this be an assassination attempt but also to protect *them* should they wilfully provoke this crowd to anger.'

He looked at his father expectantly, but Ibris still did not respond.

'The simple straight thrust is invariably the best and the least expected.' Ryllans' often given advice came back to him, and he smiled.

'Of course, with the Handira being appointed every year they may indeed simply be inept in procedural matters and you're accepting their envoy like this just to listen to what he says. However . . .' He allowed himself a theatrical pause. 'I think you hope that the absence of a violent reproach on your part will so unsettle him that, one way or another, he'll inadvertently disclose the true purpose hidden under his apparent one, or at least give an insight into their thinking.'

Ibris smiled a little and nodded approvingly. 'Convoluted and rather long-winded, Arwain,' he said, 'but interesting. I am indeed going to listen to this envoy and I'm certainly going to ensure that he isn't harmed in any way, if that's possible.' He beckoned Arwain to bend forward to that he could speak more softly. 'But heed this. Though no arrows and spears are flying here, don't be deluded. This will be as dangerous as a battle and we'll have to ride the avalanche. When we meet this man we're going to jump from rock to rock and our sole concern is not to fall. That's all. You're learning. But don't seek too diligently to guess the motives of others, you'll miss the obvious looking for the hidden. And what you need to know, you'll learn if you just listen with your whole spirit.'

'The simple straight thrust,' Arwain said, echoing his earlier thought.

Ibris nodded, then he looked a little pensive. 'Besides,' he said, almost wryly, 'you'll find in time that you don't even know your own reasons for much of what you're doing, let alone anyone else's.'

Arwain looked at him quizzically but Ibris offered no amplification of this cryptic comment. Abruptly he was businesslike. 'Stand at the back of my chair . . . here . . . between me and Aaken.' As Arwain moved between the chairs, Ibris pulled him forward again and spoke in a whisper. 'Loosen your knife and be ready but leave a clear sightline for the archers in the balcony alcoves behind us.' Then with both ducal and paternal urgency he repeated his advice. 'Don't speak; just listen and watch. And don't let the faintest shadow of your mind appear on your face.'

Arwain acknowledged the comment by a pressure on his father's arm and moved to the position his father had indicated. He was about to ask how long it would be before the envoy arrived, when the doors at the far end of the room opened suddenly and a group of the Duke's bodyguard marched in, pikes raised.

Chapter 12

There was a flurry of activity through the crowd, then an aisle opened up before the advancing guards, and the hubbub faded abruptly.

Arwain looked at the approaching group intently. There were three Bethlarii, one walking in front of the other two. Envoy and escort, Arwain presumed, judging by the insignia that the leader wore and his easier though equally contemptuous manner as he gazed freely over the watching crowd. The other two stared fixedly forward.

They were completely surrounded by Ciarll Feranc's men, but Arwain noticed that while they maintained the pace of their escort comfortably enough, they marched in step with one another and not in step with the guards. It was a simple act but it betokened a chilling discipline.

As with most Bethlarii, it was difficult to estimate their ages as they were all bronzed and weatherbeaten from their wilfully harsh life. That said, and despite their manner, they were fine-looking men, straight and limber and dressed in simple, virtually undecorated tunics. They contrasted greatly with the motley assortment of fashions, complexions and bodily shapes currently gazing at them in a mixture of amusement, distaste, plain curiosity and, in some cases, downright lust.

Arwain had to admit that even though the Bethlarii were travel-stained and patently weary, the Serens suffered by the comparison. He consoled himself, however, with the fact that the rich variety to be found in Serenstad's society had achieved far more in almost every sphere of endeavour than the stark ranks of uniform and regimented humanity that were the Bethlarii. They had also held their own against the Bethlarii army when need arose.

The Duke levered himself into a more comfortable position as the guards halted some way in front of him and the front rank opened to let the envoy move forward. Arwain willed himself to relax and watch the man calmly, though it was not easy. All three men carried themselves with such arrogance and disdain that it seemed that any form of polite discourse was out of the question.

As the first Bethlarii stepped forward, Arwain noticed that he wore a short sword and a dagger in his belt. A quick glance revealed that the other two were similarly armed. More breaches of the treaty. Arwain felt surprise and alarm taking hold of his features then he remembered his father's injunction. 'Don't let the faintest shadow of your mind appear on your face,' and, with an effort, he forced his expression into one of polite indifference.

For a moment he was tempted to work out how he might best defend his father should a sudden attack be made on him, but he rejected it. He had learned enough both from Ryllans and in the field, to know that in close quarter fighting there was no time to marshal and choose detailed plans. Awareness and single-minded ruthlessness were the watchwords. And he knew too that any rash move on his part might only impede the responses of Feranc's guards, not least the hidden archers behind him, and while a knife blow might perhaps be redirected at the last moment to avoid a friend, an arrow could not be recalled.

Watch and listen. That was what his father wanted him to do and that also would be his best defence against any attack. It was unlikely anyway that the envoy would be allowed within four paces of the Duke and he would be dead within two paces from half a dozen blades and points if he made any threatening move.

Ciarll Feranc stood up and walked forward, discreetly interposing himself between the man and the Duke. As he did so, Ibris also stood up and signalled to someone in the crowd. Arwain did not see the recipient of the signal, but, almost immediately a group of court musicians struck up. For a moment, the piece they were playing, though familiar, eluded Arwain; then he identified it as the Bethlarii AnFest, a hymn from their ancient past ostensibly written to celebrate the passing of a devastating outbreak of the plague. It was a tune which held a high place in their otherwise relatively unmusical culture.

Arwain was momentarily puzzled by his failure to identify the piece immediately. He had heard it more than once before: strident and raucous during battle; mournful and solemn afterwards as the dead were carried away under flags of truce; occasionally almost jolly, emanating from their

144

waiting, watching camps in the evening before battle. Then he realized that it was because it was being played on instruments. He had only ever heard it being sung previously. He watched the three Bethlarii closely to see how they would respond.

The eyes of the two escorts flickered briefly and they seemed to become even straighter than before. The envoy himself stopped and stood motionless while the music was played, but gave no other sign that he had heard it.

As the final chords died away, the Duke sat down again. 'Welcome to our city and our palace, envoy,' he said genially. 'Our greeting would have been a little more lavish had we had due notice of your coming. However, I understand from your message that a matter of some urgency has arisen that requires our immediate attention so we must accept a degree of informality.' He leaned forward. 'I presume, however, that the urgency has not precluded your bringing letters credential from the Handira.' He extended his hand towards Feranc.

The envoy looked from the Duke to Feranc, then turned his head slightly and made a small, curt gesture. One of his escort stepped forward smartly and handed a document to Feranc who opened it slowly and read it carefully before turning to the Duke.

'My Lord Duke, may I introduce Grygyr Ast-Darvad, head of the house of Darvad, deputed by the Handira at the behest of the Hanestra to act as envoy for the city and dominions of Bethlar.' He examined the seal. 'This letter bears the seal of the Handira, which I recognize and validate, and the same signature as the previous message.'

Ibris inclined his head in acknowledgement of this introduction then made another signal to someone in the crowd. On the instant, a small group of servants bustled forward, carrying chairs and a heavy, food-laden table which they set out in front of the Bethlarii.

'Please be seated, gentlemen,' Ibris said. 'And please eat. It's a chilly day and I've no doubt you've been travelling for some time.' He became knowingly avuncular. 'I know well enough that camp fare usually leaves something to be desired.'

For the first time since their arrival, the Bethlarii seemed to be unsettled. To have remained standing would have obliged them to conduct their debate over the table looking

145

like servants pleading before their master, while to sit would
have lessened their stern presence. Arwain found it difficult
to keep a smile from his face as he watched the envoy's brief
unspoken debate. It concluded with his sitting while his escort
stood stiffly on either side of him, but a pace back.

Added to the envoy's dissatisfaction was the fact that the
chair was large and lavishly cushioned, in stark contrast to
traditional Bethlarii furniture. But having chosen to sit, it
was not possible for him to stand again without looking
foolish. He succeeded in recovering a little of his poise,
however, by slowly and deliberately brushing the plates in
front of him to one side and leaning forward into the empty
space.

'My preference is for camp fare,' he said, speaking with
a heavy Bethlarii accent and with a voice that was guttural
and strained as if he had spent his lifetime shouting orders
on a parade ground. 'And I am indifferent to the vagaries
of the weather.' As he spoke, his eyes seemed to come
unnervingly alive.

Ibris nodded slightly in acceptance of this declaration, but
showed no reaction to the calculated omission of his title. The
watching crowd grew more silent, and Arwain could feel a
tension beginning to grow. If this day didn't end in steel and
blood it would be a miracle, he thought.

Ibris made to speak.

'Where is my messenger?' asked the envoy, bluntly cutting
across his intention.

The Duke affected a brief uncertainty, tapping his mouth
with the edge of his forefinger and frowning slightly. 'The
servants will be attending to him, I imagine,' he said. 'I
really don't know. He's probably dining. Or resting. I'll
send someone to find out and have him brought here for
you.'

Turning, he spoke softly to one of the guards behind him.
The man nodded and then quietly left the room. Ibris sat
back and waited, not attempting to speak again as if to do
so in the absence of the fourth Bethlarii would be a
discourtesy. The envoy wriggled surreptitiously on the too
comfortable chair. Carefully, Arwain felt for the man
underneath the stark image.

Eventually the guard returned, accompanied by the
messenger who went immediately to the envoy, saluted
ferociously and joined his two colleagues in their stiff array.

146

Now, Arwain thought. That's the end of the skirmishing, let's see what the attack will be like.

Apparently reaching the same conclusion, the envoy laid his hands flat on the table and prepared to speak. Ibris, however, used his own device against him, and spoke first.

'If I may, Grygyr, before you begin,' he said. 'There's a slight problem that I'd like you to clarify before we get down to your urgent message.' He did not wait for an answer, but took the original letter from Aaken and handed it to Feranc who placed it in front of the envoy.

The envoy stiffened slightly as if preparing for some kind of assault.

'I see the seal of the Handira,' Ibris went on. 'But I cannot make out the signature. I'm not concerned myself, you understand. Man to man, I've no reservations about you, but there are legal forms to be observed under our treaty, as I'm sure you appreciate, and it is our duty . . .' He waved a hand between himself and the envoy. '. . . to ensure that they are observed correctly. As on the battlefield, so here, in friendly discourse, if the forms are not observed then dishonour and treachery lie ever in wait.'

The envoy's eyes narrowed perceptibly, and he glanced briefly down at the letter. 'It's the signature of some scribe,' he said dismissively. 'His name is of no importance. The seal of the Handira needs no endorsement.'

Ibris puffed out his cheeks in reluctant disagreement. 'The treaty, as I recollect it, says otherwise. Something to the effect that your official documents shall bear the seal of the Handira, *and* the signature of the then most senior. I'm no lawyer, the exact phraseology escapes me, but that's the gist of it, I believe.'

The envoy scowled openly.

The Duke went on. 'The difficulty is, Grygyr, that this same signature graces your letters credential and if it is indeed the hand of some lowly scribe instead of the senior Handiran, then, strictly speaking, whatever we discuss is so much air, it has no binding force.' He drew in a thoughtful breath. 'Indeed, if we're being meticulous about this it also means that your very presence here is a breach of the treaty, even an act of war.'

There was a stirring among the crowd and the envoy looked set to speak again, but Ibris ploughed on.

'However,' he said affably. 'We're not lawyers, are we? It's their fault if such details haven't been attended to correctly. You've come a long way. Indeed, without our protection, it must be admitted, you've come a dangerous way. I commend you on whatever disguise you adopted, incidentally; not all our people take the broad view of our past differences that we perforce must for the general good. That being the case I see no reason why we should allow this relatively minor omission by some scribe to set your journeyings at naught.' As if seeking their support he looked round at his advisers and was greeted by much sage nodding of heads. Satisfied, he turned back to the envoy, chuckling as he did so. 'After all, it's hardly likely that the seal of the Handira could be forged, is it?' He settled himself back in the chair again. 'Now, Grygyr, if you still have no desire to eat or rest at the moment, then let's hear your message.'

Arwain stood very still behind his father's left shoulder and listened and watched. 'We'll be riding the avalanche,' Ibris had said, and, listening to him, Arwain felt the shifting ground under his feet and began to absorb the nuances of his father's performance.

Apart from what he was saying, there was the manner in which he was saying it and the small gestures and expressions that, combined, would subtly play on the Bethlarii's arrogance and must surely lead him into some indiscretion eventually. And the food and the luxurious chair were master strokes in their simplicity.

Perhaps, Arwain thought, it was because he was still peculiarly alert from his training that he was suddenly aware of these things that he must surely have seen on many occasions before. He had, after all, attended several battlefield truce meetings in the past, but by comparison with even the few exchanges that had been offered here so far, these now seemed to have been little more than a mixture of posturing displays and market-place bartering.

Perhaps, too, it was that there had never been such a strange meeting before. Whatever the reason, however, he knew that his father was teaching him something that could not readily, if at all, be taught in words, and he must have the wit to learn it.

The envoy cast as disdainful an eye around such of the crowd as he could see without wriggling incongruously in the soft chair. As his eyes met Arwain's there was a brief spark

148

of hopeful recognition which was followed almost immediately by disappointment.

Not a shadow of my mind in my face, Arwain thought. In fact, not a shadow of it in my entire posture. But I see your mind in *your* face, envoy, as clear as if it were written there. You saw me, soiled and simply clad, standing at the Duke's back, and for the moment you thought I was one of your own. Then you knew me. And now you think, they are like us, these degenerates, and it unsettles you.

'Are you sure you'll not eat?' Ibris was saying, pleasantly throwing another small handful of rounded stones under the hooves of his opponent's horse.

The envoy's face twitched and he clenched his hands tightly several times, then, as if a spasm had slipped from his control, his right arm swung out violently and sent the contents of the table crashing on to the marble floor.

There was a gasp from the crowd, but Ibris ignored the outburst apart from signalling some nearby servants to pick up the mess.

'Leave it,' said the envoy fiercely as the servants began fussing about him. They froze, looking first at the envoy and then at the Duke. Ibris nodded to them to abandon the task, then leaning to one side of his chair, casually rested his head on his hand and waited for the envoy to speak.

He had set the scene well. Grygyr Ast-Darvad looked faintly ridiculous. Ensconced in the large and luxurious chair in front of a table that was a little too high, his stern presence was lessened considerably, and in his soiled tunic he almost had the look of a dirty child; an image that was aided greatly by the food and dishes scattered about the floor around him.

Suddenly seeming to realize his position, he stood up, brushing the chair back noisily. For a moment it looked as if he were going to sweep the table to one side as a splendid gesture, but presumably noticing that it was of an extremely heavy construction, he resisted the temptation and stepped around it instead.

Ibris still made no movement but Ciarll Feranc took half a step forward and spoke softly. The envoy stopped and turned to look at him. Arwain did not hear what had been said, but, partly sheltered by his father's chair, he discreetly drew his knife. Somewhere behind him he heard the soft creak of a bow being bent. That archer would have to be spoken to, he noted.

For a long moment, the envoy looked at Feranc, who returned the gaze unblinkingly. But though Feranc's stare was without overt menace, it had an eerie certainty that had chilled braver men than Grygyr Ast-Darvad in the past and Arwain noticed the envoy breathing more deeply. He forced himself to do the same as he felt the tension in the silent room creeping into his own limbs.

'Your message, envoy,' Ibris said quietly, still as if nothing untoward had happened. His voice afforded the envoy the opportunity of escaping from Feranc without seeming to have lost the battle of wills.

'My message concerns the city of Whendrak,' the envoy said, turning sharply to the Duke. 'Our citizens there have petitioned the Hanestra complaining of abuse at the hands of the authorities. As those authorities are dominated by Serens, we consider that their treatment of our citizens is at your express wish and we demand that you order an end to this persecution immediately and take steps to ensure that the rights of our citizens are fully restored and where necessary due compensation paid.'

There was a strong 'Or else' implicit in his tone.

Ibris, however, affected a relieved indifference. 'Ah, the Whendreachi again,' he said knowingly. 'I'd not heard of any trouble there recently, but it doesn't surprise me. But I am surprised that you've come to me about it, Grygyr. Whendrak's a neutral city as you know. And not without good reason.'

He shook his head and looked up at the ceiling as if contending with a flood of old memories. 'It's been fought over so often that half the citizens are of Bethlarii stock and half of Serens, and neither knows which. And there's more than a few foreign mercenaries stamped their features on them as well. The Hanestra knows well enough that they can be a quarrelsome people who pick whatever ancestors best suit their immediate squabble. And when Bethlar and Serenstad have fought themselves to a standstill over them, as, god knows, they've done often enough in the past, what happens? They go their own way as they always have. Curse us both and solemnly vow to be neutral – again.'

There were murmurings of agreement from the crowd but Grygyr seemed unmoved. 'I'm not here to debate this matter,' he said, still assiduously avoiding using Ibris's title. 'The treaty binds us to protecting our citizens wherever they might be. I have come here openly and honourably to ask you to fulfil your obligations by restraining your people in Whendrak. If you do not do this then we will have no alternative but to do it ourselves.'

Ibris frowned paternally and waved his hand gently as if to quieten a petulant child about to commit some folly. 'Grygyr, the Whendreachi are the Whendreachi. As I've said, they're neither Bethlarii nor Serens and, apart from its strategic position, that's why their city was declared neutral when the treaty was negotiated. Declared neutral I might add with their full compliance. If either of us takes troops there, for whatever reason, and it'll need troops if they're fighting among themselves again – then it's a major breach of the treaty and will be considered an overt act of war.'

Grygyr pursed his lips impatiently. 'That is not our reading of the treaty,' he replied tersely. 'We—'

'Whose reading?' Ibris interrupted sharply.

Grygyr faltered. 'Our lawyers and scribes,' he said irritably, after a momentary hesitation.

Ibris nodded as if something had just been made clear to him. 'The same lawyers and scribes who were responsible for that?' He pointed to the letter lying on the floor amid the spilt food and broken dishes. 'Lawyers and scribes who know so little about the treaty that they didn't have our message signed by the senior Handiran? Indeed, didn't even have your letters credential signed correctly and could have had you executed as a spy as a result? So ignorant of the treaty that they breached almost every major clause, sending you here both secretly and armed, without even a token of concession towards the agreed procedures; the issuing of notices, the exchanging of heralds? You'd trust *their* reading of the treaty in this matter before mine, who helped draft it? Before your own?'

He paused briefly. 'You can read, can you, Grygyr?'

Though spoken with the concern that had filled all Ibris's words so far, the question hissed through the atmosphere like an ice-chilled dagger.

Even Arwain winced. No small part of the Bethlarii's hatred for the Serens lay in the latter's scorn for what they considered to be the impoverishment of Bethlarii culture and with it the implications of stupidity, barbarism and general oafish inferiority.

It was not without a small element of truth in that many

Bethlarii did despise such matters as reading and learning except in so far as they were associated with warfare. But it was also not an attitude that the Duke approved of, nor let go unrebuked if it was expressed in his presence. 'The simplicity in some of their art has a profundity that you'll search long to find in many a piece of Serenstad ostentation. And though their philosophy isn't ours it's valid and consistent and not without intellectual merit.'

Nonetheless, the attitude was widespread and indeed had grown over the recent years as Serenstad had continued to prosper while Bethlar had remained static and, by comparison, declined.

Maybe you came here prepared to die, warrior, or maybe you didn't, Arwain thought. But whatever you expected I doubt it was such a death by humiliation. He felt anger, pity and admiration for his father all at the same time, and knew again why he had little desire ever to be Duke in his stead.

The Duke's sudden thrust had destroyed the Bethlarii utterly. What answer could he give? No, and bring down the ultimate mockery on his head? Yes, as if he were some chastened schoolboy with an ill-prepared exercise? Both were unthinkable. Nor could he walk away with stony dignity for that would cause him to lose face in front of his own men and these gleeful enemies.

Would he perhaps strike down the offender? Would he indeed use this as an opportunity to sacrifice himself to ensure the destruction of the treaty?

No, Arwain concluded. Not unless his father had pushed him totally beyond reason. There were too many unidentified witnesses here for the truth to be hidden. The Bethlarii would know that at such a gathering there could well be visitors and dignitaries from the border communities present; people from Herion, Veldan, Nestar, any one of a score of towns and cities whose allegiance to either side was both uncertain and critical in the event of a war. No, his death would have to be away from such extremely public view if subsequent rumours were to be effective.

As these alternatives flitted instantly through Arwain's thoughts, Grygyr's eyes widened in a combination of fury and disbelief. Arwain watched him being swept away by the avalanche that his father had so successfully ridden.

His hand came out and pointed at the Duke and his mouth

opened to speak, but for some time, though his lips quivered, no sound emerged.

When it did it was raw with emotion and again Arwain found it difficult to maintain his expression of indifference.

'I read well enough, Ibris,' he managed eventually. 'I read the history of this land, *our* land, to the shores in the east, the west and the south and beyond the shores to the islands. I read enough to know of the treacheries through the ages that your forebears used to usurp our divine authority to rule here, and which you, apostate, continue.'

Released, Grygyr's rage did not spend itself, but rather seemed to gather momentum, growing upon itself, and sweeping its creator along with it.

His voice grew more powerful and a strident quality began to edge it. 'Mark this well, Ibris, vassal regent for the moment of this, our city. The day of retribution is at hand. The Bethlarii are turning again to the true way, the old way, and soon you and your corrupt ways will be swept away for ever. And so total will be your destruction that the very memory of you and all your kind will be gone utterly before the year is passed.'

There was a brief, stunned silence, then a single raucous cry of denunciation from someone released the crowd's fury and on the instant there was uproar. Immediately, two ranks of the guards that had escorted the Bethlarii through the city lowered their pikes to form a protective ring around their charge, while his three companions moved to protect the envoy himself. But they were forestalled by the other guards, who seized and disarmed them with an overwhelming suddenness that bore the hallmark of Ciarll Feranc's planning. The envoy too found himself politely but rapidly disarmed and surrounded by a double ring of guards, one facing inwards, the other outward and both with swords drawn.

The arc of guards at the rear of the Duke's entourage moved rapidly round in front of him and Arwain stepped forward, knife in hand, to be by his father's side.

Ibris watched these proceedings critically for a moment and then slowly stood up. He made no attempt, however, to shout above the din. Instead he gestured to a nearby guard, making a clapping motion with his hands. The guard nudged his fellow then the two of them swung up their shields and began beating them slowly and steadily with their swords like a great heartbeat.

Soon the persistent tattoo began to dominate the noise of the crowd, and the fury began to subside, first into a menacing rumble and finally into an awkward, expectant shuffling as all eyes turned back once again to the Duke.

Ibris nodded to the two guards and the hammering, now relentlessly loud in the silence, stopped.

He paused for a moment before speaking and when he did, his voice was calm and regretful. 'The envoy, I fear, is fatigued from his arduous journey and has misjudged a perhaps ill-expressed remark on my part. Before he leaves we shall talk again in private and go into the details of his concerns about the Whendreachi, but . . .' His voice became more commanding. '. . . you here are all witness to what has happened today. You are witness to the fact that despite many breaches of the treaty which we have with Bethlar for dealing with such matters, the envoy, Grygyr Ast-Darvad, was greeted peacefully and given due protection.' He cast about through the crowd, catching an eye here and there. 'Those of you, in particular, who are from our allied cities I ask especially to take note of this, so that truth may prevail over rumour. Further, I give you my word that he and his companions will continue to receive our protection and hospitality during their stay here, which shall be as long as they determine, and throughout their journey back to Bethlar.'

The consensus of the crowd was one of approval at this speech, though amid the applause were isolated cries to the effect that the Bethlarii should be 'Strung up' or 'Chucked off the Aphron'.

With a wave of his hand, Ibris dismissed the crowd, then turned and left the room. The envoy and his companions were ushered after him.

Chapter 13

'I don't know whether this is becoming repetitive or alarming,' Tarrian said as, head bent low, he loped steadily along beside Antyr and Menedrion's guards through the busy afternoon crowds that were thronging the wide streets of Serenstad's commercial district.

'Alarming,' Antyr replied with conviction. 'No. Terrifying. My stomach's churning. First the Duke, now Menedrion. They say he's a mad dog. Like the Duke but without his good qualities. What on earth can *he* want? I really don't think I want to think about any of this too closely . . . I think.'

'Perhaps word got round about last night. Perhaps we're becoming fashionable,' Tarrian said optimistically. 'You'll have to buy some court clothes. You'll be able to declare yourself Dream Finder by appointment to the Duke and his court and—'

'Stop it,' Antyr snapped. 'You're not helping. I told you, I'm scared.'

'You didn't have to come,' Tarrian said off-handedly.

'Oh no. Of course not,' Antyr replied acidly. 'I told them we had to see someone urgently, you heard me. And you heard him. No threats, no arguments, just "Yes sir, of course. Would you like me to tell the Lord Menedrion to wait for you, sir?" What am I supposed to say to that?'

Tarrian offered no reply and they walked on in silence for some time, each occupied with his own thoughts.

The small outburst, however, seemed to have eased Antyr's tension. 'Still, these two are pleasant enough, and at least we're not being marched along at dead of night like prisoners under escort this time,' he said eventually. 'And the Duke was a surprise. Much pleasanter than I'd imagined.'

He felt an ill-disguised wave of irritation rise up from Tarrian, but when the wolf spoke, his voice was conciliatory. 'I'm sorry,' he said. 'I know this isn't much fun but all I can think about at the moment is my pads. They're sore as the devil with all the walking I've done today. And whoever

155

thought these cobbles were a good idea must have been a shoemaker. And these crowds . . .'

He left the sentence unfinished, with an expression of disgust.

Then, like the sun appearing from behind a dark cloud, he brightened suddenly. 'Still, on the whole, I'd rather be going to the palace than to the Moras district at this time of day. We can always visit Nyriall tomorrow. And there might be more food at the palace. At least they've got some regard for a creature's needs there.' The sun retreated behind the cloud again. 'And we can get our fee from that Aaken while we're at it. Typical civil servant. Wants this, wants that, wants it *now*. But doesn't want to pay for it until he's good and ready. You take some poor artisan's wife now, she's only too anxious to pay you on the dot. It's—'

'Oh, shut up,' Antyr said, brushing the subject aside and then immediately picking it up again. 'And by "*we*" getting our fee off *Chancellor* Aaken, I presume you mean me?'

'That's normal procedure,' Tarrian replied sharply. 'What good is money to me? You're the only one who can use it. You're the one with the much prized opposing thumbs, after all.'

Despite his anxiety, Antyr chuckled at the remark. One of the guards turned to him inquiringly. 'Sorry,' Antyr said. 'Just something my Companion said.'

The guard looked at him uncertainly and then down at Tarrian. 'I didn't hear anything,' he said.

'They talk in their heads,' the other guard said before Antyr could reply, and as if he were not there. 'My mother used to use one. Swore by him. He had a cat. Big ginger thing.' He nodded to himself at the memory. 'He was all right. Bit oily, but down-to-earth when you got to know him. But that cat used to give me the creeps, especially when its eyes lit up.' He shuddered.

Antyr smiled.

The first guard caught the expression and scowled from Antyr to Tarrian. 'He's not talking about me, is he?' he inquired suspiciously.

Antyr shook his head hastily. 'No, no,' he replied. 'I was smiling at . . .' He flicked a thumb towards the second guard, ' . . . your friend . . . and the cat. Tarrian doesn't like cats either.'

'Well, him being a dog, he wouldn't, would he?' came the knowing reply.

Tarrian's groan filled Antyr's head.

'Can he talk to me in my head?' the first guard asked after a short silence.

'No,' Antyr lied.

'I'd be deafened by the echo,' Tarrian muttered.

'Will you be quiet,' Antyr snapped at him. 'This is hard enough as it is.'

'Can he hear what I'm saying in my head?' the guard persisted.

'No, no,' Antyr lied again with great conviction. 'It's not talking and hearing like we're doing now. It's a special thing, and we were both born with it. No one really understands how it works.'

'Oh,' the guard replied, mollified, though still looking at Tarrian uncertainly. He screwed up his face in concentration.

'He's shouting "Cats, boy, cats!"' Tarrian wailed in disbelief.

Antyr looked up, rubbing his slight growth of beard with casual vigour to stop himself from laughing. As he did so, he saw the familiar shape of the Ibrian monument at the far end of the long street, its spiky irregular pyramid black in the growing gloom.

'Oh, we're here already,' he said out loud, in some relief, his voice a little strained. 'I didn't realize we'd walked so far.'

Immediately all interest in Antyr's craft disappeared and the two guards quickened their pace slightly. It was to little avail, however, for the street was quite narrow and still filled with all manner of people going about their many businesses and, Duke's men or no, they were obliged to continue following the pace of the many.

In the distance, Antyr saw a bright spark dancing in front of the monument. It split into smaller sparks that danced away in their turn. For some reason he felt a fleeting lightness touch him as he saw it, then its firefly dance became just one of the Guild of Lamplighters' apprentices taking the lid off a fire bucket prior to his master and the senior apprentices lighting the torches around the monument. By tradition, the public torches of the city were lit outwards from the palace square.

'Yes,' Tarrian said, agreeing with his earlier remark. 'We're well out of the Moras for today. It'll be foggy down there by now, for sure.'

Antyr could not dispute this conclusion though he still wished he was somewhere else.

As they neared the square, the busy crowds thinned a little as the street widened and houses and buildings became larger and more spacious.

Antyr started to stride out, but one of the guards took his elbow. 'This way,' he said, pointing to a side street on the right. Antyr looked inquiringly towards the square.

'The main gate's that way,' he said, his uncertainty growing again as he followed the guard's lead.

'We're not going to the main gate,' the man replied, mildly surprised. 'Lord Menedrion's . . . guests . . . rarely use the main gate.' He nudged Antyr and winked, then both guards laughed knowingly.

'It's his women they're talking about,' Tarrian said. 'They're trying to impress you.'

'I *know*,' Antyr replied testily. 'I *can* read my own species, you know.'

'Sorry,' Tarrian said huffily. 'Only trying to reassure you.'

There were only a few people in the street, which was lined with terraces of neat, well-kept and individually distinct houses, some four and five storeys high. Expensive, Antyr mused, as the quartet followed the street round in a long, slow arc until the houses closed about in a semicircle and sealed it except for a wide, colonnaded passageway. Clattering through this they emerged into another equally quiet street which, Antyr realized, was bounded on the far side by the palace wall.

'See,' said one of the guards expansively. 'It's a lot quicker this way. Not far now.'

The street rose up quite steeply and their pace slowed somewhat until, passing under an enclosed overhead walkway, the guards stopped and one of them banged on a door set well into a deep recess in the palace wall. Antyr had not noticed the door and judged that even in broad daylight it would have been almost invisible in the shade of the walkway.

There was an almost immediate response as a small shutter behind a stout grill opened briefly then closed again. After a few dull thuds, the door opened quietly and the guard stood to one side.

Well-oiled bolts and hinges, Antyr noted, thinking immediately of his own screeching door.

'It's the Dream Finder, Antyr,' said the guard into the darkness. 'We were lucky. He was at the Guild House.'

'Excellent,' came a soft cultured voice in reply. 'His lordship will be pleased.' Then, apparently to Antyr, 'Just a moment . . . er . . . sir, there are two steps up. Take care, they're a little tricky. There's a handrail on the right.'

The voice was polite and thoughtful, but apart from the brief hesitation, it had the long-rehearsed quality of one that had spoken the same words many times to unfamiliar and uncertain ears. Similarly it was a confident and practised hand that reached out in the dim half-light to offer support.

Antyr looked at the guard who, with a flick of his head and another wink, relinquished him to the hand.

'Thank you,' Antyr said, both to the guards and to the unseen figure. Then, taking the hand, he stepped gingerly forward into the darkness. Tarrian scrabbled up the steps beside him and there was a faint exclamation from the speaker.

'I'm sorry if he startled you,' Antyr said. 'Don't be afraid.'

'It's all right,' said the voice. 'I just wasn't expecting a dog.'

As the door closed behind them, they were plunged into complete darkness, but Antyr still raised his eyebrows in surprise at the absence of any caustic response from Tarrian at this comment. Then he realized.

'Oh, it's a woman, is it?' he said, mockingly. 'I thought the voice was unusual.'

'It's a lady actually,' Tarrian replied with dignity. 'She feels very nice. And . . . Oh . . .'

'What's the matter?' Antyr asked, suddenly anxious again in the darkness.

'There's a great sadness around her,' Tarrian replied, his voice concerned and serious. 'And she's shutting it in. Like a fortress.' Fleetingly Antyr felt the pain as his Companion reflected it. But, brief though the touch was, its vivid intensity was unmistakable. It was love. Unrequited . . . but very female . . . patient . . . waiting . . . despite the pain . . .

'I'm sorry. I didn't mean to pry,' Tarrian went on guiltily. 'It just reached out and—'

Before Antyr could reassure him however, the darkness was cracked open by a shaft of light which blossomed out rapidly to illuminate a narrow stone passageway. Beside him stood a woman with a hooded lantern in her hand.

As she eased past him, Antyr took in two searching sloe

eyes set in a finely sculpted face, framed by a circle of lightly curled hair. She was handsome rather than pretty, and she was certainly no servant. He could make no guess at her age, but, somewhat to his surprise, the thought that came into his mind was: even the hood on the lantern is oiled for silence.

'Come this way, sir,' the woman said. Again, though pleasant, the words came with the bored ease of long familiarity.

Tarrian set off after her immediately. 'Oh, that's better,' he said in ecstasy. Antyr stared after him in alarm until he realized that he was talking about his feet again.

Looking down, Antyr saw that while the walls of the passageway were rough undecorated stone, the floor was completely covered by a soft and luxurious carpet which deadened their footsteps completely.

All is silence along this path, he thought.

Other, less mysterious, details struck him as they walked. At intervals the carpet was broken by a narrow slot running across the passage. The slot continued up the walls and over the arched ceiling.

Portcullises. Antyr grimaced, remembering what little training he had done for the assaulting of castles such as this. Should an enemy break down the door through which he and Tarrian had entered, they would be allowed so far in, then these great latticed gates would clang down, both preventing further progress and sealing the attackers in for disposal at leisure.

And there could be worse here. Stones that could be tilted to hurl the unwary into sealed and eyeless dungeons, or worse, below. Swinging blades so heavily counter-balanced that they could cleave a man in half, or take off his head without pause. The thought made him pull his head down into his shoulders. Then there might be sprung spears, falling stones—

Tarrian's indignant voice interrupted this grim catalogue. 'Will you stop that, and concentrate on what's happening here and now,' he said fiercely.

'Sorry, I was just remembering things,' Antyr replied.

'Well, don't,' Tarrian said tersely. 'Not unless you can remember something a little less human.'

Further debate was ended by the woman opening a door at the end of the passage and bringing the procession to a momentary halt as they were obliged to pause and allow their eyes to adjust to the bright torchlight that greeted them.

They had entered another passage through a side door. It extended in both directions into an unlit gloom, but the woman, closing and locking the door, noiselessly, Antyr noted again, nodded them towards an archway opposite.

Through this was a long stone stairway which rose upwards. Antyr's already weary legs protested at the prospect of the climb but Tarrian and the woman were already rising out of sight drawing him relentlessly forward.

The remainder of the journey was, as far as Antyr was concerned, distressingly similar to that of the previous night; an interminable maze of corridors and stairways. He made a token effort to note where they were going, but the impending future and his leaden legs soon reduced it to naught.

'Just follow the carpet,' Tarrian said eventually, in some despair at Antyr's lack of observation.

Finally they found themselves outside a small door in a dimly lit corridor lined with large framed pictures separated by elaborately arranged clusters of spears and swords and other weapons.

But despite all the gloom there was a feeling of space and great opulence about the corridor which impinged on Antyr immediately.

'Don't forget the fee,' Tarrian whispered urgently, sensing the same.

The woman tapped on the door gently. It opened silently and, after a few whispered words with someone, she stepped to one side and indicated with a wave of her hand that Tarrian and Antyr should enter.

Inside, Antyr found himself in a small ante-chamber. Despite its size, however, the sense of opulent splendour that had hovered subtly in the darkened corridor, cried out here. Landscape paintings all around gave Antyr the momentary impression that he was standing in the countryside on a bright summer's day. Plain, polished shelves bore delicate carvings of farm workers, the four chairs that guarded each corner of the room had embroidered backs and cushions that complemented the theme, and even the carpet underfoot felt like luxurious summer turf.

The soft click of the door closing behind him broke the spell and Antyr turned to speak to the woman. But she was gone. He had an image of her fading silently into the soft-footed darkness outside which he realized was Tarrian's, still unable fully to relinquish her pain.

In her place stood a tall, heavily built man with long black hair and a black beard. He exuded a power and menace which was totally at odds with the gentle pastoral quality of the little room that he was now dominating. And he was staring at Antyr intently.

Menedrion. Antyr needed no introduction. As with the Duke and Ciarll Feranc the actual presence of the man overrode the impression of all other previous, distant, encounters, exposing them as mere shadows of the grim reality.

'Not his father,' Tarrian said, his voice low even though only Antyr could hear. 'Less sure of himself. Less disciplined. Watch your step.'

It was not reassuring, but it chimed with Antyr's own response. Oddly, however, Menedrion did not disturb him as much as the strangely ominous presence of Ciarll Feranc and the truly massive presence of the Duke. This man had more the bearing of just another loutish officer and Antyr had faced enough in his time to become a fair master at handling them when need arose.

'Look tame,' he ordered his Companion, then he clicked his heels together and stood up straight.

A brief whiff of amused surprise from Tarrian pervaded him, but it was withdrawn immediately and replaced by sincere approval. 'Sorry. You know your own,' came a faint echo to him.

Menedrion, too, had apparently not expected such a response, and it seemed to unbalance him slightly.

'Parade ground or field, Dream Finder,' he said gruffly, without looking at him as he walked past towards a door opposite.

'Both sir,' Antyr replied to his retreating back. 'I was in the front rank at Herion—'

'Come through, man,' came an irritable shout. 'Let's get this over with.'

Dutifully, Antyr doubled across the ante-chamber and, with wilful deference, leaned in a little way through the open door.

The room was a more lavish version of the ante-chamber but the same decor writ large had become garish ostentation. Under other circumstances Antyr might have expected some acidic comment from Tarrian about bad taste, but he was silent. He was learning about their new client.

Menedrion was sprawled in a large chair and though dressed in a tunic and trousers that were predominantly dark green, his black hair and beard, coupled with his lowering face and hunched posture, made him look like a great black spider waiting patiently at the middle of its web.

Antyr stepped inside discreetly.

'Herion, eh,' Menedrion said, pursing his lips and nodding pensively. 'A hard day.'

'Yes sir,' Antyr replied.

'You held well,' Menedrion continued unexpectedly, beckoning him forward. 'Broke their cavalry formation and gave me the chance to mop them up.'

Antyr's thoughts were unashamedly ambivalent. Menedrion's squadron had smashed into the broken ranks of the Bethlarii cavalry as they tried to regroup following their unsuccessful charge, and then Arwain's much smaller squadron had burst out of their cover in the woods and charged the Bethlarii infantry's now unprotected flank, breaking them utterly.

The overwhelming relief that had washed over Antyr lingered with him yet, but it was tinged with shame now, a shame that seemed to grow with time, as he also recalled his rejoicing as he had stood in the still solid ranks and watched the cavalry pursue and slaughter the routed infantry.

That the same fate would have befallen him had he and his companions not held firm held increasingly less solace for him against the agonizing folly of it all. What had been a bristling line of enemy pikes and shields singing defiance and battle fury into the boiling blue sky had become a fleeing horde of sons, brothers, lovers, husbands . . .

'Yes, sir,' he said, cutting short the recollection.

'What's the matter with the wolf?' Menedrion asked curtly.

Antyr looked down. Tarrian's ears were flat against his head and his tail was between his legs. The vivid, visceral, memories of the battle had washed over to him also.

'He's nervous with strangers,' Antyr said, kneeling down and putting an arm around him. 'I'm sorry,' he said privately to Tarrian. 'Will you be all right?'

The question was pointless as he knew that Tarrian's reaction would pass as soon as his own emotional response to the memory of the battle passed.

Menedrion nodded. 'Good,' he said. 'He's a powerful-looking animal. It's as well he knows who's master around here.'

'Yes, sir,' Antyr's parade-ground reflexes had him say.

Tarrian lay down and closed his eyes. Antyr remained by him.

Menedrion fidgeted with his beard for a moment and looked from side to side about the room awkwardly for a while.

'Personally I've little time for this kind of nonsense,' he began. 'But . . .' He paused and then abandoned this approach. 'You come highly recommended,' he decided finally. 'You'd better be good. I warn you, I know you Guildsmen. I can smell a charlatan a league away, no matter what his trade.' He levelled a finger at Antyr. 'And don't think that because I'm who I am you can conveniently double your fee.'

'I understand, sir,' Antyr replied keeping his voice neutral though tempted to be mildly offended. 'The Guild have a scale of charges which you can—'

Menedrion waved him to silence. 'My counter will attend to all that,' he said irritably. 'You just tell me what it is you do and we'll get on with it.'

'I'm a Dream Finder, sir,' Antyr said, unable to keep some surprise out of his voice. 'I . . . find your dreams and . . . guide you through them . . .'

'I know that!' Menedrion said sharply. 'That's why you're here. But what do you *do*? Do you want me to go to sleep or something because you'll have the devil of a wait if you do.'

'Oh no, sir,' Antyr replied, relaxing a little and, without realizing it, beginning to take charge of the powerful figure in front of him. 'My Companion and I will need a little time to prepare ourselves but when we're ready all you'll have to do is make yourself comfortable, give me your hand and close your eyes. We can do it any time if it isn't convenient now.'

'That's all?'

'That's all, sir,' Antyr confirmed.

'How long will it take you to prepare yourself?'

Antyr was about to say, 'A few minutes, sir,' when a startled thought from Tarrian made him look down. The wolf's eyes opened abruptly, yellow and brilliant. Briefly Antyr caught a glimpse of himself as Tarrian confirmed the night-black sockets that indicated his readiness to begin the search.

So quickly, they both thought simultaneously.

Keeping his eyes downwards, Antyr said, 'We're ready now, sir, if you wish to begin.'

Menedrion replied by snapping his fingers. Noiselessly, a guard emerged from behind a large tapestry. Antyr started in surprise at his sudden appearance but remained crouched by Tarrian. The man looked impassively at him as he moved to sit in a nearby chair indicated by Menedrion, but his eyes flicked away rapidly as Antyr looked up and met his gaze.

Menedrion's reaction was more vigorous, he drew in a sharp breath and a spasm of outright fear passed briefly over his face.

'He's superstitious,' Tarrian said urgently. 'Say something quickly. He knows he's shown fear, and it'll be face-saving anger next if we're not careful.'

'I was going to ask if there was anyone you'd like present, sir,' Antyr said calmly, turning away from Menedrion and rising to his feet. 'In my experience, the presence of someone the dreamer trusts is invariably beneficial and your bodyguard would be ideal.' Then, prosaically, 'May I use this chair, sir? I'm afraid I find kneeling very uncomfortable these days.'

'Yes, yes,' Menedrion said with another wave of his hand. 'Sit wherever you want.' He leaned further back into the chair, stiffly and awkwardly, and closed his eyes as Antyr brought the chair forward and placed it in front of him.

'Would you give me your hand, sir,' Antyr said, pulling the chair closer and then showing his own empty hands to the bodyguard. Menedrion's massive hand jerked out suddenly, almost striking Antyr and making the bodyguard smile slightly at his momentary discomfiture.

Taking Menedrion's hand in his right, Antyr again showed his empty left hand to the bodyguard and then passed it gently over Menedrion's closed eyes.

'Sleep easy,' he said softly. 'Whatever befalls, nothing can harm. Dreams are but shadows and you are guarded in all places by a great and ancient strength.'

Menedrion did not so much drift into sleep as tumble into it. His whole frame sagged suddenly into the chair, his rigid arm fell limp, and his head slumped forward. Alarmed by this sudden collapse, his bodyguard started forward but Antyr stopped him with a gently raised left hand.

'He's only asleep,' he said. 'Look at his breathing. Just ease his head back and put a cushion behind it to make him comfortable.'

Despite his soft speech there was a commanding quality in Antyr's manner that made the bodyguard accept the role of nursemaid without demur.

'Have you seen a Dream Search before?' Antyr asked, his voice becoming fainter.

The man shook his head, still avoiding Antyr's gaze.

'Very well,' Antyr said. 'It's nothing very exciting, but don't be alarmed if either the lord or I speak strangely or if Tarrian whines or growls. And don't interfere or let anyone else interfere except another Dream Finder. Above all, *don't touch me*. If you do, the wolf will attack you and it's unlikely I'll be able to get back quickly enough to save you. Do you understand?'

The man nodded and mumbled an uncertain, 'Yes, sir.'

Satisfied, Antyr followed Menedriön into the darkness, although, somewhat to his alarm, he had the feeling of being drawn after him, falling uncontrollably, almost.

He seemed to touch the moment of dark silence for only the most fleeting instant, yet it was also a slow eternity, and his awareness was at once sharper and more insubstantial than he had ever known before.

And too, the shimmering lights and sounds that were suddenly there and yet which had always been there, were more vivid and intense than ever before, swirling and dipping around and about him; dancing wild formless dances, and singing wordless, broken, songs; now near, now far.

Then he was whole and at the Nexus of the dreams of Menedriön, at the heart of the myriad leaking images from the edges of his lifetime's dreams that formed the portals of entrance for those who could find them.

But only the Companion, the Earth Holder, had that skill. Here Tarrian must lead, and Antyr follow.

Then Antyr realized that Tarrian was not beside him. For an instant his hold on the Nexus wavered and his heart jolted as a choking spasm of panic began to seize him. But even before his heart could beat again, the wolf was there; unseen but whole and strong.

'So fast, so fast.' Tarrian was breathless and, for a moment, almost incoherent. 'What happened? . . . It doesn't matter . . . Hold on to me . . . Hold tight . . . I nearly lost you . . . You dwindled into the distance . . . Alone . . . Unbelievable . . .' He became quieter. 'Your talent wakens, Antyr, it sweeps all before it. Take care, I fear you can go where I can't. I hold the earth here, solid and true, but you must hold me now, for both our sakes. Hold me tight. Do you understand?'

'Yes,' Antyr replied hesitantly, countless questions forming in his mind which he set aside only with difficulty. 'And no, my control's uncertain. What shall we do? Go on or withdraw?'

Doubt hovered around them.

'Not my choice to make, Dream Finder,' Tarrian said after a moment. 'You know that. If it'll help, Menedrion's doing this at the instigation of his mother because of a strange dream he's had. It disturbed him greatly but he's also concerned that by consulting you he'll look ridiculous.'

Doubt.

To retreat now would be to face the wrath of the Duke's son, drawn into what he saw as this ludicrous, even humiliating, performance – a business for merchants' wives – and then being casually told by this charlatan that he wasn't quite up to the job today!

But, fearful though the consequences of that might be, Antyr wavered. He had been beaten and humiliated before now and survived; in the sometimes too realistic war games that had been part of his army training; at the hands of thieves and gangs of youths as he had staggered home too late at night; in drunken brawls at various inns. Fear of that must not stop him withdrawing if he felt that some greater danger for all three of them lay ahead.

But what danger could lie in a dream? None, surely – you are guarded in all places by a great and ancient power – the time-honoured pledge. But the eerie presence in the Duke's dream returned to him, and then the hooded figure with the lamp.

Yet there was pain here, too. Pain that Menedrion's undoubted courage could not contend with. Antyr did not need Tarrian to tell him that. Menedrion's embarrassment was proof enough of the man's distress.

Suddenly his motivation became important to him. The feeling rose within him that whatever decision he made, it would be the reason he made it that would be important and not the decision itself.

And scarcely had this conclusion appeared than he realized that he must go forward. Not because he was afraid of Menedrion's anger, though it was no pleasant prospect, or even because somehow he sensed that such a reverse in his life now might redirect it into bitterness and wretchedness for ever. But because of Menedrion's pain. This was what the strange gift of Dream Finding was for. Retreat would not only be failure, it would be a betrayal.

Despite the clarity of this vision, however, he knew that he was not wholly master of events and that, in some way, circumstances were shaping his deeds for him, bearing him along. Certainly he knew he could not justify his decision rationally; betrayal of what? for example. And indeed, in the wake of his commitment, other, more selfish reasons bobbed to the surface, mocking its altruism. Curiosity; what was happening to him? what could the Duke of Serenstad's son possibly have dreamt that so disturbed him? And fear; whatever was the vision of the hooded figure with the lamp that had taken him from the protection of his Earth Holder, he knew that he must hold his ground at no matter what cost, and that to break and flee was to invite both pursuit and capture . . . destruction . . .?

A weight lifted from him suddenly, and he gazed into the Nexus, shimmering and swirling, cloud-streaked with black and red like a battlefield sunset, resonating with the jangling clatter of screaming men and horses, laughing women, clashing arms and clinking goblets.

Here, he, the Dream Finder, was master. None could gainsay that. None could oppose him with impunity.

'Adept.'

The word formed somewhere, soft and transient; a chance pattern in the clamour.

He reached down and felt the unseen powerful presence of Tarrian.

There was a timeless pause, then, softly, but with the urgency of a hissing arrow, he said, 'Go, hunter. Find what has to be found. Go!'

Chapter 14

Tarrian leapt forward like the bolt from a great siege catapult. A massive and unstoppable momentum. The colours and sounds of the Nexus flew past and through them, layering and dividing, blurring with the speed of their travel yet still motionless and clear, as is the nature of things that dwell at the edges of dreams.

The colours intensified, the sounds grew. Antyr, drawn with his Companion, drew in a great breath as their tumbling pace increased.

'What's happening?' he said, though in excitement, not fear.

'We're searching the Nexus,' Tarrian said, his voice shaking with the pounding ferocity of his pace.

'No. Never like this,' Antyr shouted.

'No. Never like this,' Tarrian confirmed. 'I see more clearly, I hear more clearly. The scents . . . The scents . . .' His voice faded and Antyr was overwhelmed by the perfumes of countless grasses and trees, flowers and birds, insects and animals, all mingling yet distinct, rich and subtle; and each with its own coherent tale as clear as the sights and sounds around him, though spoken in some strange, alien tongue.

But it was gone almost before he could register what it was, though the memory of it pervaded his entire body like the lingering image of the sun behind suddenly closed eyes.

Tarrian had taken him deep into his wolf nature, something he had never even attempted, or perhaps wished to do, before; least of all when he was searching the Nexus.

The journey continued, timeless and eternal, the two travellers silent. Antyr, awestruck; Tarrian, hunting; hunting for that which only his wolf nature could know.

Colour and sounds.

'What's happening?' Antyr asked again, though it was a different question this time.

'I don't know,' Tarrian replied. 'But it's of your creating, no one else's. Just be, and trust.'

Colours and sounds.

'You are more than you seem,' Tarrian said. 'And you are guided by a great and ancient strength.'

'Guarded,' Antyr corrected.

'Guided,' Tarrian repeated.

'I don't—'

Abruptly they were still again, though the Nexus still swirled and sang around them. Colours and sounds.

'Hush,' Tarrian said. 'We're here. We're here. Yes. This is the place. The portal that we seek. Menedrion's choice.' Antyr could feel the wolf testing his many senses. Then came a doubt.

Antyr gazed around. He was himself still, and still in the Nexus, though now it was dimmer and quieter, as if a great curtain had fallen across it.

'What's the matter?' he asked. 'This hasn't happened before. Why am I not in the dream?'

A low rumbling growl formed in Tarrian's throat. 'The portal is strange,' he said.

Antyr felt the word shimmer and echo about him. 'What do you mean, strange?' he asked, anxiously.

'False . . . strained . . . distorted . . .' Tarrian gave up. 'I don't really have the words,' he admitted. Then, almost immediately. 'It's not his, not Menedrion's . . . not wholly anyway . . . it leads beyond . . .'

Antyr felt a cold wind blowing about him. A wind that had travelled over a great plain and drawn an ancient frozen chill from it.

Then he was alone, peering into the bitter darkness. He could make out a bulky form in front of him. Vague though it was, however, it was unmistakably Menedrion . . .?

Even as he formed the question in his mind, he was with Tarrian again in the strange, subdued part of the Nexus that the wolf was holding them in.

'You are guarded by a great and ancient power.' The words came to mind unbidden and unexpectedly, and he muttered them to himself almost desperately, like a prayer for deliverance.

Then, to Tarrian, his voice cracking with sudden hysteria, 'What happened? What in the devil's name happened? That was Menedrion. How could I be in the dream and not be the dreamer?'

The Nexus whirled and crackled, and Tarrian's reply was distant and frightened. 'You slipped from me,' he said, his voice shaking. 'No. You were drawn from me. Or you left. Through the portal . . . the portals.'

Antyr reached out and felt the powerful presence of his Companion. The wolf was trembling. From somewhere he found a semblance of calmness. 'What do you see, Tarrian?' he asked. 'What do you . . . sense? Describe it to me, however inadequate the words.'

Tarrian whimpered. Antyr held his unseen form close.

'What do you see?' he asked again.

'Portals within portals,' Tarrian replied, as if staring at something intently. 'Ways within ways. A rent in the fabric of the Nexus. A besieging army . . . no, that's his image . . . I think. A power from beyond. A hunter. Ah . . .!'

Tarrian's voice became a cry of horror and dismay. 'This is not the dream! This is the now. *We're at the portal of the dream that is being dreamt by another!*'

'No. That's imposs—' Antyr began, panic mounting inside him. But before he could finish, Tarrian let out a great howl, a howl that arced up and spanned the length and depths of the Nexus. And even as it rose up, it became another voice. The voice of Menedrion. A voice full of challenge and fear.

Antyr's spirit cried out in protest at the events which he felt happening around him. They were beyond anything in his experience. Beyond any of the logic and reason that sustained the Dream Finder's art. Despite Tarrian's presence, he felt lost and alone in a maelstrom of insanity. A maelstrom that he had released in some way and that he must control. But what could he do?

While his mind whirled and fretted, however, some other part of him rose and followed after the cry of the wolf.

And he was by Menedrion again, hulking in the cold darkness. Terrifyingly, Tarrian was not there, but Antyr refused to accept the paralyzing thoughts of the impossibility of this that stirred frantically in his mind. As in battle, only an immediate acceptance of the reality of his position, however strange, could help either him or Menedrion.

And Menedrion needed help. He was beset. Unarmed, he crouched, fists clenched, eyes and teeth gleaming viciously even in the gloom. Round and round he turned as dark shapes converged on him from every side.

Antyr could not make out the nature of this enemy, but he could smell their anticipation beginning to overtop their hesitancy, and he could sense their terrible hunger. A sound like a winter wind blowing through the rattling reeds filled the air.

'I am with you, Lord,' he said gently, gathering the voice from he knew not where, as if Menedrion were just another excitable client facing an unpleasant nightmare. 'Have no fear, for these are but creations of that fear. I have come to scatter them and bring you safe to the light again.'

Antyr knew the lie in his words, but knew too that in some way, Menedrion's black battle anger would doom him here if he remained.

Standing straight, he gazed around at the dark, closing horde. He had the strange sensation that within him was a flickering light that could sustain him if he knew how to use it. And indeed, as his night-black eyes swept across the approaching shapes, they hesitated.

'Who dares assail my charge?' he heard himself say, but his voice was no longer gentle. It was deep like thunder and seemed to unfold through the darkness like a great wave, sweeping the din of Menedrion's enemies before it.

'Who?' he heard himself repeat, but terrifyingly louder. The circling shapes fled abruptly, disappearing imperceptibly into the distant, deeper, darkness.

Only one figure remained. More solid than the rest.

It hissed and swayed and reached out towards Menedrion, hands clawed. 'He is mine,' it said, its voice cutting the darkness like shards of glass. 'He will join the—'

Antyr felt Tarrian beside him.

'Withdraw now, Lord,' Antyr said, still calmly, his voice a mixture of his own and Tarrian's. 'Follow the wolf. My power will protect your back like a shield. Withdraw.'

Then both Menedrion and Tarrian were gone, and Antyr was alone in the darkness with the searching figure. It let out a flesh-crawling hiss of anger and frustration and turned towards Antyr. Briefly, he felt the wash of the ancient hatred that he had felt as the hooded figure had left him the previous night. Then, abruptly, he felt . . . recognition . . . and the hatred became an overpowering lust. Its corrupt malevolence appalled him, and he raised his arms as if to protect himself from it.

The figure hesitated.

Without knowing what he was doing, Antyr reached up and drove his hands into the darkness. Then, with a great cry, he tore open its very fabric.

Light flooded in upon him like a roaring cataract, and for a timeless moment he felt himself being lifted bodily and swept along uncontrollably.

Then he was falling . . . falling . . . falling . . .

Menedrion burst into wakefulness with a great roar just as Antyr toppled over backwards on his chair and went sprawling on the luscious carpet.

As he struggled to find his bearings, Tarrian was by his side, his bright yellow eyes searching into him. In the span of a heartbeat, Antyr saw several images of himself alternating with those of Tarrian as the wolf entered and left him, almost hysterically, seeking reassurance.

'Enough,' he managed to say, as he struggled to his knees and put his arms about the animal for mutual support and comfort. 'Enough. We're back. We're—'

He stopped as he became aware of Menedrion, standing nearby, his head in his hands and swaying ominously.

'Lord!' Antyr cried, scrambling unsteadily to his feet. 'We're safe now—'

As he stepped forward however, the bodyguard, white faced and wide eyed, interposed himself. He levelled a trembling knife at Antyr's throat.

Antyr began to raise his hand in conciliation but even as he did so he became aware of the bodyguard's focus changing and in the corner of his vision he saw Tarrian, yellow eyes blazing savagely, hair bristling and top lip curling to expose his massive teeth in their flesh-tearing totality.

'Put the knife down, for pity's sake!' Antyr gasped in dismay. 'Now! Tarrian will kill you if you don't, and I won't be able to stop him.'

The bodyguard hesitated and Antyr sensed Tarrian preparing to spring. In desperation he lashed out wildly at the bodyguard's hand before the wolf launched his inevitable attack. Momentarily distracted by the sight of Tarrian, the bodyguard was unprepared for the suddenness of Antyr's slap and the knife was knocked from his hand. It twisted and glittered through the bright lamplight to fall silently on to green sward carpet several paces away.

'No!' Antyr roared, both to Tarrian and the bodyguard, stepping back rapidly and holding his empty hands out in a gesture of helplessness. Then, to the bodyguard, pleading, 'Don't move. Please. Don't threaten me. The lord's safe and when Tarrian sees I am, so will you be.'

The bewildered man looked from Antyr to Tarrian and then back at his master. Though Menedrion was still obviously in a dazed condition, he was more steady now, and his eyes were beginning to focus.

'Keep your distance then, Dream Finder, and we'll all be safe,' the bodyguard said, recovering somewhat. His voice was unsteady but purposeful. He looked back at Menedrion again. 'Sir. Are you all right?' he said urgently. 'What did they do to you? What happened? The noises you were making were fearful. I didn't know what to do for the best.'

'Leave us,' Menedrion said, after a moment.

'Sir?' The bodyguard hesitated, casting another wary glance at Antyr and Tarrian. 'The wolf—'

'Leave us!' Menedrion shouted angrily, then, relenting almost immediately, he gave an uncharacteristic smile of self-reproach and, reaching out to pat the bodyguard's arm, said, 'There's no danger here. Truly, no danger.' His smile broadened. 'None that I can't handle now I'm awake, anyway,' he added. 'Just a particularly strange and vivid dream. And I need to talk to the Dream Finder alone about it now.'

Reassured somewhat by Menedrion's easier manner the bodyguard did as he was bidden, albeit with some reluctance. 'I shall be within call, sir,' he said with quiet defiance, as he bent down to pick up his knife. Menedrion nodded.

When the bodyguard had left, however, Menedrion's façade cracked and the tumult beneath burst through.

'What happened, Dream Finder?' he said, his eyes wide with anger and fear. 'That was not the dream I had last night. The place was the same, and the enemy, but it wasn't my dream. And you were not there then. It was some other . . . person . . . and they possessed me. Somewhere between sleep and waking . . .' His final words tailed off.

'I know it wasn't your dream, sir,' Antyr replied simply. 'But I don't know what happened.'

The answer did not please Menedrion. 'I warn you, Dream Finder. Peddle me no foolishness in the hope of wringing yourself a higher fee, or ingratiating yourself at court,' he said grimly. 'I'm no empty-headed courtier's woman to be gulled by such tricks, and you'll find that life can become most unpleasant if you think otherwise. Do you understand that fully, Dream Finder?'

'I do, sir,' Antyr replied with as much dignity as he could muster in the face of Menedrion's powerful presence. 'And I've told you the truth. I don't know what happened just now. I've never known anything like it before, nor have I heard or read of such a thing. Nor has Tarrian, who worked with my father for many years before he came to me.'

Menedrion looked at him narrowly.

'You came highly recommended, Antyr,' he said darkly. 'You're a Guildsman. Dreams and all to do with dreams are your province. "I don't know" won't do. What use is a farrier who doesn't know how to shoe a horse? Or a fletcher who doesn't know how to make an arrow?' He pointed at Antyr threateningly, and spoke very slowly. 'Now, stop this nonsense and tell me what happened?'

Antyr swallowed. 'You were attacked, Lord Menedrion. I . . . we don't know how, or why, or by whom. But you were attacked here today just as surely as we were at Herion.' Released, Antyr's words became almost a babble. 'It was not a dream we found ourselves in, nor any dream you've ever had. Had that been so, I'd have been you within it. A Dream Finder can't be separate from the dreamer. That's . . .' He waved his hands in search of a word. 'Basic . . . Fundamental . . . Just not possible; any more than I could occupy your place in that chair while you're in it. We were in another place—'

'In another place,' Menedrion echoed in exasperation. 'How could we be in another place when we never left this one, man? Did we saddle up and ride there? Grow wings and fly? I warn you, Dream Finder.'

Antyr flinched at the growing menace in Menedrion's voice and his throat went dry. 'Sir, if I could say anything that would remove me from your anger, I would say it. But it would be a betrayal on my part to speak anything other than the truth—'

'Truth! What truth?' Menedrion burst out. 'If you know the truth then tell me.'

'—The truth as I see it,' Antyr finished. 'And the truth is, that I don't know what the truth is.' Menedrion stood up. Antyr raised a hand. 'Sir, I beg of you, listen to me—'

'Listen to a babbler, who doesn't even know his own trade?'

Some part of Antyr's infantry training fastened his feet to the floor in spite of his overwhelming desire to flee. An

175

unexpected twist of anger curled inside him. 'Sir,' he almost shouted. 'I didn't tout for your business like some lickspittle court tailor. You chose me. You had me sought out and brought here. You asked me to search for your dream. Sir, I *do* know my trade. Better than many. But you must let me think—'

Menedrion clenched his massive fists.

'I can't stop you doubting me, sir,' Antyr went on, still just managing to hold his ground. 'But . . .' Inspiration came, from his own remark earlier. 'Go to the Guild. Ask anyone there – anyone – if it's possible for dreamer and Finder to be separate as we were.'

The room fell very silent as he stopped speaking.

'If he attacks me, do nothing,' Antyr said privately to Tarrian, even though he knew the request was pointless.

'That's not in my choice, you know that,' Tarrian confirmed. 'But I don't think he's going to. I think you've held his charge, pikeman.' There was relief in the remark, not flippancy, but Tarrian's manner was a little distracted, as if he were listening to something very carefully. 'He's so confused I can barely snatch a coherent thought,' he said. Then he paused, and Antyr caught a whiff of his irritated concentration. 'But he's thinking as well as he's able under the circumstances.' Another pause. 'He's frightened and he wants help. But he's lucid enough to see that whether he doubts or believes you, there are problems he'd rather not face . . .'

The silence grew. 'He wants simplicity, Antyr. Battlefield simplicity—'

Antyr seized the moment even before Tarrian could finish. 'We find ourselves side by side in the same rank, sir,' he said hesitantly. 'Trust is something that perhaps we have no choice about.'

Menedrion's expression changed slightly, and his manner became quieter, less menacing.

'He thinks he's going mad,' Tarrian said quickly, as if just glimpsing some fleeting prey.

Antyr had been avoiding Menedrion's gaze so far, mindful of the lord's first reaction. Now he straightened up and looked at him directly. Menedrion flinched, but this time it was he who held his ground.

'There's a danger here, sir,' Antyr said. 'To you and, I suspect, to others. A danger that's none of our creating. A danger from . . . somewhere outside. From *someone* outside. And it's as real a threat as Bethlarii bigotry and malice. *That* I'm certain of, though I know no more, except that only a Dream Finder can help oppose it.' He hurried on before Menedrion could accuse him of self-seeking again. 'Whether me, or another, doesn't matter. And I waive any fee for this day's work. But ask the question of the Guild that I gave you before you decide my fate, or what you should do next. And if I can serve you again, I will.'

There was another long silence. 'From outside?' Menedrion said, eventually.

'Yes, sir,' Antyr replied.

Menedrion's brow furrowed and he shook his head as if to dispel too many conflicting ideas. 'How can you know that this . . . dream . . . wasn't from somewhere inside, some strange disturbance of the mind?'

Antyr in his turn shook his head, but with the confidence of a man certain in his resolution. 'How do you know when to commit your forces in battle, sir?' Antyr replied. 'You do it when your head and your stomach tell you, and they know through years of study and experience. So I know. But where a battle decision is subtle and difficult, and fraught with hazard, this is as clear to me as knowing that I'm here now and not out in the fog. And—' He stopped.

'And?' Menedrion demanded.

Antyr took a deep breath. 'And I've felt a similar assault . . . a presence . . . in the dream of another before—'

'Who? When?' Menedrion leaned forward, his eyes wide and his brow furrowed. 'What happened?'

'I can't tell you who, sir, or what happened,' Antyr replied nervously. 'Not without the dreamer's permission. Their secrets are as sound with me as are yours. But it was very recent.' Then, anxious to deflect Menedrion's curiosity, 'And I too have been . . . sought out by some strange . . . power. I was about to seek the help of another Dream Finder when your men found me at the Guild House.'

Menedrion put his hand to his head. Trust and angry doubt distorted his features. 'I don't know,' he said after a while. 'You seem honest enough. And I'm no bad judge of men usually. But all this is beyond me . . .' He clenched his fist and looked at it as if wishing to see a sword there and a problem that it could solve.

'You mentioned farriers and fletchers, sir,' Antyr said.

'You can judge their work by your own needs for what they make, but isn't the finding and casting of iron a mystery quite beyond you? And the choosing of woods and feathers?'

Menedrion looked at him suspiciously. His ownership of many of the city's workshops and forges was an object of some cautious superciliousness by certain factions of the court. However, he sensed no subtle insult. 'That's not the same,' he said, flatly.

'It's exactly the same,' Antyr risked. 'Judge me by my deeds so far. You can inquire of others afterwards, and I'm powerless before you.'

Menedrion did not answer.

'Tell me about the dream you had that sent you looking for me, sir,' Antyr said, picking up the chair he had been using, and forcing himself to relax. 'You said it was the same place, and the same enemy . . . and that someone . . . possessed you.'

Still Menedrion did not speak.

'Sir?' Antyr prompted. 'Do you want me to leave?'

Menedrion scowled. 'What will happen when I sleep again?' he asked unexpectedly.

Despite himself, Antyr grimaced. Menedrion had voiced the concern that had been hovering on the edges of his own thoughts.

'I don't know, sir,' he answered immediately and straightforwardly. Then, more insistently, 'But tell me about the dream that's disturbed you and why you sent for me instead of one of the more . . . popular . . . Dream Finders who tend courtiers, Senedwrs and the like.'

'Your name was given to me by my mother,' Menedrion said irritably, annoyed at being distracted from his main anxiety. 'What relevance is that?' he added, though in a tone that suggested he wanted no answer.

It was not, as Menedrion had said, of any relevance to their present problem, but to Antyr it was a matter for some alarm, and he recoiled inwardly from the revelation, as he felt himself take an inadvertent step into the treacherous marshland of palace politics.

No one at the palace knew him – even the porter at the Guild House didn't know him! No one except those few who had been involved in his visit to the Duke. His name could only have come to her attention through one of these, who must be among the Duke's chosen. He felt chilled at the thought of his name being bandied about such politically charged circles. Another loose piece to be discarded when the play was over!

For a moment the fear of the very real dangers that faced casual players in Serenstad's political life set aside the darker mysteries that were waiting in the shadow lands of sleep.

'Forget it!' Tarrian said, sharply, jolting him back to the present. 'The danger there is only for those who threaten others. Concentrate on the matter in hand, that's far more serious.'

'The dream, sir,' Antyr persisted, accepting Tarrian's advice. Another military analogy occurred to him. 'I must have intelligence about our enemy if I'm to decide what to do.'

Menedrion grunted, then, a little self-consciously, he retold the tale he had told to his mother a few hours earlier neglecting the assault on the girl. When he had finished, he looked at Antyr.

'And can I sleep tonight?' he asked again.

Antyr pondered what Menedrion had told him, but it gave him no insight. Rather, it raised more questions and uncertainties. He felt his feet reach the end of the road and an abyss open up in front of him. 'I still don't know, sir,' he said. 'I see two choices. Tarrian and I can stay and watch over you tonight, or I can seek out the other Dream Finder I mentioned.'

Menedrion frowned. 'What prevents you doing both?' he asked.

'Nyriall lives in the Moras district,' Antyr replied.

Menedrion's frown deepened and he looked Antyr up and down. 'You're precious little advertisement for your trade, yourself, Antyr,' he said. 'Now you tell me that this person you need advice from isn't some senior Guildsman, but someone even more impoverished than you!'

Antyr's temper flared abruptly. 'When you go into battle do you use a ceremonial sword, sir? Embossed, engraved, inlaid, beautified – useless? Or do you choose a simple well-balanced one that will hold its edge?'

Menedrion sat up and glared at him. 'Curb your insolence, Dream Finder,' he said angrily. But he answered the question. 'I use a sword I've used before. One I know I can rely on.'

And he went no further in his rebuke, nor did Antyr apologize.

Menedrion stood up purposefully. 'You'll have to stay here, then,' he said. 'Though it's damned inconvenient. I had . . . plans . . . for tonight. Still, you can't go wandering round the Moras at this time, especially with the fog coming down again, and I'm not sending an escort in, it'd start a riot for sure.' He banged his fist into his hand and swore in frustration.

'We needn't disturb your plans, sir,' Antyr said helpfully. 'We don't need to be in the same chamber, just nearby will suffice. And we can't begin our watch until you're asleep anyway.'

This seemed to mollify Menedrion to some extent, but a knocking on the door forestalled any further debate.

'Come in,' he shouted.

The door opened to reveal the woman who had escorted Antyr through the palace. She beckoned Menedrion forward and there was a brief whispered conversation.

When it was finished, the woman left and Menedrion turned to Antyr, frowning. 'Come with me. I'll find a servant to look after you,' he said. 'An urgent matter has arisen.'

Chapter 15

Menedrion looked round the room as he closed the door. His father, Aaken Uhr Candessa, Ciarll Feranc, and Arwain were seated in a wide circle and there were no servants or guards present.

His father turned towards him as he entered, and the other three stood up.

It needed no great perception on Menedrion's part to know that he had entered into the middle of a vigorous debate. Indeed, he got the impression of the last words fading into the corners of the room even as he took in the fact that his father's mood was stern. He braced himself.

'Gracious of you to favour us with your presence, Menedrion,' Ibris said caustically, before his son could offer any greetings.

Menedrion looked at him with a mixture of annoyance and bewilderment. 'What's the matter?' he asked, less than diplomatically.

'What's the matter is that I've had the palace turned upside down trying to find you all day,' Ibris replied. 'While you've been doubtless dallying in the arms of your latest paramour, we've had the privilege of a visit from a Bethlarii envoy no less. Why the devil don't you tell one of your secretaries where you're going occasionally instead of using them to cover your tracks?' He began to warm to his topic. 'My God, we could have had the whole Bethlarii army at the palace gates by now while everybody was wandering round looking—'

Aaken cleared his throat awkwardly.

Ibris cast him an irritated look but stopped his diatribe with a snort. 'Well, at least you're here now, anyway,' he concluded reluctantly. 'On reflection, it's perhaps as well you weren't at the audience.'

Menedrion's mouth dropped open as he floundered between preparing an account of his day, and shock at Ibris's news. 'What do you mean, audience? Bethlarii envoy?' he managed, eventually.

But Ibris had returned his attention to the others. 'Sit

181

down. Sit down,' he said to them with a wave of his arm. 'And Irfan, find yourself a chair and sit down as well. There . . .' He pointed a busy finger. 'Next to Aaken. He'll tell you what's happened.'

He was barely two minutes into his renewed discussion with Feranc and Arwain, however, when Menedrion escaped Aaken's telling and his voice exploded over the proceedings.

'What?' he thundered, jumping to his feet.

'Sit down, Irfan!' His father's equally loud, but more authoritative voice made Menedrion start.

Menedrion rocked back on his heels, then leaned forward towards his father. 'You hanged them all, of course,' he said.

'I hanged nobody, Irfan,' Ibris said in weary frustration. 'How many times do I have to tell you to restrain your behaviour? Will you sit down and listen, and use your head for once.'

'But you can't let them—'

'Sit down, damn it!' Ibris declared definitively.

Menedrion held his gaze defiantly for a moment then turned his face away sharply and dropped heavily back into his chair. It creaked in protest.

Ibris scowled at the chair's distress. 'Irfan,' he said deliberately. 'When you can make a chair as fine as that, you can treat it like that. Otherwise, don't.' Then, in continuing exasperation. 'I don't know how long it's going to take you to grasp this. You'll be Duke one day. You must control your tongue. You must control everything. An outburst like that could launch an army, and impetuosity like that could send it to its doom.'

'There was no one here to see it,' Menedrion protested unconvincingly.

'There's everyone who matters here,' Ibris replied angrily. 'And you'd have behaved just the same in the market place.'

Menedrion pondered a reply, then rejected it. Grinding his teeth, he folded his arms and sat back.

'Good,' Ibris said. 'That's a start. Next, learn to control your face.'

Then, placatory, 'I understand your anger, Irfan. God knows I do. My reaction was the same.' He almost snarled. 'It still is,' he added viciously. 'But there's obviously a lot more going on here than meets the eye. You're commander enough to smell an ambush and to know the importance of good intelligence and careful planning. This business needs thought and consideration before it needs action.'

Menedrion grunted a reluctant agreement.

'Aaken's told you the heart of it,' Ibris went on quietly. 'And I wanted to discuss it between ourselves before I consult the Cabinet and report to the Sened. I also want to talk to this envoy more informally. See if we can get a better idea of what they're really up to. He might be more forthcoming in private. What I've heard so far seems to make precious little sense despite our discussion so far.'

He frowned a little. 'Arwain's of the opinion that it's some religious group that's taken over and that they're looking for a full-scale war – a crusade. It's happened before, and this Grygyr's obviously a fanatic. And he's certainly been sent to provoke something. But I can't see it being a crusade myself . . . it's . . .' He left the sentence unfinished.

'Aaken thinks they're just using the Whendreachi as an excuse to distract us while they pull off some other coup such as quietly annexing Meck,' he went on. 'Ciarll's keeping quiet until he's something to say, as usual. And I'm listening to all three – silence and all. Irfan, from the little you've heard, what do you think?'

Menedrion did not speak at first.

'What do you think?' Ibris asked again.

Menedrion shrugged, though not as a mark of indifference or ignorance, but because his body was still rebelling against being restrained from dealing out summary justice to these impudent upstarts who had arrived out of nowhere to insult his father and the city.

'I don't know,' he said, looking up at the ceiling. 'The whole thing sounds preposterous to me, but . . .' He raised his hands to forestall any rebuke from his father. 'Not being there of course, I've got no feeling for it. It could be anything. Certainly they've always had their eye on Meck. It would free them from the independents at Crowhell and they could use it for trade or as a base for a navy, or both. That's why we've always kept such a large garrison there. Whendrak, I don't know. It's strategically vital for both of us, because of its location, but . . .' He shook his head. 'That's why it's neutral. They must know we'd fight them to the last man if they tried to move the army in, under whatever pretext. It would be a desperate affair. And these days I think we'd both end up having to fight the Whendreachi themselves.

After the last time I doubt they're going to allow their city to be used as a battleground again.'

Feranc nodded slightly.

'But we can talk about this until the Seren runs dry and be none the wiser,' Menedrion went on. 'We'll have to question this . . . envoy . . . to find out what they're up to. And then get up to Whendrak as soon as possible to see what's really happening there.'

Ibris nodded, seemingly pleased. 'That, we were just coming to when you arrived,' he said. He nodded to Feranc who stood up and left the room quietly.

Ibris returned his gaze to Menedrion. 'Put a chair there for him,' he said, pointing some way in front of himself. 'Then I want you to one side of him, but behind, so that he can't see your face. And you too, Arwain, other side,' he added, mindful that Menedrion should not consider himself demeaned in front of his half-brother. 'Don't speak, either of you. And don't respond in any audible way to anything he says, however provocative. I can't read him yet. We're about evens on insults so far, so I'm not going to mention any of that and hope that our protection of him in the hall has perhaps had some beneficial effect on him.'

Menedrion made a disparaging noise. 'My men would soon get it out of him,' he said grimly, standing up and moving his chair.

Ibris shook his head. 'I doubt it, Irfan,' he said. 'You forget what pride they take in their own personal courage and endurance. He could well die before he'd part with a secret. We never had much success with their spies in the field. Force won't be the way. We'll have to lure it out of him. And it may well lie in what he *doesn't* say.'

Menedrion looked doubtful, but did not argue.

'Besides,' Ibris went on. 'We've accepted him publicly as an envoy now so we've got an obligation to look after him. Arwain thinks he's come as a martyr anyway, though personally I doubt that, but whatever, we mustn't turn him into one.'

'Pity,' Menedrion muttered.

'Irfan,' Ibris said, affecting not to hear the comment. 'I'm holding you responsible for his safety and his well-being. He and his men will be treated as honoured guests and given every comfort. Believe me, that kind of treatment will unsettle them as much as any amount of beating.' He leaned forward purposefully. 'And make it clear to some of your noisier cronies that if they start talking about summary justice for these men, they'll get it themselves, parentage and patronage notwithstanding.'

'Yes, father,' Menedrion said flatly. 'And what would you like me to do if he decides to attack you here and now?'

Ibris's eyes flashed momentarily at Menedrion's tone. 'You heard me, Irfan,' he said. 'He's not to be hurt. I don't want him clubbed and stabbed whatever he does. If needs be, use your garotte to immobilize him. There's nothing like a shortage of air for making people change their minds.'

Menedrion raised his eyebrows. 'And that's the other reason you want me sitting behind him,' he said.

Ibris's face abruptly wrinkled into a smile and then he chuckled. 'There's some hope for you yet, Irfan,' he said.

The tension between father and son evaporated as they shared a brief moment of dark, family, humour.

Menedrion dropped a chair into position for the envoy, then settled back into his own. Arwain sat down next to him on the opposite side of the envoy's chair. Almost immediately, Ciarll Feranc returned, accompanying Grygyr Ast-Darvad. Once again, Arwain was impressed by the presence of the man as he strode into the room, though, oddly, in these more intimate surroundings he seemed smaller, less confident. He sensed too that the envoy was subtly wary of his companion. Immediately, Arwain's mind went back to the meeting in the hall when Feranc had moved to intercept the envoy and with a few soft words and his calm unsettling gaze had held him in thrall.

Despite almost certainly possessing considerable fighting skills, some depth in the man instinctively knew Feranc as his master, Arwain decided. The envoy had already lost any future combat with the Duke's bodyguard. There would be no trouble at this meeting.

Arwain found the realization chilling, though whether it was a new measure of himself or of Feranc he could not have said. He knew however that it was some quality in his training that had given him the insight and he congratulated himself on his assessment of the situation. Then, remembering another attribute of his training, he immediately reminded himself that he could be wrong and that the envoy was carrying his sword and knife again. He cast another quick glance at his half-brother.

Ibris had charged him with the quelling of the envoy if need arose, but Arwain suspected that, for all his fighting ability, Menedrion would scarcely have begun to move before Feranc would have finished the work himself. He found confirmation of this in the relatively casual manner in which his father had delegated the task.

With the exception of the Duke, they had all stood up when the envoy entered the room. Arwain noticed with some slight amusement that although Menedrion managed to keep his feelings from his face as the envoy passed him, he gave up the effort as soon as the man sat down, and his expression became one of undisguised hostility.

Two of a kind, Arwain thought, looking back to the envoy. They would have to come to sword strokes before any mastership was acknowledged there.

Yet somehow Menedrion was not himself. His dark, ferocious anger was muted in some way, as if part of his attention were elsewhere. Briefly Arwain found his own attention clouding with the strange events of the previous night. His awakening, apparently as Menedrion. So vivid. So intense. And the beating of the girl. He looked down at his hands. Was it Menedrion who had beaten her, or was it him doing what he thought Menedrion would do in such circumstances? No answer came.

And then the terrible truth of it all struck him fully for the first time. The truth that the chase through the cellar, Drayner's curt dismissal of his questions, and the day's bizarre events had enabled him to avoid facing squarely. The truth that *it had actually happened*! Arwain felt his mind beginning to teeter towards some whirling uncertainty. Slowly, deliberately, he took control of his breathing and forced himself back to the present. Whatever had happened last night would have to wait yet further before he could ponder it carefully.

'Grygyr,' his father was saying. 'I hope the quarters we've provided are to your satisfaction—'

'A prison is a prison be it stone or silk,' Grygyr retorted before Ibris could finish. 'My message is delivered. I have nothing more to say. As envoy I should not have been detained thus, it is in breach of the treaty.'

Menedrion's jaw tightened, but he did not speak.

Ibris opened his hands in concession. 'The treaty is a man-made thing, and thus flawed, Grygyr,' he said. 'It states that

186

I may not detain you, but demands also that I ensure your safety. The two requirements conflict in this instance and I must decide which is the lesser breach.' He leaned back in his chair.

'As I told you before, it's a considerable tribute to your . . . skill . . . that you managed to reach here unharmed, but news of your presence will be across the city by now and I wouldn't guarantee you safe conduct across the palace square without substantial protection. You saw in the hall how heated some people can become.' The envoy opened his mouth to speak, but Ibris continued. 'So, while my officers are making preparations to escort you safely back to the border, I must perforce imprison you, as it were, though I'd rather you thought of yourself as an honoured guest briefly detained at a friend's by, say, bad weather, a lame horse . . .' He smiled broadly.

Arwain could feel the envoy struggling against his father's affability.

'Also,' Ibris went on. 'I have to consider my reply to your government's message and I'd like to use this . . . unavoidable delay . . . as an opportunity to discuss this Whendrak problem with you in further detail. Away from the public gaze where we can debate ideas more freely. Men among men. Not politicians, looking over our shoulders.'

'I have nothing to debate with you, Ibris,' Grygyr replied tersely. 'The Handira's message was quite clear. Restrain your people in Whendrak and restore the rights of our citizens there immediately or we shall do it for you.'

Arwain glanced at Menedrion again. He was sitting quite still, but his eyes were boring into the back of the envoy and his hands were gripping the arms of his chair so tightly that they looked as though they would crush the very wood.

Ibris looked concerned. 'Grygyr,' he began, almost fatherly. 'This is the first news we've heard of any serious problems in Whendrak. It concerns us obviously. Whendrak is important to both of us. It can't be denied that they're a quarrelsome people, but they're not stupid. I'm sure a small delegation as provided for in the treaty will be able to help them resolve any problems they might have.'

The envoy did not reply.

Ibris went on. 'Grygyr, Whendrak is neutral. And anyone choosing to live there, renounces his own nationality. Neither you nor we have "people" there. And if Bethlar intervenes there then it will be an overt act of war, and we shall have to move against you. That's a treaty obligation. From there there's no telling where the conflict will end. As envoy, you're no mere messenger, you have both the authority and the responsibility to discuss this matter. Silence won't suffice.'

Silence.

Ibris shook his head. 'I know there's little love lost between our peoples, but I've dealt with many Bethlarii in my time and none went lightly to war.'

'My people are returning to the true way,' Grygyr said.

Ibris's expression urged him on, but the envoy offered no amplification of this remark.

There was audible concern in Ibris's voice when he spoke again. 'Your people too, have always recognized, eventually, the futility of continued conflict. We are both strong, for all our different ways, and neither can defeat the other utterly without suffering irreparable hurt in the process; destruction of the land and the farming patterns, crop failures and famine; disruption of trade and commerce, destitution; banditry; plague even. The battlefield is the way of degradation and folly, a way utterly bereft of reason.'

The envoy straightened at this remark.

'War is necessary for the reforging of a nation, and the battlefield is where men are tested and purified,' he said, his rough voice strident. 'The weak are weeded out and cast aside and the followers of the true way attain glory and honour.'

'And death,' Ibris said quietly.

The envoy sneered dismissively. 'And immortality,' he said, leaning forward. 'Their names will ring down through history in song and saga and their spirits will fight forever in the ranks of the army of Ar-Hyrdyn, and carouse in his Golden Hall.'

A cold silence descended on the room.

'The priests of Ar-Hyrdyn were ever prodigal with the lives of your young men,' Ibris said softly after a long pause. 'Should they send your army forth again then Ar-Hyrdyn can look to a great increase in the ranks of his spirit warriors.'

A knowing smile passed over Grygyr's face, but he did not speak.

Ibris looked at him enigmatically for a long moment, then he nodded slowly.

'I will ask you and your companions to accept our silken cell for a night, perhaps two, Grygyr,' he said, smiling

188

broadly, as if nothing had happened. 'Then, my son, Menedrion, will escort you back to the border stone at Whendrak. As you'll appreciate, I must report our meeting to the Sened and the Gythrin-Dy, and discuss our reply to your message. But I'll ensure that you have it before you leave our dominion. Thank you for your good offices, envoy. The commander will escort you back to your quarters now, please tell any of the servants there if you require anything.'

He gave a wave of his hand to indicate that the audience was over, and the envoy stood up awkwardly. He looked around uncertainly for a moment, until Feranc extended a hand towards the door, then, almost in spite of himself, he bowed curtly to Ibris and strode out of the room with Feranc at his heels.

As the door closed behind him, Ibris extended a hand towards Menedrion to forestall the inevitable outburst.

'Not until he's well out of earshot,' the gesture said.

Its effect was short-lived, but Menedrion's explosion, when it came, was not what had been expected. It was a mixture of amusement and bewilderment.

'I can't believe it,' he said, standing up. 'The man's a lunatic. It'd be a shame to hang him. We should put him on display in the market square.' He looked at his father, grinning broadly. 'Are you *sure* his documents were in order?'

Ibris nodded, unaffected by Menedrion's humour. 'The seal's genuine,' he said, answering the question seriously. 'Though the signature's illegible.'

Feranc returned and Menedrion sat down again. 'I'm not surprised it's illegible,' he said. 'It was probably written by Ar-Hyrdyn himself while he was possessing the body of a temple cat. What do you think, Ciarll?'

'I think we've got a very serious problem,' Feranc replied blandly.

Menedrion's eyes widened in surprise and he appealed to his father. 'From the village idiot and his army?' he said. 'Do I have to look after him, father? What if he thinks he's Ar-Hyrdyn's crow in the night and tries to fly off the palace roof?' He flapped his elbows and his laughter rose to fill the room. But while Arwain smiled and Aaken tried not to, Ibris remained unmoved.

Eventually, foundering against Ibris's silence, Menedrion's humour died down.

'I'm sorry,' he said. 'I was quite prepared to thrash the

arrogant bastard for his manners alone. But all that nonsense. He's cracked. It's ridiculous.'

'Would that it were,' Ibris said quietly. 'I'd rather join in your mirth than face the reality, but I'm afraid that Arwain's guess earlier may be nearer the mark. It seems that that grotesque religion of theirs has risen to some dominance again.' He grimaced and slapped the arms of his chair angrily. 'The black, demented bigotry of it all,' he said bitterly. 'The waste. And the arrogance of the man. He probably didn't care whether he got killed or not. He'd walked right through our domain undetected and publicly spat in our face. That was his message; utter contempt for the treaty, the peace, his life. And I took it and smiled!' It was the first time he had revealed any part of his inner feelings since the envoy had arrived.

No one spoke.

Then, he rested his head on his hand and, for an instant, looked very old.

'Ciarll,' he said after a moment. 'Your opinion.'

'Provisionally as yours, sire,' Feranc replied, carefully omitting Arwain's contribution. 'Whatever the reason, it seems that some of them at least have turned to their ancient creed again and we can probably look for widespread border provocations with a serious risk that they'll develop into a full-scale war.'

'Never!' Menedrion declared, scornfully. 'Fancy gods or not, no one's that crazy. Ever since I could handle a sword they've been pushing here, pushing there, plotting this, plotting that. Always manoeuvring for some advantage or other. And we've always sent them home with their tails between their legs whenever they went too far. They wouldn't dare attempt anything like a full-scale war. It's unthinkable. Besides, those days were dying out even before Viernce. A permanent state of war, with regular winter training and summer campaigns, almost permanent mobilization, turning the land into an armed camp? No one in his right mind wants anything like that.'

He looked around for support, but doubt hung thick in the air.

'Aaken, Arwain,' he said in appeal.

The Chancellor shrugged uneasily. 'I remember a priest we caught once, years ago,' he said, his brow furrowed as if he were looking at something in the far distance. 'He was a big man, powerful. And a tremendous . . . presence. We thought we'd caught ourselves a lord. I remember thinking as I looked at him, there'll be a fine ransom in this one.'

He paused and shook his head reflectively. 'I was already planning how to spend it. There were six of us, surrounding him, with pikes. Nowhere for him to go. No dishonour in surrender. "Come on, your highness," someone said. "Your war's over. Time to get you to market." '

He paused again, and his eyes widened. 'He just drew himself up. Looked at us as if we were so many dog turds, then he took hold of one of the pike shafts . . .' Aaken's hands came out, re-enacting the long past deed. ' . . . and just walked on to the blade. Slow as you please. Just walked on to it. Didn't utter a sound. Didn't bat an eyelid.'

He turned to Menedrion. 'That's a follower of Ar-Hyrdyn. You can forget about reason and logic. All they're interested in is dying valiantly in battle so that they can fight in Ar-Hyrdyn's legions. They're mad by any definition we know, but they're not stupid, and they're terrifying. I'll never forget the look in that priest's eyes. Triumphant even though he was dying.'

Menedrion wriggled uncomfortably.

'That envoy reminded me of him,' Aaken finished. 'Same carriage, same arrogance, disdain—'

'He's still only one man,' Menedrion protested. 'Perhaps the Handira didn't know what he was really like. We've had some strange ones in our own diplomatic corps. In fact, we've still got some, if you ask me.'

Ibris nodded and smiled faintly. 'That's true,' he agreed. 'He could be here as part of some internal political strife. But the seal was genuine and we can't plan on that hope. We can only plan on what we've seen and heard. And if the Bethlarii are going to be fighting for the honour of a place in the Golden Hall of Ar-Hyrdyn then we'll have to be in top fettle to meet them.'

He paused for a moment and rubbed his nose thoughtfully. 'Does anyone disagree with that conclusion?'

No one demurred, and Ibris became businesslike.

'We must find out what's happening in Whendrak first of all. Arwain, can you get a platoon of your guards ready to travel up there by first thing tomorrow?' he asked.

'Probably,' Arwain said, taken aback somewhat by this sudden commission. 'But it'll take most of the night.'

'Good,' Ibris replied. 'Do it. You can sleep in the saddle tomorrow. Aaken, make sure he's properly briefed on the treaty conditions concerning Whendrak. And prepare the appropriate documents. I don't want us causing the very thing we're trying to prevent through some diplomatic carelessness.'

Menedrion scowled at this abrupt development. 'I could—' he began.

'You, as my heir, will be looking after our honoured guest, Irfan,' Ibris said, cutting across his complaint before it was voiced. 'And we'll be continuing to treat him as such until he's safely back across the border.'

Menedrion rebelled petulantly. 'He needs a keeper, not a host,' he protested. 'Let Arwain do it. He's politer than I am. I can be in Whendrak before nightfall—'

'Irfan, that's an order,' Ibris said sharply. 'This is too serious for any of us to consider our own wants and fancies. Arwain's Mantynnai will see what's to be seen better than your guard, and Arwain's a better listener than you and he knows when to run away, which you don't. In addition, if something's seriously amiss then it'll only be my bastard son they've got, not my heir and one of my best commanders.' He shot a glance at Arwain. 'I'm sorry, Arwain, but you understand?'

Arwain bowed an acknowledgement.

Menedrion was still not wholly mollified. 'In addition, Irfan,' Ibris went on, his manner more conciliatory, 'I want you to get a feel for this Grygyr. Talk to him, and listen to him. See what you can smell out. It'll be much needed practice for you in controlling your tongue and it could well be important. You may have to face him in the field yet. Get a . . . company . . . ready tomorrow, with a view to starting back with him the day after.'

Menedrion gave a reluctant nod. 'And remember this, Irfan,' Ibris added. 'If their envoy returns not only alive and unhurt, but seemingly fêted and personally escorted by no less a person than my heir, it'll do little for him at home. The Hanestra is as riddled with intrigue as our Sened and Gythrin-Dy, and suspicion and jealousy are the norm. Rot from the inside will destroy a house just as effectively as flame from the outside.'

Menedrion's eyes narrowed. 'They may also just take it as an act of weakness on our part.'

Ibris leaned back with a shrug. 'Good,' he said. 'Let them underestimate us to the full.'

Menedrion's lip curled in reluctant agreement. 'Very well. Considerate host and travelling companion I'll be,' he said, sourly.

Arwain watched the exchange with some relief. His relationship with Menedrion was such that any sign of preferment by his father made him extremely wary.

Ibris turned to his Chancellor and the commander of his bodyguard. 'Aaken, Ciarll, we've a lot to do,' he said. 'The city'll be seething with rumours by now. I can avoid holding an emergency cabinet meeting until tomorrow but no longer, I think. And I'll have to have at least an announcement ready for the Sened before they finish their business tomorrow evening. But I want our basic policy decided here and now or we'll get bogged down in endless rhetoric and debate.'

Aaken frowned. 'They won't like that,' he said. 'It's not like the old days. They're used to having their say.'

Ibris was dismissive. 'They won't know it's happening if we're careful about it,' he said. 'And I still have complete command of the army as I recall.'

'True,' Aaken conceded. 'But without Sened approval for any action you take, you may have to pay them out of your own pocket.'

Ibris waved his hands. 'I'm well aware of that,' he said irritably. 'Don't be obtuse.' Then he brought his hands down on the arms of his chair with a crack. 'That's exactly what I mean about getting bogged down. This is sufficient of an emergency for me to assume all executive authority quite legally, but I don't want to do that yet; or at all, if it's avoidable. It would cause a lot of bad feeling and probably outright panic among the merchants and traders. No, we treat the Sened as we treated the envoy; gently and pleasantly. But nevertheless, we decide here, now, what's needed, then we decide what we've got to say to get the necessary approval. Is that clear?'

Aaken lifted both hands in a gesture of surrender.

'That's a detail, anyway,' Ibris went on. 'What's more important is the state of the army and the attitudes of our border allies. I want your sharpest, most loyal people out there quickly. Doing what Arwain will be doing. Looking, listening. And get someone down to Crowhell and across to

Nestar to see if any unusual groups of men have been arriving and taking ship up river.'

'If it's a crusade they're looking to start, they won't be using mercenaries, foreigners, will they?' Arwain ventured.

Ibris looked at him. 'I told you this morning about priests, didn't I?' he said, though not unkindly. 'When they're so inclined they make most politicians seem as open as little children. We've already seen one of the Bethlarii aristocracy resorting to disguise. It'll be no trouble for their priesthood to decide that anyone who wishes to fight for them for whatever reason has been led to them by the will of Ar-Hyrdyn.' His nose curled up in distaste. 'In any event, even if some religious clique has the ascendancy at the moment you can rest assured that there'll be plenty of straightforward opportunists rallying to their flag and bringing their influence to bear.'

Arwain inclined his head in acknowledgement of the lesson.

Ibris snapped his fingers. 'And talking of disguises, Ciarll—' he began.

'The matter's in hand, sire,' Feranc replied. 'I've already sent messages to the Liktors and to the garrisons to be on the lookout for unusual strangers.' Uncharacteristically, he frowned. 'I'm afraid I've been lax—'

Ibris waved him to silence. 'We've all been lax,' he said. 'I should have had the wit to realize that too long without war would have had some dire effect on their society . . .' He cast a quick, acknowledging look at Arwain. ' . . . And all of us should have remembered that the Bethlarii are our enemy and that just as nothing ever remains the same, so nothing changes.'

He nodded to himself pensively. 'We'd better start mobilizing the local garrisons at least. Let's also hope we've not been lax in our training.' It was a dark thought.

The room fell silent and the four men sat motionless for a little while, held by Ibris's concern. Then Menedrion stood up and stretched.

'Ah well,' he said. 'If I've got to get a company ready for escort duty I'd better make a start. What with that and entertaining my guest, I doubt I'll be getting much sleep tonight.'

Arwain looked at him sharply. There was an odd note in his half-brother's voice.

Fear? No, Arwain decided. It was relief.

Chapter 16

Antyr walked behind the servant in a trance. Without further comment, Menedrion had led him briskly away from his private quarters, and, with a curt dismissal and an order to remain in the palace, had abandoned him to his present guide; a round-faced old man with hunched shoulders and a worried frown that seemed to be permanent.

He also seemed to be none too pleased with his new duty and kept muttering, half to himself, half to Antyr.

'This isn't my job, you know . . . I've enough to do as it is without running around trying to find rooms for his lordship's . . .' He looked Antyr up and down critically. '. . . visitors . . . And telling the duty guards and the cooks . . . I'm in charge of the laying of tables for the whole of this wing, I shouldn't be having to do this . . . It's not right . . . He should've found one of the room servants . . . It's just typical . . .'

He rang several irritable changes around this theme as he wound an elaborate pathway through the palace, but Antyr heard hardly any of them. Nor did he notice any of the statues, pictures, furniture, tapestries and other artifacts that lined his progress and that had so impressed him the night before.

Uncharacteristically, Tarrian remained silent.

Eventually they reached their destination and Antyr was shown into a small suite of rooms. He heard himself thanking the servant absently and was vaguely aware of the old man lighting several lamps and then departing, still muttering.

As the door clicked shut behind him, Antyr leaned back on it. He felt numb all over. His body seemed scarcely his own, and his mind refused to think. Some reflex carried him towards a large couch and made him lie down on it. He was vaguely aware of Tarrian padding off somewhere.

As he lay back, his eyes focused on the ceiling, but they saw nothing, and the only movement in his mind was that of Tarrian's ancient curiosity and caution as he quickly toured the bounds of this new territory.

'We're coming up in the world,' Tarrian said when he had

finished, but the remark was empty of real meaning and the words hung lifeless and regretted in Antyr's head.

Then, from nowhere, a black wave overwhelmed him. His confrontation with Menedrion had been unnerving, but somehow it had kept him upright and sane. Now, alone, he felt the full shock of the events of the past day. The very articles of faith that suffused and supported his craft had been tossed aside, as if they had never existed, and he was adrift in an ocean of madness without star or landmark to steer by. All that was familiar and solid had become alien and menacing, like a solid shore turned suddenly quicksand.

He covered his hands with his face and squeezed as if trying to reduce himself to infinite smallness and insignificance, but the blackness sought him out and rolled over and through him irresistibly, shaking and tossing him like a pebble on that shore.

Somewhere in the middle of it, after a timeless, buffeting agony, he heard a sound; a distant moaning, sobbing. It went on for a long time, gradually coming closer. Then slowly, he realized it was himself, pouring out a great grief for some terrible, unknown, unknowable, loss.

Yet with this realization came also a faint hint of relief, and he felt the tide of blackness falter. Slowly his convulsing sobs eased and he swung himself up into a sitting position, though still his hands were over his wet face as if the sight of the reality of the world around him would shatter what sanity he still had left.

He felt Tarrian nearby, waiting, watching, with that almost frightening animal fatalism that seemed to leave him largely immune to the emotional effects of matters which he could not control.

'I'm sorry,' Antyr managed eventually.

Tarrian did not reply, but moved over to him and leaned heavily against his leg. A pack thing. One of Antyr's hands relinquished his face and reached down to stroke the soft fur. More sobs shook him.

'I'm sorry,' he repeated.

Again Tarrian did not reply. He did not understand, at least not fully, so he could not offer nothing. Yet in knowing that he did not understand, he offered everything he had. Antyr patted him, finding some solace in the purposeful presence of the wolf's powerful frame.

'I don't know what brought that on,' he said, his voice unsteady.

'You don't need to,' Tarrian said. 'It was necessary and you allowed it. It was a wise act.'

This time it was Antyr who did not reply.

The two sat in silence for some time, then, eventually, Antyr started hunting through his pockets for a kerchief.

'There are towels and water next door,' Tarrian said.

Antyr heard himself chuckle weakly as he stood up and followed Tarrian's direction. 'Thank you, Earth Holder,' he said. 'It's as well one of us keeps his feet on the ground.'

But the darkness had not left him completely and it welled up again as he worked the small, silvered pump handle and watched a stream of water splutter into a plain white bowl. The water glittered with the lamplight as it swirled and danced around the bowl, obeying hidden laws that were as immutable as those binding Antyr's craft were now capricious. The sight seemed to mock him and he felt his body begin to shake uncontrollably.

He reached out and steadied himself by leaning against the wall, as he dipped his other hand into the water and splashed his face carelessly with it.

The effort seemed to take all his strength and slowly he slithered to the floor.

Again Tarrian came and sat by him, silent, but solid.

'I'm so frightened,' Antyr said, after a long silence.

'Yes,' Tarrian said. 'You reek of it.'

Antyr gave a soft rueful laugh at his Companion's simple bluntness, but still his body was reluctant to move. Tarrian lay down patiently.

'What's the matter with me?' Antyr asked after a further long silence.

Tarrian looked at him, but did not speak.

'Too much change, too fast?' Antyr said, turning and resting his forehead against the cold, tiled wall. 'Too much foolishness. Too much weakness.'

'You're too harsh on yourself,' Tarrian said, getting to his feet and walking out of the small washroom as if he were no longer needed. 'What's happening to you is perhaps a little of all those things, but mainly it's an attack. An assault at your very soul.'

Antyr rolled his head from side to side against the tiles.

'That's what I've come to say to myself. That's what I told Menedrion. But what does it *mean*?'

He struggled to his feet awkwardly and followed Tarrian. 'What does it mean?' he repeated.

'It means you're being attacked,' Tarrian replied.

'Dammit, Tarrian,' Antyr shouted. 'Talk sense. My head . . . everything's . . . whirling.' He clenched his fists savagely and then let his hands fall limply to his sides. 'I need some clarity, not more riddles. I feel so lost. So helpless. I'm not even sure about my own sanity any more.' Then, angrily. 'And if I'm being attacked, then presumably so are you. Why aren't you frightened?'

It was a pointless question, he knew. Tarrian was an animal. He carried some human traits, just as Antyr carried some wolfish traits, but it was not in his true nature to be afraid of what he could not immediately sense. Tarrian responded to circumstances as a mirror reflects an image, even though his slight humanity made the mirror blur and shake a little at times.

'I am,' Tarrian replied. 'Your fear wakens fear in me like an echo. But that's all it is; an echo. Your fear is fear of many things. Fear of yourself, your weakness, the unknown depths inside you. Then there's fear of Menedrion, of the Duke, of your dead father's reproach, of my contempt—'

Antyr raised a hand to stop him. 'And of the hooded figure with the lamp,' he said.

'Yes,' Tarrian replied. 'Him certainly.'

'And what do I do with this grand chorus of fears?' Antyr went on, his voice hardening.

Tarrian stared at him. A cold, grey, wolf's stare. 'Live or die,' he said simply.

'What the hell's that supposed to mean?' Antyr's voice cracked into a squeak as his anger forced the question out.

'It means live or die,' Tarrian repeated.

'You're not helping,' Antyr said, dropping his head into his hands again.

Tarrian padded over to the window and jumped up to place his forepaws on the sill. 'I can't,' he said, peering curiously from side to side through the window. 'Not yet. All this is from inside you. From somewhere deep in your human nature. I can feel your pain, but its cause is beyond anywhere I can reach. You'll have to deal with it yourself. All I can do is watch and be here. But what I said is true. You have to decide whether you want life or death. If death, then jump out of this window now, and I'll mourn you. If life, then don't, in which case your next decision is fight or surrender.'

Antyr shuddered as the wolf's cold logic broke over him. He looked up at him, silhouetted against the deepening dusk outside.

Then, slowly, he stood up and walked to the window to join him. Tarrian dropped down and backed away a little as he approached. After some awkward fiddling with the catch Antyr threw the window open and leaned forward on to the sill. Tarrian watched him, motionless.

The chilly late afternoon air struck cold on Antyr's still-damp face and he blew out a long breath that misted, paused, and then silently faded. Unlike his room of the previous night, this one did overlook the city, though little was to be seen of it in the encroaching darkness.

Nonetheless, it was not without splendour. Such of the spires, domes, towers and sweeping avenues of Ibris's 'dazzling city' as could be seen from this vantage were marked out, illuminated and shadowed by a myriad of mist-haloed torches and lamps, giving them an unexpectedly delicate, restful quality. As he watched, Antyr saw other, more distant lights springing to life. The Guild of Lamplighters conscientiously pursuing their allotted task, setting at bay each night's darkness with their lights. It gave him a sudden feeling of security.

Almost abruptly he realized that though he felt blasted and empty, he also felt alive, and free, and glad to be so. Tarrian had had to state the options but they had never really existed, as both of them knew.

He closed the window.

'So much for deciding the strategy,' he said with a nervous smile. 'Tactics, I fear, may present more of a problem.'

He returned to the couch and lay down again, though this time with some relish. It was the soldier's euphoria brought on by knowing that the battle would not now be fought until the morrow; that for the next hour or so he was immortal and immune to all his ills. He had known it before.

'Before the fear and the confusion return, let's talk,' he said. 'About who and how and why and about what we can do.'

Tarrian flopped down on the floor beside the couch and rested his head on his paws. 'Who, how and why, we don't know,' he said. 'As to what we can do, we can look at what's happened and think about it and that will arm us for what happens next.'

'Perhaps,' Antyr said.

'No,' Tarrian said decisively. 'It'll arm us definitely. Don't forget that whatever's happening, we've survived so far, despite being caught totally unprepared. And too, Ibris survived, by dint of his will, and Menedrion survived his first dream by dint of . . .' He paused.

'By dint of what?' Antyr said knowingly. 'By dint of some strange intervention by some other . . . person . . . or power. It was a fair reproach he made. What do we make of that as masters of our trade, dog? As farriers and fletchers?'

Tarrian was pensive. 'Nothing,' he said after a moment. 'We just note it and remember it, like everything else.'

Antyr nodded reflectively. 'And what about me?' he asked tentatively. 'What's happened to me?'

He felt a sensation from Tarrian that he could only describe as a glow. Turning, he looked down at him, but the wolf was still lying stretched out with his head on his paws and his eyes half shut.

'What was that?' he asked sharply.

'What?' Tarrian replied.

'That,' Antyr answered in mild exasperation, then, hesitantly, 'that . . . glow.'

'Glow?' said Tarrian with amused tolerance. 'What *are* you talking about?'

'You know full well what I'm talking about,' Antyr said, leaning up on one elbow. Then Tarrian's true feelings leaked through. 'Ye gods, you're excited,' Antyr exclaimed. 'I'm being pursued by . . . demons . . . from god knows where, and *you* are excited—'

Tarrian chuckled. 'Yes. Sorry,' he said, insincerely. Antyr searched about for a suitably angry rebuke but the wolf's feelings welled up and dominated him.

Tarrian stood up and looked at him, his tail wagging. 'Didn't you feel the way we went into Menedrion's Nexus, and the way we hunted, searched it?' Briefly, Antyr was there again, amid the whirling splendour. 'The clarity, the speed, the effortlessness,' Tarrian declaimed. 'How could I *not* be excited. How could *you* not be excited?'

'Very easily,' Antyr said. 'Have you forgotten where it landed us? Or more correctly, me? In some strange place beyond . . . outside . . . the dream. Alone, separated from the dreamer and apart from you? It scared me witless, that's how I can't be excited.'

'But you survived,' Tarrian said breathlessly. 'You drew me to you, just as you did last night. You protected the dreamer and you routed your attackers.'

'But I don't know how!' Antyr said in some anguish.

'It doesn't matter!' Tarrian almost shouted. 'It doesn't matter. You won. Both times. *You* won!'

'But—'

'No buts,' Tarrian said. 'You won. And, admittedly at no thanks to yourself, and god knows how, you're ten times the Dream Finder you were a mere day ago. It's as if these . . . attacks . . . have woken something in you. Prodded something into life that was drowning in doubt and ale.'

Antyr frowned. 'But, but, but, but,' he said starkly, refusing Tarrian's optimism.

Tarrian quietened a little. 'Yes, all right,' he conceded. 'There's still more questions than answers, but we're not defenceless, Antyr. Even if we don't yet know where our . . . your . . . strength lies, it's still there when it's needed.'

Questions indeed, Antyr thought, as they surged around his mind. But they were all unanswerable and had become a meaningless circle. Somehow he brushed them aside and sat up. The euphoria was still there. He was still immortal for an hour or so.

'Well, we can't do anything now, anyway,' he said. 'We'll have to see what the night brings, and then, if we're spared, we'll go and see this . . . Nyriall . . . in the morning. One way or another we'll be wiser then, and another opinion won't go amiss. And you'll enjoy meeting another wolf, won't you?'

'Not necessarily,' Tarrian said coldly.

Antyr did not pursue the matter.

'In the meantime what shall we do?' he went on. 'I don't know what time Menedrion will be retiring, but from what I've heard it'll be late. Or at least late before he goes to sleep.'

Tarrian stretched himself luxuriously. 'I think food then our fee,' he said. 'That old moaner who let us in said to ring that bell if we wanted anything.'

A few minutes later, after receiving elaborate directions from the bewildered servant who had eventually answered their summons and seemed to know nothing about their presence there, they were walking through the labyrinthine corridors of the palace again, in an attempt to find the Chancellor's office.

'I'd have preferred to have eaten first,' Tarrian said.

'You heard the man,' Antyr replied. 'The Chancellor's office will be shut shortly. Make your choice, we either go to the refectory for a meal, and then wait another day for our fee. Another day for memories to fade,' he added significantly. 'Or wait a little for your food and get the money now.'

'All right, all right,' Tarrian replied. 'It's just that I haven't eaten for—'

'Ten minutes,' Antyr said caustically.

Tarrian maintained a dignified silence for a moment, then he turned off down a flight of stairs. 'Down here,' he said. 'I hope you're paying attention to the way we're going.'

'Right at the bottom, along the corridor, across the hall, bear right after the decorated archway . . .' Antyr began reciting.

'All right,' Tarrian interrupted unkindly, adding, 'Let's see how you manage coming back.'

'I'm not envisaging any difficulty,' Antyr replied haughtily.

Tarrian gave an anticipatory 'We'll see' grunt.

'Right, here.'

'Left!'

A little while later, and after explaining themselves to three separate servants from whom they inquired about the route, they arrived at a door bearing the worn and cryptic legend 'Chanc Gen' in ancient capital letters.

'Oh dear,' Tarrian said ominously. 'He's too mean to have the sign on his door repainted. I don't think this is going to be easy.'

As Antyr reached out to push it, the door opened to reveal a palace messenger. There was a brief dance as the two men both hesitated in the doorway and then stepped sideways and forward simultaneously. Tarrian ploughed through the resultant collision regardless, ensuring complete confusion.

'Come on,' he said, impatiently. 'I'm hungry.'

After a spluttering of mutual apologies with the messenger, Antyr found himself backing into the 'Chanc Gen' office.

'Oh dear,' he heard Tarrian say again.

Turning, he found himself standing in a large hall filled with rank upon rank of desks, each occupied by the hunched form of a black-gowned clerk. Along one of the side walls were shelves laden with heaps of scrolls and papers and dangling seals. They reached from the floor to the high ceiling, growing dustier with height, and they were complemented on the opposite wall by stacks of large drawers which also shouldered up against the ceiling as if supporting it.

As he took in the scene, Antyr became aware of a small but steady movement of clerks migrating from desk to desk, desk to shelf, desk to drawer, with the slow purposeful randomness of a mysterious but thoughtful board game. And the air was filled with the insect twitterings of innumerable scratching pens, underscored by the shuffling feet of the migrating clerks and a low hubbub of voices, though he could see no one speaking. Occasionally there was the explosive discharge of a cough.

And there was a smell . . .?

Tarrian sneezed damply.

'Dust,' he growled. 'Dusty ink, dusty paper, dusty clothes and dusty people.' He sneezed again. 'Don't just stand there, man. Speak to someone.'

Facing the massed ranks of Aaken Uhr Candessa's troops and their lowering flank guards of shelves and drawers, Antyr quailed.

'Perhaps we should come back later,' he said.

'Speak to someone,' Tarrian ordered him, pitilessly.

Goaded by his commander's blade, Antyr moved towards the nearest clerk.

'Excuse me,' he said hesitantly. 'Who do I see about . . . getting paid for—'

'Payments over there,' the clerk said without looking up, but marking the direction with a rapid flick of his pen.

Antyr turned and examined the sector indicated by his guide. It looked the same as everywhere else. He hesitated, but, sensing Tarrian's mounting disapproval, he forced his feet forward.

As he threaded his way along the criss-crossing aisles, his footsteps rose up to beat an unwelcome tattoo across the hissing murmur of the hall and he found himself slowing down and clearing his throat self-consciously. Tarrian had no such concerns, however, and he pattered ahead, sniffing at desks and occupants indiscriminately and proprietorially.

A small ripple of consternation followed their progress, until, to his relief, Antyr stumbled upon a small enclave of desks set apart from the main body. He selected an old, quite distinguished-looking clerk.

'Excuse me . . .' he began.

A familiar flick of the pen redirected him to the next desk.

Tarrian placed his forepaws on the desk indicated and stared intently at its occupant, a middle-aged man dressed identically to the others. He looked up and, unexpectedly, smiled broadly. First at Tarrian and then at Antyr.

'Lovely dog,' he said, reaching out and stroking Tarrian before Antyr could intervene.

Tarrian, however, took no exception, but half closed his eyes and moved his head from side to side under the man's hand.

'Yes, he is,' Antyr replied, in the interests of simplicity, and seizing this moment of humanity amid the quietly relentless grind of the administrative apparatus of Ibris's dominion.

'What can I do for you?' the man asked, still smiling.

'I'm trying to find someone who can pay me for some work I did last night for the . . . the Chancellor,' Antyr said.

The man raised his eyebrows, but made no comment, although his eyes flicked quickly over Antyr as if balancing the likely truth of this assertion against his appearance.

'For the Chancellor?' he echoed. 'Himself? Personally?'

Antyr nodded.

The man's smile became uncertain, and Antyr became aware of other heads surreptitiously turning in his direction. Then the man pursed his lips and became businesslike. 'Have you got a docket?' he asked.

'A docket?' Antyr repeated vaguely.

'A note authorizing payment,' the man explained. 'From the . . . Chancellor. He should have given you one.'

Antyr shrugged. 'No,' he said. 'He didn't give me anything.' Then, into the ensuing silence he began to gabble. 'The Duke told him to pay me, then Commander Feranc was going to escort me home, but Chancellor Aaken said he thought I ought to stay in the palace because of the fog, and because I was tired . . . then I think perhaps he forgot about my fee. It was all very late last night.'

'The Duke? Commander Feranc? Last night?' The man's eyebrows rose even further.

'He's thinking about calling the guard,' Tarrian said. 'You're not handling this very well, are you?'

'I'm sorry,' Antyr said, gently pushing Tarrian down from the desk. 'It is a bit complicated, I know. And I'm more used

204

to dealing with private clients, I'm afraid I don't know how you—'

His explanation, however, was ended by the sounding of a small bell.

Abruptly the sound in the hall changed, and a relieved chaos descended as pens were laid aside, books closed, chairs pushed back and casual conversations begun and ended. Antyr looked around in bewilderment. The hall was suddenly a sea of black, flapping waves as gowns of office were discarded to reveal a crowd of ordinary people in their workaday variety.

When he turned back to his own interrogator Antyr found that he too had shed his official skin and metamorphosed into a person. His smile too had returned, though it seemed a little strained. 'I'm sorry,' he said, stepping round his desk. 'You'll have to come back tomorrow. Today's not a payment day anyway, but I might have been able to sort out some of the paperwork for you if we'd had time.' He took Antyr's elbow and guided him anxiously into the flow now heading for the exit. 'You'll have to find the . . . Chancellor . . . and get a docket from him before you come back though, otherwise no one can pay you anything,' he went on. 'You know how it is. The Chancellor himself is a stickler in these matters. I'm very surprised he didn't give you one.'

Then they were at the door and, with a hasty farewell, he was gone.

'Masterly,' Tarrian said as they eventually disentangled themselves from the homegoing crowd. 'I couldn't have handled it worse myself without a lifetime's practice. He thought you were a lunatic, and I'm not surprised.'

'Be quiet,' Antyr replied crossly. 'It's not my fault Aaken doesn't know his own system. I just . . . trusted him . . . I suppose.'

Tarrian made a disparaging noise. 'Well, now you'll be dunning him instead,' he said. 'And I'm damned if I'm going to do that on an empty stomach. Let's see if we can at least find some food.'

Thanks to Tarrian's nose, it took them considerably less time to find the refectory than it had to find the chancellor's office, but again Antyr found himself in a position of some embarrassment as, after rooting through his pockets, he found he had insufficient funds for the meal being provided.

Here, however, chance stepped in to save him in the form of the old 'layer of tables' who had escorted him to his room.

'Lord Menedrion's guests. Both of them,' he said tersely to the gravy-streaked bondsman who was serving the meals. This, however, was the end of his familiarity as he wandered off immediately with his own meal to the far end of one of the long tables.

Tarrian chuckled. 'That's *your* place in the pack well marked out,' he said. 'Better than a kitchen hand but less than a layer of tables.'

Antyr, however, was occupied in rubbing a wet finger across the sign of the kitchen servitor's calling that the bondsman, with a surly but deft swing of his ladle, had just anointed his tunic with while ostensibly serving his meal.

'This is wonderful. Dream Finder to the Duke of Serenstad and his family,' Tarrian said acidly as Antyr sat down. 'Nearly thrown into Watch Pen by a clerk, confined to the palace by our client, and, but for the intervention of a table layer, starving amid plenty.'

'Eat your food and shut up,' Antyr said, frowning. 'I'm in no mood for your sarcasm.'

'Sorry,' Tarrian said, genuinely repentant. 'I was only trying to cheer you . . . oh-oh . . .'

Antyr looked up to see what had halted Tarrian's reply. It needed little finding. The head of a large hunting dog could clearly be seen above the table as it moved towards them along the aisle opposite. As it drew nearer, it caught sight of Tarrian and stopped. Then it began to move forward again, slowly and purposefully, its head lowered.

Antyr glanced round in search of its owner, but found only a group of four young men gleefully watching the dog's progress.

'Don't start a fight,' Antyr said. But there was no reply except, 'Close your ears,' followed by some garbled comment about territory and food.

Antyr knew better than to interfere, but found himself cringing nervously.

Coming within a few paces of Tarrian, the big dog stopped and glared at him malevolently. Tarrian, who was lying down and who had been eating, seemingly obliviously, stopped and, slowly looking up, returned the stare. Antyr saw his lip curl very slightly and heard a faint, low growl. Then part of Tarrian's debate with the dog leaked into his mind and he recoiled inwardly at both the menacing images of mayhem and gore, and the implacable will behind them.

The big dog presumably received the full benefit of Tarrian's wisdom as its manner changed abruptly. Its ears drooped, its tail went between its legs, and after a few hesitant backward steps it turned, trotted back to the four men and lay at their feet, to their obvious dismay. Tarrian returned to his eating.

'You certainly seem to have a way with words,' Antyr said.

'Well, I'm certainly having more success with the residents than you are,' Tarrian replied. 'You should learn how to explain yourself properly like I do.'

Antyr smiled. 'I think you're probably right,' he said. 'But I doubt either the Duke or Menedrion would appreciate that kind of language. Not to mention Ciarll Feranc or even Aaken Uhr Candessa.'

'Talking of whom,' Tarrian said, standing up. 'We'd better find him and get all this sorted out. I wasn't being sarcastic when I said we might starve to death wandering about here.'

Antyr pushed his plate to one side and wiped his mouth. The food had made him feel more settled. He nodded in agreement with Tarrian's comment. They could blunder about the palace indefinitely, relying on chance and their wits to feed and house them unless they came to some clear arrangement with someone . . . somewhere . . .

A small spark of indignation flickered unexpectedly into life inside him. After all, they hadn't asked to come here. They had been sought out by the Duke himself – and his son – and escorted through the streets by no less a personage than Ciarll Feranc himself. They shouldn't have to be buffeted about by minor clerks and splashed by kitchen servants.

He stood up with great dignity and began walking towards the door. 'You've got gravy on your chin,' Tarrian said padding after him. Antyr glared down at him, and surreptitiously wiped his face.

Outside the refectory, however, Antyr's new-found purpose faltered. On arrival, he had been following Tarrian's accelerating hunt for food and he had scarcely noticed where he was. Now he found himself in a wide brightly lit corridor, lined, as seemed to be the case throughout the palace, with magnificent works of art; pictures, carvings, tapestries. Even the cornices around the ceiling were an example of the finest plasterers' art with their elaborate interwoven patterns of branches and leaves housing strange birds and insects and occasional haunting faces.

And the lamps here don't smoke, he thought, then, unexpectedly, he felt a twinge of homesickness for his own bare room with its cracked and stained walls.

Tarrian stood silent by his side until the moment passed. 'Where do we start?' Antyr said, eventually.

At each end of the corridor there were large, open spaces and it was intersected by at least three other corridors and a staircase. 'I don't know,' Tarrian said, in a mildly injured tone. 'I can get us back to our rooms but even if I could remember Aaken's scent I couldn't find him in this lot.'

Antyr nodded. Obviously he should ask someone, but who? There were a great many people walking about, some in formal livery, some wearing what were obviously robes of office. He recognized palace messengers and Sened couriers, and there were a few black-gowned clerks, though they were more expensively dressed than those he had already encountered. Then there were various guards and servants, and a random assortment of what he would have classed as ordinary folk had it not been for their wealth being manifest in their clothing and their authority being manifest in their bearing.

Some were moving slowly in pairs and small groups, engaged in earnest conversations, some were striding out alone, others were fussing along busily bearing documents. But all were moving with confident and intimidating purposefulness.

Antyr stood motionless for a moment but no opportunity for a timely interruption seemed to present itself and the small flame of indignation guttered uncertainly as he began to feel profoundly conspicuous again.

'Ask one of the guards,' both he and Tarrian said simultaneously.

Before they could begin to implement this decision, however, a commotion at one end of the corridor brought all activity to a halt and drew all eyes.

The cause soon became apparent as Menedrion strode round the corner flanked by a bustling assembly of guards, officials, scribes and young courtiers. He was talking loudly and, each time he paused, one of the satellites would detach itself from the mass and run off, presumably to execute some command.

'Go on,' Tarrian urged, but Antyr hesitated as the group moved relentlessly towards them.

Tarrian sighed.

'Lord,' he said distinctly into both Menedrion's and Antyr's minds as the Duke's son strode past.

Menedrion stopped abruptly and turned to Antyr.

'There, that wasn't difficult, was it?' Tarrian said to Antyr. 'Go on, ask him. And stand up straight, for pity's sake!'

Antyr, however, merely gaped as he found himself not only the focus of Menedrion's attention, but everyone else's as well.

'Your pardon, Lord. But your servant neglected to tell me—' Tarrian prompted.

'Your pardon, Lord . . .' Antyr said hesitantly. 'But your servant neglected to tell me—'

'When I should attend on you—'

'When I should attend on you tonight . . . and where,' he added finally in response to another nudge from Tarrian.

Menedrion gazed at him blankly for a moment, then, as he noted Tarrian, recognition dawned. For the briefest instant, panic flitted through his eyes, then anger and confusion.

'Stand up straight,' Tarrian repeated. 'And meet his gaze, politely.'

Antyr obeyed.

Menedrion's brief confusion ended in relief. 'You won't be needed tonight,' he said curtly.

Antyr looked concerned, but this was no place to remonstrate.

'Sir,' someone said urgently, nodding significantly along the corridor. Menedrion raised an impatient hand and frowned.

'Report to my . . . private office tomorrow . . . afternoon,' he said to Antyr. 'I'll have decided what to do with you then.'

Antyr bowed then he gave Menedrion a significant look, as discreetly as he could. 'May I leave the palace in the morning, sir?' he asked. 'I have matters to . . . research.'

Menedrion stopped and returned his gaze. 'Yes,' he said slowly. 'Yes, you may.' Then he was off again, towing his entourage after him. 'But make sure you get everything you require. You'll need to be available to leave with my company the day after tomorrow.'

'Leave, sir?' Antyr managed as the tide swept by him. 'Company? Leave for where . . .?'

The question faded as Menedrion retreated but a passing figure said, 'To the border. Escorting the envoy.'

Envoy? Antyr mouthed as the corridor began to revert back to its previous rhythm. 'What's happening, Tarrian?'

Tarrian shook his head. 'I don't eavesdrop, you know?' he said, his tone mildly injured. 'Except on business.'

'I know,' Antyr said. 'But I also know that some people shout a lot. What did you just pick up from that lot?'

'It's all jumble,' Tarrian replied. 'I've been getting whiffs of something all day, there's a lot of excitement washing about.' He hesitated and his concern seeped through to Antyr.

'What is it?' Antyr said.

'It's the Bethlarii, I'm afraid,' Tarrian replied reluctantly. 'Something about a Bethlarii envoy.' He hesitated again. 'And Menedrion's mind was full of images of war.'

Antyr went suddenly cold, and the splendours around him seemed to become just so much dross.

'You're not on the reserves now, are you?' Tarrian asked gently.

'I'm well down the list,' Antyr replied 'They'd be at the gates before my turn came, I think, but—'

'I understand,' Tarrian said. 'There are no words to measure the folly of it.' He tried to offer a little solace. 'Still I might be wrong,' he said. 'Menedrion's a wild man, and he's looking for something to take his mind off his real problem. And I wasn't really listening.'

Antyr reached down and stroked him. 'Don't worry,' he said needlessly. 'I've no doubt we'll find out what we need to know in due course. In the meantime Menedrion's real problems are also *our* real problems and we'd better bend our mind to them. We'll have to find this Nyriall tomorrow and hope he can help us.'

'There's another problem now,' Tarrian said.

Antyr looked at him inquiringly.

'We can't go anywhere with Menedrion,' Tarrian answered. 'The Duke told us not to leave the city.'

Antyr caught a glimpse of a worried-looking middle-aged man across the corridor. He was stooping slightly. With a jolt he realized it was himself reflected with fearful accuracy by an elegant silver-framed mirror.

'Not pretty, is it?' Tarrian said. Antyr ignored the comment but straightened up, adjusted his robe, and smoothed down his hair.

'Well, we'd better go and speak to the Duke then, hadn't we?' he said.

Chapter 17

Antyr's encounter with Menedrion had at least overcome his hesitancy about inquiring of anyone as to where in the palace he might be and, still buoyed up, he fixed the first guard he found with an imperious stare and demanded to know the whereabouts of the Duke's private quarters.

Fortunately, the guard in question had just seen him talking to Menedrion and gave him the information without even submitting him to a suspicious look.

Now, as he walked through the palace, Tarrian's disturbing news conspired with the eerie problems mounting around him, to unsettle him again and send his mood swinging rapidly between excitement and depression.

Gradually, he brought his thoughts into some semblance of order. Practical problems first: he had to see the Duke about Menedrion's order that he prepare to leave the city. That was a conflict of instructions that he had no intention of attempting to resolve on his own! He could see that any meeting with the Duke about it might lead to complications concerning how it had come to pass that Menedrion had contacted him, but on balance, he decided that a naive craftsman's openness and honesty was his best protection; indeed, it was perhaps his only protection.

Then, though largely at Tarrian's prompting, came the problem of payment. Should he try and find Aaken and debate that with him, or should he raise it with the Duke? He quailed at the prospect of either, and decided to make his final decision when he was on the battlefield itself. As for Menedrion's fee – he was glad he'd waived it.

Then there were the other, darker, problems: the Duke's strange dream. Menedrion's even stranger one, if dream it had been. And his own frightening . . . visitation. It was difficult but he knew he must try to accept that he could do nothing about any of these until something else happened or unless the old Dream Finder Nyriall gave him some help. A siren voice somewhere down inside him still tried to lure him away from this terrifying, clinging quagmire he felt he was sinking into; get drunk! run away! But somehow he managed to shout it down.

He shook his head as he walked along. His encounter with Pandra and Kany earlier seemed like distant memories and his aching walk to the Aphron Dennai was an eternity away.

As for the possibility of war? True, it was only Tarrian's vaguely snatched impression, but his stomach plunged again, even though, of all his problems it was perhaps the one that he could do least about.

'We're nearly there.' Tarrian's voice interrupted his uneasy reverie.

Antyr looked up with a start. He had been so absorbed that for a moment he could not remember where he was. As he gazed around he was startled to see dark windows on either side of the corridor. Then he realized that they were passing over one of the palace's many high soaring covered walkways. He stopped by one of the windows and looked out.

'Tarrian,' he said softly. 'Look.'

The wolf had been walking some way ahead, his head lowered intently, but he turned without comment and came back to Antyr.

As the two of them stared out of the window, a ghostly Dream Finder and his Companion gazed back at them, but shining through these images was the sprawl of Serenstad with its fog-blurred lights expanding steadily outwards.

'I didn't realize we'd come so high,' Antyr said.

'You've been a bit preoccupied,' Tarrian said. 'We've come up quite a few stairs. And don't forget, the palace is built on a slope.'

Antyr nodded absently. It was still a breathtaking sight. What must it be like on a clear day? Glancing from side to side he could just make the edges of the two buildings that were joined by the walkway; both of them disappeared up into the darkness. And what must be the view from up there?

'Come on,' Tarrian prompted gently. 'Let's find our client.'

Reluctantly, Antyr pulled himself away from the window and set off after Tarrian again.

As they passed through the door at the end of the walkway, they emerged into what appeared to be a large foyer. It was not as brightly lit as the corridors they had been walking along, but its most striking feature was the silence as the echoing marble floor gave way to a lush carpet.

'Where now?' Antyr whispered instinctively.

'Nowhere,' Tarrian answered significantly, and even as he spoke, two large guards appeared silently in front of them.

'Have you lost your way, sir?' one of them said politely. He had a slight foreign accent. Mantynnai, Antyr deduced. These would be the elite of the Duke's personal bodyguard; men under the direct, personal command of Ciarll Feranc. Though neither of them exuded any menace, Antyr felt afraid.

'Have you lost your way, sir?' the man was repeating, a little more emphatically.

'I'm . . . I'm . . . looking for . . . I need to speak to the . . . to the . . . Duke. Sir,' Antyr stammered. He braced himself for a sarcastic response, but none was forthcoming.

'If you have a message for the Duke, it could have been left downstairs, but you may give it to me,' the guard said, still polite.

Antyr shook his head. 'No,' he said. 'I don't have a message from anyone, I have to see him personally. It's important.'

It wasn't important, he realized, as soon as he had spoken the words. It was a trivial organizational problem that certainly didn't need the personal and immediate attention of the Duke.

Then again, another part of him said, it was important, and it *did* concern the Duke personally.

Briefly the two opinions struggled for dominance, then it dawned on him that probably the worst that could happen to him would be for the Duke to have him thrown out, and, fee or no, that was not an unhappy solution to his problems. He must plough on.

'My name's Antyr,' he said hastily as he saw the guard's eyes begin to narrow. 'I saw the Duke last night. He'll remember. If he isn't . . . available, then perhaps I could speak to Commander Feranc or Chancellor Aaken.'

The guard's manner, however, changed perceptibly at the mention of Antyr's own name, making the references to Aaken and Feranc superfluous. His look of growing suspicion was replaced by a barely hidden curiosity. He turned to his companion, who nodded him towards a nearby door.

'I'll see if a member of his staff can be found to look after you, sir,' he said. 'Would you wait here.'

And he was gone, leaving Antyr and Tarrian alone with

the other guard, an older man with a seemingly easy-going manner. However, he wore a slightly different insignia on his uniform which, coupled with the fact that it was the first guard who was running the errand, identified him to Antyr as the senior in rank.

He looked at Antyr and smiled broadly though it did little to ease Antyr's trepidation.

'An unusual profession, Dream Finding,' the man said casually, his accent stronger than his companion's. 'In my time I've met many shamans and priests and so-called wise men who would listen to the telling of dreams and then foretell the future and suchlike, but I'd never heard of a skill such as yours until I came to this land.'

It seemed an odd remark, but then, for all their known loyalty, the Mantynnai *were* foreigners.

Antyr returned the smile nervously. 'We make no silk here, because we don't have the knowledge,' he said. 'And where they make the silk I understand they make no steels because *they* don't have the knowledge. Not all countries practise all crafts.'

The guard nodded and laughed softly. 'True,' he conceded. 'But Dream Finding is a strange profession, for all that. I suppose I could learn how to make silk and steel if I had to, but could I become a Dream Finder?'

'No,' Antyr conceded in turn, warming to the man a little. 'It's passed on from father to son in some way, if it's passed on at all.'

'It is a mystery then, not a craft,' the guard went on. 'A bridge to places beyond the sight of other men.'

Antyr shrugged slightly. 'A mystery to you, but a craft to me,' he said. 'Just as you are a mystery to me, but a craftsman also, Mantynnai.'

The guard smiled and nodded, though, for an instant, his eyes became distant and sad.

'Move away,' Tarrian said softly into Antyr's mind. 'You're hurting him.'

'I heard that there was a Bethlarii envoy at the palace today,' Antyr said, taken aback slightly by Tarrian's unexpected interruption and snatching at the first topic that came to mind.

'There was indeed,' the man replied.

He offered no further explanation however, and there was a finality in his answer that made Antyr loath to press him.

He glanced at the door through which the other guard had gone.

'He'll be a little while yet,' the guard said. 'Sit down. Make yourself comfortable.' He pointed to a wide bench seat in an alcove and his manner became jocular, teasing. 'Is your message *very* urgent? Have you foreseen a great Bethlarii army mustering against us in some subtle cranny of the Duke's dreams?'

Antyr hesitated. 'I must speak to the Duke certainly,' he replied. 'Or Commander Feranc—'

'Or Chancellor Aaken.' The guard finished his answer for him, nodding and laughing. 'Then you *must* have seen an army.'

Antyr went suddenly cold, something had to be stopped here and he was uncertain how to do it. He leaned forward. 'Dreams are beyond all understanding,' he said, almost aggressively. 'They spring from who knows what ancient sources deep inside us, for who knows what ancient reasons. I can foretell nothing. Nor see through mountains. I help the dreamers see their dreams again, for whatever reason they wish. And I talk to them about it if they wish. But that is all. The future is the future. Perhaps some can foresee it, perhaps not. But no Dream Finder can.'

The guard made to speak, but Antyr, committed now, continued, his mouth dry. 'Please understand,' he said. 'I may not tell you whose dreams I have searched nor what was seen there without their express permission. Duke or slave, their secrets are as safe with me as my human frailty will allow. I saw the Duke last night, but what passed between us remains between us, be it a dream search or not.' To his own surprise, he levelled a finger at the Mantynnai. 'Put no words in my mouth but what I speak.'

The guard stared at him intently for a moment, his face suddenly unreadable, then he said, 'Come with me.' And beckoning Antyr to follow him he went through the door that the other guard had taken.

Clenching his fists nervously and regretting his firmness, Antyr forced his legs forward. Tarrian padded after him.

The guard did not speak as they walked on, and Antyr noticed that he made almost no other sound either. His sword did not rattle, nor his daggers, and, for all his size, his feet fell lightly on the carpeted floor. There was just the soft hiss of his clothes and the occasional creak of his leather tunic.

Not that Antyr had a great deal of time in which to observe this as very shortly they were at another door. It was black and simple and undecorated save for a small plate bearing the Duke's emblem.

The guard knocked discreetly and, almost without pause, the door opened quietly. Tarrian waited for no invitation, but went straight in. Antyr hesitated but the guard nodded him through urgently.

The room he found himself in was in stark contrast to the ornately decorated chamber where he had met the Duke the previous night. It was large and well lit and such items as decorated the walls were maps, or plans of cities, or charts of various kinds that he could not immediately identify, though some, he noted quickly, were related to siege engines.

These, together with the utilitarian simplicity of the room, brought images of war to Antyr's mind again.

Scattered about the room were several desks manned by scribes and secretaries or surrounded by groups of officers in quiet but intense conversation, and through other doors could be seen similar rooms. People came and went and over all was a soft hubbub of voices and activity.

At the far end of the room sat the Duke behind a large table strewn with documents. There were others sitting and standing by the table, but the Duke was leaning back and talking to Ciarll Feranc, one leg thrown over the arm of his chair and the other flexing so that he was rocking to and fro on the back legs of his chair.

A young man's posture, Antyr thought, feeling a sudden and quite unwarranted sense of security pervade him.

The door closed softly behind him and the guard signalled Antyr towards the Duke. Hesitantly, Antyr set off and the guard fell in behind him.

Their arrival caused a small stir in the room, though it was largely due to the presence of Tarrian who was already wandering freely, sniffing at people and peering at documents. One or two people stroked him affectionately, somewhat to Antyr's alarm, but Tarrian paid no heed.

As Antyr and the guard reached the Duke, he looked at them and held up an apologetic finger to Feranc to suspend their conversation.

A quick glance around the room had not revealed to Antyr the presence of the first guard, and now he stood before his Duke, his present escort apparently chose not to speak. There was, however, some communication with the man as both the Duke and Feranc looked at him over Antyr's shoulder until, apparently satisfied, the Duke nodded and Antyr felt the guard move away.

Antyr had been uncertain about exactly what he should say to the Duke, not least now because his own problem seemed to be gaining in insignificance amid this muffled activity. But, like many uncertainties, this proved to be pointless as it was the Duke who began the conversation.

'You left the city today against my express order,' he said flatly, swinging his leg down on to the floor and leaning forward on to the table.

Antyr felt his mouth dropping open and only managed to stop it with a considerable effort. The question, how . . .? formed in his mind briefly but the dark presence of Ciarll Feranc and the whirr of efficient administrative activity around him answered it, at least in general terms, before he had formed it fully. The rattle of chains and the slamming of cell doors rang in his ears.

Tarrian appeared by his side, looking earnestly at the Duke.

Antyr stuttered his reply through parched lips. 'I thought you were referring to leaving the city for any length of time, sire. On a journey . . .' he managed eventually. 'I needed to think. I merely went to the Aphron Dennai to clear my mind. I—'

'You disobeyed my order,' the Duke said. 'You broke the law.'

Antyr was silent for a moment, then the faint rebellion that he had brought against Menedrion, returned. 'I didn't disobey what I took to be the spirit of your order, sire,' he said. 'I was no further from your men finding me than if I'd been at . . .' He shrugged slightly, ' . . . the market.' The movement freed him. 'I obeyed you as a matter of honour and respect, sire, and if I failed you in that then I accept your reproach and I truly ask your forgiveness.' He leaned forward. 'But I am a free Guildsman, twice served in the line. I broke no law, I can't be constrained without—'

'Due process of law,' Ibris said, completing his sentence with a brief smile of amusement.

Antyr did not feel reassured. He couldn't read a duke's smile, and due process or not; free Guildsman or not; the reality was that the Duke and his officers were to be obeyed!

Ibris, however, merely began reading a document on the

table in front of him. 'What do you want, Antyr? I'm busy,' he said casually, as if the exchange had never happened.

Antyr started slightly at this abrupt end to the interrogation, then registering the question he glanced at the others nearby.

Ibris followed his eyes and beckoned him to come round the table.

'What is it?' he said in a low, unexpectedly confiding voice when Antyr reached him.

Bending low and feeling like a conspirator, Antyr mumbled his concern. 'It's about that order, sire,' he said. 'The Lord Menedrion has now ordered me to prepare to leave with him on a journey the day after tomorrow.'

Ibris's face darkened. 'How do you come to be involved with the Lord Menedrion?' he asked.

The inevitability of the question reminded Antyr why he had not chosen to prepare an answer in advance. It was because any answer would simply be the precursor to deeper and deeper questions and increasingly difficult ethical choices for him. No inspiration came to aid him.

'Sire, this is difficult,' he said.

'Answer nonetheless,' Ibris said starkly.

Antyr took a deep breath and jumped. 'May we speak alone, sire?' he said.

Ibris frowned. 'We're alone enough here, Dream Finder,' he said.

'No, we're not,' Antyr answered with unexpected bluntness. 'Something's wrong and it involves yourself, your son, me, and perhaps one other, I don't know. I can't discuss it with you in whispers, spare me a few minutes for plain speaking.'

Ibris's frown deepened, then he let out an impatient snort. 'Very well,' he said, standing up. 'But you're beginning to abuse the regard I had for your father. I'll give you five minutes. Ciarll, come with us.

'I'll be back in a little while,' he announced to the others at the table. 'Carry on.' He indicated a nearby door to Antyr.

The door took them across a corridor and thence, following the Duke's lead, into a small, intimate room lit only by a burning fire. Feranc struck a lamp into life and Ibris strode over to the fire where he stood, staring down into it for a few silent moments.

'Speak as loud as you wish here, Dream Finder,' he said, almost angrily and turning round sharply. 'But speak quickly and to some effect, or free Guildsman or no, I'll constrain you as you've never been constrained.'

Tarrian moved across to him and curled up at his feet.

Antyr glanced at Feranc. 'May I speak of your dream in front of the Commander, sire?' he said.

'If it's relevant, yes,' Ibris replied, turning and looking at a small delicately decorated timepiece on the mantleshelf.

Antyr took the further hint. 'Sire, as I said, this is difficult. I must break a confidence which a dreamer has entrusted in me and I'll need both your understanding and your protection.'

'Get on with it,' Ibris said.

Tarrian rolled over and leaned against Ibris's leg affectionately. Seemingly without thinking what he was doing, Ibris crouched down and stroked him.

'Sire,' Antyr began. 'Why did you call me so urgently last night?'

'You know why,' Ibris replied, his tone less severe. 'I felt a . . . presence . . . of some kind in my dream. As if something were trying to enter it. Something threatening.'

Antyr nodded. 'This is not something that's happened before?' he asked. 'In my father's time, perhaps?'

Ibris shook his head. 'Usually, I consulted your father so that I could see a dream again because I felt that it needed to be thought about; that it contained some message from deep within myself that I needed to hear and couldn't during the clamour of the day. He taught me to watch and listen to my dreams so that I wouldn't need his help.' He smiled at some long-forgotten memory. 'A remarkable man your father. Strove diligently to lose his best customer. If I'd had a dozen like him, we'd have had one great, glorious and peaceful state in this land spreading up even into the barbarian tribes beyond the mountains and out across the seas to . . .'

His voice faded and he let the idea go with it.

'It's because of your father's training that I sensed that this . . . presence . . . was something from outside,' he went on, assured again. 'But I've more tangible threats at the moment, Dream Finder—'

Antyr raise his hand for silence. 'Sire, I too was assailed last night by some strange power from outside. It came to

219

me in the form of Marastrumel, the ancient personification of evil in Dream Finding lore.'

Ibris looked at him and then at Feranc.

'No one entered his room last night, sire,' the Commander said, answering the unspoken question and again telling Antyr that for at least some of the time he had been discreetly watched. 'Perhaps it was a dream.' There was a hint of humour in his voice, but the Duke did not pick it up.

'Dream Finders don't, or can't, dream, Ciarll,' he said simply. Then, to Antyr, 'They tell me that you're overly fond of ale and wine, Antyr. Could Marastrumel perhaps have come to you in a bottle?'

Antyr coloured. 'No sir. The reproach is true but the Commander ensured that I had only water last night, and drink has only ever brought me oblivion and sickness. I fear that whatever power attacked you in your dream, sensed me and is seeking me out.'

'To what purpose?' Ibris said.

Antyr shrugged helplessly. 'I've no idea, sire,' he said.

Ibris moved away from the fire and sat down slowly on a chair nearby. Tarrian crawled along on his belly and rested his chin on the Duke's foot. Ibris's face was thoughtful and serious.

'You mentioned my son and perhaps another person involved in this,' he said.

Antyr gazed awkwardly around the room, finding it almost impossible to speak the words that would break the confidence of his client.

'I'll deal with Menedrion if need be,' Ibris said. 'Have no fear on that score. You have my protection. Who's the other person?'

'I don't know, sire, I . . .' Antyr shrugged helplessly.

Ibris's irritation showed clearly and Antyr quailed. 'Which brings me back to my previous question,' Ibris went on forcefully. 'How do you come to be involved with Menedrion?'

'He sought me out, as you did, sire,' Antyr replied, finding his voice from somewhere. 'But he mentioned that he had been given my name by his mother.'

Ibris's expression changed to one of surprise, then his mouth curled into a snarl. 'That witch. Even in the Erin-Mal she sits at the heart of my dominion like a great spider,' he said, though largely to himself. He turned to his bodyguard. 'How did she find out about last night, Ciarll?' he asked.

'Assuming the Dream Finder isn't in her pay, then any one of a dozen guards or servants might have carried the information to her,' Feranc replied regretfully. 'I took no great pains about secrecy.'

Ibris waved Antyr's burgeoning denial aside before it found tongue, and he nodded in acknowledgement of Feranc's admission.

'It's of no matter, I suppose,' he concluded. 'But . . .'

He let the sentence fade out into an irritable sigh as he brought his mind back to the more pressing needs of the moment.

'I'll not pry into Menedrion's dreams, Antyr,' he said. 'But why does he need you so suddenly, and why would he want you to accompany him when he leaves? He's not a man to be frightened by shadows.'

Antyr still hesitated. Despite the Duke's obvious understanding of his position, he had not realized how deeply rooted was his need to protect his clients.

'Time isn't on your side, Dream Finder,' the Duke said bluntly. 'Speak to some purpose or leave.'

The impossibility of his situation stood stark in front of Antyr. He needed help if he in turn was to help others. But he could obtain no help if he remained silent.

He had no choice. The rights and wrongs of his breach of confidence would have to be debated later.

'I'm sorry, sire,' he said. 'But it's hard for me to do this, and I do it only because no other alternative seems to be open to me.'

The Duke looked at him, waiting.

'Lord Menedrion had a dream last night which alarmed him greatly,' Antyr said suddenly. Almost immediately he felt a sense of relief at being able to voice his concerns. 'When we searched for it, I found myself separated both from the dreamer and my Companion and in some strange place beyond the dream, where Lord Menedrion was being assailed by many enemies. Between us, Tarrian and I brought him back, but . . .' He faltered, but Ibris asked no questions in the silence. 'I don't know what happened, sire. I've never known anything like it. All I could suggest was that we keep watch on him tonight to see if anything further happens—'

'And now he'll be awake all night working and won't need

221

you until tomorrow,' Ibris said quietly, nodding slowly and turning to stare into the fire again. He was silent for a long time.

'You've heard about the Bethlarii envoy, I presume?' he said, eventually.

'Vague snatches of gossip from overheard conversations, sire,' Antyr replied. 'I don't know anyone here to discuss such matters with.'

Ibris nodded again. 'You will, Dream Finder,' he said, with some heavy humour. 'You will, I fear.'

Antyr, though puzzled by this remark, made no comment.

Ibris was silent again for a little while, then, 'Quite suddenly, and without any warning we find ourselves facing the possibility of total war against the Bethlarii. How does that strike you, twice server?'

'With horror,' Antyr answered, more quickly and definitely than mature reflection would have advised him.

Ibris continued staring into the fire, but Antyr saw his eyebrows rise at this response. 'Wouldn't you welcome the chance to find glory and adventure battling against your city's foes, Guildsman?' he asked.

'I'll fight if I have to,' Antyr replied, suddenly reckless. 'For my city and for myself. But *only* if I have to. And I certainly won't welcome it. There's adventure enough just walking the city streets at night.' He pointed to the mantelshelf. 'And there's more true glory in that timepiece there than there is a lifetime's wars.'

He sensed some kind of a response from Feranc, but the bodyguard was standing at the edge of his vision and he could not identify it properly.

Ibris glanced up at the mantelshelf. 'I wish the Bethlarii had your vision,' he said after a brief silence. Then he stood up, gently disturbing the apparently sleeping Tarrian. His manner became brisk. 'But, as ever, they don't. And, as ever, we may all have to pay the price of their blindness.'

He turned round and looked at Antyr squarely. 'I can't make head nor tail of what you're talking about, Dream Finder, but I know that *I* was attacked and I've no reason to doubt what you say about your own, and Menedrion's experiences.' He glanced at Feranc. 'Equally I can't make head nor tail of what the Bethlarii are up to. But I don't have to see spears and swords to smell an ambush, so, as far as

I'm concerned, the two events are related, and right now I'm not going to fret about the logic of it all.'

Feranc nodded, and Antyr stood very still, feeling himself suddenly the focus of terrible and unknowable forces swirling about and beyond him. Tarrian moved to his side.

'Antyr,' the Duke said, his voice calm. 'I absolve you of your oath of loyalty as a Guildsman and a reservist. I give you free choice, without reproach. Will you stand by me and help me, or take your fee and return quietly to your home to pursue your calling in peace.'

It was not what Antyr had been expecting. He had been anticipating either being thrown out or perhaps being 'volunteered' into service by virtue of 'Needs of the State'.

He hesitated. A cascade of conflicting thoughts tumbled through his head in an instant. What could he do? He didn't know what was happening. Was this some trick? Would the Duke indeed allow him to walk quietly away if that was what he chose to do? And what about Menedrion? Would he find out what had happened? And who would protect . . .? The hooded figure with the lamp appeared abruptly amid the turmoil. Who was he? And what threat did he offer? Would standing near to the Duke draw the phantom on or send it gibbering into the darkness?

And he was no courtier. He wouldn't know what to do in this place.

Then, oddly altruistic thoughts rose up to embarrass him. Who but a Dream Finder *could* help the Duke with this strange happening? And if in helping the Duke he could in some way help prevent the horror of war spreading over the land again, should he not do it? Could he sleep at nights ever again if he did not, or would he be haunted by the legions of the maimed and demented who were the true legatees of a war. He recognized his father's voice.

Tarrian was silent, though Antyr felt him prowling the edges of his mind, watching and waiting. Whatever he decided, he knew that Tarrian would remain his faithful Companion. The wolf imposed his own burden by seeking not to.

'I am your subject, sire,' he said, equivocating. 'I'll do whatever you require.'

Ibris walked across to him and placed his hands on his shoulders. Antyr felt his knees shake momentarily, then he found himself looking up into the eyes of the man, the warrior and the lover of great art and knowledge who through strength of will and strength of arms had brought a peace to the land which, though far from perfect, was longer and more prosperous than any that had been known in recorded history.

'Antyr,' the Duke said, his voice quiet. 'You are indeed a free Guildsman. What I require from you is not that you obey, but that you choose. I command many people in varying degrees in the ruling of this city and its dominions; some subtly by carefully chosen words, some . . . less subtly. But those who truly help me are not those whom I command, but those who choose to follow and know that they can walk away at any time. Do you understand?'

Antyr nodded hesitantly.

'They are few, Antyr. Aaken, my one-time shield-bearer who stood by me in the wars against my usurping kin when I was young. Ciarll here, who . . .' He glanced towards his enigmatic bodyguard. ' . . . appeared . . . one day, and turned the tide of a battle for me and says nothing about where he came from or where he learned his fearsome skills, and who bears some deep silence inside him. The Mantynnai, his countrymen, I suspect, though none will say; and their torment is newer and crueller than Feranc's. Your father, briefly, though he was a distant, aloof person who kept his own strange secrets inside him. One or two others. A few. And now you. Drawn by events to my side. Is the ground under your feet to your liking?'

Antyr stammered. 'I'm a subject. A follower of orders. Not a friend and adviser to rulers. I've frittered away much of my life in weakness and self-indulgence. My skill at my craft is not what it should be. I fear I'd be more of a burden than a support to you.'

'That is *my* choice,' Ibris replied. 'Will you help me as your father did, to the best of your ability, or not? Yes or no?'

'Face the enemy,' came a distant call in Antyr's mind.

'Yes,' he heard himself reply. 'Yes, sire.'

Chapter 18

As Feranc closed the door behind a bewildered Antyr, Ibris sat down again by the fire. He beckoned Feranc over and indicated the chair opposite.

'An act of wisdom or folly, Ciarll?' he asked.

'I think his wolf seduced you,' Feranc replied.

Ibris laughed and raised an admonishing finger. 'You're too perceptive by half, Ciarll,' he said. 'But I know that wolf about as well as I know you, which is to say, quite well, and not at all. Now answer my question.'

Feranc nodded in acknowledgement. 'It was an act of judgement,' he said.

Ibris growled disparagingly. 'Don't *you* start playing the courtier with me,' he said.

Feranc smiled broadly. It was a sight that probably only the Duke ever saw.

'It was an act of judgement,' he repeated. 'And probably a sound one, but whether wisdom or folly, only time will tell.'

Ibris's eyes narrowed. 'You're as evasive with words as you are with your sword blade when you want to be,' he said. 'What would you have done then?'

'Not have had myself made Duke in the first place,' Feranc replied. Then, before the Duke could offer him any further reproach, his manner changed, as if his brighter nature were afraid to be seen abroad for too long.

'How is the ground under *your* feet?' he asked, using the Duke's own question to Antyr.

Ibris leaned back in his chair and folded his hands quietly across himself. 'Shifting and uncertain,' he replied sombrely. 'Not through all the battles for the succession; not through all the innumerable wars and skirmishes with the Bethlarii and their allies, have I ever felt so unsure, so beset. Is it old age catching up with me, Ciarll?'

'No,' Feranc replied simply. 'Old age merely slows the thinking a little, but the quality's better. It seems that we're being attacked by forces we've never known before, and it's unsettling, not to say frightening. But your judgement about the Dream Finder is almost certainly sound.'

Surprise suffused Ibris's face. 'You accept these ramblings with considerable equanimity for a rational man, Commander,' he said.

Feranc avoided his gaze briefly. 'It's the nature of my training,' he said, almost reluctantly. 'To see what's there, and to see it and accept it for what it is. That *is* the action of a rational man.'

'Your training?' Ibris said quietly but expectantly. It was the first time that he had heard Feranc make any reference to the time before he had come to Serenstad. Feranc, however, ignored the invitation to amplify the remark and remained silent.

'What have you seen then that you're so certain of my judgement?' Ibris went on, regretting the passage of the moment.

'I've seen a Bethlarii envoy skulk into our land like a spy, in itself a profound change from their normal behaviour. I've seen at his shoulder the spectre of the threat of war on a scale that hasn't been known in generations. I've seen him behaving in a manner which virtually asked for his immediate execution and which gives us a grim measure of his religious fervour. Then I've seen the man I chose to help in his battle to bring order and civilization to this land, seek the aid of a drunken . . . practitioner of a strange and perhaps fraudulent art, and I've seen both Duke and Dream Finder transformed by their meeting; the latter especially. Now I hear that this same Dream Finder has been drawn to Menedrion, a fact even more improbable than his being sought by you.'

Feranc's delivery was flat and almost terse, as if he were a junior officer reporting intelligence to his seniors. He continued.

'The Bethlarii have turned towards the darkness of the primitive certainty of their religion. In your doubt, you've sought aid from a Dream Finder. Both actions lie beyond reason; they come as a response to something deep inside the human spirit. I've learned enough through the years to know that my head will tell me when to use my heart, and my heart will tell me when to use my head, and that while I'm prepared to use both I'll perhaps both survive and retain my sanity. I accept your judgement that the Bethlarii threat and the dreams could be related, perhaps deriving from some common source, and that being the case we must tend our Dream Finder as we'd tend our arrows and our pikes and our siege machines, even if we don't know what to do with him.'

There was a long silence.

'You never cease to surprise me, Ciarll,' Ibris said eventually. 'I'd have thought to get the sharper edge of your tongue for this last deed at least.'

Feranc raised one eyebrow quizzically but did not reply.

'Would you care to conjecture on the nature of this . . . common source?' Ibris offered.

Feranc shook his head. 'I've seen . . . and felt . . . many strange things in my journeyings. Enough to know that sometimes the *only* thing that can be done is to wait and see what happens and then accept the reality of events no matter how divorced from reason they seem. Only thus can we gain the knowledge that will give us our defence. We're like the natives who must once have faced the first arrows.'

'That's not much consolation,' Ibris interrupted. 'They probably lost.'

Feranc smiled slightly. 'A bad analogy,' he said with an apologetic shrug.

'But apt, perhaps?' Ibris replied.

Feranc moved his hand palm downwards across himself in a cutting action as if he had nothing further to add. 'Analogies are for teachers and storytellers,' he said. 'We deal with reality directly. At best, your decision about Antyr may prove crucial at some unforeseeable time in the future. At worst, the palace has another mouth, or rather, pair of mouths, to feed. And they'll do no harm. From what I've found out, Antyr fought well enough when he had to, bravely even. And so far in his life, he's been more of an enemy to himself than anyone else.'

'He's not afraid to speak his mind,' Ibris added with mild indignation.

Feranc smiled again. 'He'll need to with you as a "client",' he said. 'He'd have been counting his bruises from the palace square stones by now if he hadn't defied you when you accused him of breaking the law. I said he was changing. Personally I'm getting to like him. Underneath his doubts I think he's very sound.' He paused reflectively. 'There's

227

certainly more to him than meets the eye. And the wolf's beautiful.'

'Seduced you too, did he?' Ibris said.

Feranc's smile broadened again. 'If you'll excuse me, sire. I have duties to attend to,' he replied.

Ibris nodded. 'I'll join you in a few moments, Ciarll,' he said. 'I need to think a little.'

Feranc stood up and bowed.

As he reached the door, Ibris clicked his fingers. 'Ciarll,' he said, his brow furrowed. 'Some time tonight or tomorrow tell Menedrion I need to speak to him. And make sure that Antyr's being looked after properly before you go back, will you? Rooms and procedures etcetera.' He tapped his mouth thoughtfully. 'And that Aaken pays him for last night and makes proper arrangements for a stipend,' he added. 'You know how "forgetful" he can get about such matters when it affects the palace purse.'

'Yes,' Feranc agreed, not without some feeling. 'He can be a very zealous guardian of our coffers at times.' Then, in an echo of Tarrian's own observation, 'Antyr could well starve to death in this place if we're not careful.'

Ibris nodded. 'Him starving is one thing,' he said. 'That wolf starving is another.'

As Feranc quietly closed the door, Ibris turned and stared again into the flickering landscape of the fire with its black cliffs and crags, and its clefts and fissures glowing red and scorching yellow under the touch of invisible winds. He leaned forward, resting his arms on his knees and allowed the fire to fill his vision.

Smoke swirled hither and thither, sparks rose and scattered up into the blackness of the chimney or tumbled in cascades into the depths. Spurts of flame burst out angrily. The more he looked, the more intense and complex became the activity.

Where can such frenzy come from? he thought as he glanced at the unburnt coals at the edge of the fire, black and lifeless; just so many dull, inert stones, their appearance not giving the slightest indication of the forces bound within.

Once again, Antyr found himself following a servant in a daze. He and Tarrian had been taken from one office to another and had their names and needs noted by one officer after another. At each stage they had been treated with increasing deference, especially after a brief intervention by

Ciarll Feranc at one point, but Antyr was in no mood to notice.

Now they were being taken to their official quarters.

'What have I done?' Antyr said to Tarrian.

'The right thing for once,' Tarrian retorted. His excitement swept over Antyr. 'Working for the Duke himself,' he exulted. 'Just like your father. I never thought I'd see the day.'

The comment released a long-restrained bubble of resentment within Antyr. 'You might have mentioned that, incidentally,' he said, sourly.

'To what point?' Tarrian replied immediately. 'You felt overshadowed by your father as it was. To be constantly reminding you that he once worked for the Duke would only have depressed you further. Besides, it's none of your business, you know that.'

'Well . . .' Antyr concluded sulkily.

'Oh, come on,' Tarrian said. 'It's not important, nor ever was. But if it'll make you feel better you should know that he was never resident here, not once. Now forget it. We've present matters to concern ourselves with now. Just be thankful that the Duke will deal with Menedrion for us and that we'll be close to the heart of events where we can be of real value.'

'You'll forgive me if I don't share your enthusiasm,' Antyr replied. 'But just how are we going to be of value? I certainly don't know what's happening let alone know what to do about it. And now it seems there might be a war in the offing. Ye gods, it's awful.'

'These are your quarters, sir,' the servant said, his high, fluting voice unwittingly interrupting the silent conversation. He was holding open a door.

Antyr started, then managed to stutter his thanks as he stepped into the room.

'Nice,' said Tarrian, who was already inside and sniffing out the bounds of his new territory. 'Very nice.'

As Antyr gazed around, he felt his dark preoccupations yielding to Tarrian's continuing elation. And it was indeed a nice room. Plainly decorated and with a few pictures and some elegant furniture, it was not as lavish as the Duke's rooms by any means, but it was certainly better than those he had occupied previously.

The servant finished lighting the lamps and then withdrew

with a final fluted instruction that Antyr shouldn't forget to wear his temporary badge of office and that, if he needed anything, he was to ring the bell.

When he had gone, Antyr stood still and silent for some time. Then he felt the soft pile of the carpet under his feet and a smile sneaked on to his face. Tarrian chuckled. 'That's better,' he said. 'If we keep our wits about us, and keep well clear of politics, we can do very well for ourselves here.'

Images of unlimited supplies of food drifted into Antyr's mind and he nodded knowingly. 'I admire your altruism and sense of civic duty, dog,' he said.

'I'm impervious to your sarcasm,' Tarrian replied. 'This is splendid, and I intend to enjoy it while I can.'

Antyr sat down on a nearby chair. Suddenly he was tired. It had been a bizarre and exhausting day and he realized that both emotionally and physically he was drained.

'The bedroom's through there,' Tarrian offered.

Antyr nodded and, heaving himself to his feet again, he trudged off in the direction that Tarrian had indicated.

The sight of the bed merely increased his feelings of fatigue and pausing only to kick off his boots he flopped down on to it without either dignity or ceremony.

'I've not even got anything to wear,' he thought, vaguely as he drifted into sleep. 'I'll have to go back home . . . tomorrow . . . and . . . pick . . . up . . .'

Tarrian looked at the sleeping form for a moment and then with a noisy breath, dropped down with a thud and almost immediately joined his friend in sleep.

Nothing disturbed the dreamless sleep of the Dream Finder and his Companion that night and when Tarrian's voice woke him gently the next morning Antyr half expected to see summer sunshine pouring in through the windows so rested was he.

But the light was only that of the lamps which he had left burning all night. He glanced at the window. The sky outside was still a wintery grey.

A winter campaign. The thought came suddenly and unbidden and made him shiver despite the warmth of the room. What madness was afoot in Bethlar?

'Let's attend to our own problems,' Tarrian said, catching the thought. 'Good grief, Antyr. There's not even a war yet and you're already doing pike drills.'

Antyr was about to remonstrate with him, but the wolf was in high spirits and taking the lead. He mimicked the high-pitched voice of the servant who had acted as their guide the previous night. 'Put on your temporary badge of office . . .' then, himself again, ' . . . And let's find some food.'

'Sorry,' Antyr managed, with some sincerity, stretching himself luxuriously. He reached down and stroked Tarrian, then another cold thought struck him. The Duke! Had anything happened during the night while his newly appointed Dream Finder had been lying unconscious?

'No,' Tarrian answered. 'I've been keeping watch on both of you. Something unusual was happening somewhere, I think, I kept getting whiffs of it.' Briefly he became excited. 'I feel so sharp . . . so far-seeing . . . it's incredible . . .' Then it was set aside. 'But nothing untoward came near you, and Ibris scarcely dreamed at all.' There was an uncharacteristic note of awe in his voice. 'He's a stern man. Such control. I'm sure he knew I was there.'

'That's not possible,' Antyr said off-handedly, still stroking him.

'Maybe,' Tarrian said. 'But the impossible happened in Menedrion's dream, didn't it? Anyway, that was my feeling. We'll see if he mentions it if we meet him today.'

Antyr stood up and scratched himself.

'Really!' Tarrian exclaimed, mocking again. 'Can't you do that outside?'

Antyr eyed him narrowly. 'I think we should go and find Nyriall before we eat,' he threatened.

Tarrian did not argue. 'It just so happens that the way out passes by *our* refectory,' he said smugly. 'The *special* one for the Duke's personal assistants.'

Thus they resolved to eat before they ventured out into the streets that morning.

As they left their room, a man sitting nearby stood up and walked over to them. He had a confident and purposeful manner and obviously belonged to the palace. Antyr looked at him warily, suddenly filled with trepidation. Perhaps the Duke had repented of his appointment already. Perhaps they'd offended someone in their blunderings through the palace the previous day. Perhaps Menedrion . . . He chose not to finish that thought.

Catching his eye, however, the man smiled affably and then bowed slightly. Uncertainly, Antyr bowed in reply.

'Antyr Petranson?' the man inquired, though his tone indicated he knew the answer.

'Yes,' Antyr replied, his trepidation not being eased by the use of this formal address.

'My name is Estaan,' the man said. 'Commander Feranc has appointed me to be your escort and to help you settle into palace life.'

He had a slight accent.

'Oh,' Antyr said in relieved surprise. 'That's very thoughtful of the Commander. This is a bewildering place in every way.'

Estaan nodded slightly in agreement but did not seem inclined to continue with any conversation on the topic.

'We were just going to eat,' Antyr said. 'Will you join us?'

There was a glint of gratitude in Estaan's eyes. 'It's been a long and busy night, sir,' he said, his accent a little more pronounced. 'Breakfast would be appreciated.'

'Come on.' Tarrian's impatient voice intruded into Antyr's mind. Having satisfied himself that the newcomer was harmless, the wolf was already halfway along the corridor.

Antyr set off after him, motioning Estaan to follow.

'You know the way to the refectory already?' Estaan asked, mildly surprised.

'He does,' Antyr replied pointing after Tarrian who was disappearing round a corner.

A little later as they sat in a smaller and much more congenial refectory than the one they had used the previous day, Antyr weighed his escort. He had an oval, weather-beaten face, with alert, deep-set eyes and short, dark hair which was greying in places, though Antyr could not have attempted to guess his age. And though he was similar in size and build to Antyr, if anything slightly more spare, he had a quality about him that made Antyr feel he was much bigger. And there was that accent . . .

'Where do you come from, Estaan?' he asked eventually.

Estaan glanced at him briefly as if the question had a significance beyond its immediate content, then, discreetly, he turned his eyes away. 'Far away, sir,' he replied after a slight pause. 'But I am Serens now.'

Though there was no offence in the voice, Antyr sensed that his question had caught the man unawares and he raised an apologetic hand. As he did so, his several disparate impressions of the man fell into place. It was the lack of a uniform that had confused him.

'Don't call me sir, Estaan,' he said. 'It's not fitting. Call me Antyr. I'm just a Guildsman temporarily in the Duke's service. You're one of the Mantynnai.'

'As you wish, Antyr,' Estaan replied pleasantly, but showing no reaction to Antyr's revelation.

'Why should a senior officer of the Duke's personal bodyguard be appointed to look after a mere Dream Finder?' Antyr asked, provoked by this lack of response.

Estaan smiled disarmingly. 'I think I'll have to let you question Commander Feranc on that point,' he said with open evasiveness.

Antyr nodded knowingly and pushed his empty plate to one side.

'What do you want to do now?' Estaan asked.

'What I want to do is one thing, what I have to do is another,' Antyr replied, smiling ruefully. 'I'll need to get some of my things from home, then I'm afraid I've got to seek out a colleague in the Moras district.'

Estaan nodded. 'Well, we can ride on the first errand but we'd better walk on the second,' he said. 'And I'll need to wear something a little less ostentatious.' There was some irony in his voice as his clothes were simple and virtually unadorned. They were, however, of a high quality and would be provocatively conspicuous in many parts of the Moras.

A short while later, Antyr found himself mounted on a horse carefully selected by Estaan, and clattering nervously through the damp, grey streets towards his home.

He found the brief visit strangely poignant, experiencing an unexpected sense of betrayal as he removed some of his clothes and bits and pieces from the protection of the house's stained and worn familiarity. The front door screeched its traditional call reproachfully as he closed it, and he locked it with a peculiar gentleness.

Estaan watched his reluctant parting in silence, then he took the small package of goods from him and held out his hand to support him as he mounted his horse again.

Tarrian chuckled as he walked along by the two riders. 'It's fortunate for Serenstad that you weren't needed in the cavalry,' he said. 'I could ride better myself.' Antyr, however, was absorbed totally in remaining in the saddle and declined to reply.

Later again, and following Estaan's advice, it was a much more untidy pair that walked down through the city towards the Moras to seek out Nyriall.

Situated by the edge of the River Seren, the Moras was the oldest part of Serenstad. A mixture of warehouses, workshops and ramshackle, multi-storeyed houses, some occupied, some abandoned, it had grown out indiscriminately from the jetties and landing stages which had been built, and were still being built, to serve the ever-increasing numbers of barges and ships that carried the life-blood of trade to and from the city.

A hectic bustling area, packed with all manner of trades and businesses, it was also a congested and, in parts, largely decaying home for the people who served its needs in their turn; some permanent residents, many transient. Relentlessly, however, it drew all down to its decaying, disordered level and, inevitably, became also a haven for those who wished not to be seen, or who knew how to feed off the misery and squalor that grew there.

Though it was the artery for its wealth and well-being, the Moras was as far from Ibris's 'dazzling city' as could reasonably be imagined, and he was well aware of the horror and deprivation it housed. Yet, by a bitter irony, the very momentum of its success and frantic industry left little time and resource for its improvement, and despite considerable efforts on Ibris's part, the greater part of the Moras had remained effectively unchanged for generations.

Antyr and Estaan, with Tarrian loping along close beside them, walked steadily through the maze of narrow, crowded streets and alleyways that meandered between the tight-packed, jostling buildings.

As they moved into an area dominated by old housing, Antyr instinctively hunched his head down into his shoulders as the overhanging upper storeys of the houses began to close in overhead like watchful giants.

The lowering presence of the old buildings was made worse by the fact that nearly all of them showed signs of the settlement that was the hallmark of the area and that had resulted in the city gradually spreading up the valley's sides on to more solid ground. Indeed, hereabouts, this settlement had conspired with the original architecture to extend some of the houses so far across the narrow streets that anyone so inclined could reach from the upper windows and touch the buildings opposite.

Here and there also, crudely nailed boarding ineffectively sealed twisted doors and windows, and tattered notices pronounced buildings unsafe. While at other points, the grey sky burst through into the streets, incongruously bright, where some building had finally succumbed to the lure of gravity and collapsed completely.

Antyr was vaguely familiar with the part of the Moras in which, according to the Guild House porter, Nyriall lived, but he found that Estaan was striding through the area as if he knew it intimately.

'You seem well acquainted with the place,' he said eventually.

'Yes,' Estaan answered simply.

Antyr felt a twinge of irritation. The man seemed to speak only when he was spoken to and then he confided nothing other than what was sought of him.

'Did Commander Feranc tell you not to talk to me or something?' he blurted out abruptly.

To his surprise Estaan stopped briefly, looked at him and then shook with internal mirth. 'I'm sorry, Antyr,' he said, setting off again when it had faded away. 'I didn't mean to be rude, but I'm afraid that discretion becomes a deeply ingrained habit in the palace.'

Even as he spoke, he flicked out his hand to direct his charge into a narrow alley. Antyr followed him automatically, and for the moment he set his inquiry aside as he picked his way through the anonymous debris and filth that lined his path. He grimaced at the succession of foul smells that assailed him. Tentatively he reached out to Tarrian.

'Don't ask,' the wolf warned menacingly. 'How you creatures can live like this defies all reason. In fact, it defies *everything*! And if you'd got the remotest sense of smell—'

Antyr withdrew quickly and turned his attention back to his escort.

'Well,' he said out loud, inadvertently venting some of Tarrian's anger on to the Mantynnai. 'Why are you so familiar with this place?'

They had reached the end of the alley and Estaan led them diagonally across a noisy, crowded street before he replied. 'Apart from silks and cotton and foods, animals and timbers and all the other things that the city uses, what else comes out of the Moras?' he shouted above the din, looking at Antyr significantly.

'Plague,' Antyr said.

Estaan acknowledged the reply but waved it aside. 'Apart from plague,' he said.

Memories of violent riots and street fighting came to Antyr. 'Trouble,' he replied.

Estaan nodded. 'Exactly,' he said. 'And if guards are to be led into a place like this to sort it all out, then we need to know the terrain at least as well as the natives, don't we? What was that address again?'

Caught between the rhetorical and the actual question, Antyr stuttered briefly before he repeated the address. Estaan pointed to the entrance of a narrow street just ahead of them.

'That's it,' he said. 'Down there somewhere.'

They turned out of the crowd and into the quieter side street. Antyr puffed out his cheeks in weary dismay. Like many parts of the Moras, this had obviously been an attractive, if not select, area. Now, every little recess and alcove in the large, once dignified, houses that lined the street had been adapted by successive landlords to accommodate as many individuals and families as possible, and neglect hung almost palpably in the air.

Several ragged children were playing a hectic and noisy game, elfin voices already becoming raucous with the sharp-edged accent of the Moras. As Antyr and Estaan gazed around, at a loss to know where to look next, the children were drawn inexorably to them like stray planets to a new sun. Once in arm's-length orbit, they stopped and stared up at the new arrivals curiously.

'What y'looking for?' one of them demanded proprietorially.

'We're looking for Nyriall, the Dream Finder,' Antyr replied courteously. 'Do you know where he lives?'

There was a collective wrinkling of noses and shaking of heads, and some giggling mimicry of his voice.

'He's an old man,' Antyr offered, wilfully calm and still courteous. 'With a . . . dog . . . like this one.' He pointed at Tarrian who looked at him balefully.

'That's a wolf, not a dog, mister,' the boy replied contemptuously.

'Delightful child,' Tarrian muttered caustically to Antyr. 'I'll eat him last, I think.'

The reference to Tarrian, however, had provoked a response among the children and a huddled conference ensued with some gabbled arguments and denials, much pointing and one or two threats of violence.

'You got any money, mister,' the leader inquired after he had silenced the group.

'Thanks, men,' Estaan said suddenly to the children, briskly terminating the conference with a comradely salute, and taking Antyr's elbow.

Antyr resisted slightly but Estaan was unyielding. 'This way,' he said, pointing to a dingy building some way down the street.

'How do you know?' Antyr said glancing back at the children who were now regaling them with cries of abuse. 'He could live anywhere in any of these buildings.'

'They told us,' Estaan replied with a smile. 'You should listen more carefully.'

Antyr gave up, and contented himself with following his escort's lead.

'Wait here,' Estaan said as they reached the building he had indicated. A short flight of uneven and worn stone steps led up to an open door and into a dark passageway. Entering first, Estaan looked round for a moment before beckoning Antyr forward.

As he reached the top of the steps Antyr hesitated in the crooked doorway. Tarrian growled.

'What's the matter?' Estaan asked urgently, his eyes suddenly anxious.

Antyr shook his head as if to clear it. 'I don't know,' he said vaguely. 'Something's . . . about.' But the words were not adequate.

'What happened?' he asked Tarrian silently.

But Tarrian was no wiser than he was. 'I don't know,' he echoed. 'But I scent something nearby. Something bad. Like I felt in the distance last night, but . . . nearer. Take care.' Distaste, distress and alarm leaked into Antyr's mind. Then, unexpectedly, the wolf cried out as if a careless boot had crushed his paw, and with two bounds he was up the steps and into the building.

Estaan stepped smartly to one side to allow him past, but held out a restraining hand as Antyr, overcoming his shock at Tarrian's sudden action, ran up the steps after him.

'Careful,' he said. 'He's gone up those stairs there and they don't look too safe.'

'Something's wrong,' Antyr said desperately. 'Let me past.'

'Wait,' Estaan commanded, as he looked intently up the stairs. The sound of Tarrian's flight was floating down to them. He was half whispering, half howling.

Antyr pushed Estaan to one side and set off up the stairs two and three at a time.

'Tread lightly and keep close to the wall,' came Estaan's urgent command as he followed behind him.

On the third storey, the stairs ended, leaving Estaan breathing deeply and Antyr gasping for breath in a long corridor lit by the occasional grimy window. Tarrian was not in sight, but his yelping was beginning to fill the entire building.

A door opened nearby and a burly figure appeared, swearing foully at the noise Tarrian was creating. Oblivious, and drawn on by Tarrian's distress, Antyr tried to push by him, only to be seized roughly and lifted up on to his toes.

An angry, shouting face intruded into his alarm, filling his vision.

'Shut your blistering dog up or . . . ' it continued, but an upsweeping arm blow ended the imprecation and released Antyr abruptly.

As he staggered backwards into the wall, Antyr saw Estaan deliver an open-handed blow to the man's chest that lifted him clean off his feet and sent him skidding along the floor back into his room. Briefly, Estaan was silhouetted in the doorway as he reached in to take the door handle.

His other hand was extended purposefully towards the still-sliding figure. 'Stay there and be quiet,' he said in a voice whose authority was indisputable. Then he slammed the door loudly and, turning to Antyr, nodded him in the direction of Tarrian's crying.

Not that Antyr needed urging. The sound of frenzied scratching was now accompanying Tarrian's frantic yelping, and great uncontrolled waves of distress and frustration were so filling his mind that he barely knew which of the partnership he was.

He staggered as his arms became Tarrian's flailing paws.

'Quieten down,' he thundered into the din of his head, but it had no effect other than to add to it.

'Here,' Estaan's voice intruded.

Although not fully understanding what was happening, the Mantynnai could see Antyr's disorientation and, seizing him forcefully, he supported him as he tottered along the corridor until they came to the foot of another narrow flight of stairs. At the top was a short landing and a single door and scrabbling frantically at it was Tarrian.

Abruptly he stopped and let out a heart-rending howl.

Estaan ran up the stairs, with Antyr, still unsteady, close behind him, almost on all fours.

For a moment, he wrestled with the door handle, then he stood back and gave the door a powerful kick. The wooden landing shook with the impact, but the door did not yield. Tarrian fell silent and Antyr saw Estaan relax before he delivered another blow. He found himself holding his breath.

At the fourth kick, the door yielded and Tarrian dashed through the opening, brushing violently through Estaan's legs and unbalancing him.

Antyr, infected by Tarrian's mood, also pushed recklessly past Estaan, unbalancing him further.

Inside the room he came to an abrupt halt.

A single, inadequate lamp lit the room, and facing him was a wolf, its upper lip drawn back into a fearsome snarl. It was as large as Tarrian but it was thin, unkempt and savage-looking. And, to Antyr's horror, its eyes were glowing bright yellow.

Even as he sensed the wolf preparing to spring, Antyr took in his vision of an old man lying on a low bed behind the wolf. His hand hung down limply to trail on the floor, and his face was turned towards the door, his mouth gaping. His open eyes were like black pits.

A tidal wave of mingling emotions swept over Antyr; the unbridled death savagery of the Dream Finder's Companion, demented and protecting its charge; the instinctive animal reaction of Tarrian faced suddenly by a challenge from his own kind and with a threat to his own Dream Finder. All added to his own horror at the scene. And there was something else . . .

And amidst it all was an almost unbearable poignancy as the life and death of this old Dream Finder was borne in upon him by the simple utilitarian neatness of the few small ornaments and articles of furniture that decorated this dank, chilly room.

Then he was pushed violently to one side, and Estaan was in front of him, a long knife in his right hand. He was hastily winding his heavy cloak about his left.

The turmoil in Antyr's mind rose to an agonizing pitch as Estaan and the two wolves accelerated towards a seemingly inevitable conflict. In response, he felt some force inside him surging upwards.

It burst out suddenly.

'*No!*'

His voice rang out both audibly in the room and in the minds of the two wolves, overwhelming the hurtling intentions of the three antagonists.

The power and command in it shook Antyr, but it had a momentum of its own.

'No!' it went on, as intense and dominating as before, but calmer. 'There are no enemies here, only frightened friends.'

Following in its wake, Antyr stepped forward, gently easing past Estaan and laying a restraining hand on his knife arm. He crouched down by Tarrian and placed a comforting arm around his hackled shoulders. The wolf's responses quietened a little at his touch.

'Carry my words to Estaan, while we try to reach Nyriall's Companion,' Antyr said to him, still authoritative. 'I want no misunderstandings and sudden movements.'

As Tarrian's wolf reactions began to withdraw however, so also did those of the other although its manner was still fierce and defensive. Then Antyr felt another emotion rising up within Tarrian. And within the other wolf, he realized. It was the pain and distress that had sent Tarrian yelping through the house in a frenzy.

But now it was more coherent. And through its heart rang something else. Recognition!

Antyr's eyes widened as the revelations spread through him also. The wolf opposite was Tarrian's brother.

As the thought formed in Antyr's mind, the other wolf's expression changed suddenly, becoming placid and submissive. It dropped on to its belly and crawled towards Tarrian who bent down and sniffed it intently. Antyr withdrew from the mind of his Companion.

'What's happening?' Estaan asked softly.

Antyr stood up slowly, raising a hand for silence.

Estaan looked significantly towards the old man. Antyr

shook his head. 'Not yet,' he said. 'His Companion's still dangerous.'

Then the wolf wriggled to its feet, and for a few seconds the two animals romped and wrestled like pups. Images leapt unsought into Antyr's mind from their excitement. Images of laughter and echoing chambers. Of strange haunting song, though not, oddly, human. Images of sunlit mountains and valleys, of people and animals unafraid, of great peace and harmony. Then came sadder images of parting and . . . travelling . . . endless travelling . . .

Then the images faded as the two wolves returned to the grim present. Gradually they became still. Tarrian stood for some time with his head held over his brother's bowed neck.

Antyr waited.

Eventually, Tarrian spoke, the resonance in his voice showing that he spoke to Estaan also. He said, 'This is . . .' The word he uttered was rich in subtle meanings. Antyr had never heard the like before. 'We share dam and sire. Nyriall called him Grayle.'

Estaan looked round uncertainly then lifted his hands to his head. 'Don't be afraid,' Antyr said. 'You're being granted a rare privilege. Just listen, this is important.'

He looked at Grayle, but made no attempt to speak to him. Then he turned again to Tarrian. 'What's happened here?' he asked.

'I don't know,' Tarrian replied. 'Grayle's shocked and barely coherent. He's talking about Nyriall being separated from him. Like we were. And about being attacked in some way. Powers, forces, searching. Nothing clear though.'

Antyr nodded and looked at the old man. 'Ask him if we can attend to Nyriall, would you?' he said gently.

'You may,' Tarrian replied immediately.

Antyr nodded to Estaan who, still watching Grayle warily, sheathed his knife and disentangled his cloak from his arm as he walked over to the bed. Sitting on the edge, he lifted Nyriall's dangling arm, felt for a pulse and then laid it across his chest with a shake of his head. Almost tenderly he laid a hand on the dead man's face.

'He's still warm,' he said. 'It feels to me as if he's only just died.' He examined the body. 'I can't see any signs of violence, and he doesn't look as though he's been poisoned. Perhaps some shock burst his heart.'

Grayle started to whimper uncontrollably.

Antyr looked down at the dead man and his night-black eyes. Why had he and his Companion been prepared for the search when from the state of his clothes he had not been intending to go out?

Shapeless questions flitted darkly about his mind like gibbering bats. This was the man from whom he had hoped to obtain explanations of recent events. It had been a slender hope at best, but now where was he to turn?

He frowned.

And yet, Nyriall's strange death showed that perhaps it had not been such a slender hope after all. A frightening thought began to form.

It grew with appalling rapidity until it filled his mind like a black cloud.

'No!' Tarrian shouted at him fearfully. 'No. You can't.'

Antyr felt all his options run out. He had no choice. It seemed that all the wandering of his life had been but to bring him to this, in this tired, simple little room in the Moras.

'Tarrian, remind your brother of his duty. Grief is for later and we've little time left,' he said, sternly.

He turned to Estaan, who was trying to keep his bewilderment from his face. 'Estaan, guard the door. Make sure no one disturbs us, and under no circumstances must you touch me. The wolves will kill you, or you them, if you're lucky and fast, and then all could well be lost. If anything untoward happens, Tarrian will speak to you. If he can't, then seal this room as well as you're able and go for the Dream Finder Pandra.'

Estaan's bewilderment had become concern. 'What are you going to do?' he asked anxiously.

Antyr looked at the dead Nyriall again, then he pulled up a chair and sat down beside him.

'I must learn what killed him,' he said. 'I must enter the dead man's dream.'

Chapter 19

Ivaroth Ungwyl came to the crest of the hill and looked down at the blazing encampment. The fire was so hot that the thick black smoke was propelled to a considerable height before the cold plains' wind could begin to snatch it away and disperse it against the grey backdrop of the wintry sky.

The distant sound of screams and shouts rode on that same wind to greet him, and he smiled at both the sound and the sight. It was a familiar chorus and a familiar scene. And there would be few more such for him to relish in the future, if any; at least on the plains. When they moved south, that would be a different matter, but that was a little way off yet.

Nevertheless, he clenched his teeth in a savage leer in anticipation of the spectacle that the sack of a city must surely make. And sacked they would be until all bowed their necks to his yoke and begged to serve the peoples that their ancestors had dispossessed in the ancient times.

A powerful concussion reached him, making his horse shy a little, and rudely dispelling his vision. From the centre of the encampment below, a ball of flame began to rise into the sky supported on a pillar of black smoke.

There was a chuckle beside him. 'Well, they wouldn't have been wanting lamps this winter anyway,' said its creator.

'Indeed they wouldn't, Greynyr,' Ivaroth said. 'And the light of the Ensceini will be gone from the plains forever soon, and with it the last flicker of opposition to my rule.'

His companion nodded appreciatively. 'All the tribes united,' he said quietly. 'I'd never thought to see the like in my lifetime. These are truly times of greatness, Lord. Your shadow will darken the whole world in the years to come.'

Ivaroth smiled and, once again, the burning camp became a burning city, and the great anticipation returned.

Down below he could see figures running to and fro, vainly trying to flee from his horsemen. The sight of their flight released his predatory instinct and he turned to his entourage.

'I'm in the mood for a little sport today, my friends,' he said. 'We must make sure that the Ensceini hunters have *nothing* to return to, and our men down there may be getting weary by now, you know how Endryn's sword arm troubles him after a while.'

Raucous laughter and cheering greeted this sally and, catching it at its peak, Ivaroth raised his spear and with a shout spurred his horse forward towards the encampment.

The wind blew cold and vigorous in his face, and the pounding hooves of the galloping horses behind him filled the air with their own special thunder to accompany the lightning of his army's countless spears and swords. And all were merely extensions of his will; his to command. To launch or to stay. This was the way it was destined to be. It had been written into his soul before he had been born and with each heartbeat he drew ever nearer to its final glorious apotheosis.

Your shadow still darken the whole world, Greynyr had said.

Yes! The whole world!

A figure appeared in front of him, rising up from behind a small bush like a startled bird. It was a woman, he noted indifferently, wild-eyed and distraught in her flight. And with a child in her arms? He was unsure. Not that it affected anything.

Without thinking about the action, his practised arm spitted her on his spear, then he twisted agilely in the saddle to withdraw it swiftly and cleanly as he galloped past.

His horse did not even break step and there was a cheer of appreciation at the deed from his companions. Ivaroth joined in, waving the bloodied spear high. One of the followers reached down and seized the woman's hair as she pirouetted from the impetus of Ivaroth's blow, but such was the speed of the riders that her hair tore out by the roots and the body disappeared under the flailing hooves amid further cheering and scornful laughter.

Then they were at the camp, joining with the riders who had launched the attack. The air was full of the cries and screams of both the slayers and the slain, a tangled skein of death songs written above the bass roar of the blazing tents.

There had been little or no opposition to Ivaroth's assault. How could there have been? The men of the tribe were out wandering the plains, hunting for the food that would tide them and their families through the coming winter. The occupants of the camp were old men, young boys, women and babes.

244

They had come out offering their traditional hospitality to the approaching riders. And they had died. Slain like the animals their menfolk were hunting but with greater relish and less respect.

By an irony, however, Ivaroth's frenzied entrance into the blood-letting spared them the crueller excesses of the many forms of slow dying that stained the ways of the plains' tribes and to which a more leisured assault would have brought them.

'I want no survivors,' was his command. 'Let the bodies lie where they fall, for the foxes and the birds, and let their men see this pyre from the far ends of the plains and know then what it is to defy the will of Ivaroth Ungwyl.'

And none would have disobeyed Ivaroth's commands even had they wanted to.

After a breathless, galloping, hacking interval, a rider, shadowlike and stark against a backdrop of the blazing camp, reined his horse to a halt before his leader. 'It's done, lord,' he said triumphantly.

Ivaroth stared at him, unseeing, for a moment, then the features of his lieutenant came into focus.

'All dead, Endryn?' he asked in regretful surprise, lowering his bloodstained sword.

'All dead, lord,' Endryn confirmed. 'Now the Ensceini menfolk can do no other than come against us and perish for their arrogance in defying your will. Then your leadership of all the tribes will be beyond dispute.'

Ivaroth bared his teeth exultantly, then he jumped down from his horse, tore a shawl from the hacked corpse of a woman nearby and began cleaning his sword with it.

When he had finished, he squinted, narrow-eyed, along the blade, wrinkling his nose irritably as he fingered the edge where it had been turned in places. 'We must spare some of the city blacksmiths when we get there,' he said. 'I hear they make fine swords.'

Then, as he sheathed the sword, the cloth in his hand caught his eye and he brought it close to his face for examination in the flickering firelight. Though soiled, its fine weave and delicate coloured patterning were clearly visible and along its tasselled edge hung tiny, carved wooden figures.

'Weavers and carvers,' he sneered. 'The Ensceini would have been of no value to us anyway, with their women's ways. Better that they at least die as men.'

245

Contemptuously he threw the shawl away and remounted his horse.

'To camp, Endryn,' he said. 'Leave our sign here and make sure that our trail is clear. The Ensceini may be great hunters, but I want this matter ended quickly now, and I've no desire to be waiting about for days while they search us out. We've greater deeds to move to and the sooner we get back to Carthak, the better.'

A low red sun broke through the clouds as Ivaroth and his troop rode away from the camp. It threw long shadows across the harsh plains' grass, and until it sank below the horizon it also threw the wavering shadow of the black smoke from the burning camp along their path like a grim warning finger.

Within two days it seemed that Ivaroth's wish was to be fulfilled. The Ensceini men emerged from the morning mist carrying their battle flags.

Despite Ivaroth's arrogant dismissal of their worth, however, their sudden appearance caused a wave of alarm to spread through the camp, for they stood silent and unmoving along the broad summit of a nearby hill, appearing first as dark shadows and then as grey uncertain monoliths as the sunless dawn broke. Their skill as hunters was legendary among the tribes and none of the camp guards had heard them arrive or could say how long they had been standing there in their eerie vigil.

Thus Ivaroth was wakened by a sudden panic-stricken clamour from the alarm bell.

'They could have been on us with fire horses while we slept! Cut us down as we groped for our swords!' He could hear the words flying round the camp even as he focused on the waiting figures.

Then, chillingly, 'Why are they not afraid?'

And because of them, Ivaroth spared his guards the summary punishment they might justly have expected for such negligence, for he knew that each hasty blow to a guard would have reverberated through the camp like a clarion call, confirming the very aptness of the fears and tipping his army over into panic.

Spared all save one, that is; the guard who had sounded the alarm. Him, he felled with his own bell-striker.

'You disturb my sleep with your clatter,' he said, handing the man his striker back and kicking him casually as he rose, to let him know that he was being treated leniently.

Then he turned towards the waiting Ensceini and sniffed. They were still silent and motionless. That they had not chosen to fire the camp when they had the opportunity was yet another measure of their weakness, and too, he realized, the protection that his destiny afforded him. Now they would pay for their folly with their lives the easier and all the sooner.

'They're waiting because they're in no rush to join their womenfolk,' he said with dismissive scorn. Incongruously, his stomach rumbled in the morning stillness. He patted it and grinned malevolently. 'Mount up. We'll eat afterwards. The exercise will sharpen your appetites.'

Thus Ivaroth took his army's fear and turned it into courage and confidence once more.

The Ensceini did not move as Ivaroth's horde began to ooze from the camp like a vast, uneasy mudslide. As they began to move up the shallow hill however, one of the waiting riders moved forward, bearing a flag of truce.

Ivaroth signalled a halt and, nodding to his two companions to accompany him, continued up the hill to meet the lone rider.

As he drew nearer Ivaroth recognized the man.

'Ho, Wrenyk son of Wrenyk,' he shouted. 'Is it the Ensceini way to send a boy to do a man's work? Where is your father? You've caused me much trouble and I'd hoped to receive his apology from his own lips.'

'With my mother,' the young man replied, his voice unsteady. 'The sight of your handiwork took the life from him as surely as if you had speared him yourself.'

Ivaroth shrugged indifferently. 'It's a pity he didn't die sooner,' he said. 'Then perhaps your tribe wouldn't have been misled by his foolishness and would have joined us. And all this need not have happened.'

'It need not have happened anyway, you hell hound.' Wrenyk's passion burst out and his horse shied a little. 'What harm did we offer you or your vaulting ambition that you had to slaughter our women and children?' Ivaroth's companions closed about their leader, protectively, but he waved them aside and walked his horse forward until he was within a pace of the young man.

Wrenyk was pale, and his face was bewildered and stained with dried tears. He was covered in dust from riding, and black ash from the razed camp, and he held his reins tightly to stop their trembling as his raging inner turmoil contended with his fear before the menacing presence of the man who had become at once the unifier and the scourge of all the tribes of the plains.

'You're young and foolish, Wrenyk,' Ivaroth said darkly. 'Scarcely into manhood, for all you might think otherwise. You should have let one of your uncles undertake this task. They've cooler and wiser heads and are better versed in the acceptance of such matters. If you've come here with this sorry remnant for vengeance or reparation you'll find neither. And if you don't listen to me then the Ensceini will perish utterly this day, and in neither song nor saga will they be heard of again.'

Then he relaxed and became almost avuncular. 'But I'm an understanding man, young Wrenyk. I've children of my own – somewhere.' His two companions joined in his lecherous laugh. 'I'll forgive you your hasty tongue, and give you and your men one more chance to live. Accept my leadership and join the confederation of the tribes and together we'll sweep down through the mountains and reclaim our ancient lands to the south. Honour, glory, and battle lie by one hand, with more than enough women and . . . goods . . . to replace those you've lost. But by the other hand lies certain death. Think well, chieftain, before you speak. You have the fate of others in your gift.' He looked significantly at the still motionless riders cresting the hill.

Wrenyk fought to control his face. 'My answer is the same as my father's,' he replied eventually, his voice quieter. 'We came in our battle array not to threaten but to show you our weakness. We can't avenge ourselves nor do we seek weregild for our dead. We acknowledge your domination of the tribes of the plains, but we ask that you leave us alone. We want none of your folly. We live at peace with this land and all its creatures and its plants and its endless mystery. We have neither need nor desire to bring flame and sword to the peoples of distant lands. To bring to others the pain that we ourselves are feeling even now.'

'Desire!' Ivaroth snarled, suddenly angered by the young man's grief and his seeming lack of desire for revenge. 'My intentions for the south aren't some idle whim. They're the *destiny* of our people. The southlands were ours before the sea people drove our ancestors out and forced us to retreat to this . . .' He waved his arm across the plains about them. ' . . . this bleak wasteland.'

Wrenyk followed the sweeping arm and his eyes became

sad. 'You're as blind as you're demented, Ivaroth,' he said. 'You see only a wilderness while I, even in my youth, see true riches. And you speak of old camp fire tales and fables about the south as though they were as true and real as a quarrel about last season's hunting.' Contempt began to mingle with his sorrow. 'But, setting that aside, great leader of men,' he went on. 'Haven't your kin in the border tribes told you about the mountains with their great crags and narrow pathways where a missed footing can hurl man and horse into depths unimaginable?' The contempt became withering. 'We're a plains' people, Ivaroth, not mountain-dwellers. And horses are plains' animals. And has no one told you about the stone-faced Bethlarii who guard the passes and relish nothing more than cruel fighting in that terrain?'

He pointed to the south. 'Blood, pain and death are all that await you and all that follow you there, Ivaroth, believer of children's fireside tales and murderer of women and children.'

Ivaroth, stunned by Wrenyk's tirade, sat motionless for a moment. Then he started forward, his face livid, as if to strike him. But Wrenyk did not flinch. Instead he suddenly stared into his eyes intently. Ivaroth hesitated. Wrenyk's eyes were like his own. The irises were black, like deep pits.

'Ah,' Wrenyk said softly, his voice breathless with both fear and realization. 'I see you truly now. You have the sight as I do. You walk the dreams of others. It's *you* who's brought the demon to our nights. You who's been possessed by it. And it's you it uses for its own ends! How could I not have seen.' His voice rose to a shout. 'Abomination! I—'

Before he could finish however, Ivaroth had deftly pivoted his spear in its saddle sheath and with a powerful thrust, run him clean through.

Wrenyk cried out in pain and shock, but then he wrapped his hands around the shaft to prevent Ivaroth withdrawing it. Leaning forward on to it, he whimpered, childlike. Then, his face close to Ivaroth's, he opened his mouth and breathed in his face. Ivaroth flinched away but, held by his own grip to his spear, he could not withdraw. With unexpected vigour, Wrenyk suddenly spat at him and, releasing the spear, wiped one hand down Ivaroth's cheek. It left a smear of dust and black ash.

'By air, water, earth and fire, I curse you, Ivaroth,' Wrenyk gasped, scarcely able to speak. 'Would I had the flame here that would sere your accursed black soul, but . . .' His voice faded and he began to grope for a dagger in his belt. As he did so, Ivaroth wrenched his spear free. Wrenyk cried out again, and with one hand clutched at his bleeding wound while with the other he gripped his saddle in an instinctive attempt to avoid the rider's indignity of tumbling from his horse.

'There are others, abomination,' he whispered painfully. 'Others who walk the dreams and who will oppose—'

Ivaroth swung the spear round and struck him viciously on the temple with its weighted butt. The impact tore Wrenyk out of his saddle, but he uttered no sound other than a harsh gasp as he crashed on to the hard earth.

Deliberately, Ivaroth jerked his horse round to trample on the still form, kicking it into brief, grotesque life. Then he raised his spear high, a great cry forming in his throat.

It faltered before it left him, however, as he looked again at the ridge of the hill. It was empty. The Ensceini had gone. Drifted softly away like the morning mist while all eyes had been on the two leaders.

For a moment the sudden shock turned his stomach into ice and the trembling that had possessed Wrenyk's hands threatened to take over his own.

Feverishly he fought for control of his wilful body, keeping his face away from his men. For a moment he felt the great momentum of his destiny waver. Then, as the abyss opened before him, he was himself again.

His face furious, he rounded on his waiting riders.

'Donkeys!' he thundered. 'Blind, brainless donkeys. Is there not one pair of eyes among you?' The entire mass of riders moved back as one under the weight of his anger. Then, as he paused, sensing the declaration of a dire punishment for their neglect, they forestalled it with the same spontaneous unanimity by simultaneously moving forward with a great cry before he could pronounce it.

Rapidly gathering speed, they poured up the hillside like a great, breaking wave.

Ivaroth, standing in their path, found, as leaders have before, that he had little alternative but to lead the charge. Wrenyk's body was crushed beyond recognition by the same hooves that had destroyed his tribe.

But the furious charge was to little avail. When the leading riders reached the top of the hill, only a few of the Ensceini were

250

to be seen, and they were travelling at great speed in different directions. The rest were gone; vanished like campfire smoke into the vast, deceptive terrain that they knew so well.

Ivaroth reined his horse to a halt and wiped Wrenyk's spittle from his face. He watched the distant, fleeing figures fade into the landscape and cursed silently to himself. That had been an ill finish to what should have been the final act of his conquest of the many tribes of the plains.

The Ensceini were to have been publicly and conspicuously crushed not only for their continued opposition to his will but also to stiffen the resolve of some of his less enthusiastic allies. Now, scattered and leaderless, they could offer him no opposition, but their strange departure might ensure that part of them would linger in the minds of his superstitious followers. That, at least, he *could* crush.

'We've no time to chase wisps of dead grass over the plains.' His powerful personality washed over his now silent followers. 'The Ensceini are no more. They've paid the price of their defiance. Now, united, we shall prepare for our greater destiny.' And with a mighty cry, he turned his horse about and galloped back down towards the camp.

As the riders turned in response, the cry, 'Ivaroth, Mareth Hai! Ivaroth, Mareth Hai!' began to be heard, and as they reached the camp, it was ringing out in a great, echoing roar.

Mareth Hai. First and greatest. Great leader. King emperor. The words held many meanings with the many tribes, but above all they meant that his power was now absolute and beyond question.

The acclamation swept away the lingering remnants of dismay at the escape of the Ensceini and of Wrenyk's black-eyed sight into his soul. Ivaroth rode the sound as he might ride a string of chained horses in the Mirifest, the great annual celebration of riding skills that, hitherto, had been the only uniting element in the lives of the plains' tribes.

Faintly, like a slave whispering in his ear as he rode in triumph, however, Wrenyk's last words returned to him. 'There are others who walk the dreams . . .'

They were as nothing, however, amid the jubilation and exhilaration and it took little effort on his part to dismiss them. Many strange, terrifying things happened in his night wanderings, but with the blind man as his guide and guardian he was protected from all ills when asleep just as he was protected in his waking hours.

'Ivaroth, Mareth Hai!'

The cry seemed to hover in the air about him, all through the breaking of the camp and the return south to the huge, almost permanent, camp at Carthak that had become the base for his conquest of the tribes.

It grieved some of his closest personal allies that he seemed to be abandoning their traditional wandering ways, and there were, indisputably, many serious problems associated with living in a large fixed camp.

The concerns he eased with a mixture of blandishment and encouragement. 'It'll not be for long . . . The harder we strive, the sooner we can go our ways again . . . Are we incapable of doing what the enfeebled city dwellers of the south do?'

The problems he solved by brutal delegation. 'Deal with it,' he would say, usually to the bringer of the problem. And it soon became apparent that that was to be the totality of his involvement. After some spectacular demonstrations, few returned to their leader with excuses, however valid, about why they had not been able to achieve this or that object.

Those problems that he could not solve were those he suffered from himself. Those that were written into the very nature of the people. For the plains' people *were* wanderers, and the children of wanderers for unknown numbers of generations. To remain still was to be imprisoned.

Yet they remained in one place, held there ostensibly by Ivaroth's will and the needs of his wars of conquest, but in reality held by the strange needs of the blind man.

'This land is rich in the ancient powers,' was all that he would offer Ivaroth on the rare occasions when he was at once coherent and in a mood to explain.

Ivaroth, however, was able to use the subtle anguish produced by this defiance of the tribespeople's basic natures to weld together the savage and angry heart of his huge army.

'When we are done, we shall have the entire world to roam in and none shall gainsay us.'

It was the elder Wrenyk's querying, and subsequent rejection of this promise that had led ultimately to his death and his tribe's downfall.

As the caravan neared Carthak, Ivaroth looked at the sprawling, ragged jumble of tents appearing on the horizon, their curved, peaked roofs seeming to mimic the mountains behind them to the south.

Carthak was built on the site that his tribe had been camping on when he had been expelled, and he could never approach it now without recalling his return from that brief exile, riding Ketsath's horse through the low morning mist and carrying the strange, cowled man behind him.

A child gathering water from a stream had been the first to see him. She had looked up, wide-eyed and alarmed, as his horse had clattered on the stones fringing the curve of the opposite shore. There had been a brief pause and then recognition had dawned and she had turned and fled, calling out to her father. The pitcher she had been using rocked for a moment then tumbled over slowly to return most of its contents to the stream.

Ivaroth splashed his horse through the shallow stream and, bending low from his saddle, swept up the pitcher. With a grim smile he drained the small amount of water that remained, then threw the pitcher on to the rocks nearby where it smashed. He did not offer any to the cowled man.

The child's shrill cries roused the camp more effectively than any amount of clamouring bells, and Ivaroth soon found himself walking his horse along an alleyway of hostile, shouting people. Whether intimidated by his arrogant manner or just curious to see his fate at the hands of others, however, none tried to lay hands on him.

When he reached the heart of the camp, the elders of the tribe were already gathering to meet him.

He did not wait to be addressed, however. 'I come as your chieftain to take your obeisance, and to lead you and all my people to our greater destiny,' he said before any of them could speak. Then, swinging his leg over his horse's neck so as not to disturb his companion, he dropped down on to the ground solidly and stared about him.

After a momentary, shocked silence, shouts of abuse and scornful denial began to rise from the crowd.

'Be silent,' Ivaroth shouted immediately. His voice was unexpectedly powerful and seemed to echo across the whole camp. The cries faded as rapidly as they had arisen.

The elders were less intimidated. 'Your right to be chieftain in your brother's stead is forfeit, as is your life, Ivaroth Ungwyl,' one of them said, stepping forward. 'Not only for defying the sentence of exile given to you for the slaying of your brother, but for the murder of Ketsath.'

'That's not for the likes of you to determine,' Ivaroth said unabashed by this opposition. 'Ketsath was sent to provide me mount and sustenance, for that alone his name will be honoured by future generations.' He glanced round the crowd until he saw some of Ketsath's kin. 'And he died well,' he said to them. 'A true man. No yielder. He should have been buried thus.'

This comment and the dignified manner of its delivery caused a faint murmur of approval from parts of the crowd.

'No!' shouted the elder, his voice shocked. 'You add a blasphemy to your crimes, Ivaroth. You speak as though Ketsath were a sacrifice from the gods. He was a green youth that chance brought across your path in your moment of need. And he was no match for your cruel skills—'

Ivaroth pointed at him. 'Do not purport to tell me the ways of the gods, old man,' he said. 'They *guide* my steps while they toss you hither and thither like seeds in the wind.'

The elder stepped forward furiously, but stopped abruptly as he met Ivaroth's gaze.

'I didn't return to bandy words with old men,' Ivaroth said, waving his hand dismissively. 'I returned to fulfil my destiny.' Then, without losing any of his commanding presence, he became conciliatory. 'But I shall not disregard the ways of my people,' he shouted. 'Set out the gauntlet. And make haste. I weary of this needless chatter.'

The remark was greeted first with silence and then uproar. His brief sojourn in the wilds had softened his brain and a death madness was now upon him, was the immediate opinion of most.

No one could survive the gauntlet! Most accused men willingly accepted banishment or slavery rather than run it.

Within minutes, the two lines of men had formed, facing one another and swinging their weighted staves. Ivaroth watched with a look of amusement on his face. Then, as the crowd fell silent, he turned to the cowled figure still waiting quietly on the horse, and held out his hand to him.

The man moved his head in an unsettling, unnatural manner, then his hand came out, its fingers curling and uncurling expectantly. At once hesitantly and deliberately they wrapped themselves around Ivaroth's extended hand.

Then, abruptly, they released him, and waved him sharply towards the waiting lines as if they too were weary of waiting.

Ivaroth approached the two lines. Twenty men in each. By tradition they were the forty fighting men nearest to the challenger at the moment of his challenge, but he noticed that they were without exception drawn from his fiercest opponents.

A figure stepped out of the crowd. 'This is unjust,' he cried out to the elders. 'These are all his enemies, to a man. Men who would benefit from his death. Why am I not there, I was within ten paces of him when—'

'Be silent,' the chief elder said, rounding on him. 'Ivaroth has no entitlement to trial by gauntlet at this stage. His life is already forfeit. This is merely to be his execution.'

The man's face twisted in rage, but to have opposed the elder's word further would have brought Ivaroth's fate down upon himself as well. But turning round, he snatched a staff roughly from a man nearby and threw it to Ivaroth.

Catching it, Ivaroth looked at it, and then at his would-be ally. 'I'm indebted to you, Endryn,' he said. 'You shall ride by my side when this is over.'

'In the same burial cart,' someone shouted, releasing the crowd's tension into jeering laughter.

Ivaroth, however, kept his eyes on Endryn. Then he threw the staff back to him and, with a last look at his hooded companion, walked towards the waiting lines.

'Remember this day,' he said as he strode forward purposefully. 'I shall not be so merciful to my enemies in the future.'

The hooded figure swayed from side to side as if moving to some rhythm that only he could hear, and as he did so, Ivaroth's voice rose above the din of the crowd like a great rolling thunderclap.

Then that was all that was left. Ivaroth the storm. His roaring voice like thunder, his movements as swift as the wind, and his terrible power, that of the lightning itself. Men, bigger and stronger than he by far, seemed paralyzed by his scything progress as with fists, feet, and murderous hurling grip, he dodged and smashed his way through the mass of flailing staves and jostling bodies with the unstoppable ease of a mountain boulder crashing through a forest.

And throughout, the hooded figure swayed to and fro, revelling in his own, obscene, music.

Abruptly, it was over. The lines had broken and fled before this whirling, elemental force could complete its work, and Ivaroth stood triumphant amid the groaning, dying wreckage of his short journey.

The sound of the conflict seemed to roll away into the distance, like messengers carrying the news across the plains, then there was silence.

Ivaroth turned and looked at the watching elders. 'Thus I abide by the ways of our people,' he said. 'And thus shall I lead them ever. This is my vow. No longer will we quarrel among ourselves like bickering children. All the tribes shall become as one under my hand.'

'To what end, Ivaroth Ungwyl?' one of the elders managed to say, his voice faint with shock at the sight of what had just passed, but still defiant.

Ivaroth looked at him and then round at the stunned crowd. 'To vengeance and our destiny,' he said, his voice rising. 'We go to the land where there are fields and pastures and slaves for all. Where the wind doesn't strip faces and hands raw. Where the snow doesn't cover the earth for half the year and the sun doesn't hang low in the sky like a weeping maid's face . . .' The elder stepped forward as if to oppose him, but Ivaroth's words were bludgeoning their way into the hearts of the crowd. ' . . . We go to the rich land beyond the mountains that the sea people so foully tore from our forefathers in times long forgotten.'

He crouched low and picked up a fallen staff, then he stood up suddenly, holding it high. 'Now!' he demanded. 'Who rides with me? Your chieftain by blood and by ordeal? Who rides with Ivaroth Ungwyl?'

As the crowd's roar of acclamation rose up into the cold morning air, the hooded figure's swaying became faster and faster, until it was almost an ecstatic trembling.

'Ivaroth Ungwyl!' the crowd roared. 'Ivaroth Ungwyl!'

'Ivaroth, Mareth Hai! Ivaroth, Mareth Hai!'

The echo of the memory merged with the present as Ivaroth started out of his reverie, and found himself leading his caravan into Carthak amid excited milling crowds. Repeating the gesture of that distant day, he drew his spear from its scabbard and standing high in his stirrups, lifted it triumphantly over his head.

Now, we are ready, he thought. The last threat to his own power was gone. Now the people could be told the truth about the imminence of the assault on the south. Except for his closest aides, none knew how advanced were the preparations. And no one, save he and the blind man, knew of the strange, unwitting, allies that they had.

Chapter 20

Estaan sat down. He had positioned his chair so that he was in the shade, and, with a turn of his head, could look through the grimy window, or at the broken door, which he had wedged shut with another chair, or at Antyr and the two wolves sitting and lying by the dead Nyriall.

He drew his knife and slipped it under the folds of his cloak. Then he steadied his breathing. A silence filled the room which seemed to act as a focus for the random noises that reverberated through the tired fabric of the old building. A distant door slammed; a dog barked; voices, unclear, came and went, some conversational, some angry, some laughing; the thin sound of the children in the street filtered through occasionally; footsteps too, came and went, pattering, pounding, running. And boards creaked treacherously. But Estaan remained still; watching, listening, guarding.

Antyr's instructions had been unequivocal and he had repeated them more than once. Do not interfere. If anything goes amiss, seal the room and seek out the Dream Finder Pandra. Do not interfere.

Then, his eyes black and frightening, he had taken Nyriall's hands, while the two wolves had lain at his feet and seemingly gone to sleep.

Estaan waited; watching, listening, guarding, learning.

Though motionless in the darkness of Nyriall's mind, Antyr was hurtling forward almost recklessly.

He could not afford the luxury of thinking too closely about the folly of what he was doing. His father had died searching for the dreams of a *dying* man. Nyriall was *dead*. It was as if some inner force had taken control of him and was propelling him onward under the urging of some desperate need that he could not begin to fathom.

Tarrian was by him, nervous and unsettled, but faithful and trusting; and grimly determined; the hunter in him wild and hungry. And with him too was Grayle, quiet and strange, barely perceptible, running by the side and in the shadow of his newly found brother; his older, more powerful brother.

Yet though Grayle was not the dominant Companion, he was, ironically, foremost in this precipitate chase; his slight, silent presence disturbing; eerie even.

Then how could it be otherwise? Antyr thought. Prepared by Nyriall for a search of a dreamer who was not there. Then torn from his Dream Finder by death under who knew what circumstances.

And, more prosaically, searching with a new Companion was always a strange, unsettling experience, so intimately linked were their thoughts and emotions.

'Don't fret, I'm with you, and whole.' The voice startled Antyr. So much of its tone and aura was Tarrian's, yet it was very different. And it was hung about with grief and the dreadful turmoil of emotions that follow in its wake.

'I will grieve when my duties are done.' Grayle answered the unspoken question, though Antyr could sense all too human traits of vengeance fringing the wolf's words.

'We will all grieve, Grayle,' Antyr replied. 'But now we must hurry. Run with your brother to wherever your instincts take you. My faith in you is total—'

'Yes,' Grayle said, interrupting him. Antyr sensed Tarrian's surprise. 'Your faith *is* total, and it strengthens mine and sharpens my every sense. You're stronger and more skilled even than Nyriall, and I'd have judged him almost a Master. You above all can search out what has happened; and what has been happening. My brother and I will guard you where we can, and will watch and call for you when you go from us. Have no fear, you are guarded in all places by a great and ancient strength.'

'What do you mean, go from you?' Antyr asked.

But Grayle did not reply.

On through the blackness they sped. Antyr alone and motionless yet drawn along by the surging, hunting, wolves; a nothingness in the darkness save for his bright, sharp awareness, intangible yet as purposeful as a flying arrow.

On they plunged.

No familiar flickering wisps of light and sound came to greet them; to dance and shimmer and whisper. For this was the inner realm of a Dream Finder and there were no dreams to leak into the darkness of his hidden nature and form the bright and shimmering nexus to draw the Companions forward.

Yet Antyr had set off in pursuit of the dream that could not be. Fear began to buffet him, a stinging, dust-laden wind in his face.

'No,' he cried out, denouncing it. Each step we take through life is into the darkness, he knew. It cannot be otherwise. And fear of the darkness was fear of life. Knowledge alone could light the way and we must not fear to enter the darkness to seek it. And where knowledge stopped while need yet existed, then we must follow the deeper reasoning that our prattling minds make us deaf to, until we reach the light again.

His thoughts seemed to be part of a huge chorus of other voices, coming from both within and without.

Then he was alone!

The wolves were gone. Gone utterly. No sound. No faint, lingering hints of their presence. Just silence. And darkness.

They had been gone forever. Indeed, they had never been.

And he was in a bright sunlit field, strewn with swathes of white flowers like the stars on a clear summer's night. Above him a scattered flotilla of small white clouds drifted leisurely across a blue sky at the behest of some scarcely felt wind.

A few paces in front of him, a figure was crouching with his back towards him. He was looking at the flowers; touching them gently. Antyr coughed. The figure started violently and, turning, stood up, almost tumbling over in the process.

Antyr drew in a sharp breath. The figure was Nyriall, his face fearful and his eyes still like pools of night.

'Who are you, Dream Finder?' Nyriall said, his voice shaking and his posture defensive despite his age. 'And why do you pursue me?'

'I'm sorry I frightened you, Nyriall,' Antyr replied hastily, concerned at this response from the old man. 'Please don't be afraid. I mean you no harm. I'm Antyr, son of Petran. I'm not pursuing you. I came after you to find out what had happened.'

Nyriall looked at him narrowly for a moment then put his hand to his head as if trying to remember something. 'You came to find . . . ' he muttered vaguely.

Antyr waited.

'I remember now, I think,' Nyriall said slowly. 'Grayle was suddenly no more. Not torn from me. Just no more.' He took Antyr's hand anxiously. 'Where is Grayle, how is he?'

259

'He's safe,' Antyr said, as reassuringly as he could. 'He's lying in your room with my own Companion, his brother, Tarrian, by his side. And I'm there too. And one of the Duke's own Mantynnai guards the door.'

Nyriall touched his head again. 'Room?' he said, puzzled, then, 'Mantynnai? Mantynnai? Yes . . . The Viernce mercenaries . . . Serenstad . . . Ibris.' His voice grew louder. 'What are you doing here?' he burst out suddenly.

'We found you . . .' Antyr hesitated. 'We found you, in your room, in the Moras. You were . . .' He changed direction. 'You were . . . unwell . . . but searching . . . and with no dreamer. I was anxious about you so I followed. With Grayle and Tarrian. I don't know how I came here. I was hoping you might be able to tell me.'

Nyriall seemed to be recovering from his confusion. 'You found me?' he said. 'Unwell?' Antyr nodded unhappily. Then, very calmly, Nyriall said, 'I was dead, wasn't I? They killed me. Severed me from Grayle and from that reality.'

Antyr felt suddenly cold, but there was no comfort to be found for him. 'Yes,' he said, reluctantly, after a moment. 'I'm sorry. There was no sign of life in you . . . your body . . . when we arrived. And Grayle was greatly disturbed.' He retreated into the reassuringly practical. 'Tarrian managed to calm him somehow. He didn't hurt anyone.'

Nyriall was silent for some time then his mouth dropped open and he looked at Antyr. 'And you followed me?' he said in disbelief. 'I'm a Dream Finder, I don't dream. And you followed me? Into a dream that I couldn't have had? And a death dream at that? What possessed you?'

'I don't know,' Antyr said, a little irritated at Nyriall's tone. 'And I didn't question. I just followed some impulse. Tell me what happened to you, Nyriall. I don't know how much time I have. Where are we? How did you come here? Who . . . killed you? . . . and how? Your room was empty and Grayle uninjured.'

Nyriall looked around at the field. Sunlit meadows and forests rolled into the distance towards white-topped mountains. He breathed in deeply. Antyr copied his actions. The air was sweet and cool and laden with the scents of rich grasses and flowers. It was a beautiful place.

'I don't know where I am,' Nyriall said softly. 'Nor can I answer any of your questions. My mind is still . . . scattered

. . . confused. Something to do with dying, I suppose,' he added with an unexpected flash of humour.

It faded rapidly however. 'And if I could answer, how would you return to . . . Serenstad . . . with the knowledge? This is no dream, man. I think this is . . . one of the dreams beyond dreams. A place that only the likes of us can reach, and then perhaps only by chance.' He took Antyr's arm, unexpectedly excitedly. 'I think this is part of the Threshold, the ante-chamber of the Great Dream itself.'

Antyr grimaced. 'I want no children's tales,' he began. 'I want an explanation—'

Nyriall rounded on him before he could continue. 'Children's tales!' he said angrily. 'Look around you, man. Do you doubt what you see? Ask yourself why I'm here, when you say I'm lying . . . dead . . . in Serenstad? And ask why you're here, real and solid, crushing the grass beneath your feet and feeling the sun on your face, when you're sitting next to my corpse?' He reached out and slapped Antyr's face lightly as he spoke. 'And if your Earth Holders rest in my room with you, where are their dreamselves, Dream Finder?'

His brief anger gave way abruptly to near panic. 'Maybe you're right,' he said fretfully. 'Maybe this isn't the Threshold.' He shook his head. 'But wherever it is, we're lost. I know no way back for either of us. And if you say a Mantynnai guards our bodies somewhere, then he may soon find he's guarding two corpses and coping with two demented wolves. What possessed you to follow me?' he said again.

'A way back will be found for me,' Antyr said urgently, suddenly determined to take control of this rambling debate. 'Perhaps even you. I don't know. All manner of strange things have happened to me these last few days.' He, in turn, began to ramble. 'A presence in the Duke's dream. A visitation from a figure that looked like Marastrumel. A separation from both Companion and dreamer with Menedrion. And menace in all cases. Some evil's afoot that I seem to be being drawn to. And now I'm here, as a result of who knows what impulse, perhaps to find out what had happened to you, perhaps because you have knowledge that I need. To help myself and to help others. I don't know—'

Nyriall took a pace back during this tirade, then lifted his hands to stem it.

'I hear you, Antyr,' he said, almost apologetically. 'You look a poor soul to be Dream Finder to such wealthy and powerful men, Antyr. But I hear you. And I believe you. Calm down. I understand. Truly.'

'But—'

Nyriall waved him to silence. 'I understand because I too have felt strange things,' he said earnestly. 'But not just recently; over many years. Small things. As you said; a . . . presence . . . in the dreams, as if there were another Dream Finder there, watching, listening.' He shook his head, his brow furrowed. 'And occasionally . . .' He hesitated, searching for words. 'The feeling that the dream was being . . . changed . . . manipulated. It wasn't good.' He looked at Antyr. 'I know my craft, Petran's son. And I practise it well, and with caring.' He curled his lip derisively. 'Not like the clowns and dandies who fop around the Guild House, dancing to the whims of courtiers' foolish women.'

Antyr winced slightly at Nyriall's suddenly vitriolic tone even though he sympathized with the comments. Then he found his conscience pricking him. Perhaps if he'd spent more time practising and studying his craft and less time carousing he too might have felt what was happening the sooner. He dismissed the reproach quickly. Whatever had been, was no more. And now was now.

A cloud drifted briefly over the sun, bringing a momentary chill to the two men.

Nyriall let his passion subside before he continued. 'It's been getting worse, I'm sure. Then a week or so ago, it broke out like plague. And always this feeling of someone searching, or worse, someone changing things for some reason. I had one client, a middle-aged man; a sensitive, I suspect. All of a sudden, nightmares. Appalling things. As bad as any I've ever searched. And unequivocally from outside. I feared for his life; certainly his sanity.' He shook his head, his black eyes looking at some other place far from this pastoral idyll. 'Then . . . today, I suppose . . . I was resting, very still, very quiet. Thinking about him. What I could do or say to help him. It wouldn't be putting it too strongly to say that I was desperate. Then I felt something, nearby, and before I knew what was happening, Grayle and I were prepared.' He turned and looked at Antyr, his voice suddenly awed. 'We moved into a dream . . . but not a dream . . . when no dreamer was present. I've heard of such things. And not only in children's tales,' he added. 'Gateways through into the Threshold of the Great Dream. Accessible only to Dream Finders who had become Masters of the craft—'

He stopped and looked down at his hands. 'But I'm no Master,' he said. 'Competent, yes. Perhaps above average. But no Master. Where a Master might walk with careful step, I suspect I tripped and blundered in.'

'To here?' Antyr asked.

Nyriall shook his head. 'No,' he said grimly. 'Some other place. Dark and barren. A great bleak plain with a bitter wind blowing across it.'

'And figures, shadows, waiting for you?' Antyr said, unable to contain himself.

Nyriall nodded. 'Two,' he said. 'And they radiated the menace that had been haunting me. Without thinking about what had happened or where I was, I just challenged them.'

He wrapped his arms about himself and his face became drawn. 'They seemed surprised as they turned to look at me . . .' His voice became hoarse and he shuddered at the memory. 'I panicked. Suddenly I was aware that Grayle was gone and that I was in this . . . awful place . . . with these strange, frightening people. I had to escape. I ran. They followed, hissing, whispering. Then I felt . . . hope . . . in front of me. I ran towards it and suddenly I was in the bright daylight.'

He caught Antyr's look, but shook his head. 'No, not here. It was bright and sunny, but I was on the fringes of a terrible battle. The air was full of screams and clashing arms. I carried on running, and then the . . . hope . . . was there again and I ran to it again.' He stopped and shrugged. 'And here I am,' he concluded. 'In this beautiful place. No longer pursued, but ignorant, lost and now, you tell me, dead.'

Antyr puffed out his cheeks. Nyriall's brief bewildering saga had raised more questions and provided no answers to the ones he already had. He did not know where to start.

Nyriall straightened up and looked out over the countryside. 'It is the Threshold,' he said quietly. 'Scorn the idea how you will.' Antyr raised a hand of denial. Nyriall's tale had shaken loose much Dream Finding lore that he had either long forgotten, or dismissed as old-fashioned foolishness.

When a Dream Finder's knowledge and understanding became sufficient, it was said, he could find the Gateways in the dreams of others, or sometimes directly, without the aid of a dreamer. Gateways into the worlds beyond the dreams. The myriad worlds that jostled and mixed together, yet were separate, and which were the Threshold of the Great Dream itself.

'And as the Nexus is but the echoing shadows of the dreams, so the dreams themselves are but the echoing shadows of the worlds of the Threshold. And, too, these worlds are but the echoing shadows of the Great Dream that lies beyond the Inner Portals and contains all things.'

Nyriall looked at Antyr. 'Treatise on the Ancient and Wondrous Art of the Dream Travellers,' he said, identifying the book that had for many generations been regarded as the definitive work on Dream Finding lore. 'It's a long time since you've read those words, I suspect,' he said.

Antyr nodded.

'Don't forget the rest,' Nyriall went on. 'And a Master may pass through the Gateways into the Threshold, and there journey through the Doorways between the worlds. But only if his skill be great, and his courage high. For he must go alone, separated from his Earth Holder. And he must suffer the travails of these worlds, even unto death.'

Antyr let out a great breath. 'But only if his skill be great and his courage high,' he repeated. 'I'd have thought both those attributes precluded me.'

Nyriall shrugged. 'Me also,' he said. 'But who can say what forces lie within us? Or, for that matter, manipulate us. I'm no Master. I came here perhaps by an inadvertent talent, perhaps by mischance and ignorance, and, seemingly, died for it. You, I suspect, might be different.' He looked at Antyr regretfully. 'But I can tell you no more than I have. Perhaps that's all you needed to learn. To be reminded of what you already knew.'

Antyr returned his gaze, but did not reply.

'Cry out for your Earth Holder, Antyr,' Nyriall said, encouragingly, then, correcting himself, 'Your Earth Holders. Perhaps there is a way back for you if you trust yourself enough.'

'But what about you?' Antyr said.

Unexpectedly, Nyriall smiled. 'This looks like a nice place. It's certainly better than the Moras. I wonder if there are people here?' He opened his arms wide. 'A new start at my age, Antyr. To be blunt I'd have considered myself fortunate if I'd survived another winter of Menedrion's smoke-laden fogs; I've got a cough that tears me in half. I'll see what this place has to offer. Perhaps even learn how to find the Doorways, and see what else is here.' He paused. 'I'll miss Grayle, though,' he said sadly. 'I'll miss him a lot. Look after him if you get back. Tell him I'm sorry to leave him, but it'll probably be for the best. And thank him, I couldn't have had a finer Companion.'

Antyr nodded. 'I will,' he said.

Then, on the soft breeze came a distant sound. It was the howling of wolves.

'Listen,' Antyr said, leaning towards the sound urgently. 'Grayle and Tarrian are searching. Somewhere in the darkness they're seeking me. And they're drawing nearer.'

Nyriall cocked his head on one side, listening intently. 'Yes,' he said. 'I recognize Grayle. And that's his brother, you say? Such wonders—'

He stopped suddenly, his eyes wide and afraid, and fixed over Antyr's shoulder.

Hesitantly, Antyr turned. The landscape behind him was darkening. Black clouds were building, mountainous and massive in the blue sky. A low rumble of thunder rolled ahead of them. But the objects of Nyriall's attention were two figures . . . or was it one? And the coming darkness seemed almost to emanate from them.

Antyr screwed up his eyes to clarify the vision. There *were* two figures.

The thunder came again. Antyr frowned; the storm had come from nowhere, and its apparent association with the two figures was disconcerting. He looked up at the clouds. They seemed to be both far and near and the effect was disorientating.

'I think they bring it,' Nyriall said, following his gaze and nodding anxiously towards the two figures.

'Who are they?' Antyr asked, though he already knew the answer. Without any prompting by Nyriall, he could feel the menace, the evil, that radiated from them.

One of the two figures waved his hand and there was a dazzling flash of lightning, followed immediately by a deafening thunderclap. As it rumbled into the distance Antyr heard a high-pitched hysterical laughter, and it seemed to him that one of the figures was swaying and bending in some obscene, motionless dance.

Antyr felt a wave of nausea overtake him. The enemy was

in sight and he wanted to flee. Then he remembered Nyriall, and anger filled him at the sight of the old man's new domain defiled by these corrosive intruders.

'Run!' he said suddenly to Nyriall. 'They mustn't find you. This is your world now.' He looked around. 'Quickly. Hide in the trees over there. I'll protect you, somehow.'

So urgent was his tone that Nyriall set off immediately. He had gone only a little way, however, when he turned as if to come back. 'But—' he began.

Antyr waved a hand across the still sunlit land spread out in front of them. 'This is yours now, Nyriall,' he repeated, then, turning and pointing to the two figures, shadows now, in the ominous clouds. 'And they are *my* enemies now. Go, and my thanks for your wisdom and guidance and your brief friendship. I shall tend to Grayle.'

Nyriall still hesitated.

Antyr waved him on. 'Live well and light be with you,' he said, the words coming unbidden.

Nyriall tilted his head on one side and looked at him curiously. 'And with you . . . Master,' he said after a long hesitation. Then, raising his hand in salute, he turned and ran towards the trees that Antyr had indicated.

Antyr smiled slightly. Nyriall was making good speed for an old man with a bad chest.

But the lightness passed almost immediately as the import of his actions dawned on him. He turned again to look at the two figures.

The sight made him draw in his breath. It was as if the lowering, lightning-shot clouds had drawn together and descended to focus around the strange couple totally so that they carried their own storm-tossed night with them. Antyr felt that he was looking through into another world, so intrusive was the sight amid the sunlit landscape that still fringed it at the edges of his vision.

Menacing peals of thunder rolled out to surround him, and amid the awful din, he heard again the faint strains of the shrieking laughter he had heard before. It stirred deep and frightening emotions within him and he felt his flesh crawling.

Somewhere, too, into his hearing, came again the distant howls of the two wolves. Not searching for him, though, Antyr realized. Just singing out to say that they were there, in their home, their territory, singing out to say that all was safe and to tell their kin that they could return and to tell others not to approach. And their song was louder.

'To me, Earth Holders. To me!' Antyr shouted silently in reply.

Then, glancing quickly at the now distant and still-retreating figure of Nyriall, he started walking slowly towards the darkness.

As if his cry to his Companions, or his purposeful movement, had caused some great disturbance, the two figures turned towards him, and though Antyr could not see their faces, he knew that they were now watching him intently. He could feel their malevolence.

He walked on.

Then the attention wavered, and one of the figures raised a hand to indicate the fleeing Nyriall. Antyr sensed the storm whirling, darkening, gathering itself to launch some power against the old man. Shadowy shapes began to form in it, sinister, predatory.

'Ho!' Antyr cried, lengthening his stride, in spite of an inner voice asking him very earnestly what he was doing. The shapes faltered.

The sound of Tarrian and Grayle grew louder.

He called again. 'You do not belong here,' he shouted. 'Who are you and why do you bring this uproar and destruction with you? Why do you pursue the innocent and why do you search for me?'

Abruptly, it seemed that the storm was rearing up like a ravening animal, battering frenziedly against some flimsy barrier in an attempt to reach and rend him.

The demented laughter, however, had stopped. In its place, Antyr heard a sound like the gurgling, lusting anticipation of some evil child. It was worse by far than the laughter.

And he had felt it in Menedrion's dream.

Somehow, he maintained his progress forward, though the sound of the thunder was pouring about him now with the pounding intensity of a rock fall and he felt that at any moment it might crush him utterly.

Then he was in the darkness. A darkness lit blue by cascades of forking lightning, and riven by a howling wind that snatched and tore at his cloak, thrashed his hair into his face and momentarily buffeted him to a standstill. The strange dark shapes flitted about him, circling, swooping suddenly and veering away. Watching, waiting for the moment to pounce.

Antyr straightened up and, gritting his teeth, forced one foot in front of the other.

'This is folly,' cried his inner voice, louder now. 'You don't know who or what these creatures are, but you see their power, and you feel their evil. You can't stand against them. Run while you can.'

'I will hold. I will hold.' He muttered the phrase to himself like a litany. It had sustained him in battle, it would . . .

'There you had companions at your side and your back, and a spear to your front,' came the reply. 'There you fought for your homeland. There you faced men . . .'

He faltered. The thundering storm raged about him. The shadows danced, faster and faster, lusting.

'Nyriall,' said some other part of him. 'He is lost in this place and he is in your care.'

His feet began to move again.

Looking ahead, he caught occasional glimpses of the two figures; stark black silhouettes in the purple, lightning-lit darkness; watching, waiting, also.

Was he being drawn to them? Or pushed? Either way, it seemed to him that his feet were being moved by some will other than his own.

And what he was doing was folly, beyond a doubt.

Desperately, he thrust his hands into his pockets. They were full of their usual clutter and he realized that he was in this place exactly as he had been when he had left Nyriall's room in Serenstad. And the only thing he had that could be used as a weapon was a small knife and that would be of little use against anyone, let alone these . . . creatures . . . and their seemingly elemental powers.

It came to him, unhelpfully, that the ancient traditional formal dress of the Dream Finder included two knives and a sword. He knew why now!

His hand went to his belt, but he did not even have his weighted club with him. That had been left behind when Feranc had called to bring him to the Duke, and set him on this increasingly terrifying slide into the unknown.

And was that barely two days ago?

Momentarily, he was in two places at once. Here, in this thunderous, haunted turmoil, and sitting in Nyriall's room in the Moras, Tarrian and Grayle whimpering and twitching at his feet, and Estaan sitting on the edge of his seat by the window and staring at him wide-eyed.

'And a Master may pass through the Gateways into the Threshold, and there journey through the Doorways between the worlds. But only if his skill be great, and his courage high. For he must go alone, separated from his Earth Holder.' Nyriall's quotation from the Treatise came back to him. A Master must be his own Earth Holder, he realized suddenly, though again, the knowledge was of no value to him.

'And he must suffer the travails of these worlds, even unto death.' The final sentence brought him sharply back to his present situation.

One of the shadows made a movement and Antyr saw a sword blade glisten in the flickering lightning. It was oddly reassuring. Some part of these creatures was mortal despite the darkness they had brought. Then he felt a will reaching out to him, greedily, wanting him, needing him. It was repellent.

He stopped. 'Who are you and what do you want?' he shouted above the din.

There was no reply, but the noise and power of the storm increased. And the searching will increased in intensity. Antyr felt an anger forming within him. 'Speak, or go from here and trouble us no more,' he heard himself saying.

Then the skin-tearing laughter returned, this time low and loathsome with dark glee.

Anger and terror rose to fill Antyr's mind in equal proportions.

'Tarrian! Grayle!' he roared inside his head. 'To me! To me!'

It seemed to him that the figures and the shadows retreated a little before his call, but he could not see clearly enough in the constantly shifting light.

He cried out again.

This time, he felt the storm itself lessen in intensity, though a sudden flash of lightning revealed the figures to him. Still motionless.

Faintly, he could still sense Tarrian and Grayle howling, searching for him. But he did not know how to reach them.

His feet started to carry him forward again and he found a soldier's thinking guiding him. Whatever powers these creatures possessed, he had not been struck down. Indeed, only a sword had been drawn against him. They could not destroy him. Or chose not to!

Long-forgotten memories of sweaty training yards returned

to him. Manoeuvres formed in his mind. All he had to do was get inside that sword, then . . .

'And he must suffer the travails of these worlds, even unto death.' The rest of Nyriall's quotation brought him to an abrupt halt.

The lust reached out to him again.

He had not been struck down because he was wanted, he realized chillingly. He might perhaps be able to defend himself unarmed against a swordsman – perhaps, he emphasized to himself – but could he truly defend himself against whatever had the power to cause this dreadful tortured darkness? Could he prevent himself from being bound if that was its desire?

'Tarrian, Grayle,' he whispered, desperately. 'To me. To me.'

Still faint, but nearer, the wolves' calls filtered into his mind; urgent, running; that leisurely lope that could carry them effortlessly for league after relentless league.

Then the figures were but a few paces from him.

They were indeed in the heart of the storm. More than ever, the lightning-etched darkness danced and whirled about them. It was like a frenzied pack of hounds, yelping and barking; waiting on their will.

Yet even so close, Antyr could not make out any details of the appearance of the two figures. As the lightning came and went, it seemed that they were like two grim, black monoliths; carvings rather than men; like ancient, enigmatic standing stones; windows into another, eternally dark place.

Though the sword was still of this world, glinting menacingly.

And the will and the desire were there too. He felt them as clear and stark around him as he could see the black silhouettes in front of him.

'Who are you? What do you want?' he asked again, shouting into the storm, but barely able to hear his own words.

'Ah . . .'

A long grasping sigh of fulfilment reached him, and one of the figures slowly extended its arms towards Antyr as if offering him an embrace. The gesture was peculiarly monstrous and again Antyr felt the hairs on his arms and neck rise up in revulsion. He tried to step back, away from this apparition and its foul intent.

But his feet would not move.

'Mine,' said a soft, enfolding voice that seemed to freeze Antyr's limbs.

'Tarrian, Grayle. To me. To me,' he cried out again, clinging desperately to the faint calls still ringing in his head.

'Ah . . .'

The figure, its arms thrown wide, like a black abyss, was closer to him, filling his vision, though he had not seen it move.

Antyr's eyes flicked from side to side, but he could see nothing except the tormented darkness and the shadows closing around him. And, try as he might to prevent it, his eyes were drawn inexorably forward until he could do no other than stare into the widening embrace of the figure.

'Even unto death.' The words of the Treatise came to him again.

'No,' he managed, first as a first thought, then as a word, then as a denial with his whole being. The figure halted. But still it dominated his sight.

'You will be my Guide,' said the chilling voice again.

'No!'

'No!'

Another voice coincided with Antyr's and he was aware of the flash of the sword blade.

'Tarrian, Grayle!'

Then he was plunging into the darkness, nostrils full of the familiar, homing scent, powerful limbs pushing him forward, towards the call, towards the desperate need, towards . . .

Himself! Standing alone, and menaced.

Antyr felt the wolf spirit of his two Companions rise up from within him and take possession of him. His limbs were free, his eyes widened and his mouth gaped, and, predator now, he leapt with a roaring snarl at the abomination that was his prey.

He had a fleeting impression of a hand in front of him, tearing something away. Rescuing it? Then, in a time less than the blink of an eye, the menacing will and its desire vanished, and with them the storm and all its whirling horrors; dwindled to a tiny black clamorous vortex, and then, with a last frenzied, high squealing shriek like finger nails drawn down glass . . . nothing; just warm sun, blue sky, white clouds . . .

'Don't move! Don't move!'

The voice was Estaan's, powerful and commanding, yet frightened. The place, Nyriall's cramped room in the Moras.

Antyr put his hands to his head and blinked several times, his eyes momentarily dazzled by the brief brightness of the summer meadow.

As he focused again, he saw the dead body of Nyriall on the bed in front of him, and the memory of the old man scurrying across the sunlit grass returned to him. He touched the pained face tenderly.

Then he became aware of Tarrian and Grayle snarling and, looking up, he saw Estaan, holding two knives now, watching him wide-eyed and fearful.

'No, no, no,' Antyr said hastily to the two wolves, at the same time lifting a reassuring hand towards the Mantynnai.

Estaan, however, did not relinquish his defensive stance. Further, Antyr noted, he was standing with his back to the door, holding it shut in addition to the chair that was wedged there. He could have fled from whatever had frightened him, but he had chosen to remain, and, presumably, to face and kill it if necessary.

'What's the matter?' Antyr stammered, alarmed at the man's demeanour.

'Who are you?' Estaan said, his voice strained. Then, without waiting for an answer, 'What have you been doing?'

Tarrian, no longer snarling, but with his upper lip drawn back angrily, and his hackles lifted, wriggled forward a little towards Estaan's left. Grayle, standing, moved one very slow step in the other direction. Antyr felt a subtle hunting communication between the two, somewhere below his normal awareness. Estaan's eyes flicked between the two.

'No!' Antyr shouted again both into his Companion's mind and out loud, for Estaan's benefit. 'He means no harm. He's frightened. The evil we've been through must have reached him in some way. He'll hurt no one if we don't move. Come back to me.' Neither of the wolves moved. 'Come back, damn you!' he thundered.

With an oath, Tarrian slithered back to Antyr's feet, and Grayle sat down, though neither took their unflinching gaze from the Mantynnai.

'He's on the edge of killing all three of us,' Tarrian said, unequivocally, his voice resonant so that Antyr knew he was speaking also to Estaan. 'Something's bubbling out of his past. A dreadful guilt—'

'Shut up,' Estaan shouted. 'And get out of my mind.'

Tarrian growled menacingly.

'We're not going to harm you, or anyone,' Antyr said, hastily, still struggling to quieten his own inner turmoil. 'We're going to sit very quiet and still until you can explain what's . . . distressed . . . you so.'

Antyr's words seemed to calm Estaan a little, but like the wolves, his dangerous posture remained. 'Distress,' he echoed, bitterly. 'A poor word for . . .' He stopped and looked around the room as if searching for some unseen foe. 'But it's gone.' He nodded to himself in confirmation. 'The evil's gone. I'd never thought to feel its like again. I thought it had died with . . .'

He left the sentence unfinished and, like a great shield, the impenetrable composure that, above all, typified the Mantynnai, closed about him. He sheathed the knives.

'I'm sorry,' he said simply. 'But you must tell me what happened. You're dealing with forces of great power and great evil that I . . . we've encountered before. You must not . . . face it alone or unwary.'

'I'll tell the Duke,' Antyr said quietly. 'Then I'll tell you what I can if it'll ease your pain. But you must tell me what it was you saw or heard.'

'Saw? Nothing. Heard?' Estaan shrugged. 'Mutterings, whimperings, yelps, the occasional bark. But *felt*.' His hand came up in emphasis. 'Suddenly, for an instant, the room was full. Full to choking point with the evil that turned us against our own and brought us to this benighted land . . .' He stopped abruptly.

Antyr grimaced at the pain in his voice, but even as he did so, Estaan was calm again.

'We must attend to the old man,' he said. 'Then I'll take you to the Duke straight away.'

Antyr stood up slowly. He felt weak and, for a moment, the room spun around him. 'No,' he said. 'We must find Pandra first—'

He was interrupted by a sudden pounding on the door.

'Open up,' came a commanding voice. 'Open in the Duke's name.'

Chapter 21

Arwain looked up into the grey sky, then down at the damp grey stones of the palace courtyard, then he yawned monstrously and with complete disregard for any propriety.

In answer to his father's question, could he get a platoon of his guards ready to ride to Whendrak first thing the following day, he had answered, 'Probably.'

It had proved optimistic.

'Is it an emergency, sir?' Ryllans had asked, when Arwain had entered his private quarters a little more unceremoniously than he had intended, and blurted out his instructions, rather than calmly issued his orders.

'No,' Arwain conceded. 'But it's urgent, and it *is* my father's express command.'

Ryllans nodded sagely, his expression gently nudging Arwain into a fuller explanation of the Duke's decision.

'First thing?' he asked, when Arwain had finished.

'First thing,' Arwain confirmed.

Ryllans blew out his cheeks.

'What's the problem?' Arwain asked, his brow furrowing at this familiar display.

Ryllans stood up and looked around. 'Where are my boots?' he asked. He spoke the question largely to himself, but involuntarily Arwain found himself gazing round the room in search of them.

'There,' he said irritably, pointing to the offending items, lying askew by the door, where they had obviously been kicked off. Ryllans' gracious gesture of thanks reproached him for his impatience more than any words could have.

'Nothing insurmountable, sir,' Ryllans said, answering the question as he picked up one of the boots and began pulling it on. 'But we'll want our best men for that kind of a journey and they're all on different duties at the moment. Some just starting, some just finishing.' He paused and looked thoughtful for a moment. 'And I think some are taking rest days.'

Arwain nodded as he listened to this information, but his

attention was taken totally by the way Ryllans, instead of sitting, was casually standing on one leg as he pulled on his boot. He did it calmly and quietly and without any staggering or wobbling.

Ryllans caught the look. 'Balancing exercise,' he said, answering the unspoken question. 'Stability is everything.' He placed his now booted foot very gently on to the floor and equally gently transferred his weight to it. 'And sensitivity.' Up came the other leg. 'Training isn't just for the yard, and what we learn there isn't just for fighting.'

Arwain frowned a little. 'I don't understand,' he said.

Ryllans inclined his head. 'It doesn't matter. You train diligently and you gain the attributes you need even though you're not aware of them.' He smiled broadly and briefly took on his authority as Arwain's instructor. 'But don't let me see you sitting down to put on your boots again – sir.'

Arwain looked at him narrowly. 'And don't you distract me with your Mantynnai games, Ryllans,' he said knowingly. 'I didn't come here for training, and besides, I've no desire to become a heron. Come back to the point. What's the difficulty about getting the right men together for a patrol up to Whendrak tomorrow?'

'None, really, sir,' Ryllans answered, lowering his other foot. 'Though we'll have some sour faces to deal with. And purses to fill for the extra duty, and you know what Chancellor Aaken's like.' He took down his jacket from a hook. 'Also it'll be fairly hard riding to get there before nightfall and, with respect, I don't think it would be too wise to go thundering into Whendrak exhausted and covered in lather and sweat if there's likely to be any . . . problems . . . to be dealt with. If I have the duty guards relieved early, and we arrange to leave a little later, then they can get some rest and if we make a short camp tomorrow night we can ride in, slow and fresh, on the following morning. Perhaps pick up a little intelligence on the way.'

As usual, Ryllans' advice was sound, and Arwain bowed to his judgement, though not without some scowling.

It was not, however, the minor logistical problems of gathering men and materials together that had protracted Arwain's preparations, though it had taken longer than he envisaged. It was Aaken's briefing on the diplomatic formalities of approaching this neutral city and its spiky, wilful people.

Now he was by Arwain's stirrup. 'You're certain you have the procedures clear, Lord Arwain?' he said. Arwain stifled another yawn and managed a polite answer to this further repetition of the question.

'Yes, Aaken,' he replied. 'And where some detail eludes me, I'll smile and crave their indulgence.' He demonstrated by smiling down at the narrow, worried face of the Chancellor.

'Safe journey, Ibrisson,' Aaken grunted by way of response. 'Stay alert.'

Then Arwain signalled to Ryllans. The Mantynnai gave a soft-spoken order, and the platoon clattered forward across the courtyard and out through the wide gates. Aaken's worried look returned as the riders disappeared from view. He had never found it easy to let others do what he considered to be his work; especially young people.

'A failing,' the Duke would reproach him. 'The young take power if you don't give it to them. You should know that.' He would laugh. 'We did.'

Aaken took such comments with an ill grace. 'My head knows it, sire,' then he would pat his stomach. 'But my belly . . .?'

Still, he mused, turning away and walking up the broad steps that led back into the palace, the head was right and the belly did not object too strongly to remaining in the warm palace while others bounced in their saddles through the wintry chill.

Almost the exact thought was passing through Arwain's mind as he passed the Ibrian monument and set off down the long avenue that led from the palace square. The weather was cold and raw. Autumn becoming winter was not his favourite time of year; neither scented mists and dusty sunsets, nor sharp, ice-sparkling cold with the prospect of smothering snow and the glittering anticipation of the Winterfest at its heart.

A breeze started to blow, taunting him as it lowered the temperature even further. With a grimace he drew his cloak tighter about him then glanced at Ryllans. The Mantynnai too was adjusting his cloak, but he seemed to be largely impervious to the weather, riding now just as he would on a warm summer's day; relaxed and easy.

Arwain resolved to do the same. He did not pretend to understand all that the Mantynnai tried to teach him, but he had already learned that just copying them was often worthwhile.

Despite the fact that the places of power and gossip in the city were alive with talk about the Bethlarii envoy and his outrageous conduct, the appearance of a platoon of palace guards passing through the streets in casual, not to say ragged, formation, caused no great stir among those who saw it. Such comings and goings were unexceptional; there were always new recruits being taken out on training patrols, or groups going to relieve soldiers garrisoned out in Serenstad's dominion cities.

Their route out of the city took them down towards the river and through the busiest part of the Moras district. The press of people, riders, pack horses, and every conceivable type of cart and wagon, travelling in every direction, coupled with the efforts of the Way Liktors to control this disorderly throng at the many busy junctions along the way, reduced their progress to less than walking speed.

Ryllans turned to Arwain with a grin, after a while, and shrugged his shoulders. Then he let his reins fall and, sitting back, gently urged his horse on with his knees as opportunity permitted. Arwain looked skyward in reply. He really should speak to his father about these Way Liktors. Whenever they appeared to take up their duties at the busiest time of the day, they always seemed to bring the admittedly slow-moving traffic to a complete halt in every direction.

Still, he consoled himself, it *would* only be a few minutes' delay, for all it felt like much more, and it would make no difference to the time when they would reach Whendrak. It was not as if he were expected.

'Ho, Ryllans.' A voice reached him above the noise of the crowd as they waited. Arwain looked around but could not at first identify the caller. Then he caught sight of a man nearby, waving urgently. He was being escorted by two large Liktors. So apparently was his companion, a scruffy-looking individual with two large dogs.

One of the Liktors remonstrated with the man, who, after a brief debate, waved again to Ryllans, beckoning him forward.

Ryllans turned to Arwain. 'It's Estaan,' he said. 'He seems to be having some problem with the Liktors, may I . . .'

Arwain signalled his agreement before the request was made. Briefly, Ryllans tried to turn his horse towards the beleaguered Estaan, then he gave up and dismounted.

278

Arwain watched Ryllans' rolling gait and gently sweeping arms carry him as smoothly through the press as if he were swimming in a calm lake. Making landfall, as it were, at his destination, there was some explanation from Estaan followed by some debate with the Liktors, during which Ryllans appeared to be vouching for Estaan, opening his cloak to reveal his field uniform and insignia, and discreetly pointing back to Arwain once or twice.

There was some earnest pouting and brow-furrowing by the Liktors, but seemingly Ryllans succeeded in his plea as the two eventually nodded to him and, after turning and saluting to Arwain, allowed themselves to be drawn into the crowd again.

Arwain smiled slightly. Though not a talkative person, Ryllans could be most persuasive when the need arose. He did not, however, immediately start the journey back to his horse again, for Estaan took hold of him vigorously by the arms and began speaking to him with some passion.

Despite himself, Arwain leaned forward as if he might hear the conversation over the din of the traffic. It was, of course, impossible, but he found it difficult to draw his attention away. He knew Estaan by sight, but had never spoken to him and had no idea how the man normally behaved. Perhaps he always gesticulated and spoke with such fervour. Perhaps not all the Mantynnai were quiet and restrained. But he knew Ryllans, and it was his response that reached to him over the heads of the crowd more eloquently than any speech. He started back from Estaan, and even at this distance, Arwain could see that his face was shocked.

He wiped his hand first across his forehead and then across his mouth. Fear! Arwain read. Fear! What words could have frightened Ryllans into such a public display, such a lapse of control?

Arwain looked at Estaan's companion, the man with the two dogs. He was standing motionless, looking puzzled. And there was something strange about his eyes.

Then Ryllans was returning and Estaan and his companion were making their way through the crowd again. Arwain watched Ryllans as he drew nearer. His eyes were wide and preoccupied giving him an expression that Arwain had never seen before, nor thought to see ever, and his progress through the crowd was rough and awkward. Something had unsettled him profoundly.

'What's the matter?' he asked urgently as Ryllans reached him.

The Mantynnai started then looked at Arwain blankly for a moment before recognition came into his eyes. 'I'm sorry, sir,' he began, flustered, almost. 'May I . . .' He drifted off again briefly. 'May I speak to . . . my men.'

'Yes, of course,' Arwain replied, resisting the strong temptation to repeat his question.

Then, still on foot, Ryllans was talking to his men – not the entire platoon, but *his* men; the Mantynnai.

Reading Ryllans' response as Arwain had, the Mantynnai had surreptitiously gathered together and they bent low in their saddles to hear his message.

Arwain listened shamelessly, but it was to no avail. Ryllans was talking in what was presumably the Mantynnai's native language. It dawned on Arwain that he had never heard it before; not even when he had come upon groups of them unawares when they might reasonably have been expected to be speaking in their own language.

And it was beautiful and resonant, like something that might have come out of an ancient saga. But even to Arwain's ears there was an occasional harshness rasping through it, and its effect on Ryllans' listeners was dramatic. Without exception, the men stared at him with expressions of disbelief and denial; all composure gone, making them very ordinary men. One or two of them made a brief circling hand movement over their hearts which was obviously reflexive, while others went pale and muttered to themselves.

There was a brief attempt at debate by some of them, but Ryllans cut it dead with a few terse phrases and, as he returned to his horse, the quiet stillness of the men descended over them, though to Arwain it was now not an outward manifestation of some inner resource, but a shield behind which they were withdrawing in the face of some fearful attack.

'What's happened?' Arwain demanded, Ibris's son now, and shaken by the response of the Mantynnai.

Before Ryllans could reply however, the traffic started to move forward again and there were some cries of abuse from the riders and carts behind them.

Uncharacteristically, Ryllans turned round and abused the abusers before clicking his horse forward. It was an action that gave Arwain a further measure of the man's turmoil.

'What's happened?' he asked again as the platoon began to move off, though this time his voice was concerned rather than commanding.

Ryllans' face was grim and he stared resolutely forward in silence for some time. Arwain sensed that he was debating what to say, perhaps even whether to lie or not, and he knew that, whatever he was told, he had no way of judging its truth. He reached out and laid a hand on Ryllans' arm, the hand of a friend.

'The truth will probably be the wisest and safest,' he said. 'If it's frightened you then it's dangerous. But if it offers no threat to this city or this land then keep your peace and I'll not press you, though I'll listen if talking about it will ease your burden. But if it *does* offer a threat, then the more we know about it the better we'll be protected.'

Ryllans glanced at him, his face riven with regret. 'I doubt there's any true protection against this,' he said. 'We'd thought it . . . long dead . . .'

Despite himself, Arwain turned away from the pain in his face. He looked up at the untidy, hectic buildings of the Moras that lined their route. A patchwork of windows, gantry hatches, chains and ropes, large signs, small signs, painted signs, carved signs, all manner of commercial paraphernalia carried his eyes up to the jumbled clutter of uneven gables and eaves that fringed the skyline. Pock marks of decay and neglect, patched repairs and bright paintwork jostled for his attention.

Here and there, carved gargoyles gazed down unblinkingly with squint-eyed indifference on the shuffling stream of human endeavour below.

Nothing offered him release from Ryllans' pain however, and he turned back to him again.

Ryllans was looking round at his companions. Abruptly he seemed to come to a decision.

'Estaan's been escorting your father's Dream Finder on some errand,' he began, with preamble.

'Dream Finder!' Arwain exclaimed. 'My father?'

Ryllans waved a disclaimer. 'I know no more than that,' he said hastily. 'Your father's Dream Finder.'

Arwain gave a slight, resigned shrug.

'They went to see a . . . colleague . . . of the Dream Finder's for some reason,' Ryllans went on. 'But apparently the old man was dead when they arrived and in trying to help him, this Dream Finder . . . released . . . found . . . something . . .' He stopped, seemingly unable to continue.

'Something you'd thought long dead,' Arwain offered, using Ryllans' own words.

Ryllans nodded. 'Yes,' he said slowly. 'Long dead. Well dead.' He put his hands to his eyes and blew out a long, trembling breath.

'What was it?' Arwain said softly.

Ryllans, however, shook his head. 'The tale's not mine to tell,' he said.

'But—'

Ryllans continued shaking his head. 'I'm sorry, sir,' he said. 'I shouldn't have mentioned it.' He affected a casualness that was patently false. 'Possibly Estaan was distraught. Misunderstood something. Dream Finding's an odd business by all accounts, and not one most of us are familiar with.'

Arwain's eyes narrowed. 'Don't trifle with me, Ryllans,' he said angrily. 'Either as your pupil or your lord. You insult me and demean yourself. Mantynnai don't go faint at the sight of a dead man. Tell me the truth. If there's a danger here, we need to know. Perhaps the army may need to be mobilized and prepared. Weapons forged, horses and waggons—'

He stopped as Ryllans turned towards him, his presence stern and hard. 'An army will be of no avail,' he said categorically. 'Vaster and finer armies than any this land could muster, have trembled before the presence of this . . . power.' Seeing the effect of his words however, he held up a reassuring hand. 'Have no fear though,' he said. 'We've learned. We'll know if it's truly here. It uses men. We'll feel it this time before it grows and takes root, and if we can't tear it out, then . . .' He hesitated and took a deep breath. 'We'll find those who can.'

Arwain frowned and made as if to speak.

'Truly, I can tell you no more,' Ryllans said quickly but politely, and with almost a plea in his voice. 'And if we fret about this strange . . . perception . . . of Estaan's when we should be thinking about the Whendreachi and the Bethlarii, then we might find ourselves walking into more trouble than *we* can handle before this journey's out.'

Arwain looked at him earnestly for a moment, then nodded. 'You're right,' he said acknowledging both the plea and Ryllans' unassailable defences. 'But school yourself to the idea of discussing this further when we get back from Whendrak.'

Ryllans looked at him enigmatically.

'I'd be a poor pupil if I asked less of you, wouldn't I?' Arwain said.

Ryllans bowed.

And I'll find out about my father using a Dream Finder, too, Arwain resolved.

They rode on in silence through the rest of the Moras district until they passed through the main western gate to the city and found themselves on the crowded and bustling waterfront of Serenstad's harbour; a man-made extension to a natural lake, with rows of green-stained groynes and causeways jutting out into it to provide the moorage that the city's trade needed.

Ships and barges were being loaded and unloaded. Wagons, pack horses, people, were arriving, leaving, queuing, wandering lost, and the air was full of voices; crying orders, shouting abuse, making bargains, singing even, the whole shot through with the clatter of horses' hooves and iron wheels on stones, rattling chains, creaking beams and pulleys, and occasional anonymous thuds and crashes.

It was colder here than in the crowded streets, and Arwain felt the open aspect and the energy of the place washing away the lingering concern he had about Ryllans' unusual behaviour.

Vaster and finer armies, he thought with some amusement. What peoples, what power, could bring to the field anything finer than the army of Serenstad? Or for that matter, Bethlar? The discipline and skill of such forces could overcome any foe should need arise.

The last darkness fell from him and he breathed in the cold river air and patted his horse encouragingly. Ryllans caught his eye and smiled slightly.

At the north end of the harbour was the largest of the bridges that served the city. A dozen or so arching, elaborately carved, masonry spans came from each shore and culminated in a soaring latticework of iron and timber, to carry a wide road high over the river. It was a matter of considerable pride to Ibris that this bridge had been built in his time and at his behest to replace its crumbling and dangerous predecessor. It was a matter of considerable pride to Menedrion that his forges and workshops had formed much of the iron.

With its building, yet more trade had come to the city, and like the harbour and the Moras, it was invariably crowded with all manner of traffic.

Thus when the riders turned on to it they were still obliged to move at the same leisurely pace they had been maintaining through the latter part of their journey.

When they were about halfway across, Arwain paused for a moment to look out over the busy harbour with its boats and ships plying to and fro through the cold grey water. From there, his eyes rose inevitably to the city, its rooftops and towers and spires rising above the wall and the ragged confusion of the Moras, and then disappearing up into the soft mist that clung to the sides of the valley.

Thousands of people beyond his sight would be pursuing their untidy, everyday lives there, carrying their myriad, personal, grumbling burdens, be they real or imaginary. And while many would deny that they achieved a great deal with their day's toil, the city slowly became more beautiful, lives slowly became more easy. Greater happiness and contentment were approached.

And, Arwain mused, his actions now, his awareness, his touch on affairs, might help draw these souls out into bloody and fearful conflict. There would be progress there too. Into his mind came the picture of his wife, smiling to hide her concern as she kissed him at their parting scarcely an hour before. The memory hurt him.

'It's only for a couple of days . . .'

'Take care, my love . . .'

But the progress that grew from conflict was the progress of grim necessity, of men struggling to climb out of the mire that their darker nature and foolishness had led them into. There were better ways by far.

Arwain realized that he was resting his hand on his sword hilt. A grim paradox. Without the sword, Serenstad, its peoples, its buildings, its questing knowledge, would fall, beyond a doubt, just as would any man unarmed among villains. Yet, having it, did it not draw forth the swords of others?

He made no attempt to answer the question. He had tried before, walking over victorious battlefields, amid the bodies of friends and enemies alike. Seeing ghastly wounds, trampled faces, strewn entrails being squabbled over by carrion. Listening to terrible sounds; some, high, shrieking; others, soft, nauseating. And then there was the awful dispatching of the too grievously hurt . . .

And in his exhilaration, he had wrought such horror himself with triumphant relish.

There were better ways by far, indeed. And whatever the answer to the question, if answer there was, it was part of his lot to have both the knowledge of his sword and the knowledge of those ways. One could not be found without the other, nor could anything survive without both. That much he *had* learned.

Gently he pulled his horse's head about and clicked it forward. He was aware of the platoon moving after him, but as he looked into the throng ahead, two approaching figures caught his attention.

Why they should have, he could not say. They were just two riders among many and they were making no special stir in their progress.

As they drew nearer he watched them carefully; puzzled at what impulse might have drawn his eye to them. Certainly there was nothing immediately apparent. They were bare-headed and wearing simple, unostentatious riding cloaks, though, he noted, these seemed to be of a high quality and a slightly unusual cut. And they rode well; very relaxed and easy in their manner; even more so than the Mantynnai perhaps.

And their horses were magnificent, he noted, as the animals too came more clearly into view. Then he became aware that the two men had also attracted the attention of Ryllans.

'Fine horses,' he said.

Ryllans started, almost violently. 'Yes,' he stammered.

Arwain stared at him. His face was even more alarmed than when he had spoken to Estaan.

'What's the matter?' Arwain asked urgently.

'Nothing,' Ryllans said quickly. 'I thought it was someone I once knew, but . . . it wasn't.'

He was lying, Arwain knew, but he knew also that having taken the trouble to lie so readily, Ryllans would not part with the truth until he was ready, no matter what demands were made of him.

The two men were alongside. Still for no reason that he could see, their fine horses notwithstanding, they made an impression on Arwain. One of them turned towards him and, catching his eye, gave a slight nod of acknowledgement at this seemingly inadvertent happening. Then his gaze turned to Ryllans, who was looking wilfully forward. There was inquiry in the stranger's eyes, and a brief touch on his partner's arm.

Discreetly, Arwain watched the two men as they passed by the platoon. They seemed to be looking at the guards with open but casual interest.

Foreigners, he surmised. Curious to look at our famous soldiers. But the conclusion was unsatisfactory. He turned in his saddle and peered after them. They were talking to one another and pointing towards the city. Foreigners, definitely, Arwain decided. But as he turned back, he caught a ripple of unease among the guards. No; among the Mantynnai. It was gone before he could truly register it.

Something stirred within him. He had the feeling of events moving that he could not identify. Ryllans visibly shaken by a few brief words from one of his own, then deliberately lying about the two strangers; two strangers who also provoked some response from the other Mantynnai.

It could only be something from the past of these men; these still, watching, men.

With an effort he set the ill-formed questions aside. Ryllans' earlier remarks were still pertinent. They were on a delicate, perhaps dangerous mission to Whendrak. Whatever lay in the past lay in the past. The present was all that mattered now. And if that were fouled, then the future might be truly grim.

Still . . .?

He cast another quick glance backwards, but the two men were out of sight amid the swaying wagons and the bobbing heads of other travellers on the bridge.

'Trot!'

They had reached the end of the bridge and the congestion was easing as the traffic spread out like a river delta, each strand going its separate way out into the widespread dominions of Serenstad.

Ryllans' command brought Arwain to the present again and in line of column, the platoon set off along the road to Whendrak.

Chapter 22

'Oh god, he's got two of the damn things with him now,' was Kany's greeting as Pandra opened the door to Antyr and Estaan.

Tarrian's ears went back, and his tail drooped, as did Grayle's.

'Now, now, Kany,' Pandra said reproachfully, before Antyr could explain their errand. 'They are what they are, just as you are what you are.'

Kany gave a scornful growl and muttered something inaudible, concluding, gracelessly, 'Still, I suppose you'd better let them in. You'll freeze the place out leaving the door open.'

Then he sniffed, and a faint hint of sympathy entered his voice. 'And they seem a bit fraught about something.'

Pandra gave an apologetic smile as he picked Kany up, put him in his pocket, and motioned his guests to enter.

He pointed towards a half-open door as he lingered briefly to see the two hesitant wolves safely in. Antyr stepped through it to find himself in a warm, well-lit room. It was small and rather cluttered, but it was homely and pleasant, and, like the outside of the house, indicated that the old Dream Finder had had a modestly successful career.

Pandra joined him and, for a few moments, scuttled about fussily, unnecessarily moving cushions and picking up an odd book and a few papers from the chairs and placing them on a table.

'Sit down,' he said finally to Estaan and Antyr. 'And come in, you two,' he added to the two wolves who were peering nervously around the door.

'It's all right for you, but this place is going to stink of wolf for weeks now. How I'm supposed to get any rest with my nerves permanently twitching at the scent, I don't know.' Antyr caught the loud whisper from Kany, but Pandra shushed him hastily.

'I got your address from the Guild House,' Antyr began,

sitting down. 'We . . . I've . . . a problem and I didn't know where to turn, to be honest. I . . .'

Pandra waved him silent. 'Just tell me what's happened,' he said. 'I'm glad to see you again. I must admit, you've been constantly in my mind since we met in the library, and one doesn't have to be a Companion to see that you're disturbed about something.'

The latter part of his remark was obviously spoken for Kany's benefit, but it provoked no response, and Antyr could feel the three Companions talking urgently at some level below his awareness.

Pandra leaned forward confidentially. 'That miserable porter at the Guild House said you'd been arrested by the palace guards. Quite smug he was about it. I was most concerned . . .' He tailed off absently, then, 'And I've been thinking about your story . . . That separation from your Companion . . . One gets into such a rut, one forgets . . . It came to me last night, though I'm hesitant to mention it, it sounds so foolish . . .'

'I've been into one of the worlds of the Threshold,' Antyr said starkly, before Pandra could continue.

Pandra stared at him blankly at first, then his face became a mixture of excitement, disbelief, and alarm. He looked at Antyr intently. 'You feel no madder than you did yesterday,' he said with unexpected bluntness. 'And I don't think I am. We must talk . . .' He flicked a significant glance towards Estaan.

'Shall I wait outside?' Estaan said, intercepting the look.

Antyr shook his head. 'This is Estaan,' he said to Pandra. 'He can stay, for the moment, at least. He's been a witness to today's events and he . . . felt . . . something himself. And he's one of the Mantynnai. He was instructed to look after me after . . .' He looked about the room self-consciously. 'After I was appointed to be the Duke's Dream Finder.'

Pandra scrutinized Estaan carefully for a moment. 'Mantynnai, eh?' he said. 'Kany?'

'He is,' the rabbit replied after a brief pause. Pandra nodded.

Estaan shifted uncomfortably as this unseen judge announced his verdict.

Pandra turned again to Antyr and raised his eyebrows. 'Your fortunes seem to be rising, young Antyr,' he said with some irony. 'Arrested one minute, Dream Finder to the Duke next. And now escorted personally by the Mantynnai.'

'I wasn't arrested,' Antyr said, shaking his head. 'I was being sought out by another . . . important . . . client.' He waved his hand irritably. 'But that doesn't matter at the moment.'

He frowned and looked at the frail old man. 'How well did you know Nyriall?' he asked.

'Hardly at all,' Pandra replied. 'I've met him once or twice at Guild meetings, but it was a long time ago. An unusual man. You could feel that, just by speaking to him. But a bit too much of an idealist from what I've heard. Seemed to think he could do something about *everybody's* unhappiness . . .' He shook his head. 'But you've got to accept reality sooner or later, haven't you? There's only so much you can do for anyone. And you'll do no one any good by starving to death for them.' He paused, then said, 'I gather from the past tense in your question, that he's probably done just that.'

Antyr shook his head. 'Not quite,' he said. 'But I'm afraid he *is* dead. Though far more strangely than by starvation.'

Pandra waited.

Plunging in, Antyr told of his visit to Nyriall and the strange events that had passed there.

The old Dream Finder was silent for a long time when Antyr had finished.

'Then they're truly there.' The voice was Kany's, and it was subdued, awe-stricken almost. 'The worlds of the Threshold. Truly there. Just like it says in the Treatise. I'd never given it two minutes' serious credence; this is an age of reason, isn't it? And now you've been there. And even drawn your Companions after you. All three of you there, for a brief moment . . . I didn't believe you, Tarrian, Grayle. I'm sorry . . .' His voice faded.

'But what does it all mean?' Antyr asked. 'And why's it happening to me? I'm no . . . Master. I've had no special training. Nor done any special study. In fact, if the truth be told, I've neglected my craft as diligently as others have pursued theirs.'

Pandra shook his head. 'You ask unanswerable questions, Antyr,' he said. 'It seems you are a Master, regardless of your application to your craft. Your . . . great . . . talent is perhaps as chance a thing as any Dream Finder's ordinary one. And there's neither rhyme nor reason as to why that's handed down to some and not to others. At least, no reason that we can see.' He paused thoughtfully. 'Perhaps you went . . . astray . . . *because* of the extent of your ability. Great talents are not always a blessing. I've a client who's a fine painter; brilliant even. His work is much praised and some of it is actually hung in the palace. But he sits far from easy in his life. He's a peculiarly tormented individual.'

Antyr grimaced. 'Master,' he muttered to himself in denial. 'Maybe you're right. I don't know. I certainly don't feel like one.' Wilfully, he set the subject aside. 'But, whatever I am, I've still to find out what's happening, and why. I have to find out who those two figures were and what they were doing there, creating such havoc and . . .' His face went grim as the thought formed in his mind. ' . . . *Murdering* Nyriall!'

The words hung in the air like acrid smoke and for a while no one spoke.

'You can walk away,' Pandra offered tentatively. 'It might have been something that Nyriall brought on himself and it may have died with him.'

Antyr shook his head. 'No. I don't think so,' he said. 'The evil in it was something I'd felt before. And I've got the feeling that if I run, it'll follow me.'

Silence returned to the room.

'We must look in the Treatise first,' Kany said eventually, his voice determinedly calm. 'You've been thrashing about so frantically in your fatigue and fear, and Tarrian's been so full of guilt at what he sees as his responsibility for failing to stop your seemingly relentless decline, that you've failed to consider the most obvious source of information.' He paused. 'As have we, if I'm honest. Too old. Too stupid. Go and get the book, Pandra.'

Pandra hesitated.

'Go on,' Kany snapped, his normal manner reasserting itself. 'It's on the top shelf in the back room.'

'I know,' Pandra replied testily. 'But I don't see what good the Treatise is going to be. I don't remember anything in it about how to become a Master; how to *reach* the Threshold or . . .' He paused as if suddenly recollecting something.

'No, you never read it properly,' Kany shouted into his reverie. 'Dream Finders never do. Learn a few tricks then think they know it all. Now go and get it. You, Mantynnai, go and help him, it's heavy and it's on a high shelf. We can't afford physician's fees if he falls off something and injures himself.'

Estaan stood up uncertainly, still unsettled by this strange conversation that was half spoken out loud and half echoing in his head. He looked at Antyr who, despite his own confusion, could not prevent himself from smiling.

'Yes, it is a rabbit who's ordering you about,' he said. 'Don't fret about it. Look at Tarrian and Grayle.'

Estaan glanced at the two wolves, both sitting still and subdued in a corner.

Still preoccupied, Pandra took the rabbit out of his pocket and, putting him on the floor, nodded graciously to Estaan who had already moved to open the door.

'Pick me up,' Kany said sharply to Antyr as the two men left. 'I want to get a close look at you.'

Antyr did as he was bidden, taking the rabbit in both hands and lifting him up until he was opposite his face.

'You *are* a ruffianly looking creature,' he said as he surveyed the rabbit's battered features.

Kany's nose twitched vigorously. 'You're no Buonardi sculpture yourself, Dream Finder,' he replied.

Tarrian got up and moved over to them. He put his forelegs on the arm of Antyr's chair and intruded his nose anxiously between Antyr and the rabbit.

Kany's eyes narrowed. 'Do you want a third nostril, bonzo?' he said brutally.

Hastily, Antyr transferred the rabbit to one hand and put the other reassuringly on Tarrian's shoulder.

'Kany, behave yourself.' It was Pandra, returning, followed by Estaan who was carrying a large book and several smaller ones. Without ceremony, Pandra took Kany from Antyr and dropped him, none too gently, back into his pocket.

'You have to be firm with him at times,' he said. 'He's got a very domineering streak if he's allowed too much of his own way.'

Antyr nodded, understandingly. Tarrian dropped back on to the floor, but lay across Antyr's feet.

'A fine searcher though,' Pandra added, as a small hedge against future recriminations, 'A fine searcher.'

He sat down and reached up to take the large book from Estaan. 'Been in the family for generations,' he said, running a finger along the engraved leather spine.

'Never mind the history lesson,' Kany said, impatiently, struggling out of Pandra's pocket. 'Turn up the section on the Threshold and the Rites of Mastership.'

Pandra settled the book on his knee, opened it reverently, and began squinting at the ornately scripted index. Slowly he turned over a page. Then another.

'What are you doing?' Kany asked irritably.

'I told you, there's nothing in the main texts,' Pandra said, without pausing in his search. 'Contrary to your opinion, I *have* read most of them at one time or another, and I'd have remembered if there was anything there that dealt with anything like this. I'm looking for the appendix that deals with the Mynedarion.'

Antyr winced. 'What for?' he asked nervously.

Pandra looked at him. 'Because that's what's come among us,' he said simply.

Antyr's mouth went dry. He wanted to speak, but could not, and for a moment his stomach felt hollow and ghastly.

'I don't pretend to understand what you've just told me,' Pandra said. 'And to be honest I'm still a little . . . disoriented . . . by it all. But one thing rings out.' He tapped his finger on the page absently. 'Change,' he said conclusively. 'This Nyriall figure that you met, whoever or whatever he was, spoke of change. Something that came into dreams and changed them. Can *you* do that, Antyr?' he asked rhetorically. 'Can *any* of us? And the figures you met changed the weather. Made their own storm seemingly. And more.'

He levered the book open and thumbed through several pages before finding what he wanted. He read for a moment then reached up and selected a volume from the pile that Estaan was still holding.

'But the Mynedarion are a myth,' Antyr said hesitantly.

'So is the Threshold these days, supposedly,' Pandra replied as he thumbed through the second book. 'And even the Great Dream itself. Just colourful creation myths for children, and esoteric lore about our ancestors for the study of learned scholars.'

Antyr closed his eyes. The memory of the storm that appeared out of nowhere returned to him; whirling dark thunder clouds streaked with lightning, a howling wind, full of purposeful shadows, a nerve-shredding laugh. And at the focus of it all, two motionless figures.

He opened his eyes and looked down at his hands. They were trembling.

A hand touched his arm gently. 'Don't be afraid of your fear,' a voice said softly. Antyr turned and found himself looking up into Estaan's face. 'What I felt in that room, I've felt before,' the Mantynnai went on. 'It was no illusion, no trick of the mind. And fear is the true response. But it *can* be faced and defeated. That I've seen also.'

Antyr shook his head. 'Maybe,' he said. 'But not by me. I . . .' He stopped abruptly, realization dawning on his face. 'I escaped because one of them wanted me to. Before Tarrian and Grayle came, one of them said, "You shall be my Guide." ' He shuddered at the memory of the malevolent desire in the voice. 'But the other one cried out, "No!" and . . .' He closed his eyes again in concentration. 'Put his blade between us . . . I'm sure.'

Pandra, however, did not appear to be listening. 'Yes,' he muttered to himself as he ran his finger down successive pages rapidly. 'There's a lot of ifs and maybes and buts here. Mynedarion are manifestations of aberrant streams in the flux of the Nexus, whatever that means. They're distortions in the dreamer's Nexus ordering produced by adverse Companion reaction . . . blah blah . . . Typical academic guff. They'll say anything bar "We don't understand." ' He gave a disparaging snort. 'I don't think some of these people would know whether they were in a Dream or a hay cart. But . . .' He jabbed the page forcefully. 'They say more than they realize. They all accepted that Mynedarion, whatever they are, need a willing Dream Finder if they're to reach into dreams and beyond. It says here that they have a power, an old power of some kind, it's not clear. Magyk's the word they keep using, but lots of things were magic when this was written which are understood properly now.' He shook his head. 'Anyway, this . . . power . . . can be used to change things here . . . in this world. But it's multiplied many times in the worlds of the Threshold, and is . . .' He brought his face close to the page. 'Beyond limit . . . in the Great Dream itself. From there they can change all things . . . Even the past itself. And it's there that they always strive to reach.'

He fell silent.

'A power, beyond explanation, to rend and change, does exist.' It was Estaan again. His voice was dark with certainty.

'I have felt it. Seen its work. As have all the Mantynnai. It's why we're here. Have no doubts about such a thing whether you understand it or not. It was mingled in the evil in that room today.'

Antyr and Pandra looked at him as if for a further explanation, but none came.

'Which leaves us where?' Kany said, after a moment, his voice subdued.

'Couch it in whatever language you like,' Pandra replied. 'It leaves us with an evil power stalking the worlds of the Threshold. An evil that can enter and change dreams at will. And one guided and protected by a Dream Finder of consummate skill; a Master.'

Antyr looked at him. 'There are no such Dream Finders in Serenstad,' he said, looking for solace in practicalities.

Pandra nodded. 'One would think so from the general state of our craft,' he said. 'But there are Dream Finders throughout the land. Even in Bethlar. It's an ancient craft. Many people are Dream Finders without even realizing it. And distance in this world will mean nothing to someone who can walk in the Threshold.'

Antyr looked down. The urge to flee was seeping into him again.

'What can it . . . they . . . want?' he managed to say.

Pandra shrugged. 'From what you say, there seems to be both madness and malice in one or both of them. Who can say what they want? But I've lived long enough to know that power always seeks more power. It needs no reason.' He looked significantly at Estaan. 'I think we must talk about . . . Guild matters for a moment.'

Antyr was more straightforward. He turned to the Mantynnai. 'Estaan, we must discuss the dreams of others. I'm sorry. Can you wait outside.'

Pandra stood up, placing the books on the floor. 'Go into the back room,' he said, with an apologetic smile. 'You'll have to forgive our discourtesy, but I doubt we'll be long.'

'I understand,' Estaan said. 'Perhaps I'll learn a little about Dream Finding from your books while I'm waiting.'

Pandra snapped his fingers and took Estaan by the arm to escort him from the room. 'I'll find you the very book,' he said. 'An excellent little apprentices' manual.'

When he returned, he was sombre-faced and serious, however. 'Power lies with the Duke here,' he said, without preamble. 'And all of a sudden he seeks out a poor spark of a Dream Finder who turns out to be a Master. Very strange. Tell me about his dreams and why he sought you out.' Then, nodding towards the two wolves and lowering Kany on to the floor, 'And you three listen and exchange whatever you need as well.'

Antyr recounted the events of the past two days and described the dreams of both the Duke and Menedrion. Pandra listened in silence, but his old face seemed to grow older as Antyr continued, and when, finally, he spoke, there was a marked tremor in his voice.

'Menedrion as well,' he said. 'And drawn into the Threshold apparently. Power seeks power. I was right. I hoped that perhaps it might have been you that brought all this about in some way, but it seems not. It seems that, whoever these two are, they're trying to possess the dreams of our leaders, or worse, draw them into the Threshold . . .' He paused as if reluctant to continue.

'Where they can be killed, or perhaps possessed themselves,' Antyr said, remembering the shadows that closed about him.

Pandra closed his eyes and nodded. 'I fear you're right,' he said. 'If the Treatise is correct, and it seems to be from what you've said about that storm's suddenly coming from nowhere, then they already have great power in the Threshold. If they're choosing to assail our leaders then they must be seeking power in this world.'

His voice jerked the words out unhappily.

'What are we to do?' Antyr asked after a long silence.

Pandra shook his head reflectively. 'Your father's shadow is reaching down to us, Antyr,' he said. 'Good flows from good. Just a conscientious man with his client was your father, but the trust he built up in the Duke has sustained him and given him self-knowledge enough to protect himself when the need arose, albeit without realizing it.'

'Yes, perhaps, but what can we do?' Antyr repeated, impatiently.

Pandra shot him a mildly reproachful glance. 'Because of your father's work with the Duke, we can tell him the truth,' he said sternly. 'And we must tell him about Menedrion's dream too. Under the circumstances it's a necessary breach of confidence. From what you say, I'm sure he'll believe us and he may well have his own ideas about what's happening.'

It took them little time to reach the palace from Pandra's house, but it proved no easy task to gain an audience with the Duke.

'There's been a noisy cabinet meeting, by all accounts,' Estaan said, returning from his first attempt. 'And he's due at the Sened shortly to make some kind of statement about this envoy. There's all manner of people clamouring to see him; merchants, Gythrinwr, diplomats . . .'

Antyr looked around. The wide hallway they were standing in was indeed busy with guards, messengers, officials bustling to and fro urgently.

'What about Aaken and Feranc?' he asked.

'They're no use anyway. We need to speak to the Duke,' Pandra said, before Estaan could reply. He turned to the Mantynnai, unexpectedly resolute. 'Young man. You're a soldier. Cut your way through to him, at whatever cost, and tell him that his Dream Finder must speak to him, immediately, on a matter of the utmost importance.'

Estaan hesitated.

Pandra took his arm, urging him forward. 'You say you felt an evil that you've felt before,' he said. 'That makes you the wisest here. Be your own judge of the urgency of the matter.'

Estaan rubbed his chin briefly, then nodded and set off again.

It was some time before he returned, and he was looking somewhat flustered when he did.

'Come on,' he said, breathing noisily. 'I've got you five minutes. And it's cost me five years of growth the mood the Duke's in!'

Antyr could appreciate Estaan's concern as soon as he stepped into the Duke's room. The figure before him was not the affable, almost fatherlike, figure that had greeted him on their previous meetings. This was a powerful leader of men . . . leader of armies . . . preparing for battle. That it was predominantly a political battle at the moment, rather than a military one, made his manner no less formidable.

'Five minutes,' he confirmed, holding up his fingers, before Antyr could speak. He glanced at Pandra and the two wolves. 'And don't abuse my regard for your father and respect for your craft by expecting to bring in all your drinking cronies.'

As much to his own surprise as anyone else's, Antyr, grim-faced, strode towards the Duke. The Duke's eyes widened angrily in response to his manner, but Antyr did not wait for any reproach. 'The old man I went to see for advice is dead,' he said. 'Murdered, I think, by the same . . . people . . . power, that tried to enter your dream.'

'Murdered, you *think*?' Ibris said with heavy and impatient emphasis. 'You've seen corpses enough in your time, haven't you?'

'Murdered I'm certain,' Antyr returned. 'Though not by any means that either you or I have seen before.'

'I want no riddles,' the Duke retorted. 'Speak plainly. And who the devil is this anyway?' He flicked his head towards Pandra.

Pandra stepped forward hesitantly to introduce himself, but Antyr did it for him. 'This is Indares Pandra, sire. A Dream Finder who knew my father and who still respects and knows the old ways. I sought his help.'

Ibris grunted dismissively. 'You set my own bodyguard on me, Dream Finder,' he said. 'I don't know how you managed that, but this matter of importance had better be just that or—'

'It is, sire,' Antyr said, cutting across him. 'What do you know of the Threshold?'

Ibris scowled at the interruption, but Antyr's abrupt question provoked an automatic answer. 'It's part of your Dream Finding mythology, isn't it?' he replied. 'Worlds beyond the dreams. Real worlds like this one. Worlds within worlds. And beyond them again is supposed to be the Great Dream.'

'Not mythology, sire,' Antyr said, without giving him pause. 'But truth. I've been to one of the Threshold worlds twice, perhaps three times, these last two days. And met the power that tried to enter your dream—'

'Enough,' Ibris said fiercely, his face set. 'I haven't time for this.' He rounded on Antyr. 'I had some reservations about seeking your help in the first place, Antyr. Now I see they were right. You're not your father's son, you're just another charlatan hoping to find an easy living by gulling me with woolly-headed nonsense.' His lip curled. 'Travelling to other worlds! What kind of a fool do you take me for?' He turned towards the door. 'Estaan!' The Mantynnai appeared almost immediately.

297

Ibris turned back to Antyr. His presence seemed to fill the room. 'Out of regard for your father you'll not be punished for this pathetic chicanery, but make sure you never cross my way again, and keep your tongue to yourself if you don't want to lose it. Get them out of here, Estaan. I'll speak to *you* later.'

Estaan stepped forward. There was regret and dismay in his eyes but the purposefulness of his stride was clear enough.

Antyr held out a shaking hand to stop him. Estaan hesitated and glanced at the Duke. 'Sire,' Antyr said, his voice trembling like his hand, but nevertheless, intense. 'Do as you wish. I'm well content to go back to my old life. I'm a wiser man by far than I was two days ago, and I want no more adventures such as I've had today. But be alert tonight, for everyone's sake. Whatever my father taught you, hold to it, and above all be yourself and trust yourself. There *is* a threat to you. And have someone, anyone, guard your son's sleep. He has neither your knowledge nor your will. He's already been drawn into the Threshold, and it's only by a chance intervention by someone else that he hasn't been . . . overwhelmed, perhaps killed, yet.'

Estaan took his arm firmly, lifting him up on to his toes, but Antyr held Ibris's gaze.

Ibris raised his hand and Estaan paused.

'Tarrian,' Ibris said. 'I felt you prowling the edges of my sleep last night, for which my thanks. Am I to believe this tale?'

'I've mixed with humans long enough to learn how to lie, Ibris,' Tarrian replied. 'My word's no better than his. Use your nose when your wits fail you, pack leader.'

Ibris frowned, then motioned Estaan away. 'Five more minutes,' he said tersely.

Nervously, Antyr recounted his tale once more, as briefly as he could.

When he had finished, Ibris looked at Estaan. 'And you felt some of this . . . presence?' he asked.

Estaan nodded. 'I was terrified, sire,' he said simply. 'There was a . . . power . . . there that I've felt before and have no wish to feel again.'

Ibris looked at him narrowly. 'From before your arrival here?' he said. Estaan bowed by way of reply, but did not speak.

Ibris's manner softened slightly. 'Wait outside all of you, I need to think for a moment,' he said.

As the door closed behind the three men, Ibris stepped over to an alcove and drew back the partly closed curtain.

The tall figure of Ciarll Feranc stepped out of the shadows.

Chapter 23

Ibris put his hand to his head wearily. 'What did you make of all that, Ciarll?' he asked.

Feranc shrugged slightly. 'Very strange,' he replied. 'Estaan's Mantynnai, he sees things the way they are better than most. If he admits to being terrified then it was for some good reason. What did the wolf say to you?'

Ibris smiled. 'Told me to use my nose,' he replied with a chuckle. 'Called me a pack leader.' He sat down and stretched his legs wearily. 'Fair comment I suppose and, for what it's worth, I don't think the Dream Finder's lying, or trying to ingratiate himself. But his tale is so preposterous.'

'Dream Finding is something I've no experience of,' Feranc said. 'But there are many strange things in the world and the wolf's advice is sound under the circumstances.'

Ibris nodded thoughtfully. 'Strange indeed,' he said. 'I can't avoid feeling that events are moving quite beyond my control. As if some . . . outside . . . power were forcing them along.'

Feranc waited impassively.

Then, rather awkwardly, Ibris said, 'The Mantynnai came much later than you, but they *are* your countrymen, aren't they?' He looked at Feranc, almost plaintively. It was a subject he had touched on lightly at times, but Feranc had never responded and he had never pressed the question.

Feranc nodded. 'They are,' he said, without deliberation. 'But I know none of them, nor why they're here. And, clear-sighted though they are, I doubt any of *them* know me for one of their countrymen.'

Ibris rested his head on his hands. Feranc's almost casual admission was in itself oddly unsettling. As if in some way it implied further the importance of events far beyond his knowledge or his will.

'You understand that nothing would have made me pry into this but a great sense of unease and Estaan's specific reference to his past,' he said. 'You know that I accept them for what they are, here and now, and for what they've been since they came to this land. Just as I've always accepted you.'

Feranc nodded again.

'But tell me what you can, that might give me some guidance,' Ibris went on. 'Tell me what there is in your country that could terrify one of my Mantynnai.'

Feranc sat down opposite the Duke, his face unreadable. 'This is my country, Ibris,' he said. 'But I understand your need.' He took a deep breath. 'I know of nothing in my birthland that could produce such a reaction. It was a country with a strong . . . soldierly . . . tradition. But it wasn't warlike. It was civilized, peaceful, well governed, and above all free. A rare balance, as I've found on my travels since. Strength doesn't bring freedom, but freedom can't survive without true strength; the strength that comes from inside a people. The strength to see your neighbour wearing a sword and to be glad of it, knowing that he is well capable of using it, and will draw it to protect *you* if need arises.' He paused and his eyes became distant and unfocused.

'Why did you leave?' Ibris asked, almost immediately regretting the haste of the question.

Feranc started slightly from his reverie. 'The countries on our borders were very different from us, but similarly blessed with peace and order, and self-knowledge. Then one of them was attacked. Hordes of barbarians came to their shores, burning, killing, destroying . . .' He shook his head. 'We went to their aid. We could do no other. I was a . . . King's man . . . like I am now, albeit more lowly. But my . . . regiment . . . was special; very highly trained; the eyes of the King's army, and a secret dagger in the heart of the enemy. There weren't many of us.'

He stopped. Ibris remained silent.

'I saw such things . . . did such things. Things that must inevitably change the direction of a man's life ever after.' He shook his head slowly and pensively. 'When word reached us that the enemy was routed and had fled back to the sea, I think I just wandered away, out of those freezing mountains.' He wrapped his arms about himself involuntarily. 'I scarcely remember. I just knew I couldn't go home. I was defiled in some way.' Ibris grimaced at the distress his request had caused.

'I just wandered and wandered. South. Away. Anywhere,' Feranc went on. 'From land to land, people to people. Until I came here. Saw a faint shadow of my homeland in this city and its dominions. And you, striving relentlessly to better it all. Here I'll stay, I thought. Put my peculiar skills at the service of this man. Build the heart of my country here anew.'

Ibris reached across and touched his arm gently. 'I'm sorry, Ciarll,' he said. 'I didn't mean to disturb such painful memories.'

Feranc smiled slightly. 'There's little or no pain in them now,' he replied. 'Even though they're with me every day. I couldn't be of any value to anyone if they weren't. Now I'm more whole. And Serens. Besides, your need is great, and I was lucky. I was taught by wise men so while I did foul things, they were none of them truly avoidable. I have at least the consolation that I can face my conscience. I can account for my deeds.'

He fell silent.

'And the Mantynnai?' Ibris asked, tentatively, after a moment.

Feranc frowned thoughtfully. 'I don't know,' he said. 'They've not been trained as I was, very few were. But they've all been in the King's service at some time, I'd say, or at least been trained by his men. It's difficult to say exactly, they're a very mixed bunch.'

Ibris looked surprised. 'That's the last thing I'd have said,' he remarked. 'It doesn't need much of a soldier's eye to pick one of them out of a crowd.'

Feranc nodded. 'True,' he said. 'But what you see is the unifying effect of whatever drove them from . . . their country. *I* see many different traits in the way they conduct themselves. And their fighting techniques are fascinating. They reveal a great deal. I can recognize the basis of all of them but, quite independently, they've also developed them in the very direction that I was trained to. I had a teacher once who said that all paths become the same eventually if pursued for the right reasons. I didn't know what he meant then, but I do now.'

'But why would they leave their country?' Ibris asked gently as Feranc fell silent once more.

Feranc shook his head. 'I don't know,' he said. 'But I feel that they left bearing an even greater burden of guilt and pain than I, and that, for all their calm and quietness, most of them are a long way from being truly at peace with themselves. They're driven by something. That's why they stood and died at Viernce. Even now I think they'd form a ring around you and die to a man if need arose.'

'And you, Ciarll?'

'I *might*,' Feranc replied, with an unexpected smile.

Ibris smiled too, but his face was soon dark again.

'It's just occurred to me,' he said, very slowly. 'That perhaps once they followed this evil that Estaan spoke of.'

'A sad thought,' Feranc replied softly. 'But perhaps apt. Though I can't imagine what it could have been. For the most part, even the barbarians who invaded our neighbours were not evil. They were misled and ignorant, and by virtue of their ignorance, they did evil deeds which warranted armed opposition. But that wouldn't frighten a man like Estaan. It would make him reach for his sword.'

'So presumably something happened in your land since you left?' Ibris said.

Feranc nodded. 'Presumably,' he echoed. 'But I doubt the Mantynnai will tell you, me, or anyone. Nor do I think we should ask. If they know of some strange threat, then they'll take steps against it. I think we must watch them and learn that way, until perhaps an opportunity for an open question presents itself.'

Ibris sat silent for some time. 'You're right,' he said. 'We must trust them. They'll do nothing that will allow any harm to happen to Serenstad. God knows, they'd no reason to stand and fight at Viernce, but they did, and if they hadn't, then we wouldn't be here today. And they *would* fight to the death for me if need arose.' He looked at Feranc. 'As I would for them,' he added deliberately. 'Whatever they did and whatever drives them, they're fine and true men now, by any measure. Perhaps like you, they see some . . . what was it you said? Some shadow of their homeland here. But whatever it is, we owe them a debt beyond measure.' He paused. 'We must just be careful that we don't allow them to sacrifice themselves to assuage some long-past misdeed.'

Feranc bowed his head in acknowledgement.

'But I still don't know what to do with this Dream Finder and his wild tales of worlds beyond,' Ibris said, in some exasperation.

'Nothing's changed much since last night,' Feranc said quietly. 'Except that the Dream Finder seems to be growing in stature almost as we watch him.'

Ibris nodded in agreement. 'Yes,' he said. 'He's a more powerful spirit than he realizes. A true Serens.'

'A true man,' Feranc corrected.

'Yes,' Ibris said softly.

'Take him seriously,' Feranc said, uncharacteristically authoritative. 'If only for the effect he had on Estaan. He's no charlatan, we both feel that. He believes what he's seen and he's struggling with something, beyond a doubt.'

Ibris nodded uncertainly.

Feranc leaned forward, suddenly almost animated. 'Consider the worst, however improbable,' he said. 'A strange, malign power loose among us. Attacking us through our dreams in some way. You can raise an army to face the Bethlarii and many of us can help you lead it. But who can fight a foe that can come through the darkness into our sleeping minds and perhaps kill us there?'

Ibris watched him.

'You can't charge cavalry against a city wall,' Feranc went on. 'And you can't tunnel under an infantry line. Tactics and troops change with circumstances. If we need someone to . . . fight . . . in dreams then we must have someone who understands dreams, who can enter them, and who's no coward. And heed his warning about Menedrion. I've already told him that you want to see him today. You must tell him about all this and ensure that he's . . . guarded . . . in his sleep, however these people do that kind of thing. And speak to the man again now. Question him. Listen to him. And give him immediate access to you at all times.'

Ibris's eyebrows went up.

'At all times,' Feranc repeated. 'I'll be honest, the man intrigues me. He's the kind who springs up from nowhere in a broken pike line and somehow pulls it together again. And it *is* only another mouth or so to feed at worse. If he becomes troublesome or foolish he's easily dealt with.'

'You're right again,' Ibris said, sitting up. 'Find Menedrion and bring him here immediately, no matter what he's doing – or to whom – then bring them all back in. And you may as well stay yourself, I doubt there's any point trying to hide you from those wolves. They probably knew you were there all the time.'

Menedrion needed little persuasion to leave his duties as host to the Bethlarii envoy.

'Father, my face is aching with smiling at that black-hearted, intolerant bigot,' he blustered as he entered the room. His clenched fist came up. 'The sooner we . . .' He stopped as he saw Antyr.

'What's he doing here?' he demanded.

'He's here for the same reason you are,' Ibris said, curtly. 'Because I told him to be.'

Sensing his father's mood, Menedrion held his tongue, but he gave Antyr a look of such menacing suspicion that Ibris was obliged to speak again. 'You can rest assured he's done you no ill-service, Irfan,' he said. 'And since he attended you he's been appointed as one of my senior advisers.' He looked narrowly at his son.

Menedrion seemed to be considering some comment but in the end he just sniffed loudly, and sat down heavily on a nearby chair.

Ibris turned to Antyr. 'Tell me everything again,' he said simply.

Antyr was less than happy at being the object of dispute between Ibris and Menedrion, and far from certain about his status in such a gathering following the Duke's earlier outburst. He stepped forward however, and did as he was bidden; telling of his visits to both the Duke and Menedrion, and ending with his experience at Nyriall's, adding this time, Pandra's conjectures about the Mynedarion.

There was a brief silence when he had finished, then Menedrion gave a blast of disgust. 'What blithering nonsense,' he burst out derisively. 'Wondrous worlds in the great beyond. Magicians conjuring thunder and lightning out of nowhere. I didn't believe tales like that when I was three. What's it going to be next? The Winterfest Giver with his red cloak and white beard? What are we doing here, father? We've all got *important* matters to attend to.'

He leaned forward in his chair, but before he could continue, Ibris intervened. 'Look in the mirror, Irfan,' he said sharply. 'When did you last have any sleep? And what drove you to your mother seeking a Dream Finder?'

Menedrion's jaw jutted out angrily and, for a moment, it seemed almost that he was going to leap up and strike his father. Then he turned away abruptly, and slumped back morosely in his chair. It creaked in protest.

'Have you ever known me to play foolish games, Irfan?' Ibris said, his voice mildly conciliatory. 'I can't pretend that I believe this business of the Threshold and strange real worlds beyond where dead men can be alive again, but I'm satisfied that *I* was menaced in some way in my dream. And I've enough experience of Dream Finding to know that a Dream Finder can't be separated from the dreamer as you were. We don't need to know exactly what's happening to know that something's badly amiss. And I intend to take action to protect our flanks by using the only troops we have to hand for the job.'

Menedrion looked up and the two men gazed at one another silently for some time, the one fatigued, beneath his air of angry bluster, the other determined and concerned. Eventually Menedrion lowered his eyes and nodded slowly.

'Whatever you say, father,' he said. 'I'll own to the fact that I was frightened in that . . . dream. Wherever it was, it was as real as here.' He slapped the arm of his chair. 'And so was the threat that I felt. It was like no dream I've ever had. I don't know who protected me the first time, but he and the wolf saved me the second time.' He nodded towards Antyr.

Ibris nodded in some relief, a danger accepted was a danger that could be met. He turned to Antyr. 'You must advise,' he said, holding out his hand. 'We can't go without sleep or our ordinary old-fashioned enemies in the here and now will defeat us.' He was almost light-hearted.

Antyr, finding himself suddenly the focus of attention, froze. Under other circumstances he might have expected a spine-straightening rebuke from Tarrian for such dithering, but the wolf was silent.

The Duke nodded at him expectantly.

Desperately, Antyr took refuge in the truth. 'I don't know what to do, sire,' he said, eventually. 'I've no experience in such matters. Nor do I know anyone who has. I don't know what powers this . . . Mynedarion . . . or his guide have. What their intentions are . . . who they are . . . where they are . . . anything . . .'

'Nonetheless,' Ibris said, levelling a finger at him. '*You* must advise. Useless though you feel yourself to be, you're still the only one here who's made real contact with this enemy. Think. You'll find you've come away with more information than you've realized.'

Antyr stared at him vacantly.

Ibris leaned forward. 'Firstly, you survived,' he said simply. 'You say this . . . creature . . . raised a great wind, darkened the sky with thunder and lightning. That's a power beyond anything that even our artillery machines, or Menedrion's great forges can achieve. But still you survived—'

'Because he wanted me,' Antyr interrupted, without thinking.

Ibris nodded. 'Further information,' he said. 'Which I'd forgotten myself. And also you thought that you noted a division in their ranks.'

Antyr shrugged. 'It was only a thought, sire. An impression,' he said.

Ibris cast a glance at Feranc, who smiled slightly. 'Battles have been won and lost on far less than that, Antyr,' he said. 'That's one of the reasons why it's a good idea not to have them if they can be avoided. Too much rests on random chance.'

Antyr opened his arms in a gesture of inadequacy.

Ibris became more stern. 'We cannot see a danger and do nothing,' he said. 'You are the only one who can help. Trust your judgement. Advise.'

Antyr looked at Pandra and then at Tarrian and Grayle. The two wolves looked at him unblinkingly, but neither spoke. A pack thing, he thought grimly.

There was a long silence.

Then he looked squarely at Ibris. 'You've never had a dream such as you had the other night, sire?' he asked.

'Never,' Ibris replied.

Antyr turned to Menedrion. 'Nor I,' Menedrion replied, before the question was asked.

Antyr closed his eyes. He felt an abyss opening before him again.

'We are guarded in all places by a great and ancient strength,' he said resolutely and, releasing a long slow breath, he stepped into the darkness.

Walking over to Menedrion, he stood over him and stared at him intently. Menedrion met his gaze unflinchingly, but with some suspicion.

'You are Irfan Menedrion,' Antyr said, his voice unexpectedly commanding. 'Son of Serenstad's greatest Duke. A man who will be Duke himself, one day. A great leader of men in battle. Where you are, men rally, lines re-form, and enemies quail. A great warrior. None opposes you willingly.' He reached out and placed his extended forefinger in the middle of Menedrion's forehead. 'Remember all this. Remember it as you would remember the battlefield earth, firm and solid, under your feet, supporting you faithfully as you swung your sword. Remember it as you would remember the weight of your lance, the movement of your horse. Remember. You are master of yourself. You cannot be moved if you do not wish it. Sleep with the sword that you've used before, beside you; the one you can rely on. It will remind you of your power. Sleep brings you no threat. Dream in peace.'

Menedrion made no movement as Antyr removed his hand, but all hostility had gone from his face.

Antyr turned to the Duke and fixed him with the same, black-eyed gaze. 'You understood these things well already, sire, although you did not realize it,' he said. 'Now you understand them more. Sleep brings you no threat. Dream in peace.'

The room became very still and Antyr moved softly through the silence like drifting smoke.

He looked at Estaan. 'You are not of this land,' he said. 'You are tortured, but you have strange deep strengths from another place. Dream in peace.'

Finally he came to Ciarll Feranc. He looked up into the Commander's enigmatic face for a long time.

'And even deeper strengths yet,' he said, finally, very softly. He bowed slowly. 'Dream in peace.'

Feranc bowed in reply.

Antyr turned back to the Duke. 'If Pandra is willing, he should accompany the Lord Menedrion, to guard his dreams, sire. His Companion is a kindred spirit to the lord. Very fierce.'

Ibris glanced at the old Dream Finder, who nodded hesitantly.

'Menedrion, take Pandra as part of your entourage,' Ibris said. 'But he's no sapling. See that he's looked after properly. Comfortable wagon, comfortable quarters. You understand? And listen to him.'

Menedrion looked warily at the old Dream Finder and then nodded. 'I'm sure he'll be better company than that Bethlarii bigot with his damned preaching and his endless prayers,' he said. 'But who's going to pay for him? Aaken's already been complaining about the cost of this envoy and—'

Ibris scowled. 'We'll discuss that later, Irfan,' he said sharply.

Menedrion grunted suspiciously and then stood up. 'Well, if there's nothing else to be decided for me,' he said, somewhat caustically. 'May I get back to my duties? There's still a lot to do if we're to leave tomorrow.'

When he had left, Ibris stared at the door for a moment and then turned to Antyr. 'For a man who minutes ago didn't know what to do, you seem peculiarly confident all of a sudden,' he said.

Antyr shrugged. 'You're my Duke and Commander. Your order left me no choice. So I spoke the truth as I felt and as I spoke I realized that what I felt was the truth.'

Ibris made to reply, but Antyr continued. 'Besides,' he said. 'The . . . attackers . . . failed to reach you when you weren't even aware of them. Now that you are aware, your strength and control are magnified many times. Add to that the fact they've fled before Tarrian and me, twice already, my feeling is that they'll not be too anxious to return too quickly.'

'But if they do, what of my son?' Ibris asked.

'I've no unequivocal answer for you, sire,' Antyr replied. 'But we're indeed protected in many strange ways. Someone, somehow, protected Lord Menedrion in his moment of need. Probably a close relative who might not even have known what he was doing. Someone accidentally sucked in by the disturbance in the Dream Ways. He, or she, probably thinks it was just a nightmare. But now your son has accepted his own fear and vulnerability, he too will be stronger by far. And should there be any assault on him, Pandra and Kany will waken him on the instant.'

'But—' the Duke said, catching a doubt in Antyr's tone.

Antyr pulled a wry face. 'But who they are. What they want. Why they want it . . .' He shrugged. 'All the questions that clouded my sight before, must still be answered sooner or later, because they *will* return eventually. There was a malevolence there that will not rest until it's . . .' He paused as a grim image came to him suddenly. He voiced it hesitantly. '. . . until it's walked with relish through endless fields of our dead, calf-deep in blood and flesh.' His eyes narrowed, then closed. Faintly, at the edge of his mind, the word formed. 'Vengeance,' he said softly. 'A dark and ancient malice is seeking vengeance.'

310

A deep stillness filled the room again. No one moved, no one spoke.

A lamp spluttered noisily, breaking the spell.

'And you, Antyr?' Ibris said, clearing his throat. 'What of you? Who will protect your nights?'

'Tarrian and Grayle, and my own wits and awareness,' Antyr replied. 'And I shall have my sword and daggers sharpened, and carry them with me from now on in case I'm drawn away unawares.'

'But still, questions, questions,' Ibris said.

'Yes, sire,' Antyr agreed. 'But all we can do now is wait for the night and sleep. We've done all that can be done here. Now, with respect, I think that you have more pressing problems with the Sened and the Bethlarii envoy.'

Ibris stood up. 'Indeed,' he said. 'A timely reminder.' He glanced at a timepiece on the wall. 'And I'll have to hurry. The Sened will be less than pleased if I drag them into an evening sitting.'

Taking Antyr by the arm, he moved towards the door. Feranc fell in beside them. 'You must keep me informed of anything untoward that occurs in this strange business,' he said. 'I've arranged for you to have access to me at all times, for that purpose. I know it's not a privilege that you'll abuse. Likewise I must know where you are at all times. And go nowhere without Estaan. Do you understand? There are other, more prosaic, forces than dream demons and Bethlarii who have little love for me, and to be of value to me is sometimes to attract unpleasant attention.'

'Yes, sire,' Antyr replied, bowing as he opened the door to let the Duke and Feranc through. As he passed by, Feranc looked at him briefly, and gave a small, satisfied nod.

'You've made an impression on the Commander,' Estaan said, when Antyr had closed the door.

'I've made an impression on myself,' Antyr replied ruefully as he sat down again. 'Ye gods, my legs are shaking. What possessed me to speak to the Duke and Menedrion like that? And now I'm involved in palace politics.'

Tarrian and Grayle moved over to him and Tarrian sat down and leaned against him. He did not speak, but his satisfaction and approval filled Antyr's mind. He reached down and held both the wolves tight.

As he did so, he looked up at Pandra, standing silent by the wall. Remorse struck him at the sight of the frail old man.

'I'm sorry,' he said. 'If I've done you a bad service, perhaps I can still remedy it. I'm sure someone else can be found to guard Menedrion if you think it'll be too much.'

The remark galvanized Pandra. 'No, no,' he protested. 'This is splendid. I've spent my whole life pottering about through my craft always feeling that something, somewhere, was missing. Always half wondering whether I wasn't in fact just a charlatan myself. Now I'm walking by the side of a Master. The Threshold itself beckons. No, you did me no disservice.'

Antyr's remorse did not recede. 'They killed Nyriall, you know,' he said. 'Killed him.'

'Killed him here,' Pandra said. 'But not there. There he was alive. Moving from world to world—'

'Because they were hunting him,' Antyr exclaimed.

Pandra, however, was not to be deterred. 'But he escaped,' he declared. 'Besides, he went there by accident. I may not be a Master, but if I'm drawn there inadvertently, at least I'll know what's happening. And *I* shall be carrying my sword and daggers too in future.'

Antyr sighed and sat up. 'Kany, what do you think of your Finder's enthusiasm?' he asked.

'Oh, nice of you to ask,' came the instant, and peevish, reply. 'Do feel free any time to volunteer us to wander about the Threshold tackling sinister Master Dream Finders and cracked Mynedarion dragging thunderstorms and legions of shadows in their wake. It's just what we need to while away the tedious hours of our retirement.'

Antyr opened his mouth to reply, but Kany continued, gathering momentum.

'And what do you mean by calling me a kindred spirit to that lout Menedrion?' he went on. 'That's very respectful of you.'

'He'll get used to the idea,' Pandra intervened reassuringly.

'You are only guarding Menedrion,' Antyr said by way of mitigation.

'Make your mind up,' the rabbit snapped. 'Are you glad or sorry you talked us into this job?'

Antyr made to reply again, but no wisdom came to guide him and he wilted before Kany's displeasure.

'Take no notice,' Pandra said. 'You'd no choice but to do what you did, and I'm well pleased at the prospect. As is Kany, really. Though he's loath to admit it. Besides, I can't see that there's any danger in just guarding, but, to be blunt, if there is, I'd rather go with a flourish than a long sigh. Old age doesn't suit me.'

'A long sigh suits me well enough,' Kany muttered. 'The desire for death or glory is one of many human traits that I consider myself fortunate not to understand.'

Antyr decided to let the matter lie. Another matter occurred to him.

'What about the Liktors who arrested us?' he asked Estaan. 'I'd forgotten about them. I should have mentioned it to the Duke.'

Estaan shook his head. 'I'm glad you didn't,' he said with a smile. 'I don't think he'd be too impressed by my care for your welfare if he heard we'd been arrested for assault and being involved in a suspicious death.'

Antyr was not reassured. 'Your friend vouching for you only got us Liktor bail, you know,' he said. 'We're technically under arrest.'

Estaan laughed. 'And rightly so too,' he said. 'What would you have done with two disreputable individuals found with a dead body and claiming to be there on the Duke's business?'

'Well I suppose—' Antyr began.

'Don't worry,' Estaan said dismissively, but sympathetically. 'I'll sort it all out when I arrange for Nyriall's body to be collected. There'll be no problem.'

The mention of Nyriall's body, however, brought dark thoughts back to Antyr. 'I find it hard to imagine that he's still alive somewhere, right now, wandering through those sunlit fields, while at the same time he's lying cold and stiff in that poky little room.'

'Do you think they'll still be hunting for him?' The voice was Grayle's and it was fretful. Antyr reached down and stroked the wolf. 'I don't think so, Grayle,' he said. 'I think that my intervention gave them more serious things to think about. Don't be too concerned. He was pleased at the prospect of a new start in a new world. He said he doubted he could have survived another fog-choked winter.'

A wave of sadness passed over him. It was the wolf's, he knew.

'He was sorry to part from you though,' he went on. 'Said he'd miss you a lot and that I was to thank you. He couldn't have had a finer Companion.'

Grayle let out a little whine, and then lay down, resting

his head on his forepaws. Antyr continued to stroke him.

'I let him down at the end,' Grayle said. 'He slipped from me somehow. I don't know how. He was there, then he was gone. In an instant. Just gone.'

Before Antyr could reply, there was an interruption from Tarrian at a level beyond his awareness. He reached out to them tentatively, then withdrew, leaving the two brothers to their own discourse.

'Well, I suppose the rest of the day's my own,' he muttered ironically.

Scarcely had he spoken, however, when the door opened and the Duke reappeared. 'A thought just occurred to me, Antyr,' he said. 'I'd like you to watch the Bethlarii envoy's dreams tonight. Is that possible?'

'Yes, sire,' Antyr said with a slight shrug. 'Providing he's not far away.'

Ibris nodded. 'I thought so,' he said. 'I'll arrange it.' He looked at Antyr, stern again. 'And, Antyr, this concerns the needs of the state. You owe this man no duty of confidentiality. I want to know whatever he dreams about. Does that present you with any difficulties?'

Antyr recalled his protestations to the bodyguard when he had sought out the Duke the previous evening.

'Yes, sire,' he replied. 'It's contrary to all my teachings. But war is a greater evil by far, and if I can give you information that might prevent one, then I'll do it.'

Chapter 24

Tarrian and Grayle walked some way ahead of Antyr and
Estaan through the busy afternoon crowds. Grayle kept a
fraction to the rear of his brother, but matched his stride
exactly.

Antyr looked up. The grey clouds had been lightening all
day and were now breaking up to reveal a watery blue sky.
Occasionally, bright waves of light from the low sun washed
over the city, patterning the streets with long unsteady
shadows and cutting golden chasms through the haze.

The small procession had no goal at the end of this journey.
Antyr had expressed a need to walk and think for a while
and this was the consequence. Pandra had remained at the
palace to rest a little and to luxuriate in the rooms and the
new status that had been allotted to him.

Both Antyr and Estaan, however, were now rapt in
thought.

Antyr was surprised at his own easy acquiescence with the
Duke's suggestion – order – that he spy on the Bethlarii
envoy's dreams. A dreamer allowed a Dream Finder access
to his or her deepest and most private thoughts and however
the craft might have declined over recent years, the respect
for confidentiality was as strong as it had ever been, even
gaining protection under Serenstad's law.

And it was deep in Antyr also. That fact he had never
doubted throughout his ragged, sour career. The idea of
divulging a client's dreams was unthinkable, physically
distressing.

Now, quite willingly, he had agreed not only to divulge
the contents of a man's dreams, but to enter them unasked;
an even greater breach of his craft's time-honoured
constraints. What surprised him most, however, was that he
felt not the slightest twinge of remorse or hesitation.

The logic of his case he had stated spontaneously and with
great clarity when the Duke asked him to undertake the
covert search of the envoy's dreams, but he felt strangely
uneasy about the fact that he was suffering no emotional

rejection of the idea. Indeed, he was actually looking forward to the venture.

Who am I to set aside the practice of centuries so casually, even for such an important need? he thought.

'Probably the first who's had the chance.' Tarrian was unequivocal in his opinion. 'Ibris is nothing if not an original thinker. Besides what *are* you fussing about? What he's asked you to do is no different from crawling through hedges and ditches to see the strength and disposition of an enemy's forces. You don't all march to battlefield wearing blindfolds, and then whip them off and start fighting on the stroke of the hour, so that no one has an unfair advantage, do you?'

Antyr rebelled at Tarrian's mockery. 'No,' he began. 'It's not the same at all—'

'Of course it is, you jackass,' Tarrian said brutally. 'This envoy hasn't asked you to search his dreams so you're not betraying any special confidentiality. You're merely peeping into his documents. Under other circumstances, it'd be tortured out of him, you know that. This is a war you're talking about, and spying's an infinitely lesser evil. We might find things that'll save hundreds of lives. Look around you. Some of these people will be killed if there's a major war; particularly the young ones. Many of them will lose someone they know or love, and every one of them will suffer some form of hardship, whether it's shortage of food or just extra taxation. Where's the problem?' He did not wait for a reply. 'And if we come across nothing worthwhile, then where's the harm?'

'Yes, I know,' Antyr admitted, looking round at the late afternoon crowds. 'You're only echoing my own thoughts, but it still feels strange that I don't feel strange about it.'

'Too complicated for me, I'm afraid,' Tarrian said with a dismissive grunt. 'I suggest you enjoy the fresh air and the walk, it might be a busy night.'

Antyr nodded. There was no point in prolonging the debate. If debate it was, with so little being spoken for the defence of the envoy's rights. He would do what the Duke had asked for many reasons, but high among them was a determination that if he could use his skills to spare others the experiences that he had had on the battlefield then he would use them. Perhaps, indeed, that was what such skills were truly for.

His left hand moved across to his right, not for the first

time, to fiddle with the ring that Feranc had given to him before he had left the palace. 'This is a token of high office, Antyr,' he said. 'Don't hesitate to use it when you need it.' Surreptitiously, Antyr glanced at it again. It bore the Duke's insignia.

'Yes, you're right,' he said out loud.

'I beg your pardon,' Estaan said, starting from his own reverie and turning to him in some surprise.

'No, I beg yours,' Antyr replied hastily. 'I was talking to Tarrian privately. I won't do it again. *We* won't do it again, will we, Tarrian?'

'No,' echoed Tarrian's voice in his head. 'I'm sorry, it was thoughtless of me to leave you out, Estaan.'

Estaan shook his head slightly and then looked at Antyr. 'It's a strange sensation this speaking into the head without sound. How do you do it?'

Antyr laughed and raised his hands in an admission of ignorance. 'How do you walk? How do you breathe?' he asked. 'I've no idea how we do it. It's just something we were born with. An ability to see a little way into one another's minds, and to speak without talking. Many things about Dream Finding are profoundly strange and not remotely understood.'

Estaan's eyes narrowed. 'You *can* see into people's minds then,' he said, as if confirming a suspicion. There was a slight edge to his voice that made Antyr suddenly nervous.

It was Tarrian who answered however. 'No, he can't,' he replied. 'Except in so far as I enable him to. But I can.'

'How much, how easily?' Estaan asked, almost sharply.

'It depends,' Tarrian replied quietly. 'Sometimes the house is open, lights blazing, and I can wander easily from room to room. Sometimes it's locked up tight and I can scarcely peer through the windows.' His voice became firm. 'But I don't look unless I'm asked to, or unless I think someone represents a danger.'

Estaan looked down at him suspiciously. 'How do I know you're not searching my mind right now?' he asked awkwardly.

'You don't,' Tarrian replied bluntly. 'You have to trust me. You have to ask, is this wolf an honourable man? and then weigh the implications of your answer.'

Estaan paused and looked at Tarrian again. 'You're teasing me, I gather,' Estaan said.

'Only a lot,' Tarrian said, with a laugh. 'But, I'll answer your real question if you wish.'

'What do you mean?' Estaan said defensively.

'I mean that there are times when I hear people without intending to. As I am with you now,' Tarrian replied.

The group was broken up momentarily by a boisterous crowd of apprentices emerging from a building. They ran off down the street, laughing and shouting.

'What do you mean?' Estaan repeated as the apprentices receded, at the same time lifting his hand to shield it from the suddenly brilliant sunlight flooding the street.

'I can hear you when you shout,' Tarrian replied. 'It's a common problem with humans, they're invariably shouting. They seem to have little or no control over their minds. We spend most of our time trying not to listen.'

'I don't understand,' Estaan said, becoming almost agitated in his manner.

'The answer to your question is, no, I know nothing of your history before you and the other Mantynnai came to this land,' Tarrian said firmly. 'If it's any consolation to you, it's in some dark, closed portion of your mind which, believe me, nothing would possess me to enter. And such bits as leak out, I refuse utterly to heed. Does that answer your question?'

Estaan stopped walking and put his hand to his mouth pensively. 'Yes,' he said, after a moment. 'I'm sorry I doubted you, but what did—'

'Ask him yourself. That was nothing to do with me,' Tarrian interrupted brusquely.

As if compelled against his will, Estaan turned to Antyr. 'What did you mean when you said I was tortured?' he asked.

Antyr met his gaze. The sun struck the faces of the two men throwing half of them into deep shadow. 'I don't know,' he said. 'I spoke as I felt. I meant you no insult or pain. I said also that you have strange deep strengths within you. All of this I still feel. What do you want me to say?'

Estaan let out a deep breath. 'Nothing,' he said, after a long pause. 'I'm sorry. So many strange things are happening. Old memories, old feelings, are rising to the surface that we . . . I . . . had thought long buried. It's as though some great force is beginning to shake the whole world, and do what we may, we'll not be able to avoid the consequences.'

Antyr offered no reply. Estaan's thoughts chimed too much with his own.

318

Abruptly Estaan straightened up, as if the simple speaking of his concerns had released him from them. 'Still, we can do no more than fight the fight we find ourselves in, can we? And stay alert and aware if we want to survive. Nothing worse can happen to us than has already happened. And this time we'll be ready.'

Antyr let this enigmatic remark pass. He had not relished this inadvertent excursion into the dark reaches of the Mantynnai's mind, brief though it had been.

'Talking about survival,' he said, snatching at the word. 'When I was in the Threshold I had everything with me that I had had in Nyriall's room.' He rattled the contents of his pockets to demonstrate. 'The traditional formal dress for a Dream Finder includes a sword and two daggers and that must be why, so that they'd be armed if they entered the Threshold. In future I intend to wear a sword and carry at least two daggers, so that I can defend myself if need arises. Will you help me choose some weapons and give me some advice about using them?'

Estaan looked uncertain whether to be concerned or amused. 'Tut tut,' he said, opting for the latter and turning to the regulations governing the military responsibilities of Serenstad's citizens. 'Every adult male Serens is supposed to keep and maintain . . .' He began to count on his fingers. ' . . . A pike, a bow and three score arrows, carry at all times a serviceable sword, and—'

Antyr raised a pleading hand. 'I'm serious,' he said. 'I need your help. That was a real world I found myself in and apart from the storm, that was a real sword that someone drew against me. And Nyriall said that he found himself on the edge of some great battle at one stage.' He became earnest. 'I've done basic swordwork and I've had to use one once or twice in combat. I didn't kill anyone, I don't think, but I just need—'

'I'm sorry,' Estaan said, recanting his light-heartedness. 'I'll help you in any way I can.' Antyr looked relieved, but Estaan looked at him solemnly. He took his arm, fatherly almost. 'You must understand, Antyr. Fighting alone, man to man, is different from fighting in the line. A weapon doesn't make a warrior. That comes from inside. Reliance on a weapon can literally prove fatal. Without the true knowledge of your worth to yourself, carrying a sword may only mean that you're carrying it for your enemy to take and use against you. It may be that you're stronger and better protected, unarmed.'

Antyr looked at him uncertainly. 'I think I understand,' he said cautiously. 'And the reason I haven't got a sword is *because* I've had to use one in the past; I left it on the field. But now I'd like one about me again, and such advice as you can offer about how I should use it.'

Estaan smiled the sad smile of the professional warrior for the reluctant amateur. 'You shall have both,' he said. 'And the best I can find.'

The sinking sun began to turn red, turning Ibris's dazzling city into one of glittering ruby and garnet. A few delicate pink clouds drifted idly overhead, but on the horizon they were lowering black. Antyr twisted the ring on his finger again and then turned back towards the palace.

Later, he prepared himself for the clandestine observation of the Bethlarii envoy. Feranc showed him the envoy's quarters. The man's bed was in a corner. 'I've had the rooms behind and to the side, emptied,' Feranc said. 'Choose whichever you feel will be the best for your vigil.'

Tarrian and Grayle sniffed around the room curiously. Antyr looked at the bed. Its sheets and covers were obviously of the finest quality and delicately decorated with embroidered patterns. But they had been pulled back and meticulously folded in a manner that could only have been done by a soldier.

The sight brought memories back to him of his own time in barracks and the strange mixture of loneliness and close companionship that the disciplined communal living had inspired. For the first time since he had accepted the Duke's order, he felt a twinge of remorse at the 'ambushing' of this man, virtually alone among his enemies. It did not deflect him from his intention to fulfil the order, nor set aside the reasons for it, but, ironically, it made him feel a little easier.

'It'll make no difference,' he said. 'Choose the one which will be the least disturbed during the night.'

Feranc placed him in the side room. It was furnished identically to that of the envoy, but Tarrian and Grayle nevertheless examined it just as thoroughly.

'What time will he retire?' Antyr asked, sitting on the edge of the bed.

Feranc smiled slightly. 'Fairly soon, I think. He's responded to lord Menedrion in largely the same way that the lord has responded to him. There's certainly no anxiety by either to be longer in one another's presence than necessary.'

He paused in the doorway. 'Is there any danger in this . . . procedure?' he asked.

Antyr shook his head. 'No,' he said. 'It's very common. Usually it's done when someone's been having serious nightmares. You can either wake them up, or, preferably, talk them through it to remind them it is only a dream and make them feel in control. Besides, with Estaan guarding the door, two Companions guiding me, and this sword by my side, I've never been so well protected.'

Feranc glanced at the sword dubiously. 'Will that actually be . . . there . . . with you? In the dream?' he asked.

Antyr shook his head. 'Not in the dream,' he said. 'But if somehow I'm drawn into the Threshold again, then it'll be with me there, I'm sure.'

'I won't pretend to understand,' Feranc said after a thoughtful pause. 'Just . . .' he shrugged. 'Take care.' He seemed to dismiss his concerns and became practical. 'That's a Mantynnai sword, you realize. Longer and differently balanced to the standard infantry issue. Can you use it?'

Antyr shook his head again. 'Not well, I should imagine,' he replied. 'But I'd rather have it than not. Estaan has lent it to me.'

Feranc nodded doubtfully then looked intently into Antyr's darkening eyes. 'If you find yourself in danger, you must follow the *true* warrior's way. Listen, avoid, fly if you can, fight only if you must.'

He spoke very quietly and without any dramatic emphasis, but the words seemed to break over Antyr like a great wave, imparting meanings to him that were far beyond the apparent content of the words.

'Thank you,' he stammered, resting his hand awkwardly on the hilt of his sword. 'I'll remember.'

'And if you have to draw that thing, keep it simple,' Feranc went on, nodding at the sword. 'Straight lunge, straight cut, basic parries. And fly as soon as you can.'

He was gone before Antyr could speak again.

Estaan, standing nearby, blew out a long breath. 'I couldn't have taught you that much in a year,' he said. 'What a man. I told you that being a warrior came from inside.' He turned to Antyr. 'How did you feel when he spoke?' he asked.

Antyr dithered. 'Ineffective,' he said after an unhappy search for the right word.

Estaan patted his stomach. 'So did I. And I understand what he's talking about. Remember how he was, when he did that to you, and be the same,' he said. 'I know I will.'

Feranc's influence seemed still to fill the room, and the two men spoke very little as they waited for the envoy to be brought to his room.

'Let go of him now,' Tarrian said softly to both of them after a while. 'Or we'll carry his presence into the dream and be detected for sure. He's only done what any good teacher does; shown you what you already knew.'

'Yes,' Antyr said simply, swinging his legs up on to the bed and self-consciously adjusting his sword.

'What do you want me to do?' Estaan asked.

'Nothing.' The two wolves and Antyr replied simultaneously, making Estaan start.

Antyr laughed. 'Just guard the door and don't allow anyone in, except Pandra,' he said.

The sound of voices coming along the passage outside ended the exchange.

'It's Menedrion and the envoy,' Estaan whispered.

Antyr nodded then looked down at Tarrian and Grayle. The eyes of both the wolves were bright yellow. Briefly he was looking up at himself, his eyes black and cavernous. It happened twice as each of the wolves exchanged with him. Grayle's body felt different from Tarrian's but the exchange was too rapid for him to search out where the differences lay.

He lay back and motioned Estaan to silence.

The Mantynnai relaxed back into a large chair from which he could see both the bed and the door. The two wolves both circled a little before spiralling down gently to lie by the bed.

Menedrion's forced heartiness could be heard even through the closed door, as could its failure to impinge upon the envoy, whose harsh voice spoke only once, briefly, before the door to his room closed.

It was followed by the sound of further muffled speech and footsteps which Antyr identified as Menedrion leaving and the guards taking position outside the envoy's room.

He reached out to Tarrian and Grayle. 'Very gently,' he said. 'Be very aware; very still.'

They waited in silence for a long time. All four listening and still. No sound came from the adjacent room except the occasional anonymous bump, until eventually a low murmuring began to seep through to them.

'He's praying,' Antyr said. Somehow the sound hardened his heart. He knew a little of the Bethlarii religion and its simplistic demands for mindless obedience that sent its more zealous followers into murderous fighting frenzies on the battlefield, as careless of their own lives as of their enemies'. He had lost friends and come near to dying himself at the insane hands of such people.

He carried too, he knew, a portion of his father's moderately intolerant attitude to religions in general. 'Religions illuminate no truth, it's truth that illuminates religion,' he would say, adding forcefully, when he began to get heated, 'and we're all responsible for our own actions. Looking to blame some invisible deity for what we do is neither logical nor acceptable in a civilized people.'

The murmuring ceased as if at the command of Petran's long-dead voice.

Within minutes, Antyr felt the enveloping blackness that told him that the envoy was asleep. Tarrian and Grayle carried him silently into it.

For a long time nothing happened as the envoy passed to and fro through different levels of sleep. Images and random thoughts came and went. Coherent arguments and plans began to form, only to disappear into rambling nonsense. Violence against a sycophantic image of Menedrion was predominant. Antyr smiled slightly; doubtless Pandra would experience the converse of these thoughts when he came to guard Menedrion later.

They waited. Here there would be no search for the Nexus, no hunt for the dream. Here they would merely observe.

It's coming.

Antyr felt the whispering approach of the dream almost as soon as did the two wolves. The sensitivity and speed of his response gave him, for the first time, a measure of the changes that had happened to him over the past days. It was truly startling, but his control too, was growing equally and no ripple of surprise reached up from within him to reveal his silent presence in the envoy's mind.

Then they were there. Dream Finder and the Dreamselves of his two Companions at one with the Bethlarii envoy, Grygyr Ast-Darvad, walking slowly down a long avenue of columns. Tall and ghostly in the brilliant moonlight, the columns soared up dizzily into the night sky until, somewhere far beyond his sight, great arches would join them together to support the star-loaded heavens. On these arches and winding, snakelike, down the columns were carved the epic tales of the battles that Ar-Hyrdyn had fought on his way first from man to hero, then to god and, finally, to the conquest of the ancient gods themselves, to learn that he himself had been the original creator of all things, treacherously tricked and bound in the world of men by his jealous offspring.

Now, all bowed their heads before him, obedient to his every whim.

Beyond the columns, dark trees stood, solid, black, and eternally patient. In the depths of these forests waited the myriad red-eyed hunting beasts of Ar-Hyrdyn. These he used to hunt down the spirits of those who had died fleeing the battlefield, or who had betrayed their companions. Terrible and long was the rending fate of such souls.

Grygyr could feel the relentless stares of Ar-Hyrdyn's creatures, but he was safe. No such fate awaited him? Was he not true to the faith in its every particular? Was he not, even now, in the midst of his enemies, stern, aloof, fearless of death, and unyielding to their effete and decadent lures?

The envoy's self-righteous anger and corrosive hatred was repellent to Antyr, but he made no stir.

Turning to his left Grygyr looked up at the moon. It was the moon of this world. Larger and brighter by far than the moon of the waking world, it dominated the sky so oppressively, that he felt he could reach up and touch it.

Its face was scarred and pocked, giving it a diseased and bloated appearance.

Even the heavens had felt the touch of Ar-Hyrdyn's wrath.

Grygyr returned his gaze to the journey before him. He had travelled it many times.

Ahead, the roadway gleamed white in the moonlight. But it was not paved with marble as it might be in some temple. It was a continuous mass of bones; human bones. They were more numerous than the pebbles on a storm beach, and they sloped up on either side of him, forming a shallow valley. At the centre, where he walked, the bones were crushed and broken, and with each footfall, white dust rose to powder his booted feet.

Grygyr exulted. Thus ended all those who opposed the one

and only true god; crushed utterly beneath the feet of his invincible army. The army that would one day open its ranks and greet him, Grygyr Ast-Darvad, as one of their own when finally he fell in battle. He stood tall and proud at the prospect of such glory.

In the far distance was a light like a low, brilliant, star. This was his destination. The great Golden Hall of Ar-Hyrdyn, where his army would be singing and carousing after their day's fighting. This time he would come to it.

His stomach tightened with desire and determination, and he started to stride out. Apart from his lust to come to the Golden Hall, Grygyr knew that the god had no welcome for the slow and tardy.

Despite his best efforts, however, the journey became as it always had before; the distant light seemed to come no nearer. Yet the road under his feet bore increasing evidence of the passage of Ar-Hyrdyn's army. So vast must it be and so fierce its tread, that the bones which formed the road here had been crushed to a dust so fine and deep that his feet began to sink in it, making each step an ordeal.

Onward, relentlessly, he moved; his legs first protesting and then screaming with pain as he dragged each foot from the yielding yet clinging dust. His face, however, remained set and emotionless. The journey was ever thus, and to show distress would be to find himself rejected ε* the very threshold of the Golden Hall itself.

Thus, though his pace slowed, he held his posture tall and proud.

A breeze came purposefully, mockingly, out of the night and began to blow the stinging dust into his face. It stuck to his sweating face, caking his dried lips, clogging his nostrils, and sealing his eyelids.

He wiped his eyes. Still the golden beacon was ahead of him; blurred and streaked, but a little nearer, perhaps?

At the thought, his legs sank suddenly to their calves in the dust.

He looked up. The moon had grown larger, more oppressive, adding its mighty weight to his burden.

The sound of his gasping breath and pounding heart filled the universe. Then came the despair. Would there be no end to this?

'Did you think that the journey to the Golden Hall of Ar-Hyrdyn would be so light a journey?' came a voice within him. It was his true self taunting his weakness. He accepted its rebuke.

Yet his legs slowed in their rhythm. Slower . . . and . . . slower . . .

They must not stop. To seek rest here would be to die. And to die here, a mortal, chosen as Ar-Hyrdyn's messenger and allowed to this most sacred of places, would not only be to die away from the battlefield, it would be the foulest sacrilege. His days for all eternity would be filled with the terrible sound of Ar-Hyrdyn's hunting horn and the howling of his beasts as they pursued and tore at him forever.

He sank now almost up to his knees, but still he moved, wrenching his legs free from the clinging dust. And still the golden light drew him on.

Faintly, on the stinging breeze, he thought he heard the sound of Ar-Hyrdyn's warriors; encouraging him? Or were they just singing and laughing, unaware of his fate, his presence even? It made no difference. This time he would be among them; one of them. He would not yield. No pain, no fatigue could keep him from such fulfilment; could keep him from his destiny.

Abruptly, and not knowing how he came there, he was on all fours, his hands sinking into the dust. Anger welled up inside him at his body's silent treachery. He must not crawl, like some craven slave! He must stand, and walk.

Somewhere in the dark forest beyond the columns, something howled in anticipation.

Antyr felt Tarrian's and Grayle's wolf spirits responding to the call, but his will helped them to keep silent and still.

Somehow, Grygyr came to his feet, goading himself forward with the memories of ordeals he had survived before. He opened his mouth to cry out, 'I will come there, Lord, I will come there, though it take a myriad lifetimes for each step.' But the dust blew into his mouth, acrid, gritty, choking.

Then the whole world shook.

He closed his eyes in a mixture of fear and expectation.

When he opened them, it was to see the terrible figure of Ar-Hyrdyn himself before him. The great god of the Bethlarii towered high into the night sky, black against the huge glaring moon which, drawn by the god's presence, had swollen even further and swung silently behind him to form a ghastly backdrop.

As it always did, a fascinated terror filled Grygyr at the sight of this apparition.

'Did you think that the journey to the Golden Hall of Ar-Hyrdyn would be so light a journey?' the figure said, echoing Grygyr's own thoughts, in a voice that sounded like rolling thunder and that shook Grygyr to his very soul.

The god extended his hand and the distant light rose into the air until it passed in front of the moon and Grygyr could no longer look at it, so bright was the moonlight.

'Lord, I will do whatever is your wish, to gain your favour,' he said, trembling and lowering his eyes.

'You will do whatever is my wish,' the figure announced definitively.

Face still set and resolute, Grygyr came to attention. The ground was now hard under his feet.

There was a long, timeless pause, then the voice rumbled, 'Still you live.'

Grygyr's eye widened. 'The Duke is a cunning and devious foe, Lord,' he said hastily. 'He fights like a poisoning woman, not a man. He has ignored my insults and issued loud public promises for my safety, so that only by attempting his life can I make the Serens end my own. And to act thus now would be to broadcast my treachery across the land and turn the wavering cities against us—'

'This I know!' the voice thundered savagely. 'This I ordained so that in living when you strove to die, you would learn the subtle ways of your enemy.'

The black form became alive with a billowing thundercloud movement, shot through with flickering lightning.

'Forgive me, Lord,' Grygyr said hoarsely, looking down again.

The thunder subsided. 'Your loyalty is known and will be rewarded, my priest,' the figure said, almost conciliatory. 'And you have done in Serenstad all that was required of you. Whendrak now will be the lure. Return home now and note what you would note as a soldier as you pass through their land for when you pass through it again with a victorious army at your back.'

'I shall, Lord,' Grygyr replied fervently. 'I have already learned much. I—'

'Go now,' the voice said.

Grygyr hesitated. Was he to be denied tonight? He ventured, 'Lord, may I not look again upon your domain so that I may better describe its wonders to your followers?'

There was a strange silence, an unexpected hesitation. Then the huge figure seemed to grow in size until it filled the entire sky. Grygyr quailed before it.

'You presume,' came the terrible reply. 'Go now before you anger us further with your mortal folly. You are put in the balance again. We shall return at some other time and consider your worth then. Be faithful and true, priest.'

'Your justice is boundless, Lord, I—'

Before he could finish, a great horn call rang out and the air was suddenly filled with the cries of countless hunting animals. Grygyr looked in terror from side to side. All around, dark shapes were running out of the dark shadow of the forests. He looked up at the figure, but it was gone. Only the monstrous moon remained, and it was slowly turning red.

'Go now,' said an echoing voice out of the emptiness.

Grygyr screamed.

'No! Lord!'

He raised his hands to protect his head as the shadows closed in on him. He felt their hot, fetid breath. He screamed again.

Then the ground under his feet became dust again, sucking him down, down, down. He thrashed his arms in flailing panic, but still he sank. And still the black creatures neared. The dust rose up past his chest, his throat. It poured into his edges of his closed mouth, forced itself into his nose, his eyes, his ears, and finally closed over his head.

He felt the cold breeze blowing through his clutching fingers, then savage jaws closed about them . . .

Antyr opened his eyes. There was a bumping sound from the adjacent room, as if the envoy were drumming against the wall.

Antyr grimaced as indignation and horror swept over him. It was partly his own, partly that of Tarrian and Grayle. The power, the terrible skills of the men, that had murdered Nyriall, that had been at the heart of all the events of the past days, stood clear in the envoy's dream.

Scarcely one jot of it had been of his own making. They had taken his most primitive fears and desires and woven them into the images of their will, to use him like some grotesque puppet. To the Dream Finder and his Companions, it was obscene beyond belief.

'Mankind unfettered is beyond all understanding,' Tarrian said, scratching at the floor in bitter frustration.

'What's the matter?' Estaan asked, yawning.

'The envoy's had his dream,' Antyr replied quietly, wiping his forehead. 'Poor devil.' He sat up and swung his legs on to the floor. The two wolves stood up and came close to him. He stroked them both.

'You seemed quiet enough,' Estaan said, wide awake now. 'Not like at Nyriall's. Did anything interesting happen?'

Antyr, however, was still in quiet communion with his Companions. 'If I had the power that these creatures have, I'd shine a great light into the souls of these benighted people,' he said, voicing his thoughts. 'Turn them away from their grim beliefs, turn them to knowledge and beauty. Not use it to deepen and darken their ignorance still further.'

He took the two wolves by the scruffs of their necks and shook them both gently. 'What say you, dogs?' he said.

'Whoever they are, they're powerful and skilful,' Tarrian replied. 'Who knows what devilment they intend. We must hunt them down and destroy them.'

'And you, Grayle?' Antyr asked.

'They took Nyriall from me at a whim,' Grayle replied. 'I need nothing other than that to kill them.'

The wolf's single-mindedness was chilling. Antyr patted him.

'Please, tell me what's happened,' Estaan said plaintively.

'We must waken the Duke,' Antyr said, ignoring the plea.

'At this time of night!' Estaan exclaimed. 'Is it essential? I doubt he's had much sleep these past two nights. What's going on?'

Antyr looked at him thoughtfully. 'You're right,' he said, then he looked at the two wolves, their eyes yellow, their postures expectant.

He nodded, and lay back on the bed. The two wolves lay down also and, with a knowing nod, Estaan relaxed back into his chair.

'Find the Duke,' Antyr said to the two wolves.

The Dreamselves of the two wolves hurtled into the darkness.

Chapter 25

Darkness. Twittering wisps of fading dreams.

'Sire?'

Recognition.

'Antyr? How . . .? I'm not dreaming. Am I?'

'No, sire. But you are asleep. I've sought you thus to tell you that the men who slew Nyriall and who have troubled us these past nights, have visited the envoy.'

'Visited?' Alarm. Guards! 'How?'

'Rest easy, sire. They came through his dreams. They conjured the form of the Bethlarii god Ar-Hyrdyn from him, and tormented him cruelly. He is Ar-Hyrdyn's priest.'

'I feel your pain and anger, Dream Finder. Are you certain it was they?'

'Beyond doubt, sire. Their presence is unmistakable. And they faltered and then punished him when he asked to see their domain again.'

'I do not understand.'

'They have perhaps tempted him before with some joy in the Threshold, but since my arrival there to protect Nyriall, they are uncertain about their mastery there.'

Appreciation. 'To what end was this visitation?'

'I cannot say, but it was to no good one. He was to have died here, at our hands, seemingly, but *your* will prevailed. Now, he is to live and return home.'

'Why?'

'They say his task is finished . . . or changed. He has been spying, and he will spy further.'

Indifference. 'He is a soldier.'

Silence.

'What did you learn of these . . . men . . . who can enter and change dreams thus?'

'They are powerful, skilful, and malevolent.'

'What is their intention?'

'I do not know. But it is evil beyond anything we have known before. They said that Whendrak is now the lure.'

The lure . . .? 'To what?'

'I do not know.' Anger. 'I know only that they must be sought out and destroyed.'

Surprise. 'There is the law yet, Dream Finder.' A reproof.

'They are demented in their evil, and beyond all law, save kill or be killed, Ibris.'

'I hear you, wolf, and shall weigh your judgement in due time.'

'I am not of your pack or your kind, Ibris, and thus am beyond your judgement, just as they are beyond your reach. They are also beyond all reason and too dangerous to live. When we meet, they or we shall die. Their deeds dictate their sentence.'

Silence.

'I hear you still, wolf. And trust you. What shall *I* do?'

'Lead your people, pack leader. War is coming.'

'And what shall you do, Antyr?'

'Find them.'

'How? Where?'

Silence.

'And when you find them?'

'I am changed.'

'Indeed. I feel your power. But—?'

'Lead your people, sire. I shall tell you what I can, when I can, if I can. Guard our bodies as need arises.'

'But—'

'Do this, sire.'

Silence. Doubt. Resignation.

'Rest now, sire.'

Snuffling, searching, finding, wolfish chuckling. 'A gift, Ibris. An old and joyous dream. Sleep in peace. You are guarded in all places by a great and ancient strength.'

Darkness.

Chapter 26

Arwain looked along the broad valley towards Whendrak.
Rooftops, towers and pinnacles floated on a light morning
mist which was turning yellow in the rising sun. The air was
cold and damp, but fresh and clean.

Whendrak was no Serenstad, but it was a fine, lively city.
Its architecture mingled the spartan Bethlarii style with that
of the ebullient, adventurous, Serens, and showed an equal
irreverence for both. It was distinct and unmistakably
characteristic. As were the Whendreachi; honed by the
generations of warfare that had passed over them.

Rising out of the mist, the city was a beautiful sight, but
for those who knew it, the valley carried too many memories
for the scene to be observed untainted. Throughout the long
history of the land, bitter battle after bitter battle had been
fought there over Whendrak, and where the birds were now
rising in song with the burgeoning day, the awful screaming
song of battle had many times held sway. And the dew-soaked
grasses now darkening under the horses' hooves had as many
times been prodigally drenched in blood.

Arwain had a great sympathy, and no small affection, for
the Whendreachi, though it was not to be denied that they
were a hard, obdurate and abrasive people. They seemed to
possess an uncanny knack for self-destruction which was
matched only by their seemingly relentless will to survive.
And these two attributes they bound together with an acidic,
graveyard humour. They tended to be both the delight and
the despair of thinking people.

Arwain shook his head as he looked at the city. What the
devil was going on there now? Would it prove to be no more
than a little local political intriguing? Or would it be some
ugly burst of tribal anger threatening to bring riot and terror
to the streets and striking the sparks that could lead to war.
Or . . .

He dismissed his conjectures. He would find out soon
enough when he reached the city and he would have to think
on his feet then, unclouded by too many prior judgements.

Nonetheless, he was still uneasy. It was true that of the travellers they had passed on the road, more than usual seemed to be entire families moving wholesale, and many bore a harassed, if not fearful, look about them. But that, though ominous, was not the main cause of his present concern. That came from the conduct of the Mantynnai among his guard.

In the night he had half woken from a fitful sleep to hear the low murmur of voices nearby. Turning, he saw that it was a group sitting around the campfire. They were talking softly but earnestly – agitatedly even – from their gestures. His eyes closing of their own volition, Arwain had made no effort to listen to what they were saying, but words had floated over to him. Strange foreign words, resonant and strong, that in some way made him feel a poor, inadequate creature. The men were the Mantynnai, he realized as he drifted into sleep again. And they were holding this soft, anxious debate in their own language.

Now, in the cold morning, he saw the incident as yet another in the strange chain of events that had started with their chance meeting with Estaan in the crowded Moras street, and gone on to the equally chance encounter with the two riders on the bridge. Seemingly trivial incidents which had left the unshakable Mantynnai uncertain and even defensive.

On an impulse, he signalled the platoon to halt, then motioned Ryllans forward, out of earshot of the others.

'You disturbed me with your debate last night,' he said, looking intently at him.

Ryllans did not reply immediately. 'I'm sorry, sir,' he said flatly after a moment.

'Ryllans, it's not enough,' Arwain went on, fighting down a twist of anger at this offhand reply. 'In all the years I've known you, I've never heard you use your own language, even in private when you were alone with your compatriots. And I've never seen you so . . . uncontrolled . . . so unsettled. We may be riding into great danger here, as you yourself pointed out. I must know what's happened that could so unman my father's finest guards before I risk entering Whendrak.'

Ryllans met his gaze unflinchingly. He opened his mouth to speak, but Arwain spoke first.

'Elder to younger, Ryllans,' he said. 'No deceit, no equivocation.'

334

Ryllans' expression softened and he almost smiled. 'An excellent throw, sir,' he said. 'A finely judged lack of opposition to overwhelm me. You're an apt pupil.'

'And none of that either,' Arwain said sternly. 'I want the truth. Now!'

Ryllans turned towards the city and shook his head regretfully. 'I'm sorry,' he said. 'I told you yesterday, it is truly not my story to tell.'

Arwain's eyes narrowed, but Ryllans reached out and took his arms, almost fatherlike.

'You're correct,' he said. 'We are . . . disturbed.' He hesitated. 'Echoes from our past have reached us. Rolling out of nowhere like thunder out of a cloudless summer sky.' Pain came into his face but he crushed it. 'Echoes of a past of guilt and shame for which we try ever to atone. Two great blows came yesterday. Separate. But coming together like hammer and anvil. The evil we . . . followed.' He forced the word out. 'And thought dead, is perhaps with us again. And those we wronged are come to seek us out.'

'The two riders?' Arwain exclaimed, his face disbelieving. 'Two men! How could two men exact retribution from you? Besides, you have the protection of all of Serenstad if you need it, you know that. And whatever you may have done, it's long atoned for by your service here.'

'They have the law of our homeland with them. And right,' Ryllans said simply. 'And they will seek an accounting, not retribution. Punishment will lie in the hands of others.'

His voice and his whole manner were oddly fatalistic. Arwain put his hand to his head. 'I don't understand,' he said. 'We have our own law here. And no one can—'

Ryllans' hand tightened about his arm. 'I told you this, because our shock had infected you and was likely to mar your judgement,' he said. 'What I told you yesterday about Whendrak is still also true.' He pointed towards the city. 'There is what must occupy your full attention now.' There was a hint of anger in his voice. 'We are not unmanned. We are warriors. We move as an attack demands, when it demands. Where there is no foreknowledge, there can be no forethought. And there is never true foreknowledge. *That* you should know already. We are your Mantynnai, you have our hearts, spirits, and sword arms unimpaired, here and now. Serve us and Serenstad similarly in Whendrak, Ibris's son. All other things in their due time.'

Though softly spoken, Ryllans' words impinged on Arwain powerfully. He struggled to find words of his own that would answer the Mantynnai's ruthless logic, but none came.

Instead, he laid his hand on the hand that was holding his arm and gripped it powerfully in acceptance, then he signalled the platoon forward.

They approached the city at a leisurely walk and with the Duke's pennant well displayed, if a little reluctant to flutter in the still morning air.

'They're extending their walls,' Ryllans said as they drew nearer. He pointed.

Arwain followed his finger and saw the cobwebs of scaffolding blurring the line of the walls. 'They're a neutral city, they can do what they want,' he said with a slight shrug. 'But it's not good. The Whendreachi wouldn't spend money like that if they weren't very concerned about something.'

They continued in silence until they came to the first gate. It was closed, and a small crowd of people were gathered in front of it, waiting with surly patience for it to be opened. A large burly man sitting on a rock by the side of the gate looked up as Arwain's platoon arrived. Seeing them, he shook his head wearily and stood up, taking hold of the leading rein of a string of donkeys as he did so.

Muttering to himself, he walked over to a wicket door in the gate and began beating on it with a massive clenched fist.

'Come on!' he bellowed, in the unmistakable Whendreachi accent. 'Get off your lazy backsides in there. I've got this lot to deliver, there's two midwives, three joiners, a ruptured mason and god knows how many other folk out here with a living to earn.' He banged again. There was some laughter among the crowd at his manner, and voices were raised in support of his plaint.

'And there's a fortune-teller who's beginning to look decidedly worried,' the man went on, rising to the crowd. He winked at Arwain. 'And now the posh folks are starting to arrive. That's how late it is. Shift yourselves!'

Arwain lifted his hands to his face to disguise his amusement at the man's antics. Ryllans laughed openly.

Suddenly there was an angry rattling of bolts and chains, and the wicket was slammed open noisily. A guard emerged, catching his pike on the lintel and nearly tripping as he struggled to release it. He was quite short and he looked decidedly harassed. He was also unimpressed by the applause that greeted his ungainly arrival.

'All right, all right. Stop all this row,' he said in a voice full of command and indignation until it cracked into a squeak.

'You get this sodding gate open and we'll stop, Erryk,' said the burly man. 'Some of us have got jobs to do, you know. Can't sit around the guard house brazier all day.'

The guard cleared his throat. 'It's not my job to open the gate,' he said, hoarsely. 'The gateman's not turned up. And neither's the Exac.'

There was a spontaneous cheer from the crowd.

'You can't come in without paying your Gate Tax,' the guard protested.

'Nothing to do with us, Erryk,' the man continued. 'If he's not here, that's his problem. If he had an honest job he wouldn't be so reluctant to get up in the morning and do it.' He flicked a thumb towards the sun. 'Gate's supposed to be open at sun-up, not sun-down. That was the law before taxes were even thought of; part of the Ancient Rights, you know that. Come on, stop messing about, get this gate open.'

The crowd, though good-humoured, grew noisier in support of their impromptu leader, shouting and cheering with increasing vigour. Someone started to bang an iron pot, and others soon followed suit.

The guard dithered for a moment, then with an extravagant gesture of resignation, struggled back through the wicket gate. A moment or two later, after further bumping and rattling, the gate began to swing slowly open. Led by the burly man and his donkeys, the small crowd quickly surged forward into the widening opening. It was a rare event for the Gate Exactor to be absent, and not an opportunity to be missed.

'Thanks, Erryk,' the burly man shouted as he disappeared through the gate. He pointed to his donkeys. 'First egg that one of these lays today is yours.'

The guard drove the gate's large bolt into its housing with some venom then looked up at the retreating figure. Waving his fist, he shouted something that was too fast and too colloquial for Arwain to understand, thought it was patently not complimentary. Without turning, the burly man raised his hand in friendly acknowledgement.

'And stop calling me Erryk,' the guard managed irritably, as a parting shot, adding futilely, 'my name's—'

'Oi!'

Arwain had dismounted and was approaching the guard as this cry rang out. He started, thinking it was addressed to him.

'What d'you think you're doing? You can't do that,' the voice continued, laden with disbelief and righteous indignation.

Arwain identified the speaker. It was a short, stout individual, running, with some difficulty, towards the gate, and waving his arms. He was panting heavily when he eventually arrived.

'Can't do what?' the guard said crossly.

'Open the gate,' the stout man spluttered. 'Open the gate. You can't do that. That's a gateman's job. I'll . . . I'll have to report this—'

'Report your over-sleeping while you're at it,' the guard snapped peevishly. The stout man's chin came out defiantly, but the guard was not to be gainsaid. He levelled an angry, prodding, finger at the gateman. 'I had half the countryside outside here, threatening hell and all, because you couldn't shift out of your bed. What was I supposed to do? I'm responsible directly to the Council for the peace here, you know, not some sodding Guild contractor. If anyone's reporting anything here, it's going to be me.' He was beginning to warm to his subject. 'And that lazy Exac's no better. He—'

Arwain cleared his throat loudly. 'Excuse me, gentlemen,' he said, stepping forward.

The guard stopped and looked up at him.

'You haven't heard the last of this,' the gateman said spitefully, slipping this blow into the sudden silence, before scurrying off, grumbling to himself.

The guard snarled something after him then turned back to Arwain. 'Yes?' he said, frowning a Whendrak welcome at this newcomer.

With an effort, Arwain forced himself to remember Aaken's instructions.

'I am Arwain, son of Ibris, Duke of Serenstad,' he said formally. 'I have letters patent confirming this, and matters that I need to discuss with the leaders of your city. May I have your permission to enter with my escort?'

The guard's mouth slowly sagged open during this speech, and when it was finished, he began to execute a small, agitated dance, shifting his weight from foot to foot, his pike from hand to hand, and turning his head from side to side as if searching for help or escape.

He accompanied this dance with rhythmic stutterings which eventually merged into fairly coherent speech which, summarized, indicated that he didn't know what to do . . . And his officer was late . . . and . . . the Exactor . . . and the gateman . . . and he shouldn't be doing this duty really . . . he was supposed to be off sick . . .

He was rescued by the appearance of another guard; the tardy officer, Arwain judged. With a nod the new arrival dismissed the floundering guard into a nearby sentry post, then turned to Arwain inquiringly, at the same time casting a rapid glance over his escort.

Arwain repeated his introduction and request to enter the city.

This time he was successful.

Shortly afterwards, while the rest of the platoon waited in the forecourt of the Council's Meeting House, Arwain and Ryllans were being escorted by a group of guards into the presence of Whendrak's Maeran, the leader of the city's council, and its most powerful citizen.

As was allowed under the treaty, both men were still armed, but the waiting platoon had been obliged to leave its weapons at the city's gate.

Somewhat to Arwain's surprise, the Maeran was quite a short, inconsequential-looking man who exuded none of the power that Arwain had come to expect from leaders of men. Indeed his first impression was that the man looked more like a successful merchant than a politician.

'Sit down, gentlemen,' he said affably, indicating two chairs. Arwain noted that they faced the window, while the Maeran sat facing them with his back to it. He began to reconsider his first impression of the man.

He bowed. 'I have letters patent here for your inspection, Honoured Maeran,' he said, before he sat down. As he pulled out the documents, a large guard quietly appeared in front of him, his hand extended to receive them.

'They'll not be necessary, Lord Arwain,' the Maeran said, giving the guard a reassuring nod. 'I recognize you well enough. And this, if memory serves me right, is Commander

Ryllans of the Duke's Mantynnai, seconded to your own personal bodyguard.'

Arwain's surprise showed.

The Maeran smiled. 'I've been to Serenstad many times, lord,' he said. 'I'm well acquainted with the city, the palace, and, at least by sight, your father, yourself and your brothers.'

Arwain looked disconcerted. 'Honoured Maeran. I'm afraid I've no recollection of a visit by Whendreachi dignitaries ever,' he said, awkwardly.

The Maeran made a conciliatory gesture. 'Please, my title's a little cumbersome. My name's Haynar. I'm just a humble merchant,' he said. 'I go to Serenstad and many other places simply on matters of trade and business.' He nodded to himself. 'It's a marvellous, bustling place. Full of vigour and opportunities, for those who can seize them. Besides, formal receptions aren't to my taste, if I'm honest.' Then he shrugged. 'And as a neutral city, we like to avoid any actions that could be construed, however wrongly, as being partisan.'

'Do you travel also to Bethlar?' Arwain risked.

'Oh yes,' came the unhesitating reply. 'Though not as much. They do precious little in the way of trading and they aren't the happiest of people to be among.' He laughed. 'I don't suppose I should say that really in view of the fact that I'm at least three-quarters Bethlarii myself.'

The man's informality and joviality were infectious, but Arwain carefully avoided relaxing too much. He had seen his father use precisely the same technique to lure information gently from some unsuspecting individual.

'Anyway,' Haynar continued. 'I've sprung my little surprise, now perhaps you could spring yours.'

'I have nothing to spring, I hope, sir,' Arwain said, blandly. 'I was asked to come here by my father to seek information.'

Briefly he outlined the message that the Bethlarii envoy had brought to Serenstad.

As he spoke, Haynar began to tap his foot agitatedly.

'This is appalling,' he burst out, when Arwain had finished. He jabbed his forefinger into the arm of his chair. 'We won't tolerate it. Never again will we allow ourselves to be used as some kind of a pawn in the eternal games that Bethlar and Serenstad play,' he said fiercely, now very much a leader of men.

Arwain was taken aback. 'We play no game, sir,' he said earnestly. 'You said yourself, our city is a marvellous place, bustling with vigour and opportunity. The only opportunities in war are death and survival, and it was war that the Bethlarii envoy spoke of as a result of what was happening here. If you know Serenstad and its people at all, you know that we seek no war. We'll fight if we have to, but *only* if we have to, and with every reluctance. That's why I'm here, almost within a day of hearing them, to tell you of the Bethlarii's words and to ask you what truth lies in them, if any.'

Haynar's eyes narrowed. 'Let's not be naive, lord,' he said. 'There are other opportunities in war. Your brother's factories forge weapons as well as ploughshares and coach wheels. And he's a wild man. War might well suit many of his ends. And you've more than a few problems with some of your people that a war might judiciously alleviate.'

Arwain felt anger flare up inside him. Desperately he forced the image of his father into his mind; his father sitting calmly while the Bethlarii envoy had publicly insulted him. Sitting calmly and prevailing.

Surreptitiously he took a deep breath and released it slowly. 'I can't deny that there's a considerable element of truth in what you say, sir,' he said, as quietly as he could manage, though it made his tightened jaw ache. 'But if you feel that is the predominant element, then I must return to my father and confess that I have failed in my mission here, and advise him to send others, perhaps better suited to diplomacy.'

Haynar put his hand to his mouth casually, hiding further his already shaded face. He did not speak.

Arwain made to rise, but Haynar gently motioned him to remain seated. After a long pause, he stood up and walked over to the window.

'Did you notice the work on our walls as you arrived?' he said, almost absently, after a further pause.

Arwain replied that he had.

'Expensive,' Haynar said, shaking his head. 'And wasteful. Time, effort, resources. All could be better spent. But we intend to emulate your father, lord. We intend to be strong.' He turned to look at Arwain. 'Neutral,' he insisted, raising a hand in emphasis. 'But strong, resolute. Not aggressive.' He gave a short, grim laugh. 'The last thing we want is control over others. We're a people shaped through countless generations by the warfare of others, and we intend to use the peace that your father began to become a third force in the land. A force that will bind, us, Bethlar, Serenstad, *all*

341

the cities and towns, with a myriad of tiny bonds of trade, trust and blood, so complex and intricate that war will cease to exist as a practical alternative in solving disputes.'

Some merchant! Arwain thought.

'I commend you,' he said. 'As would my father, if you would not consider such a commendation to be demeaning.'

Haynar returned to his chair. 'Wouldn't your father be concerned that such a third power might combine with the Bethlarii to form an army that could take Serenstad's dominions from it as from a child, and then finally sweep the city itself aside?'

Arwain thought for a moment. 'He would consider it, I'm sure,' he said, with a slight smile. 'And he would watch, and listen. Which is no more than he does now. And should he see such a development beginning to occur, then he would ask you about it, probably very straightforwardly. Just as I asked you about the truth in the Bethlarii envoy's claims about the treatment of those they call their people here.'

Haynar raised his emphatic finger again. 'There are no Bethlarii people here. You know that,' he said. 'Nor Serens. There are only Whendreachi. What I just said; the work to the walls; the intention to be strong. This is their will.'

'Your vision though, Honoured Maeran?' Arwain said.

Haynar nodded. 'Possibly,' he said. 'But *their* will nonetheless.'

'Then what did the envoy mean?' Arwain asked simply. 'Was he lying? And if so, to what end?'

Haynar leaned forward and frowned. 'He was and he wasn't,' he replied. 'And the end they seek is war, without a doubt, which is why we're accelerating the work on our defences.' He looked straight at Arwain. 'But as to why . . .?' He shook his head.

'I don't understand,' Arwain said. 'How can he lie and not lie?'

Haynar pulled a rueful face. 'The same way that I just did,' he said. 'It's true there are no native Bethlarii and Serens here, except perhaps for a few who've come here following marriage. But adherence to your two states brings constant trouble to our streets.' He began to gesticulate as he spoke. 'Like Serenstad, we have our factions, Guilds, political parties, various cartels of influential people, businesses, malcontents. And where there is such variety there is, inevitably, confusion, inefficiency, mistrust and, sadly, corruption; and progress towards better times is at best . . . uneven. Then, the ignorant become impatient. They weave flights of fancy about the possibility of some simple sovereign remedy for all ills being at hand. Some will follow an eloquent and persuasive leader. Others will follow the holy writing of some confounded god or other. They come and go leaving varying amounts of emotional debris behind them, but, at the moment, we are suffering badly from those who, like me, are largely Bethlarii by blood, but who, unlike me, take an over-weaning pride in it and imagine that a return to Bethlarii puritanism and . . . harsh warrior training . . . will bring about a new age of prosperity and dignity.'

Arwain nodded. 'As you say, troublesome factions are not uncommon in Serenstad, too,' he said. 'In what way are these people causing special problems?'

Haynar leaned back. 'They're violent,' he said bluntly. 'Very violent. They march through the streets intimidating people, they disrupt Council meetings, Guild meetings, they attack people whom they consider to be "too Serens". And when we take action against them, they send messages off to Bethlar saying we're victimizing them.'

'And has Bethlar replied?' Arwain asked.

Haynar looked at him and then at a large, old-fashioned time-piece hanging on the wall. 'Come with me,' he said. 'There's an emergency Council meeting in about an hour. I think you'll find it interesting and informative.'

The Council Chamber was smaller than Arwain had imagined, being used to the large Sened Hall and the even larger hall of the Gythrin-Dy. Nonetheless, it was impressive, with semicircular rows of seats laid out in tiers raking gently down to a raised platform at one end of the hall. The walls were covered with intricately carved wooden panels showing significant scenes from Whendrak's history, but as they were led in, both Arwain and Ryllans found their eyes drawn inexorably upwards. Instead of the smoothly polished wooden beams and plastered ceilings that would grace such a hall in Serenstad and most other cities, the ceiling seemed to grow naturally out of the wall panels and consisted of a complex, interwoven web of tree branches. They were of every conceivable girth, and they rambled their twisting way across the hall and up into an impenetrable darkness without any semblance of regularity of pattern.

Here and there, lamps were hanging from the lower branches, but there were also several shining high up within the labyrinthine structure, so that they looked almost like stars shining down through a forest canopy.

'It's like being under the roots of a great tree,' Arwain whispered to Ryllans, involuntarily awed by the sight.

Ryllans nodded. 'Remarkable,' he said. 'And an assassin's paradise if there's access to it.'

Arwain shot him a reproachful look, but the official escorting them, unabashed by the remark, said, 'The only way in is well guarded, sir. It's a long tradition.'

Ryllans bowed in acknowledgement.

'Must you always have such dark thoughts?' Arwain said to him when the official had left. 'I've never seen anything like it, and you fuss on about assassins.'

This time it was Ryllans who offered the reproach. 'I never have dark thoughts,' he said, smiling a little to show the lie. 'It is indeed a rare sight. Beautiful, remarkable, intriguing, *full* of question . . . *and* . . . an assassin's paradise. If you can't see that, then you're not aware, and if you're not aware, then you can't see the true beauty. Every rose has a thorn.'

Arwain searched briefly for a reply then gave up.

He reverted to their interview with Haynar.

'What did you make of the Maeran?' he asked, settling back in his seat and watching the Councillors arriving.

Ryllans shrugged. 'Hard to say,' he answered. 'Just being Maeran of Whendrak means he's a shrewd, devious, ruthless individual, to say the least. And he's a horse trader. Says as much between his words as he does with them. He told you he knew a lot about you and that you knew nothing about him in his very first sentence.'

Arwain nodded. 'How did I manage?' he asked.

'Very well, I'd say,' Ryllans replied. 'Your straightforward approach was probably the best response against someone like him. And you certainly won us a hearing, perhaps more, by not losing your temper when he provoked you. We must listen very carefully to what's going on here.'

Arwain looked around and frowned. 'Listening's one thing, hearing's another,' he said.

The remark was prompted by the growing noise in the Council Chamber which was now filling rapidly. Much of it consisted of noisy greetings and banter, the latter brought about mainly by the apparently early hour of the meeting.

There was, however, a general air of concern and anxiety about the place, which gradually began to deepen as the Chamber filled.

Little here that he hadn't seen in many a Sened meeting before over some storm in a wine glass, Arwain mused, but, abruptly, the atmosphere changed, becoming suddenly tense and watchful as a group of men entered and, without offering any greeting to anyone, or even looking around, marched directly to their places.

They were dressed identically in grey uniforms and, to a man, their demeanour was arrogant and their expressions emotionless.

'No debate about where they look to find their "sovereign remedy",' Arwain said, using Haynar's words.

Any further discussion about the newcomers was forestalled, however, by the entrance of Haynar and several others on to the raised platform at the front of the Chamber.

The Chamber fell silent almost immediately, but a formally dressed guard on the platform raised his pike and dutifully struck its butt three times on the wooden floor.

The sound rose into the air and then echoed back down from the branches overhead, greatly magnified. As the sound died away, Haynar rose to speak.

He made little preamble.

'My friends. May I first apologize for the short notice given for this meeting and for its ungodly hour. May I also thank you for your attendance.' Arwain noticed immediately that his voice was carried evenly across the hall by some quality in the strange ceiling.

Haynar took a document from his gown and laid it respectfully on the lectern in front of him.

'I have here a letter that I received yesterday. I called this meeting as I felt that you should all be made aware of its contents and be given an opportunity to discuss it fully as soon as possible.' He looked down at the document. 'It bears a signature that I can't decipher, but the seal is authentically that of the Bethlarii Council of Five, the Handira.'

A murmur rose from the Councillors, but Arwain could not detect the dominant mood in it. He cast a discreet glance at the stern group that had just arrived. They were all sitting bolt upright, as if to lean back would represent some display of weakness or disrespect, confirming his initial impression that they were representatives of those Whendreachi who looked to Bethlar for the answer to such ills as their city suffered. They were all staring fixedly at Haynar.

'"Vassals," the letter begins,' Haynar read. He put no inflection into the word, but the murmur rose again, unequivocally angry. He ignored it and continued.

'"It has been made known to us that our citizens living within your bounds are being ill used by your people. They are being deprived of their livelihoods, homes, liberty, right of access to your courts, and, above all, the right to pursue their religious observations. You will cease this persecution immediately and make full reparation of all hurts before the solstice. You will also commence dismantling the new fortifications and defences that you have built about your city. If these instructions are not implemented immediately, then a military governor will be appointed in your stead."'

There was a brief pause after Haynar finished, then uproar broke out. Sitting motionless amid the cries of outrage and anger, Arwain found himself back in Serenstad, standing behind his father as the Bethlarii envoy had approached him in a similar vein.

Haynar did not move or make any attempt to stop the noise for some time, then he nodded to the guard standing nearby.

Once again the guard banged his pike on the floor. The sound rose above the din and echoed down from the tangled branches overhead. It had little effect initially, but at a further nod from Haynar, the guard repeated the action with greater force, and the Chamber fell suddenly silent as the brief tattoo boomed out overhead like thunder.

Arwain and Ryllans exchanged appreciative glances. The Whendreachi Councillors were markedly more disciplined than either the Sened or the Gythrin-Dy.

As the sound faded, a flurry of hands rose into the air, but Haynar ignored them.

'Allow me the first word, my friends,' he said. 'I'll be brief.' He tapped the Bethlarii document. 'I'll gloss over the tone of this missive, which, frankly, defies me. Let us consider just two facts. One: is it true that any of our citizens are being persecuted? Answer, no. Rather it is that certain factions which seek to take us under Bethlar's grey sway have provoked violence against the persons and properties of those it sees as enemies to its cause; namely those whom they cannot defeat in debate here, in this Chamber. And they have brought to their aid those criminal and deranged elements which plague any community and who care nothing for any cause save violence and destruction. Two: the fortifications we have undertaken were at the agreed will of the great majority here. We are a neutral city under the Treaty between Bethlar and Serenstad and in this particular, while we do not ally ourselves with either, we may do as we wish.'

Haynar's manner throughout this short speech was calm but resolute, though a snarl of defiance permeated his final sentence. It captured the mood of his listeners and there was a loud burst of applause and cheering.

Haynar waited for it to subside. 'My friends,' he began again. 'It has long been the wish of our people that we should never again be caught between these two great cities and their endless wars. And to this end we have striven to become strong enough to be independent of them both.' He leaned forward on to the lectern. 'And we have succeeded, my friends,' he said slowly but with great power. 'We have succeeded. We seek nothing but friendliness and trade with all the peoples of this land, be they allied to Bethlar or Serenstad, but we will destroy utterly anyone who turns his sword against us, from within or without.'

More applause greeted this affirmation, but as it faded, a lone voice emerged. It was one of the grey-uniformed group. He was waving his fist angrily.

'Haynar, you lie,' he shouted. 'You lie, and you lead this city to perdition with your ambition and folly.'

Cries of protest greeted this outburst.

'No, I will be heard,' the man went on, shouting louder, his voice echoing raucously from the strange ceiling.

'You'll be heard more clearly, if you speak a little more quietly, Garren,' Haynar said ironically, sitting down and casually extending a hand towards him.

The comment caused some laughter, which did little to improve the man's temper. He raised his fist again. 'You accuse us of violence against our opponents, but we have only armed ourselves because of the violence that was offered to *us* in the first place. When we are allowed to meet and worship in peace then we will no longer need this protection. You say we wish to bring the city under the protection of Bethlar. This is another of your lies. Rather it is *you* who wishes to bring us under the sway of Serenstad.' His lip curled arrogantly. 'A city riddled with corruption and decay, and ruled by merchants, Guildsmen, and an effete aristocracy.

347

Whendrak is, by ancient right, a Bethlarii protectorate. Only when we return to that state and to the ways of our ancestors can we begin to root out the decadent and degenerate elements that have brought so many ills upon us, and move forward to our true place in the land.'

Arwain's eyes narrowed in distress at the vehemence in the man's voice.

'Enough!' Haynar's voice rang out in exasperation as Garren gathered his breath for another onslaught. 'We've heard all this nonsense before, Garren. You seem to think that if you tell a lie often enough and loudly enough, it will become the truth. Whendrak has been under the sway of both Bethlar and Serenstad many times through its history. Now, by their treaty, we're a neutral city.' He paused and put his hand to his head in a gesture of concern. 'Even at this stage my old friendship for you and your family prompt me to offer you a word of personal advice.' He leaned forward and his voice became unexpectedly passionate. 'You're a clever, capable man, Garren,' he said. 'You must surely see the rabble, the mad dogs, who follow your ridiculous baying, for what they are.' Garren made to speak, but Haynar lifted a hand to prevent him. 'Ponder this. How you are going to control them when their usefulness to you has passed? It's far easier to unleash a wild animal than it is to recapture it.'

'I will not listen to my supporters and friends being thus maligned,' Garren shouted, his voice booming unpleasantly about the Chamber again.

'And I'll not listen to any more of your ranting, Garren,' Haynar said, his voice softer than Garren's, but somehow overtopping it. He slapped the document lying on the lectern. 'This is directly due to your treachery . . .'

He hesitated, and his concern surfaced again briefly. 'And do you imagine that the Handira give a fig for your petty, crawling obeisance and your ridiculous scheming? The only value that Whendrak has for them is its strategic position as a base to move against Serenstad. They're using you to do their dirty work for them, that's all.' Anger and frustration burst through into his voice. 'You're not stupid, man. What do you think the Bethlarii are going to do with you and your troublesome followers? Honour you? Laud you?' He struck his chest. 'You know what they think about us with their fatuous tribal pride. We're just so many mongrel half-breeds, marginally superior to their dogs, but fit only for use as slaves and arrow fodder.'

Garren leapt to his feet furiously. 'Speak for your own kind, Haynar,' he shouted. 'We are all pure-born Bethlarii for ten generations—'

'Not according to what my uncle says about your mother, Garren,' came a voice from somewhere, with a sharp Whendreachi accent. The Chamber erupted in laughter, as much to release the tension built up by Garren's manic utterances as at the humour of the comment.

Arwain watched Garren waving his fist and shouting, though he could hear nothing above the din.

The laughter splashed to and fro for some time until Haynar, smiling himself, eventually managed to wave it to silence.

'I will waste no more time on this pointless debate,' he said, sobering. 'You have the facts before you and you must decide upon what we shall do. I ask you to confirm the policy which we have followed these past years. That we will stand firm and oppose *anyone* who would try to impose their will upon us. To help you in your discussion I have used my authority as Maeran to make a special decree.'

The Chamber became very still. Ryllans nudged Arwain gently and with a slight nod directed his attention back towards Garren and his group. Guards were entering quietly and standing along the aisle behind them.

'We have food and water to sustain us through any siege,' Haynar went on. 'Arms to defend ourselves. And above all, newly strengthened walls that soon will repel even the heaviest artillery, the tallest towers, the deepest sappers.' He paused. 'But such walls are in truth only as strong as their gates. And gates are only as strong as the man's arm that can draw the bolts. *Treachery* will be our greatest enemy in any conflict with the Bethlarii.' He paused again. 'My decree therefore is that Councillor Andreth Garren be deprived of his office and confined to his house pending formal impeachment and trial. So also his senior lieutenants. And for those of his followers who will not disavow their allegiance to him, and renew their allegiance to this Council, expulsion from the city.'

The guards behind Garren and his group moved forward and one of them bent down and spoke to Garren. Across the Chamber, Arwain saw him casting about as if for help from

349

his fellows or for some route to escape. To no avail, however, and, after a further word from the guard, he and his entourage rose to their feet and, with returning arrogance, marched out of the Chamber escorted by the guards.

The announcement and the removal of Garren and his followers were greeted by the Councillors with a stunned silence.

As the door closed behind the departing group, Haynar spoke softly but purposefully. 'Debate what you have heard, my friends,' he said. 'And choose well. Freedom and progress, with the responsibility that goes with both; or stagnant Bethlarii overlordship. I will return to hear your will in due course.' He bowed his head for a moment, then turned and left the platform.

As he left, the silence began to disintegrate around the two watching Serens. At first gradually, then with a great rush like a breaking wave. Several Councillors left the Chamber hastily while all those that remained began talking urgently, and seemingly indiscriminately, to their neighbours on every side.

'Gentlemen.'

Arwain turned. It was the official who had brought them into the Chamber. 'Would you follow me, please.'

Though his voice was soft, his manner was urgent and Arwain and Ryllans followed him without question.

He led them out of the Chamber by a different door to the one they had entered through, and as they followed him along passageways and down stairs, Arwain felt an increasing urgency in his pace.

'What's the matter?' he asked.

'The Maeran will explain,' the man said, politely.

Then they were walking rapidly down a narrow stone stairway and being ushered into a small courtyard. Their horses were waiting, saddled and ready, along with the platoon and a small group of mounted Whendreachi guards.

Haynar was there also. He stepped forward. 'You must leave immediately,' he said. 'If I'm allowed I shall report your visit to the Council.'

'If?' Arwain queried, taken aback by this sudden change in events. He pointed back towards the Council Chamber. 'I thought you were in charge here.'

Haynar smiled ruefully. 'I am and I am not,' he replied.

350

'The decree I've issued against Garren is a considerable risk—'

'You could have done nothing else,' Ryllans interrupted unexpectedly.

'You and I know this,' Haynar said, leading them to their horses. 'We study our history. But . . .' He shrugged. 'We've got more than a few self-servers and weak-kneed appeasers in the Council. The vote's going to be close. I can't guarantee that we'll stand against Bethlar even though we ought to.'

'Don't you have emergency authority as Maeran?' Arwain asked, as he mounted his horse.

Haynar smiled again. 'Garren's a considerable orator. And his followers hold real power on the streets here. My authority's only as effective as my ability to impose it if need arises. As I said in there, our security is no more than the strength of one traitor's arm.'

He waved aside any further debate. 'You must go now. There's liable to be serious disturbances when the news of Garren's arrest gets out and I can't guarantee your safety. Tell your father what's happening here. Most of us are with you and we'll do our best to oppose Bethlar, but . . .' He changed direction. 'These guards will escort you to the gate. Go now.'

Arwain looked down at him. 'Do you want our help, Maeran?' he said significantly, laying emphasis on the last word.

'No, damn it. We want neither of you,' Haynar said bitterly. 'But better you than them. And the treaty's going to be no more than smoke in the wind soon if you *don't* help. But tell your father to be careful. This is just a ploy, I'm sure.'

Arwain reached down and took Haynar's hand. 'I understand,' he said.

The sound of shouting floated into the courtyard. Haynar nodded. 'Go,' he said, then he turned and ran back into the building.

As their escort led them out of the walled courtyard, the truth of Haynar's words became apparent. There was an unmistakable tension in the air. Groups of young men were running about wildly while other people in the street were running to avoid them.

'Ar-Hyrdyn, Ar-Hyrdyn.' Arwain looked round to see where the chant was coming from.

'Serenstad scum,' came a cry.

A rock struck Arwain's temple. He slumped forward on to his horse's neck, blood pouring from his head.

Chapter 27

Ivaroth stared up at the southern mountains. His horse was restless, responding to his unease. He was a man of the plains. He did not like mountains. They dominated, hedged in, constrained travellers to narrow, often precarious, pathways with giddying heights both above and below. They were no place for a race born to ride free across the endless plains, flat and wide and open, where the weather could be seen and judged and did not turn from bright sunlight to dank freezing mist without warning, where the sun did not rise late and set early amid ominous, judging shadows.

'Ivaroth, I will follow wherever you lead, but . . .' There was a head-shaking pause. 'I have misgivings.'

The speaker was Endryn, one of the few who had stood by Ivaroth when he was accused of his brother's murder and who had spoken out, at no small risk to himself, against his expulsion from the tribe.

The need to answer these doubting words gave Ivaroth the power to dispel his own concerns. He turned to Endryn with a yellow-toothed grin splitting his flat, scarred face.

'You mean you've got bellyache again,' he said, leaning across and swinging his clenched fist in a backward blow at Endryn's stomach. Used to this attack, Endryn nimbly kneed his horse sideways so that the blow missed, but the prospect of the impact made his muscles tense and, placing his hand on his stomach, he winced and laughed simultaneously.

'I knew it,' Ivaroth said. 'You always get the bellyache before a battle. That's what makes you worth having by me in a fight, old friend. Your bad temper.'

Exposed, Endryn openly hugged his stomach with both hands. 'Thank you, Mareth Hai,' he said with some irony. 'It seems you have the vision of the healer as well as the warrior. But we don't have a battle in front of us at the moment.'

Ivaroth laughed loudly and then waved his fist at the waiting mountains. 'Of course we do,' he said. 'Look at them. Row upon row of enemies. And they'll kill more than a few of use before we're through them.' He seemed to relish the prospect. 'Still, our real battle's going to be keeping the men going when they start bleating about the cold and the endless wind and their aching legs.'

'That may happen sooner than you think,' Endryn said. 'All the signs down here are that winter's coming early, and there's already snow on some peaks that wasn't there a few weeks ago. A lot of the chieftains will be clamouring for the expedition to be left until the spring.'

Ivaroth turned on him, his face suddenly angry. Endryn flinched, though he knew that the anger was not directed at him.

'No,' Ivaroth said, savagely. 'Not by all the powers in this land.' This was a strange new oath that Ivaroth had taken to using since he had returned from the wilderness with the old man and started on his great rise to power. Whenever he used it, something in his voice seemed to make the very ground shake, and a deep, rumbling unease would pass through Endryn. '*Now* is the time,' Ivaroth went on, his voice becoming more impassioned. 'The only time. All will move against us if we delay.' He held up his fist, clenched tightly as if to prevent something slipping away from him.

'You're so certain,' Endryn said, unable to still his doubts before the dark presence of the mountains.

Ivaroth bared his teeth. 'Yes, I am,' he said. 'I've been given the vision to see the tide that our people can ride to reach our destiny, and we shall ride it, no matter what the cost. We shall ride to avenge our ancient ancestors and to regain the rich land of the south that is rightly ours. I tell you, Endryn, if we do not do this *now*, then we'll be doomed to the plains forever until we decay and fail and become weak and scattered like the Ensceini.' He took in a deep breath. 'I'll allow nothing and no one to stand in front of this venture, if we have to pull those mountains down stone by stone. As for the men . . .' He drew his sword and held it menacingly in front of Endryn. 'I'll cleave from neck to groin anyone who shows even a moment's hesitation once the march begins.'

The two men looked at one another. 'Including me?' Endryn asked.

Ivaroth laughed. 'Of course including you,' he said, striking Endryn a great slap on his shoulder. Then he

354

smacked his own chest. 'I'd cleave *myself* if I faltered on this road.'

Abruptly he stood up in his stirrups and brandished his sword at the mountains. 'Hear my voice, ancient rocks,' he shouted. 'Grow used to it, because it is the voice of your lord. I shall lead my men through your valleys and over your ridges, and split you asunder if you defy me. Do not doubt either my will or my power, because the one is green and strong and the other was ancient even before you began your journeys to the sky.'

He ended his echoing harangue with an ear-splitting war cry. Endryn, caught up in his fervour, joined in, then the two turned about and galloped back towards their camp.

As Endryn had said, however, there was opposition from some of the chieftains to Ivaroth's scheme to march through the mountains, especially in winter. His principal advisers sat with him in the assembly circle in his great tented pavilion.

'Mareth Hai, a man may ride his horse in any direction he chooses until it dies of exhaustion, but he will still have covered only the merest fraction of your domain. Already your fame is such that your name will ring down in history and legend as the greatest leader the plains have ever known. Do not cast this away so lightly on such a reckless throw—'

'The winter comes early. Such passes as there are will be blocked with snow—'

'We'll barely be able to carry the food we need as it is. If we are delayed—'

'The mountains were set there by the gods to bar our way. To flout their will is to court a fearful retribution . . .' This was Amhir, as much a shaman as a chieftain and a constant thorn in Ivaroth's side with his religious utterances. There was a brief, but uneasy pause after he had spoken.

Then, the discussion continued. 'My tribe has fought often against the southlanders, the Bethlarii. We raid them regularly. In their villages and farms they're but men . . . and women,' he added to appreciative nods and laughter. 'But when the word is out that we're among them again, they fetch up their army and those of us who wish to return again next season, retreat while they can, without dishonour. Their wall of shields and spears cannot be breached and they show no mercy . . .'

Ivaroth listened attentively to many similar speeches, nodding thoughtfully on occasions, until eventually the circle

of chieftains fell silent and the sounds of the camp outside
began to seep into the pavilion.

'I hear you all,' he said quietly. 'You speak much that is
worthy, and you give me sound advice. I'd not have it said
that the Mareth Hai disdained the counsel of his chieftains;
of those that he has entrusted with the leadership of his
people; of those that have ridden and fought by his side.'
He paused. 'But also, I cannot have it said that I allowed
myself, who am but the will of our peoples, to be deflected
from our true destiny by timorous, shivering fears.'

His voice grew in power and intensity as he spoke, and,
though no one dared move, it seemed that the circle shrank
visibly as each tried to avoid that insignificant movement or
sound that might suddenly bring down the fearsome,
unpredictable anger of their Mareth Hai, like the last gentle
breeze that finally topples a teetering boulder.

Ivaroth looked at each in turn. 'You ask me to look at what
has been achieved.' He flung out his arms contemptuously.
'Everything so far has been a mere sharpening of our swords
in anticipation of the true battle. Hard at times, but no more
than a pruning of the weak and ailing. My name is *nothing*.
Our achievements are *nothing*. Vague echoes on the plains'
wind. But when the sound of our horses thunders across the
length and breadth of the rich southlands, then will my name,
and our achievements, truly ring down through history.'

Stillness.

'You talk of the winter, of the snow and wind, of going
without food.' He gave a gesture of jocular disbelief. 'How
can you, the leaders of my people, fret about such nonsense?
What else is *every* winter but snow and wind and going
without food? Each year we wait through the dreary gloom,
stomachs rumbling, hands and faces raw, fearful in case this
time the sun doesn't return, until the days . . .' He drew out
the words and made an incongruous flapping motion with
his hands. ' . . .slowly lengthen, and the birds return . . .'
Then with an angry snarl he cut through the momentary
lightness he had brought to his speech. 'This time we do not
wait for such slight glories. This time we travel towards a
glory of our own.'

He looked round the circle again. 'As for the mountains
being placed there by the gods.' He shrugged fatalistically.
'Who am I to gainsay such matters. Perhaps they were,
perhaps they weren't. But I know that they weren't placed

there to bar our way. They were placed there to challenge our fitness to return to our true land. Can you truly say that we, the greatest tribal federation the plains have ever known, are incapable of scrambling over a few rocks?'

Still no one attempted to speak.

'And as for the Bethlarii.' He pointed to the two who had spoken about them. 'I value your words. Not only do your people have the knowledge that will ease our way through the mountains, but you've met the enemy face to face, sword to sword.' He beckoned his listeners forward and the circle craned inwards. 'But listen. Dismiss your concern about walls of shields and spears. Formidable they may be against a raiding party, even a large one. But we're no raiding party. We're an army. An army so vast that we could trample them underfoot and scarcely falter in our advance . . .' He waved a hand to dismiss his own exaggeration. 'Not that that will be necessary. Walls can be ridden round, can't they? Ask yourselves, how fast can these walls of shields and spears wheel and turn to protect their flanks and rears? And how fast can they run when we ride past them towards their homes and unprotected wives?'

A tentative but relieved laughter greeted this remark. The Mareth Hai's ambition and ranting oratory were fine in their place, but a glimpse of the down-to-earth fighting tactics that he was evolving for the prospective conflict was reassuring.

His face darkened, and the laughter faded. 'We go over the mountains,' he said, looking at each in turn again, as if his black eyes could see into their souls. 'We go to sweep away those who usurped our ancient land. This and this alone is why we paid the blood debt that has made us now one, where once we were many.' He leaned forward. 'I will not allow anyone or anything to thwart this intent. When your people come to you with their innumerable plaints, give them this as a lodestar to dominate their vision and guide their will.' He drew his sword and pointed it towards the centre of the circle. Lamplight flickered off its polished blade as he turned it slowly from side to side, sending brief, bright stars hurtling across the curving canopy of the tent. 'I will solve all weariness, all doubt, all discomfort, with this edge if I have to. Many ways seem to exist for the wayward and the weak, but in truth there is only one way. My way. Forward.'

'No!'

The stillness of the circle became suddenly taut with tension at the cry, and all eyes moved from Ivaroth's hypnotic blade to the speaker.

It was Amhir. He was swaying to and fro and clearly in the grip of some religious fervour.

Ivaroth looked at him coldly, but did not speak.

'You blaspheme, Ivaroth Ungwyl,' Amhir said, his voice hollow and distant. 'As we near the mountains, more than ever do I know that you will be defying the gods themselves if you seek to lead the people through to the south.'

Ivaroth's grip tightened around his sword hilt as his every instinct prompted him to deliver summary justice for this defiant interruption. A surreptitious and unseen touch from Endryn restrained him, however. The many religions that the tribe followed had been the greatest source of their division and antagonism. So much so that it could be said that, after his fighting skills, Ivaroth's greatest attribute as a leader was his meeting this problem squarely, insisting that all should be allowed to worship as they wished.

But he was an unequivocal, simple reformer, offering no subtle arguments. 'We have problems enough right here that need our swords and courage. In future, those among you who choose to quarrel violently about the merits and flaws of your many gods I will personally dispatch to them for a final judgement.'

It took but a few summary executions to demonstrate the deep wisdom and effectiveness of this policy.

Nonetheless, mutual intolerance was still a substantial threat to the new-found unity, and religious matters had to be handled carefully. Endryn's discreet reminder was timely. Slaying Amhir for impertinence would cause some stir, but not for long. Slaying him while he might be considered as speaking the will of his gods could give rise to serious problems.

'Amhir,' he said, menacingly, hoping that his manner alone might reach through to the man before he committed some greater folly. 'Never before has any leader allowed such freedom for people to worship as they wish. And while I allow that freedom . . . indeed, enforce it . . . then the gods have what is their due and they must allow me what is mine; the right to lead my people unhindered. You forget that you sit here as a chieftain, not as a shaman. Keep your visions to yourself. I forgive you your outburst as I know your heart is as sound as your sword arm, but speak no more of this foolishness.'

'No,' Amhir said loudly. 'I cannot remain silent. The mountains have spoken to me. They have shown me the future and it is full of darkness and bloodshed if we do not turn from this path. You are led by a demon, Ivaroth, and it leads you to its own purpose, not yours.'

All eyes turned towards Amhir fearfully. His voice was powerful and convincing, and instinctively he fanned the smouldering embers of superstition that lay deep inside the plains' people. Ivaroth felt the doubts of his chieftains forming around him. At their focus was the ancient, primitive challenge to leadership that they all subscribed to wittingly or unwittingly: surely no one could thus openly oppose the Mareth Hai unless he were truly possessed of some great truth?

Amhir had sealed his own fate. Ivaroth's question was now simply one of deciding the most expedient way for his disposal.

A figure behind Ivaroth stirred, and a bony, unclean hand emerged to close about his arm. It squeezed it longingly several times as though its owner were overcome by some great desire that only Ivaroth could satisfy. It was a repellent gesture, but Ivaroth merely inclined his head slightly towards the figure as if he were listening to something.

Slowly he nodded and the hand slid away very gradually, its long fingers trailing over Ivaroth's arm with a lingering reluctance to leave him. Again Ivaroth ignored the intimacy of the gesture.

Amhir levelled a hand towards the figure, his eyes wide with what was now obviously an uncontrollable passion.

'Silence!' Ivaroth thundered, before Amhir could speak. 'You have the temerity to tell *me* that you know the will of the gods? *I* am the will of the gods. How else could I have become Mareth Hai and brought together the tribes as I have?'

'I have seen what I have seen, Ivaroth,' Amhir said, seemingly impervious to Ivaroth's anger. 'I feel the power of the land growing as we near the mountains and the gods have spoken to me. They have shown me the future. They have shown me the demon on your back. They have—'

'What future did they show you, Amhir?' Ivaroth said, smiling; suddenly intrigued, conciliatory even.

At the sight of the smile, several of the chieftains began quietly to ease away from their leader and the shaman. The circle grew perceptibly wider.

But still Amhir seemed unaware of the danger. 'In a dream, I stood on a high place and saw there remnants of our army returning from the mountains, broken and destroyed. I heard the plains filled with the weeping of countless widows, and the cries of children, starving because the hunters were all gone.'

'You heard all this? You saw it? In a dream?' Ivaroth said, his voice softening and his smile broadening.

The tension around the group became unbearable. Ivaroth's temper was explosive and swift, and invariably fatal for someone. He had once run a sleeping sentry through with his own sword, declaring to the shocked officers with him, 'I left him as I found him.'

Now, despite the tremors that Amhir's voice was sending through their dark and bloody souls, most of the watchers expected a similar fate to befall him and were watching Ivaroth's sword closely, ready to dive for cover when it swept suddenly into action.

But instead, Ivaroth sheathed it with a grim laugh. 'I'd thought to strike you down for bringing your religious ranting to this assembly, Amhir,' he said. 'But I see the gods are merely toying with you.' He shrugged casually. 'A fate which you have justly brought on yourself by your endless meddling in their affairs, seeking to interpret this omen and that portent in your arrogance.'

Amhir opened his mouth to speak but Ivaroth raised his hand. 'They've doubtless sent you such dreams knowing that your folly would lead you inexorably to death at my hand just to show that any future *you* had seen yourself in could only be a delusion. However, when you are yourself, you're too fine a warrior to lose, and I'll be no party to their antics. If they wish an end to you, then they must attend to it. Leave us now. Come to me in the morning and tell me what other visions you've had.'

Amhir's mouth worked agitatedly.

'Go, before I recant,' Ivaroth said menacingly. 'I'll do their work if I have to.'

As if being pulled by unseen hands, Amhir stood up unsteadily and, without any leave-taking, staggered from the tent. In the ensuing silence, only a low, ecstatic breathing from the figure behind Ivaroth could be heard.

Endryn looked alarmed. 'Mareth Hai, fine warrior or no, he must be silenced,' he said urgently. 'If he goes wandering the camp talking like that he could cause havoc.'

Ivaroth shook his head. 'Let him speak to whomever he wishes. The more who hear him, the more will know of his folly,' he said. Then, with almost fatherly regret, 'He meddled where he shouldn't have, my friends, and now there's a price to be paid. We must keep away from him if we don't want to share it. Frankly, I doubt he'll see the night through.'

Then, addressing the unspoken conclusion which came immediately to the minds of his listeners, he said, 'Arrange an honour guard about him tonight. He's to be protected. I want no assassin's blade entering this affair.'

Later, Ivaroth sat alone in the tent. He had dismissed the assembly shortly after the departure of Amhir, telling the chieftains to meet with him again the following day. 'When we'll discuss the detailed plans for our passage through the mountains and our assault on the southlands.'

They were both confused and subdued as they left, not least as Ivaroth's final words had been to confirm his earlier order. 'See that Amhir is well guarded this night. Put your finest men around him.'

Now, Ivaroth stared into the flame of a solitary lamp; the whites of his eyes turned as black as the moonless night outside in preparation for his entry into the dream world. The flame flickered occasionally, or bent slightly this way and that, following the promptings of some unseen force.

How different am I from you? Ivaroth thought. Moving here, moving there. Whose plaything am I?

He was not normally given to such introspection. He was a warrior. Destiny was for those who saw it and seized it; by word or by sword, by truth or by treachery, it mattered not. The gods, if gods there be, favoured the bold.

And yet . . .

There were things that were hidden from him. Why should he be able to visit the dreams of others, to watch, to listen, to revel and, lately, to learn? Wrenyk had spoken of it, but he had never known of others. He rubbed the cheek that Wrenyk had spat on.

And how could it be that he could move into the strange worlds beyond the dreams? Real worlds, filled with real lands and real people . . . and real danger! Worlds where he had soon learned to carry a sharp sword and walk softly, and into which he never strayed too far.

And who was the blind man, with his mysterious and terrifying powers who had been drawn to him in the deserted wastes of the north?

More than ever this question taxed him now. Amhir's words returned to him, 'They have shown me the demon on your back.' It was a long time since anyone had dared refer even obliquely to the strange hooded figure that had come out of exile with him to become like his shadow, frequently at his side and even present in some eerie way when he was absent.

Only Ivaroth knew of his strange, dangerous powers: that he could sometimes see into minds, and even speak into them without sound; that he could, as he had when Ivaroth had faced the gauntlet, fill others with great power and strength, making them invincible against all opposition; that he could make objects move, conjure fire from the air, and even make the earth shake; a deed which seemed to excite him beyond all reason.

And he was patently insane, muttering and gloating to himself in a soft, repellent whisper. A blind drivelling old man, with eyes as sickly milk-white as Ivaroth's were now black; yet who could see into the spirits of men? A man who never seemed to eat or sleep, but who seemed to be kept alive by some strange power that he drew from who knew where? And a man who seemed to possess no fleshly appetites at all, not even for the occasional woman.

But he could lust, and lust more than any man could for a woman. Indeed, his every action seemed to radiate gross and unholy desire. He lusted to use his power. Though not so much in this world. It was in the worlds beyond that he wanted to use it, for there it was multiplied a hundredfold.

And he had known of these worlds from the first moment he had stared into Ivaroth's eyes!

Mutual need had bound the two men together. 'Take me through the dreams and into the worlds beyond, Ivaroth,' he had said, at the same time filling Ivaroth's body with burning fingers of pain. 'And all you desire here shall be yours.'

At first, Ivaroth had taken him out of mortal fear of his strange powers, regarding the promise as a mere taunt. But his natural opportunism had soon shown him that the blind man's craving to visit the worlds beyond and use his power there was almost uncontrollable, and as such was a weakness that could be used to control and manipulate him.

And as he began to get some measure of the blind man's powers, his own ambitions began to grow with an equal lack of restraint. With such powers at his behest, nothing could stand in his way. This grotesque old man was indeed his destiny.

Thus one day, out in the cold, bleak wastes where they had met and were then subsisting, Ivaroth had refused to take him into the worlds beyond.

For a brief, but seemingly eternal moment, the blind man's fury had been beyond belief and Ivaroth found himself the centre of pain that he could not have thought imaginable. But he was no coward and was truly willing to sacrifice his life for the ambitions he saw opening before him with the blind man's powers at his command.

Whether he spoke the words, or merely formed the thoughts, he never knew, but even as he fell to his knees, he shouted defiantly into the pain. 'I am Ivaroth Ungwyl, a son of the sons of warriors since time began. Death holds no fear for me, old fool. Slay me and you will lose all, for there are no others like me throughout all the tribes of the plains.'

The pain had stopped almost immediately but, roaring with hatred and fury, Ivaroth had lurched to his feet and struck the blind man a ferocious blow in the face that sent him sprawling on his back in the rough grass. He had scarcely struck the ground when Ivaroth's sword was pressing into his throat.

'Slay me and *you* lose all,' the old man had said, cringing away from the purposeful point, fearfully.

Thus was their bargain struck.

Now, however, like the guttering flame before him, it was faltering again. The blind man had used his power surreptitiously to protect and strengthen Ivaroth in battle, making him the invincible leader of his own tribe, and subsequently of all the tribes as he pursued his relentless ambition to become Mareth Hai and form an army that could carry him through the mountains to seize the southlands. In return Ivaroth had taken the blind man into the worlds beyond to run amok for a while with his greater power.

But Ivaroth had always been deeply suspicious of the blind man. Often, like a cunning child, he would turn to Ivaroth and say, 'Take me to the other place, the place beyond here, where the true power can be found.' He used no threats, but he was endlessly persistent, his blind eyes watching Ivaroth carefully each time he spoke thus. Ivaroth, however, did not understand him. He would take him from world to world, but always there was the same peevish shaking of the head, and the plaintive squeezing of his arm. 'This is not the place. Please look again, search inside yourself, it is there. I feel it.'

The tone sickened Ivaroth, but he learned silence. A little disgust was a small price for the benefits that the blind man's cooperation brought him.

And in more conciliatory moments, he would say, quite sincerely, 'I would find this place for you if I could.'

'But you must search, you must, you must . . .'

Then had come the great discovery.

They had left one of the worlds beyond and, seemingly accidentally, entered the dream of one of the Bethlarii Handiran. It was a dream full of images of perpetual, ritualized warfare, of dying and being reborn to fight again. And over all hovered the image of some tedious deity, Ar-Hyrdyn. The blind man took little or no interest in dreams and, himself indifferent, Ivaroth had been about to withdraw from it when the blind man's Dreamself had touched him with repellent glee.

And he had changed the dream! Twisted it somehow to his own fancy, and sent the dreamer hurtling towards a screaming wakefulness.

The blind man could use his power to change dreams!

Even now, Ivaroth still felt the emotion of that realization. To the blind man the torment to the Bethlarii had been no more than a passing and gratuitous spite; the slow, pointless crushing of a harmless insect. To Ivaroth, the manner in which it was done and the person to whom it was done, revealed his road to the south and the fulfilment of his wildest ambitions.

And their bargain had been made anew. Ivaroth promised that he would carry the blind man further into the other worlds in search of this 'other place', while the blind man would bend and shape the dreams of the Bethlarii leaders to Ivaroth's will.

It was work that the blind man grew to relish, for the

Bethlarii were a people who worshipped pain and suffering and their minds were a rich storehouse for his cruel humour. Soon, one man actually died from sheer terror as a result of his handiwork. Ivaroth noted the incident well, and, as he learned more about the Bethlarii, used it on several carefully arranged occasions to remove opposition from their hierarchy and also to consolidate the power of those he could best manipulate by giving them the sight to prophesy such deaths.

So it had gone for many months. Ivaroth ruthlessly forging his federation and the blind man gleefully tormenting the Bethlarii through their dreams to prepare the way for Ivaroth's coming. On occasions they took some of the Bethlarii into one of the worlds beyond where the blind man's power could weave a magic quite different in its conviction from that within the dreams.

But now, a strange opposition had arisen. First, the strange old man who appeared from nowhere in one of the worlds, to challenge them and then flee from world to world, through the doorways that Ivaroth thought only he could find.

The lamp flame spluttered momentarily as the memory returned to him. His black eyes narrowed uncertainly. He and the blind man had nearly been killed in that battle the old man had led them to.

And then he had led them to the other one. The one who had arisen to protect him like some avenging demon. It had looked like a man, but it had walked towards Ivaroth's sword and into the blind man's insane storm apparently unafraid, calling and challenging them . . .

Ivaroth turned away from the memory of the savage rending power that had suddenly surged out of the howling darkness, like some great predatory animal. Terrible eyes . . . teeth . . . And the blind man had stood there, his blank eyes gleaming with lust, and his arms extended as if to embrace the terror. Only by main force had Ivaroth torn them both back to this world.

Had it all been a trap? he thought. And if so, by whom?

He did not dwell on the idea. He remembered only the blind man's wild clamouring as they had crashed into the consciousness of this world.

'He can take me there. He can take me there,' he kept saying, alternately fawning and raging, one moment grovelling at Ivaroth's feet, the next wildly seizing and pummelling him. Used to physical combat, and himself full of battle anger following the unexpected and terrifying assault in the world beyond, Ivaroth was unaffected by the blind man's futile attacks and after a little while he ended the matter with a savage blow to the jaw.

Crouching down by the crumpled form, he was sorely tempted, for a moment, to end the cloying mutual reliance that bound them together, by crushing him underfoot. But calmer counsels prevailed and he waited for the blind man to stir.

When he did, Ivaroth held a knife against his throat.

'The worlds beyond are dangerous, old man,' he said. 'When we are there, you obey me absolutely, or I shall abandon you there and return to slay your form here. Do you understand?'

'He can take me there . . .' The litany began again, but stopped abruptly as Ivaroth's knife pressed harder.

He clutched at Ivaroth's sleeve and Ivaroth felt a spasm of pain forming inside him. His eyes widened in fury and seizing the blind man's wild matted hair he yanked his head back violently forcing the knife up under his chin.

'No more,' Ivaroth said through clenched teeth. 'Or I'll drive this blade through your brain before you can blink.' The blind man became rigid, and the pain faded, but Ivaroth did not release him. Instead he drew his face closer. 'That apparition you're blubbering after, wanted only our deaths. You can't be so blind that you didn't see that. I don't know who or what it was, or why it came for us. I've never met the like of it before. Perhaps it's always been there, perhaps your power drew it there . . . I don't know. But I've no intention of returning to the worlds beyond for some time, so school yourself to that. We continue with the conquest of the south first. Then and then only, will I take you back to seek your "other place". Do you understand me?'

The blind man had seemingly accepted this ultimatum and since then had fawned about Ivaroth more than ever, like some child seeking favour. But Ivaroth had made and slain too many enemies and allies in his time not to understand what was happening.

Just as in the blind man's ability to change dreams, Ivaroth had seen his ambitions unfold before him, so, in that demon that had attacked them, the blind man had seen the spirit that could take him to this elusive 'other place' that he was eternally fretting for. Nothing now would quench his desire.

And, Ivaroth realized starkly as the flame in front of him finally flickered out, he would indeed fulfil his promise and one day carry the blind man into the worlds beyond again, to seek this 'other place', because he would need the blind man not only to conquer the south but to rule it, and to maintain his rule over the tribes.

The blind man was power, and power must be a close-watched ally not a captive, or it would bloom in secret and then turn on its captor.

Their mutual needs and desires bound Ivaroth and the blind man more completely than any lovers, and, in the end, only death would separate them.

That night Ivaroth led the blind man into Amhir's dreams.

The shaman's screams could be heard around the camp, but he could not be wakened.

In the end, he died.

None could look on his face.

Chapter 28

Ryllans seized Arwain to stop him falling from the saddle, at the same time searching through the milling crowd to see who had thrown the rock and whether more were likely to follow.

The rest of the platoon closed in around him rapidly, while the Whendreachi guards, drawing short staves, charged into the noisiest group of youths, scattering them briefly.

Like skirmishers, however, the youths merely dodged and weaved between the horses and the flailing weapons, and whenever opportunity presented itself, stood their ground to throw more stones and other missiles at the platoon and its escort.

It took Ryllans little time to realize that they were in considerable danger. Except for himself and Arwain, the platoon was unarmed, which effectively left them only with their horses as weapons. But the street was crowded not only with attacking youths but also many other people who were obviously innocent of any ill intent; indeed some had already been injured by the indiscriminately thrown stones. If he led the platoon out at the charge, many people would be badly hurt and, in any event, he was not sufficiently familiar with the city to know which would be the best way to flee.

A screaming woman, with blood running down her face, bumped into his horse to emphasize his dilemma.

He looked around again and, somewhat to his relief, saw that the Whendreachi guards seemed to be familiar with this type of problem. After their initial charge they were working in groups to pick out and deal with individual offenders. This tactic not only lessened the intensity of the assaults, but made the guards the new focus as the youths sought to rescue their compatriots.

'This way!' an officer shouted to Ryllans. He was pointing to a narrow alleyway nearby. Instinctively, Ryllans looked up at the rooftops for would-be ambushers, but the officer shouted again more insistently.

A figure surged from between two horses and grabbed at

Ryllans in an attempt to unhorse him. For his pains he received a snakelike flick of the Mantynnai's fingers across the end of his nose which sent him reeling backwards, howling in pain, but uninjured.

The next assailant was treated less charitably and caught the heel of Ryllans' thrusting boot squarely on the jaw. He collapsed without a sound.

Others among the platoon were dealing similarly with such of the youths as reached them, and a degree of reluctance was beginning to show itself in their attackers. It was no victory however: the youths merely fell back and increased their stone-throwing.

'Hurry. Follow me,' the Whendreachi officer shouted urgently, riding into the alleyway. 'My men will form a rearguard. We can reach the other street before they can get around.'

Still supporting Arwain, Ryllans rode after him, and the rest of the platoon followed. The alleyway was barely wide enough for two horses to ride side by side, and Ryllans had to lean forward awkwardly to support Arwain as they clattered along it. Shouts and screams followed after them.

The street they entered at the far end was quieter, and such people as were there seemed to offer no threat, though seeing the horsemen emerge from the alleyway at speed, several of them began to scurry away, obviously in anticipation of trouble. Ryllans handed Arwain to one of his comrades as he checked the rest of the platoon leaving the alleyway.

All arrived safely without serious injury, though there were several with cuts and bruises. He noted, however, that several of the Whendreachi guards were missing.

'Your men?' he said, catching the officer's arm as he rode by.

'They'll keep them occupied for a while,' the officer replied. 'Don't worry, they're used to this kind of thing. And the Watchguards will be along soon. But we must keep moving.' He nodded towards the bleeding Arwain. 'We can't stop to look at your man. Just keep him in his saddle and follow me.'

He made no further delay but galloped off immediately, beckoning Ryllans to follow.

As they swung to the left at the end of the street, a group of youths came running from the right.

This time, seeing his attackers clearly, and unhindered by

passers-by, Ryllans led a group of the Mantynnai wide and scattered them without losing speed. The Whendreachi officer gave him a wave of thanks.

There were no further incidents as they galloped through the city, but it was apparent to Ryllans that the officer was avoiding the larger streets. Despite the urgency of their flight, he noted that many of the buildings they passed were similar in style to those in the Moras district, although they were clean and well maintained. He felt a slight twinge of regret that he had not been able to spend more time looking at the famous Whendreachi architecture.

As they neared the gate, it became clear that, though rapid, their pace had not been rapid enough; a crowd was already gathering. And people were arriving from every direction. Again they were mainly youths, though Ryllans saw several older men among them, and many were wearing the grey uniform that Garren and his supporters had worn. A small force of guards was struggling to keep the gate open.

The officer swore softly to himself. 'We'll do our best,' he said to Ryllans. 'But I can't guarantee your safety.' There was anger in his eyes as he looked at Ryllans. 'You'll understand what it costs me to say this, soldier. These are my people and my problem, and we neither want nor need you here. But do what you have to do to survive if we can't hold them for you. Try not to kill anyone if you can avoid it.'

Ryllans nodded. 'Triple file, and trot,' he shouted to the platoon. 'Follow the guards and defend yourselves as needed. Minimum effective force.'

As they moved forward, Ryllans jumped from his horse on to Arwain's and, pushing him forward, covered him with his own body.

The crowd began shouting and throwing stones as they drew near and the group trying to shut the gate increased its efforts.

Unexpectedly, the Whendreachi officer signalled a halt and then walked his horse forward a little way.

Ryllans, fearing treachery, discreetly positioned himself to draw his sword quickly and to lead his men through at the charge.

The officer conspicuously returned his staff to its loop on his saddle, then he held up his hand for silence. The stone-throwing stopped and the shouting died down a little.

'These people are official representatives of Duke Ibris of

Serenstad,' he said, authoritatively. 'They're here unarmed, bar two of them, in strict accordance with both the letter and the spirit of the treaty. They're entitled under our law to courtesy and safe passage.' The crowd grew quieter, as the majority tried to hear what he was saying. Their general demeanour, however, was still hostile and abusive.

Someone gave a cry of command and the group by the gate began trying to close it again.

The officer stood in his stirrups and pointed to the group. Then, in a voice that had obviously rung out across many training yards, and through which a marked Whendreachi accent was breaking, he bellowed, 'Shut that if you want, but be advised. If you do, we'll have no alternative but to hand our weapons to the Serens so that they can fight their way out. And whatever they do to you will then have the sanction of our law and the treaty. It's your choice.'

The group around the gate faltered. Some stood back, though others began redoubling their efforts to close it, jeering and catcalling raucously as they did. The officer gave a resigned shrug and casually drew his sword. He nodded towards Arwain. 'You surprise me,' he said. 'This man here wasn't struck down by some hero. He was hit by a stone, as were several passers-by.' Carefully he took hold of the blade of his sword with his left hand and, holding the hilt forward, glanced around as if looking for someone to whom he could hand it. 'I think you should know, however, that stone-throwing will be no defence against these men. They're less than pleased at being attacked for no reason, and many of them are Mantynnai; you know . . . Viernce.' He paused briefly to allow the significance of the words to sink in. 'So if you wish to lock yourselves in with them, armed and angry and with free rein to do whatever they have to to defend themselves, then feel free. It'll save me and my men a great deal of trouble.'

The crowd fell silent, and the group by the gate thinned still further, some of them now actively dragging others away.

Seeing the opportunity in the lull, the gate guards moved quietly forward, and opened a passage through the crowd. There was no resistance.

The officer sheathed his sword and motioned the platoon forward. Cautiously, Ryllans moved back on to his own horse. But the balance of mood within the crowd was almost palpable. A careless gesture now could tip them over into riot regardless of what individuals among them might think about tackling the Mantynnai.

'Eyes front,' he ordered calmly and formally. 'Walk.'

As he passed the officer standing in the gateway, he saluted him but did not speak. The officer returned the salute. The only sound to be heard was the leisurely clatter of the horses' hooves on the stone roadway.

Then they were all through the gate. The palace guards closed in quietly behind them, blocking the gateway with their horses while the members of the platoon began quickly recovering their weapons from the gatehouse.

For the first time Ryllans was able to examine Arwain's injury. There was quite a lot of blood, but the wound appeared to be only superficial.

He dismounted. 'A little water to bathe this?' he asked the officer.

The man glanced back through the crowded gate and regretfully shook his head. 'I'm sorry. You see the way it is,' he replied. 'You mustn't stay here. We've been lucky. The crowd's getting bigger and I haven't the men to defend you.' He looked straight at Ryllans. 'I don't want you taking swords to them despite what I said, and that's what you'll have to do. Whendreachi slaughtered by Serens, however justifiably, will tear the city apart, and bring the Bethlarii down on us like wolves. Please go now, there are good streams not far along the road.'

'I understand,' Ryllans replied. And to give truth to the officer's words, the noise of the crowd began to grow again. Suddenly a single figure wriggled between the horses and, evading the lunging guards, charged, screaming, towards Ryllans. He was wildly waving an axe.

Ryllans stepped away from the officer with a quick shake of his head to indicate that he should not interfere. Then, as the demented figure reached him, the axe raised for a skull-splitting blow, he stepped casually aside as if nothing untoward were happening, and swung up into his saddle.

His attacker, unable to stop because of the timing of Ryllans' movement, ran through the place where he had been standing and straight into the gatehouse wall. His hysterical screaming ended with an abrupt and incongruous 'Erk!' as he struck the wall. Staggering back, stunned, he dropped the axe on to his foot and flopped down on to the ground with a winding thud.

Ryllans ignored him and, with a final salute to the officer, signalled the platoon forward. The officer was grinning broadly at the Mantynnai's treatment of his attacker, and quite a few of the crowd were also laughing. It was as good a gift as he could give them under the circumstances.

The platoon moved to the canter almost immediately. Glancing back, Ryllans saw that the gate was being closed.

They maintained the pace until they came to the first stream, where they stopped and Ryllans began treating Arwain's injury.

He could not keep the concern from his manner. Cleared of blood, the gash, as he had thought at the gatehouse, did not seem to be deep. But Arwain was showing no signs of consciousness.

He shook his head. Arwain needed attention more skilled than he could give, but the nearest city where such help could be found was now Serenstad itself. 'We can be there before midnight if we ride hard,' someone said.

Ryllans shook his head. 'A journey like that might kill him for sure,' he said.

'So might the delay,' was the reply.

'I can't risk it,' Ryllans said. 'We'll have to travel slowly. But if we can't get to the city quickly, we'll have to bring the city to us.' Without further delay he selected three men to travel to Serenstad as fast as possible, with instructions to return with the Duke's physician, Drayner, and a suitable vehicle for transporting Arwain.

As the men galloped into the distance, Arwain was carefully lifted back into the saddle and the platoon moved off again, leaving a further three men to act as rearguard in the event of pursuit from Whendrak for any reason.

Ryllans grimaced as he mounted up behind Arwain to give him as much support as possible. Nothing he had done could have avoided the injury, but . . .

He let the self-reproach go, it served no useful purpose. Nevertheless, walking when his lord and friend needed urgent help, would be agonizing, and there was little or no consolation in the fact that he knew that this decision also was correct.

Help, however, was nearer to hand than Ryllans had thought, as late in the afternoon the three messengers encountered Menedrion and his company escorting the Bethlarii envoy back to the border.

Where Arwain's platoon had been dressed in simple field uniforms and had moved quickly but with alert discretion, Menedrion's company was moving at a leisurely pace and was dressed with formal pomp. It was a blaze of colour even in the dying daylight.

Alert for any excuse to leave the sour presence of the envoy, it was Menedrion himself who made his way through the vanguard that had halted the three riders. He was wearing a black fine-linked chain mail and a red surcoat emblazoned with his own eagle crest, and he looked like some hero from Serenstad's ancient literature. He was, however, a soldier of the present, and after a quick glance at the breathless riders and the foam-covered horses, it took him but a few questions to find out what had happened and to determine his course of action.

Within minutes, three of his own men, fresh mounted, were galloping back towards Serenstad, while his company physician and an escort were galloping towards Whendrak, followed by the hospital cart, moving as fast as it safely could.

Menedrion returned to the envoy's side, but did not speak.

You can ask if you want to know, you bastard, he thought.

To his annoyance, however, Grygyr was as impassive as ever, seemingly quite indifferent to the commotion that the arrival of the three riders had caused.

Not that the lack of conversation distressed Menedrion immediately. His mind was now full of questions following the brief account given to him by the messengers. Arwain hurt in Whendrak by rioters? Serious disturbances in the streets? He had not asked why; had there been some pursuing danger, the messengers would have volunteered the information.

His father's words came back to him ominously. ' . . . if something's seriously amiss then it'll only be my bastard son they've got, not my heir . . .' Ibris had been thinking in terms of hostages, Menedrion knew, not injury.

Once upon a time, and largely due to the influence of his mother, Menedrion would have been quite happy to see Arwain come to grief, but since he had been named his father's heir and he, Arwain and Goran had sworn oaths of loyalty to one another he had mellowed a little towards him.

It helped too that Arwain showed not merely no outward inclination to rival him for the Dukedom, but a positive disinclination, though Menedrion did not have his father's sight in this. Ibris knew that if Arwain wished to oust Menedrion then he was quite capable of doing it both effectively and quietly.

However, Menedrion's concern as he tried to settle back into this leisurely diplomatic escort, was, somewhat to his own surprise, quite genuine, and the stony indifference of the envoy seemed to increase his need to speak in order to put a stop to the whirling, repetitive thoughts that were besetting him.

With an effort, he forced himself to speak of other matters.

'It'll be an hour or so before we can pitch camp,' he said. 'I confess I'll be glad to stretch out tonight. I find this kind of slow progress more wearying than a forced march.' He turned towards Grygyr. 'I suppose you'll be glad to get back to your own field quarters again after sleeping in our effete feather beds.'

Menedrion made the remark in all innocence, adopting a 'companions in adversity' manner. He was startled therefore at the envoy's expression as he turned sharply to face him. Throughout his brief stay, Grygyr's face had borne no other expression than contempt and indifference. Now fury and alarm mingled unashamedly.

'What do you mean?' he asked, hoarsely.

I don't know, Menedrion thought. But if it's stinging your backside I'm going to find out, and mean it again.

'Nothing special,' he said blandly, as if the small outburst had not happened. 'I couldn't help noticing that you seemed tired this morning. I presumed you hadn't slept well.'

Grygyr's control reasserted itself. 'I slept well,' he said, tersely.

Menedrion persisted, the soldier in him felt a weakness in his enemy that needed to be probed. 'I'm glad,' he said. 'Sleep is important. Lack of it is apt to mar the judgement and can lead to serious mistakes.' He paused. 'Mistakes that envoys and soldiers can't afford, eh?'

'I slept well,' Grygyr said again, looking stonily forward.

'As I'm sure you will tonight,' Menedrion said, nodding.

Later as the company began to make camp, he sought out Pandra. Mindful of Ibris's instructions about the old man, Menedrion had established him in a covered living wagon with a soft bed and many cushions. When he found him, however, Pandra was alternately rubbing his back and banging the bed.

'What's the matter?' Menedrion asked in some concern. 'Is the bed too hard?'

Pandra shook his head. 'No, sir,' he replied. 'I'm afraid it's too soft. I need a hard bed. I'll lie on the floor tonight. I'll be fine.'

The incongruity of the frail old man's reply released some of the tension from Menedrion, and he laughed loudly. 'I'll have one of the pioneers find a couple of planks for your bed,' he said. 'I can't have my father finding out that I made you sleep on the floor.'

He laughed again as he leaned out of the door of the wagon and shouted orders to someone.

'Did you want something from me, sir?' Pandra asked when Menedrion came back inside. He was puzzled by the mirth he had unwittingly caused.

Menedrion became more serious and motioned him to sit down. 'Yes, I do,' he said, lowering his voice. 'Something's disturbing the envoy. Something about sleep, I think. Do you think you could . . .' He gesticulated vaguely. ' . . . get into his head tonight and see what's happening?'

Pandra looked at him. 'No, sir,' he said carefully, shaking his head. 'It—'

Menedrion scowled. 'I thought you could enter dreams without the knowledge of the dreamer,' he interrupted.

Pandra raised a hesitant hand. 'That's true, sir,' he said. 'But I can tell you already that you're right about the envoy. Antyr kept watch on him last night and he spoke to your father about what he encountered there. He didn't tell me anything except that it was useful and that I should keep clear of the envoy's dreams myself.' Briefly he held Menedrion's gaze. 'He was quite emphatic about it, sir. My task is to protect you, not to venture into regions where I might well be lost, and you with me.'

Menedrion's jaw tightened. Nothing untoward had happened while he had slept the previous night, and the subtle presence of Pandra and Kany had been oddly reassuring, but though he was still uneasy about going to sleep, it unsettled him in some way to have this odd pair in his entourage as 'protectors'.

Pandra noted his returning tension. He became confidential. 'But he also said that, though we should not

377

lower our guard, he felt the danger to you and your father had actually become less because of his own encounter in the Threshold.'

Menedrion shook his head. 'I don't understand any of this,' he said finally. 'My bodyguards carry swords and shields. And *I* need enemies that I can take a sword to, not all these . . . shadows . . . vague images.'

He fell silent, his face perplexed.

'This whole business is unmanning me,' he said eventually, lowering his head. 'And I've actually got a stiff jaw being . . . diplomatic . . . to that stone-faced Bethlarii, knowing that he's as anxious as I am to try knocks with me.' He looked up, his face frustrated. 'Now I have to have my sleeping hours patrolled by an old man and a rabbit.'

Under other circumstances, Pandra might have chuckled at such an observation, but it needed no great sensitivity to see that Menedrion was in a dark mood, and would have to be handled carefully. Before he could speak, however, a face appeared briefly round the door of the wagon.

'Who wanted their bed making harder?' it said irritably, then, without waiting for an answer, it disappeared and several wooden boards were precipitated noisily through the door followed by a large canvas tool bag. The wagon shook under the impact as it landed. 'You civilians don't know you're born,' continued the face, as its owner followed and plunged straightway into the bag. He raised his voice to make himself heard over the noise of his rattling tools. 'Everyone else is moaning because the ground's too hard, as if it was my fault, for crying out loud. And it's fetch this, fetch that, as if I didn't have my own duties. And now *your* bed's too soft. I've more important things than this, you know—'

He stopped suddenly as he looked up from his bag in search of the culprit and found himself staring into Menedrion's face. There was a brief, confusing flurry as he stood up hurriedly and saluted; not easy in a low, crowded wagon and with a large saw in one hand. Both Pandra and Menedrion were obliged to take evasive action.

'At ease,' Menedrion said grimly, when the wide-eyed man came to a shaking stillness at last, but before he could find the words to fill his desperately working mouth.

The man's stamping foot shook the wagon again.

Menedrion seemed to be holding a brief debate with

himself, then he stood up. 'Tell him what you want and then join me outside,' he said tersely to Pandra.

A few moments later, Pandra climbed carefully down the steps of the wagon; behind him a desperate hammering began. Despite himself, Pandra could not forbear smiling.

Menedrion, however, seemed still to be preoccupied by his own thoughts and Pandra laid his amusement at the pioneer's antics on one side. He seemed to have established some rapport with this wild, dangerous son of Ibris, but he had no illusion about understanding him, and knew only too well that an injudicious familiarity might bring down a dire punishment, if not on his head, by virtue of the protection his age and Ibris's will offered him, then on some other innocent's such as the churlish pioneer.

Falling in beside Menedrion he looked about him at the purposeful activity of the company establishing its camp around them. All manner of noises filled the air: hammering and banging, shouted commands, laughter, oaths, some vigorous but tuneless singing, the occasional bark of a dog somewhere, the neighing of disturbed horses . . .

And it smelt of damp, newly crushed grass, savoury meats from an impromptu kitchen somewhere, smoke from the dozens of torches that were transforming the camp into a flickering world of brightness and shadows.

'May I speak, sir?' he said eventually.

Menedrion started slightly and then nodded.

'I don't think you should concern yourself with what's happening in the dream worlds,' he said. 'There's nothing you can do except follow my, or Antyr's, advice. There's some Dream Finder blood in your family's veins without a doubt, that's why you sensed the Bethlarii's pain. But the true skill hasn't been given to you and you're helpless there. As helpless as I'd be these days in an infantry line.'

'Does this have a point?' Menedrion said.

Pandra felt the edge in his voice, but continued.

'Strange forces are moving against us, sir,' he said, watching Menedrion carefully. 'Forces that none of us understand, but which will destroy us if we don't accept their reality. And the reality is that they're attacking you through your dreams and *only* a Dream Finder can truly protect you.'

A twitch of impatience made a fleeting appearance on Menedrion's face, but Pandra went on, his voice unexpectedly forceful.

'You know the truth of that, sir,' he said. 'You've felt it and you're too clear-sighted to deny it.'

Menedrion did not reply.

'The cavalry trust the infantry to split the enemy line so that they can drive into it,' Pandra continued. 'The infantry trust the cavalry to guard their flanks and rear. If you climb a siege tower you trust your engineers know their work and that it won't collapse under you. So it is here. You must trust me and get on with the tasks that are yours. I'm your shield-bearer in the dream world. Kany and I might be just a rabbit and a frail old man here, but our Dreamselves are not so. We've more than enough skill to protect you. Kany on his own has spirit enough to quell a wolf; you've felt that too, I know.'

Menedrion stopped and looked at him, doubt beginning to replace his angry impatience.

'You must fight where you fight best, sir,' Pandra said, almost reckless now. 'Not cloud your judgement with matters beyond your knowledge and training. Your task is to help your father avoid war with the Bethlarii, or, if that fails, to arm his army from your forges and lead it against them. If you fail in this, then we're all lost.'

'And if you or Antyr fail against these . . . powers . . . as you call them?' Menedrion asked soberly.

Pandra looked into his eyes. 'Then, too, we're probably all lost,' he replied slowly.

'This isn't easy,' Menedrion said, expelling a noisy breath.

'Have you ever fought a battle that was?' Pandra retorted. 'Or one that wasn't different from every other? Or one that didn't cause you pain and loss even when you won?'

Menedrion did not reply.

Pandra went on. 'Each new weapon that's invented, each new tactic that's thought of, always breeds its own reply. Defences are invented that were never dreamt of before. So it is here. Despite feeling the reality of what's happened to you, you still rebel at the idea of strange forces assailing us through our dreams. Yet, just as they came from some place beyond our knowledge, in response to them comes an equally strange, improbable defender; a poor spark of a man, seemingly hell-bent on destroying himself for most of his life, suddenly thrust forward by . . . fate . . . chance . . . who knows?' He echoed Feranc's words. 'Just like some inconsequential pikeman who somehow rallies his comrades when they're about to break.'

He hesitated. 'I think perhaps we must accept, sir, that we may not be the principals in this conflict. We may be unwitting participants in some greater battle. But whatever, we must each face the enemies that we *can* face and trust others to do likewise.'

Menedrion looked up into the night sky. It was too dark to see the clouds and the air was full of rising sparks and a swirling haze of smoke from fires and torches. 'I concede your conclusions,' he said. 'They're scarcely profound. But let's not pretend this is some "battle of the gods" we're involved in, Dream Finder. Somewhere at the back of it all are *men*. What you could be usefully doing is finding them. Once you've done that . . .' He slapped his sword hilt. 'I'll need no magic skills for dealing with them.'

Then with an abrupt though not discourteous nod, he dismissed Pandra and strode off through the hectic camp, his heavy form black in the torchlight. Pandra watched him go, then turned to head back to his wagon.

'You handled that very well,' came a patronizing voice in his head.

'Thank you, Kany,' he replied. 'And thank you for the support you gave me by pretending to be asleep all the time.'

The rabbit ignored the jibe. 'Spirit to quell a wolf, eh?' he preened. 'Very poetic. And very true.'

'No. Just very poetic,' Pandra replied caustically. 'I've a professional and patriotic obligation to keep up the morale of my client, and that allows me a little . . . licence . . . with the truth at such times.'

Kany gave a dismissive snort, then, abruptly serious, he said, 'Do you think he understands?'

Pandra shrugged. 'Why should he?' he replied. 'We don't. Nor, for that matter, does Antyr. I just hope I told him the truth when I spoke about Antyr as our unheralded defender. What he can do awes me, but I'd feel a lot easier if I could see a little more technique and a little less luck in the proceedings.'

'Technique? Luck?' Kany burst out scornfully. 'I despair of you creatures. You're so . . .' He struggled for a word. ' . . . so . . . cluttered . . . disjointed . . . unaware . . .' He gave up. 'Of course you told Menedrion the truth. You just weren't listening! How you ever survived as a species, being so deaf, blind and stupid, defies me utterly. I suppose it's MaraVestriss's idea of a joke.' His mood darkened. 'In which

381

case, with a sense of humour like that, he must be human himself. That's a grim thought I could well have done without.'

'Would you like a carrot?' Pandra said into the inky silence that followed this revelation.

Later, Pandra lay down luxuriously on his hard bed and prepared to search out the sleeping Menedrion's mind. Had he chosen, he could have reached it instantly, but he preferred to allow his Dreamself to wander through the great cloud of whirling night thoughts that rose from the camp, rather as a general might survey the terrain he was in before moving his forces against a particular foe; though to Pandra this preliminary excursion was more like entering a great library or a beautiful garden than preparing for a battle.

Just as the smoke from the fires and torches rose into the sky and diffused and reflected their light to form a hazy, orange dome over the camp, so the thoughts and dreams of the company hovered like a shimmering golden cloud around Pandra as Kany carried him forward on the search. It was a skill that had grown immeasurably since they had met Antyr, and both revelled in it.

They drifted, timeless, weightless, unhindered.

Where they chose to listen, the noise was clamorous, and where they chose to look, the scenes were hectic and boisterous. But all was well; the company *was* predominantly male; and no strange shadows moved through the haze, nor untoward sounds or movements disturbed it.

Very tentatively, and despite Kany's stern disapproval, Pandra touched the Bethlarii's mind. It made him start: it was raw with swirling emotions, dominant among which was fear. But there was nothing untoward and Pandra abandoned it feeling slightly ashamed at his intrusion.

Then he *did* sense a presence. It was faint, like a star in the corner of his eye, appearing fitfully between slowly drifting clouds. It was, however, quite definite.

Without speaking, Kany brought Pandra instantly to the fringes of Menedrion's night thoughts.

Nothing was amiss.

Although Menedrion was not dreaming, Pandra knew that the tide of his sleep was carrying him into the dreamlight of the Nexus.

Then the presence was there also; still faint, but

nevertheless sharp and hard. Pandra sensed Kany's cruel fighting instincts preparing to defend their charge, but feeling no immediate menace himself he gently breathed a soft word of patience.

Silently, but very alert, Dream Finder and Companion waited, as Menedrion drew nearer to his dream. The presence waited also.

Pandra began to feel a sense of loss about it. Helplessness. Confusion.

Then, as he had always been, he was Menedrion. He was alone and desolate, and sitting on the Ducal throne amid a deserted and decaying palace. A group of crows were bickering noisily around a gaping hole in the ceiling; the floor was littered with debris and the remains of broken furniture; pictures were defaced and statues smashed, and beyond the lichen-stained walls, he knew, lay a country ravaged by plague, famine, and war.

Pandra did not speak, but let his reassuring presence be felt. The scene, though grim, was no more than might be expected from a leader facing unknown responsibilities.

And yet, there was more. The presence was there also, but now it was in the dream; of the dream; he, Menedrion, felt it. Yet still it had no menace.

Kany waited. On the instant, he would snatch Menedrion back to wide-eyed wakefulness.

Then he was outside the palace, walking through the wrecked streets of Serenstad. Some of the houses were burning, and the air rang with the cries of the sick and the dying. Here and there, groups of people were running from building to building. Looters.

Pandra reeled. He was no longer Menedrion! He was. . . Arwain!

And yet he was Menedrion!

He was both! He was inside the palace, surrounded by decay, and he was outside, walking the ruined streets.

Sensitives. Kany formed the word in his mind. Ibris's bloodline. The dreams of the half-brothers had come together. Arwain it must have been who unwittingly rescued Menedrion from the Threshold three nights ago, Pandra realized.

What shall I do? Pandra thought softly to Kany.

Nothing, came the reply. Watch and wait. There's no danger . . . so far.

Menedrion rose from the throne and walked down the steps of the dais on which it stood. Dust and rubble crunched under his feet. Angrily he kicked away a silver goblet and it clattered noisily along the floor until it came to rest against an overturned table.

Arwain wandered, bemused and lost. Beggars held out their arms to him; mothers, their sick children. Smoke drifted into the street adding an acrid edge to the sweet smell of decay and death. He felt so weary, so sick. Somewhere was an answer to all this; but where? All the streets were familiar, but they were not where they had been; it was as if they had been shuffled and rejoined like the pieces of some child's game. He moved from place to place that should not have been together and yet were; and always had been.

Menedrion stepped up on to the fallen gates of the palace and looked across the palace square at the jagged, broken remains of the Ibrian monument. The square was surrounded by broken walls and charred ruins.

Rage boiled up within him. 'No!' he thundered. 'I will not have this.'

He started to run.

Arwain also began to run. His head pounded.

Menedrion felt the city streets moving under his feet as though he were motionless on a great treadmill. It came to him that, run as he might, he would not be able to escape.

Arwain, however, ran faster and faster, his breath gasping, his heart racing. He had to escape the destruction around him, the pain in his head. He had to escape.

Then a strange feeling of hope seemed to be just ahead of him.

Pandra felt Kany stiffening then releasing himself for movement. Nyriall had run towards hope in the Threshold, and moved from world to world!

'We must waken them,' Kany said urgently.

'No,' Pandra replied. 'Not yet. They need each other.'

'I don't understand . . .'

Arwain reached a small archway. It was a focus; the end of his chase. He reached out his arms to touch both sides then he leaned forward into it.

Beyond, brilliant against the begrimed horror of the destroyed city, was a beautiful land, with rolling countryside and forests through which great rivers flowed, shining silver and gold under the bright summer sun. He breathed in the heavy scents of grasses and trees that came to him softly on a warm summer breeze. Two paces more and he could lie down and rest his pulsing head among flowers and clovers.

Menedrion began to turn and turn, making the city whirl about him.

'No!' he shouted again. Then, 'Arwain! To me! To me! This must not be. To me!'

Abruptly, he stopped.

Arwain turned.

Ibris's sons faced one another. Behind Menedrion lay ruined Serenstad like a crumpled map. Behind Arwain stood the archway, blue with summer sky and bright with the hope of a world beyond that of men.

Arwain beckoned Menedrion forward, gesturing towards the archway.

Pandra, bound to each of the Dreamselves, found their two desires, needs, resonating with his own. This was, beyond a doubt, a Gateway to the Threshold. How it came to be found by a dreamer unaided was a question that could perhaps never be answered . . .

He is sensitive, he is injured, and he has travelled here before, came Kany's thoughts, colder, less awed, than the Dream Finder's, but fearful for all that.

. . . but he *had* found it, and just as Arwain, bruised and hurt, sought the seeming solace of the world it opened on to, so Pandra, the Dream Finder, was drawn almost irresistibly to step through into the world he knew he might never find again. Yet too he knew that dangers lay beyond the Gateway with which he was not equipped to contend. And to step through would be to enter a world from which he might not be able to return, leaving his body perhaps to perish here.

And it was not the way, Menedrion knew. Here was where they both belonged. Fighting to bring the beauty of the world beyond to this world here. Fighting to prevent the horrors about them. Not chasing after vague shadows; resting while their people suffered.

Pandra was surprised at Menedrion's perceptiveness and his deep feeling for his future role.

The situation, however, was dangerous and, to his horror, caught in both Dreamselves, Pandra knew he could do nothing. He could speak to either, but he could not instruct the dreamer; the Dreamself was not the real self and would not necessarily be directed by reason.

And, in any event, he was as torn as they were. The desires of the half-brothers began to mingle. Both felt the lure of the beautiful world beyond, both knew that they did not belong there.

Then the archway began to grow larger. Arwain staggered towards the brightness.

Menedrion's hand closed about his brother's in the instant that Kany's powerful reflexes, beyond all conscious control now, tore away the veils of sleep.

Chapter 29

Pandra dashed through the camp, accompanied by the guard who had been posted outside his wagon. The air was cold and damp and, after only a few paces, the dew-sodden grass had soaked his feet and the hem of his robe.

The dull red remains of camp fires, and the guttering efforts of a few torches were all that lit their way, though, to the east, the sky was greying slightly.

The guard, still bewildered by Pandra's abrupt and explosive emergence from the wagon, was leading the way.

'There, sir,' he said, pointing towards a large tent.

Menedrion's tent, however, needed no identification, for the entrance flap had been thrown back and the Duke's son was standing there, illuminated by lamplight from within. He was berating two sentries who were making a desperate attempt to rekindle a fire.

Pandra stopped and raised his hands in relief.

'Sir!' he shouted. Menedrion started and peered into the gloom. Pandra stepped forward and without any courtesies took Menedrion's elbow and guided him back into the tent.

Inside, Menedrion yanked his arm free. 'I was about to send for you, general,' he said acidly. 'I have the feeling that you left our retreat a little late there, or am I mistaken?' Then, angrily, 'What in thunder's name is going on? And why was Arwain there? And where is he now?'

Pandra dropped down into a nearby chair and leaned forward, breathing heavily.

'Give him a chance to catch his breath, man,' Kany's voice snapped angrily into Menedrion's mind. 'He's older than your father, you know. He shouldn't be being bounced about the countryside in a cart like a pig going to market. And even less should he be running around at this time of night to be roared at by ungracious louts. He'll be lucky if he doesn't catch a chill.'

Menedrion raised his hands apologetically in response to Kany's commanding tone, then he clenched his fists and, after taking a long breath, burst out furiously, 'I won't be spoken to like that by a . . . a . . . *rabbit*! By a . . . pie filling!'

Kany struggled out of one of Pandra's pockets. Pandra was still catching his breath, but he placed a restraining hand on his Companion's indignant head. It was to little avail.

'I'd give *you* a rare belly ache, Irfan Menedrion,' Kany retorted angrily. 'It's me you can thank for getting you out of there at all.'

Menedrion's jaw came out and he raised a menacing finger.

'Enough, enough,' Pandra managed at last. 'No more, please. It's like being in a sack with a cat and a dog with you two. Please give a moment then we'll talk quietly, and calmly.'

Kany, his nose twitching ferociously, scrambled awkwardly round into Pandra's lap where the old Dream Finder stroked him gently. Gradually both began to breathe more easy.

'I don't know the answer to any of your questions, sir,' Pandra said eventually. 'My hope is that you saved your brother, but in all honesty I don't know.'

Menedrion sat down on the edge of his bed, his angry face becoming bewildered.

Pandra did not wait for him to speak. 'You and your brother are both sensitives,' he said. 'It was probably him who became tangled in your dream and brought you back from the Threshold the other night; drawn to you unknowingly in your danger.' He shrugged. 'By some quality in your bloodline, just as you were drawn to *him* tonight.'

Menedrion, however, was hardly listening.

'The world through the archway seemed so real,' he said, his voice unexpectedly soft and distant. 'So bright, powerful . . .'

'It *was* real, sir,' Pandra said. 'And viewing it from the grim darkness of your dream made its brightness all the more vivid.'

'You wanted to go into it as well, didn't you?' Menedrion said, looking into Pandra's eyes.

The old man nodded. 'Oh yes,' he said, without hesitation. 'But it would have been too dangerous.' He paused. 'Every world has its sunny days.'

'Why didn't you warn us?' Menedrion asked.

'I couldn't,' Pandra replied. 'I'm not a Mynedarion. I can't change things. I can speak, reassure perhaps, and certainly wake you if necessary, but dreams pursue the course the dreamer sets at some level beyond his knowing or controlling.

Besides, I've never encountered even a shared dream before, let alone found one of the Threshold Gateways. I took risk enough in making Kany wait until I saw . . . felt . . . what was happening.' He looked down at Kany. 'It may be that I stayed too long. It puts a great strain on a Companion to leave a dream like that.'

Menedrion nodded. 'I felt it,' he said. 'A great surge of power. I sat bolt upright, wide awake. I've been drowsier waking to a night ambush. It was . . . very strange.'

Tentatively he reached out and stroked Kany with his thick forefinger and the three fell silent.

Their reverie was disturbed by the entrance of a guard.

'Look-outs report that Lord Arwain's platoon is in sight, sir,' he said quietly but urgently.

'Saddle my horse,' Menedrion said, standing up quickly.

He looked at Pandra as he struggled to fasten his tunic in haste. 'We'll wait, sir,' Pandra replied to the unasked question. 'Whatever's happened, there's nothing I can do now.'

Within minutes, Menedrion and two guards were galloping towards the approaching platoon. A dense, ground-hugging mist gave them a ghostly quality in the greying dawn and as he looked at the slow-moving hospital cart and its shadowy escort seemingly rising up out of this soft cloud-carpet, Menedrion wondered for a moment whether he was not dreaming again, and that he would wake up suddenly to find himself in his tent, or perhaps even in his rooms at the palace.

Hailing outriders dispelled his fancy, but Menedrion ignored them and rode straight to the cart. The driver made to halt, but Menedrion waved him on and swung from his saddle directly on to the small platform at the rear.

Inside, the hospital cart was lit by a swaying lamp, and sitting opposite him as he entered was his company physician. He could not see the man's face in the dim light, but his head was bowed slightly and Menedrion presumed he was asleep.

Baring his teeth, he stepped forward to shake him awake angrily, but a voice stopped him.

'Irfan, what's happening?'

Menedrion turned. It was Arwain. He was lying on a low bunk, a bandage about his head. His eyes were open and inquiring. He was alive! Menedrion knelt beside him and as he did so, Ryllans entered.

'Lord Arwain needs rest, gentlemen. Please don't disturb him further.'

It was the physician. He was standing behind the two men, very much awake. And his voice and manner were unequivocal. He outfaced the two warriors.

'He woke up sharply a few minutes ago,' he said, answering the unasked question. 'Don't ask me why or how. Head injuries are peculiar and such recoveries aren't unheard of; a lot depends on the individual's inner resources. I think he's out of whatever danger he might have been in, but he does need rest and a little natural sleep, so I must ask you to leave, or at least remain here in silence.'

Arwain's hand came out and caught Menedrion's sleeve. 'What's happening?' he asked again.

'You were struck by a stone as we left the Council hall in Whendrak,' Ryllans replied softly.

Arwain waved the answer aside and drew Menedrion lower. His face was anxious. 'For my sanity, Irfan. Did you dream as I did just this moment, and was there another present?'

'Yes,' Menedrion replied simply. 'The city in ruins, the archway. We shared the same dream, and an old Dream Finder and his Companion saved us from some danger at the arch.'

Arwain lay back, his manner easier. 'Dream Finder,' he muttered. 'Dream Finder.' Then he frowned. 'What were you doing using a Dream Finder?' He put his hand to his head, agitated again. 'And father. He's been using one. What—?'

Menedrion anticipated the physician whose hand was coming out to end the discussion. 'Rest easy,' he said. 'There's nothing to worry about. You're on your way home now and father will tell you what he's been up to when you get there. I'm escorting the Bethlarii back home.'

Arwain looked doubtful, but a long, loud yawn possessed him before he could pursue the matter, and his eyes started to close, albeit reluctantly. The physician took Menedrion's arm and with a glance motioned both him and Ryllans to the door.

Outside, Menedrion shivered. It was the first time he had noticed the morning cold.

'Ryllans, I got the bones of this affair from your messengers, but what the devil's going on?' he demanded angrily, taking the reins of his horse from one of the guards.

He mounted. 'And why the devil didn't you look after him properly?'

Ryllans ignored the criticism, but related the events at Whendrak accurately and quickly. His telling was too insistent and detailed for Menedrion not to pay attention and, when the tale was finished, his mood was quieter. At least here was something he *could* deal with; enemies with weapons and all too human malice in their hearts.

He pulled his cloak about him. 'We have to go past Whendrak with the envoy, Ryllans,' he said. 'What's your advice?'

'Avoid the city and the nearby routes,' Ryllans said, without hesitation. 'The problem must be serious if such fanatical Bethlarii supporters have actually been appointed to the Council, and another Serens' presence so soon will almost certainly cause more unrest.'

'The ridge way then?' Menedrion said.

Ryllans nodded. 'And take some of my company with you. They can drift into Bethlarii territory when the envoy's left. We need to find out how far their army's been mobilized.'

Menedrion looked at him in some surprise. 'As bad as that already?' he asked.

'I think so,' Ryllans replied. 'And that's what I'm going to report to your father when I get back. The Bethlarii can mobilize more quickly than we can, we can't afford to delay. We can always stand down again if I'm wrong.'

Despite the grimness of their conversation, Menedrion chuckled. 'You'll be popular with Chancellor Aaken,' he said. 'Have you any idea how much it costs to mobilize the army to its attack strength? All the wages and compensation for taking men from their trades? And the disruption to commerce? We'll need no formal challenge, they'll hear Gythrin-Dy howling all the way to Bethlar.'

Ryllans blew out a steamy breath into the cold morning air and, his own mind still dark with his recent concern about Arwain, answered the remark seriously. 'I know how much it'll cost both in money and lives if the Bethlarii move on Whendrak and we're caught with unprepared companies and regiments scattered all over the land. And I know which way some of our less enthusiastic allies will jump as well.'

Menedrion, sobered by the cool response, nodded in agreement. 'Anyway, *that* decision is my father's, fortunately. You choose the men you want to go over the border and give them their instructions.' He paused thoughtfully. 'I think it would be better if they didn't join our company, but continued on with you for a while and then returned quietly and shadowed us. That envoy doesn't miss much and he'd certainly notice your field uniforms suddenly appearing in the middle of all our fancy dress.'

Ryllans saluted. 'I've chosen and instructed them already, sir,' he said. 'If you don't require me further I'll go and confirm details with them right now.'

Menedrion nodded and then, dismounting, returned to the hospital cart. He remained quietly by his sleeping half-brother, his erstwhile rival, for a little while after the platoon had moved quietly past the awakening camp.

Later that day, the company, strung out to some length along the narrow ridge way, passed by Whendrak. The weather was cold, misty and damp, but occasionally the mist lifted and the city could be seen in the distance below.

Pausing on a grassy knoll, Menedrion stared at it in some distress. Columns of black smoke were rising from it at many points, and, as far as he could see, the various gates were all closed. He was not certain whether or not it was his imagination, but he thought he heard the faint sound of clashing arms and shouting crowds wafting on the chilly mountain air.

Grygyr Ast-Darvad joined him. With an effort Menedrion made his face impassive. With considerably less effort, the envoy's face remained so.

'Did you think to keep the persecution of our people away from my sight by taking this route?' Grygyr asked. 'Ar-Hyrdyn's breath blows away the mist of your deceit.'

Surreptitiously, Menedrion took a very deep breath and drove his fingernails into his palms to remind himself of his father's instructions.

'As I told you, envoy,' he said, slowly and carefully. 'We received word that there's been some rioting in the city, and that the mood of the Whendreachi was uncertain. As my first responsibility here is your safety I deemed it necessary to take a route that would keep us well away from the city.' Then, letting his restraint slip slightly, he added, 'And if you can see any of your people, as you call them, being persecuted from this distance, I commend your eyesight.'

Without waiting for a reply, he pulled his horse away and rejoined the company.

The brief remainder of the journey was without incident. They dropped back down into the valley and eventually came to the tall standing stone that had been placed there to mark the formal boundary between the territory of Bethlar and the neutral region around Whendrak. It was a bleak, desolate area, and apparently deserted, but Menedrion had little doubt that, somewhere amid the crags, Bethlarii eyes would be watching keenly.

Bearing in mind his father's remark that it would do the Bethlarii envoy little good to be seen to be being fêted by the Duke's son, Menedrion drew the company up in formal array on the east side of the stone, and offered them for inspection. The envoy refused, as curtly as he had refused every other courtesy, but Menedrion rode close to him and obliged him to move along the line while he bombarded him with fatuous pleasantries so that, to a distant observer, it might seem that they were in earnest conversation.

Then, by way of a finishing touch, he reached across and embraced him before easing his horse back and saluting. The whole company saluted and then gave a formal cheer. Grygyr glared at Menedrion furiously. 'Until we meet again, Serens,' he said, through clenched teeth, laying his hand on his sword hilt.

It was the first recognizable emotion the envoy had shown since he had arrived and it heartened Menedrion considerably. 'Until we meet again, envoy,' he echoed, with a bow and a broad, satisfied smile.

The envoy and his three aides galloped off quickly, but Menedrion had the company remain at its station until they had passed out of sight. Then he had them rest and eat, and finally he sent out several small parties ostensibly foraging for firewood and fresh water, but in reality providing a source of confusing movement which might be of value to the Mantynnai following on behind.

Not that he knew where Ryllans' men were. Deliberately he had not asked how they would enter Bethlarii territory and Ryllans had not volunteered the information. They might be in this very section of the valley right now, or they might be high on the ridges. But it did not matter. By keeping the company active for some time he was ensuring that they and not the silent trespassers would be the focus of attention for any watchers.

Finally they left. Menedrion risked taking one of the lower

routes, but skirted wide when they came again to Whendrak. As they passed by the city, however, the fires were noticeably worse and this time there was no doubt about the sound of fighting.

Grim-faced, Menedrion led the company past at a steady trot.

It was night when the remainder of Arwain's platoon arrived back at Serenstad, and the fog was descending again, yellow and sulphurous.

Ryllans had set an easy pace and they had been met eventually by a concerned Drayner. Arwain, however, after a few hours' sleep, had woken free from headache and all other ill effects of the blow he had received, save the pain of the wound itself. He pronounced himself fit to ride.

Drayner differed. 'I'm here as the Duke's representative,' he said at the first sign of reluctance by Arwain to submit to examination. 'To dispute with me is to dispute with him.'

Arwain glowered at him for a moment, but he was no match for the physician's moral authority under such circumstances. With an ill grace he submitted, confining himself to a small gesture of childish defiance, by swinging athletically from his horse directly on to the hospital cart.

Ryllans caught Drayner's eye, and the two older men smiled briefly.

Inside, Drayner spoke to Menedrion's physician as though, after the manner of physicians, Arwain were not there. Then he examined the wound, peered into his eyes, down his ears and, opportunely, in the middle of an increasingly angry inquiry from his patient, down his throat, all with a similar detachment.

In reply to Arwain's questions about the sudden appearance of Dream Finders in the middle of this crisis, Drayner maintained a steady litany. 'I know nothing. You must speak to your father about it.'

In the end, however, he had been obliged to agree that Arwain would probably suffer more harm fretting about returning home as, ' . . . part of a damned baggage train!' than by riding, and it was in this position that Arwain finally led his men on to the bridge over the river Seren.

There were no other travellers on it that night and it was a very different sight from when they had left two days earlier. The hovering firefly lights of the torches strewn about it emerged out of the gloom first, haloed and streaked, and giving it the atmosphere of a dimly lit cave; an atmosphere scarcely lessened by the gradual appearance of sections of its latticed sides which faded upwards into the yellow vagueness above like great cobwebs.

And the river itself seemed to be moving more slowly, its surface black and glistening and dully throwing back such of the torchlight as reached it.

No one spoke as the platoon rode slowly across the bridge, cloaks pulled protectively across their faces. The sound of the horses' hooves, and the occasional cough, fell flat and dead in the stillness.

'This is intolerable!' Ibris thundered as he yanked the great curtains together brutally, to blot out the sight of the smothered, suffocating city. 'It's been getting worse for a decade now.' He waved his arms vaguely as if signalling his own futility in the face of this massive assault on his demesne. 'And it's all Menedrion's fault,' he continued, half-heartedly. 'With his stinking workshops and factories. We didn't have fogs like this when I was young. If we had them at all they were grey and damp, not yellow and slimy!'

He sat down heavily in a large chair and pointed at Aaken. 'And don't bother defending him,' he said with a significant look. 'He's more than capable of doing that. And I'm well aware of the weapons we need and all the other trade implications.'

He fell suddenly silent and his expression changed to one of concern. 'When this Bethlarii business is over, if we're spared, we'll have to do something about it seriously,' he said, after a moment. 'This stuff's doing more harm to our people and the city than all the wars we've ever fought.'

It was an unequivocal judgement, and one he had never made before in such clear terms, although he had inveighed against the annual fogs often enough.

Aaken followed his Duke's advice and said nothing. The builder of the dazzling city needed no allies to his great cause and, having now voiced his new intent, would give short shrift to any who chose to oppose him. Besides, his outburst was not truly at the choking fog. It was at the Sened, with its bickering factions: some, for the most part safely beyond the chance of conscription, indignant and blustering, reproaching him for not summarily executing the Bethlarii envoy for his insolence and breach of the treaty, and demanding that war be declared on Bethlar immediately; others, whingeing and appeasing . . . we must compromise, give them this, give them that; while yet others, shrewd-eyed, were scenting the air like predators, looking for what advantage they might gain for themselves by agreeing with one side or the other.

And the Gythrin-Dy was different only in the emphasis of its rhetoric: Who's going to pay for all this? What about the disruption to trade and commerce? Special pleas for special trades, and their counterpart, 'Would the Duke ensure this time that men will be drawn equally from all trades?' And so on.

His own vision and will so clear, Ibris found the collective blunderings of others difficult to sympathize with and, particularly in times of emergency, would frequently remark in private that he was hard-pressed to know which of the many groups he despised the most.

On such occasions he regretted having delegated so much power to the two bodies, and it was little consolation to him that he knew he had had no alternative if his city and its dominions were not to be torn apart, either now or later, by the bloody tribal and family strife that had been the dominant feature of the land's long history.

Nevertheless, despite their failings, both houses had, reluctantly and after much noisy debate, given him the financial authority to mobilize the full army if need arose, 'which need to be reported to this house immediately'.

Without that, he would have had to risk bearing the initial costs of the mobilization himself and had it proved unnecessary he would have received little or no compensation. Such a financial loss could have weakened his and his family's position so seriously as to jeopardize their rôle as, effectively, the city's hereditary leaders. Some among the Senedwrs, he knew, had looked to that in opposing his request. He would remember them in due course.

Familiar with his lord's moods at such times, Aaken remained silent; glad that his irritation with the day's proceedings had found some kind of a voice in abusing the fog. He knew also, however, that Ibris's anger was compounded with concern for Arwain following the news of his injury brought by Menedrion's messengers. And too there were the alarming implications of the street violence in Whendrak.

The two men sat in silence for some time, Ibris lounging back and staring sourly at the faint halo around a nearby lamp.

Then, with a subdued snort of self-reproach at such idleness, he leaned forward and placed his hands on his knees, preparatory to standing up. As if on cue, the double doors at the far end of the room opened and Arwain entered, accompanied by Ryllans and Ciarll Feranc. The sound of busy activity washed in with them from the corridor beyond. It was cut off abruptly by the closing of the doors and the three men approached him.

Ibris rose quickly and without the old man's leverage on his knees he had been intending.

Embracing Arwain briefly but warmly, he nodded towards his bandaged head, and with an unsuccessful attempt at curtness, asked, 'Has Drayner seen that?'

'Yes, of course,' Arwain replied with the slightly patronizing tone of the grown child towards its over-anxious parent. 'And he's declared me fit for duty.'

Ibris grunted suspiciously, and then led Arwain over to the fire, motioning Ryllans and Feranc to follow. He looked at his son's damp hair and wrinkled his nose.

'You stink of the fog,' he said. 'Sit down, both of you and give me your report. All I've heard so far is that you were hurt in some street fighting.'

Arwain told such of the tale as he could and Ryllans completed the remainder. Ibris, leaning against the mantelpiece, asked few questions, and nodded approvingly at Ryllans' sending some of the Mantynnai into Bethlarii territory.

When they had finished, Ibris lowered his head thoughtfully and stared into the fire. Then, after a long silence, he looked up and turned to Feranc.

'How near are the local garrisons to being fully mobilized?' he asked.

'Very near,' Feranc replied. 'But despite the gossip about the Bethlarii envoy, the feeling is that it's an exercise.'

Ibris nodded. 'Well, none of us likes to face reality,' he said. 'But I want them ready for a forced march to Whendrak within the week, with first and second reserves standing by.' He turned to his chancellor. 'Aaken, what's the position with our mercenary groups?'

'Most of them have signed for winter duty, but I've no

doubt they'll be clamouring for extra payment if there's actual fighting to be done,' Aaken replied.

Ibris frowned slightly. 'Keep an eye on that, Ciarll,' he said. 'An agreement's an agreement, and they've had precious little to do these last few years. Let me know if you're not happy with anything, I don't want any of them suddenly changing sides in the middle of a battle.' Feranc nodded in reply but did not speak.

Ibris paused to push a smouldering log back into the fire with his boot.

'Send to Meck and ask them to mobilize also, with a view to watching for incursions south, just in case this is only a diversion after all. And *tell* them at Herion, Nestar and Veldan. Any havering there and invoke the Treaty right away. And find out if there's been any unusual Bethlarii activity in their areas recently. And tell our divisional commanders at Tellar and Stor what's happened so far, and that I want them ready for a march on Whendrak at a moment's notice. It'll cause some flurry, but impress the urgency of the matter on them.' He looked at Feranc significantly. 'And I think they'd better mobilize their reserves also, if only for domestic protection. We'll review the situation when Menedrion and the Mantynnai get back.'

Feranc nodded silently again, but Aaken fluttered slightly.

Ibris spoke: 'You know how fast the Bethlarii can mobilize if they want to, Aaken,' he said. 'Their whole society's built around the procedure. They could field an army ready to march into Whendrak in half the time it takes us. And it'll cost a damn sight more than mobilizing a few reserves if they do that.'

'I wasn't going to quibble about the cost,' Aaken replied defensively. 'At least, not now we have Sened backing. But what you're doing could be construed as a provocation and give the Bethlarii the excuse they've been looking for.'

'No,' Ibris said, definitely. 'They need no provocation from us, they've made up their minds, I fear. Their envoy having survived, they're going to use the trouble they've stirred up in Whendrak as an excuse for whatever large-scale military adventure it is they intend. I don't know what it will be, and I certainly don't know why, except that it's something to do with that damned religion of theirs . . .' He stopped abruptly and his gaze drifted thoughtfully towards the fire.

'Although it occurs to me now, that what they're doing

is not more than self-defence in a way,' he said softly, after a long silence.

Arwain looked up, his bandaged forehead wrinkled into a surprised frown. 'We don't threaten them,' he said, almost indignantly. 'We've been meticulous in observing both the letter and the spirit of the treaty.'

Ibris nodded. 'True,' he conceded. 'But nevertheless we threaten them, and will continue to do so increasingly.' He was speaking half to himself, as if to clarify his thoughts. 'We've grown and prospered through this long peace. Gained wealth, and won increasing influence in the land. Spread knowledge and invention and beauty. While the Bethlarii have clung . . . remained true, they'd say . . . to their old ways . . . to their ancient traditions. And stagnated as a consequence. Just by being what we are, we've struck at their very heart. Blow after blow after blow. And to oppose us in kind would be to change: to accept our way, and destroy their old ways even further.'

'You'd be the last to denounce tradition,' Arwain said. 'The rope that joins our shifting present to the solid anchor of the past.'

Ibris smiled slightly at this use of his own past rhetoric. 'In its place,' he agreed. 'While we know why we're following it . . . for remembering and learning from the past . . . for harmless pleasure, even.' His smile faded. 'But never blindly. Never just because it *is*. We all seek security and safety from the world's crueller ways, but change is the natural way of things no matter what we think about it, and the only true security is to accept that and act accordingly. The Bethlarii have sought to deny it; to deal with growing knowledge and complexity with ignorance and wilful simplicity. Now, in contrast to the light we've brought to ourselves, they've turned back to the dark centre of their nature, of all our natures, manifest in their savage old god and his bloodthirsty ways. They seek the annihilation of our whole way of life whether they realize it or not, and we must be prepared to seek theirs if we're to survive.'

Arwain frowned. 'A grim conclusion,' he said.

Ibris nodded regretfully. 'One prevails in combat only by being willing to be more ruthless than your enemy,' he said. It was the dark adage that had pervaded all Arwain's military education and that encapsulated the true horror of combat, be it between individuals or nations.

Briefly, visions of a war of conquest and the suppression of a people passed through Arwain's mind, but it was Ibris himself who dispelled them before they found voice. He let out a noisy breath. 'Still, it probably won't come to that,' he declared. 'If we can hit them hard enough, their very rigidity may bring the whole thing down about their ears.' He became brisk. 'And I've spent enough time conjecturing. Gentlemen, I'm detaining you from your duties.'

Arwain remained behind after the others had left.

Ibris became preoccupied again, standing staring into the fire. For all the hectic activity of the past days, it was the information that Antyr had brought to him in his strange, dreamlike visitation that loomed largest in his thoughts.

Without preamble, Ibris told his son of the strange events that had drawn Antyr and Pandra and their strange Companions into his confidence.

In so far as he had considered the matter Ibris had half expected Arwain's reaction to be one of rather caustic suspicion, but when he had finished, his son was silent and wide-eyed.

Ibris looked at him narrowly. 'Have *you* had any strange dreams recently?' he asked anxiously.

'Two. Both involving Irfan.' Arwain answered without hesitation, his voice hoarse.

Ibris stood up and tugged urgently at a bell pull by the fireplace. Almost immediately a servant entered.

'Ask Antyr and his Companions to join us immediately,' Ibris said, sharply. The servant disappeared even more quickly than he had appeared.

'You'll tell Antyr all about your dreams, and answer any of his questions fully and truthfully,' Ibris told Arwain.

His manner forbade any debate.

A few minutes later, Antyr was shown into the room accompanied by Tarrian and Grayle.

The two wolves moved to Ibris, their tails wagging, and he bent forward to stroke them. Arwain, however, stood up suddenly and pointed at Antyr. 'You were the one in the Moras the other day, with the Liktors and the Mantynnai . . .' He clicked his fingers. ' . . . Estaan.'

Antyr stepped back slightly. 'Yes,' he said, suddenly nervous. 'But I thought that that had all been attended to.'

Ibris laid a hand on Arwain's arm and eased him back into his seat. 'I heard about your little encounter,' he said with

400

a smile. 'But we've more important matters to deal with at the moment.'

The sight of Antyr, however, had brought all Arwain's concerns about the Mantynnai flooding back.

'More important than Ryllans hearing something that left him openly afraid and had all the Mantynnai holding late-night discussions *in their own language*?' Arwain replied in a low, urgent voice.

Ibris frowned briefly. 'I know something's disturbed them badly,' he said. 'But I'm not prepared to question them about it. My trust in them is total.'

'But—'

'Total, Arwain!' Ibris said definitively. 'The Mantynnai won't let anything threaten this land. In this matter we must wait on their will. However—' he motioned Antyr to sit down. The wolves circled down to rest at his feet. 'Their . . . unease . . . is duly noted and I'll be giving them every opportunity to talk about it.'

'And the two riders on the bridge that they recognized and who disturbed them as much as Estaan's message?' Arwain added, his voice still soft and urgent.

Ibris hesitated at this news, then, 'Tell me later,' he said, a flick of his hand ending the conversation. 'Right now, just tell Antyr about your dreams.'

Arwain hesitated, loath to have his concerns set aside so lightly.

'Now, Arwain!' Ibris said quietly but unequivocally.

Arwain hesitated again briefly, then with some awkwardness recounted the two dreams he had seemingly shared with Menedrion.

When he had finished, Antyr turned to Ibris and shook his head. 'I've no explanation,' he said. 'But your sons are sensitives, just as you are, sire. When Menedrion was threatened, Arwain was drawn to him and saved him. When Arwain was in danger of slipping into the Threshold, Menedrion was drawn to him in turn. I'll speak to Pandra, and Tarrian and Grayle will speak to Kany, but I doubt we'll find an explanation.' He raised his hand to prevent Ibris's pending interruption. 'However, I feel no danger here. Something deep inside your sons draws them to protect one another. They're bound by some old tie of blood. It's good.'

'But why was Arwain attacked in his dream?' Ibris asked anxiously.

'He wasn't,' Antyr replied. 'I don't know how he came to find the Gateway to the Threshold. Perhaps it was something to do with his earlier contact through Menedrion's dream, perhaps it was his injury . . .' A thought occurred to him. People often died from apparently slight head wounds. Could it be that some injuries led them towards and through a Gateway? He left the idea unspoken. 'But there was no power drawing him forth, no malign presence. He felt none and had they been aware of one, Pandra and Kany would have snatched him away on the instant. He was in danger, but he wasn't attacked.'

Ibris looked uncertain. He turned again to Arwain. 'How do you feel?' he asked.

Arwain was quietly battling for self-composure. Had it not been for his own experience he would not have given any of the current proceedings a moment's credence. Now, however, he had no choice but acceptance.

'Oddly enough, both more and less bewildered, more and less alarmed,' he replied. 'Less, because I'm reassured that I'm not going mad; more, because it seems to make both us and the Bethlarii part of some game between players who are beyond our reach and beyond our measure in power. How can we protect ourselves from such . . . creatures?'

'People,' Antyr corrected. 'One with a gift like my own, though greater, and one with a rarer, stranger, gift still. But people nevertheless. Not mythical creatures, not gods.'

'But as powerful as gods, from your telling,' Arwain replied. 'And I ask again, how can we protect ourselves from them?'

'After our encounter with them, I don't think any of you will be assailed again,' Antyr said. 'I think they'll be reluctant to wander indiscriminately through the Threshold again, judging by their treatment of the envoy.'

'But if?' Arwain persisted.

'Then knowledge will be your best protection,' Antyr replied. 'Knowledge of who you are and who they are, and that dreams are but shadows of your own making. In addition you should remember that even in ignorance, you and your brother watched over one another. And now Pandra and Kany will be watching you as well.' He pointed to the two wolves, seemingly asleep across Ibris's feet. '*We* will watch for the Mynedarion and pit ourselves against him if we come upon him. *You* must turn your mind to the enemy you *can* face – the Bethlarii.'

'But—'

Antyr waved him silent. Ibris raised an eyebrow in some amusement as he noted the growing confidence of Petran's son.

'The Mynedarion *will* come. Have no doubt about it,' Antyr said, his black eyes peering into Arwain's powerfully. 'He is mad with power and desire. That much I've felt for myself. And though he pursues an end we cannot see, *you've* no choice now but to cut off his sword arm – the Bethlarii army. That done, if it can be done, then perhaps his intention may become clearer.'

'Sound strategic thinking,' Ibris said to Arwain, with a slight smile.

When Antyr had left, Ibris summoned Ryllans and Feranc again.

'Two things,' he began. 'Firstly, take especial care of my son here. With all the confusion of mobilization there's a great deal of unusual coming and going about the palace and for all we're preparing to meet the Bethlarii, we'd be ill advised to ignore our normal enemies, not least my wife. Her reach and malice are considerable . . .' He raised a hand to forestall an interruption by Feranc. 'I know you've increased the guard on the Erin-Mal, Ciarll, but Nefron has many friends who're not my friends, and many of my friends who are caught in her grip, and my stomach says caution, so I mention it to you. Take what action you see fit and keep me informed.'

Feranc bowed.

'Secondly, there is the disturbance among the Mantynnai,' Ibris went on.

Ryllans stiffened slightly. Ibris looked at him squarely. 'I have no doubts about your loyalty,' he said quietly. 'And I'll press you on no matter. But I gather that you've encountered . . . aspects . . . of these recent happenings in the past. Before your time here. Arwain will tell you and Ciarll everything that's happened here tonight with Antyr, then I want you to talk with your companions and come to me with what you feel I need to know.' He cast a brief, significant glance at Ciarll Feranc to impart the message.

'Remember this,' he said, placing his hands on Ryllans' shoulders. 'You are all Serens now, while we still struggle to be Mantynnai. You have not only my trust, you have my protection.'

403

Chapter 30

Antyr sat alone in his room. A fire, lit by a servant, burned cheerily in a corner grate, and several lamps, also lit by a servant, complemented the fire's earnest efforts. Heavy velvet curtains, drawn by Antyr himself, stood solid and purposeful between the light and warmth of the room and the yellow, dank darkness, moving softly and treacherously through the city streets outside.

Antyr was oblivious to the comfort of his surroundings, however. He was rapt in thought. Save for his attendance on the Duke to listen to Arwain's dreams, he had done little else but think since reporting the details of the envoy's dreams to the Duke in person following his more unorthodox nocturnal visit.

Ibris had listened, asked a few questions, thanked Tarrian with a knowing smile for the dream that the wolf had retrieved for him, and then dismissed them politely.

'What am I supposed to do now?' Antyr asked Estaan surreptitiously after he had left the Duke. Estaan had laughed. 'You're a Ducal adviser now,' he said. 'You don't do anything.' Then recanting a little. 'Sorry, I couldn't resist that,' he added, insincerely. 'But you've no specific duties, so if the Duke hasn't asked you to do anything, then you can please yourself what you do until he sends for you.' He raised a cautionary finger. 'Then, you run, and you prepare to go without sleep. If you'll take my advice, you'll make the most of whatever leisure comes your way.'

They had spent some time wandering about the palace, with Estaan generally continuing to instruct Antyr in the ways of the vast sub-culture of palace life. In particular, he introduced him to those who held the real administrative power and responsibility in the palace, and whose friendship would be 'worthwhile'. He also advised him about various individuals who were 'best avoided', and also what to say and do if he was accosted by any of the guards. 'It'll be some time before they all get to know you.'

It was a bewildering lesson for the Dream Finder, though

had he paused to consider, he might have realized that the ways of his own lifestyle up to the last few days would seem no less complex to a stranger thrust suddenly into it.

He did not consider it however, being for the most part preoccupied by the events that had brought about this improbable change; events that had surged out of nothingness to overturn his bleak, pointless life and thrust him into the circles of Serenstad's most powerful as some kind of a principal player.

But what kind of a player was he? That his life of ale-swilling and corrosive self-pity now seemed to belong to someone else, long ago, was a source of both surprise and satisfaction to him, but with his new-found well-being and increasing excitement about his strange burgeoning skills, came darker thoughts. It was as if he had struggled at last from some great, clinging morass, but finding himself safe on firm ground, armed and armoured even, gradually realized that he was on the enemy's shore. An enemy whose numbers, weapons and intent he knew nothing of. And there was no retreat open to him; he could move only forward. It was not possible for him to return to his old ways now, to plunge back into the morass. Too much had been awakened inside him.

Thus, sensing his charge's preoccupation, Estaan had eventually gently abandoned his instruction for the day and advised his pupil to, 'Go back to your quarters and sit and think. I'll attend to the other matter you wanted me to look at.'

And thinking for the most part was what Antyr had been doing, though, he mused, shifting position slightly to relieve a stiff leg, to little avail. He had spoken to the Duke and Arwain with great confidence about the possible intentions of the Mynedarion and his guide, and indeed he felt confident. But who was he to interpret the motives of such creatures, such men?

Yet even on reflection, his conviction did not waver. The Mynedarion and his guide would not return lightly to the Threshold for some time. This had been confirmed when they had faltered at the prospect during the Bethlarii envoy's dream. But why . . .?

The thoughts circled again.

The Mynedarion's longing for him had been beyond dispute; 'You shall be my guide,' the dark figure had said amid the din of the storm, and the memory of the cloying desire that had surrounded the words, hung in Antyr's mind like a sickness. But the guide, the Master who had brought the Mynedarion to the Threshold, had been afraid; afraid enough to draw his sword, despite the awesome power of his ghastly companion.

Of what he had been afraid, however, Antyr could only surmise. Was it simply the sight of a stranger approaching him so purposefully? Unlikely, Antyr decided, remembering Nyriall's reference to a battle he had encountered in one of the other Threshold worlds. Some at least of the Threshold worlds were obviously well populated. And the sword had been drawn before Tarrian's and Grayle's hunting spirits had merged with him to make him truly formidable.

Suddenly it came to him that the guide had been afraid to lose his charge. He had been afraid that the Mynedarion would, for some reason, discard him in favour of this new arrival . . .

An ill-focused power struggle formed in Antyr's mind. Not only was he now a player in the affairs of Serenstad and the Duke, he was a player in the affairs of the Mynedarion and his guide, and who could guess at their intention beyond seemingly fomenting war between Bethlar and Serenstad?

The revelation felt like a step forward, but he could clarify the matter no further. And other thoughts still bewildered him. What had possessed him to venture after Nyriall, to seek out a Dream Finder's dream; the dream that couldn't be; and a dead man's dream at that? And then to walk into that storm, towards the heart of that raging darkness? And as for how he had escaped . . .? It was beyond Tarrian's or Grayle's ability to tell him. The whole experience seemed to be beyond all analysis.

His thoughts circled and swirled, and his moods came and went; now fearful, now courageous, now sad, now happy. But he arrived at no conclusions.

He looked down at his two Companions stretched out asleep in front of the fire. Tarrian was on his side with his nose close to the fire, while Grayle was on his back with his front legs daintily crooked in the air and his back legs splayed wide. Had he been awake it would have been a deliberate posture of submission, but now it was simply a brief unstable equilibrium, and very soon he would roll over into some other position.

So relaxed, Antyr thought. Just to watch them motionless was to learn about the true nature of movement.

Then an imp took hold of his foot and poked Tarrian with it.

'Hedonist,' Antyr said. 'Why can't you fret awhile like I am instead of hibernating?'

Tarrian did not move but a patronizing sigh filled Antyr's head. 'We don't need to fret,' came the reply. 'You're doing more than enough for us all.'

Grayle chuckled and slowly rolled over.

'Thank you for your support,' Antyr retorted caustically.

'Our pleasure,' the two wolves replied simultaneously with some mirth.

Antyr shook his head and smiled.

'You've both been suspiciously quiet these last two days,' he said. 'What have you been up to apart from finding every eating hall and kitchen in the palace, and ingratiating yourselves with cooks and servants?'

'Thinking, like you. And talking, and listening,' Tarrian answered.

The reply was more serious than Antyr had expected and for a moment he did not know what to say.

'Talking and listening to whom,' he said, eventually.

Tarrian struggled to his feet and stretched himself luxuriously before lying down again. 'Talking to each other. Listening to you,' he replied.

'To me?' Antyr said, in some surprise.

'Oh yes,' Tarrian replied. 'We're as confused as you about everything that's happened. We need to know what you've made of it all.'

'Precious little, I'm afraid,' Antyr said, wearily. 'My thoughts simply go round and round, but reach no conclusion.'

'You misjudge yourself,' Tarrian said. 'Your whirling thoughts are necessary to feed the true knowledge that lies deeper inside you.'

'In my wolf self?' Antyr retorted ironically; the topic was not unfamiliar.

'Indeed,' Tarrian replied, in like vein. 'In your wiser self. The part of you that truly knows, when the mind alone cannot. I've told you often enough, just follow your nose.'

Antyr rubbed his eyes for no particular reason. He did not disagree with his Companion. Dream Finding was a born gift and while, to those possessing it, techniques could be taught and learned, it was at heart beyond rational explanation. And the strange bond between Dream Finder and Companion was rooted in trust; a trust that could only come from some deep inner certainty.

And it must still be so, he realized abruptly. In doing the things that he had done, he had acted correctly. Just as the two wolves, in doing what they had done, had acted correctly. That logical reasons could not immediately be found to justify their actions was irrelevant. Dream Finding came first from within. Whatever attributes had awakened in him must be no different in their nature from those that were already there and which he took for granted. Just like roots hidden in the dark soil. Unseen they grew and changed, and from them, into the light, came trees and flowers and grasses for all to see. And they, in their turn, sustained the roots.

'See. You got there in the end,' Tarrian said. 'Laboured away and arrived at the answer you've known all your life.'

Antyr looked at the wolf narrowly, but the comment was straightforward and quite without irony. After a moment he nodded. 'True,' he said. 'But it's not enough. I still feel I must have reins in my hands. Knowledge of what I'm doing. Control over it.'

He faltered and, sitting upright, became agitated. 'Who knows what these people can do? What powers they can bring against us? Faith in my ordinary Dream Finding skill is one thing. I have experience – past knowledge to guide me. But this . . .!'

Tarrian crawled along the floor towards him and flopped across his feet. Grayle did the same. Antyr leaned forward and stroked the two wolves. For the moment, it seemed that nothing else could be said about his concerns.

With a brief touch of remorse he turned to the needs of his Companions. 'I'm sorry,' he said. 'I've been so preoccupied with my own problems I've ignored you entirely, haven't I?'

Under other circumstances such a comment might have provoked an acid response from Tarrian, but all Antyr felt was a wave of understanding and support.

'It's all right,' Tarrian said. 'We've had a great deal to talk about and we could do nothing to help you.'

Antyr bent right forward and embraced the two wolves in silence for a long time. 'Brothers reunited,' he said eventually. 'I'm happy for you.' Then, without thinking, he intruded, 'How did you come to be separated?'

He tried to call the words back even as he spoke them, but the wolves showed no dismay. 'It's the way of things,' Tarrian replied quietly. 'We were pups together, in the care of others, learning. Then when we had grown, and learned, as we thought, enough, we went our separate ways.'

There was a strange quality in Tarrian's speech that Antyr could not identify. Homesickness . . .?

Antyr could not keep the next question from his mind. 'Where do you come from?'

Then, like birds released from a cage, others came; how had Tarrian learned of his strange ability, how had he met his father, how had the two wolves come together in the city and not known of one another?

Flustered by his indiscretion, Antyr struggled to set the questions aside, but Tarrian began to answer them, as if the time was now appropriate.

'We come from a land, far, far away,' he said, his voice oddly resonant with meanings that Antyr felt inadequate to grasp. 'We were born, suckled, and orphaned, in the darkness, nurtured and taught in the Great Song, and let free to roam blessed mountains and wide lands unhindered by the men who lived there; men who took joy in our being; saw us for what we were and were unafraid.'

The images in Antyr's mind were vivid and alive, though the words told him nothing.

'And we left unhindered. Drawn away by curiosity—' Tarrian stopped abruptly. 'It was a mistake,' he said. 'There is no other land or people to compare with . . .' Again, Antyr felt and rejoiced in the images, but found he could not form the words that he heard.

'When this is over, perhaps we will return,' Tarrian concluded.

The words struck Antyr like a spear thrust. He knew that Tarrian was, above all, a free spirit; he could, and would, do as he wished. Yet Antyr had never even contemplated being without his Companion. The joy faded and he went suddenly cold inside. But reassurance came, though unasked for.

'Just a fancy,' Tarrian said. 'A human trait we've picked up. Don't fret. It's only humans who live in the past and the future. We live here, in the present. All futures are unknown.'

Antyr made no reply except to stroke the wolf's upturned head.

'How did you come here together?' he asked, in spite of himself.

'Who can say?' Tarrian replied. 'We parted in the wilds as

we became wolves again and gathered and guided our own packs. But who knows what powers took us from our packs and led me to your father and Grayle to Nyriall and yet kept us apart?'

There was a mixture of conflicting emotions in his voice, and the soft knock on the door that ended their discussion was not unwelcome.

Antyr's thoughts darkened again, however, as he identified the knock as Estaan's. Not because it was the Mantynnai but because the knock was one which Estaan had told him to expect, despite the fact that he had left a guard outside Antyr's room while he was away. It was one of the small tokens that reminded Antyr that now he stood close to the Duke and that he was part of the endless political dance that skipped and stepped through the corridors of the palace and the Sened and the Gythrin-Dy. A small part, admittedly, but nonetheless perhaps a part to be manoeuvred by bribery, calumny, gossip, or even assassination if matters grew more heated. Both words and shadows would become different now, and he must learn to listen and watch more carefully. And whether he liked it or not, some of the steps he would have to dance himself.

Then he dismissed the thoughts angrily. He would follow the advice that Ciarll Feranc had given him before his first fraught meeting with the Duke. Be honest and straightforward. And, where possible, silent, he added to himself. He had already learned that for himself watching the conduct of Estaan. What was not said could not be disputed.

Grayle and Tarrian wagged their tails faintly at the sound of the knock, but otherwise did not move.

'Thanks for leaping to my defence,' Antyr said with heavy reproach.

'Go and open the door, and stop moaning,' Tarrian retorted. 'Estaan's got a gift for you.'

'Come in,' Antyr shouted, turning in his chair slightly to see the door better. Estaan entered quietly. He was smiling and carrying a sword and sheath. Antyr stood up to greet him.

'I think this will suit you better than the one I lent you,' the Mantynnai said. He held out the sword to Antyr who took it gingerly and after a brief hesitation looped the belt about his waist.

The two wolves grudgingly clambered to their feet and ambled across to inspect the weapon. 'Just something else for me to trip over when I'm in there, I suppose. As if walking on two legs weren't hard enough as it is,' Tarrian concluded after subjecting the sword to a thorough sniffing. 'I hope that thing's not sharp, he'll cut something off himself for sure,' he added.

Antyr did his best to ignore the remark, and cautiously drew the sword. The two wolves scurried away at speed, with mock cries of alarm, to sit side by side against the wall furthest away from him.

'Very droll,' Antyr said, glowering at them. Then he brandished the sword at them, making Estaan wince and take a pace backward himself. Tarrian laughed.

Antyr blushed and apologized to the Mantynnai. Estaan waved the apology aside, but looked at Antyr doubtfully.

'I've no choice,' Antyr said, answering the unspoken concern. 'I know you can't make me into a swordsman, but I need to be armed, and I need to . . . loosen up what I can remember of my sword drills . . .'

Estaan nodded. 'I understand,' he said. 'But it's here and here, you need to loosen up as well.' He tapped his stomach and then his head. 'Would you like to come down to the training hall for a while?'

Antyr accepted the offer uncertainly. At least it would be something to do other than brood. Besides, despite Tarrian's mockery, he already felt easier with a sword by his side.

The training hall was small and deserted, though, dutiful as ever, the Guild of Lamplighters had done their work, and it was brightly lit. Countless feet had worn the wooden floor smooth and shiny in places and the characteristic smell of years of heated endeavour pervaded the place. Tarrian muttered something uncomplimentary but Antyr did not catch it.

The walls were without ornamentation and exuded a dusty, no-nonsense utilitarianism indicative of too long without decoration. Completing the exclusively functional appearance and aura of the place were racks of worn and battered training weapons at one end of the room, a series of fading mirrors along one side, and several items of mysterious, but equally worn, equipment crowded carelessly into a corner.

'Oh, I brought you these as well,' Estaan said as he inspected his pupil. He produced two daggers; one, to Antyr's eyes, very large, and one of a more conventional size. Antyr looked at them, unsure of what response he should make apart from a vague, 'Thank you.'

Estaan clipped the large one on to Antyr's belt and then

412

disappeared behind him to fit the other one horizontally into a sheath at the back of the belt. Then he led Antyr to a chair by the wall.

'Sit down,' he said.

Antyr did as he was bidden. Estaan watched the awkward performance critically, then beckoning Antyr to rise, made further adjustments to the various sheaths.

After two or three attempts, Antyr protested mildly that, 'They're all right now, I'll get used to them.' But Estaan had survived because he knew the importance of small things.

'Riding, walking, running, sitting, standing, lying, you must be comfortable,' he said, gently brushing the remark aside as he continued adjusting straps and loops on Antyr's sword belt.

And when he had finished, some considerable time later, Antyr was just that. He had run, jumped, walked, sat, lain, and – thanks to some of the equipment in the corner, which, despite its aged appearance proved distressingly effective – demonstrated that he could climb and also sit a saddle without losing his new weapons or tangling himself in them.

'Good, we'll begin,' Estaan said eventually, just as Antyr was hoping he would say, 'We'll finish for now.'

His dismay showed, and Estaan chuckled softly. 'Just a little practice to give you something to think about,' he said, walking over to the weapons rack and selecting a stout wooden sword.

'Draw your sword,' he said, as he returned. Self-consciously, Antyr obeyed.

'Now attack me,' Estaan went on. Antyr frowned and looked at the gleaming edge of the sword in his hand. He was no expert in such matters, but he could see that it had recently been ground and sharpened and he had seen enough on the battlefield to know what appalling injuries a sword could inflict.

'Not with this,' he replied, making to sheath it. 'I might make a mistake. I might hurt you.'

Estaan nodded. 'That's true,' he agreed. 'But training is mutual learning. This is for our benefit, not just yours. If you hurt me, the fault is mine.'

Antyr shook his head and did not move.

'Don't worry,' Estaan said, smiling. 'I didn't survive so long by taking risks with novices. As soon as you're anything like proficient, *you'll* be using the wooden sword, and I'll be using the real one.'

413

Despite this reassurance, Antyr still hesitated.

'A straight lunge is invariably the best attack,' Estaan offered, encouragingly. 'Do it slowly if you're worried.'

With an effort, Antyr brought the sword up and lunged weakly towards his mentor. Estaan did not move, and the point stopped half a pace in front of him. He looked down at it wryly, 'Hardly fatal I think,' he said. 'Try again.'

Embarrassment and nervousness vying with one another, Antyr lunged again, a little more purposefully. As the point approached, Estaan walked quietly around it and tapped the extended blade with his wooden training sword. His movement alone took him out of any danger, but the blow further deflected Antyr's lunge and, lightly, but definitely, Estaan drew the edge of the training sword along Antyr's throat.

'Don't stop, lunge again,' he said as Antyr was about to lower his sword and wait for criticism.

After a few minutes of similar futile effort, Antyr, despite himself, began to grow angry at this elusive figure casually avoiding his lunges and poking him with the training sword or drawing its rounded edge across his throat, his wrists, the back of his knees and ankles, and various other places.

Eventually he lowered his sword in frustration. 'This is a waste of time,' he said, irritably, thrusting the weapon back into its sheath.

'No it's not,' Estaan said quietly. 'I need to see where you're strong and where you're weak if I'm to help you.'

'What do you keep running away and hitting me with that damned thing for, then?' Antyr burst out, gesturing towards the training sword and involuntarily denouncing the Mantynnai's calm with his own agitation. 'Show me something!'

Estaan looked straight at him, his gaze penetrating. 'First rule when training and practising is to remember that there's no such thing as training and practising.'

Antyr's forehead furrowed.

'There is no trying, only doing,' Estaan went on before Antyr could protest. 'There's not one way of fighting in here and another out there. If I just drop my guard and debate with you after I've avoided each of your attacks, because this isn't . . . real . . . then I'm teaching my mind and my body to do just that, and that's what they might do against a more serious attack.' He stepped close to Antyr. 'As it is, I teach my mind

414

and body only how to kill or immobilize you after *every one* of your attacks. And you will learn to do the same.'

Antyr looked uncertain.

Estaan's manner became unexpectedly stern. 'No,' he said, taking Antyr's arm firmly. 'Have no doubts about this. Grasp it if you grasp nothing else that I tell you, and it'll help you towards the knowledge that might save your life one day.'

'I *have* used a sword in combat, you know,' Antyr protested defensively.

Estaan nodded, but there was denial in his expression. 'You told me you left your sword on the field because of what you'd done with it,' he said. 'Injured someone badly, I suppose.' Despite his sternness, his voice was sympathetic. 'Saw your flailing, panic-stricken efforts to tear him open and heard him scream. Saw a wild enemy suddenly become an ordinary man who never wanted to be there and who wanted nothing more than to flee. Saw wife, mother, children.'

Antyr closed his eyes in a vain attempt to shut out long-dormant memories suddenly re-awakened. 'It was a battle, man,' he said, scowling. 'We'd no choice. They were through the pikes and splitting the ranks. We had to draw swords and fight or . . .' He stopped.

'They'd have killed you.' Estaan finished the sentence. 'And many more.'

Antyr turned away from the Mantynnai's gaze. 'You don't have to justify yourself,' Estaan said. 'Least of all to me.'

There was such pain in his voice that Antyr's own concerns faded.

'Your salve for your memories is that you did what you did to save yourself or your comrades,' Estaan went on. 'That's all you're ever going to have. That's all you can possibly have. And if that's insufficient for your pain, then take the sword off now. You'll be safer unarmed.'

His manner was unequivocal.

Antyr gazed at him helplessly. 'I can't go unarmed,' he said eventually. 'But I can't face . . .' He grimaced. 'I can't face that horror again.'

Estaan nodded again and, looking at Antyr very intently, said simply, 'You can.' He brought his face close to Antyr's. 'Because some part of you enjoyed the butchery . . .'

There was a brief, agonizing silence in the old hall. Antyr tried to speak out an angry denial, but the words would not form.

'It's in all our natures, Antyr.' Estaan pressed on, softly relentless. 'And your only salve for that is that having seen it, you learn to accept it for what it is, and know that when need arises, it is right that it be given rein.'

Antyr gazed from side to side, like a trapped animal looking for escape. But Estaan's brutal honesty permitted no flight. Antyr felt tears filling his eyes.

'You've no right to speak like that,' he managed hoarsely and pathetically.

'I've no right not to,' Estaan replied softly. 'If I'm to give you such a weapon and show you how to use it. If I'm to let you go to face unknown enemies, while you're not aware of the realities of your own nature . . . of combat . . .'

With a desperate effort, Antyr found his voice. He tore away from Estaan. 'I need no lectures from anyone about the realities of fighting,' he shouted angrily. 'I may not be any great soldier, but I've stood in the line and held, with arrows and missiles falling all around. And people and horses screaming and dying.' He shook his head as if to dispel the sound. 'I've seen . . . comrades, enemies . . . who cares . . . whimpering and howling, with limbs half hacked off . . . bodies trampled under countless hooves . . . brains and guts leaking into the mashed earth, great feathered arrows sticking out of gaping faces and barbed heads sticking out through backs . . .'

He fell suddenly silent. The pain of the old memories made him want to lash out, to strike someone down. He raised his hand towards Estaan. 'Why do you pursue such a calling?' he asked, his face almost scornful.

Estaan started slightly.

Antyr felt a gasp in his head and then the word, 'Gently', followed in its wake. Tarrian and Grayle spoke simultaneously, and with such feeling that, despite his own pain, the judgement he had offered Estaan for his cruel honesty seemed to fly in his own face.

'I'm sorry . . .' he began, but Estaan waved his apology aside sadly.

'I do it because it's the right thing for me to do,' he said simply. '*How* that came to be, I won't discuss with you. But I learned long ago that such skills and self-knowledge as I have I must place between those who are possessed by their destructive natures and those who cannot adequately protect themselves.'

Antyr made to speak again, but Estaan continued. 'I look at Ibris and his great city, so full of beautiful things, and I watch him strive endlessly to make it more beautiful, and to tear the whole land away from its obscene and bloody history into a future where war becomes a sick and distant memory.' Passion seeped into his voice. 'Creation is the work of lifetimes, Dream Finder, destruction the work of moments; a knife, a hammer, a flame. I take pride that I can use my own dark skills in the ways of destruction *to protect creation from destruction*.'

Antyr looked at the Mantynnai and for a brief moment, felt the man's wholeness, his inner balance. Felt his understanding of the terrible deeds that lie within the depths of all men, and felt the will that had accepted them and that strove to use them as servants not masters. Here indeed, he realized, was a man from whom he could, and should, learn much.

'I'm sorry,' he said again, after a long silence. His demeanour added content to the inadequate words. 'I was wrong to reproach you. I'll do as you say. I'm ready to learn whatever you're prepared to teach.'

Estaan smiled slightly and bowed.

The brief outburst had been in some way cathartic and Antyr seemed to feel that both his mind and his body were moving more easily now.

Without speaking, they resumed their practice, Antyr gradually gathering the courage to attack more purposefully, and Estaan continuing to avoid the attacks effortlessly and deliver his painless but lethal counters.

After a little while, Estaan called a halt and they sat down on the floor.

'I'm not telling you anything you don't know when I tell you that you're no sword master, am I?' he said.

Antyr, breathing heavily and wiping his forehead with a kerchief, shook his head.

'Still,' Estaan went on. 'I've seen worse, by far, and there are one or two little things – simple straightforward things – that we can work on, that you'll find helpful, as well as . . .' He tapped his forehead with a smile. 'Also you need more exercise. You're not in the best of condition.' His smile broadened as Antyr looked at his sweat-soiled kerchief. 'The heart of your personal combat strategy is going to be flight, you understand that, I know, and you'll need to be as fit for that as for fighting.'

Antyr lay back on the hard, wooden floor and nodded again,

'I'd forgotten how hard all this business was. Can't I be excused effort, on compassionate grounds?' he pleaded faintly.

'I have no compassion,' Estaan replied, grinning.

Antyr groaned softly.

'Don't worry, I've not lost a trainee yet,' Estaan went on, unsympathetically and getting to his feet. 'But I've seen enough, and you've done enough for now. What I want you to do now is think.'

With a remarkable lack of both grace and dignity, Antyr managed to struggle to his feet. 'I understand,' he replied.

Estaan took his arm and began leading him towards the door. Tarrian and Grayle padded after them.

'Think about the question you asked me,' Estaan replied. 'And apply it to yourself. Why do you wish to carry a sword? Turn it round and round, and don't turn away from your darker nature.'

Later, washed and rested, Antyr lay back in his bed and did as he had been told. A single lamp on a nearby table threw comforting shadows about the room.

It took him a little thought, however, to reach a conclusion and see the implications. In his anger he had demanded that Estaan justify himself for being what he was, and, almost to his distress, he had received an answer. This must now be his own, though the motivation was more selfish than the Mantynnai's.

He was entitled to carry a sword and, should need arise, protect himself from the strange, armed figures who stalked the Threshold. He would seek no confrontation, but if it were forced upon him – forced upon him – then the consequences, however horrific, were not his responsibility. He must harness the will of the darkness within him, keeping at bay its bloodlust if he could. He must strike; strike hard, strike fast; strike without pity; strike unencumbered by screaming bloodstained memories, past or future; strike from that most ancient need, the need to survive. Then and only then should he stay his hand.

'Very complicated creatures, people, aren't they?'

Tarrian's voice intruded into his conclusion. 'Rambling round and round just to reach the blindingly obvious.'

Antyr reached out and lowered the lamp's flame to a tiny point. 'Go to sleep, dog,' he said, and, much more quickly than he had for several nights, he drifted gently off to sleep.

Chapter 31

Apart from continuing to familiarize himself with the palace and receive instruction from Estaan and some of the other Mantynnai, little of any great import happened to Antyr over the next few days.

They were far from quiet days, however. The palace was alive with activity, both frantic and ordered, while the Sened and the Gythrin-Dy were alive with rhetoric, both self-seeking and sincere.

And looking to the spiritual needs of their flocks, Serenstad's many priests offered a similar variety of choices. Some sat in silent, mysterious meditation, some spoke with quiet, caring reasonableness, while yet others railed, with various degrees of coherence both for and against war against the Bethlarii. The citizens of Serenstad did not lack for opinions to discuss.

And of course, there was the inevitable clamour of Guild officials besieging the mobilization offices pleading for this, that and the other special case. To no avail, however; the law permitted no exceptions for the able-bodied. Early in his reign, Ibris had abolished almost all forms of exemption from military service, not least the long-established practice of allowing individuals to purchase it. The proposal had met with a great deal of opposition from some of the powerful trading houses, but it had found much support from both the people and the ruling families and he had won the day. Such pleas by the Guilds were thus, in many ways, as ritualistic as any of the priests' activities, but, their prayers passionately rendered and duly rejected, the Guild officials were able to depart with *their* civic consciences clear.

'One of my better decisions,' Ibris would remark from time to time. 'Whatever a man is born to in this city he can strive to change it and have my blessing, but arrow storms and cavalry charges are no respecters of either birth or worth and I'll have no one sheltering behind money bags while he expects others to shelter behind shields.'

Following the orders for mobilization, there was a short but spectacular increase in the unlicensed markets that were a feature of Serenstad street life, as the shrewder traders began to sell old swords, pikes, bows and other military paraphernalia, to those who through the years of comparative peace had . . . forgotten . . . that they were required by law to possess and maintain such equipment. These suddenly blooming commercial toadstools were known as wagon marts, as the participants invariably chose not to set up the traditional decorated street stalls, but to trade directly from their wagons . . . to which their horses also remained harnessed.

In the spirit of the military thinking that begat this activity, the traders would post lookouts so that due warning of the approach of Liktors – or worse, the market Exactors – could be reported in sufficient time for them to institute an orderly retreat with a view to regrouping elsewhere. The particularly shrewd, however, held their ground and produced grinding and whetting stones so that they would be found, 'Performing a public service, sir,' when discovered. 'No tax liable under mobilization.'

Almost inconspicuously among this mounting hubbub, Menedrion returned. He was well pleased with himself for his treatment of the envoy, but angry and concerned about Whendrak and anxious to be 'doing something'. With him returned Pandra and Kany to confirm to Antyr the details of Arwain and Menedrion's strange and shared dream, and the finding of the Gateway into the Threshold.

Despite the fatigue of the journey, Pandra was in a state of some elation.

'To come across such a thing,' he waxed. 'It's thrown a light across my entire life as a Dream Finder. I feel as if I were just starting again, like some excited apprentice. To know for certain that all those worlds truly exist.' He waved his hands to prevent Antyr interrupting. 'I know you told me about them . . . but to actually see one . . . To be on the edge of it.'

Antyr, however, could not forbear sounding a warning note above this eulogy. 'Take care, Pandra,' he said. 'We're stumbling about blindly, or worse, perhaps being moved at the whim of some power we can't perceive. What we both learn, we must teach each other, but we must take no risks. Both Arwain and Menedrion must be told of the danger the Threshold presents to them. They have a strong natural resistance, and knowledge will make it stronger. But you and Kany must guard both of them now. And if either comes near a Gateway again, wake them on the instant.'

'I will!' Kany averred, before Pandra could reply, in a manner which clearly indicated that any response from Pandra, however worthy, was to be viewed with the utmost suspicion.

A couple of days after the return of Menedrion, the remainder of Arwain's escort returned. They brought with them the dark news that Whendrak was still sealed and apparently torn by civil strife and that the Bethlarii were indeed gathering an army somewhere to the west of Whendrak.

'We couldn't venture in as far as we'd have liked,' they reported. 'It was too dangerous. There were patrols everywhere.' They had, however, seen sufficient supply convoys, camps, infantry and cavalry activity, to know that the army being gathered was far in excess of anything needed to take Whendrak.

It was enough. Ibris summoned his senior commanders and gave them the news.

'This, and other intelligence that I've received, convinces me that the Bethlarii are intending a major military adventure against us,' he announced. 'Regretfully, I see no alternative but to move an army up to Whendrak immediately. We may be too late to prevent them from taking the city, but we must stop them taking the valley at any cost. The sealing of the city prevents us from serving the appropriate notices within the terms of the treaty and thus we've been manoeuvred into the position of using the same pretext as the Bethlarii themselves. Doubtless they'll quote that fact freely if they try to sway some of our less enthusiastic allies.'

He paused and looked out of the window. Beyond the walls of the palace he could see the busy streets of his city. When he turned back to his audience, his face was uncharacteristically angry.

'However, I don't intend to give them even *that* advantage, gentlemen. As you know, the major treaty cities allied to us are already mobilizing, but I've also sent messengers to every town, village, and hamlet, explaining everything that's happened so far and requesting full voluntary mobilization—'

An almost universal gasp of surprise interrupted him, but he continued. 'Within the next day or so I intend to send more senior officials to add strong persuasion to that request.'

421

Then he yielded to his listeners. With varying degrees of deference and bluntness, they reminded him that full voluntary mobilization was a historic relic carried down from the times when there had been only a handful of towns in the land, when armies were smaller and less disciplined, and when loyalties and boundaries were far more fluid than today. It had been retained as an idea almost for sentimental reasons and, paradoxically, it was both too heavy a response to the present crisis and also quite an impractical option for meeting a real conflict.

Except for politely curtailing those who drifted into details of what should be done, Ibris listened in silence until everyone who wished to speak had spoken.

'You're correct, of course, gentlemen,' he agreed. 'And incorrect also. Correct in your history of the idea, and, conceivably in saying that it's not a particularly practical option. However, you are incorrect in thinking that it's an excessive response to what's happening.'

He raised a hand to forestall opposition.

'Why are the Bethlarii doing this?' he asked bluntly. 'Why, after all this time, are they preparing to launch a major war against us?'

'They hate our guts,' someone said, to some laughter.

'True,' Ibris acknowledged, smiling. 'That's probably always been the real reason. But they've always had enough political sense not to admit that openly. They've always sought an excuse that will at least give them a veneer of more civilized justification for unleashing mayhem.'

He looked across the watching faces and shrugged. 'Where are their long-winded diplomatic notes setting out reasons why this or that territory is by rights theirs? Where are their complaints about "bandits and outlaws" raiding their farms and hiding on our side of the border? Where are their complaints about our traders competing unfairly with them? Our fishermen entering their waters? And so on.'

There was an uncertain silence, then, 'They sent an envoy to complain about what was happening in Whendrak,' someone offered.

Ibris nodded and frowned. 'And a grotesque venture that was,' he replied. 'Almost every aspect of it was contrary to the treaty. The man wilfully behaved in a manner that could have got him killed. And his visit only became public knowledge because *we* made it so. Their complaints in the past, I need hardly remind you, have usually been loud and public. From my discussions with him, and from other information I've received, and not least, bearing in mind that not even the staunchest of Bethlar's allies would give any credence to the idea that they were entitled to protect ''their citizens'' in Whendrak, I can only presume that *his death at our hands* was intended as the pretext for the war. He was to be a sacrifice to Ar-Hyrdyn.'

Everyone looked uncomfortable, but no one raised a voice in disagreement. The envoy's conduct had been the topic of considerable debate and gossip, and the Duke's conclusion was as good as anyone else's.

'The fact is, gentlemen,' he went on, 'that their actions are wholly out of character with anything they've ever done before. My belief is that their society has been corrupted by a fanatical form of their state religion and that the war they're intending to unleash is, to them, a crusade; a holy war to be waged in his name.'

This conclusion, however, did provoke a response, albeit mixed. Some, who knew their history, grimaced at the prospect. There had been religious wars in the past and they had been distinguished from all other wars by their unremitting savagery and brutality. It seemed that fighting under the aegis of divine inspiration served only to rob men of any semblance of restraint and humanity. Others in the room shook their heads as if to deny the possibility.

Ibris did not argue. 'I'm open to alternative suggestions, gentlemen,' he said, looking round.

'It could be no more than an elaborate ploy to distract us while their real move is made elsewhere,' someone said.

'My own feelings at one stage,' Ibris replied. 'But the Mantynnai say that the forces massing near Whendrak are very substantial, and there's a . . .' He gesticulated, searching for a word. 'A feeling almost of nightmare . . . insanity . . . about all that's happening. No logic. However,' he raised a reassuring hand to the speaker, 'the cities along the southern Bethlarii border have been alerted to such a possibility, Meck especially.'

A silence descended on the room. Ibris looked around at his men.

'This is why I've called for full voluntary mobilization from every community in the land,' he said bleakly. 'If the Bethlarii are about to launch a holy war . . .' He stopped abruptly and lowered his head thoughtfully for a moment. When he looked up, his face was set. 'There is no "if" about it, gentlemen,' he said, unequivocally. 'The Bethlarii *are* going to launch a holy war and the *whole* land must be made ready to face it. From Rendd right down to Lorris I want no one unaware of what's about to happen and I want no one thinking that they can avoid playing some part in opposing it. I want all petty feuds and squabbles laid to rest.' His manner became grim. 'And god help *anyone* who tries to use this business for some power game of his own! The hearts and minds of the whole land must be with us.' The room became very still. 'And, too, the Bethlarii must learn that they'll be facing not just armies, but an entire people.'

'And if you're wrong, sire?' a lone voice asked.

'I'm not, commander,' Ibris replied. 'Believe me, I'm not.' He looked at Menedrion, and then at Arwain before turning back to the questioner. 'But, in answer to your real question, I'd rather end my rule of this city and its dominions in ridicule and bankruptcy than risk seeing them suffocated in the obscene bigotry of Ar-Hyrdyn's priests.'

It was a phrase that brought behind him such waverers as there were in the room, and the discussion turned rapidly towards the details of the operations that were to be mounted.

After the meeting, Ibris drew Ryllans and Feranc on one side.

'Now is the time,' he said quietly. 'Walk with me.'

The two men walked beside their Duke in silence as he wandered through the halls and corridors of his palace. From time to time he stopped and looked at a painting, a statue, a rich ornate mosaic, until eventually he led them out on to the flat stone roof of a high crenellated tower.

The air was cold and damp, but fresh, and free from any taint of the yellow, acrid fog that had choked the city streets so recently. High, grey clouds reduced the sun to a bland, white disc.

Below them they could see the walls and courtyards of the palace, and beyond them, the rooftops, spires and domes of the city rising up to the cliffs of the Aphron Dennai and sloping down to the rambling disorder of the Moras district by the river. Grey mists merged land and sky in the distance.

Ibris leaned on the parapet and gazed over his city in silence for some time. 'What do you think of my interpretation of events, Ryllans?' he said, without turning round.

'Accurate,' the Mantynnai replied, without hesitation. 'And your response is appropriate.'

Ibris turned round. 'What do I need to know about these events that I don't already know?' he asked.

Ryllans looked at him. 'I've no great revelations for you, sire,' he said.

'Tell me what you can, nevertheless.'

Ryllans nodded and began without any preamble. 'The presence that Estaan felt when the Dream Finder . . . entered . . . the mind of the dead Nyriall, was one that he'd felt before. One we'd all felt, long ago.' An involuntary spasm of pain distorted his face momentarily. It was reflected almost immediately in Ibris's; the Duke had never seen the Mantynnai so openly distressed. But Ryllans continued without pause. 'It was the presence of . . . someone . . . that we'd all once served. I'd like to say, someone who misled us, but we were then, as now, free men . . .'

He fell silent and for a moment stood looking out over the city.

Then he shrugged, as at some inevitability. 'An evil came to our land. An ancient evil as it transpired, although to us it was merely a man; a good friend and helper to our ailing king, as we thought.

'Over many years, he was the king's faithful adviser and physician, and as the king became progressively weaker he took upon himself more and more of the burdens of state; and with them, inevitably, the reins of power. And, too, he did countless small, seemingly worthwhile things that in reality began subtly to undermine the qualities that made our people strong and free.

'Eventually, as his truer nature came nearer the surface, and voices began to be raised against his conduct, some of the most loyal lords complained directly to the king. But he was almost insane with his illness, and, in a rage, he had them imprisoned.'

He shook his head at some memory. 'Then a man came from another land close by and exposed the evil for what it was.'

He closed his eyes and shook his head again, but his voice was calm when he continued. 'Great harm was done to our city that day. Buildings broken and crushed like so many children's toys. Hundreds died.'

'This man came with an army? Laid siege to you?' Ibris

inquired, confused by the remark and also anxious to say something that might relieve Ryllans of some of his burden.

Ryllans turned and looked straight at him. 'No,' he said simply. 'He came with only one companion, and faced the king's . . . physician . . . on the palace steps. The damage to the city was wrought by no more than a wave of the hand.'

Ibris's brow furrowed and, despite himself, he glanced at Feranc. His bodyguard, however, made no response, and his face was unreadable.

'A wave of the hand, Ibris,' Ryllans repeated, stepping outside the protocol of their relationship to emphasize the truth of what he was saying. At the same time, he pointed to his eyes. 'I was there, wearing the livery of the man as he did the deed and showed himself for the demon he truly was, and showed us the power that he commanded and that could be ours also.'

Ibris could not contain himself. 'I know neither gods nor devils, Ryllans. Only men with godlike and diabolical ways—'

Feranc laid a hand gently on his arm and motioned him to silence.

Ryllans looked at him again. 'The word was ill chosen,' he said. 'It came from my stomach, not my head. Such as I've learned about him since is that he was indeed a man but that his . . . soul . . . was wholly corrupted by his possession of a great and ancient power.'

He paused briefly.

'After this terrible meeting, he slew the king and took possession of the land, with such as ourselves at his side. Then came civil strife and all the horrors that that implies; kin against kin; treachery, mistrust; darkness. And in the end the loyal lords raised an army and marched to meet us.' He shook his head reflectively. 'Some said that his crushing power was bound in some way, but, whatever the cause, he withheld it and we were defeated. The lords broke our army and he fled. Fled into the cold mistland to the north with us at his heels.'

He fell silent again for some time, and his voice was very soft when he spoke again, as if afraid it might be overheard. His slight accent became more pronounced.

'There we learned that the one we followed was but the servant of another. A great source of evil that felt as if it had come from the beginning of all time.'

'A man?' Ibris asked, his eyes wide at the continuing pain in Ryllans' voice.

426

The Mantynnai made a dismissive gesture. 'No one ever saw him, or even his citadel, but his will was everywhere . . .' He looked at the Duke. 'Both feeding on and nurturing the devils in men. It was said that his malevolence had spanned the ages and had once spanned the world, and that, reawakened, he was preparing to do so again.'

He shuddered suddenly, and swayed violently. Instinctively, both Ibris and Feranc reached out to support him, but he set them aside gently.

'But the lords and their allies followed us with a great army. Larger than anything this land has ever known.' An expression almost of pride came on to his face. 'As it stood against us, it stretched far beyond the sight into the dank mists and teeming rain. Rank upon rank. They, like us, were drenched and chilled and their colourful pennants and flags hung limp and lifeless, but we could feel their will assailing us across the plain even as we waited. Waited with many times their number in savage readiness, and with his will charging our spirits. Soon the enemy would be utterly defeated and we would sweep out into the world and to power and wealth.

'But it was we who were defeated, despite our numbers and our cruel troops. And somewhere, beyond our seeing, our master and his master were . . . taken from the battle . . . I don't know . . . suddenly, they were gone, and we were lost.

'Then, we scattered and fled, over mountains and plains, through deserts and wildernesses. Through the years. And as we fled, we gained a little wisdom. And finally we came here, and saw a faint echo of our homeland and its king, and resolved that here we must stand, and seek to serve where previously we had sought to rule.'

Ryllans fell silent, his eerie tale finished. Ibris wrapped his arms about himself as if infected by the chill mists and rain that had fallen on that last battle. There had been such power in Ryllans' telling that for a moment he felt himself small and utterly defenceless; a pawn in some greater game; his life's achievements mean, tawdry and pathetic.

He held out his hand and looked at it, then at his city. That men, even good men, could follow evil leaders, he knew all too well. But could a man possess a power that could crush a city with the merest wave? It wasn't possible . . .

But he could not dismiss such a witness as Ryllans. And the Mantynnai had not spoken in allegory and metaphor. He had seen what he had seen and he had told of it truthfully.

Ibris's thoughts whirled. Feranc offered no support. Indeed, his whole manner seemed to have become more distant and enigmatic than ever as he had listened to Ryllans' tale.

Not possible! The words echoed around his head, clung to his thoughts like a crawling, suffocating creeper clings to a tree.

His knowledge of Ryllans hacked at them. Just as his city seen from this tower was not the city that would be seen from the streets below, so he knew that he had to stand where Ryllans stood to see what he saw.

Had not he himself believed Antyr with his tale of worlds beyond this one, where a dead man lived again, and strange men possessing a power to change by means not understandable to ordinary men, moved freely and manipulated his enemies? Had he not believed him strongly enough to mobilize his entire country for war as never before, and to jeopardize his own position as ruler?

'Your story verges on the unbelievable, Ryllans,' he admitted simply, at last. 'But I've known you too long to do other than believe you totally. Time will perhaps reconcile me to the strangeness of it.'

To break the unreal atmosphere pervading their high eyrie, he became practical.

'You fear that this . . . man . . . and his master are perhaps come here after fleeing the field?' he asked.

Ryllans frowned thoughtfully. 'No,' he said, shaking his head definitely. 'They were gone utterly. Not just fled. Gone from inside us, never to return. There were other powers fighting that day. We were but part of a greater battle. My master and the one he served both fell to some other hand, I'm sure, but I could not say they were . . . dead . . . slain. Could you slay the sky, the wind? But they were gone.'

'Then what's so distressed you all?' Ibris asked.

'The power is there for all to use, who can master it,' Ryllans replied. 'And there were darker followers than we in those days. Disciples.'

'And one such might be here?'

'Someone with his . . . skills . . . *is* here,' Ryllans answered.

His unequivocal tone seemed to strike Ibris clear through and he felt a whirl of fear twist in his stomach. In spite of himself he exorcized it with a reproach. 'How could you and the others have followed this . . . man . . . when you learned the truth?' he asked.

Ryllans bowed his head slightly, then looked at him squarely. 'We followed,' he said, though with neither excuse nor plea in his voice. 'Now we atone as best we can.'

As he knew it would when the question left his lips, Ibris's reproach rebounded on him. 'You are punished *by* your sins not for them,' he had once heard a philosopher say scornfully to a priest extolling the punitive wrath of his deity.

Thus is Ryllans punished, and so am I now, he thought.

He reached out and took Ryllans' arm. 'Forgive me,' he said.

Ryllans laid his hand over the Duke's in acknowledgement. 'There is more,' he said.

'Tell it,' Ibris said quietly. 'Then we will gather it all and consider.'

He was aware of both Ryllans and Feranc looking at him sharply, but the moment was gone before he could question them, and Ryllans was speaking again.

'When our army broke and scattered, no pursuers were sent after us to cut us down in vengeance and hatred. Our opponents . . . our own people and their allies . . . were savage and fearsome in combat, but they stayed their hand in victory.' He paused thoughtfully. 'Perhaps it was there we began to learn,' he said softly.

'But it is the way, the law, of our people to demand an accounting from wrongdoers, and they will allow neither time nor distance to remit that.'

Ibris frowned. Arwain's remark about the two men returned to him. It had slipped from him in the turmoil of the past few days.

'The men that Arwain spoke of,' he said. 'The ones on the bridge. They're your countrymen?'

Ryllans nodded. 'From their bearing, their clothes, their horses, they were king's men, beyond a doubt.'

Feranc turned away suddenly but Ibris did not notice the movement.

He opened his arms in a gesture of dismissive indifference. 'This is *my* domain, Ryllans,' he said, almost angrily. 'You, all of you, probably above all my subjects, are under my protection. I cede my jurisdiction to no foreign monarch.'

He turned to Feranc before Ryllans could reply. 'Have these . . . king's men . . . made any representations at the palace for audience?' he demanded.

Feranc shook his head, but did not speak. Ibris turned back to Ryllans. 'Could you have been mistaken?' he asked, his voice softening. 'Many people come to the city. Perhaps they were simply foreign merchants. You'd not long received Estaan's news. You were upset . . .'

'There was no mistake,' Ryllans replied. 'They were king's men, and they must surely be here searching for us.'

Ibris spun on his heel and slapped his hands down violently on the stone parapet. A large part of him wanted to curse the intruders into oblivion. Two men, in the name of sanity! Come to *his* city to drag *his* Mantynnai back in chains! *They'd need their mighty army!*

But the wiser part of his nature recognized his anger as fear. Fear at whatever it was about these king's men that could so disconcert – not frighten, he noted – his Mantynnai. The men who had fought and died for him. The men whose gradual influence had improved beyond recognition the fighting qualities of his army. The men whose loyalty had given him the sureness and stability to lead his people forward, away from the endless debilitating cycle of internecine warfare and futile, waiting peace.

His anger left him suddenly, and when he spoke, his voice was calm and even.

'Ciarll, find these men urgently. It shouldn't be difficult, by all accounts. Bring them . . . ask them . . . if they would be kind enough to attend on me as soon as possible.'

He turned back to Ryllans. 'I note the pain that this tale has cost you, my friend, and, as ever, I stand in debt to your courage and honesty,' he said. 'But we're on the verge of war. Organizing the greatest mobilization ever, to face who knows what strange dangers. I can allow nothing . . . *nothing* . . . to interfere with our preparations. Thousands of lives depend on us. Whatever your countrymen want, I shall listen to . . . *we* shall listen to. And *we* shall decide what action must be taken.' He levelled a forefinger at the Mantynnai. 'But these are ancient sins and your . . . accounting . . . having kept this long will keep a while longer. Whatever they wish, whatever you wish, *nothing* will be done until this war is over and the peace well begun.'

Ryllans bowed and Ibris turned towards the tower doorway, beckoning the two men to follow him.

As they walked down the tower's stone steps, Ibris welcomed the clatter of their feet as it further dispelled the

430

disturbing atmosphere of Ryllans' tale and, he realized abruptly, Feranc's deep withdrawal.

'Do you wish me to begin looking for these men immediately?' Feranc said, his voice matter of fact, and giving the lie to Ibris's thoughts even as they occurred.

'Yes,' he said, with a slight start, then, 'no. No. Not yet. I think we should talk to Antyr first. This old enemy of Ryllans is assailing us, and the Bethlarii, through our dreams, for some end of its own, and while Antyr's quite frank about not understanding what's happening, he's nevertheless the one who knows the most about it, whether he realizes it or not. I think we, you, Ryllans, should tell him all that you can.'

'Yes,' Ryllans replied.

They left the tower through a heavy wooden door carved with a great battle scene; two huge armies locked in conflict, and the air above them full of fighting birds. The carving was extraordinarily vivid and lifelike and spread out from the door across the stone jambs that framed it.

Ryllans pulled the door shut with an echoing boom which resonated around the hall they had entered. He looked down at the door's great iron ring, then briefly squeezed it, as if for comfort, before letting it fall. As it struck the door, it made an unusually melodic note which seemed to linger in the air and follow the trio as they strode away.

Gradually, the corridors they followed became more busy and Ibris felt the new, hectic routine of the palace beginning to close around him – a familiar armour.

He did not allow it to seal him off from his new revelation, however. Indeed he allowed his thoughts about Ryllans' tale to eddy to and fro freely, knowing that this alone would enable them to find some equilibrium in time. For the moment he resolved to consider only the simple practical matter of the two foreigners searching out his Mantynnai.

The whole affair seemed to him to be at once both trivial and profound. The wish of some distant and unknown monarch for retribution for offences committed so long ago, was not worthy of the slightest consideration when set against the present dangers now threatening the land. Even the Mantynnai's offence, presumably treason, was of no great import in the context of a civil war. All countries had such conflicts at one time or another, and generally only the principals suffered punishment when they were resolved.

And what could two men achieve?

Yet these two who had come quite openly and yet so quietly to his city, had disturbed the Mantynnai more than he had ever known.

They reached the small hall where Estaan had been training his charge, and Ibris set his conflict aside for the moment.

As they entered, Antyr, red-faced and panting, was laying about him with a wooden training sword and Estaan was parrying and avoiding the blows. Antyr had eventually overcome his reservations about attacking correctly, and, for the most part, his blows were accurately placed and purposeful. Estaan moved around and through them with an ease and quietness which, while frustrating, not to say, infuriating, for Antyr, was wholly deceptive.

Ibris placed his finger to his lips for silence as they entered and, for a little while, the three of them watched the two protagonists. As they did so, Tarrian and Grayle sidled stealthily over to them and began fawning about the Duke.

Feranc smiled slightly.

'That's enough, you rascals,' Ibris said, bending down to stroke them. 'Don't think that I don't know how to deal with flattering courtiers . . .'

At the sound of his voice, Estaan turned slightly and Antyr slipped past his blade and charged him heavily. The Mantynnai went sprawling across the floor. Both Ryllans and Feranc laughed and clapped spontaneously, but Antyr, startled either by his temerity or his success, stopped suddenly and put his hand to his mouth like an errant child.

Immediately, Ryllans cried out, almost as if in pain. 'Don't stop! Finish him! Finish him!' he shouted, striding forward urgently. But it was too late. Estaan had rapidly regained his feet, and before Antyr could respond his sword had been brushed aside and the Mantynnai's sword run across his midriff.

He looked set to compound his mistake by apologizing, but Ryllans had wrapped a strong arm about his shoulders and was instructing him before he could speak.

'That was a good move . . .'

Estaan, rubbing his ribs, nodded in agreement.

' . . . but you forgot what you were doing. You weren't fighting him for fun, for exercise. You were fighting him to stop him from killing you. The instant that threat was dealt with you should have looked to ensure he did not repeat it. In this case you should have had your foot on his sword and your blade at his throat. *Then*, perhaps you might have been able to pause a little, if it was only him you were dealing with.'

'I know, I know,' Antyr managed to stammer.

'Only here,' Ryllans said, tapping Antyr's head. 'You've got to know it here.' He tapped his stomach. 'Or you're dead.'

Antyr nodded energetically.

'Learn this, Antyr,' Ryllans went on, still holding Antyr tightly as if to squeeze the lesson into him. 'The most dangerous time in close-quarter fighting is when your opponent goes down. You relax, thinking it's over. He's galvanized by his danger and . . .' He drew his finger across his throat. 'Fighting is cruel and horrible beyond belief. The difference between living and dying depends on your willingness to accept and implement *immediately*, whatever your survival demands. You must understand this totally if you're going to carry a sword with a view to defending yourself with it.'

He released his pupil, who muttered an awkward acknowledgement.

'How is he?' Ryllans asked Estaan bluntly. 'I see he's graduated to a training sword.'

Estaan smiled and nodded. 'He's no swordmaster, nor ever likely to be, but he's better than average,' he replied. 'And much better than he was a few days ago. I think he has a more realistic measure of his own worth now. He knows to run away unless he's cornered and he's had enough battle experience to realize that other resources will come to his aid if that happens.'

Ryllans nodded. 'Good,' he said. 'Keep him at it.'

Antyr glanced from one to the other as they spoke, like someone awaiting sentence, then he turned to the Duke as if to a higher court.

But Ibris deemed the matter beyond his jurisdiction. 'I apologize, Antyr,' he said. 'I should have known the Mantynnai would knock you into shape when I gave them the job of looking after you. They take it as part of their protection for you that you have to be trained to look after yourself.'

'I think I volunteered for it, sir,' Antyr replied.

The Duke seemed doubtful. 'Maybe,' he said. 'But you'd have ended up doing it anyway.'

He signalled an end to the discussion with a gesture, and then motioned Antyr towards a bench at the side of the hall.

'I want you to listen to Ryllans' tale,' he said, as he sat

433

down. 'I doubt you'll understand it any more than I did, but ask him any questions you like and don't feel obliged to make any comment about what you hear. I just want you to know everything that I know about this business. Whether or not it's important remains to be seen.'

Later, the Duke spoke privately with Feranc.

'Have *you* anything to tell me that I need to know?' he asked.

Feranc shook his head. 'No,' he said, simply.

Ibris looked at him anxiously. 'Your land has suffered greatly and strangely since you left, Ciarll,' he said. 'Armies raised, battles fought, civil war. Strange powers at work. Haven't you to tell me that you regret leaving; that perhaps if you'd stayed, events might have been different?'

Unexpectedly, Feranc smiled, though sadly. 'I've no regrets,' he replied, shaking his head. 'Events *would* have been different if I'd stayed, but for better or for worse, who can say? Who can say which side I'd have joined? I'd no close kin, and I was young and tormented.'

Ibris opened his mouth to speak, but Feranc continued. 'I'm curious to know what happened, very curious, and perhaps one day I'll be able to speak with Ryllans and the others about it at leisure. But it's of no importance.' He turned to the Duke. 'More important at the moment is the presence of the two men that Ryllans saw.'

'Could they be your countrymen looking to bring their old enemies to justice?' Ibris asked incredulously.

Feranc nodded. 'It's possible,' he replied. 'But we'll know for sure if we find them.'

'*If* we find them?'

'If they've come so far, then they're no ordinary king's men and if they're who I think they are, then if they don't wish to be found, they won't be,' Feranc said.

A brief look of irritation passed over Ibris's face. '*You're* their kind, Ciarll. Just find them. And soon.'

Feranc looked mildly surprised at Ibris's tone.

'Yes, it's that important,' Ibris said sharply, answering the implied reproach. 'Despite my curiosity about these shades from times long gone, my real concern is still for the problems we have here and now. And these people – *if* they're Ryllans' people, your people – have faced and defeated this . . . power . . . that assails us. We must recruit them as allies.'

434

Chapter 32

It was a cold, bright, sunny day when the first divisions of Ibris's army marched out of Serenstad on their journey to Whendrak. The sky was bright blue, and empty of clouds, and a slight breeze fluttered the buntings and pennants that had been draped about the city for this occasion.

A flag-draped podium had been erected on a rocky outcrop on the far side of the river and from it, Ibris and various other dignitaries were reviewing the troops as they passed over the bridge.

A large crowd had gathered and the many boats in the harbour were also crowded with spectators. There was a comforting amount of cheering and applause, but it was encouraging in tone, not joyous, and the predominant mood was one of anxiety.

After so many years of comparative peace and growing prosperity, the sudden flaring of Bethlarii hostility had come as a peculiarly awful shock to the Serens, and many could still not yet properly accept it.

It did not help that nothing had presaged this adventure; no increasingly acrimonious exchanges between envoys, no rumours of villages being raided, or trades routes blockaded, no formal denunciations, challenges or declarations. In fact nothing which would serve to rouse the population into a mood unequivocally in favour of military action.

But it was the possibility that the reason for the aggression might be religious which caused the real concern. Trade and land were matters that the Serens could understand fighting for if need arose. But some bizarre deity . . .?

'This is the information I have received, and it is beyond dispute,' Ibris told a subdued and hushed joint meeting of the Sened and the Gythrin-Dy following the return of Arwain's Mantynnai with their unhappy confirmation of the Bethlarii's intent.

'I need hardly mention that when many of us here were younger, fighting the Bethlarii was almost an annual occurrence, on one pretext or another. Fortunately, times have changed and we've all become a little wiser. Indeed, I'm sure that, despite our many differences, no one here will dispute that these are *enlightened* times. Times in which the sword and the bow are no longer regarded as acceptable tools of disputation. Fortunately too, however, despite this absence of hostilities, we have remembered that no city, no community, no man even, can lightly set aside those same tools or turn completely away from the idea of such conflict, as there will always be those who would seek to impose their will upon us by such means.'

There were murmurs of agreement about the chamber.

'Thus we have continued to give due note to martial skills, maintaining our army and making service a necessary social duty for all our young men. Not to menace our neighbours. But to show that as we value the hope of the future, so, by maintaining our strength, we remember the lessons of the past.'

He had concluded his speech by an appeal for unity between the many quarrelsome factions of the two governing houses and the other city institutions.

'This conflict, however, my friends, will be like no other there has been within our lifetimes. The Bethlarii have turned away from light, and reason, and knowledge, and have been possessed by a dark and ghastly bigotry. They will know no rest until they have spread this monstrous creed across the whole land unless they are shown the folly of their ways. And they will know that folly only when they have been decisively, conclusively, stopped.'

He paused and looked slowly over the silent, watching, representatives of his people.

'It will be a grim conflict we send our young men to,' he went on, after a long pause. 'And we must stand as they stand. Shield to shield. Stirrup to stirrup. We ask them to stand and suppress the weakness of their flesh in the face of missiles and charging cavalry. To stand even when their comrades fall wounded and dying about them. Thus we too must suppress our own weaknesses and petty differences and stand firm in the face of those among us who would seek to use this tragedy for their own ends, or worse, who would seek to appease this tyranny of ignorance which the Bethlarii have chosen to accept.'

There had been a little uncomfortable shuffling at these last remarks, but Ibris had won the unanimous support he had asked for.

'For now,' Aaken added cryptically.

'Now's the important time,' Ibris replied.

He had been obliged, however, to make a sacrifice of his own in the wake of this appeal, and standing beside him now on the podium was his wife, Nefron: 'Much recovered from the long and exhausting illness which had confined her to the Erin-Mal, and standing true and strong beside her husband in the land's great time of need.'

'Just keep an eye on her,' Ibris told Feranc and Ryllans with prodigious emphasis.

'But . . .?'

'Don't worry, I'm not leaving her at my back. She'll be accompanying us to the front,' Ibris said grimly, answering the question before it was asked. 'For the morale of the army,' he added significantly. 'Or at least as near as will seem seemly of me to the people.'

Neither Ryllans nor Feranc demurred openly at this decision. Nefron gaining public esteem by such 'courage' was probably better than Nefron left to her own devices back in Serenstad.

'So thoughtful of you to bring me out in this bitter wind, my dear,' Nefron said quietly to him as she smiled and raised a waving hand to the passing troops.

Outwardly, Ibris ignored the barb, though, as they both knew, it struck home, and, despite himself, long-buried memories of their earlier passions stirred to reproach him.

'Another cloak for the lady Nefron,' he snapped unnecessarily at a nearby servant.

'Winter's in the air,' someone said.

The remark made Ibris cast a brief but anxious look at Feranc, standing nearby. Though the Commander of his bodyguard never spoke of it, Ibris knew that he had a particular horror of winter combat.

Ironically, however, this was to the benefit of the army, as Feranc had imagination enough to put himself in the place of those he led. Thus he was meticulous in ensuring that clothing was appropriate and that supplies were adequate and thoroughly organized. More importantly it drew on his every dark resource to the full, to ensure that the conflict would be over as soon as possible.

Menedrion, standing beside his mother, shifted uneasily. He had little time for such ceremonies and was anxious to be with his troops.

Not that there was a great deal of ceremony about this march past. Apart from battalion and company colours and a liberal sprinkling of favours and pennants on pikes and waggons, there was no other concession to the traditional, more formal, departure of the army from the city. The matter was too urgent for such niceties and the men were in their field uniforms and setting their faces towards a rapid march to Whendrak.

Others would follow in due course, and others had already left. Except for his immediate personal guard, Ibris's elite bodyguard, equipped with the minimum of supplies, were already well on their way, by forced march. They were under the command of Arwain, with Ryllans as his aide. What they found when they arrived at Whendrak would be carried back by gallopers and would form the basis of the tactics for the army proper.

The baggage train and its flank guards were now rumbling past.

Menedrion shifted again.

'Be patient, Irfan,' Nefron said. 'I'm sure Arwain will be able to manage without you for a little while.'

'Go and take up your position in the column, Irfan,' Ibris said, before Menedrion could reply. Then with a nod to the officer in charge of the ceremony, he turned, said a few farewells to the various dignitaries, and, taking his wife's arm, gently escorted her down the podium steps. At the bottom he left her in the charge of her own small entourage and bodyguard.

Below them, the crowd was beginning to head back across the bridge towards the city. Some remained, however, as the rearguard passed by, and for some time after even the Duke and his party had left. Mothers sent their love and hopes after their sons and tried to keep their fears from their faces. Wives held babies close and clutched young, uncomprehending hands tightly and did the same. Young boys felt the weight of the adult fear, however, and did not play and roister with the toy swords and spears they had brought in support of their departing brothers and fathers.

Ibris and Nefron parted without speaking.

'Galloper!'

'Let him through!'

Arwain looked up with a start and cursed himself silently.

How long had he been walking along in a trance? The relentless marching pace was both exhausting and hypnotic; he must have been almost asleep on his feet!

That wouldn't happen again, he resolved, as he searched for the approaching rider.

The man soon came into view and Arwain saw that he was driving his horse hard.

There was little semblance of rank and file in the column, as each individual made the best pace he could to keep in contact with the leaders, but there was still a clear order of march, and the straggling vanguard parted to let the rider through. He came to a staggering halt beside Arwain.

The horse was lathered in sweat and the rider was little better. He accepted Arwain's supporting arm as he slid, exhausted, from his saddle. A trooper ran up and took the horse.

Ryllans appeared at Arwain's side.

Before either of them spoke, the messenger said, breathlessly, 'The Bethlarii have surrounded Whendrak. Two full divisions, I'd say.'

Arwain's heart sank. Two divisions! Ten times the men he had. The scale of the Bethlarii's intent and the speed of its execution, chilled him. And what could he do against such odds?

'Surrounded, or taken?' Ryllans' calm inquiry cut across Arwain's dismay. He offered the messenger his water bottle. The man seized it eagerly.

'Surrounded,' he confirmed. 'There were still signs of fires inside the city, but it must still be sealed, the Bethlarii were making towers.'

'Good,' Ryllans said. 'While Whendrak holds out against them, they'll not be anxious to move on through the valley. Were you seen?'

'No. I kept to the south ridge and it was deserted.'

Ryllans nodded, but said nothing. Then, dismissing the messenger, he spoke to Arwain quietly. 'If they've not occupied or put lookouts on the ridges then they're either not expecting us yet or they just don't care. It's not like them to be so careless, but . . .' He shrugged. 'This whole business is out of character . . .' He thought for a moment.

'We've got to keep them in the valley until the main column arrives,' Arwain said. 'And there's no saying how long Whendrak will hold with them on the outside and some kind of uprising on the inside. They could be on the move even now.'

It was a grim thought. 'We can't meet them with a force this size,' Ryllans said, mouthing the obvious to clear his mind. 'Not anywhere in the valley, it's too wide. But we can harass them, slow them down, if needs be.' He nodded to himself.

'We'll need to hold the ridges for that,' Arwain said.

Within the hour a rider was heading back to Ibris's army with the news and details of Arwain's intention, a company of the bodyguard was moving forward at full speed, with a view to securing the ridges during the night, and Arwain was forcing his complaining limbs to meet the renewed pace of the column.

They rested for a little while during the night. 'We'll be at the valley tomorrow,' Ryllans said. 'Perhaps fighting. A little food and sleep is essential now.' Though it seemed to Arwain that the Mantynnai himself got little of the latter. Certainly he was always either awake or absent on the several occasions that Arwain was jerked awake by one physical discomfort or another.

He made a note to mention Ryllans' apparent self-neglect in the morning with a view, perhaps, to a mild rebuke, but it was he who was bleary eyed, stiff and shivering, and Ryllans who was wide awake and quietly mocking when the camp roused itself in the pre-dawn darkness.

It was an eerie awakening. Silence would be essential from here on, and the chilly gloom was alive with whispering shadows and hooded lamps, as weapons, supplies and equipment were checked, stiff joints massaged, blistered feet given their final attention before being pressed back into duty.

Then they were marching again, not as quickly as before, and more carefully. It was more important now that the column did not spread out too far.

Trudging through the darkness, surrounded by so many companions, Arwain felt suddenly very alone. He had commanded before, but not such a lightly armed, swiftly moving and independent group. True, he had Ryllans beside him and he was content to note the Mantynnai's unobtrusive advice, but he knew that he must bring to the fore everything that he had ever learned about fighting, about tactics, about people, about the terrain, everything, if he was to be anything other than a hindrance, or worse, to the group.

He stared into the darkness around them. There was no moon and the stars appeared only fitfully through a light haze of cloud. And it was nearly freezing; the air was misty with the clouded breath of the walking men and filled with the muffled sound of careful treading and the occasional rasp of a foot slithering on a damp rock.

He glanced up at the sky again and as he did so, two thin spears of light skimmed briefly across his vision.

He smiled. Chance, he thought. Starflies were not common at this time of year, and they shone for barely the blink of an eye. Yet he had looked up at this one moment just in time to see two of them perform their flight across the heavens.

Thus was it going to be from now on until this cruel affair was over. There would be plans, strategies, tactics, but always chance would be there to divert the course of any combat with its arbitrary and featherlike touch; an arrow caught in a breeze, a pebble under a foot, a cry to distract the attention, a spark from a burning brand.

'In battle, as in all things, you must learn from what was, you must look to what may be, but your mind and your body must be neither clouded nor ruled by either. You are here now, and now you will live or die.'

The advice had not been Ryllans', but Ciarll Feranc's when one day he had seen Arwain training and chosen to speak for some reason.

Ryllans had stood back respectfully. 'I try to understand him,' he had said when Feranc had left and Arwain had turned to him for an explanation. 'Just remember what he said, and think about it. He's twenty times the warrior that I'll ever be.'

Arwain took the advice and, occasionally, just like the brief faint flaring of the starflies' flight, he thought he understood.

Then, without realizing how it had come about, he felt differently about the stiffness in his limbs, about the cold striking into his hands and feet, about the burdens of leading this group, about the endless options that lay ahead. None of them was in any way diminished, but in some way he accepted rather than resisted them and they became no more onerous to him than the weight of his mailcoat and boots.

And he knew where they were. The bewildering darkness became subtle shapes and shadows that he recognized.

'We're near the mouth of the valley,' he said softly to

441

Ryllans. 'About two hours' hard marching from the city, I'd say. We'd better halt and send out scouts.'

The Mantynnai nodded, and sent out the whispered command to halt.

The column closed ranks in the darkness and after a brief discussion with the officers, Ryllans sent a small group ahead to reconnoitre, and then ordered the column forward again, slowly and battle ready.

The silence that had pervaded the marchers thus far became tense now and was permeated with whispers of 'keep together' and 'keep quiet'. There was an occasional muffled cry and flurry as someone was startled by a scurrying night animal, or low swooping bird.

After a while, there was a flicker from a hooded lamp ahead and, after a whispered challenge, two of the scouts returned to announce that the road ahead was clear for some way and that they had left markers. The other scouts were continuing ahead. Then the two men were gone again.

Ryllans did not increase the speed of the march, however, as haste was no longer needed, and it was important that the column kept together.

Gradually the eastern sky began to grey, but like a grim parody of a sunset, the western horizon became noticeably red. 'Let's hope that's just camp fires,' Arwain said.

As they eased forward, successive scouts returned to say that the road was still clear, and then, finally, that the city was still untaken. Further, the Bethlarii were not attacking; their camp was at rest. Less heartening, though, was the news that further Bethlarii troops appeared to have arrived.

Ryllans called another halt and led Arwain aside.

'We've no idea of the state of affairs in Whendrak,' he said. 'They might be secure and comfortable, or they might be on the verge of defeat. From what we saw while we were there, they're badly divided among themselves and I fear the latter's more likely, if only by virtue of treachery at the gate. However, that may well be academic. If the Bethlarii are bringing up fresh troops, they may be planning a major assault, or they may be intending to leave a force here to contain the city while their main army moves on through the valley. In which case they could be moving at dawn.' He nodded towards the greying east.

'Go on,' Arwain said into the silence.

'We can wait and see if they intend an assault,' Ryllans

442

continued. 'But if they don't, if they move on, then they'll march right into us.'

'From the silence I presume that we've occupied the ridges,' Arwain said. 'We could harass them if they move, as we decided.'

Ryllans shook his head. 'It would've been risky against two divisions, even allowing for a couple of battalions being left around the city. But if they've been building up their numbers while we've been marching, we've no idea how many would be coming through. It may not be possible for us to delay them until the main army arrives. In which case we could lose a great many men and perhaps even find ourselves cut off for no great gain.'

Arwain breathed in slowly. They had no information on which to make a rational decision, but Ryllans' comments were sound and, with or without information, the decision had to be made.

'That leaves us with retreat or . . . an immediate attack,' he said, after a long pause. 'And as retreat would be worse than just standing here, that means we must attack. Now. Before dawn.' He felt at once sick and excited.

Softly, Ryllans summoned the officers again and laid the same conclusion before them. It was greeted with an uneasy silence and Arwain was glad of the darkness concealing his face. He became aware, however, of the faces of others, pale in the darkness, turning towards him.

'I see no other alternatives,' he said, surprised at his own calmness. 'There are people in Whendrak fighting both their own and the Bethlarii, and every moment we wait, we jeopardize them and we allow the Bethlarii to increase their force. My father's finest troops didn't make a forced march across the country to act as mute witnesses to the death of Whendrak or to stand by like keening widows as the enemy brushes us aside.' He paused.

'They have numbers. We have surprise.'

The die was cast.

Ivaroth Ungwyl brought his horse to a halt as he reached the ridge. A bitterly cold wind struck him suddenly, making him tighten his cloak and swear to himself.

Overhead, an unbroken sea of grey clouds moved southward, as if, whey-faced, they ran to tell the lands there of his coming.

443

Ivaroth glared at the lowering peaks above and around him. Here and there the higher ones disappeared up into the clouds, and some were capped and streaked with recent snow, making them brilliant even in the prevailing greyness. The scene would have moved a less jaundiced spirit with its stern splendour and majesty, but to Ivaroth, the massive, ageless, and immovable presence of the mountains was an affront. These stones mocked him.

'Who are you, Mareth Hai?' they seemed to say. 'And of what worth is your vaulting ambition in the span of our time? 'Tis but a heartbeat since your long-dead kin fled through our valleys into the north, and the merest shake of our hoary heads would sweep your great army into oblivion forever. And who will remember you in but a handful of summers?'

Ivaroth snarled and fought to set the thoughts aside.

I am Mareth Hai, he shouted in silent defiance. As I conquered the plains so will I tear you rock from rock if you defy me. Level your cliffs, span your ravines, choke your rivers and waterfalls.

His inner spleen, however, gave him little solace. The mountains had taken a toll already and, he knew, would take a further before his army rode out into the southlands.

He looked back. The army was spread out along the trail. Men were toiling with horses and waggons loaded with tents and food and equipment, struggling with tow ropes and under heavy packs and panniers. The rambling procession dwindled into the distance where it disappeared from view, swallowed by the rugged terrain. He knew, however, that it was spread out far beyond his sight like a great dark serpent, moving relentlessly forward at his will.

'It is good.'

The voice both echoed and interrupted his triumphant reverie. It was the blind man. He was, as ever, standing nearby, seemingly as oblivious to the biting cold as he was to all the other rigours of the journey. Ivaroth suppressed a shudder. The old man seemed to be drawing some unholy sustenance from the rocks themselves as they moved deeper into the mountains. Now he was running his hands over a flat slab of rock as though he were a tender lover with his bride. Only his own consuming need for the man prevented Ivaroth from cutting him down in disgust.

However, it was rare for the old man to speak unless either spoken to, or to express some need, and, almost in spite of himself, Ivaroth felt drawn into a conversation. 'What is this power you draw from the rocks?' he asked. It was a long time since he had asked such a question, though even as he did, he expected nothing more than the reply he had always received in the past: silence.

The blank white eyes turned towards him, unreadable as ever, though Ivaroth sensed a dark amusement. The long, bony hands closed around the edge of the rock in a repellent embrace.

'It is the power,' he said, unexpectedly and with a mild hint of surprise in his voice. 'The old power that is in all things. Since the beginning of all things. Since before the beginning. My master taught me its use.' The hands began to caress the rock again. 'And here it is rich with the memories and skills of those who went before. Soon I will be as I was before *he* came. Came with his cruel sword and slew my . . .'

His voice tailed off in a strangled snarl, and his face became a mask of rage.

Ivaroth's eyes widened in alarm at the sight and, instinctively, he slid his hand under his cloak towards his knife.

But even as he touched the hilt, calmer counsels prevailed. The blind man had never before talked about his past, and the hint of defeat in the few words that he had just spoken, addressed themselves to the tactician in Ivaroth. He might . . . no, would . . . need to defeat the old man himself one day, and while he was being so forthcoming . . .

He was about to ask, solicitously, who this master was, and who the cruel swordsman, when, to his horror, he saw that the blind man's fingers had dug into the rock as if it were no more than damp sand. Ivaroth felt the hairs all over his body stand on end.

Then the old man seemed to recover himself, and, casting a sly, sightless glance at Ivaroth, he withdrew his fingers from the rock, and with a longing pass of his hands, made it whole again.

'It is a power beyond your knowing or understanding, Ivaroth,' he said, reassuringly. 'But through me, it will give *you* the power that you seek, the victories, the wealth, the worship of your people, the vengeance of your race.'

'And what will it give you?' Ivaroth asked, pulling his thick kerchief over his face to disguise the hoarseness of his voice as it struggled from his fear-dried throat.

The old man's face became alive with anticipation. 'More,' he said, simply.

It was a chilling answer, but Ivaroth felt himself drawn inexorably forward. 'And then?' he pressed.

'Then . . .' The old man paused. 'Then, I shall return and seek my master, and his master in turn. And restore . . .'

His voice faded again and, though still powerfully curious, Ivaroth did not choose to pursue his questioning. The image of the torn rock hung in his mind. Whatever masters the old man had served in the past, he had no wish to learn of them. At least not at the moment.

Turning away, Ivaroth clicked his horse forward a little way and then dismounted. Peering ahead he could just make out in the distance the red flags that his scouts had positioned to guide the army.

Drawn from the southern tribes who had regularly raided the northern Bethlarii outposts, their mountain lore, though limited, had proved invaluable. 'The gods favour us, Mareth Hai,' they had said when they reported to him at daybreak. 'They bring the cold wind, but they keep at bay the mists. We'll move well today.'

And they had. Indeed they had moved well almost every day since they had left the plains. Mindful of Ivaroth's injunctions, complaining had become a discreet affair throughout the army, confined to low voices and close friends, though few were at ease with the alien terrain.

And not without cause. There had been several fatalities and many injuries as the plains' people learned about this new, unyielding domain. Unwary feet which dislodged rocks on to those following below; narrow and treacherous paths and too steep slopes that claimed waggons and horses and also those who struggled too long to restrain them; savage winds which toppled the incautious down buffeting crags and into screaming voids.

At the same time a new breed had appeared amidst the disparate tribes that Ivaroth had welded together in this great venture. Men who had looked at the terrain, and at the sweating, straining effort of their fellows, and who had directed their own effort into acquiring skills unknown in the plains: widening and strengthening pathways, fixing ropeways, using levers and pulleys.

Ivaroth watched this remarkable metamorphosis but hid his elation as each new piece of ingenuity spared his fighters and moved his army forward. He hid also his distrust for these men with their strange, clear-sighted vision. What did they see when they looked at him? Still, they were like the blind man, they were but men, and susceptible to blade and point.

'Good. You have done well,' he would say impassively. And they went away aglow with his approval.

A hand caught his elbow. He did not respond, the blind man's cloying grip was all too familiar.

'Soon,' the old man said, lifting his face upwards as if scenting the air. 'You are nearer to your old lands than your new.'

'How long?' Ivaroth asked.

The blind man did not answer. His head was swaying from side to side hypnotically.

Ivaroth did not press his question. It would be to little avail; the old man seemed to have either no concern for, or conception of, time and distance. It was as if part of him, perhaps the greater part of him, existed in some other place.

Later, as the great caravan rested, draped like a thin dark scarf about the shoulders of mountains, Ivaroth amazed his scouts by telling them what they had been about to tell him. A few days, the weather continuing to favour them, and they would be out of the mountains and moving across the rolling foothills. Ahead of them then would be the rich lands of the south.

'Tonight we must visit our allies,' Ivaroth said to the blind man. 'To ensure they are still resolute in their purpose.'

The blind man smiled.

Ivaroth turned away from the sight.

Chapter 33

As Arwain dispatched the gallopers to carry the news of the intended attack back to Ibris, his thoughts became as dark as the surrounding night.

'It's no worse than any ambush,' part of him said.

'It's murdering sleeping men,' said another.

'You'll not murder many. You'll be lucky if you reach the camp unseen, and if you do, the alarm will be sounded within minutes. Then you'll be fighting for your lives. Outnumbered more than ten to one now they've brought new troops up.'

'But killing men unshriven—'

'There's no good way to die in battle. And they've done it to us often enough in the past.'

'We aren't them.'

'Ah, are we not? We've *never* done it to them in the past?'

'We've changed.'

'Indeed?'

Silence.

'But you've just sanctioned this deed? Will you account for it when the time comes?'

'The time is now, and I account for it now, to the one who matters the most; myself.'

'Too easy.'

'Killing them may save us, and many others.'

'May is a frail word on which to place this dark and joyless burden; from which to claim necessity.'

'It's all we have. All I have. The treaty, the paper wall that kept us apart, is breached. Breached by them, utterly, and without a vestige of provocation.'

'Not enough.'

Stillness. Then, 'The last religious war was savage beyond belief. We must defend ourselves.'

'But an unprovoked attack?'

'The assault on Whendrak is provocation by virtue of treaty and historical fact. Serenstad must defend itself, and we, here, cannot risk waiting the enemy's pleasure.'

Silence.

'They'll come definitely, if you attack.'

The arguments began to circle. 'Yes, but probably quickly, with a small force that we may be able to contain. And if they send a large force, it'll have been delayed and it'll move more slowly.'

'May? If?'

Arwain closed his eyes. For a moment, his mind was choked by a great, entangled, knot of causes and effects which disappeared back into time and beyond the boundaries of his knowledge.

They ceased suddenly as if they had been severed by a swift sword cut.

'What we do *is* necessary. It's necessary because we're here, and all other alternatives that we have from here lead . . . may lead . . . *as far as we can see*, to destruction.'

Unsought and unexpected, a vision of his wife, and a great longing for her, intruded on his thoughts and made him falter. But his debate had a momentum of its own, and the vision was swept away even as Arwain reached out to it.

'What myriad happenings brought us here, brought the Bethlarii here, is beyond my sight and my understanding, let alone my unravelling. What we're going to do is necessary and its necessity is the true measure of war.'

The debate faded. Arwain reached up and wiped his brow. It was damp with perspiration despite the morning's chill.

And this necessity was also a measure of his father, he realized. His father, who had determinedly turned his face against the ways of the past and led the Serens and their allies away from such necessities for so many years.

Standing alone in the cold darkness, Arwain resolved that should he and Serenstad survive, he would try to be a better pupil at the feet of this man. Now, however, he must guard his father's life's work by following his teaching and tending to this cruel necessity.

Then Ryllans was by his side. Arwain felt his urgency. The east was greying relentlessly. The mountains would slow the arrival of the morning light at Whendrak, but the attack must not be delayed further or it would be impossible to effect the clandestine retreat that was vital to their intention.

'I'm ready,' Arwain said, turning towards the Mantynnai.

Silence was to cover the vanguard of the Serens' attack. A great roaring charge might possibly panic the first of the besiegers that they reached, but the Bethlarii were hardened fighters and the very din of battle would probably help them to recover and regroup quickly. In addition, the noise would certainly rouse those in more distant parts of the camp, bringing them to the scene armed and savage.

Thus those among the bodyguard with the skills for the task were now moving silently ahead to kill the sentries as quietly as possible. That done, the main force would move equally silently into the camp, killing and destroying all they could, and then retreat quickly at the first sign of the Bethlarii recovering.

The action had to be swift and lethal, and it was essential that the Bethlarii gain no measure of their true size or they would counter-attack recklessly at first light and Arwain had no illusions about the ability of his battalion to withstand what would surely be a massive and infuriated onslaught by a vastly more numerous army.

Slowly, crouching low, the Serens drew nearer to the camp. Almost ritualistically, as if for comfort, Arwain's hand kept testing the metal buckles on his belt and scabbards to ensure that the cloths binding them were firm and secure, to prevent them from rattling.

The force had been divided into small groups, each of which could fight as a close formation team in the event of unexpected opposition. At the same time, the groups would maintain close contact with their neighbours to minimize the risk of being separated and cut off. The use of such groups would also help to maintain a better standard of discipline.

'This is an action to cause damage and delay,' Ryllans emphasized. 'It's not a battle we can win. The last thing we want is anyone running amok, screaming and yelling like some berserker. The Bethlarii will be doing enough of that in due course, and the sooner the camp's roused, the sooner we have to retreat, and the sooner they'll regroup and come after us. Is that clear?'

The shadows around him nodded silently.

'Right. Just remember. Keep quiet, keep your wits about you, advance cautiously, keeping contact with your neighbouring groups, and do your jobs. That way you'll survive.'

Soft, whispering orders sighed through the darkness and the advance stopped. Arwain tightened his grip about his sword. He looked back to see that his group was in good order. They were very near to the camp now.

Presumably not anticipating an attack from either the city, or from along the valley, the Bethlarii had posted few sentries, though several were guarding a partially constructed siege tower. A few lamps revealed their vigil and it was the rapid destruction of these particular guards that Arwain had taken as the task for his own group.

There was a short, high-pitched cry from some way ahead, to the left, followed by some grunting and scuffling. Arwain started, as did several of his companions. The noise seemed to ring like a trumpet clarion through the darkness and Arwain felt his already racing heart pound even harder. Deliberately, he took in and released several slow breaths to calm himself, forcing himself to look at the men around the tower.

No stir came from the camp, however, though some of the guards looked about to see what had caused the noise.

Unnecessarily, Arwain held up his hand for both silence and stillness, but after a long moment, the tower guards fell back into their casual watch.

Then, like a poison-tipped arrow, the codeword he had been waiting for and dreading hissed at him out of the night. *The lone sentries are down, move in.*

Arwain nodded to his two immediate companions and the three of them stood up and began walking forward casually. The remainder vanished into the darkness.

As they neared the tower, Arwain's companions put their arms about his shoulders, and he drooped his head as if he were sick or injured, and in need of support. They did not speak, but they made no attempt to walk quietly.

As they drew nearer, Arwain scuffed his feet along the ground and coughed.

The sound galvanized the tower guards. 'Halt,' one of them called, advancing, his spear levelled.

'It's all right,' one of Arwain's companions called back with what they had agreed was a passable attempt at a Bethlarii accent. 'Our mate's cracked his head open, we're looking for the—'

The accent was not good enough.

'Ye gods, they're Serens! Sound the—'

At the first exclamation, however, Arwain had relinquished his supporters and moved forward. He reached the man in three long, swift strides. The movement was so sudden and purposeful that the guard faltered momentarily, and, side-

452

stepping the extended spear, Arwain drove his sword through the man's throat, silencing his cry instantly.

The guard's hands dropped the spear and came up reflexively and futilely to grip the lethal blade. For an instant, Arwain lost his balance. As he struggled to recover it and also retrieve his sword he felt his two companions move past him and engage the other guards. Then the rest of his group were there, at the rear of the distracted guards.

Even as Arwain registered this fact, a figure lunged towards him. Without thinking, he twisted sideways and felt the terrifying draught of a blade passing in front of him. His attacker lurched forward under the impetus of his missed blow and Arwain drove the palm of his free hand into the side of the man's face ferociously. He felt a bone crack, and heard the man utter a strange cry as he staggered under the blow. Arwain tore his sword free from the dying man and struck the reeling figure a blow on the shoulder. The man went down and Arwain struck him again.

Then there was a flare of light. A lamp had been knocked over and the spilled oil had ignited violently. Arwain took in the scene as if it had been some vivid picture hanging in his father's palace. A mass of shadows and men, swirling and moving in some unholy dance, something far away from him, aesthetic almost, to be viewed dispassionately, at leisure.

In the same instant he heard again a score of Ryllans' training yard reproaches.

'Move, Arwain! Move!'

The distant vision passed from his mind and he saw the scene as it was: shadows and men swirling and moving in terror, rage and bloodlust. He saw too that the guards were losing, and that the fire would probably ignite the whole tower.

Good, he thought, as he drove his sword into a Bethlarii about to bring his foot down on a fallen figure. That'll be useful to the Whendreachi. He pushed the struggling Bethlarii off his sword with his foot and reached down to drag the downed Serens to his feet.

A glance showed him the last guard falling and that all his men were standing, though some appeared to be injured.

How long had it all taken? Scarcely twenty heartbeats something told him, but time had no meaning here. Here there was only now.

Quickly he checked that those injured could continue, then

he looked out in the darkness away from the flickering flames beginning to rise up the tower. The night was alive with the shadows of his battalion, moving silently into the Bethlarii camp like a great, engulfing, black tide. Where it passed it would leave only death.

He pointed towards the nearest tent. A figure was crawling out of it. At the sight of the blazing tower, he, like the first guard, faltered, and like the first guard, he died for it as a single blow from Arwain almost severed his head. Then swords cut open the tent, and in a brief orgy of stabbing and hacking, killed the bewildered occupants, before moving swiftly to the next tent.

The deed was repeated along the whole of the Serens' line. And repeated and repeated.

Arwain did not count how many died. He thought mainly of his next stride forward, knowing that to do otherwise could bring death to him as easily as he brought it to the surprised Bethlarii. Once he thought of those that this cruelty might save, but the thought vanished as he was obliged to deal with an armed Bethlarii who was more quickly aroused than his fellows.

Gradually the night silence began to fill with the cracking and snapping of the burning tower, the sounds of pounding feet, hacking effort, and, increasingly, agonizing cries of bewilderment and terror.

Then it was rent by the shrill alarm cries of escaping survivors. First one, then another, then many, dashing through the camp and rousing whom they could in their flight.

As this clamouring news of the assault began to outpace the progress of the attackers, so the first rush of the black tide began to peter out, and the Serens found themselves meeting increasing resistance.

It was necessarily disorganized however, and by maintaining their close groups, the Serens were able to continue pushing relentlessly forward for some time, ruthlessly cutting down those Bethlarii who attempted to stand their ground.

For a brief period, and quite by chance, several of the groups came together to form a continuous marching line reminiscent of the traditional pike line in formal battle array. And for that same period, it seemed that panic would indeed overwhelm the Bethlarii as they fled before it.

454

The Serens' line advanced triumphantly.

By the light from the burning tower, Arwain saw the group nearest his own accelerate and surge off into the darkness.

His stomach went cold. 'Close up, close up. They've separated from us,' he hissed to his own group.

Over to his right he heard the mounting noise of the wakening camp. He and Ryllans had discussed the many dangers inherent in this attack. The greatest, they concluded, was not the possibility of being overwhelmed by direct resistance, but in fact the contrary. It was the possibility that the Bethlarii immediately in front of the attack would crumble and that as a consequence, the Serens would move too far forward, perhaps even breaking through the Bethlarii circle, only to find it closing about them in awakened force and leaving them with their backs to the city wall.

And this was what was happening.

Arwain did not hesitate.

'Sound retreat, quickly!' he shouted urgently to his signaller.

Even as the horn call rang out, it was echoed by an identical call from Ryllans' signaller at the other end of the attack line. It did not surprise Arwain. The tactic was one of many that had been agreed in advance of the attack, in the knowledge that communications between the two principal officers would be impossible once the enemy was engaged.

Arwain peered anxiously into the darkness.

'Sound again, and keep sounding!' he said.

'Lord!' A hand seized his arm and turned him round. His companion was pointing back to the blazing tower. Against its light, Arwain saw a large group of Bethlarii forming around it, spears and swords silhouetted clearly. They were in some disorder, but even as he looked he saw the group's attention drawn towards the darkness from which came the invader's horn call.

Arwain's immediate response was to retreat, but now his group were effectively the rearguard to a large part of the battalion and these Bethlarii were the unwitting vanguard of the encircling movement that must inevitably cut off the Serens' force if they did not retreat quickly.

'Form up around the signaller,' he ordered. 'Lock shields and hold.' Then, to the signaller, he hissed, 'Blow as you've never blown.'

The signaller needed no such instruction but acknowledged

it with a glance of his whitened eye and a nod which made his horn call waver slightly.

Arwain's attention returned to the now cautiously advancing Bethlarii. They were visible against the light of the tower and, occasionally, a point or an edge reflected the firelight ominously. If they closed, then his small group would not be able to hold for more than a few minutes. He glanced over his shoulder. Other fires were springing up through the camp, but still there was no sign of the neighbouring groups returning.

Briefly a surge of self-reproach washed over him. Would this venture prove to be no more than the reckless loss of Ibris's famous bodyguard? The finest of Serenstad's troops massacred under the command of his bastard son?

He had a vision of the endless disastrous consequences of such an outcome and once more his wife's face appeared to him.

But the relentless sounding of the horn kept him anchored firmly to the present and the vision of his wife merely served as a centre around which he formed a stern resolve.

'Shout,' he cried to his men. 'They can't see us as well as we can see them. Shout! Swords and shields!'

The men obeyed, banging their swords on their shields and roaring fiercely. The advancing Bethlarii hesitated slightly, their leaders crouching slightly and peering into the gloom.

The horn blew.

'The charge chant!' Arwain shouted to his men.

The shouting faded suddenly and was replaced by a rhythmic chanting punctuated by equally rhythmic tattoos of foot stamping and swords against shields. At this change, the Bethlarii halted and some of them began to edge back a little, though others, Arwain noted, began to close ranks.

As the chanting increased in intensity, Arwain desperately looked again into the darkness behind him. For the most part, the Bethlarii were still only a loose-knit crowd; they *might* scatter at the climax of the chant in anticipation of a solid line of shields and spears emerging out of the darkness towards them, but . . .?

Should he risk a short charge? Line abreast, he and his few men would look more numerous than they were.

The decision, however, was made for him. The Bethlarii might only have been a loose-knit group, but they were an angry one and their anger was growing in proportion to their hesitation. They needed only the slightest touch to release their building energy.

It came in the form of a tall figure who broke through to the front of the crowd and began haranguing them. Arwain noticed that he was dressed differently from the rest.

One of their damned priests, he thought.

But scarcely had the thought formed than the priest let out a great shriek, full of hatred and fury, and began to charge. Without even the slightest hesitation, the Bethlarii followed him.

'Lock shields! Hold the circle!' Arwain shouted.

Cries of 'Hyrdyn! Hyrdyn! Hyrdyn!' reached him as his own men fell silent.

His legs began to shake.

'Hold,' he said, commandingly. 'The others will be retreating back towards us. We mustn't fail them.'

He braced himself for the impact.

Then, to his horror, he was aware of the circle breaking; space at his back. Before he could turn to confirm this, however, a spear flitted across his vision and struck the Bethlarii priest full in the mouth. His shrieking battle cry stopped in a stomach-churning squeal and the impact of the spear coupled with his forward movement sent him crashing backwards, his legs flailing in the air.

Two more spears followed, one striking another Bethlarii, the next narrowly missing a third. Just as the priest's arrival had ignited the crowd, so his abrupt demise doused it, and the Bethlarii began to retreat.

'They're back,' one of Arwain's companions said, looking over his shoulder.

The remark was unnecessary.

'Retreat,' Arwain ordered. That too was unnecessary.

But in the darkness the retreat proved more dangerous than the advance even though there was no immediate pursuit. Then, they had approached quietly and carefully in close formations, placing each foot with care. Now, they were carrying their dead and badly wounded, and with hatred and anger howling behind them, and retribution waiting in the near future, they were all fighting the urge to flee. Despite the best efforts of the officers, they did not maintain a pace slow enough to be safe in the difficult terrain and several were injured in falls.

Eventually, as the dull grey dawn began to etch out figures

and landscapes, they gathered on a level area some way from the road that meandered down the centre of the valley.

They were greeted by the battalion's companies of archers. The assault on the camp had been too scattered for them to be used effectively, and they had been left to try and establish ambush positions to deal with the inevitable Bethlarii response.

While the returning infantrymen tended their injured, Ryllans sent scouts forward to report on the movement of the Bethlarii and conferred with the archers about their dispositions.

Arwain joined him. 'How many dead?' he asked.

'I don't know yet,' Ryllans replied. 'But not many I think. We were lucky. I never expected that we'd come so close to breaking through the line like that. A little later with the retreat and it would've been a very different tale.'

But there was little time for either reminiscence or analysis. The attack had nearly foundered by virtue of its success. Many Bethlarii had been slain and no small amount of damage done. Whatever their intention had been for this day, it would now be radically different. Arwain still could not fault the original surmise; it would be a small force quite soon, or a large one much later. But, that *was* surmise, and until it became reality, Ibris's bodyguard must be prepared for any outcome.

Arwain sent another galloper back towards his father's approaching army with details of the outcome of the attack, then returned to his men.

There was a strange quietness about the cold field. Some of the men were talking softly; some were resting, as well as they could on the rocks littering the dew-sodden turf. Others were comforting or being comforted. Many were at the edge of a nearby stream, washing blood from their weapons and themselves with its icy water. Arwain moved through them all, encouraging, sustaining, quietening; an unwitting copy of his father when himself a young commander.

Finally he came to the lee of a large rock where the battalion's physician was doing what he could for the seriously wounded.

As he drew near, his eye was caught by several lines of hummocks in the grass by the rock. It was not until he was almost upon them that he identified them as bodies.

458

Even as he watched, two men helping the physician brought another and laid it gently by the others. One of them wrote something on a piece of paper.

Against the rock-face, several lamps and a small fire etched out a bright, colourful tableau in the morning greyness. At its edges were the wounded, lying and sitting, some alone, some with companions to sustain them, while at its centre was a huddle of kneeling men. Arwain wanted to turn away, but forced himself forward.

The physician, his face strained and gaunt in the cold, unnatural light of the lamps and the burgeoning daylight, was routing into an open wound in a man's leg from which protruded part of an arrow shaft. The man was struggling desperately.

Catching sight of Arwain silhouetted in the half light, the physician snapped, 'Don't just stand there, man, help hold him down.'

For a moment, and, to his immediate regret, Arwain found he was looking for an angry rebuke for the physician for this insolence. Then, in atonement, he did as he was bidden and seized the man's legs which were coming free from the ropes that had been used to secure them to two posts driven into the ground.

The man's eyes were wide with terror and agony, though he did not make any attempt to relinquish the heavy leather belt that his teeth were biting into.

There was a sudden grunt of effort and then a sigh of relief from the physician and the arrow's barbed head was drawn reluctantly from the wound. Then, briskly, the physician snapped his fingers at one of his assistants by the fire. Almost before Arwain realized what was happening, the assistant, his hand protected by a thick cloth, had drawn a metal rod from the fire and given it to the physician who plunged its red-hot end resolutely into the wound.

The sound and the smell turned Arwain's stomach, but clenching his teeth, he clung to the still struggling legs, focusing his gaze on the round hammer marks in the splayed top of one of the posts to which the man's legs had been bound. He seemed to feel every blow that had been struck to drive the post into the hard ground. Then, at last, the injured man gave a convulsive heave and then went limp. After a moment, Arwain released his legs. His head was spinning and he was shaking.

'Sew him up quickly before he recovers,' the physician was saying to someone. 'Then get him up to the road with the others. There's nothing else I can do for him here. His war's over for some time.'

With an almost incongruous gentleness, the two men picked the man up and carried him a little way away to attend to this injunction.

The physician bent down and washed his hands in a bowl nearby. Arwain caught the sweet, pungent smell typical of Drayner's surgery. Then the physician was shaking his hands vigorously and beckoning his helpers to bring the next victim forward.

He glanced at Arwain while he waited. His gaze was one that Arwain had seen before in the faces of field physicians; practical and detached but underlain by a deep anger. It contained a cruel vision.

But who knows what my own gaze tells, Arwain thought, and, as if in confirmation, a brief look of self-reproach passed over the physician's face.

'I'm sorry I spoke harshly, lord,' he said. 'I didn't recognize you.'

'It's of no consequence,' Arwain said, laying a hand on the man's arm. 'Tend your charges.'

The physician turned to the man being laid in front of him. The men carrying him were being impeded by an anxious-looking trooper who was holding the wounded man's hand, but neither offered him any reproach.

Gently, the physician unwound the bloodstained rag that had been used as a makeshift bandage about the man's head. One of the helpers brought a lamp closer. It revealed a livid and gaping wound that had obviously been done by a battle axe. The physician's brow furrowed slightly. Arwain tensed his stomach and forced his own face into immobility. Then the physician looked at the man's waiting friend, and shook his head.

'If he wakes, he'll not live. And there'll be nothing but pain for him until he dies,' he said softly. 'What do you want me to do?'

To Arwain's horror, the man turned towards him, his eyes pleading. 'He saved my life,' he said. 'That was meant for me.'

There was a similarity in the features of the two men that indicated they were related – brothers, perhaps. Man and commander fought within Arwain. The man sought for soft words, compassion, understanding, for time in which this tragedy could be accepted. But the commander knew their situation was too dangerous for the celebration of grief. That must come later.

The two needs merged. 'He's your kin,' Arwain said quietly. 'Do for him what you'd like him to do for you if you were in his place.'

The man looked down at the mangled head, his eyes filling with tears. Tenderly he ran his hand over the blood-clotted hair.

Then, his mouth taut, he nodded towards the physician. 'Do it,' he said hoarsely.

The physician glanced at Arwain and flicked his eyes towards the distraught brother. Arwain stood up and took the man's arm. 'Come on,' he said, gently, helping him to stand. 'He'll be tended with respect and there are others needing the physician.'

The man nodded slowly, then suddenly yanked himself free from Arwain's grasp and dropped to his knees by his brother. The physician signalled his helpers, but Arwain held out his hand to stop them.

The trooper bent forward and put his head by his brother's. Arwain heard him whispering something to the dying man, then he was standing again, wiping his hands down his crumpled tunic. Without a word he strode off into the grey anonymity of the field of waiting soldiers.

Even though the man was gone, the physician kept his long-bladed knife from view as he drew it. It was a well-practised gesture.

Arwain turned away and left the lamplit scene.

Coming towards him was Ryllans.

'Any news?' he asked, for want of something to say that would distance him further from this one death.

'Only from the company on the ridges,' Ryllans answered. 'They met no opposition and they're well placed to defend their positions.'

'And us?' Arwain asked, looking round at the broad field that sloped gradually up from the road until it petered out in dense vegetation and scree. Adequate as a rallying point, it was not remotely defensible against a large force.

'The archers have found a narrower, rockier section further

461

back,' Ryllans said, pointing down the valley. 'It's not perfect, but it's as good as we're likely to find.'

A little later, the surgeon's work finished, one of the two waggons that had accompanied the battalion, began its journey back to the main army, bearing those wounded too seriously to continue.

The straggling column of retreating men opened to let it pass, and then closed behind it like a dark, silent river.

As they trudged steadily forward, a dull sun rose to greet them, throwing long, faint shadows up the valley. Grim black columns of smoke scarred the western sky.

Antyr moved to the front of the enclosed waggon that he was sharing with Pandra. He was still not wholly used to its relentless, rocking motion and frequently stepped outside to join the driver and enjoy the cold morning air.

Tarrian and Grayle were already there, lying in the footwell, their paws draped over the kicking board, and their inquisitive heads held high as they peered around at the rumbling train and the quiet countryside preparing for winter.

'Another storm brewing, sailor?' Tarrian scoffed, as Antyr's head emerged from the waggon.

'Shut up, or I'll ride my horse and you two can run beside me like dutiful hounds,' Antyr replied brutally.

'You forget I've seen you ride,' Tarrian retorted, unabashed by the threat.

Antyr contented himself with a grunt and sat down by the driver. He was joined almost immediately by Pandra, who carefully placed a large cushion on the hard wooden seat, before sitting down.

'A hard bed, I like,' he said. 'But not seats.'

'Are you all right?' Antyr asked. The waggon was, in many ways, remarkably lavishly appointed, but Pandra was an old man to be undertaking such a journey.

'Yes, I'm fine,' Pandra replied, shuffling himself comfortable and rubbing his hands together. 'I'm enjoying this. It makes me feel quite young again.'

Antyr caught a whiff of some caustic comment by Kany, but Pandra merely smiled smugly and patted his pocket gently.

Well wrapped against the morning cold, they sat in companionable silence for some time.

'Dream Finders are you?' The question came from the driver. Both Antyr and Pandra turned to him. He was a man whose grey hair and weather-beaten face made all attempts at guessing his age futile, but even if his face had not confirmed him as a countryman, his patient, placid manner would have. Antyr and Pandra's surprise, however, was due to the fact that throughout the journey so far he had spoken very little to his two passengers, confining himself mainly to puffing on a carved wooden tobacco pipe and clicking affectionately to his horses from time to time.

'Yes,' Antyr replied.

The driver nodded sagely, and removed his pipe from his mouth as if to speak.

Then he put it back again. Antyr and Pandra exchanged glances, and the driver clicked at his horses and puffed contentedly on his pipe.

'Bannor,' he said after a while.

He held out his hand to Pandra, who, after a brief hesitation, shook it and introduced himself in turn. The hand moved to Antyr who did the same. It was large and muscular, but its grip, though positive, was gentle and careful, and, despite the cold morning, its touch was warm.

'You're a farmer, Bannor?' Antyr asked.

Bannor shook his head slowly and took his pipe from his mouth again. 'Labourer,' he said. 'Traveller. Farm to farm as season needs.' He pointed the pipe stem over his shoulder. 'My waggon,' he added.

The revelation left the two Dream Finders at somewhat of a loss as to what to say next.

'It's very . . . comfortable. And kind of you to let us use it.' Antyr's reply was a little awkward. He was fairly certain that the waggon would have been commandeered, and that they were about to be subjected to some acrimony on that account.

Bannor, however, simply inclined his head slightly in acknowledgement. 'My pleasure,' he said. 'Known the Duke a long time.'

'You *know* the Duke?' Antyr could not keep the surprise from his voice.

Bannor nodded again, but did not amplify his observation immediately.

'Good man,' he said, after another long pause. 'Asked me to look after you.'

There was a chuckle from Tarrian. 'Deep one, this,' he said. 'And quiet. Pleasure to be with. Not like you rattling townies.'

Antyr ignored the jibe.

'How do you come to know the Duke?' he asked, speaking slowly in an attempt to make his curiosity seem less strident against Bannor's patient demeanour.

'Fighting,' Bannor answered.

Antyr nodded. How else? he thought.

'And you?' The echo of his own question from Bannor, albeit leisurely, caught Antyr unawares. He had a fleeting image of slow plodding feet following a plough; feet that would neither quicken nor slow with the terrain, but would continue relentlessly until the whole field was turned, and would then carry their owner to his hearth at the same pace.

'He . . . sent for us,' Antyr replied eventually, fiddling with his ring of office.

Bannor nodded slightly and sucked on his pipe. 'Knows his men, the Duke,' he said. 'Always did.'

And that seemed to be the end of the matter; at least for the time being. Antyr was quietly relieved. He made a note to himself to be careful with this seemingly slow countryman. He sensed no malice in him, but realized that his relaxed manner might extract confidences more readily than the craftiest Liktor. He wondered how many more ordinary people the Duke bound with old ties of personal loyalty. Probably a great many, he decided.

He turned his gaze to the baggage train ahead of them. Many of the waggons were of a standard army design, but the majority were obviously modified farm vehicles, although there were also hospital waggons and several specially made house waggons to accommodate the administrative personnel that were an integral and vital part of Ibris's army.

He leaned out and glanced back at the train behind them. In the distance he could see the lavish waggons that housed the lady Nefron and her entourage. It added an unnatural sense of incongruity to the scene. Like most Serens he knew the rumours about the reason for Nefron's confinement to the Erin-Mal, but official pronouncements had always resolutely maintained that she was 'plagued by ill health'.

Now she was suddenly recovered and trailing dutifully after her husband, 'for the morale of the troops'.

Not for mine, though, Antyr thought, remembering that

it was her unseen touch that had brought him to Menedrion. He sided with the current refectory wisdom; Ibris had released her to guarantee greater unity among the various factions that comprised the city's government, but he didn't want her left to her own devices in Serenstad.

Antyr shrugged the conjectures aside. Whatever their truth, he had more urgent matters to occupy him.

'Double your guard on myself and Menedrion,' Ibris had said to him and Pandra before they had left Serenstad. 'I know you feel I'm strong enough to protect myself, but we're all of us going to be increasingly tired and preoccupied and this bond between Menedrion and Arwain is too vague for me to rest easy with; especially as they're a long way apart now. Besides, with this matter coming to a head, who knows what . . . they'll . . . do before it's finished.'

Antyr could not dispute this precautionary recommendation, though he had expressed some concern that, not fully understanding what was happening, he might prove inadequate to the task.

Ibris could well have replied that, inadequate or not, Antyr was all they had to oppose these strange attackers, but instead he just looked at him and said, bluntly, 'You won't be.'

It had done little to reassure Antyr, but he had done as he was bidden and, with Tarrian and Grayle, had assiduously guarded the Duke's sleeping hours, while Pandra and Kany had guarded Menedrion's. In addition, they had wandered through the night thoughts of the camp in search of the untoward. It had been a disturbing experience, full of doubts and fears and longings for home, shot through with red and screaming strands of madness and bloodlust. But they had found nothing unusual and had reported the same to the Duke.

Ibris had nodded knowingly. 'They're waiting,' he said. 'Waiting to see what happens at Whendrak. Don't lower your guard.'

What guard? Antyr mused wryly, as the comment came back to him, but he did not voice the question.

Alongside the baggage train, the infantry flank guards were walking stolidly on in loose order, some alone and silent, others in groups, talking and laughing; above all, laughing.

The sound brought back memories to Antyr of his own time in the line; there were few things to compare with the camaraderie brought about by a common discipline and a common danger. And it lingered long after grimmer memories had sunk into the darker recesses of the mind.

Perhaps it was this selective recollection that helped keep such monstrous folly as war alive in the world, he thought with a mixture of irony and bitterness as he looked at the young faces walking beside his waggon. Always it was the young who paid the price of their elders' greed and pride and foolishness.

Yet people were predominantly forward-looking and hopeful, and by their nature they could not, would not, burden themselves constantly with the horrific memories that were necessary if such folly was to be prevented in future.

Balance was all. To remember all was to choke the future with the vomit of the past. To forget all was to leave the ground fallow for its re-creation.

'A deci for your thoughts,' a voice said, interrupting his reverie. It was Estaan. He jumped up on to the waggon.

He was smiling broadly and Antyr responded as he moved along the seat to make a space for him. 'They're worth more than that,' he said with a profound shake of his head. 'I've just solved all the world's problems.'

Estaan declined the seat and remained standing on the edge of the platform, supporting himself by holding the corner upright of the waggon. He drew in a hissing breath laden with reservation. 'We'd better recruit another army then,' he said. 'It's people like you who start wars.'

Then he laughed loudly, infecting Antyr and Pandra and even raising a soft, shaking chuckle from Bannor.

As he subsided, it occurred to Antyr, not for the first time, that here *was* balance. The Mantynnai knew, remembered, and progressed. They protected the weak and they taught the less able to protect themselves where they could. Much of his time training with Estaan had been spent in considering the harsh logic of violence, and the insight derived from that revealed many other things. Indeed, it was a defensive weapon as potent as any sword and any amount of instruction in its use.

'It's a fine day, gentlemen,' Estaan went on. He lifted his head and scented the air. 'The fields are preparing for rest. Winter's on its way, sharp and clear.'

'We *are* going to war,' Antyr said in some surprise at this enthusiasm.

'We're not there yet, and it's still a fine day whether we

have a war or not,' Estaan retorted, smiling again. He leaned out from the waggon and made an expansive gesture. 'Look at those birds, those trees, everything.'

Further debate on the matter was ended, however, by the arrival of a messenger. Antyr judged that he was scarcely of an age to be serving his compulsory army duty. Probably lied about his age, he thought, and, with the thought, he had a vision of fretful parents moving about their house in awkward silence, unable to look at one another for fear that they would see in each other's eyes, the spectre that the boy had invoked.

'Lord Antyr,' the boy began, breathless and flushed. 'Would you attend on the Duke immediately, please.'

Tarrian chuckled at the boy's wide-eyed promotion of the Dream Finder to the aristocracy. 'He's probably misheard,' he said. 'The Duke probably said old, not lord.'

'We'll be along straight away,' Antyr replied to the messenger, poking Tarrian with the toe of his boot.

Estaan jumped down from the waggon and Antyr followed him. He unhitched the horses from the back of the waggon and handed Antyr the reins, then he watched with quiet approval as Antyr carefully adjusted his sword before he mounted.

Tarrian and Grayle jumped down also and, weaving nimbly through the infantry, disappeared at speed into the fields.

Kany's stern, and very loud, injunction followed them. 'No rabbits!'

The 'or else!' implicit in the tone made even Antyr quail.

It took the two men some time to reach the head of the long, marching column, and when they did, there was little of Estaan's appreciation of the day to be found.

The interior of the large waggon that the Duke was using as his march headquarters contrasted starkly with the surroundings in which Antyr had previously seen him. Its lines were simple and functional and it was undecorated and contained nothing, as far as Antyr could see, that was not absolutely necessary.

Antyr took in the whole ambience of the place instantly as he and Estaan were ushered in by a guard. Yet he belongs here just as he belongs in one of his lavish staterooms, he thought as he saw the Duke sitting facing the door at a small, robust table.

Looking up, the Duke nodded an acknowledgement to

them, as did Menedrion and Ciarll Feranc who were sitting at the sides of the table.

A slight frown crossed Ibris's face and he gestured to the guard who had admitted Antyr and Estaan.

'Arrange for Antyr's waggon to be brought to join the advance train here. It's too far away,' he said. 'Attend to it immediately, please.'

'I want to keep you up to date with everything that's happening,' he said to Antyr, as the officer left. 'I don't know how you ended up in the baggage train, but . . .' He shrugged dismissively and picked up a paper from the table.

'We've had word from Arwain,' he went on. 'When he arrived at Whendrak he found two full Bethlarii divisions surrounding the city and more troops arriving. To delay them from moving down the valley, he launched an attack last night which inflicted quite heavy casualties on the enemy, and he's now taking up a defensive position in anticipation of their response.'

A battalion against two divisions! Antyr thought. He could not read the Duke's impassive face, but either Arwain had taken leave of his senses or the situation at Whendrak was truly desperate. A scuffling outside the door interrupted his conjecture.

Antyr's head suddenly filled with characteristic abuse, then there was a loud bark and the door was pushed open roughly.

'Sorry. He didn't seem to know who we were,' Tarrian said to everyone as he and Grayle padded noisily across the wooden floor. An indignant and flustered guard appeared in the open doorway.

Impassive at the heroism or folly of his son, Ibris allowed his irritation to show at this trivial incident. 'He didn't,' he said crossly. 'It's just another administrative oversight.'

He waved to the guard. 'It's all right,' he said. 'These animals are quite tame, they're to be allowed to roam where they please.'

'Tame!' Tarrian's indignation, however, was for the Duke and Antyr only.

Ibris ignored the protest and continued. 'See that that is clearly understood by *everyone*. Interfering with them will be a disciplinary offence.'

The guard saluted and left.

Ibris levelled two fingers at the two wolves. 'That is not

468

carte blanche for you to raid every kitchen tent in the column,' he said sternly. 'I shall regard that as looting. Is that clear?'

'Yes,' came a rather sulky reply after a short pause.

Ibris nodded, and the sternness fell away from him. 'Keep away from the men,' he said. 'There's endless scope for misunderstandings and accidents in these circumstance and I don't want either of you injured.'

Antyr gave Tarrian a sharp, private command to stay silent, and Ibris returned to his message from Arwain.

'As a result of his action we're sending two divisions up at speed, to meet with one from Stor.' He looked at Antyr, who was wondering what relevance all this activity was to him. 'They'll be under the command of Menedrion, and I'd like you to go with him. Pandra can stay here and keep an eye on me.'

The relevance explained, Antyr's stomach sank; he had no desire to be rushing towards a battlefield behind Menedrion's banner. He'd done his part when it was needed, he shouldn't be asked to do it again. It was too much.

But other thoughts came through the fear. Despite the seeming quiet of the past few nights, the Duke's eldest son still needed to be protected. And with Arwain, Menedrion and the Bethlarii in close proximity, who could tell how vulnerable this would make them to the Mynedarion and his guide? Antyr felt again the weight of his own ignorance about these unseen assailants.

However, Pandra couldn't do it. Not the journey, nor, in all probability, any defence of the dreamers against a serious assault.

Somewhere he felt choices falling away from him. Felt his feet being drawn down a path determined by others.

But to where? Into what darkness?

'Tarrian? Grayle?' he reached out to them silently.

For a brief instant he was surrounded by sensations and a deep, ancient knowing, that were at once profoundly familiar and utterly alien to him. And they were sharp and intense.

I am wolf, a fading, distant part of his mind thought before it vanished.

All around was fear and reluctance; and a terrible longing to return to·a place far, far away. A place of endless freedom and light, of great beauty, where a great harmony prevailed.

And, too, the place of his birth, the place of the song, of the . . .

He was himself again.

'We have some measure of your burden as you have of ours, Antyr,' Tarrian said, his voice subdued, shocked even. 'We'll stay with you to the end, or until our strength fails us.'

Antyr looked at the Duke. 'We'll do whatever you wish, sire,' he said.

Chapter 34

Efnir was a small hamlet of perhaps twenty families situated in the shadow of the mountains that marked the far northern edge of Bethlarii territory. It was an isolated, self-sufficient community, far from the mainstream of Bethlarii life, but its people were of a traditional, old-fashioned disposition, and it was a matter of some pride to them that when the Hanestra called on men for the army, Efnir would always play its full part, and would not stint on its duty.

Thus it stood now empty of men, other than the very young and the very old.

Not that this greatly affected daily life. The departure of the men was not particularly welcomed, but it was not uncommon in any Bethlarii community, 'The army must be kept in good order', and life was arranged accordingly.

Now, more than ever, any distress at the leaving of the men was thoroughly hidden beneath stern, determined faces, for this time it was no training exercise that the men had gone to, it was war. This time, sons and husbands had been sent off by their proud mothers and wives with an embrace and the time-honoured edict, 'Return with your shield, or on it.'

'The Serens have assailed our people in Whendrak, in breach of the treaty, and the city is to be returned at last to its true allegiance.'

There had been some slight, extremely polite, questioning . . . requests for clarification . . . of the priestly acolyte who had brought the news, but, as was fitting, he had not been pressed, and, as had become the way these days, he had confined many of his answers to, 'It is the will of Ar-Hyrdyn.'

Despite this divine reassurance, there had been some unease . . . suspicion? . . . among the men that all was not as it should be. Such of them as travelled at all, knew that the Serens had gone their own way for many years now, seemingly indifferent to rekindling the flames of old conflicts. And surely there would be no Bethlarii community at Whendrak? It was a city mired in trade and commerce. There might well be Serens there, of course; they were a mongrel

471

breed quite without honour and pride, and capable of anything. But there would be no Bethlarii there, surely? Certainly no *true* Bethlarii.

And, too, there was some concern about the . . . intensity . . . of the priests who seemed to be rising high in political power up there in Bethlar . . .

But these doubts had scarcely found voice, other than obliquely. For as each man looked at his neighbour he saw only a reflection of his own face with its expression of a grim willingness to observe the ancient, trusted code of unquestioning submission to the Hanestra. At such times, even to *show* doubt was to preach dissension and that would surely bring about public or worse, private, denunciation and thence, disgrace, banishment, perhaps even death.

Thus the men of Efnir, full of confidence and bravado, left their homes and their wives and mothers, 'for the good of the state', which, of course, was above them all.

Magret and her ten-year-old son, Faren, went over the field towards the place from where they normally drew their water. It was a cold day, a bitter wind blowing down from the mountains that dominated the tiny hamlet.

Magret adjusted her shawl. 'When we've done this, we must go up to the forest with the others to help collect firewood; we'll be needing plenty soon,' she said to her son, pulling the wide collar of his tunic up about his red ears.

With an accurate imitation of his father's scowl, Faren pushed it down again and straightened up to face the cold wind; a man should not concern himself with such discomforts.

Magret smiled to herself at the gesture, but, unwittingly, a little sadly, as pride at her son's spirit mingled with those deeper currents that told her, far below the well-learned patriotic responses that passed for thought, that these men and their warring, strutting ways, were fools beyond description.

The stream was wide and slow-moving where they stopped to fill their earthenware jars. It had bubbled and cascaded down rocky channels and over steep edges before it came here, and but a few paces further downstream it would chatter off again on its way down to the lowlands and the great rivers. But here it was slow and placid, as if gathering its breath after such a journey, and readying itself for the next.

It was not quiet, however, as all around, the sound of water rushing towards this resting place filled the air.

It was the noise that prevented Magret from hearing the approaching riders as she laid down her yoke and began showing Faren how to fill the jars without putting his hands into the almost freezing water.

Even when they were on the opposite bank she saw them before she heard them, or rather, she saw their reflection in the gently eddying water of the stream.

She looked up with a start and took a step back as she stood up. The jar she had just been filling teetered slowly and then fell over and rolled into the stream with a soft splash. Faren, who was neglecting his task and leaning over the low bank pulling faces at his reflection in the water, looked around at the noise.

His mother stepped forward and, seizing his arm, pulled him to his feet and put him behind her before he could say anything. Normally he would have protested at this treatment, but there was a power and urgency in his mother's hands that forbade all resistance.

Magret met the gaze of the first rider. He was a powerful-looking man with a flat, scarred face, and a beaklike nose that made him look like a bird of prey. Standing by him was a thin figure in a soiled cloak, his face hidden in the depths of a large hood.

The rider was smiling, though the smile merely increased the menace which his very presence seemed to generate. But the hooded figure was worse. Though still and silent, it sent shivers of fear deep into Magret the like of which she had never known before. Fears that plunged down through nightmare into those same currents that told her and all women of the folly of men. Now they swirled and heaved and reminded her that men could be murderous fools as well.

Her eyes flicked beyond the two men. Other riders were arriving. Two, three . . . a group of . . . six . . . and more, many more.

They all reined to a halt behind the leader as if waiting for something. Magret felt Faren clutching at her skirts, tugging slightly. Without taking her eyes from the watching men, she reached down to comfort him.

It was not easy. She knew that both she and the boy were in some danger. These men were foreigners, tribesmen from beyond the mountains. As a child she had seen their kind when they raided her father's village in search of food, weapons . . . women.

But they'd never been this far east before.

They'd always been routed easily enough once the villages had been raised.

But the village was empty of men. As were virtually all the others between here and Bethlar.

The villagers would have to flee into hiding in the woods until the raiders had gone. But they had to be warned before they could do that.

Suddenly the stillness was broken as the leader's horse lowered its head and began to drink from the stream. Others followed.

Moving as the horse moved, Magret bent down to Faren and whispered to him. 'Don't be afraid,' she said. 'Walk away until you can't see them, then run as fast as you can back to the village and tell your grandfather what's happened. Tell him they're raiders from over the mountains and that everyone must get out of the village right away.'

Faren gripped her skirts tightly. Gently she prized his fingers free and putting all her courage into meeting his fear-filled eyes, she said firmly, 'Go now, straight away. It's important. I'll be all right.'

Reluctantly he turned and began walking away. After a few paces he turned and looked back. Magret smiled at him, and he went a little further. Then, she bent down calmly and picked up her yoke as if nothing untoward was happening.

'Stop there, boy!'

The voice, heavy and harsh with its alien accent, rang out above the noise of the stream. Faren stopped and half glanced back at his mother.

Magret spun round. The caller was the first horseman.

She held his gaze defiantly. 'Go on home as I've told you, Faren,' she said loudly, keeping her eyes on the foreigner.

'Stay there, boy!'

The leader turned to the hooded figure at his side, who, without speaking, mounted up behind him. Then he eased his horse forward into the stream.

Magret, too, moved forward and stood on the bank opposite him. She pointed at him. 'Stay where *you* are, northerner,' she said. 'You've picked an ill place and an ill time for your raiding. Turn about and leave now before our menfolk find you're here.'

The leader's smile broadened, and he continued walking his horse across the stream. Reaching Magret, he bent forward towards her.

'Your menfolk have all gone to the war, haven't they, my sweet?' he said. 'And we've come to take back our land.' He swept his hand slowly in a broad encompassing gesture.

Magret felt the blood draining from her face. She was about to denounce his words with scorn and derision, but she knew her voice would betray her just as her face had.

What did this man mean, take back the land? And how did he know the men were gone to the war?

She fought down her fear somehow and forced a note of maternal concern into her voice to stand in the stead of her defiance. 'Go home, northerner. I've seen your kin before, seen them die for their foolish bravery. All you'll get of this land is your length to lie in forever. Go before the winter seals you here.'

The rider looked at her thoughtfully for a moment, then he seemed to dismiss her and turned and signalled to his men. Leisurely, they began to move forward across the stream. Magret walked backwards ahead of them, up the sloping embankment as they advanced. As before she tried to count them, her mind running to the possibility of a message to the nearest town. When she reached a point which overtopped the embankment on the other side, however, she stopped, and her eyes widened in disbelief. Beyond, were riders as far as she could see – hundreds of them! Thousands even! This was no raiding party. This was an *army*! A vast army of horsemen!

Scarcely realizing what she was doing, she reached up and seized the rider's bridle. He reined his horse to a halt and stared down at her angrily.

Vaguely, Magret had thought that she might find words that would somehow turn this man around, but now, against such numbers, she knew that nothing but another army could prevail. An ancient instinct took command. She might not survive this encounter, but . . .

'Run, Faren!' she shouted at the top of her voice. 'Run! Warn the village! Run . . .'

Her cry stopped abruptly as Ivaroth's spear ran her through. It was a swift and skilful thrust but it was also one that nearly cost him his life. Magret's eyes rolled back in shock and terrible realization, then her lips curled into a savage snarl and the shock vanished, displaced by hatred and rage. Gripping the shaft of the impaling spear, she swung her full weight on to it suddenly, almost unhorsing Ivaroth, then she twisted round and producing a long knife from somewhere within her copious skirts she lunged at his thigh as he struggled to keep his seat.

It was a murderous and powerful blow that would have cut Ivaroth to the bone and probably emptied his life blood in moments, but the reflexes, borne of a lifetime spent fighting and killing from the saddle, saved him as they released his grip on the spear, and pushed its shaft upwards and sideways. The action destroyed Magret's swinging balance and she staggered backwards for several paces before toppling over with a cry of pain.

As she hit the ground the knife bounced from her hand. Ivaroth watched her struggling to recover it for a moment. A timely reminder, he thought, as he remembered advice given to him by men who had raided into Bethlarii territory before. 'Take care with their women, Mareth Hai, they're usually armed, and nearly as dangerous as the men.'

He edged his horse forward and leaned forward to retrieve his spear.

Seeing her death approaching, Magret made a desperate, scrabbling effort and at last reached her knife. 'Run, Faren! The village . . .' she managed to shout as she seized it, but even as her grip tightened about its hilt, Ivaroth's expert hand wrenched his spear free with a practised twist, and both knife and voice slipped from her again. With a soft, almost whimpering moan, she rolled over on to her face and lay still.

Ivaroth glanced at her indifferently and sniffed. He was about to hold up the bloodied spear to his men as a sign of what was to be in this land, when a fearful scream rang out.

It was Faren. He had watched open-mouthed and paralyzed as his mother had been struck down and killed, but now something had released him and he was running across the field shrieking incoherently.

Ivaroth made a swift gesture to his companion, who slowly nodded his head in acknowledgement.

Then there was a soft, but deep rumbling, and small ripples like those across a wind-blown field of corn, ran through the very ground itself towards the fleeing boy. As they reached him, their impact knocked him into the air and he crashed down heavily.

Ivaroth trotted towards him, but the boy did not rise. Yet he was shrieking more than ever. And wriggling.

Ivaroth frowned and slowed his horse to a walk. When he reached the boy he saw that both of his arms were embedded in the ground up to the elbow. At his back, he heard the blind man breathing; an unholy descant to the boy's frantic screaming.

Ivaroth clenched his teeth. Sport was sport, but the relish the old man took from such deeds disturbed him at some depth within himself that he could not fathom.

Drawing his sword, he finished the terrified boy with a single stroke. 'Your noise is frightening my horse, boy,' he said as he did the deed, lest it be misconstrued as an act of compassion.

Then his army moved forward again. Freed at last from the narrow constraints of the mountains, they spread out across the wide fields like a river reaching a delta.

As a further demonstration of his insight as Mareth Hai, Ivaroth had led the journey through the final valley personally, allowing none of the scouts to go ahead.

'None will oppose us. This is our destiny,' he said, in answer to the concern of his advisers. 'Have I not told you repeatedly that their men will be elsewhere?'

Now, to confirm this prophecy, he sent a few scouts ahead to find the village the woman had spoken of. His confidence infected everyone and the tribes' entry into this new land was like the return of a successful hunting party rather than the first intrusive steps of an invading army. Besides, had they not completed the greatest journey in the history of all the plains' people? Nothing now could stand against them.

Over the next few hours the leisurely, walking hooves and wheels of Ivaroth's army fouled the quiet stream resting in its dell and trampled the bodies of Magret and her son beyond all recognition.

It was late morning when a scout returned to Ryllans with the news that a Bethlarii force was leaving the camp.

'Three battalions of infantry and a few dozen riders,' Ryllans said, echoing the scout's message. The Bethlarii's response made sense: the terrain was unsuitable for large-scale cavalry action and three battalions was a substantial enough force to engage almost any opposition in the relatively narrow confines of the valley. The riders would be there perhaps as advance scouts, skirmishers maybe, or, more likely, as messengers, and, judging by the speed at which the force had been mobilized, reinforcements from the camp would not be slow in arriving if needed.

'They must have been preparing to move, after all, to be able to put so many men in the field so quickly,' Arwain said, speaking to the same thought. 'We were right to attack when we did.'

Ryllans nodded and glanced up at the watery sun. It was impossible to say how long it would be before Ibris's army arrived. All they could do now was hold until there was a serious risk of their being overrun. There would be no easy decisions this day.

Without any further debate he and Arwain moved to their respective posts to advise their officers of the news and to confirm the tactics to be adopted.

The archers were to play the major part in slowing the Bethlarii column. During and since their integration into the Serens' army, the Mantynnai had made many quiet changes to traditional weapons and tactics, and among these was the adoption of a larger, more powerful bow, and the training of men in its use.

It was said that the archers were a truly formidable force now, but today was the first time they were to be tested in a major conflict.

Firing from such cover as the valley sides offered, the first platoon launched its arrow storm – one, two, three volleys – into the advancing column. The effect was immediate as the heavy iron-tipped arrows penetrated stout leather breast-plates and, to a lesser extent, the more robust leather shields.

The soft winter silence that filled the valley, broken menacingly by the hissing flights of Serens' arrows, began to be rent open by the sounds of wounded men screaming as they struck home.

The column came to a hasty and ragged halt and the archers maintained their fire until the Bethlarii regrouped, threw up a shield wall and sent their own archers forward to reply. However, their bows having a lesser range than the Serens' and their target being smaller and more dispersed, the Bethlarii archers had little serious effect until a shield wall was provided which enabled them to move further forward.

At the same time, two groups of Bethlarii infantry separated from the main column and began moving up the valley sides with the intention of out-flanking the Serens.

These, in their turn, found themselves under fire from other archers and were obliged to retreat hastily. For a long time the Serens succeeded in holding the Bethlarii column.

After a while, however, the flanking Bethlarii suddenly split into smaller groups and with a great roar charged forward to pursue the archers at speed. Small targets now, and moving quickly, they were too difficult for the archers to pin down, or even seriously delay.

The suddenness of the manoeuvre took the archers by surprise and many were slow in responding.

Arwain heard Ryllans catch his breath as they lay in their distant vantage watching the scene. 'Move, move, move,' he whispered to himself urgently. 'They're fit, fast, and angry. *Move*!'

And in confirmation of these words, several archers, standing too long, and then encumbered by bow and quiver as they tried to flee over the awkward terrain, were caught and slaughtered by the Bethlarii.

Arwain and Ryllans watched the rising and falling swords and axes in silence.

Then there was a brief lull, until, now with loose-knit skeins of flank guards moving along the valley sides, the Bethlarii column began to move forward again.

Ryllans and Arwain glanced at one another. The loss of the archers had been a grim reminder of the ferocity and courage of their opponents and, although the Bethlarii response was broadly what they had envisaged, both were concerned that they now had only one more delaying tactic before they must make the decision whether to stand or retreat.

Ryllans looked down the valley. Everything was still and calm. No sign of even a galloping messenger, let alone a relieving army. With an effort he put from his mind a persistent thought urging him to calculate the probable position of the main force. It was not possible with the information he had, and in any event would serve no useful purpose. His and Arwain's task was to keep the Bethlarii in the valley for as long as they could, but not to jeopardize the bodyguard to any serious degree. If, as a result, the Bethlarii took possession of the valley, so be it. At least they would have been slowed down.

Then the final part of their trap was sprung, as two companies, half the battalion, emerged from the confused rocky cover on one side of the valley to sweep down on the scattered Bethlarii flank guards in as near close formation as they could manage.

One or two groups of Bethlarii attempted to join together and lock shields against this onslaught, but to little avail, and the majority, finding themselves too far apart to develop an effective defence, fled back to the main column. On the opposite side of the valley, the guards there too began to close up and retreat in anticipation of a similar attack, although none came.

In the face of this assault on one flank and the risk of one on the other, the column stopped and again began to establish a shield wall, only to see the Serens withdraw as suddenly as they had attacked, and to find themselves under further arrow fire, even more intense than before.

Despite the intensity, however, the effect of the arrow storm was less than previously as many shields came up overhead immediately, and within a very short time, scattered groups of Bethlarii emerged as before to deal with the archers, though this time they were followed at a well-calculated distance by larger groups in closer formation who could protect them from another attack by the Serens' infantry if need arose.

Ryllans and Arwain exchanged another glance, this time of resignation. 'It's a pity the Bethlarii don't put their considerable skills to better use,' Ryllans said, allowing himself a brief moment of reflection, then, 'Time to leave.'

A short horn call rang out above the shouting men and whistling arrows, and those groups of archers that had not already been obliged to fall back, did so with alacrity.

This time, none was caught by the Bethlarii, though there were some narrow escapes, and one man, confused by the terrain, was separated from his companions and found himself alone on an exposed ledge with a rock-face at his back, a dangerous drop on two sides and approaching Bethlarii on the third.

He looked up the ragged cliff-face behind him and then over the edge in front of him, then, as calmly as if he were at a quiet evening's practice with friends, he took an arrow from his quiver, nocked it, drew it slowly, and shot the first Bethlarii to reach him at close range.

The arrow tore through the man's throat with such force that it knocked him backwards and embedded itself in the chest of his companion following close behind. Pinned together in their death embrace, arms and legs flailing like some grotesque insect, the two men tumbled off the ledge, air-foamed blood hissing noisily from the awful throat wound and whirling in the air around them like coloured ribbons in a children's dance.

A third Bethlarii hesitated at the sight and received an arrow square in his chest. He tottered backwards for several paces before his knees buckled and he collapsed. A fourth Bethlarii fled.

Watching him flee, the archer took careful aim and shot him also.

There was a strange, timeless interlude in the battle, around this beleaguered figure, as the Serens retreated and the Bethlarii column moved forward, inexorably cutting him off.

The companions of the dead Bethlarii stood well back, prowling like predators waiting for their prey to weaken; discipline swept aside for the moment by the need for personal vengeance against this one representative of their enemy.

Seemingly indifferent to their presence or what must surely be his impending death, the man waited, an arrow nocked and the string of his bow slightly drawn, again as if he were merely waiting at the shooting line for permission to shoot.

At one point a group of the Bethlarii ventured nearer, shields raised. But still the archer waited, motionless, until they charged along the ledge, then with the leisure that had hallmarked all his previous actions he shot the leader in the leg. The barbed-iron point, crafted and hardened in one of Menedrion's workshops, entered the man's thigh and emerged, blood-red, at the back. He crashed down with a terrible cry, his shield and sword flying from his grasp. Even before he struck the ground, however, the archer had nocked another arrow and raised his bow to take his next victim. The other Bethlarii dropped down behind their shields immediately.

Rolling over in agony, the injured man looked up at the waiting archer.

Their eyes met. Then, without lowering his bow, the archer shouted, 'Take him away.'

There was a hurried discussion among the waiting Bethlarii,

then two of them scuttled forward, still crouching behind their shields, and dragged their companion away.

Below, the Bethlarii column moved relentlessly on and the Serens retreated before it.

Interest in the lethal archer flagged gradually, as the gravity of events below eventually drew the Bethlarii away, albeit reluctantly. They left him with menacing gestures and grim promises that they would return.

When they had gone, the archer remained where he was for a little while, and then slung his bow over his shoulder, turned round, and began scaling the rock-face.

The Serens were now in ordered but complete retreat, the archers acting as rearguard and still taking a sufficient toll of the Bethlarii to slow their progress. It was dangerous work, and two more archers lost their lives in the process.

Then the valley broadened out and, for the first time, the Serens stood exposed in their entirety. The realization that they had been struck such a savage blow, and delayed so severely in their pursuit, by such a small force, fuelled the anger of the Bethlarii to near frenzy, and they began to move forward at speed.

Marshalling the archers, both Arwain and Ryllans noted the change immediately and simultaneously reached the same conclusion. Their own men were tired, cold, and hungry after the forced march, the nerve-wracking assault on the camp and the equally nerve-wracking retreat. They could not outrun the much fresher Bethlarii for very far.

'They'll hack us down piecemeal if we continue,' Ryllans cried above the din of the nearing Bethlarii. 'We'll have to stand.'

It was something they had planned for but had desperately hoped to avoid. The Bethlarii, however, had adjusted to their harassing tactics more rapidly than they had envisaged, and this was the inevitable outcome.

Arwain nodded and gave the order to his signaller.

At the sound of the horn call the Bethlarii faltered momentarily, fearing some further ambush, even though there was patently no cover for ambush, nor any larger force waiting for them.

It seemed to Arwain, as he and Ryllans ran back with the archers, that the retreating infantry halted almost with relief at being given the opportunity to stand and fight. This was also a factor they had ignored in their calculations, and it put some heart into him. Retreat was intrinsically debilitating and Ibris's bodyguard were not chosen for their stupidity; all of them knew the consequences of being caught in loose formation by a superior force while together, tired or not, there was at least *some* chance of survival.

Arwain cast about him quickly to ensure that none of the archers was straggling, then, like a dutiful sheepdog, he followed after them, urging them forward while his mind repeated his wife's name over and over, like a protective litany.

The already forming shield wall opened to admit the returning rearguard and closed behind them rapidly. A single glance showed Arwain that the contingency orders were being obeyed meticulously. The men were forming a triple-ranked square with some four platoons at the centre ready to move to any threatened section of the wall.

Still breathless, Arwain and Ryllans moved round the square rapidly, bringing power and energy from their very depths to fire the men.

'Hold! Whatever happens, hold! Time is everything. The army's coming. Hold!'

'Archers! Select targets of opportunity. Especially priests and officers.'

Then the Bethlarii were on them.

Despite the array of spear and sword points darting and thrusting into their front ranks, the Bethlarii pressed forward in their anger and, almost immediately, the shield wall yielded a few paces. Men from the centre rushed to the weakening section, some helping their comrades to push their spears forward or to hold their shields, others using their own spears and swords to lunge and hack at those Bethlarii who had managed to force their way to the wall.

Archers, as ordered, waited, searching the heaving throng of roaring men for those on whom to best spend their remaining arrows.

The square held, but only just. It had been the right decision to stand and fight. The Serens were faring far better in this close-ranked defensive position than they could possibly have done had they been fallen upon from behind by the far more numerous Bethlarii. But it needed no fine judge of men or military tactics to see that their defeat, and possibly total annihilation, was simply a matter of time.

Their first furious charge having failed, the Bethlarii

withdrew a little way and began to spread out to surround the square on all four sides.

Arwain and Ryllans took the opportunity to renew their exhortations to the men, 'While they wait, while they think, while you hold, Ibris and the army draw nearer.'

Inwardly, however, Arwain knew that the next assault would be far more dangerous than the first. Then, the Bethlarii had struck in almost blinding anger and passion. It had cost them several men killed and many badly hurt and they had inflicted virtually no harm on their enemy. Now, however, their officers had obviously gained control again and the Serens could look to a much more disciplined and methodical attack.

Archers, long pikes, or delay, he thought to himself. The long pike was the weapon for massed shock troops and, not unexpectedly, he had seen none at any time during the pursuit. And the passions of the Bethlarii were too high for them to wait until the Serens were too tired, cold and hungry to stand. That left . . . 'Archers.' It was Ryllans, calling to their own men and also drawing their attention to the Bethlarii's next tactic. Bowmen were rapidly assembling along the Bethlarii front opposite one side of the Serens' square.

Ibris's archers needed no detailed instructions, they knew well enough what was about to happen and that they were the only ones who might stop it. A sustained arrow storm would break the square more surely than any charge.

They pushed through to the front rank and began their own assault before the Bethlarii were properly prepared.

Mantynnai-trained, Ibris's personal bodyguard were marksmen. They released no arrow storm of their own, but merely a handful of well-aimed shots before retreating to the back of the line again. Most of the arrows struck their targets, killing some of the Bethlarii archers and wounding several more.

Briefly the rage of the Bethlarii surged through again and there was an angry move forward. Some frantic shouting halted it quickly, however, and after withdrawing a little further for a while, more archers were brought forward again, this time behind a strong shield wall.

The square quivered as the first volley came over. High-held shields and a forest of waving spears stopped or brought down many of the arrows, but three men were injured.

The physician rushed to help the men, the reserve guard

and the archers hurriedly picked up such of the fallen arrows as they could, and Ryllans and Arwain moved hither and thither, encouraging the men.

Another volley came, and another. With each one, jeering cheers rose up from the Bethlarii ranks. Two more Serens fell.

Somehow, Arwain managed to transform his terror at this fearful rain into anger. As he did so, he felt his vision clear and, almost to his surprise, he saw the attack for what it was, namely, not very effective. The Bethlarii had insufficient archers to end this matter quickly and, despite the casualties, the atmosphere in the square was becoming one of participating in a dangerous sport rather than defending against an attack.

'This isn't going to break us,' he said to Ryllans. 'They must see that by now. Do you think they're waiting for more archers from the camp?'

Ryllans shook his head. 'No,' he said. 'They want us *now*.'

Then he took Arwain's arm. '*They're* going to charge soon,' he said, nodding to the Bethlarii forces on the flanks of the square. Another volley came over, to be met again with waving spears and high shields. This defensive response was possible because the enemy before them was some distance away. However, it left the front vulnerable and, Arwain realized, it was possible that the Bethlarii at the side could charge in when a volley was released and penetrate the temporarily weakened line. It would need careful timing, but . . .

Ryllans shouted to the officer in charge of the archers. 'Time to send them their own back. Deal with them one at a time.'

The officer nodded and the Serens' archers moved forward again to retaliate.

Using the enemy's own arrows, groups of them began to shoot simultaneously at the shields protecting individual Bethlarii. It was a tactic that was wasteful of arrows, and not many of the Bethlarii archers or their shield men were hurt, but it was profoundly intimidating and soon their line was badly disrupted, and the lethal rhythm of their volleys, broken.

'Fast!' Ryllans shouted when he was satisfied with the disarray among the enemy. 'Reserves move forward and replace centre ranks.'

Arwain shot him an alarmed glance. This was no time for

parade-ground exercises! Before he could protest, however, the changeover was under way and the weary front-rankers were retiring thankfully to the centre.

A strange silence suddenly descended on the battlefield as the Bethlarii too watched this unexpected manoeuvre.

A light came into Ryllans' eye. 'Go and negotiate,' he said suddenly, to Arwain.

'What?' Arwain responded in disbelief.

'Go and negotiate,' Ryllans repeated. 'And take your time. Quickly man, while they're wondering what's happening.'

The Mantynnai seized his lord's arm and pushed him towards the front of the square. 'Something green . . . white, something white, for a flag of truce,' he shouted to the men around him. A soiled rag was thrust into his hand and he tied it around a spear shaft and pushed it into Arwain's hand.

'Give me your sword and shield,' he said, taking them before Arwain could demur. 'Say anything, but say it slowly. And confidently! The archers will cover you.'

The front rank opened to let Ibris's bemused son through.

Arwain felt the focused anger and hatred of the watching Bethlarii like a physical impact. He stepped forward a little way and then slowly looked along the enemy line, as if he were a visiting dignitary conducting a formal inspection. Then, raising the spear with its ragged flag, and taking a surreptitious deep breath, he stepped forward again.

The valley turf was damp and crushed, and in places had been torn into muddy strips. After about twenty paces he stopped and drove the spear into the ground. Then he waited.

Each heartbeat brings my father nearer, he kept repeating to himself, though his eyes were still scanning the Bethlarii front line, waiting for one of the archers to draw his bow. His legs were shaking and he had to remind himself that this was so that they could move the quicker if need arose. The knowledge did not help a great deal.

The strange, waiting silence continued for some time, then a figure emerged from the Bethlarii ranks. He was tall and powerfully built and his dress identified him as a priest.

This religion must pervade their whole society, Arwain thought as the man walked towards him.

He stopped after some twenty paces, as Arwain had done.

Wait, Arwain thought. Let him set the pace, I'll follow as slowly as I can.

486

The Bethlarii priest spoke immediately, however, and his words offered little hope of delay.

'We will allow you some time to make your peace with whatever pagan gods you worship, Serens,' he called out, his voice loud and commanding. 'Then we shall end this foolishness and crush you as we would crush any irritating insect.'

Arwain ignored the taunt. 'I am Arwain, son of Duke Ibris, priest. I do not debate with underlings. Return to your prayers and leave this matter to soldiers.' He made a dismissive gesture and, looking past the priest towards the waiting solders, shouted loudly, 'Someone fetch an officer of my standing so that we may speak together with authority.'

The priest angrily came forward several paces. Arwain moved forward also.

'Careful,' he heard Ryllans hiss behind him.

'I am one of the chosen of Ar-Hyrdyn, unbeliever,' the priest said, his eyes blazing. 'We have his authority in all things. But the lowest among us here has authority greater than that of the bastard son of a usurper and his band of murderers.'

Again, Arwain ignored the priest and shouted past him towards the soldiers. 'I have never heard it said that the Bethlarii were either dishonourable or foolish? Surely such a great warrior people as you will not allow itself to be led by these prating charlatans, like so many sheep?'

He paused briefly and waited until the priest was about to reply. Then he continued. 'You men all know that Whendrak is a neutral city. Some of you might even have been there when this was solemnly agreed between my father and your Hanestra, *and by acclamation of your army*, many years ago. You know that to attack it as you've done is to break your most solemn and binding oaths, and our actions last night were but to remind you of the consequences of pursuing such wickedness. Withdraw now or the further consequences will be a thousand times worse. Your land will ring with the keening of your widows and mothers, their losses made doubly awful by the knowledge that their men were oath-breakers and, worse, fools, for following these black-hearted priests and their ignorant superstition.' Abruptly, he sneered. 'Ask yourselves, men of the spear and the sword, what kind of men are they that say they speak to your great war god in *dreams*? Once you would have stoned them as blasphemers, or banished them as lunatics—'

At the word, dreams, however, the priest had started violently and, to Arwain's surprise, the front ranks of the Bethlarii actually retreated a few paces.

'Enough,' the priest roared furiously. 'It is *you* who blaspheme, impugning his chosen. We will allow you no such further opportunity.' Then, turning and striding back to his own line, he shouted, 'Kill them all!'

There was no debating or preparing the order of battle. Instead, the Bethlarii levelled their spears and, with a roar, began charging towards the square on all four sides. Arwain forced himself to walk back, taking up the spear as he passed it. The shield wall opened to admit him and as it closed behind him, he found himself facing Ryllans. He shrugged apologetically.

Ryllans took his arm reassuringly and gave him his shield and sword back. There was naked fear in his eyes as the din of approaching Bethlarii increased. 'Forget your training now,' he said. 'What you've truly learned, you'll use without thinking. Anger and determination are your only true allies.' And, as he spoke, the fear disappeared.

'Hold your positions!' he bellowed. 'They'll tire soon enough. Let them break themselves like waves against our rocks. Hold! Hold!'

The impact of the Bethlarii charge, however, was terrible. Arwain felt the ground shake under his feet. Two sides of the square buckled inwards, several men falling, and it seemed for a moment that they would break entirely. But again the reserves in the centre ran to the weakened sections and succeeded in beating back the encroaching enemy.

For a while there was a desperate and bloody stalemate, with the Bethlarii, like a storm-tossed sea, rearing and screaming as they struggled to beat down the bristling hedge of thrusting spear-points and hacking sword edges that was the Serens' shield wall.

Arwain and Ryllans strode around the square, directing the reserves, hurling back the enemy's spears, and, above all, encouraging the men ceaselessly.

Gradually, however, the fury of the Bethlarii seemed to become increasingly demented, and the square began to contract under the weight of the onslaught. Twice, individuals actually succeeded in mounting the shields and spears to leap screaming into the square. A reserve officer dealt with one, and Arwain the second, pinning him to the ground with a spear.

Desperately Arwain glanced at Ryllans as the square began to waver. A lord's son, he had fought previously as a cavalryman, and he was unfamiliar with this close-quarter combat. But he could tell that this was no ordinary infantry battle. The Bethlarii were possessed; fighting as if their lives were of no import; fighting as a crazed rabble. It was the very antithesis of the disciplined, ordered infantry fighting that had been the hallmark of such confrontations in the past and which could guarantee individuals on the victorious side, at least, a high probability of survival. This thunderous riot around him was madness! Truly the unreasoned product of some grotesque religion.

Ryllans, however, was teaching, as all good teachers do, by example. He was moving unerringly to those parts of the wall that were weakest and laying about him with a purposeful, cold-eyed savagery that made all who met his gaze, falter and grow sane for the moment.

'War is an evil because, to survive, the victim must become as bad as the aggressor,' he would often say when Arwain rebelled against some technique he was being shown. 'It is an evil because it places men in a position where their only ethical choice is kill or be killed, and by whatever means is quickest and most effective. If, in such a position, you do not have the knowledge . . .' He would shrug and leave the conclusion unspoken.

Prior to the attack on the camp, Arwain had silenced his inner debate with the realization that he had no alternative but to do what he was about to do, simply because he was there. Now, in the midst of falling spears, clashing arms, and roaring, screaming, dying men, he understood at a deeper level by far.

His eye lit on a large Bethlarii beating down a shield with a great battle axe. When Arwain stepped forward to kill him, another Mantyannai had joined the square.

Then after a timeless interlude of bloodstrewn, whirling mayhem, the air was abruptly filled with horn calls.

Bethlarii horns. Arwain's heart sank. Reinforcements! As if they needed any. More from the camp, come to see the sport. But his grip tightened around his sword and even as the thoughts taunted him he reached over the shields and

489

struck down a Bethlarii trooper with a blow that cleaved clean through his helmet.

As he struggled to wrench the blade free, he was searching for his next adversary. But there was none. A space had opened between the Bethlarii and the shield wall. Groping pathetically at his head for some futile measure of the terrible injury Arwain had done, the Bethlarii fell back, not into the arms of his still fighting comrades, but on the heaped bodies of the dead he was soon to join.

'They're retreating,' someone next to Arwain said, his voice low with disbelief.

The noise of the avenging army faded and that of the calling horns rose to dominate the valley. The gap between the two forces widened.

'They *are* retreating,' came needless confirmation from several voices simultaneously.

Arwain became aware of his own raucous breathing and gradually his mind slowed sufficiently to accommodate this new pace of events. The army must have arrived, he realized ecstatically. But turning round, such of the valley that he could see was still deserted.

Then a hand took his elbow and he found himself looking along someone's pointing arm up on to the southern ridge. Clearly visible in the pale wintery sun was a long marching column.

'And the north ridge too, look!' someone called.

A cheer began to rise up from the square, but a powerful voice stilled it.

'Hold your positions! Strict battle order! Archers; priests and officers, targets of opportunity.'

It was Ryllans, teaching still.

Chapter 35

'Got yourself in a fine mess there, brother,' Menedrion said as he unexpectedly embraced Arwain. Then he looked him up and down appraisingly. 'How much of that is yours?' he asked.

Arwain followed his half-brother's gaze, looking first at his hands and then at his clothes. In common with his companions, he was covered in blood. Tentatively he felt about himself.

'None, I think,' he concluded after a moment. 'Or not much anyway.'

Menedrion shook his head and reached up to touch Arwain's helmet. He ran a finger along an indentation. 'It's a wonder,' he said. 'You're supposed to be the thinker, Arwain. Has it never occurred to you that blocking stones and sword blows with your head is not the wisest of things to do?'

There was little time for such exchanges, however. Menedrion's reaction on hearing of his half-brother's intention to launch an attack on the vastly superior Bethlarii force had been the same as everyone else's, namely, considerable alarm, and this had manifested itself in the speed at which he had led his two divisions to Arwain's aid.

However, it had been no mindless charge and, noting Arwain's information that the ridges had not been taken by the Bethlarii, Menedrion had sent gallopers ahead to tell the infantry from the approaching Stor division to move along the north ridge, while the infantry from one of his own divisions moved along the south. The remaining infantry and all the cavalry were to follow them along the valley floor.

The tactic was intended to look like a large-scale encirclement of the forces around Whendrak, and would indeed have served as such had opportunity presented itself. Menedrion, however, harboured only moderate hopes that this would happen, as the ridge routes were not easy and were too visible from below to allow surprise. Further, the mountain weather was, untypically, clear that day.

Nevertheless, the prospect of such an assault had been sufficient to make those Bethlarii attacking Arwain withdraw at full speed.

Now, it was essential that the three arms of the attacking force continue towards Whendrak, the valley force in particular chasing the Bethlarii back to their camp and, with good fortune, causing panic there that might lead to a precipitate withdrawal from the valley.

'I can't see that happening, to be honest,' Menedrion said to Arwain. 'But at least they'll have to pull back from the city before they make a stand and that'll be *some* gain. Wait here until father arrives or until you hear from me.'

Briefly Arwain had considered protesting at being left behind, but the thought expired almost as it was born. He was exhausted, thirsty, hungry, shocked, and now cold, as the frenzy of the battle faded away. His men were the same and they must be looked to before he himself could even think of rest.

Menedrion left some of his pioneers and commissary staff behind as he moved off along the valley. Soon they were pitching tents, lighting fires, rigging kitchens, and, the most wretched of their tasks, clearing the battlefield.

Later, their men tended as their needs demanded, Ryllans and Arwain sat leaning against a rock by an open fire.

'How are you?' Ryllans asked, looking at his pupil.

Arwain was about to utter a conventional platitude when he caught Ryllans' eye.

'Sick,' he answered truthfully. 'And bewildered. My head is still ringing with the noise, my arms twitching with hesitant sword and shield strokes, and my eyes and my legs are still watching for arrows and spears falling out of the sky. And thoughts are circling my mind as relentlessly as the Bethlarii did our square. It's as if the least slip on my part would bring them crashing down on me.' He picked up a small twig from the edge of the fire and tossed it into the flames. 'I want to be back home with my wife, fretting about my training and my duties and palace politics . . .'

Ryllans smiled slightly and nodded. 'Good,' he said. 'Don't be concerned about your thoughts. While you can see them, and while you're that honest with yourself, they're not going to hurt you. Your mind has to twitch just like your body after such a shock. And you're not alone, Duke's son.'

He held out his hand. It was shaking.

Arwain looked at it in some surprise. 'Every time I looked at you, you seemed so calm,' he said.

'As did you,' Ryllans replied. 'Indeed, as we both *were*, given the circumstances. But being calm in battle isn't the same as being calm by one's fireside.'

Arwain remembered his own legs shaking as he had confronted the Bethlarii priest between the two armies. 'You've a way with the obvious,' he said with a slight laugh that cracked and died.

Ryllans' head came forward a little and he stared at Arwain intently. 'You're right, I do have a way with the obvious,' he said. 'And for good reason. One man's obvious is another man's ignorance.' He reached out and took Arwain's arm, to catch his attention. Arwain turned and met his gaze. 'All the battles you've fought before have been as a cavalry officer, Arwain,' he went on. 'You've no measure of what it's like in the line, no measure of the obvious. So I'll tell you now, I've been in battles longer and bloodier than this by far, but I've never known anything as terrifying. Not even at Viernce. Never been so frightened of that random arrow or spear, of my own weakness, my inadequacy. The thoughts circling *my* head are saying, "How did we hold so long?" Over and over.' His grip on Arwain's arm tightened. 'They'll pass, I know, but believe me, tales of this brief little battle here will ring down through history. Storytellers will eat well, making their listeners sweat and shiver with the excitement and the bravery of it.'

Arwain continued looking at him as this revelation broke over him. It should not be thus; it should be the terror and horror of it that persisted, not the vicarious excitement and misunderstood bravery. But that, he knew, was a matter beyond any controlling.

Then a dark thought emerged into the light. 'The stuff of tales it might have been, but it was a mistake for all that,' he said.

Ryllans did not respond.

'I misjudged completely the speed of their column and the speed at which we could withdraw.' Arwain's guilt found words. 'We should never have had to stand and face them.'

Ryllans seemed unconcerned. 'We *both* misjudged them,' he said abruptly. 'But we were neither foolish nor careless and that's all the solace you're going to get. War is misjudgement writ large, and chance, let alone misjudgement, runs riot. That's why we train. So that we *can* respond to the unforeseeable with some hope of surviving. Just concentrate on learning what's to be learnt.'

His guilt cauterized by Ryllans' words, rather than purged, Arwain sat silent, gazing into the crackling fire.

Ryllans stared out over the empty, scarred ground that had been so bitterly fought over but an hour ago.

He scowled.

'We've got nine dead and twelve, maybe fifteen, seriously injured,' he said, half to himself. 'But they must have lost perhaps seventy or eighty dead, including at least one of their precious priests. And god knows how many more were badly injured.'

Arwain turned to him. Ryllans' words stirred something that was on the edge of his own thoughts.

'It was a cruel ambush we launched against them,' he said.

Ryllans nodded. 'But their response was absurd nevertheless. All those men killed for virtually nothing. All they had to do once we chose to stand was to surround us, bring up more archers from the camp, and use us for shooting practice.' He shook his head. 'They could have destroyed us utterly without losing a single man.' He gave a slightly bitter smile. 'They'd even have got all their arrows back afterwards.'

'They didn't have time with the army so close,' Arwain offered, glad to be exercising his mind with practicalities.

'It wouldn't have taken long,' Ryllans answered, brutally. 'And anyway, *they* didn't know the army was coming. If they didn't even bother to post proper sentries, it's highly unlikely they'd done any reconnaissance beyond the valley.'

Arwain had no reply. Ryllans was right. The Bethlarii had been well disciplined in the defence of their marching column, but wildly reckless in their assault on the square. And no amount of anger, however justified, should have turned disciplined fighters into such a disordered rabble.

Ryllans' eyes narrowed. 'They're possessed utterly by this religion of theirs,' he said. 'Logic and reason have gone and they're going back to what they must have been centuries ago: ignorant, vicious barbarians.'

Arwain held out his hands to the fire.

'No attempt to secure the ridges, no lookouts along the valley, inadequate sentries. It's certainly bad, and it's certainly not typical of them,' he mused. 'But I'm not sure what it tells us, except that such carelessness will be to our advantage.'

'It tells us that they're unpredictable and thus perhaps more dangerous than they've ever been,' Ryllans said starkly. 'I've seen religious fanatics take a score of arrows and still kill people before they died. It's not good for morale I can assure you. But . . .' He raised a finger to forestall a question. 'While we're aware of the problem, we can deal with it. Thought and calmness in action, coupled with a steadfastness of purpose . . .'

'Murderous ruthlessness, you mean,' Arwain interrupted.

Ryllans nodded and continued. 'Yes,' he agreed. 'Thought and calmness and murderous ruthlessness will give us the day.'

The two men fell silent and, after a moment, Arwain drifted off to sleep. Ryllans reached across and pulled his cloak about him, then settled back against the rock and closed his eyes.

To a casual observer, it would have appeared that the Mantynnai had fallen asleep like his lord, but at the sound of a soft footfall nearby, a thin bright line appeared under the seemingly closed lids.

He was surrounded by his own kind and those that they trained, but his hand eased itself inconspicuously into his cloak and towards one of his knives. There was something odd about the sound; it was too soft, and there was no call for stealth in this place.

The reason for the softness manifested itself almost immediately as a woman emerged into view around the rock. It could have been one of the nurses from the medical corps, but Ryllans' hand did not move from his knife, and for an instant there was a flicker of surprise in his eyes.

'Lady Nefron,' he said.

The woman drew in a sharp breath and lifted her hand to her heart as she turned quickly towards him. 'You startled me,' she said.

Ryllans made no apology, but he stood up and stepped towards her, placing himself between her and the sleeping Arwain.

'What are you doing here?' he asked, politely, but authoritatively. 'This may yet be a battleground again. Do you have the Duke's permission to be here?'

Nefron's eyes blazed. 'Of course,' she said through clenched teeth. 'Do you imagine I'm free just because I'm no longer in the Erin-Mal? I can do nothing without his word, nor go anywhere without an escort of stone-faced troopers following me. But you'd know that, wouldn't you? As you and your kind trained them.'

'Yes,' Ryllans replied.

Nefron flinched as if her own venom had rebounded from Ryllans' blunt reply. 'I asked to come because I thought I'd be able to help your wounded,' she went on. 'That's what I've been dragged along for, isn't it?'

'The Duke does not consult me on such matters,' Ryllans said. 'But the men will appreciate your concern. Fighting is a cruel matter, all solace is welcome.'

Nefron looked at him intently.

'I cannot read you, Mantynnai,' she said after a moment. 'Most men I can read, manipulate if I have to. But not you; none of you. Always you elude me. What are you thinking? Why are you the way you are? Foreigners dying for this land, this man, my husband?'

'We are what we are,' Ryllans answered. 'Who can say why?'

'You can,' Nefron answered unequivocally.

Ryllans did not reply.

Nefron blew out a long irritated breath, then shivered. She hunched her shoulders and pulled her cloak about her tightly. Involuntarily, Ryllans' hand reached out to help her.

'Careful, Mantynnai,' she said tartly, her lip curling. 'That was a touch of humanity.'

There was a brief flash of terrible anger in Ryllans' eyes. 'You waste your life in this futile railing at your own pain, Nefron,' he said, his voice quiet but very powerful. 'You ask who I am, who we are, the Mantynnai. You should first ask who you are, before you concern yourself with others.'

Nefron's eyes widened at this unexpected rebuke, and she drew herself up angrily. Before she could respond, however, Ryllans was standing in front of her with a knife in his hand. He had drawn it with a movement so swift and skilful that she had scarcely seen it.

Terror replaced the anger in her face, but the hand that came up was as defiant as it was defensive.

Ryllans grasped it forcefully and placed the knife in it, his own hand tightening her fingers around its hilt.

'Kill him,' he said with a casual nod towards the sleeping Arwain that belied the immovability of his grip. 'Have your

496

heart's desire. The object of your endless scheming. Fulfil your darkest ambitions. I'll not hinder you, on my word.'

Nefron's lean, handsome face had become contorted with shock and bewilderment and she began to sway. Ryllans put a powerful arm around her and jerked her upright. 'No, Nefron, there's no escape on the battlefield, you kill or you are killed,' he said, his foreign accent suddenly strong. The hand holding the knife in hers pointed it towards Arwain.

'Kill him now,' he said. 'As you've always wanted. Destroy the product of your husband's divided, perhaps foolish, love; his few stolen couplings with your sister.' He bent her forward. 'What's a little more blood this day? It's soon done. I can show you how to do it. Show you where to plunge the point, turn the blade so as not to make too much mess, see . . .'

The knife was almost at Arwain's throat.

With a strangled cry and a prodigious effort, Nefron wrenched herself upright and stepped back. Calmly, Ryllans released her hand and stood staring at her.

She hurled the knife away with a mixture of fury and revulsion, then she turned on her unexpected tormentor. Her mouth was working, but no sounds came. A lesser woman, a mere lord's wife, would have screamed and sobbed, protested about such unwarranted and brutal handling. But instead she managed to gasp out, after a long, agonizing struggle, 'How did you know?'

Ryllans held her gaze. 'Mudstains over the bloodstains on your elegant cloak. Fine-crafted shoes soiled beyond repair. Blood on your hands . . . and on your face.' He pointed, and Nefron lifted a hand to her face, though she lowered it before it reached its destination.

'You've been wandering this field, oblivious to where you were. Doubtless you rushed here on the pretext of comforting our wounded for some subtle, scheming reason of your own. Perhaps you even came as a mother anxious about Menedrion. Or perhaps you came to see if your long, wearisome vengeance had been wrought at last, and Arwain killed.' Nefron could not turn away and Ryllans continued relentlessly. 'But you've seen the dead and their fearful mutilations. Seen men's entrails and precious limbs scattered across the mountain turf, with birds and animals waiting to snuffle among them, but hopping and scuttling to one side as you approach; deferential, fearful in the presence of one of the *great* predators. You've seen the faces of the dead, with their shocked, unbelieving eyes. And you've seen the terrible, screaming wounds of the maimed.' He leaned forward towards her. 'But worst of all, you've seen into their eyes, and into the eyes of *all* the men who fought here.'

'How did you know?' She mouthed the phrase distantly, as if it were all she had left to hold on to.

'It's in *your* eyes now,' Ryllans said. 'But I know because I myself am not yet returned from the raw, bloody edge of today's events. I'm still in the killing vein. Life, death, a flick of the wrist.' He made the gesture in front of her face. 'My sight is still too sharp, too clear. It sees into your soul and cannot do other than kill the monstrous folly it sees dwelling there.'

There was a long silence.

The noises of the crackling fire and of the camp, eddied idly around the two motionless figures.

Then Nefron bowed her head slightly, and, without speaking, turned back towards the camp.

Ryllans watched her retreating figure until she was completely out of sight, then he sat down again, his face unreadable. His hands were shaking again.

Arwain slept.

Lying in the camp nearby, drifting in and out of sleep were Antyr, Tarrian, and Grayle. They had arrived with Menedrion somewhat the worse for wear: Antyr sore and weary through the long-sustained ride, Tarrain and Grayle footsore and thirsty with the relentless pace that Menedrion had set.

Despite his tiredness, however, Antyr's increasing sensitivity felt Arwain's sleeping thoughts and he was with him on the instant. The dreamselves of Tarrain and Grayle joined him almost as quickly.

Estaan, sitting near Antyr's rough bunk and idly flicking through a book, noted the change in the demeanour of the three sleeping figures. Increasingly familiar with the ways of the Dream Finder and his Companions, he knew that beneath the closed lids, Antyr's eyes would be black as night, like deep pits, while those of the two wolves would be yellow, wild, and all-seeing. Quietly he moved his chair to the entrance of the tent so as to prevent any incautious entry.

Arwain's sleep was slight and flimsy, and, like Ryllans, his sensitivities raw. In the mists he felt the presence of Antyr and the wolves and he grimaced inwardly. Discreet and intangible though it was, their attention felt intrusive. The all-too-real horrors of the day had driven the strange happenings of recent nights from his mind completely, and now that he was reminded of them in his shallow, twilight slumber, they seemed to have lost any semblance of significance.

'Leave me. No sleeping thoughts can harm me after today.'

'We are here by your father's will, and such a judgement is not yours to make.'

'Leave me!'

Silence.

'Leave me!'

'We cannot. Rest, lord, that we may rest also. This field is a distressing place for my Companions. Human barbarism frightens them at levels far beyond my comforting.'

Anger and disbelief. 'Wolves, frightened by killing?'

Rasping scorn. 'We kill to eat, *lord*. What do you kill for? You'd soon put a spear through *my* ribs if you found me eating your dead, but you made them thus, and you'd let them rot here.'

Arwain's mind filled with the complex maze of reasoning that he had struggled through during the day, but it foundered in the light of the wolves' contempt. Not because it was flawed, but because it was human, and could not hope to stand against the deep wisdom and knowledge of these wild creatures.

Gently, Antyr's will stilled the wolves' fears and they slipped to the boundaries of Arwain's thoughts, beyond even his most sensitive seeing.

Stillness.

Then, in the far, eyeless distance, he sensed the long mournful howl of the two wolves, rich and subtle in harmony and rhythm, rising and falling in accordance with some spirit unknowable by the listener.

In the dark stillness of his mind, Arwain looked at his image in the shining blade of his sword, now cleaned of the day's gore.

'I want to be home, at peace, with my wife, my friends. This is no way to be . . .'

Hesitation. 'Yet not for anything would I have been anywhere other than here this day. Standing with my companions and holding the line. Fighting the demons in myself as well and the enemy beyond. Learning.'

The howling drifted further and further away, beautiful, longing, lost.

From under Arwain's closed lids, a tear emerged. It slid down his cheek, a bright, slender strand, cutting its way through the grime of battle that stained his face.

Then, far beyond even the wolves' howling, he heard a faint, ground-shaking thunder . . .

He listened. It was important.

But it was gone.

Ivaroth's army moved relentlessly southward. Certain though he was of the absence of most of the Bethlarii menfolk from the northern regions, he did not proceed rashly. The sudden, unexpected, ferocity of Magret had reminded him vividly that these were a stern and warlike people, well steeped in the ways of combat, and that to trifle with them was to risk disaster.

Sooner or later, the knowledge of their arrival in the land would spread faster than they could move, but Ivaroth determined that this would be as late as possible, and that when, finally, major resistance was mounted against him, he would be operating from a territory extensive and secure enough to sustain his army without the need to rely on lines of supply through the mountains.

Accordingly, the land to be passed over was well scouted before the army moved forward. Small communities and isolated farms were destroyed without hesitation, as were lone travellers, or any other potential carriers of news who found themselves in Ivaroth's path.

Thus the city of Navra was taken completely by surprise.

'It's many times bigger than the villages we've seen so far, with great buildings, taller than the highest trees,' Ivaroth told his scouts as they prepared to leave. 'And a great stone wall about the whole of it.' They looked at him in respectful silence. The Mareth Hai's knowledge of this land and these people was as strange as it was accurate, but this wild oratory provoked some discreet sidelong glances from the scouts as they rode off.

'Ha!' he laughed grimly as they returned, wide-eyed. 'You took your Mareth Hai for a rambling storyteller when you left, didn't you? But tell us what you found.'

A flurry of anxious denials met this ominous rebuke, and details of the city with its great buildings and surrounding wall poured out over the amazed listeners.

'It is thus, I tell you. We all saw it. The Mareth Hai's sight is beyond understanding.'

Airily accepting this adulation, Ivaroth turned his officers' minds to the practical problems of taking such a place.

From his travels through the dreams of the Bethlarii, he had learned a great deal about their art of war, and he knew that while it might be possible to lay siege to a city such as Navra, it would be difficult, and debilitating for his men. Further, it would tie down too much of the army and risk their premature discovery. Despite the ingenuity that had been shown in the passage through the mountains, he also had little faith in the ability of even his cleverest men being able to build siege towers and rock-throwing catapults.

No. The most effective way to take a city was by surprise, or treachery. He had no friends within the city who would open the gate, so he must ensure surprise.

And he did. A few men, posing as benighted travellers, gained access at one of the smaller gates and, quickly disposing of the unwary guards, threw the gate wide open.

There then followed a night of slaughter and terror as the citizens of Navra were awakened by the crackle and roar of burning buildings, the clatter of hooves galloping through their stone-flagged streets, and the screams of the dying mingling with the triumphant cries of their murderers.

The many men and women who snatched up swords and spear from their bedsides, and dashed into the night to face this unheralded and nightmarish invasion, fell like wheat before the scythe under the hooves of Ivaroth's rampaging army. Sluggards and dreamers survived.

Those who managed to reach one of the gates found all of them sealed by these strange and savage mounted men who seemed to be without number.

Dawn came to a crushed people. Some resistance was being offered hither and thither, not least by a company of reservists, but their obliteration was merely a matter of time, and such of the city fathers as had survived the night, accepted Ivaroth's terms . . .

'Kneel or die.'

A proud people, many of the citizens secretly denounced this spineless submission by the city's old men, but it did not take Ivaroth long to demonstrate that he was not only a man of his word, but one of instant execution. To deter opposition to his will, he had ten people chosen at random and then killed publicly, with the announcement that for every one of his men that was attacked, ten more would die.

With the city sealed and the invaders present in such overwhelming numbers, overt resistance ceased almost immediately. The Bethlarii were not a cowardly people but, apart from Ivaroth's ruthlessness, they were shocked almost to stupefaction by the sudden, hammerblow occupation of their city.

And too, there was a quality about the old man who was Ivaroth's constant companion that chilled utterly those who came near him.

Then, as his forces quelled the immediately surrounding countryside, and the citizens began to recover, Ivaroth splintered any consensus against him by showing unexpected and arbitrary flashes of mercy and kindness: executing some of his own men for rape and for looting, and punishing others in various ways for lesser offences. He appointed a new council of citizens to advise him, and began recompensing *some* of the citizens who had suffered loss or bereavement during the invasion.

Also, many of the city's most respected priests, those too old to be with the army, began to speak of dreams which revealed to them that this seeming scourge was nothing less than the will of Ar-Hyrdyn and that the Bethlarii's true future lay with those who had the vision to see the true worth of this great and powerful leader from the cold plains beyond the mountains; this Mareth Hai.

'Who could have brought such an army through the mountains without the blessing of Ar-Hyrdyn?'

It was thus a completely subdued Navra that Ivaroth left behind when he set off with an army towards his next goal, the river town of Endir.

Nonetheless, he took a liberal sprinkling of hostages and left a substantial garrison to tend the city.

Ibris frowned a little at Feranc's news.

'The two men have left Serenstad and are believed to be going to Viernce.'

'You said they'd not be found if they didn't wish it, didn't you?' Ibris said.

502

'They're not hiding, or they'd have disappeared without trace,' Feranc replied. 'They've been quite open and straightforward in their movements, the Liktors only missed them because of the confusion of the mobilization. I've sent messages on to Viernce asking for them to join us here. I'd be surprised if they didn't come.'

Ibris's irritation showed. 'What the devil do they want in Viernce?' he said angrily.

'Probably more information about the Mantynnai,' Feranc answered. 'From the reports I've had about them, that seems to be why they're here.'

Ibris slapped his hand on the table impatiently. 'Dammit, I'm not prepared to have these strangers . . .' He stopped and levelled a finger at Feranc. 'Are you sure you're looking for these countrymen of yours properly?' he demanded.

Unexpectedly, Feranc smiled and then chuckled in the face of this unwarranted reproach. 'I am, sire,' he said with some mild irony around the title. 'But admittedly not with the urgency that I'm helping you prosecute this war.'

Ibris scowled by way of apology. 'I feel the need to talk to them, Ciarll,' he said, more soberly. 'Particularly after this.' He fingered a paper on the table in front of him. It was a message from Menedrion. The Bethlarii had decamped from Whendrak with scarcely a token resistance. 'It makes no sense.'

Feranc gave a slight shrug. 'They may have misjudged the size of the forces coming along the ridges,' he said. 'Arwain said that their dispositions around Whendrak, and their general discipline, showed a remarkable degree of negligence.'

'Maybe,' Ibris replied. 'But remember, according to what Antyr saw in the envoy's dream, Whendrak is the lure. They may be retreating to draw us forward, extend our lines and then cut them and encircle us, or begin their true offensive in another region.'

Feranc looked at Ibris, but offered no comment.

'Yes, I know,' Ibris said into the silence. 'We've been over this twenty times if we've been over it once, and all the precautions that can be taken *have* been taken, but . . .' He blew out a long, unsettled breath and tapped the paper again. 'The Bethlarii don't yield like this. It all seems too easy.'

Feranc's expression changed. 'Not for Arwain and Ryllans it wasn't,' he said sternly. 'That was a rare stand they made.'

503

Ibris nodded and waved an apologetic hand. 'Yes. But you understand what I mean.'

'I think you're too concerned,' Feranc replied. 'There's a limit to the amount of guessing and out-guessing an enemy that can be done sensibly. From what Arwain and his officers have said, my feeling is that in their rise to power, these priests have had to purge much of the army's officer elite and install their own people. Ignorance won't tolerate knowledge. And now the army's paying the price in incompetent leadership.'

'You're probably right, Ciarll,' Ibris said. 'But I'd like you to raise the search for these two men a little higher in your priorities, if you would.'

Over the following days, Ibris's army, reinforced by the force from Tellar, moved westward along the Whendrak valley towards Bethlarii territory. Reports reached him from all over the land about the progress of the full voluntary mobilization. Generally it was proceeding well, though not without opposition of varying degrees in certain cities.

'I notice that apathy increases with the distance from Bethlar,' he said acidly, looking at two almost identical returns from opposite ends of the land, Torrenstad and Lorris. 'And I see the Guilds are organizing marches against it in Lingren.' He paused and then became abruptly angry. 'These people aren't fit to be fought for! What chance would the Guilds have of surviving if Bethlar took control?' His anger mounted explosively. 'Ye gods, we've had good men killed already. Ciarll, send to Aaken, tell him to have the leaders of this opposition arrested and conscripted under whatever war regulation he can find. If they want the power and benefits of leadership, then they can earn them by leading from the front. And tell him to make the Sened and Gythrin-Dy's displeasure well known in Torrenstad and Lorris . . .' He sent a sheaf of papers scattering across the table. 'And all the others who're dragging their feet and hiding behind our shields.'

Then, as suddenly as he had erupted, he became calm. 'And send our thanks and congratulations to the others. Especially Crowhell.'

He smiled and shook his head. 'They're rogues to a man down there, but they're realists. *They* know what Bethlar would do to their vaunted independence, not to mention their sea trade. They've done well. Money *and* men!'

Reports also reached him from Meck and Nestar and other cities along the border. Still no surprise Bethlarii incursions had occurred. Increasingly it seemed that they were gathering their forces somewhere west of Whendrak for a major battle.

Before moving the main part of his army past Whendrak, however, Ibris observed the letter of the treaty meticulously, going in person unarmed to the city gate with a small, flagged escort.

He was greeted by Haynar. The Maeran's face was drawn and weary, and his eyes were full of anger and bitterness.

Ibris had carefully memorized the formal greeting that was required of him in these circumstances, but when he looked at Haynar, he said simply, 'If you will allow us, we will give you whatever aid you need to repair the damage that has been wrought on your city and your people, Maeran. And we will help you deal with your internal dissension if you wish.'

Haynar's angry look did not soften, but no anger reached his voice when he spoke. 'Part of me would bring down a curse on both your camps for this horror, Duke,' he said. 'But I judge this was none, or little, of your doing, and I accept your help for our wounded and sick, with thanks. As for our . . . internal dissension . . . as you choose to call it; little now remains.' His mouth became a hard line. 'The instigators have been sent to their precious deity for his judgement in the matter. Whendrak can . . . and will . . . tend its own problems of government.' Before Ibris could reply, Haynar went on. 'You have our permission for your army to pass by the city.'

These were the words required of the treaty.

Ibris bowed, but instead of departing, he clicked his horse forward until he was by Haynar's side. He laid a hand on the Maeran's arm.

Haynar met his gaze forcefully and a grim determination filled his face. 'This will never be again, Ibris,' he said. 'This city has not survived this ordeal to risk being at any time again a pawn in the ancient madness between your two peoples. I give you due warning that we shall fortify our city and arm our people, and use every device at our disposal to increase our power and influence, until we become the third great power in this land.'

Ibris nodded. 'This you told my son,' he replied. 'It is your right; your duty, even. And while your sword hangs by your door and not at your belt, you'll have nothing other than friendship and help from Serenstad.'

'This your son told me,' Haynar replied.

Eventually, the army reached the end of the valley, and Ibris found himself looking out over the fertile plains that marked the eastern extremity of Bethlarii territory.

There he waited until he received word about Hyndrak to the north. Hyndrak was a substantial garrison city, and divisions from the cities of Stor and Drew had been sent there directly to seal it and prevent any assault on Ibris's supply lines as he moved towards Bethlar. This action would also protect their own cities from any direct assaults by the Hyndrak regiments through the mountains.

'Hyndrak has been surrounded. There has been no resistance,' the message said when it came, adding significantly, 'We suspect that the Hyndrak regiment has decamped and that there are only reservists here.'

'Excellent,' Ibris acknowledged flatly. 'Send word to remind the commanders there that there's to be no attempt to take or subdue the city.'

Feranc bowed. 'All is clear then,' he said flatly.

Ibris pulled open the flap of the command tent, and looked out across the rolling Bethlarii pains.

'All is clear,' he echoed.

Chapter 36

The busy confusion of the large camp gradually grew quieter as the last light of the setting sun faded. Dark strands that had been staining the red and pink clouds stretched across the horizon, slowly spread to make them cold, grim and distant.

Stars began to appear in the purpling sky, while more homely lights were struck inside the rows of tents and wagons. Fires were stoked to help keep the chill of the coming night from bearing too hard on the many sentries posted about the camp.

Lamps, too, were lit in Ibris's command tent, reshaping its dull greyness with new and warmer shadows. Ibris was lounging back in a large chair while Menedrion, Arwain and Ryllans were sitting to one side of him. Ciarll Feranc, silhouetted against a particularly bright lamp, was bending over a table, examining a map. A large fire burned in the centre of the tent, its fumes rising into a decorated cowl that carried them out into the night.

The group's deliberations were interrupted discreetly by an announcement from the guard at the door and Antyr entered, accompanied by Estaan. They brought with them a brief swirl of cold air, and the fire flared up momentarily, releasing a soft puff of smoke into the tent. Menedrion scowled at the decorated cowl and then leaned forward to strike it with the flat of his hand.

Behind Antyr and Estaan came Pandra, his posture a little self-conscious, as it invariably was in the Duke's presence.

Ibris motioned them all to sit down, then stroked the heads of Tarrian and Grayle which appeared suddenly on his knees. As usual the two wolves flopped down across his feet.

'To continue, gentlemen,' Ibris said. 'It seems that we're ready to begin our march towards Bethlar. Politically, the attack on Whendrak gives us the right under the terms of the treaty. Militarily, our force is large enough and growing daily, and we've received no indication that the Bethlarii are using this as a diversion while they mount a major attack elsewhere. Morally . . .' He shrugged sadly. 'Who can say? We've lost two of the three heralds we sent out with messages for the Hanestra asking for a meeting, and the third only escaped because someone shot at him prematurely.' He paused and shook his head slowly. 'It's unbelievable,' he said, almost to himself. 'Killing heralds now . . .'

Then he let out a sharp breath and pressed on. 'All the evidence that our advance patrols are bringing back confirms that the Bethlarii seemed to be mobilizing the entire people. In theory we could just wait, fight a defensive war until their country collapses about them, but we may be more vulnerable than they are to such a sustained drain of men and women from their normal lives. Besides which if we let them finish their mobilization we'll be facing a truly huge army. Attack now is no more than self-defence . . .'

His doubt hung heavy in the air, but no one spoke.

He dispelled it himself. With a dismissive wave of his hand, he sat up in his chair, disturbing Tarrian and Grayle.

'How are things on our second front?' he asked Antyr abruptly.

Antyr hesitated briefly and then said, 'Nothing untoward has happened recently, sire.'

Ibris's eyes narrowed. 'But . . .?' he asked, catching a doubt in the Dream Finder's voice.

Antyr hesitated again and looked round awkwardly at the listening group. 'I don't know,' he said. 'Nothing *has* happened, but there's an unease in the . . .' He moved his hands vaguely.

'In the what?' Ibris asked, before Antyr could continue.

'In the mingling of the dream ways . . . the . . . night thoughts . . . over the camp . . . it's difficult to explain,' Antyr answered. 'It's as if a great storm were going on somewhere . . . or were about to arrive. The atmosphere's jagged, tense . . .'

'Several thousand men expecting to march to war soon are hardly going to be at their most relaxed, Antyr,' Ibris said.

'No,' Antyr said, shaking his head. 'That's nothing unusual, as you say. But this is beneath and beyond. Faint and distant, but all-pervasive. I can't say what it is or what it means, I've never felt anything like it before. It worries me.'

Ibris frowned and turned to Pandra. 'Have you noticed this . . . strange . . . atmosphere . . . pervading the, whatever they are, the night thoughts?' he asked.

'I feel nothing but the doubts and fear that you yourself described,' Pandra replied. 'But I don't have either Antyr's skill or his sensitivity. My not noticing something doesn't mean it isn't there.'

Ibris's frown deepened. 'Wolf?' he said in some irritation.

'Listen to Antyr, pack leader,' Tarrian replied. 'And don't be so angry just because you didn't get the answer you wanted. You hired him to do a job and he's doing it.'

'I *appointed* him,' Ibris interjected sharply, thrown off balance by Tarrian's offhand manner.

'Oh, so that's why Aaken's so slow paying his wages? It's an honorarium? Prompt payment isn't dignified. I understand now. Very complicated, humans.'

Despite the grimness of the moment, Ibris found his irritation evaporating at Tarrian's tone. He chuckled softly.

'I'm sorry, Antyr,' he said after a moment. 'I wouldn't rail at a messenger because he couldn't see through a mountain, so I should have listened and thought before I spoke. Tell me what you can, however vague. I'm still concerned about the warning that Whendrak is the lure. I see no military traps waiting for us so I'm waiting for some other revelation.'

Antyr's forehead furrowed with effort. 'I've no reason for saying this,' he said softly. 'No logic, no observed sightings, intercepted messages. But I can't help but feel that the trap, whatever it is, is already beginning to close.'

All eyes turned to him. Even Ciarll Feranc inclined his head towards him as he maintained his scrutiny of the map on the table.

'Somewhere, something dire is happening,' he went on before anyone could speak. 'But it's not here. Here you must do what you can see to do. Wherever this trap lies, it's beyond your finding for the moment. I . . . we . . . will watch the dreamways and give you what warning we can, and what protection we can.'

Ibris leaned back, his face anxious. 'I'm at a loss,' he said. 'You tell me to go to battle with the Bethlarii while some other ambush is under way. What am I to make of that?'

Antyr met his gaze. 'Just that, sire,' he said, his voice quiet but unequivocal. 'You've an enemy that you can see. Fight him with all your skill, or you'll be defeated. You've also an enemy you can't see.' He waved a hand across Pandra and the two wolves. 'We will watch for him, and advise you as

509

well as we're able. Until that time, you can do nothing about him. *Nothing*!'

'Your mind is clear enough about that, I see,' Ibris replied. Then he looked round at the watching faces.

'Do any of you wish to add anything to this advice?' he asked.

Ryllans indicated Estaan. 'We've been constantly on the alert for . . . strange . . . happenings ever since Antyr's encounter with the Dream Finder Nyriall, but we've felt nothing.'

Ibris glanced at Feranc. 'I've sent further messengers to Viernce,' he said, without looking up from the map.

'Enough of all this,' Menedrion burst out impatiently. 'We're all agreed about this dream nonsense, and we're wasting time pursuing it further. Nothing's happened so far, and if something's about to then we can't do anything else but wait and rely on . . .' He waved vaguely at Antyr and Pandra.

'More importantly . . .' The vague gesture became positive, and pointed in the general direction of Bethlar. 'There's an army of lunatics out there, growing day by day, and if we don't deal with them very soon, we'll none of us have any dreams to worry about in future.' He leaned forward, clenching his fist to make his point. 'We should move against them immediately. Hit them hard, hit them fast, hit them *now*! Then, we can fret about our dreams at our ease.'

'Succinctly summarized, Irfan,' Ibris said, smiling to take the edge off the irony in his voice. 'Anyone else got anything to say?'

There was no reply.

'Very well, gentlemen,' he said, standing up. 'We march tomorrow.'

Captain Larnss yawned mightily. Ye gods, this was a boring job. Nursemaiding all these volunteers and reservists at the back of beyond on the offchance that the Bethlarii might spring a sneak attack across the northern border while the army was looking for them at Whendrak. Some hopes!

He was beginning to wish they would. Anything was better than this trial by tedium.

'A good career move for you, Larnss,' he had been told. 'Not many captains of your age get such a responsibility.'

510

'Career move,' he had retorted, somewhat indiscreetly. 'I'm hardly going to cover myself in glory in front of the Duke while I'm up there, am I?'

'Men in the right place can prevent a battle, captain, and staying alive is glory enough for most people in a war. Besides, the Duke knows the value of those who wait prepared at the edge of the conflict.'

'That's very poetic. But I'd rather have my present responsibility and be in one of the divisions marching to Whendrak.'

'Here are your orders, captain. Safe posting.'

As if it could be anything else up here. Rendd, of all places. Serenstad's most northerly ally. Sheep, sheep, more sheep, and a goat. Give him city life any day. An up-and-coming officer already moving into the fringes of court life, he shouldn't have been dumped up here. Not for the first time since his arrival he began to search through the names of his superiors for the most likely culprit.

'Companies one to five ready to commence patrol, sir.'

The voice made him turn a further yawn into a taut-lipped expression of acknowledgement and, fastening up his tunic, he stepped out of his tent to examine his charges.

Companies indeed! They were scarcely more than glorified platoons. As he walked along the waiting ranks, he tried to work up a sneer for these local volunteers, gathered traditionally into companies by family and district. But they'd been reliable and conscientious so far, and more than anxious to oblige this young fellow from the city. He could not deny that it made a refreshing change from the ambitious back-biting that often typified life in the Serenstad force.

They're not such a bad lot really, he admitted grudgingly. Just farmers and artisans looking to do their bit. Not exactly the legendary warriors of heroic saga, but they were his to make what he could of. It could've been worse. He could have been sent to Farlan and been given the job of trying to organize sailors and fishermen into a fighting unit.

He was about to take his horse from a waiting groom, when, on a whim, he dismissed the man. Be prepared to do as your men do. That much he'd learned from studying Ibris and Menedrion. This patrol was to be a comparatively short one and was to be made on foot, so he too, would walk. It would do him no harm. Indeed, the walking might help him shake

511

off the lethargy that the slow pace of this place seemed to be inducing in him.

The Rendd reservists set off on their patrol.

Once or twice during the day, Larnss regretted his decision to walk, as the locals, used to the hilly terrain, maintained a very commendable pace. It took him some effort to keep his discomfort from showing in his face.

The patrol was, of course, uneventful and they began pitching camp beside a wide, boisterous stream, just before sunset.

While the work was proceeding, Larnss walked up a nearby hill and surveyed the countryside. There was little to be seen except rolling hills in every direction, although to the north – north-east? – he fancied that the sky seemed red. Endir was it, over there? He could not remember, and without giving the matter any further thought he turned back towards the camp. A fine drizzle started to fall.

As he strode down the hill, he frowned in a mixture of irritation and dismay. Before him lay a rambling string of tents spanning across a sharp bend in the stream.

Orders from Serenstad had been quite explicit; all camps in border areas were to be laid out with a defensible perimeter, and appropriate sentries mounted.

Managing to control his initial response he took the officer responsible on one side and explained to him the inadequacy of his response to orders that might well have been initiated by no less a person than the Duke himself.

'Letting the men put their tents up where they want, won't do,' he concluded. 'Apart from the standing orders, this is a border area. What if there's a sudden attack?'

'Sudden attack, sir? Here?' the man interrupted, laughing good-naturedly.

Larnss' face hardened and he levelled a finger at the suddenly solemn officer. 'Yes, a sudden attack, here,' he said angrily. 'We're at war, for your information. It's not for us to decide what might happen, it's for us to behave like soldiers and be ready for whatever *does* happen. Groups like us are spread out all along the border in case of some Bethlarii treachery.' He modified his own commandant's words. 'The Duke knows the importance of those who wait prepared at the edge of the conflict, that's why I've been sent all the way from Serenstad.' He glanced up into the increasing rain. He'd had enough doing as the men did for one day, and he certainly didn't intend to get soaked with them while they repitched the camp. However, the matter couldn't be let lie . . .

'Now you can go back to the men and tell them as our perimeter's been doubled, so has sentry duty. Perhaps then, tomorrow, they'll appreciate the value of observing the Duke's orders and lay the camp out as a proper defensible enclave. And if there's any complaining, we'll put stakes around it . . . or a ditch . . . or both. Dismiss.'

Do them no harm, he thought later, as he extinguished the lamp and lay back in his blankets. In fact, it had been very useful; given him a chance to display his authority quite legitimately. And he'd done it quite well, he decided.

He toyed with the idea of waking early and making a spot inspection of the doubtless negligent sentries, but his aching legs and admittedly not unpleasant fatigue told him that this was little more than idle dreaming.

He yawned and stretched, then closed his eyes. The blankets were warm and though the ground was hard, he was both too weary and too contented to care. This might not be such a bad posting after all.

The sound of the rain on the canvas was oddly comforting and as he drifted off to sleep, its steady drumming rose to fill his mind and displace all other . . . sounds . . . distractions . . . thoughts . . .

Drumming, drumming.

Drumming.

Grey wakefulness slowly penetrated into the sound.

And more!

Shouting!

Larnss leapt up, suddenly wide awake, just as the flap of his tent was torn open by a wide-eyed and breathless reservist.

Larnss did not wait for him to find his voice, but pushed past him and out into the dawn.

For an instant he thought he was dreaming. Pouring around the broad shoulder of the hill, and making for the camp at full gallop, was a vast horde of horsemen. The drumming hooves filled the air, almost drowning the shrill cries of the sentries dashing through the camp desperately rousing their companions.

Larnss' mouth dropped open. He had seen the Serenstad cavalry at practice and that was a formidable sight, but this . . .

This was unbelievable.

513

But it was there! And it would be on them in minutes. Stark reality swept aside Larnss' initial shock.

Drawing his sword, he ran through the straggling camp, slashing open tents and brutally kicking awake any who had not already been wakened.

'To me! To me! Spears and shields! Form up, as you value your worthless lives. Form up!'

His junior officers frantically following his lead, the five companies attempted to form a line across the bend in the stream, but the speed of the approaching horsemen and the size of the widespread camp resulted in their only having time to form three ragged squares; two against the banks of the curving stream, and the third in between them.

Larnss, in one of the outer squares, was petrified. Questions flooded into his head. Who were these attackers? Bethlarii surely. But with such a huge cavalry force? He squinted into the approaching mass, but he could see none of the characteristic markings that he had been told typified the Bethlarii regiments.

And how could they hope to stand against such a force? Their position was surely impossible against such numbers. The horsemen could move through the gaps between the squares and surround them almost completely. And the stream, though quite fast and deep, was certainly fordable and of little real defensive value.

'Hold!' he shouted, trying to beat down his terror.

Then, to his horror, he saw the centre square waver ominously.

He had a vision of them scattering and splashing through the stream, to flee across the countryside while the great tide of riders surged through the opening they had left.

Without thinking, he forced his way through the uncertain shield wall of his own square and dashed across the gap towards the centre one.

Matching the speed of his arrival at the centre with shouts of encouragement interspersed with imprecations, curses, and blows, he stilled the mounting panic.

'Hold or die. It's that simple!'

Then, suddenly. 'Look, they're slowing.'

Somehow he managed to make this sound like an angry reproach to his quavering men rather than the cry of surprise that it actually was. A glance around, however, showed him the cause of riders' loss of momentum.

They were charging into a narrowing field. Already, he noticed, some of the side riders were drawing back to avoid being edged into the stream, while the remainder were having to rearrange themselves to avoid collisions with each other.

The Rendd reservists, Larnss' first command, had been given a little time.

Larnss seized two men. 'You, left flank at the double. You, right. Anyone who's got a bow there is to defend the gaps. Shoot for the horses. The more we bring down, the less room they have for manoeuvre. Move!'

The two men needed no encouragement and scurried across the gaps as the few in the centre square who had bows began stringing them and preparing to implement Larnss' shouted instruction before he ordered them to.

'Shoot when you're ready,' he shouted. 'Targets of discretion. Aim at the horses.'

There was a brief lull as the archers waited for the riders to come within effective range.

Larnss gripped his sword until his hand throbbed.

Then the archers began to shoot. Almost immediately, the front riders in the charge, already in some disarray, began to break up. The relentless thunder of the horses' hooves faltered and the air began to fill with the sounds of men cursing and horses screaming in terror and pain as the iron-tipped arrows struck home.

Many stumbled, bringing down their riders, while many others reared high, forelegs flailing in an attempt to flee this cruel assault.

Larnss watched this unexpected enemy carefully. Who were they? he asked himself again. There were flags flying among the host, but still he could see nothing he recognized. And the horses were sturdier and slightly smaller than those used by either the Bethlarii or the Serens. But, most bewildering of all, was the sheer number of riders, and, he noted, watching the line disentangle itself, brilliant riders at that, for all that their formation discipline was not particularly good.

He'd heard of a land beyond the mountains in the far north which was said to be populated by wild tribes of horsemen, but surely. . .?

'Fast!' he shouted to the archers as the great charge came to a shambling and chaotic halt, with the front riders turning to retreat running into those at the rear who were still advancing. '*Fast, damn it!* Save your arrows for when they're advancing, not retreating.'

At the top of the hill, Ivaroth and his senior officers watched in dismay and disbelief as the charge squeezed itself to a halt in the corner formed by the stream, and then began to retreat raggedly under the arrowfire from the three squares.

Angrily, Ivaroth seized the reins of his horse and braced himself to charge down among his men. A hand reached out and caught his arm. He turned angrily. It was Endryn. His reaction had been automatic and he was about to express the concern that arrows were no respecters of person when wiser inner counsels prevailed. 'They've spent too long fighting women and old men,' he said softly so that only Ivaroth could hear. 'It's time they were reminded how dangerous these people can be and what a journey lies ahead to the fulfilment of your vision.'

Ivaroth's jaw worked agitatedly for a moment, then he nodded grimly. 'You're right, Endryn,' he said. 'A few dead will be a salutary lesson.' His eyes narrowed. 'And it'll save me the trouble of executing some of those blockheads myself,' he added.

Despite this routinely cavalier attitude towards his followers however, anxious, more conservative thoughts were increasingly occupying him. Effectively empty of fighting men, Endir, like Navra, had been subdued with ease, and now stood occupied by his army. The army too patrolled the river that ran between the mountains and Endir so that, as far as he knew, no clear news of his invasion had passed westward. Thus he was now in a position to move down into the territory of Serenstad, taking first the small city of Rendd and then the much larger city of Viernce.

There was no reason why the tactics of careful scouting and surprise that had worked so well at Navra and Endir, and indeed, at all the smaller settlements they had encountered, should not work on Rendd and Viernce also.

Yet it unsettled him that his knowledge of Serenstad was only a mixture of travellers' tales, tribal lore, and such as he had been able to learn from the Bethlarii whose dreams he had ravaged. He would have preferred to have taken emotional possession of the Serenstad leadership as he had the Bethlarii, but his few attempts had been oddly unsuccessful. Further, they had shown him, albeit briefly, a vision of a people whose society was far more complex and diverse than that of the Bethlarii, and one much harder to control through the fear and superstition of a few leaders.

Thus, with an increasing part of his army being left behind to control the conquered territory, and with a more uncertain foe and therefore the most dangerous part of the invasion before him, Ivaroth was concerned by the seeming incompetence of his men now attacking the camp below.

Rendd, small and sleepy, from what he had heard, should present little or no problem, but Viernce was different. Large, walled and almost certainly garrisoned, it had loomed large in Bethlarii minds as the source of a great defeat brought about by an unexpected resistance on the part of a few brave and ferocious soldiers. It would therefore have to be approached and taken with the utmost skill and speed. But taken it must be. Taken and crushed so that no vestige of resistance lay in its people and so that it could be maintained thus by a comparatively small force. He would need every one of his men to complete the most important stage of his conquest of these rich and lush southern lands, for only when Viernce was quelled would he be able to venture safely westwards towards Whendrak to annihilate whichever battle-weary army had survived the war that he and the blind man had so painstakingly engineered. After that, the pacification of the rest of the country could confidently be left in the hands of his officers while he turned his mind to the running of his new kingdom.

The culmination of his long-planned ambition rising before him dispelled the momentary anxiety that Ivaroth had felt at the folly of his men in attacking so incompetently this small force they had come upon. Endryn was right, they'd been too long fighting women and old men. He'd bang a few heads together later, and that, coupled with the casualties these southerners were inflicting on them, would soon give them their edge again.

Even so, came the persistent cautionary note, he must keep a careful eye on what was happening. Good horses were good horses and too valuable to be casually thrown away. The local horses were no good.

Unaware of the brooding presence of the creator of his troubles, Larnss moved restlessly about the square, doing what he could to keep up the heart of his men.

'Hold firm. No horse is going to charge a solid spear line.

517

They're not as stupid as men. Archers, save your arrows for the leading horses. Take your time. Don't miss!'

But if every arrow killed a dozen horses and a dozen men, it would be to no avail, he realized, as the brief interlude following the first charge gave his training an opportunity to exert itself and he did a quick estimate of the massive force ranged against them. It was a chilling deduction. The attackers, whoever they were, seemed to have neither archers nor infantry with which to soften up the squares, but it was asking a lot of even the finest foot soldiers to stand firm against charge after charge.

'You can't suppress the flesh,' someone had once told him when he argued the impossibility of cavalry breaking up disciplined infantry. 'You wait until you've stood there holding your pike with a line of horses charging at you. It's a matter of whose nerve goes first.'

And there was no question about whose nerve would go first here.

Nevertheless, the only protection that his company had was to stand as long as they could, and to use their few archers to break up any charges while their arrows lasted. Then . . .

The question was replaced by another before he could form the grim answer. What were these people doing here? This was clearly Serenstad territory, and they had attacked his force without any semblance of warning. They must be what the Duke had feared when he ordered full voluntary mobilization and alerted all border cities and towns to watch for surprise attacks . . .

Rendd!

The vision of the little city – his responsibility – being overwhelmed by these invaders suddenly filled his mind. With a large part of its defending force tied down here, Rendd could not hope to stand against such an army.

He must get a warning to them.

Scarcely had the thought occurred to him than a darker one formed. Viernce! After Rendd this must surely be the destination of these riders. And from there . . .!

He cursed himself for not bringing his horse.

A cry drew his attention back to the riders. They had regrouped and were starting to gallop forward again. This time they were coming in two wide columns, presumably with the intention of sweeping through the gaps between the squares and wheeling to attack on all sides.

It was an awesome sight and Larnss felt the panic mounting in the men around him.

'First man to falter, *I* kill,' he roared spitting out his own terror into the words. 'They're riders, not cavalrymen. Look at them! A mob! Archers, take those leading horses! Bring them down! If any get through seize the horses, we must get a message back to Rendd.'

Roughly he yanked a junior trooper from the rear ranks.

'You can ride, I've seen you,' he shouted into the young man's frightened face to make himself heard above the mounting din. 'If we can get a horse, you're to ride to Rendd and tell them . . .' He looked around desperately. Rendd was too big to evacuate and too small to stand against this invader. '. . .Tell them what's happened here and to make whatever peace they can with these people; delaying them as much as they can. Then get a fresh horse and get to Viernce and warn the garrison there.'

The trooper nodded vaguely, but the approaching horsemen now drew all attention.

As much by coincidence as by intent, several archers from the three squares loosed their arrows at the same time and a dozen or more horses at the head of each column came crashing down, unseating their riders violently and bringing down several of the horses immediately behind them.

Nevertheless, many riders leapt over – or moved around – the chaos and reached the squares. There was a brief savage interlude as the reservists wielded their spears frantically, unhorsing many of the riders and killing or injuring several others.

The squares held again, but only just, and the riders began to retreat in disorder once more. Dragging the trooper with him, Larnss pushed through the shield wall and seized the bridle of a riderless horse.

'Get on it and go!' he roared. 'Rendd and Viernce! As you've never ridden before!' The young man hesitated, then leapt into the saddle when he saw the fury rising in Larnss' face.

Larnss slapped the horse and, with an awkward salute, the trooper spurred it forward towards the stream.

'They're coming again!' came the cry.

Larnss, however, was watching the receding rider, now guiding his horse into the hectic stream. Then to his horror, he saw two riders splashing down the stream after him. An arrow took one of them, but the other continued.

The young trooper saw the impending danger and tried to urge his horse on, but it slipped and stumbled, unseating him.

Without thinking, Larnss sheathed his sword and set off down the slight slope at full tilt. Both horse and trooper had regained their feet and, with one hand clasping the horse's reins, the trooper was struggling to draw his sword to defend himself against the approaching attacker when Larnss hurled himself from the bank of the stream and brought both horse and rider crashing down heavily in a flurry of spray and flailing limbs.

Holding his victim's head under the water, Larnss shouted to the trooper who was wading towards him.

'Go, man! Take this horse as well, and go!'

The trooper did as he was bidden, at some speed.

Then, still holding the struggling rider under water with one hand, Larnss drew his sword and he thrust it into the submerged body. There was a brief, bloodstained thrashing, then stillness. He relinquished his charge and the current caught it and carried it a few paces downstream before it wedged on a rock.

Larnss paused and looked for a moment at the first man he had ever killed. He felt numb.

But the commotion of the greater battle asserted itself over his own needs almost immediately.

'No!' he cried out desperately as he looked back towards his beleaguered command. His precipitate flight to help the messenger had been misunderstood and panic had struck the middle square even before the riders had. Now they were scattered and fleeing, with triumphant horsemen pursuing them, cutting them down with swords and axes, and skewering them on lances. The other squares, now heavily beset, were crumbling also.

Larnss staggered out of the steam and ran towards his tent nearby. Outside it stood the flag of the Rendd reservists. He seized it and held it high.

'To me! To me!' he roared.

A rider emerged from behind a tent and, with a malevolent grin, answered his call by levelling a lance at him. Hardly aware of what he was doing, but possessed by a terrible anger, Larnss held his ground until the last moment and then stepped to one side, at the same time bringing the standard down on the lance. Its point dipped and then plunged into the soft earth and the rider was hurled over the top of it to land several paces away with a sickening thud.

Larnss, wrenching the spear from the ground, heard both the wind and the life go out of the man, but it was of no more interest to him than the knowledge the grass on which he stood was green. All that mattered was the next attacker.

He was impaled on his comrade's weapon as Larnss again stepped aside and thrust the spear straight up under his chin and then released it. He heard, sharp and clear in his now profound awareness, the clink of the point striking the inside of the man's helmet as it passed through his skull.

'To me! To me!'

Another rider fell, this time to a savage sword cut that almost severed his arm.

Fleeing men gravitated to Larnss' powerful call and the waving standard. He looked around. The camp was a sea of galloping horsemen, swords rising and falling, strange, alien flags fluttering, and here and there were islands of men standing in groups, in pairs, alone, hacking and fighting.

And the noise: the shouting, the screaming; a great paean of hatred and terror and pain.

You are finer men than any legendary warriors of heroic saga, Larnss thought, as he slashed at the face of a nearby horse. And you deserved a better leader.

The injured horse reared in panic and threw its rider, but its flailing hoof caught the Rendd reservists' acting commander in the face and killed him instantly.

High on the hill, Endryn and the others watched the massacre enviously.

Endryn nodded appreciatively. 'They fought well, these southlanders,' he said. 'No cowardice at the end. They fell like stones, each man in his place.'

He turned to Ivaroth. The Mareth Hai, however, was in no mood for singing the praises of a gallant foe. His face was livid. Endryn involuntarily edged away from him.

'Stop him,' Ivaroth was saying, his trembling hand pointing towards the retreating figure of Larnss' messenger. 'Stop him.'

'We can't. He's too far away,' Endryn exclaimed, immediately wishing he had simply galloped off on the futile errand instead and bracing himself for a savage rebuke, if not worse, for his folly.

But Ivaroth was not talking to him, he was talking to the old man standing by his saddle. The old man, his face hooded, looked up at him and slowly shook his head.

Ivaroth bent down and hissed at him. 'If he reaches Rendd, then the news of our coming reaches Viernce also. And you see how these people fight. Without Viernce secure at our back we can't move to destroy whoever's left at Whendrak and *all fails*. Stop him.'

Still the old man did not move.

Ivaroth lowered his voice further, his black eyes peering relentlessly into the dark void of the hood. 'If we do not win this land, then my own kind will kill me, let alone the enemy. And without me, you'll not be able to reach the places beyond or the *other place* you're so anxious to find.'

The blind man seemed to ponder for a moment, then he looked up and turned towards the fleeing messenger. Slowly, reluctantly, he raised his hands, as if reaching out to him.

A low rumbling filled the air, and the riders at the top of the hill found themselves struggling to control their mounts as the ground beneath them began to shake.

The rumbling faded, or rather, retreated. Watching the distant rider, Ivaroth saw a swathe of destruction following after him. Soil and turf, shrubs and plants were torn up and thrown bodily aside as if by some unseen giant hand. The messenger reached the top of a small incline and looked over his shoulder briefly.

Then he disappeared in a cloud of dust.

Ivaroth's eyes shone with satisfaction.

'Mareth Hai!'

Ivaroth turned round sharply at the alarm in the voice, but before he noted the speaker, he felt the old man leaning against his leg.

Then the mentor and dark angel, who had brought him this far, slithered to the ground.

Chapter 37

The atmosphere in Ivaroth's camp was tense and uneasy. What should have been a raucous celebration of the destruction of the Rendd reservists was dampened by Ivaroth's fury at the losses they had sustained.

But Endryn knew that the fury, justified though it might have been, was not what it seemed. In reality it was a transmutation of the fear that had struck Ivaroth when the old man had collapsed.

Pacing up and down his tent, he tried to push the memory of the fear in Ivaroth's eyes from his mind as, yet again, it returned to torment him. He could not remember ever having seen Ivaroth afraid before. Even when they were children together, it had been Ivaroth, the younger, who had been the leader, riding the wildest of the horses, taking the hardest of the falls, sneaking close towards the camps of hostile tribes, and unflinchingly, contemptuously even, accepting whatever punishments the adults had meted out from time to time.

Endryn wiped his brow. Two questions bayed at his heels. Who else had seen the look in the Mareth Hai's eyes and, worse for him personally, did Ivaroth know that he, Endryn, had seen the look?

He had flicked his eyes away from Ivaroth's face on the instant, and turned them to the collapsing man, for fear of Ivaroth's dreadful response to the witness of such weakness, but. . .?

And who was this old man, with his blind white eyes and his flesh-crawling presence, to induce such a reaction in Ivaroth? The oft-asked question rose to set aside Endryn's immediate concerns. It came now with an urgency more pressing than ever before. Not that he had ever dared to ask it. Such few as had, had received no answer other than Ivaroth's terrifying black-eyed gaze, and those foolish enough to misinterpret this and to press their inquiries had died for their pains.

Yet it should be addressed, with the camp seething with rumour, their advance halted without any reason being given, and the Mareth Hai sitting, unapproachable, by the cot of the grotesque companion he had brought out of the wilderness.

Part of the answer he knew: the old man was power — real power. Not for him the noisy conjurings of the swift-fingered shamans to gull the superstitious. His was a way of dark, watchful silence that would not grace such antics even with contempt; the way that went straight to its goal and crushed anything that stood in its path. An ancient, a . . . Endryn's mind hesitated at the word . . . a magical power; one beyond all understanding.

Yet, though he had no understanding of this power, Endryn was well content to accept the evidence of his own eyes and be grateful that he stood near to the man to whom the command of it had seemingly been granted.

He could not begin to guess at the bargain that Ivaroth might have made to make this creature his own . . . if that indeed was the case. But now, as mysteriously as he exercised his power, the old man had been stricken; over-reached himself in some way perhaps, as he sought to destroy the fleeing messenger.

And now the great drive south was halted. The camp idle and the men festering.

With each passing day there was the risk that random refugees who had avoided their patrols and scouts, would reach Bethlar or Serenstad and reveal what was happening. He must do something. He was Ivaroth's closest confidant. The ties that bound them were rooted strongly in their pasts, they should protect him . . .

He took a deep breath as he reminded himself that Ivaroth had killed his own brother.

Still, family was family, these things happened. He and Ivaroth were saddle companions. That was different. . .?

Composing himself, he went to the door of his tent and, after a brief hesitation, yanked it open and strode out into the cold wintry gloaming.

'Sirs, sirs. Please, sirs . . .' The two riders had seen the woman bustling along the track which crossed the field, but were nonetheless surprised as, arms waving agitatedly, she almost hurled herself in front of their horses.

She was middle-aged and stout, and her flushed face and heavy breathing confirmed that she had not run anywhere in many years. Her shoes were soiled with mud and she was wearing no cloak or gown to protect her from the cold weather. What was presumably her good house pinafore was crumpled and grimed.

Without pausing, she seized the bridle of the nearest rider; the younger of the two, a man with a round, worried face which, for all he was no boy, had a touch of innocence about it. She leaned heavily on the bridle for support. 'Please help me, sirs. I don't know what to do,' she managed to gasp out eventually.

The man bent forward and laid his hand on her shoulder gently. 'Quietly, mistress,' he said. 'What's the matter? Have you been attacked?'

The woman hesitated, taken aback by the man's heavy foreign accent. Then she looked into his face intently and seemed to reach the conclusion that she could still seek his help.

'No, sir,' she said, a little more calmly. 'But I've a hurt man at my cottage, and my husband's . . . over the fields . . . and the man needs help. He's raving something terrible. And I can't even ride to the village for a physician.'

Without waiting for an answer, she started to lead the horse towards the track she had just run along. The two men exchanged a brief glance, and the older man nodded.

Keeping pace with the woman's anxious tugging, they soon found themselves passing alongside a carefully cut hedgerow draped with drop-laden cobwebs. Passing through a gateway they came into the garden of a farm-worker's small cottage; it had the high-pitched, thatched roof and broad, overhanging eaves typical of the area.

'This way,' she said, releasing the horse and bustling off towards an already-open door. The two men dismounted and followed.

The woman had disappeared into a room off the small hallway as they entered, but her whereabouts were revealed almost immediately.

'Oh, you shouldn't be out of bed,' came her anxious voice. 'It's bitter out there. You'll catch your death with that fever. Lie down, please—'

'But I must reach . . . Viernce . . . Warn them . . . The horsemen . . . It's following me . . . tearing the ground . . .' the speaker gave a brief, fearful scream. '. . . run . . . run . . . I must . . .'

The second voice was a man's but it was weak and barely coherent. The two men stepped quickly into the room. The woman was trying to prevent a young man from rising from a bed. His tunic and trousers were obviously a uniform of some kind, but they were soiled and torn and his face bore signs of a futile attempt to wash mud and blood from it. His eyes were wide with fear.

'Oh sirs, he's been like this since he woke up,' the woman volunteered, vainly trying to push the man down. 'Ranting about a message and something chasing him. I can't handle him, clean him up, or . . .' She shrugged and resorted to soft reproach in an attempt to silence the man. 'Lie still now. Look at the mess you're making of my bed.'

The older of the two men moved to the other side of the bed and sat down on it. 'Lie down, trooper,' he said, gently but firmly, putting his hands on the man's shoulders. 'Nothing pursues you here, you're safe among friends and I'll take your message in a moment. Be still.'

The young soldier's eyes widened further and he seized his comforter's arm. 'It tore the ground up . . . tore it up . . . raced after me . . . burst my horse . . . burst it . . . like a rotten fruit . . .' His voice disappeared into a fearful wail, and he began shaking violently.

The man frowned and glanced at his companion whose brow furrowed in response. 'Enough, trooper,' he said, this time sternly. 'You're still on duty and this is no way for a Duke's man to behave. Lie down and be still. That's an order.'

His tone seemed to reach through to the soldier in the man and he became a little quieter. Hesitantly he lay back, though his eyes were fixed on his new commander.

'Who is he? Where's he from?' the man asked the woman.

'I don't know,' the woman replied. 'He sounds as if he might be from Rendd . . .' She gestured vaguely over her shoulder, adding, 'Up north, I found him sprawled in the field just outside, his horse dead . . . dying . . . beside him. He'd ridden it to death. It was foaming and sweating something awful. I managed to drag him in, but he needs proper help, and I can't . . .'

The man nodded and raised a hand to stop her. 'I understand,' he said. 'We'll help you.' He laid his hand on the distressed soldier's forehead and frowned again. 'Get me the medicine pouch.' he said to his companion.

The younger man left the room and returned shortly with a leather case which he handed across the bed.

The woman followed the two men's actions anxiously. 'Are you physicians?' she asked.

'No,' replied the older man, with a faint smile as he carefully examined the contents of the pouch. 'Just travellers. We know enough to look after ourselves, and this was given to us by a . . . most . . . remarkable healer.'

Her immediate concerns now transferred to the charge of others, the woman examined her two saviours. Almost immediately, her hand came out to touch the cloak of the man standing beside her. Then realizing what she was doing, she snatched it away. 'I'm sorry,' she said, flustered. 'But it's such lovely material. I . . .' A blush lit up her already flushed face further. 'Who are you?' she asked, to dispel her embarrassment.

'In your language, I think you'd call me . . . Jadric,' the younger man said. 'And he's . . . Haster. We're just travellers come to see your great cities.'

'You've picked a sad and dangerous time, sirs,' the woman said. 'We'd all hoped that we'd see no more wars again, but . . .'

'Ah!' Haster's voice cut through her lament as he held up a small ornately carved stone jar. He removed its lid and shook some tablets into his hand. Picking one up he touched it gingerly with his tongue and pulled a wry face.

'Feverfew?' the woman asked.

'Similar, I think,' Haster replied. 'Fetch him some water to take these with, would you.'

Happy to be doing something, the woman scuttled out of the room.

Haster bent forward and, putting an arm around the young man's shoulders, eased him into a sitting position. The woman returned with an earthenware cup.

Haster placed one of the tablets in the man's mouth and offered the cup to him. 'Swallow this,' he said. 'It'll help ease your fever.'

His eyes still fastened to Haster's face, the man did as he was bidden, then lay back.

'Now, tell me your message,' Haster said after a moment.

The young man's agitation threatened to return, but a raised eyebrow from Haster stilled it.

'We were attacked,' the man began, rapidly.

'We? Who?' Haster intervened quietly but firmly.

The young man looked bewildered for a moment as if the simple question had driven all memories out of his head. 'The reservists,' he managed eventually. 'From Rendd . . . companies one to five . . . under Captain . . . Larnss, from Serenstad.' Haster nodded and motioned him to continue. 'We were on routine border patrol . . .'His eyes widened suddenly and he reached out and clutched Haster's arm. 'Then they attacked us . . .'

He fell suddenly silent.

'Who attacked you?' Haster asked, after a moment, laying his hand over the soldier's comfortingly.

Bewilderment returned to the man's face again, but this time it was different. He shook his head. 'Bethlarii, I suppose,' he said. 'But . . . they didn't look like Bethlarii . . . and I've never seen so many horses. There were thousands of them—'

'How many, trooper?' Haster asked, stern again.

The man met his gaze. 'Thousands,' he repeated unequivocally. 'Thousands and thousands. The hillside was black with them. Coming and coming.' His calm slipped away from him again. 'And they killed everyone . . . we were in bad order, but we managed to form squares . . . but they broke . . . I saw it. All five companies destroyed, wiped out. Everyone.' His face began to distort as grief started to assert itself. 'All my friends. I—'

'Later, trooper,' Haster said quickly. 'Tears later. Tell us how you escaped and what your message was.'

Words spilling over one another, the young soldier told of Larnss capturing the horse and saving his life in the stream.

'Where am I?' he said abruptly, breaking into his own narrative, his face shocked. 'I was supposed to go to Rendd . . . to warn them . . . then go to Viernce . . .' Agitated, he tried to sit up again, but Haster held him. 'Where am I . . .?'

'You're in a farm house near Viernce,' Haster said reassuringly. 'You rode your horse to death, and almost killed yourself in the process. But you're safe here. Tell me what killed your other horse. It tore up the ground, you said.'

The young man's agitation increased violently and his face became white with terror. The woman stepped back in alarm and Jadric moved forward hastily to help Haster hold him down if need arose.

It was some time before the soldier was quiet enough to

speak coherently again. 'It came after me.' He lifted his arms over his head as if to protect himself.

'What did?'

'I don't know . . . I could feel it . . . full of hatred and evil . . . but I couldn't see anything . . . the ground heaved and lurched underneath it . . . soil and shrubs were thrown up into the air . . .' His eyes looked upwards as if he were still watching the destruction. Then he looked at Haster and seized his arm again. Haster winced at the force of the grip and with a deceptively gentle movement, pulled his arm free. 'I jumped off my horse . . . rolled down the hill. My horse . . . burst . . . burst . . . a great shower of . . . blood . . . and . . . bits. Terrible sound . . .'

Haster and Jadric looked at one another over the distraught storyteller. Both of them were pale.

'I must have caught the other horse . . . I suppose . . . I don't know . . . I just remember . . . pounding, pounding . . . fleeing . . . and the hatred . . . the horror . . . following me . . .' He began shaking violently again.

Haster nodded to Jadric to hold the man down while he began searching through the medicine pouch again. Retrieving another small stone jar he hastily pushed a second tablet into the man's mouth and then held it shut. After a moment, the man's trembling diminished and his eyes closed.

The two men stood up as he relaxed. 'He'll sleep for some time now,' Haster said to the woman. His face was strained and, as if to reassure himself about something, he drew his hand across his forehead.

'Where's his horse?' he asked.

'It's out in the field at the back. Where it fell,' she replied. 'I'll show you.'

A little later, the two men rode into the nearby village and sought out the local liktor.

'I'll send someone up to the cottage to tend the man straight away,' the official said after they had recounted the young messenger's tale, omitting only his telling about the destruction of his horse. 'But all this business about an attack by horsemen on Rendd and then the city . . .' He shook his head and pulled a knowing face. 'Everyone knows the Bethlarii don't have that kind of cavalry. And they certainly wouldn't attack Viernce with it if they had; it's fortified. I think perhaps—'

There was a brief flash of impatience on Jadric's face, but

529

a quick, almost imperceptible, gesture from Haster made him keep silent.

'They're not Bethlarii, officer,' Haster interrupted, his voice authoritative. 'Though they might be in league with them as they must have passed through their territory. They're tribesmen from beyond the northern mountains. We travelled through their land to come here and the horse the lad rode is one of theirs without a doubt. Go and look for yourself. You've not seen a horse like that in these parts ever, I'll guarantee you.'

'I haven't seen one like yours, if it comes to that,' the liktor retorted with some indignation. 'But I'm not going to make an invasion out of it. And I can't go rousing the garrison on the strength of a dead horse, and the gullibility of two strangers for the tale of a fevered reservist who's probably nothing more menacing than a deserter.'

Haster fixed the man with a cold gaze, his presence suddenly powerful and dominant. 'You won't rouse the garrison, officer,' he said. 'The commander there will, when he's considered all the relevant information which I would ask you to deliver as soon as possible. If it's a mistake, which I doubt, then no harm's been done, and if the lad's story is accurate, then every moment is vital.'

Despite a good effort, the liktor could not hold Haster's gaze, and he glanced down quickly at some papers on the desk in front of him. Haster continued before he could speak. 'As for being strangers, you're quite right. We're both strangers and outlanders, visiting your land for the first time. We've no desire to become involved in one of your wars.' He reached into his cloak and pulled out a document. 'However, we're travelling this road at the request of a Commander Ciarll Feranc to see the Duke with the army at Whendrak. As a result of our encounter today *we'll* now be travelling there as fast as we can. The danger's real, no matter what you might think about it. Please take the lad's story to the commander at Viernce with the same dispatch.'

He offered the document to the officer sufficiently long for him to note the Duke's insignia, then, with a salute, he turned and strode out of the office. Jadric followed him, his face set.

When the liktor, discomfited and flushed, stepped outside after them, it was to see them galloping down the village street. 'Reckless riding,' he muttered to himself crossly, adding peevishly, 'and you'll not get to Whendrak at that speed, my lords, fine though your horses are.'

'We'd better do as they say, corp. They sounded like Mantynnai to me.'

The intrusion came from a cadet liktor who had sat silently in the background during the discussion and who now emerged behind his senior to watch the outcome. Part of his training today included learning when to keep silent. The liktor scowled down at him ferociously.

'Have you finished those mobilization reports I gave you to do, yet, cadet?' he thundered.

Ivaroth looked down at the blind man, lying on the rough bed. He was torn as ever. Part of him wanted to finish the old man off; rid himself of this fearful creature. That's what it'll come to in the end, he thought yet again.

Yet still he watched the rising and falling of the man's chest anxiously, like a mother with a new-born child.

Still he needed him. Needed him to sustain himself with the personal power that made him the greatest and most feared warrior among all the tribes.

He cursed himself for his folly in driving the old man to so outreach himself in attacking the fleeing messenger. But he had become so used to the old man using his power directly on physical objects as well as firing his own inner fighting spirit, that it had never occurred to him that it was anything other than effortless. The old man had broken spear shafts and sword blades, shaken the earth, causing horses to stumble, lit fires with a flick of his hand. And, of course, there were the wild, almost unbelievable excesses he indulged in when they visited the worlds beyond. Nothing Ivaroth had seen had prepared him for the toll that destroying that messenger had seemingly wrought on the old man.

The old fool must have known what would happen. A memory of the slowly shaking head returned to Ivaroth reproachfully. Yet the old man had obeyed!

His need for me must be greater than mine for him, Ivaroth concluded. Despite his concerns, the thought elated him.

It must indeed be so. The old man had stuck to their bargain faithfully; making no demands – still less, threats – that he should be taken into the worlds beyond to search for this other place he had so lusted after at one time. He had obeyed all Ivaroth's orders without question or delay;

tampering with the occasional dream to quell some rebellious lieutenant, or some doubting Bethlarii priest; strengthening his arm so that he could deal with some offender spectacularly; many small things.

I've beaten you, old man, Ivaroth concluded. You're prepared to destroy yourself at my whim because of the fear that I won't take you to the worlds beyond again.

It was a good feeling.

Yet Ivaroth still had his own needs. And they were considerable. He could not keep his army idle here for much longer. Tight though his grip was on the captured territory, it was only a matter of time before news of his invasion would leak out, and then the vital element of surprise would be lost. He wanted no major encounters until the two great armies beyond Whendrak had fought one another to a standstill, leaving him only the weakened and battle-weary remnants to deal with. And, too, a sudden faltering in their advance might well turn his own people on him. And without the old man's power he was virtually defenceless.

Something had to be done. And he could not ask the aid of any of the tribal shamans; that would seal his fate utterly.

The sound of voices outside the tent broke into his thoughts. Then, the door flap was pulled open and Endryn entered.

Instantly, Ivaroth felt his lieutenant's doubt and fear, screwed tight into anger. He went cold. It was as if the thoughts he had just had of his downfall had somehow reached out and begun their own fulfilment. Endryn was like the sudden icy wind that presaged the blizzard.

True to his character, however, Ivaroth struck first, straight to the heart, and without hesitation. Endryn had scarcely taken a step into the tent when Ivaroth beckoned him forward urgently.

'As ever, you read my mind, Endryn,' he said, taking his arm in a powerful and urgent grip. 'I was about to send for you.'

He led him towards the old man. 'He needs my aid, Endryn,' he said. 'He's done much for our people that cannot be told, but now he's been stricken by his too-zealous help to our cause.'

Endryn looked uncertainly from Ivaroth to the unconscious form on the bed.

Ivaroth finished his kill. 'I can't abandon him now,' he

532

said, before Endryn could speak. 'He's been too faithful a servant.' Then, lest this loyalty sound too implausible, he added pragmatic self-interest. 'And he'll be even more so if I can save him.'

'I don't understand, Mareth Hai,' Endryn managed at last. He ventured into the tacitly forbidden territory of Ivaroth's relationship with the old man. 'What has he done?' he risked.

The question provoked no rebuke, however. Instead, Ivaroth placed a hand to his forehead and sat down on a chair by the bed. 'Many things,' he replied. 'Things beyond simple understanding.' He looked earnestly at his lieutenant. The black irises of his eyes had spread to give him the terrifying gaze of the Dream Finder. Endryn, despite himself, turned away. 'He's a bridge to the powers that shape our destinies, Endryn.'

'The gods?' Endryn exclaimed incredulously, despite himself. 'He's a shaman?'

Ivaroth shook his head irritably and waved an angry and dismissive hand. 'Tricks and deceits for controlling the ignorant and the foolish, Endryn,' he snarled; an unwitting echo of Endryn's own thoughts but minutes earlier. 'There are no gods, you know that. This man knows the ways of the *true* power. The power of the wind and the thunderstorm, the power that carved out the valleys and peaks of the mountains, that levelled our own endless plains. And the power that can shape the minds of our enemies.'

Endryn, taken aback by this unexpected revelation, gazed about almost vacantly. Then, habit drew him back inexorably into his old patterns of thought and tribal loyalty.

'What do you want me to do?' he asked.

'Guard me,' Ivaroth replied, simply. 'I must go after him and I'd have you wait beside me while I'm searching.' Endryn began to frown uncertainly, his mind turning incongruously to horses and search patrols. 'Allow no one to disturb us,' Ivaroth continued. '*No one*, I'll seem to be asleep, but you're not to attempt to wake me, whatever happens or however long it takes. I shall return. And he with me. Do you understand?'

Endryn shook his head then straightened up. 'No, Mareth Hai,' he answered bluntly. 'But I'll obey your orders.'

Ibris's army moved relentlessly deeper into Bethlarii territory. Increasingly, reports were coming back to him that the

Bethlarii were gathering in force to meet him and, increasingly, his own doubts grew. There was a wrongness about all this.

It's hardly surprising that Dream Finders are involved in this, he thought with dark amusement. It has all the qualities of nightmare about it. The unannounced and seemingly demented envoy, Grygyr Ast-Darvad; the explosive deterioration of government at Whendrak; the news of the Bethlarii's massive mobilization, and his own response to it. The killing of heralds . . .

He shook his head. So many things, large and small.

And not least among these was the presence of Antyr with his strange, burgeoning powers and his fears and doubts. And too, the mysterious shadow from the past that so unsettled the Mantynnai.

Each day, he and his advisers efficiently and skilfully dealt with the many and complex problems that arose in the moving of a great army and the simultaneous ruling of a land. To his relief, much of the internecine squabbling between his dominion cities had indeed faded in the face of this common threat. Yet for all the reassurance he found in this, he had the feeling, as he had remarked to Arwain at the arrival of Grygyr Ast-Darvad, that he was actually riding an avalanche, and that he was doing no more than keep an unsteady balance. One slip and. . .?

Somehow, from somewhere, he – and the Bethlarii – were being manipulated. And all of them were trapped.

He called Antyr to him.

Antyr was pale when he entered the command tent. And Tarrian and Grayle remained watchfully beside him where previously they would fawn mockingly about the Duke. Estaan stood a discreet distance away. Despite his Mantynnai control, he looked tense and uncertain.

Ibris's broader concerns slipped from him. 'What's the matter?' he asked immediately.

Antyr shook his head. 'I don't know,' he replied. 'All through the day I've felt . . . a tension . . . an unease, growing.' There was fear in his voice, and his hand was opening and closing nervously about the pommel of his sword which was now always about his waist.

Ibris stood up and moved towards him, but there was a hint of a curl in Tarrian's lip, and Antyr raised a hand to keep him away.

'I feel I'm being . . . drawn away,' he said. 'Nyriall said something like that happened to him . . .' He grimaced. 'I don't know what it is. But . . . whatever happens . . . just put some men around me . . . under Estaan . . . he understands as well as anyone. If I fall, just guard me. That's all. Don't touch me. The wolves can do no other than protect me, though they die for it, and if they die, then wherever I am, I too am lost.'

Concern filled Ibris's face. His mind swam with questions, but he knew that Antyr had told all he could.

'I'll do as you say,' he said as reassuringly as he could. 'You'll be ringed with spears and shields at all times. As safe as I can make you. I—'

Ryllans entered the tent, cutting Ibris short. Uncharacteristically, his face was flushed. He hesitated as he caught sight of Antyr and his face became anxious as he noted his demeanour. The momentum of his news however, drew him back to the Duke.

'They're barely half a day away,' he said without preliminary. 'Shuffling around, picking their battle order. Waiting.'

The Duke closed his eyes and drew in a long breath. Avalanche or no, he knew beyond doubt what had to be done now.

'Antyr, go to your quarters and wait . . . for whatever it is.' He glanced at Ryllans. 'His own battle is starting. He's to be as closely protected as if he were me, and he's to be given whatever he asks for. Estaan will be in absolute charge of the guard.' Ryllans nodded in acknowledgement and Antyr and Estaan left.

Ibris looked at him. 'Senior officers' meeting, now,' he said. 'We'll have to go through the different responses to—'

He was interrupted again. This time it was a guard who entered. Ibris nodded to him impatiently.

'Two strangers, foreigners, have approached the west perimeter of the camp, sire,' the man said. 'They're asking to see you, sire, and they've a letter bearing your insignia and what seems to be Commander Feranc's signature, but I thought I'd better check before I brought them to you.'

'You did right, guard,' Ibris said. 'Tell me what they're like before you bring them here.'

The guard pursed his lips. 'Hard to say, sire,' he replied. 'They've been riding like the devil. But under the grime, there's fine clothes and fine horses . . . very fine horses.' He hesitated. 'They seem polite enough, but they've got . . . a way about them . . . a fighting man's way . . . a little like Commander Feranc. And, with respect,' he nodded to Ryllans. 'They sound like Mantynnai. But with very strong accents.'

Back in his quarters, Antyr dropped wearily on to his bed. 'Do you want anything?' Estaan asked.

Antyr shook his head as he closed his eyes. 'No,' he said, absently checking his sword. Then, opening his eyes, now black as night, he said, 'Thank you, Estaan. For our instruction and your patience.'

Estaan smiled a disclaimer. 'You were easier to teach than many I've had to deal with,' he said.

But Antyr did not hear the reply. A great wind had drawn him into another place.

Chapter 38

Amid the ghastly flickering and screaming chaos of the blind man's Dream Nexus, Ivaroth waited. Hitherto he had had to pause there for only the merest instant, scarcely a heartbeat, before the way would become apparent and his spirit, now bearing the blind man's Dreamself, would leap towards it.

He had never questioned the nature of this strange conjoining. It was just one more strange quality among the many that this profoundly strange old man possessed. And, in any event, he had found that little about the blind man responded to thoughtful analysis. It was sufficient for Ivaroth that it happened the way it did and that he was the blind man's only vehicle into the dreams of others, or the worlds beyond.

The only vehicle, that is, except for the man, if man it was, they had encountered on their last long rampage there.

Ivaroth had seen him advancing relentlessly, and he had quailed before the murderous savagery that had suddenly exploded from him as he had come within sword range. But the old man had seen something else. The way to the other place that he so lusted for.

It was a death sentence for someone.

Ivaroth would not be taken unawares again. Should he again carry the old man into the worlds beyond as widely as he had been wont to do, and should they again happen upon this stranger, then Ivaroth would strike him down on the instant. And the old man too, if necessary. Better dead than someone else's.

But these were thoughts now far from him as he waited at the Nexus. It was frantic and crazed beyond any he had ever found before; streaked through with countless alien images and desires, and awash with terrors. Terrors that flooded out of the long past dreams with the fearful uncontrollability of vomit.

And beneath all, relentless and ever-present, like the funereal bass note to some terrible dirge, was a dark and evil . . . memory? . . . presence? . . . will? . . . that made even Ivaroth blench.

The blind man's Dream Nexus was no place for a sane man. Yet he must remain there. Remain until a way became apparent. Or until . . .

Scarcely had the conjecture begun to form than he felt the old man's Dreamself with him; silent, watchful, expectant. Suspiciously, no sense of injury or illness lingered around it.

Then the way appeared and, motionless, he followed it. Followed it into the shimmering clouds of dream thoughts that pervaded the camp, and the land, and . . . everywhere.

All around him, amid the myriad tumbling thoughts of men and women and children, Ivaroth saw, felt, the ways into the worlds beyond, the gateways to the worlds of the Threshold.

Untutored, untrained, Ivaroth did not even know that in this land he would have been called a Dream Finder. Still less did he know that he was a natural Master of the art. One who could enter dreams, enter the Threshold worlds, without the aid of a Companion.

He knew, however, that the skills he had, had been increased manyfold since his contact, his unholy communion, with the blind man.

'You must tell me what happened if I'm to bring you back,' he said to the silent spirit beside him.

'Beyond your understanding, Mareth Hai. What you asked was too much for this frame in this world.'

'But you obeyed.'

'I obeyed.'

There was no reproach in the statement, nor rancour.

The old man was beaten!

Ivaroth could scarcely contain himself. But still, it would be a futile victory if the old man was lost to him. He had to be brought back.

'What are your needs?' he asked.

Silence.

Longing.

Ivaroth felt abruptly generous. Holding the old man's spirit, he moved into the Threshold.

He screwed up his eyes in the dazzling glare, and, his hand on his sword hilt, turned around quickly, taking in the entire scene. He relaxed almost immediately. They stood alone on the slopes of a snow-covered mountain. Above them a brilliant sun shone in a clear blue winter sky.

Behind the two tiny figures, great white mountains disdained their insignificance and peak upon peak reached out to both horizons, while in front of them lay an undulating plain, its whiteness broken only by the scar of an occasional rocky outcrop and scattered clusters of trees. High above them, mountain birds circled leisurely, following their own, unseen pathways.

The old man threw back his hood and raised his sightless eyes wide to the sky. He let out a long, ecstatic sigh, as his arms slowly spread out and his mouth opened into an expression of gaping fulfilment.

The long bony hands uncurled so slowly and painstakingly that it seemed they would go on for ever and ever. To Ivaroth, it was like watching the unfolding of some grotesque plant.

As he watched however, unease began to replace his habitual disgust. The old man's recovery seemed to be both total and very rapid. Instinctively, he glanced around again, warily looking for any other figures in the eye-straining whiteness, but still no one was to be seen.

Neither man moved for some time. Ivaroth, still and watchful, the blind man, arms extended, face stretched up to the sky.

Then he laughed. His sinister, gleeful, and nerve-tearing laugh.

Ivaroth smiled slightly. All was well.

The blind man brought his arms down and then briefly closed his eyes. The snow some way in front of him erupted in a great white cloud. Opening his eyes he stared, unseeing, at his handiwork. The fine snow settled slowly and gracefully, then it erupted again . . . and again . . . and again, as if the very presence of such harmony were an offence in itself.

Sustained by the old man's will, the snow rose higher and higher into the bright sky, twisting and turning, whirling and swooping, seemingly obedient to his least whim, though Ivaroth, as ever, could see no outward sign of how this power was manipulated.

Then, as the snow moved faster and faster, there came the sound of a great wind. Though no breeze struck the two watchers, it grew in intensity until, screaming and howling, it was like the worst of winter's bleak excesses marching to and fro along the mountainside at the behest of its creator. The blind man's laughter increased frenziedly to mingle with the din.

Ivaroth's unease returned.

'You're soon recovered,' he shouted.

539

The old man did not reply immediately, then, 'Yes, Ivaroth Ungwyl,' he said. Ivaroth's eyes narrowed dangerously. 'Mareth Hai,' the old man added, conciliatory.

'These worlds are nearer the heart of the power. It has weakened me to be so long from them, but now . . .'

He turned towards a nearby outcrop. As Ivaroth followed the sightless gaze, the air shimmered as it would over a fire, then there was an ear-splitting crack and a massive slab separated from the rock face. Slowly it tumbled down into the snow, fragmenting as it did so. Ivaroth staggered slightly as the thunderous noise of the collapse reached him, and the impact of the collapsing mass shook the ground.

In these worlds beyond, he had seen the old man create storms, rend trees, make the earth shake and buck like a tormented horse, even create monstrous likenesses of Ar-Hyrdyn to bind the minds of the Bethlarii priests. But he had never seen such a display of elemental power as this. Two things came to his mind simultaneously. The old man must die sooner rather than later. Whether he had always had such power and had only now decided to reveal it, or whether he had suddenly acquired it, did not matter. What mattered was that the possessor of such power in one world would not rest until he had found it in another, and with such power he would be beyond all control. The other thought, he spoke out loud . . .

'You could bring down the walls of a city with such power,' he cried excitedly.

The blind man, however, did not seem to be listening. He was staring into the streams of snow and rock still sliding and clattering down the mountainside.

'I shall be as him,' he said, though to himself. 'I shall be the earth shaker.' Then he paused and a look of realization spread across his face that made Ivaroth lay his hand on the hilt of the knife in his belt.

The old man turned to him, his face alight ecstatically. Ivaroth found himself fixed by the terrible sightless eyes. 'We must find the other place, now,' the blind man hissed his demand. 'If I can be as my mentor here, then in the other place *I shall be as his master*.'

He began rubbing his hands together and his voice fell to an awestricken whisper. 'Yes, yes. That is my destiny. It is fitting. My blinding, my wandering, but trials. All is clear. I am to displace *him*. I need only the key, and . . .'

Ivaroth quailed inwardly under the dreadful gaze. What did this creature see with those blank white eyes? What shadowy recesses of the soul did he peer into? And what terrible ambitions had now been struck alight in him?

Ivaroth did not dwell on the questions, however. Instead, he drew his knife. It was an unfamiliar weapon taken from the body of the man who had led the soldiers at Rendd, but Ivaroth adapted to weapons quickly and his move was so swift that the point was at the blind man's throat before he could finish his sentence.

'You forget yourself, old man,' Ivaroth said menacingly. 'The search for that place you seek will be *after* we have conquered our enemies in the real world. This was our agreement. There are enemies here as well as the way to this . . . other place . . . you're so desperate to find, and it would be folly to loiter here unprepared. I brought you here now only in the hope of curing whatever ill you'd done yourself. That done, we leave.'

Then his voice became persuasive, though the knife point did not move. 'The sooner our conquest is finished, the sooner I can bring you here to seek what you want at your leisure. Now you're recovered, and have found even greater power, you can smash the walls of Viernce and any other city that opposes us, and our progress will be all the quicker. None will be able to stand against us.'

The old man's manner changed as Ivaroth spoke. He lifted his hand pleadingly. 'I do not have this power in the world you call the real one, Ivaroth Ungwyl. It is my birth world.' He waved towards the scarred rock-face. 'Such a deed would rend me asunder. Only in the place beyond here will I find the heart of the power. Only there will I be able to reach out across the worlds and protect my body from such harm.'

Ivaroth wavered. The old man was lying, using him, that was obvious. What was not obvious was the extent of the lying. Keep it simple, he concluded, as he glanced at the damaged outcrop.

'One tenth of that will destroy a city wall,' he said. '*That* you can do. We return, now!'

Antyr screamed.

He was falling.

No. He was not moving. Yet he was being hurled along. Tumbling uncontrollably like a missile from some great siege

541

engine, yet tossed and buffeted like a broken twig in a winter storm.

All around him, scenes flickered and streaked by and through him incoherently; rolling sunlit countryside, bleak winter plains, great smoking mountains, monstrous storm-wracked seas, black clouds streaming across blood-red skies, huge tracts of barren, sand-strewn deserts. Countless strange and eerie landscapes.

But none there for more than the blink of an eye.

If they were there at all.

And he was in all of them. Forever.

And voices tore at him; beckoning, fearful, anxious, angry, demanding. A gibbering, meaningless cascade, full of burning urgency filled his ears, his mind, his whole body.

And amid it all, he felt great forces searching for him; battling for his soul . . . his skill?

They would tear him apart!

'*No!*'

At his cry, the din stopped. And had never been.

A powerful blast of cold air hit him and, abruptly, he was himself again, in a solid, real world. Gasping and sobbing with rage and fear, he dropped to his knees.

They sank into snow. He slumped forward and felt his ungloved hands sinking into the cold wetness. The chill jolted him into sharp awareness and, struggling to his feet, he gazed around in confusion. He was in a snowstorm!

The biting wind cut through his tunic and, in a bizarre reaction to his terrifying passage there, his first thoughts were ironic.

I practise with my sword, I carry it with me constantly for fear of enemies. Now I'm going to freeze to death for want of a coat.

The light, however, was oddly bright for a winter storm and, further disorienting him, the wind faded away suddenly leaving the airborne snowflakes to continue on their urgent paths for a little while, and then float gently down to earth.

Ivaroth turned, like an animal who, from some inner depth, had sensed the presence of a predator.

The blind man's storm had stopped, and the whirling, subsiding cloud of snow was alive with rainbow colours and strange dark shadows.

542

Then the shadows merged. And out of the greyness, a figure emerged.

Ivaroth felt a chill possess him, colder by far than that of the mountain snow around him.

'Ah!'

The figure halted as it heard the blind man's loathsome sigh of desire.

Then all about them, the sound of hunting wolves could be heard.

Ivaroth, warrior and assassin, reacted. He seized the blind man's arm and at the same time hurled his new-won knife at the motionless figure.

Antyr saw the whole movement as if it had been stretched through an infinity of time. Around him, he was aware of each and every snowflake with its own endless variety of points within points within points. And he was aware of his assailant and his companion. The one, short and powerful, his face like a bird of prey, was hurling the knife. Antyr felt his ruthless cruelty in his very posture, and quailed before it. But the other was worse by far. He seemed to have a presence beyond the immediate, like ominous, flickering shadows reaching back into unknowable and fearful planes of existence.

This was the Mynedarion!

White, sightless eyes sought him out. Visions of desire and power filled him. Wells of limitless ambition opened within him and gushed forth. All things could be his. Here was his guide.

'Reach out and seize your destiny, Dream Finder.' A myriad voices filled his head. 'Towns and cities and all their peoples will bow down before you at your least gaze . . .'

Sunlight caught the blade of the knife as it left Ivaroth's hand, and the bright light dimmed the vision. Antyr's gaze turned to his attacker. Night-black eyes possessed him.

And then he was the attacker; gripping his treacherous wilderness companion with confused and murderous hatred and launching the blade towards the heart of this apparition that the . . . creature . . . had drawn here, before returning to . . .

There was a fleeting vision of a huge camp. And horses . . . so many horses. And a great army . . . brought over the mountains. Cities taken. Battles fought. And a land to be conquered . . . and, deep, deep below, beyond the knowledge of the man, a chorus of whispering voices demanding . . . vengeance!

And he was himself again. Powerless to move as the circling blade arced relentlessly towards him. The Mynedarion began to reach out towards him, and his mouth opened to form a cry . . .

Antyr's mind urged his body, but it was too slow, too sluggish, too clouded . . .

Then there was clarity and simplicity. He was wolf. Traversing the strange world between and beyond the dreams and the Threshold, where the Companions waited and watched and hunted.

Untrained, unhindered reflexes possessed his body.

It twisted and swayed to one side and its hand reached out and seized the hilt of the passing blade with almost contemptuous ease.

With a great cry of rage, Ivaroth caught the blind man and the two fell back, fading and dwindling into nothingness.

Antyr stared at the place where they had stood, then at the knife in his hand.

'Where did you get that?'

The question was Estaan's.

Antyr swung up from his bed in confusion, stumbling over Tarrian and Grayle who were also struggling to their feet.

Tarrian was full of excitement. 'Those paws of yours are really awkward,' he said. 'And *are you slow*! You nearly got yourself killed, standing there like that.'

Antyr, however, could not speak. He gazed vacantly at the knife in his hand and then let it fall. Then he sat back on the bed and embraced the two wolves, silently and passionately.

Estaan, white-faced, bent down and picked up the knife. 'Where did you get this?' he asked again. 'It was in your hand, just as you woke up, but it wasn't there before.' His whole manner was alive with concern and confusion.

Antyr shook his head and raised a hand in a plea for a brief respite.

'It's an army knife,' Estaan went on, unable to restrain himself. 'A captain's . . .?'

'I must see the Duke, right away,' Antyr said, ignoring Estaan's agitation and standing up again. Estaan pushed the knife into his own belt and reached out to support Antyr.

There was some considerable activity in and around the Duke's tent when Antyr and Estaan arrived.

Uncharacteristically, Antyr pushed his way through the guards at the doorway and entered the tent without announcement. Estaan and the two wolves followed in his wake.

Ibris turned angrily towards the interruption. The look on Antyr's face however stifled the oath that his mouth was forming.

Antyr waited on no ceremony.

'A great army of horsemen,' he blurted out. 'From the mountains. I have seen the Mynedarion and his guide. I have *been* the guide. They've come to conquer the land. Take it for their own.'

His message delivered, Antyr felt strangely emptied, then words came to him unbidden.

'The Mynedarion is an abomination,' he said. 'He is in many places at once. His power is fearful, and his ambitions unfettered. He must be found and destroyed.'

He shivered and then, his mind clearing, he braced himself for a rebuke.

To his horror, however, the Duke's eyes widened in fear and, his own composure returning steadily, he became aware of the tension that pervaded the atmosphere of the now-silent tent.

'The trap closes,' he said softly, then, his fear becoming surprise, 'How . . .?'

Antyr shook his head. 'I was drawn there. By the Mynedarion. I think he has . . . need of me. His guide is a strange Dream Finder. For an instant I was him. I saw all these things. Then he tried to kill me.'

'He awoke with this in his hand,' Estaan interjected, stepping forward and proffering the knife to the Duke. 'It's standard issue. A captain's knife. It came from nowhere. Just appeared.'

Ibris looked at the Mantynnai and then at the knife. Then he put his hand to his head and sank back into his chair.

'No more!' Menedrion's powerful voice shattered the dreadful silence. 'I don't know what all this trickery's about, but we've got a real enemy only a day away and we're wasting precious time listening to this nonsense.'

'With respect, Lord, this is not nonsense, as, I suspect, you well realize.' The speaker was Haster. His face showed fatigue and his clothes were stained with the evidence of a frantic journey, but his voice was calm and quiet. Behind him stood Jadric.

Menedrion rounded on him furiously. 'Speak when you're spoken to, stranger,' he said savagely. 'It's bad enough that you sneak into our land, at the behest of some far distant king, to judge our finest warriors for some alleged crime committed years ago. Now you burst in here, ranting about an invasion from the north. By horsemen from over the mountains . . .'

He stopped abruptly with an angry gesture as he realized he was recounting Antyr's message.

Haster withstood the onslaught without showing any signs of emotion, holding Menedrion's gaze patiently.

'Our monarch is a Queen now, Lord,' he replied quietly. 'The King was slain. And we did not come to judge the Mantynnai, as you call them. We came to find them and to tell them that an accounting is required of them.' He turned to Ibris, still sitting with his head bowed. 'But now, far more urgent matters are to hand.' He pointed to Antyr. 'This man is of your land, I presume, and I've no idea how he's learned what he's learned. None could have travelled here from Viernce as fast as we did. But what he says accords with what the soldier told us. Weigh both of us as you see fit, then decide. But do it quickly.'

Menedrion started forward angrily at Haster's abrupt and authoritative conclusion.

'No, Irfan.' It was Ibris. Menedrion stopped, reluctantly, but maintained a relentless glare at Haster. The Duke looked up. His face was weary, but the tone of his voice was unequivocal. 'These men are guests and have ridden hard to bring this news. That, you can see for yourself. Now Antyr comes to tell us the same, unasked, and stricken himself in some way if you care to look at him.'

Menedrion did not reply, but looked suspiciously from Antyr to Haster.

'But there's more, isn't there?' Ibris said, returning to Haster. 'You can have learned little of us from your short stay here, and an unexpected army at our backs is of no concern to you as foreigners. Something the reservist said told you not only that he was telling the truth, but also that some greater danger threatens us all. Is that not so?'

Haster turned to Ryllans and then to Estaan and the other Mantynnai who were in the tent.

'Your answer is important,' Ibris said. 'Weigh it well.'

Haster nodded slowly. 'Yes, I understand,' he said. 'You're correct. The danger that threatens you is the power that ravaged our own land and carried us into war many years ago.'

Ibris looked at him narrowly. 'Is there fear in your voice, Haster?' he asked.

'There's fear to my very heart, Duke,' Haster replied. 'But it doesn't cloud my vision. What is, is, and must be faced as such, however much I'd rather sit by my hearth and have everything otherwise. I am heartsick and weary of fighting and travelling.'

Ibris glanced at Ryllans. 'I've been told a little of this before, but I'd been told too that your army had destroyed the source of this power.'

'Our army destroyed only its army of men,' Haster replied. 'The wielder of the power was destroyed by others who came to our aid.'

'How then is he alive again, and come here?' Ibris asked, his voice hardening.

'He isn't,' Haster replied. 'But there were not only followers who fled at the end. There were disciples too. Few, but skilled to some degree in the ways of their Master, and, doubtless, vengeful, after his destruction.'

'And we have one such here, now?' Ibris asked.

'An old man, lean and cadaverous, blind, his eyes white,' Antyr said before Haster could reply.

Jadric caught Haster's arm and there was a short exchange between the two men.

Haster nodded. 'That one, I fear, we know of,' he said, a brief flash of pain and distress suffusing his face.

Ibris glanced from Antyr to Haster. 'Can we face this power?' he asked.

Haster did not answer immediately. 'I don't know,' he said eventually, shaking his head. 'From the mere hands of this blind man's master, it tore apart one of our greatest cities. Though afterwards, he was strangely bound.'

There was a murmur of disbelief from the listeners, but Ibris silenced it with a flick of his hand. The memory of this same tale being told to him by Ryllans, high up on one of the palace towers, echoed through his mind like a waking nightmare.

547

Haster seemed a little surprised at Ibris's immediate acceptance of this statement and he paused until Ibris motioned him to continue.

He looked intently at Antyr. 'We found that other forces beyond our understanding had awakened at the same time as the evil. In the end though we had to face the armed might as best we could, others faced the power. Perhaps it will be so here also.'

Imperceptibly, his tone had lightened a little, as if his own thoughts were just clearing and a faint hope had glimmered briefly. He looked again at Antyr.

'You may well be right,' Ibris said. 'For the first time since Grygyr Ast-Darvad appeared, I feel an order, a pattern, emerging, albeit malign.' He fell silent for a moment, his face anxious. 'But it's little consolation. With what others have told me and with Antyr's tale, I must accept your story of these invaders from the north. But that being so, our position is truly grim. We're caught between two armies. One is just ahead, and known to be ferocious, while the other is already ravaging our land and is both many days away and completely unknown to us. And above the whole a sinister will hovers, wielding a power we can't begin to understand.' He looked at Haster and Jadric. 'Will you help us further?' he asked simply.

Haster nodded. 'We have no choice, Lord,' he replied. 'But we're only two swords to add to your many. We know little or nothing of your army, its organization, its arms and fighting methods, and still less do we know anything about your land . . . its roads, passes, terrain—'

Ibris waved the reservations aside. 'You have knowledge of this power,' he said.

'Only to recognize it,' Haster interjected quickly. 'Not of how to oppose it. That task will lie with your man here.' He pointed to Antyr, who started violently.

Ibris nodded. 'I know,' he said. 'He's no great warrior by our normal measure, but he's stronger and more gifted than he knows.'

Antyr spluttered. 'Sire, I can't—'

Ibris cut him short. 'You've less choice than any of us, Antyr,' he said. 'You've been lifted . . . snatched . . . from obscurity and decadence, against your will and your inclination, to find yourself among my closest advisers. Your skills have increased beyond your imaginings in a matter of only weeks. Twice now, perhaps three times, you've been drawn into the Threshold to face this . . . Mynedarion. Whether you like it or not, you'll be drawn to him again to . . . Get him a chair someone.'

Antyr had turned white, and was swaying uncertainly. The Duke's sudden command seemed to steady him a little. 'No, no, I'm all right. I can stand,' he said, suddenly embarrassed by his public display of weakness.

Ibris stared at him intently, his look both fatherly and full of the icy calculation of a commanding officer committing his troops. 'I told you before, Antyr, that whatever happens to you, you'll be protected here completely. And whatever happens to you . . .' He raised a finger vaguely. '. . . there, don't forget, you've met him before, and survived. And he's at odds with his guide. You're facing a divided enemy, Dream Finder. Remember. That's important.'

Embarrassment or no, Antyr closed his eyes and began breathing deeply to quieten his quaking insides. He wanted to run away, to be sick, to shout and scream, to be back in his old wasted ways, to be anywhere other than here, to be anything other than what he was; the sole hope of the Serens against this unseen, insane, and malevolent foe; the single tiny pivot bearing so crucially such a crushing burden.

Into his darkness, however, other thoughts rose to sustain him, albeit faintly.

Don't break. Hold your ground, hold your ground. Or die.

He *had* survived. He hadn't been casually swept aside by this unholy power. And, indeed, as Ibris had cruelly summarized, *he had no choice*. He could not knowingly enter the Threshold, but the Mynedarion could seemingly draw him there at will.

He felt Tarrian and Grayle leaning against his legs slightly, as if for comfort. The wolves' fears reached out to mingle with his own. In turn he reached out to be with his two Companions. Ironically, their fear reassured him; it gave him a measure of the rightness of his own emotions. Both the animals were pack leaders by nature. But they were thus *only* because they were not afraid of their fear, and faced danger wholeheartedly when need arose. Indeed it was necessity, and necessity only, that was the driving force of their terrible ferocity and courage.

And, threading through their fear, Antyr felt that necessity asserting itself. From their own inner well-springs the two wolves had drawn Ibris's conclusion before he had spoken it to Antyr. They were trapped, cornered. Now they must hold their ground. Fight or die.

Antyr became angry. *And he had started* none *of this!*

He opened his eyes and met the Duke's gaze forcefully.

'Make what dispositions you must to face this new enemy, Ibris,' he said. 'Tonight, to aid you, Pandra and I and our Companions will assail the Bethlarii as best we can.

'Then I shall turn about and hunt those who so far have seen fit to hunt *me*.'

Chapter 39

There was stunned silence in the tent as, with a stiff, almost military bow, and without seeking the Duke's permission, Antyr turned and left.

Estaan hesitated for a moment uncertainly before following him.

Then uproar broke out. Menedrion strode forward to confront his father.

'Who the devil does he think—?'

Ibris laid a gentle hand on his shoulder, at once restraining and reassuring. With the rest of the gathering he was more abrupt.

'Silence!'

His voice rose above the noise and descended on it like a great bird of prey, extinguishing it completely.

'The man goes to fight alone against an enemy about whom he knows *nothing* except that he possesses a terrible power. He bears a greater burden than any of us, but he's Serens, perhaps even Mantynnai now, he'll do what he must and what he can though it destroy him. We can do no less. The lapse of a few niceties of protocol are forgivable.'

He beckoned Arwain forward and placed his other hand on his shoulder.

'We here have to help him by concerning ourselves with the enemies *we* can see. With the strategy and tactics we're going to need to deal with two enemies instead of one.' He glanced round at his listeners, his look and voice designed to stamp out their alarm and replace it with stern purpose.

'We don't know where this force of northerners is, save that it's somewhere between Rendd and Viernce. We may assume that if its leader – a Dream Finder, I'd remind you – is at this moment tending the needs of his . . . client . . . then the force is presumably camped.'

Arwain made to speak, but Ibris, still holding his shoulder, shook him silent gently, and continued.

'That situation may, and probably will, change rapidly now

that there's been this encounter with Antyr, but still we have a little time, and we must use it to the full.'

He released his two sons and walked across to a table littered with maps and charts.

'Obviously we can't move a large infantry force so far across country either quickly enough or without giving the day here to the Bethlarii. Equally obviously, we can't allow this force to fall on Viernce.'

Arwain's question escaped. 'Surely they'll not attack a walled city with just cavalry?' he said.

Ibris nodded pensively. 'One would imagine not,' he said. 'But from what little I know about the plains' people, there are many tribes, and they spend much of their time quarrelling among themselves. It's fair to assume, therefore, that if a leader has arisen capable of uniting these tribes *and* bringing a large cavalry force over the mountains, then he's a man not to be underestimated. My immediate feeling is that such a man will use stealth and cunning where he can. Good tactics against a walled city. But he may have siege engines and skilled sappers for all we know.'

He tapped a chart absently with his finger, his face grave. 'Besides, perhaps walls are no hindrance to this . . . Mynedarion . . . and his strange power.'

Menedrion frowned and, stepping close to Ibris, half whispered the thought that no one else dared to voice. 'You don't believe this nonsense about him being able to destroy a city with his bare hands?'

'I can do no other,' Ibris answered starkly but equally softly. 'Twice I've heard it and the first time was from a witness whose word was beyond dispute.'

Menedrion stared into his father's face, for an instant his eyes were those of a frightened eight year old. Ibris nodded in understanding. 'One step at a time, Irfan,' he said, taking his son's arm in a purposeful grip. 'I don't know what game is being played here, or by whom, but I know that your part is to smash the Bethlarii army. I know also that you're the only one who can do it.'

Menedrion's face hardened again as the grim leader within him gradually began to reassert itself. He stepped back with a curt bow of acknowledgement and Ibris continued.

'However, their intended tactics at Viernce are of little relevance. What *we* must do is stop them reaching the city.'

He raised his hand to forestall the inevitable questions.

'Accordingly, tomorrow, or as soon as is possible, the army, under Menedrion, will march at full speed against the Bethlarii and engage them immediately with a view to winning as rapid a victory as possible.'

The announcement swept away the uncertainties cloying the atmosphere.

Ibris ploughed on. 'And, tonight, leaving as soon as they're ready, my personal bodyguard will ride across country to oppose this new enemy. They'll be under the command of Arwain, and accompanied by Haster and Jadric if they're willing.'

There were murmurs of concern.

'To move so fast, such a force could carry little in the way of weapons, what use would they be against a large cavalry force?'

'Your bodyguard is the heart of our army.'

'Gentlemen,' Ibris said sternly, before the debate gathered momentum. 'The bodyguard will take their bows and as many arrows as they can carry. That's the only practical defence against both cavalry and infantry. They'll seek out the enemy and hold him for as long as they can. At the same time messengers will be sent to Viernce, Drew, Stor and Serenstad to warn them to levy all remaining reservists to go to their aid.'

'That's damn near the women and children,' someone muttered, but Ibris ignored this remark.

'As for the Bethlarii, they're obviously preparing for a set-piece battle. They've not harassed us or our supply lines, tried to sway our weaker allies by either force or argument, launched diversionary assaults elsewhere along the border.' His voice became bitter. 'Their actions still make little sense, but I imagine they're looking for one huge, and *final*, encounter. Something that will be looked on with favour by Ar-Hyrdyn.' He paused for a moment to let his anger subside. 'Such a battle, *as you know*, will be won by the most disciplined side, and my bodyguard could add little to what we already possess. On the other hand, *no one* other than they could move overland and oppose these new invaders with any semblance of a chance of holding them until larger forces can be raised.'

There was silence when he had finished speaking. Whatever reservations any of his advisers might have had about his decision, they were insufficient to overcome the combination of his analysis and his will.

Pandra listened to Antyr's tale with increasing distress.

'What can *I* do?' he asked when it was finished.

Antyr pulled his chair closer to the old man and leaned forward urgently. 'Just help me tonight, Pandra,' he replied. 'We have to set aside everything we've ever held precious about our craft. We have to go into the Bethlarii dreams and tell them the truth about how they've been misled.'

Pandra shook his head anxiously. '*We're* not Mynedarion, Antyr,' he said. 'We can't change what they're dreaming. We—'

'We can enter their dreams, and speak to them,' Antyr interrupted. 'Nothing more.'

'Speaking to a dreamer to reassure him when he's asked you to be there is one thing. Blazing in like some sweating messenger is another,' Pandra rejoined. 'Anyway, they'll probably just wake up.'

'Maybe,' Antyr agreed. 'But we must do it nonetheless. I promised Ibris I'd do something before I went hunting for the cause of all this . . . horror.'

'Before *what*?' Pandra exclaimed, half standing.

Antyr repeated his intention awkwardly.

'High time too!' The voice was Kany's.

'Shut up,' Pandra said sharply, slapping his pocket.

'And how do you propose to hunt this . . . creature?' he went on, returning to Antyr.

Antyr reached out and placed a hand on Pandra's arm. 'I don't know,' he answered. 'But somewhere there's a way to him other than being drawn in by him. And I must find it. My every nerve feels alive and raw with expectation. It's as if the whole dreamscape around us is crying out under some assault. Since I saw that abomination so close, so clear, I've felt a terrible presentiment. I feel powers gathering like those that must have shaped the world itself.'

Pandra's face creased into unhappiness. 'You're imagining things,' he said, without conviction. 'You're just tired and frightened. After all—'

Antyr shook his head. 'No,' he said simply. 'I'm frightened, certainly. But I'm imagining nothing. My mind's clear and sharp. Bars are being forged that will cage us all, or beat us into nothingness, and only I can do anything about it.'

Pandra fell silent.

'What am I to say?' he asked after a moment.

Antyr shrugged. 'I don't think there's anything you *can* say,' he replied. 'Just help me tonight, and then keep watch as you've done every other night.'

Pandra allowed himself a small sigh of resignation. 'Very well,' he said. 'But I'm not even sure I can reach the Bethlarii from so far away.'

'You will.' It was Tarrian who answered his doubts. 'Your skill has grown from its closeness to Antyr. As has Kany's, and ours. His very presence clears the ways, strips away our blindness and confusion, opens up vistas . . .'

An impatient snarl interrupted his eulogy. 'Never mind the poetry, dog. Let's get on with it. Let's get our teeth into those Bethlarii behinds and give them a good shaking.'

'Ah. Ever the sensitive observer of our condition, Kany,' Pandra said as Tarrian's ears went back before this onslaught.

Quite suddenly, his eyes filled with night and he looked at Antyr. 'At your pleasure,' he said.

Estaan watched the two men, Pandra lying motionless on a rough camp-bed, Antyr seated on a chair beside him. Pandra, eyes closed, was apparently asleep, but Antyr's eyes were wide open, as if he were both present in the tent and flitting through the night ways at the same time. He was an oddly fearful sight.

Worse, however, were Tarrian and Grayle. Their eyes too were wide and watching, their bright sun-blazing glare seeming to penetrate into his very soul. Wherever else they might be, they were unequivocally here as well and profoundly dangerous. After a while, he turned away.

The dreamscape around and through the Bethlarii camp was like a great shimmering mirage; a glittering, iridescent cloud of shifting colours and images that were there and not there; silent sounds that rang and clamoured, incoherent yet full of meaning; time that was and that will be, and that never could have been . . .

Pandra breathed a long, low sigh of wonder at this vision.

'Now.' Antyr's will formed silently within him.

Throughout the night, sleeping Bethlarii snapped sharply into wakefulness, their dreams untypically fresh and vivid in their minds, and words, *sacrilegious words*, ringing in their ears.

'You have been deceived by false prophets. The horsemen

from the north ravage your land while you dally here, facing an enemy here only at your provocation. Abandon this field, tend to your true needs.'

Endryn waited outside Ivaroth's tent. In front of him the vast camp was almost invisible in the darkness. A few fires burned here and there and an occasional torch flickered as someone moved about between the rough lines of tents, but there was nothing that indicated the true size of the force waiting there.

Endryn, however, had little thought for such images. Fiercely he seized one hand with the other in an attempt to stop them both from trembling. He was glad of the enveloping darkness; he had little doubt that fear was written all over him.

There was silence in the tent at his back now, but nothing could have persuaded him to look into it to see the outcome of the turmoil that had erupted so terrifyingly.

In a time less than the blinking of an eye, a great blast of bitterly cold air had filled the tent, and two motionless figures had sprung screaming to life; Ivaroth's black eyes like pits of doom in his vengeful face, and the old man's sightless orbs ablaze with hatred and anger.

The old man's hands were reaching clawlike towards Ivaroth, while the Mareth Hai was drawing a knife from his belt, as Endryn retreated, full of superstitious terror.

Inside the tent, however, the pandemonium had fallen to the merest whisper, and Ivaroth was resealing his bargain with his erstwhile wilderness companion.

His murderous reflexes had brought his knife blade to the old man's throat at almost the instant of return.

'Your need for me is greater than mine for you, old man,' he said. 'If need arises my army can conquer this land without you now, while you will never find your special world without me.'

The blind man had not replied. It was not necessary. Regardless of the truth of Ivaroth's words, both knew also that, act of folly or no, Ivaroth *would* kill now, on the least whim, regardless of regrets later. The blind man became very still.

'Seek to deceive me like that again, and you'll die before your next heartbeat, old man,' Ivaroth said. 'Seek to disobey me, and you'll die no less quickly. Obey me, and, despite

556

your treachery, I'll still take you to look for this place you cherish so.'

'But the true power lies there, Ivaroth Ungwyl. With it, we can conquer worlds beyond your—'

Ivaroth bared his teeth. 'The true power lies *here*, old man,' he said softly, pressing the point of his knife into the blind man's throat. 'Tomorrow, we'll hold a brief ceremony, to celebrate your recovery,' he went on. 'Then we march to Viernce. I'll look to take it by stealth at night if possible, but if not, your . . . special skill . . . will be used to destroy its walls. If it takes a toll of you, I'll see you're properly tended, have no fear.'

Slowly, he removed the knife from the old man's throat. Then, casually, he tossed it into the air. Flickering in the lamplight, it reached its zenith and began twisting downwards. Abruptly, Ivaroth seized it and brought it plunging down towards the old man. It tore through the soiled blankets and embedded itself in the planks below, its edge just touching the old man's throat.

It was a brief but terrifying display of his natural prowess and speed with such weapons.

Without speaking, he yanked the knife free, and walked out of the tent.

Endryn started at the sound behind him.

'He's quite recovered,' Ivaroth said, almost affably. 'All is well. Tomorrow we begin preparations for the taking of Viernce. The men have rested enough.'

Again, Endryn was glad of the darkness to hide the riot of conflicting emotions on his face. Contradictory though it was, not least among the prayers he had uttered into the night was that Ivaroth would have slain this . . . demon . . . that had battened on to him.

'As you command, Mareth Hai,' he replied briskly.

Ivaroth turned to return to the tent, then paused.

'There are people in this land who ply a trade known as Dream Finding, Endryn,' he said thoughtfully. 'Send to Rendd and our other cities. Anyone practising this peculiar skill is to be executed immediately. See to it now.'

Estaan raised a cautionary hand to the messenger who had entered Pandra's tent.

'Stay where you are, and make no sudden movements,' he said.

The messenger needed no prompting, having seen the two yellow-eyed wolves immediately on entering the tent. He bent forward and whispered in Estaan's ear.

Estaan frowned slightly, and, thanking the messenger, cast a glance at Antyr.

'What's the matter?' Antyr asked, his voice, distant but clear, echoing in Estaan's head.

The Mantynnai drew in a sharp breath. 'I thought you were . . . asleep,' he said, out loud.

Antyr chuckled. 'I'm in other people's sleep,' he said. 'But I can see your concern. What was the message?'

Estaan hesitated for a moment. 'Arwain and the bodyguard are preparing to leave for Viernce,' he said. 'I—'

'Should be with them.' Antyr finished his sentence for him. Estaan looked pained. 'Yes . . . No . . . I—'

'I'll come with you,' Antyr said. 'Give me a moment.'

Inside the dream thoughts of the Bethlarii, Antyr watched the startled Estaan, and at the same time touched Pandra, diligently pursuing his task.

'I must leave you, Pandra, Kany,' he said. 'I'm needed elsewhere. Keep on with this task for as long as you can. The truth must lighten their darkness eventually. Thank you for your help and friendship.'

Pandra's anxiety washed over him, but only the words, 'Take care,' formed.

Kany's farewell was more robust. 'Scent him out, bring him down, hunters three,' he said powerfully.

'*You* can't go,' Ibris said, his face flushed with the effort of pushing his way through the bustling activity of his bodyguard as it prepared to leave.

Antyr finished tightening his horse's cinch then turned to the Duke. 'Estaan said that, Arwain said it, everyone I've met so far has said it.' He nodded towards Haster and Jadric who were standing nearby and watching the exchange. 'Even those two are thinking it, though they're too polite to say anything. I'd be obliged, sire, if you'd tell everyone that I'm going with the bodyguard to Viernce and I'd value their help instead of their opposition.' His voice was strident.

'Steady,' Tarrian whispered to him.

Ibris met Antyr's black-eyed gaze squarely, torn between anger, respect and concern. He waved a hand at the gathering group of men.

'These are hard, highly trained men,' he said. '*Young* men for the most part. My best. They'll be riding like the devil and fighting a dreadful battle against who knows what odds at the end of it. They won't be able to nurse you along the way or protect you when you reach the enemy. If the journey doesn't kill you, the—'

'*He* is there,' Antyr said, resolutely interrupting his lord. 'I've no relish for this but I have to find him before he comes for me again.' He looked down for a moment. 'And it may be that I'm the only one who can protect your men, Serenstad's men, from his power. And, at worst, while he has to deal with me, he can't deal with *them*.'

Ibris wavered.

'They can tie me to my horse if I look like falling off,' Antyr pressed.

'And the wolves?' Ibris asked. 'They can't run all that way.'

'Throw them in panniers,' Antyr replied shortly.

'What!' Tarrian's indignation was considerable.

'Throw them in panniers,' Antyr repeated firmly. 'They can sleep. They'll need to be fresh when the hunt starts.'

Tarrian's indignation faded slightly.

Haster walked across to them. 'If it's your wish that he goes, lord, we'll tend him,' he said. 'He can ride between us, he'll be no burden.'

'But you must be exhausted yourselves,' Ibris protested.

Unexpectedly, Haster smiled. 'We're tired certainly, but we've finer horses than yours, lord,' he said. 'And we've learned the art of sleeping as we ride.'

Ibris grimaced and then gave a resigned shrug. 'As you wish, Dream Finder. You must go where your heart leads you. Take care. And my thanks to you.'

A little later, Antyr found himself mounted between the two strangers, with Tarrian and Grayle ensconced in panniers. Tarrian had protested more than a little at the indignity of being lifted into his, but was now almost asleep. Grayle was as silent and deep as ever.

Antyr watched Ibris and then Menedrion embracing Arwain, then, almost before he realized what was happening, Arwain had swung up into his saddle and, with a stomach-turning lurch, his horse surged forward into the night.

Chapter 40

The day was full of winter brightness. A cloudless blue sky, brilliant sun, and a windless cold.

It was a day for brisk walking through ragged, leafless country lanes or along hilly ridges or across manicured parks. A day for warm reassuring clothes and a warm fireside and warm company to return to.

It was a day especially apt for celebrating life, but, albeit reluctantly, Ibris's army had risen to a misty dawn, to celebrate death. It had risen shivering with the cold and the fear: the fear of impending battle, the fear of showing fear, the fear of failing in command, the fear of edges and points, of missiles and flailing hooves, of looking into the face of the unthinking, fear-spawned, *personal* hatred of the enemy and, worst of all, of random, cruel chance.

Quickly the army had drawn noise and bustling activity over its nakedness like a familiar blanket.

And now it moved across the rolling Bethlarii landscape in battle formation; the sun glinting off spear points and armour, shields and harness, and brightening the surcoats and the pennants and flags emblazoned with their many devices.

The air was filled with the soft clatter of marching and riding men, punctuated occasionally by shouted orders to maintain the line, and made purposeful by the ominous tattoo of the pace drums. A dark-green trail marked the passing of the host as the dew-damped grass was relentlessly crushed under hoof and foot.

Visibility being good, and being some way from the Bethlarii position, Ibris and Menedrion rode at the front of the line with several other senior officers and aides. No one spoke.

A small group of riders appeared in the distance. Ibris motioned a signaller to halt the advance.

The pace drums stopped with startling suddenness and for a moment it seemed to Ibris that the ensuing silence was absolute.

561

As the riders drew nearer, the noise of the thousands of now waiting men began to assert itself.

'It's Feranc's patrol,' Menedrion said.

Ibris nodded and clicked his horse forward, motioning Menedrion to follow him.

As Feranc's men reached them, Ibris sent the men back to the waiting officers to make their reports. Even as he did so, he saw Feranc's eyes flicking along the length of the waiting army.

'Your bodyguard, the Mantynnai, Arwain?' he asked as Ibris turned back to him.

Ibris told him what had happened the previous night. After he had heard the tale, Feranc lowered his head. Ibris waited for his reaction, concerned.

'The Dream Finder has gone with them?' Feranc said, after a long pause.

Ibris nodded awkwardly, somewhat taken aback at this unexpected response.

Feranc grimaced in sympathy. 'It'll be a bad journey for him,' he said. 'A dark grim night he'll not forget.'

'You'd rather you were with them?' Ibris said, cutting across this digression and anxiously voicing what he felt would be Feranc's unspoken reproach.

Feranc looked up at the blue sky, thoughtfully. 'Your reasoning was sound, lord,' he said eventually. 'And it was a decision only you could make.'

The two men looked at one another.

'Thank you,' Ibris said softly.

'Talking of difficult decisions . . .' Menedrion broke the silence and gave Feranc a significant look. 'As commander I've decided that you, father, will take command of the reserve cavalry . . .'

Ibris turned to him, his face darkening.

'You're too old for the front line,' Menedrion said hastily, and more bluntly than he had intended.

'I can ride and fight you into the ground yet,' Ibris blustered noisily.

'Not these last ten years, you can't,' Menedrion retaliated vehemently, leaning forward towards his father, chin jutting.

Feranc coughed.

Ibris turned to him. 'Ciarll?' he appealed.

'Commander's decision,' Feranc replied simply.

'Ciarll!'

'Please, father. Your will has brought us this far. You're the heart of all our dominions. If you fall today, then . . .' He flicked his head towards the waiting army. 'They'll evaporate, disappear. We'll *all* be lost. And city after city will fall in our wake.'

Ibris looked at his son narrowly. 'Think you can out-talk me as well, do you?' he said darkly.

Menedrion scowled impatiently. 'No, damn it,' he said. 'I'm trying to tell you what you already know. I want all eyes forward. I don't want anyone risking themselves and their companions playing unofficial bodyguard to you.' His expression became embarrassed. 'Besides I've told all the company commanders you'll be protecting the rear, and that's what they've told the men. Everyone's happy with that. It'll not help their morale if they see you at the front. They'll think it's because Arwain and the others leaving has seriously weakened us.'

Ibris's eyes narrowed further and his mouth tightened.

'Yes, I know,' he said abruptly.

Menedrion started at the unexpected reply.

'Do you think I don't know what's going on in my own army?' Ibris continued, not without some relish. 'I was just wondering when you were going to get round to telling me about it, that's all.'

Menedrion looked as if he were considering a wide range of replies to this revelation, but in the end, without taking his gaze from his father, he spoke to Feranc.

'Tell us the enemy's latest dispositions, Commander,' he said.

Feranc replied without preamble. 'Substantially unchanged from earlier reports. The traditional Bethlarii battle order. Predominantly heavy infantry in phalanx, with cavalry and light infantry protecting the flanks and rear. At least twice our number in all.'

'Anything unusual in the line?' Ibris asked. 'Chariots? Artillery? Cover for ambushing cavalry? Treacherous ground?'

Feranc shook his head. 'Nothing,' he replied. 'Nor anything to be seen in the surrounding countryside. Though there seemed to be quite a lot of activity along the line. Messengers running to and fro.'

Menedrion shrugged slightly. 'Probably last-minute

563

preparations,' he suggested. 'They know we'll be on them before noon.'

He looked at Feranc and then his father. 'I can see no reason to alter any of the tactics we've decided on. Can you?'

Ibris looked at him quizzically. 'Why the uncertainty?' he asked.

Menedrion frowned. 'I'm uncertain because I still can't believe they're doing this,' he said reluctantly. 'Throughout this whole campaign they've shown none of the war-craft that we know they have. Even now, at the end, they've made no special effort to choose advantageous ground, there's no evidence of flanking forces in the area, nothing that seems to indicate a will to conquer. *It makes no sense.*'

Ibris could offer him no clearer vision.

Feranc spoke. 'They're preparing to fight the battle of the end of the world,' he said. 'The final battle in which all other conflicts will be resolved and from which Ar-Hyrdyn will choose those destined to join the great heroes of legend who occupy his Golden Hall.'

Menedrion puffed out a long steaming breath into the cold air. 'It's as logical as anything else I've heard,' he said resignedly. 'But where does that leave us earth-bound souls?'

'Facing an enemy that's liable to fight to the death, rather than break and run,' Feranc replied starkly.

Menedrion's lip curled. 'You can't suppress the flesh, Ciarll,' he said. 'Fear is fear. We'll see how their faith sustains them when our arrows are falling about them.'

Feranc nodded. 'True,' he said. 'But we mustn't underestimate them. This day is going to be long, hard, bitter and bloody.'

'Yes,' Ibris agreed, his voice sad. 'And it *will* be the end of their world. Whatever corruption in their society has brought them to this, all will indeed be resolved today.'

Menedrion cut the discussion short. 'It's still *their* choice, father,' he said. 'Don't forget the heralds they killed. If their . . . sickness . . . can't be swayed away with reason and logic, then we must do it the physician's way. We must lance it. And quickly, if there's another enemy at our back.'

He reached up and pulled down the visor of his helm, then held out his mailed hands to Feranc who took them in both his own.

'Strength to your arm, Feranc the shield, Feranc the slayer. Here's to tomorrow's sunrise.'

'Light be with you, Irfan Menedrion,' Feranc replied, then, taking the Duke's hands, 'And with you, my lord. Guard our backs well. And put me to the sword if I flee.'

Finally, Menedrion embraced his father in silence.

Then the three parted to ride to their allotted positions.

As he rode back towards the army, Menedrion drew his sword and waved it high above his head with a great shout. His cry echoed over the Bethlarii plain and into the bright sky and the cry of the entire army rose to follow it.

They had stopped. But the world was still filled with pain. He had never known anything but pain, nor ever would for all eternity to come.

No part of Antyr's body gave him any other message. Who would have thought that the human frame could travel so fast for so long, or that men could remain in the saddle throughout?

He had vague recollections of an occasional voice penetrating the haze of agony with the advice that he should, 'Just relax, don't fight the horse.' Then, more sternly. 'Relax, you're *tiring* the horse.' He had recollections too, that there had been other brief pauses punctuating this lifetime of pounding impact he had been living, though, as now, they had offered little comfort.

Even the dawn had brought no relief. Indeed the bright golden wash that had splashed into his face seemed to pass straight through him and illuminate his pain, so frail had he become.

He had *no* recollection of the strong hands that had reached out and supported him as he slithered into the unconsciousness from which he was now emerging.

'You've done well,' an echoing voice was telling him from far away.

Mysteriously he floated out of his saddle and propped himself up against something . . . a tree, he realized, as he managed to look up through the intricate tracery of winter-bared branches.

Something damp and cold touched his face and sniffed inquiringly, then there was a vigorous splashing sound nearby.

'That's better.'

Antyr winced as Tarrian's relieved voice boomed into his head like a cascade of tumbling boulders. 'That wasn't too bad a journey after all, was it? Slept most of the way. If you

565

ever get a horse I think I'll travel more like that. It's very comfortable. And quite stylish in its way.'

Antyr felt stirrings of malevolence deep inside, but it was beyond him to formulate it into purposeful abuse and he let it lie.

'Are you awake?' Tarrian said with deplorable heartiness, his paw poking Antyr with reckless disregard. Antyr stared at the hands that came up in front of him to deflect this unwanted attention. After a timeless interval he recognized them as his own. At the same time, his voice began to return.

'No, I don't think so,' he replied. 'At least I sincerely hope not.'

Slowly the pains wracking his body began to fragment and take up residence in various limbs and joints, and the memory of the purpose of this journey returned. It stood like a dark, evil forest, barring his way to the future.

He felt sick.

What madness had prompted him to join this demented dash across country to face some unknown enemy? What madness had drawn him into this whole business? He felt an overwhelming nostalgia for the familiar sounds and smells of his favourite inns, and the familiar, torchlit streets he had staggered along so often.

He put his hand to his head in imitation of the gesture he had made many times through his life on waking and finding himself regretfully reviewing his recent follies.

'Are you all right?' someone asked.

Carefully, Antyr turned a protesting neck to see who had spoken. It was Estaan. He looked desperately weary. Under other circumstances Antyr might have replied with some mildly acid rejoinder, but he too was too weary to find solace in humour.

'Come on,' Estaan said, bending down and unceremoniously hauling him to his feet. 'You can take some pride in having survived this journey. We lost a few on the way.'

'Lost . . .?' Antyr asked vaguely.

'Just exhausted,' Estaan replied. 'No fatalities fortunately. Come on, you'll feel better if you keep moving.'

Antyr's legs were reluctant to respond and he tried to slither back down on to the ground. Estaan held him upright however and then dragged him forward roughly, leaving him no alternative but to walk or fall.

Antyr uttered a feeble cry of protest and pain and there was a faint growl from Tarrian.

'Never mind growling at me, wolf,' Estaan said brutally. 'Get into his head and wake him up properly. If he falls, he's finished.'

Another face swam into Antyr's view before Tarrian could respond. It was Haster. He peered intently into Antyr's face for a moment and then he was gone. Abruptly, powerful hands from behind him began seeking out stiffened joints and muscles and manipulating them purposefully.

Antyr cried out again, though more loudly this time, but Tarrian did not interfere.

'It's for the best,' he said awkwardly into Antyr's slowly clearing head. Then he was gone, and Grayle with him.

Then Haster was peering into his eyes again and driving thumbs into his shoulders. 'I'm no expert at this,' he said. 'But that should help.' He repeated Estaan's advice. 'Keep moving.' Adding, 'Stand up straight as well.' Then he too was gone.

A memory of Tarrian uttering the same rebuke when he had first met Ibris returned to Antyr and, as then, he found himself obeying without conscious thought. It helped; a little.

Tentatively, he began to test out his protesting limbs and to look beyond himself. All about him were weary-looking men, most of whom, he noted, were also trying to ease life back into stiffened limbs. The sight of this common discomfort made him feel a little ashamed of his complaining.

To a man they were grimy with travel, and their bedraggled condition was heightened by the brilliant sunshine that flooded over the scene. Steaming breaths, however, confirmed the temperature that he himself was just beginning to be aware of.

Looking around he saw that they had stopped at what appeared to be a deserted farmhouse. Beyond it lay bleak rocky countryside which gave testimony as to why it had been deserted. A little way away a rough road wound down a shallow incline between two small hills and dipped straight down into a river. A ford, Antyr presumed.

In the distance, dark clouds were building.

Antyr took a long draught from his canteen. It was cold and it seemed to etch out his insides, almost painfully, as he swallowed. He drew in a sharp breath. The jolt helped to clear his mind further and the darkness looming ahead of him came into sharper focus. So too did his own position. Whatever happened now, there could be no way back to anything that had ever been before; neither the bad nor the good.

'Where are we?' he asked Estaan after a moment.

'Somewhere south of Rendd,' Estaan replied. 'The farm's called Kirstfeorrd.'

'And the enemy?'

Estaan shrugged and motioned Antyr to follow him. As they wended their way through the resting men, Antyr noticed the horses being corralled at the rear of the building. A small wave of guilt passed over him. Ibris's bodyguard, he knew, took pride in tending their horses before themselves.

'My horse?' he asked, a little shamefacedly. 'I didn't—'

Estaan patted his arm and smiled appreciatively. 'It's been tended. Don't worry about it.'

He walked on, but Antyr stood watching the horses. Splendid, trusting creatures, he thought. Would it ever enter your heads to treat *us* as slaves? To lead us into mayhem and slaughter for some whim of your own?

As he watched, one of them staggered and fell over. For a moment it thrashed about on the ground in distress, scattering the other horses. Then it lay still, foam trickling from its mouth and its eyes white and wild. Almost immediately a soldier was by its side, stroking the frightened head. Another joined him, and there was a brief discussion.

Antyr turned away, knowing the outcome. As he looked at the retreating form of Estaan, the sound of a powerful axe blow reached him. He flinched involuntarily.

Arwain was leaning over an old table examining a map when Estaan and Antyr entered the farmhouse. Ryllans and other Mantynnai were with him.

For an instant, the enormity of what had happened swept over Antyr. At his word, the finest of Ibris's army had been torn from what would undoubtedly be a fearful and vital battle, to exhaust themselves in a dash across the country to face an enemy he thought he had seen in a brief exchange with the strange warrior who was guiding the Mynedarion.

He felt cold.

Then he recalled that the two strangers, Haster and Jadric, had brought similar news at the same time and his immediate concern eased a little. He noticed that the two men were standing a little apart, watching quietly, though their manner was politely diffident rather than aloof.

He wished Tarrian and Grayle were here; he would have liked to learn more about these two men who seemingly came to threaten the Mantynnai with retribution for old misdeeds, yet who were now followed by them. And, also, who had secured the respect of the Duke almost on the instant.

They looked as travel-stained and weary as everyone else, but then, they *had* undertaken this journey *twice* within the last few days.

'This is the most likely route for a large force moving south from Rendd.' Arwain's voice interrupted his reverie. 'And there's no evidence that anything of any size has passed this way so far. We'll just have to hope this is the way they'll come and prepare accordingly.'

Antyr went cold again. If the army came that he had seen, he'd probably be wiped out with all the others. And if it didn't come . . .?

The memory of the great horde in Ivaroth's mind was still vividly with him, but despite that and despite the confirmation of Haster and Jadric, he still felt disturbed by the weight of the decisions being made on the strength of his vision.

'We can send scouts out when the horses have rested a little,' someone said.

Arwain nodded unhappily. Then he turned to Haster and Jadric. 'We're indebted to you for your message and your help in carrying us through the night. There's little more I can offer you by way of thanks under these circumstances, but I can't ask you to stay with us here. This isn't your war, this isn't your battle, I—'

Haster raised his hand. 'It *is* about our war and our battle, lord,' he said. 'Had you chosen not to believe us then we'd have had to fight it alone.'

Arwain frowned and then smiled uncertainly, glancing round at the Mantynnai to see if he could find some indication of how he should respond to this strange utterance, but there was only acceptance and agreement to be read in their faces.

'I don't pretend to understand,' he said with a dismissive lift of his hands. He echoed his father's words to Antyr. 'You must do as your hearts bid you.'

Unexpectedly, both Haster and Jadric smiled. 'Our hearts bid us flee,' Haster said. 'It's our knowledge and our duty that tells us we must stay. If we don't stand now, then someone else will have to in the future, and far more will then perish. This we know from the past. And if we, soldiers by calling, don't stand now, to protect those less able, what worth are we to anyone, not least ourselves?'

Arwain bowed slightly. 'You teach me my own duty,' he said, without rancour. 'You honour us with your help. I'll not deny that two more swords will be of value. Though I'm still far from certain how a force this size is going to stop the horde you've all described.' He nodded towards Antyr. 'I suppose we'll have to go out and find them and start—'

There was a commotion outside.

'I don't think that will be necessary, sir,' Antyr said. As he spoke, Tarrian and Grayle burst into the room and took shelter under the table.

'They're here!' Tarrian's voice sounded simultaneously in the heads of all those present. 'Minutes away.'

Haster and Jadric started noticeably, both raising their hands to their heads in disbelief. There was no time for explanations, however, the two wolves were followed by cries from outside carrying the same information.

Arwain was the first out of the farmhouse, his face dark and grim. Emerging from between the two hills on the other side of the river came a column of riders. They were walking, and in loose formation.

'String your bows,' Arwain shouted unnecessarily as he strode through his men towards the small wall that ringed the farmhouse. 'I'm going to try and talk to them, for what it's worth, but if we have to engage them, you know what to do: standard procedure; bring down the horses first, then the men, as need arises.'

Antyr looked at the lengthening line of horsemen and then, for the first time properly, at the soldiers around him. His eyes widened. 'How many of us are there?' he whispered to Estaan.

'A hundred and six,' the Mantynnai replied. 'We lost thirty-three on the way.'

Antyr felt the breath leave his body and for a moment he thought he was going to suffocate. He mouthed the number to himself in disbelief. He had not realized they were so few. When he had set out with them it had been dark and all had been confusion and uproar.

Ivaroth's vision returned to him.

His message to Ibris must have been misunderstood!

'There are *thousands* of them!' he hissed to Estaan. 'Didn't

Ibris understand? I presumed he was sending the whole regiment of the bodyguard. Why didn't he send more?'

For the first time since they had met, a flash of anger passed over Estaan's face. 'The *Duke* understood perfectly,' he said. 'He sent those who were best fitted to this task and whose absence would not disturb the strength of the army too greatly. It was no easy decision. We trust him. See if you can.'

Antyr raised a shaking hand to wipe his mouth. 'I'm sorry,' he said. 'I—'

Estaan gave a small grimace of self-reproach at his outburst. 'So am I,' he said. He looked at Antyr pointedly. 'We're all weary, sore, and frightened, but for what it's worth, it's some measure of my regard for you that I forgot you're not one of us.'

Arwain had mounted his horse and was about to spur it forward when he paused. 'Whatever happens, I want no heroics today. We're here to slow this . . . army . . . down, and we'll only do that if we survive.' He pointed at Antyr. 'Above all, though, the Dream Finder and his Companions are to be protected. That is a duty beyond all others today. Is that understood?'

Under battle orders, the men acknowledged the question in silence, then Arwain, accompanied by Haster and Ryllans, rode off to meet the vanguard of Ivaroth's horde.

Menedrion raised his hand and the army at his back came to a lumbering halt.

Silence hung over the field. No birds sang, nor animals stirred. Only the breathing and shuffling of the thousands of waiting men, like the sea breaking on some distant shore, intruded on the peace of the cold, sunlit scene.

From somewhere, a tiny breeze rose and briefly fluttered the pennant at the end of Menedrion's lance. He looked up and listened to it. It was a lonely, defiant sound. Then it fell still.

He looked forward again. The Bethlarii army was spread before him. Unusually, it was not as still and ordered as he had seen it in the past, but it was huge. Feranc's estimate of their numbers had, as he expected, been distressingly accurate. It was at least twice the size of the Serenstad army.

And they would be no disordered rabble. Some of them would be reservists, of course, and some newly conscripted. They were probably what was responsible for the movements in the line. Nonetheless there would be a substantial core of hardened ghalers and officers waiting to oppose them.

Feranc's words returned to him; the battle of the end of the world. Whose world? he wondered. Serenstad and its dominions were unlikely to be the same after this, whatever the outcome. Ibris's call for full voluntary mobilization in the face of the Bethlarii threat had caused political problems which would doubtless persist for many years *if* Serenstad survived the day. But it had also, with one blow, cut a great swathe through the innumerable, squabbling factions, and conspiring cliques that hitherto had made political life in his dominions so complex and difficult . . .

Menedrion tore his mind from the future and brought it to bear mercilessly on the present.

Like the final flutter of his pennant, however, his mind lingered briefly on the waiting enemy in front of him.

The Bethlarii were a splendid sight, he conceded, with their ranks of shields, coloured and patterned with tribal and family emblems. Their colour on the battlefield was markedly at odds with the greyness of their normal lives. Granted it was so that Ar Hyrdyn could readily identify the most valiant in the fray, and name them correctly when his messengers brought the spirits of the dead to him afterwards for due honour in the Golden Hall, but that did not alter the splendour of the sight.

He turned and looked at the Serenstad army. The emblems and flags of families, traditional regiments, allied cities, even some of the great trading houses, made them no less splendid to look at than the Bethlarii.

Then all the musing was done and Menedrion became only the will that must galvanize these men and destroy the enemy. The Serenstad cavalry was more numerous than the Bethlarii and more skilled in their riding, though the Bethlarii were formidable fighters with their double-headed lances once contact had been made. The infantry was markedly less numerous and, discipline for discipline, there was little to choose between the best of both sides. The Serens, however, were now using a longer, iron-pointed pike and that, he knew, would cause the Bethlarii ghalers severe problems. Then too, the Serens' archers were better equipped, with longer range bows.

Nevertheless, it had to be assumed that the Bethlarii would be unlikely to break in the face of a direct frontal attack and, with such a long line, they had men enough to swing round and attack the Serens' flanks. Should that happen, it was unlikely the Serens' cavalry could defend them against a sustained cavalry and infantry assault.

The main plan, therefore, discussed at length with Feranc, his father, Arwain, and all the senior officers, was to advance behind a screen of elaborate cavalry manoeuvres and feints, and then, using mounted archers to disrupt the flanking cavalry, launch the full attack against the Bethlarii left flank with the hope of breaking it and sending it panicking into the rest of the army.

Various contingencies had been planned for also but once the battle was under way, individual company commanders would be responsible for implementing these as circumstances arose.

Nothing had changed. As expected, no heralds had come from the Bethlarii to quote terms or complaints and, following the deaths of his own heralds, Ibris had sent no more. Nothing now was to be gained by delay.

Menedrion lowered his lance, prior to giving the signal to advance.

Abruptly and unexpectedly, Feranc was at his side, pointing. Menedrion followed his arm. A rider was moving along the front of the Bethlarii line. It was too far away to see clearly, but he appeared to be gesticulating wildly. Feranc frowned and leaned forward as if by so doing he could hear what was happening.

The persistent, uneasy, movement in the Bethlarii line seemed to ripple behind the man as he moved along.

'A berserker,' Menedrion said dismissively. 'He'll be charging us on his own next. Nothing that a couple of archers or good pikemen won't be able to deal with.'

Feranc shook his head. 'I think not,' he said. 'Look.'

Even as he spoke, a figure emerged from the centre of the ranks and seemed to be remonstrating with the man. The line in the immediate vicinity of the incident broke up in disorder.

Menedrion and Feranc watched in silence, unable to interpret such events as they could see.

Then more riders were moving along the line and the disorder spread.

Menedrion gripped his lance tightly. What chance had brought this about, he could not hazard but this was the moment. This was the loose pebble that would begin the avalanche.

'Now,' he whispered to himself. 'Now!'

He lifted his arm.

Arwain, Ryllans and Haster positioned themselves across the road in front of the advancing riders.

There was a momentary confusion then the troop came to an uncertain halt and a group of six riders galloped forward.

Arwain had never seen their like before. Flat-faced and swarthy-skinned, they were clad in a random assortment of tunics and trousers made predominantly of leather and fur, though he noticed one or two decorative items that were conspicuous by being unmistakably Bethlarii or Serens in origin. Plunder, Arwain presumed, and a deep anger began to stir in him.

The horses they were riding were as mixed in colouring and style as their clothes, but though all the animals were quite small they were very sturdy-looking. Arwain had never seen their like before, but he judged them to be both manoeuvrable and capable of great endurance. Further, each rider sat his mount as if he were a natural part of it.

An array of swords, knives, spears and lances completed a motley whole, but Arwain spoke his immediate reaction to his companions. 'These people must be able to ride and fight from the saddle like the very devil. I wouldn't want to meet them in the field without a good row of pikes in front of me.'

Both Haster and Ryllans nodded in silent acknowledgement of this judgement.

The six riders reached them and spread out in an arc. One of them spoke to the others in his own language and there was some raucous and derisive laughter. The arc opened and curled round a little further. Haster and Ryllans gently eased their mounts sideways.

'Who are you and why do you ride in armed force into my father's land?' Arwain said.

There was a brief debate among the six riders and some pointing at Arwain and the others.

'They're deciding who's to have what booty after they've killed us,' Haster said.

'You know their language?' Arwain asked in surprise.

Haster shook his head and his lip curled into a brief,

humourless smile. 'No,' he answered. 'But what they're saying is the same in any language.'

'Fetch your leader here,' Arwain demanded powerfully.

'Ryllans, take the three on your side, I'll take the others,' Haster said quietly. 'Lord Arwain, stay back unless we need you, and prepare to retreat quickly.'

Arwain was about to dispute this order with some indignation, when the six riders, without any apparent signal, spurred forward.

There was a cheer from their watching comrades.

It faded rapidly, however. At the first movement of the riders, Haster and Ryllans surged forward also. So fast was the response that they had almost closed with the attackers by the time Arwain had drawn his sword to join them.

Haster, however, had approached his first attacker empty-handed. Turning in the saddle at the last moment, he avoided a spear thrust and, seizing the shaft of the weapon, twisted it in such a way that his opponent was lifted clear from his saddle and hurled violently into his neighbour, unseating him. It looked like a display of prodigious strength, but despite the speed of the action, Arwain noted that Haster had seemed to use virtually no effort.

Without pause, however, and even as the two men were still falling, Haster swung the spear around and hurled it at his third target. It struck the man in the upper arm with such force that it pinned it to his body. He let out a great scream, and it was only some deep reflex that kept him mounted as he turned to flee. It served him little, however, as he had scarcely gone a dozen paces when he slithered from the saddle to be dragged along the rocky road by his now panic-stricken horse.

Ryllans in his turn had dispatched two of his attackers, a little more slowly, but just as effectively, with only two savage sword blows. Arwain struck down the third.

Haster rammed his horse sideways into the two men he had unhorsed, as they were struggling to their feet.

Both fell heavily and one of them stayed down, but Arwain swung low out of his saddle and seized the survivor by the collar of his tunic. He yanked him up on to his toes and placed his smoking, bloody sword blade at his throat. It was shaking. But not as much as the white-eyed tribesman.

'My father's a merciful man, that's why you're alive,' he snarled. 'But this is how it will be for all of you if you do not return whence you came. Pick up your dead and injured, and leave.'

He pushed him away violently and then the three of them turned rapidly and began galloping back to the farmhouse.

The sudden, explosive response by the three riders, and the rapid dispatch of their comrades, had stunned the watching tribesmen, and for a moment there was a deep and profound silence in the wintry stillness. Then, with a roar they charged forward as one.

Estaan handed Antyr a knife. It was Larnss's. 'This belongs with you, not me,' he said. 'Now break out those packed arrows and make sure everyone's well supplied.' He looked at his charge earnestly. 'I'll do my best to watch you, Antyr, but keep your wits about you. I—'

'Grayle and Tarrian will guard me,' Antyr said, in an unsuccessful attempt at reassurance. 'I'll be all right. You look to yourself.'

As he ran towards the small storage area in front of the farmhouse, Tarrian and Grayle emerged, ears laid back and tails between their legs. They ran straight to Antyr. He knelt down and put his arms around them.

Responsibility for them and their fear helped him to turn away from his own terror as the thunder of the approaching hooves and the cries of the riders grew louder.

'I'm sorry,' he said, desperately and inadequately. 'If I'm killed, then flee, live your lives as you should and my thanks and blessings go with you for ever.'

The sinister sound of flying arrows began to punctuate the din, followed almost immediately by the screams of terrified horses and injured men.

Antyr tightened his grip about the two animals, both trembling violently. 'Your very natures bind you here with me, and *I* have no choice but to stay. I'm sorry. Let that part of you which is human guide and control that part which is wolf. And let that part of you which is human be at its worst. Remember; this day goes to the most terrible.'

From out of their whirling, tormented fears and doubts, the wolves' voices emerged as one. 'We understand,' they said. Then, abruptly they were themselves again; strangely calm and alert.

Antyr released them and, with shaking hands, began to cut open the packages of arrows.

Chapter 41

Ivaroth struck the messenger a vicious backhanded blow that knocked him from his horse.

'Endryn, Greynyr, to me,' he shouted, and pausing only to sweep the blind man up behind him, he spurred his horse forward.

His two lieutenants caught up with him as he ploughed recklessly through the crowds of riders, striking out and swearing profusely at anyone who was slow in moving out of his way.

His face was a mask of fury and it was some time before Endryn dared risk a question.

'What's happened?' he asked eventually.

Ivaroth waved a clenched fist forward. 'Those donkeys and asses in the vanguard have got themselves ambushed,' he shouted angrily. 'Thirty dead before they knew what was happening according to that whingeing messenger!'

'We must be careful, Mareth Hai,' Endryn said tentatively. 'We saw at Rendd what damage these people can do . . .'

'Careful? *Careful*?' Ivaroth's fury spilled over. '*They've stopped the advance.*' He drove his spurs savagely into his horse's flanks, making it leap forward. 'I'll not have my way barred further by *anything*. We'll make an example of whoever's caused this. If any survive I'll have them flayed alive for a month and then feed their remains to the people of Viernce.'

Endryn looked at Ivaroth strangely. The savagery of his response was nothing unusual, but there was a quality about his speech and his manner that alarmed him; a lack of control, a rage; the word came unasked for; a madness. It was something that he had seen growing ever since that fearful confrontation with the blind man.

He looked surreptitiously at the old man sitting behind Ivaroth, his face hidden by the hood of his ragged gown. One day soon, I'll rid us of you, you monstrosity, he thought. Ivaroth may dismiss the gods as he chooses, but I know a demon when I see one. Whatever bargain he's struck with you, the price is too high.'

Slowly the hooded head turned towards him, and Endryn felt himself unable to tear his eyes from the darkness that faced him.

His throat began to tighten as if a great hand were squeezing it. And he could do *nothing*! Not even cry out.

He was going to die.

'You will show these creatures what power truly is,' Ivaroth shouted over his shoulder.

The grip vanished from Endryn's throat and he took in great draughts of the cold winter air.

Ivaroth glanced at him, his face suddenly curious. 'What's the matter?' he asked abruptly.

Endryn shook his head. 'Nothing,' he said. Then, mustering a grin from somewhere, 'Just battle bellyache.'

Ivaroth let out a great laugh, though, Endryn noted, that too was laced with madness.

For the remainder of the journey he kept his mind well away from any further such considerations.

Then a group of riders came towards them.

'Where?' Ivaroth said grimly, before any of them could speak.

A shaking hand directed him towards a nearby hill. 'They can be seen from up there, Mareth Hai.'

Ivaroth crashed past the speaker and urged his horse brutally up the hill. Endryn and Greynyr followed.

As they reached the crest, the small farmhouse below came into sight. In front of it lay the dead and dying bodies of horses and men. Behind a small wall surrounding the farmhouse stood the defenders who had halted his advance on Viernce.

'A handful,' he said, his voice hoarse with disbelief. 'A mere handful.'

He looked back at the blind man. 'Destroy them,' he said. 'Bring that house down, tear up those trees, rend them as you rent that messenger's horse, sink them into the hard earth as you did that boy – for our later sport.'

The blind man, however, seemed distracted. He dismounted and moved forward, his head turning from side to side like a predator sniffing for prey. His hands reached out, clawlike.

*　　*　　*

578

Crouching silent beside Estaan, Antyr looked up at the figures that had appeared at the top of the hill. Adding to the fear that already pervaded his entire being, an ominous tremor began to develop. It was as though some dark and terrible eye were searching for him.

He reached out and took hold of Estaan's arm, childlike almost.

But Estaan himself was staring up at the figures, his face wrinkled as though he were trying to remember something. As were Haster and Jadric and the rest of the Mantynnai.

Then the figure standing at the top of the hill reached out both arms as if to embrace the entire land.

'Aaah!'

Ivaroth heard the end of his world in the blind man's sigh.

No! He would not allow it. Not now. Not after so much.

'*Destroy them all!*' he screamed to his waiting army below. '*Crush them utterly.*'

Then he brought his sword down on the old man's head.

'It's him!' Antyr gasped, rising to his feet and staggering backwards, his arms raised as if to protect himself from some unseen assault.

Ivaroth's horde poured out from between the hills in a vast, black, screaming tide.

The blind man turned and brushed aside Ivaroth's descending blow as if it were no more than a falling leaf.

'Come, Ivaroth Ungwyl,' he said, his voice ecstatic with triumph. 'Come and know your destiny. You are my way to the power that is the power of my master's master. His mantle *shall* be mine. He shall bow before me and I shall be all. Earth-shaker, weaver of the winds, and mover of the great tides. I shall rebuild his great places of power. His enemies shall be mine, and I shall destroy all their works so completely that their memory will not linger even in the least grain of dust. Then I shall build the world anew in my image.'

Ivaroth slid from his saddle and crashed to the floor. His eyes were black, like shafts down into mines of some unknowable, stygian depth.

As too were Antyr's, as he fell back and lay motionless on the winter-chilled grass.

Estaan knelt down by his side, his face desperate, but he

was pushed to one side by a charging blow from Tarrian. When he recovered his balance, Tarrian and Grayle, eyes blazing yellow and feral, were pacing a watch about the Dream Finder's body.

Ivaroth's men fell like corn before the scythe as the arrows of Ibris's bodyguard relentlessly found their marks. Wounded horses stumbled, throwing their riders and bringing down the horses pressing close behind them. The air was filled with the screaming of men and horses: in pain, in fear, in battle frenzy, in death.

But the black tide was vast and as men and horses fell, others replaced them. And those who were only unhorsed, charged forward on foot. Soon sections of the wall were alive with cruel hand-to-hand combat.

Endryn and Greynyr stared at the downed body of their leader, then, as one, reached for their swords. Both were skilled and hardened warriors, and, for all they were not young, mercilessly swift at killing when need arose.

But they knew they were defeated even as they formed their intent.

The blind man held out his hands to them. Endryn was lifted from his saddle and hurled some twenty paces away. His body bounced twice then rolled down the hill and under the hooves of the frenzied army below. Greynyr clutched at his throat, then, eyes bulging, crashed face-down on to the ground by his erstwhile master.

Arwain swung his sword down on the skull of one of the tribesmen who had reached the wall. The man tumbled forward and Arwain wrenched his blade free with an effort. With an even greater effort he wrenched his gaze from the dying man's face.

He looked around. A dozen small birds flew across the sky intent on their own needs, and bright sunlight lit the surrounding countryside with winter clarity and mocked the bleak, struggling, pageant being enacted around the old deserted farmhouse. The storm clouds drew nearer.

Despair welled up inside him. So far few of his force had been hurt, while the enemy had suffered severely. But the odds were overwhelming and these invaders fought as if death meant nothing to them.

And it was only a matter of time before all their arrows were spent. Then . . .

'Lord.' It was Haster. He pushed a bundle of arrows into his hand. 'These are the last,' he said simply.

Arwain's order passed along the hard-pressed line. 'Prepare to fall back!'

It was a world of whirling darkness and noise, lit only by lightning from a tormented, lowering sky. Lightning that forked from cloud to cloud. Lightning that vented its terrible spleen on the trembling ground below. Lightning that flared silent and ominous within the clouds themselves, like the gas from some long-decayed marsh. Lightning that was searing white and fevered yellow and red like the fires of some sword-forging furnace.

Antyr gazed around. His terror seemed to resonate with the very air about him.

In all the dreams he had walked, he had never seen such a fearful place as this. And he was alone! There was no sign, no hint of the presence of Tarrian or Grayle.

A dark, luminous mist hung over the shaking ground, obscuring it completely.

Shadows flitted around him, now clear and vivid, now vague, like wind-caught smoke.

Yet they were familiar.

As was the sound that mingled with the rolling thunder.

Then sound and images came together in Antyr's mind to form a ghastly whole. It was the battle! Wherever he had been thrown, it was no Threshold world. It was near the heart of that terrible conflict in his birth world; some tortured realm created as nightmare and reality began to merge.

'Tarrian! Grayle!' he shouted, but though his words rang through his head, he made no sound. The shadow-filled air jibbered at him in reply.

He turned around to search for something that might help him focus his swirling, panic-stricken thoughts.

Then, scarcely a dozen paces away, he saw a figure, silhouetted dark and ominous against a frenzied, lightning-lit background.

Yet it was another person, another human, in this demented place. Antyr reached out to it in appeal.

The figure inclined its head inquiringly, then stepped

forward. The sky flared red and lit the blade of the sword he was carrying. Then, Antyr felt his menace.

He stepped back. 'Who are you? What do you want?' he asked wordlessly.

But the figure did not reply, it moved relentlessly forward through the flickering shadows of the battle in the other world.

Trembling, Antyr drew his own sword and, holding it with two hands, offered an uncertain guard. The figure stopped and a voice full of scorn and grim humour passed through Antyr.

'And I thought you were a demon,' Ivaroth's voice said. 'You're just a man, as I am. It seems your guardian is as lost as mine.' He gave a low, sinister laugh. 'I don't know where that old fiend has plunged us with his vaunted power, but he's lost himself somewhere, for ever I hope. While you, his lusted-after prize, the cause of all this, are here, defenceless, for me to spit like a pig.'

Antyr tried to remember Estaan's teaching but all his knowledge seemed to have evaporated. Fear dominated him.

'Tarrian! Grayle!' He tried again, but there was no response.

Ivaroth paused for an instant at the cry, then with a roar he swung his sword at Antyr's head.

Antyr jumped back desperately, thrusting his own sword forward to parry the blow. Ivaroth's powerful cut, however, simply swept his blade aside, sending him staggering.

The shadows of the battle swirled and flitted between the two men as Ivaroth cut again and again at the elusive Dream Finder.

Antyr's every instinct was to flee. But to where? Could there be any shelter in this place? This fearful half world that seemed to have been created just for the two of them.

Ivaroth came again, his anger mounting at this scuttling, pathetic opponent from whom he had once fled. Abruptly, Antyr's terror overwhelmed him and swinging his sword furiously from side to side he charged, screaming, at Ivaroth.

Ivaroth retreated before the onslaught, though in cold caution, not fear. His moment of triumph was near now, he knew. Many a terrified creature had swung at him thus in the past. He revelled in the stink of Antyr's fear.

And there it was!

With a whirling twist of his blade, he entangled Antyr's

and sent it soaring high into the dark air. The screech of metal against metal overtopped the noise of the thunder and the battle, and the blade flickered red and white and yellow as it turned and spun under the rumbling sky.

Antyr staggered back under the impact of Ivaroth's sudden counter-attack, and tumbled incongruously on to the ground. The clinging mist billowed around him.

Ivaroth levelled his sword at him, then set it to one side and bent forward, bringing his face close to Antyr's.

'Know, Dream Finder, that it is an honour to die on the sword of Ivaroth Ungwyl, lord of all the tribes, Mareth Hai. Know.'

Antyr quailed before the night-black eyes and the night-black void that was Ivaroth's mouth. Then, scarcely aware of what he was doing, he spat into the dreadful mask of his impending death.

For an instant it seemed that all noise and movement had ceased.

Then, through the silence, Antyr saw his left hand seize Ivaroth's sword arm.

And the tumult was alive again.

Antyr's right hand drove Captain Larnss' knife brutally up under Ivaroth's ribcage.

The blackness vanished from Ivaroth's eyes and Antyr hesitated at the bewilderment and pain he now read there.

But even as he did so he felt a response from his victim and saw their message change, to frenzied murderous rage. And, too, he heard the cry of Ryllans in the training hall.

'Don't stop! Finish him! Finish him!'

Then, Estaan's *true* training came forth as Antyr's whole being accepted the reality of his needs and did what was necessary for his survival.

Tightening his grip on both Ivaroth's sword arm and Larnss' knife, he swept through his hesitation and doubts, and, levering himself up from the misty ground, he charged forward into his enemy, pushing, pushing, pushing, though his voice screamed and screamed as if that could erase forever the memory of the deed.

Then they crashed to the ground.

Antyr saw Ivaroth's life leave him as surely as he had seen his sword bounce from his hand.

And for an instant the shadows were whole and solid again. Around him the bodyguard, arrows spent, had formed a defensive ring, and images of flailing hooves, whitened eyes and hacking blades flooded into him. And with it, the terrible din.

Yet through the din came another sound. Reaching out to draw him back.

'No, Antyr, Dream Finder, my guide. That world will be no more. Your destiny lies elsewhere. You are to be my most favoured when the inner portal is found.'

Antyr hung in timeless, featureless greyness.

Before him, white, sightless eyes seeing all, was the blind man.

'Mynedarion,' Antyr said hoarsely. 'Abomination. I—'

The blind man reached out to him and Antyr's voice left him. 'It was well you triumphed,' he said. 'Else I had been lost. Ivaroth was treacherous to the end. But the power knew of my coming, and preserved me.'

'Tarrian! Grayle!' Antyr tried to scream, but a gesture of the long clawed hand seemed to silence even his thoughts.

'Nothing but my will prevails here, Dream Finder,' the blind man said. 'And my will is that you find the inner portal that will bring me to the power. It is near this place. For it has drawn you here. That I know. That I can feel. But you must guide me.' His voice became seductive. 'That done, then all will be yours.'

Antyr again found his mind filled with images of wealth and luxury and power. It seemed that every desire he had ever had was but a hair's breadth away from him. Some simple act away. Everything he had ever wanted.

But the mayhem of the battle and the death of Ivaroth were too close. No wealth, no luxury, no power could stand the bloody comparison with such truths.

And abruptly, he was free. Free and running through the greyness.

Yet not free. For somewhere, he knew the blind man was pursuing him.

Antyr ran and ran. All was greyness, but about him he sensed many different ways.

And then, though all was still greyness, he knew that the blind man was close upon him. Pursuing. Or following? He felt his terrible menace reaching out to seize and bind him again.

He turned suddenly. There, ahead of him, was his escape. Hope swept over him. He dashed forward towards it.

As he passed through the inner portal, the blind man's triumphant hand closed about his shoulder.

Carried on high, distant winds, the dark storm-clouds swept in front of the sun, bringing sudden and premature night to the battleground.

The battle faltered momentarily.

Then, as if emulating the clouds themselves, Ivaroth's hordes pressed forward again. Ibris's bodyguard fought now over a terrible redoubt of dead and dying men and horses, but still the tribesmen came, an endless black tide beating at this tiny resolute rock.

Two crawled from the heap and threw themselves toward's Antyr's motionless body. Estaan, bloodied and exhausted, pinned one to the ground with a spear he had wrested from someone. Grayle tore the throat out of the other in a killing frenzy.

Hackles raised like armoured spikes, teeth bared in all their bone-crushing power, eyes brighter than the noon sun, Tarrian turned to Estaan.

'Take no more of our prey, human, friend though you be.'

Estaan returned to the fray. It was the lesser terror in that circle.

'He is here . . . He is here . . . He is here . . .'

The voices echoed through Antyr.

'The Adept . . . The Adept . . .'

Antyr was whole. He stood beside the blind man on some strange vantage.

But he looked about him with eyes that were not eyes, and saw with a sight that was not sight. Around him he knew a myriad worlds in their entirety; shifting, changing, merging. All the planes of existence that were, that could be, that would be.

And the countless worlds of the Threshold, necklaced and joined about the hurt that was his birth world.

He could reach and touch and know. Know everything. From the least to the most.

This was the Great Dream.

Wonder and terror overwhelmed him.

He felt his mind unhinging.

'Where is the power?'

The blind man's words were jagged and querulous, like

shattering crystals amid this wonder, but they gave Antyr his centre again in this place of infinities.

'We have the power,' said the voices. 'The Adept is our way. You, our instrument, faithful one.'

Antyr's soul froze at the touch of the will behind the voices.

'Through the long ages we have waited since we were chained here. Now we shall be free. Now, in you, we shall return to that desecration you dwell in and right its vile wrongness.'

'Who are you?' Antyr managed.

There was dark amusement in the answer.

'We are the spirits of those who occupied the land and were driven from it. Those who learned of the true power and used it against our enemies. Those who lingered in the mountains before our people deserted us and fled to the plains, and *they* came to pinion us here, beyond all things.'

The voices stopped.

'But now we are wiser. For there are others here. Now we see our travail was but part of a greater ill. Now we shall avenge ourselves and be also the vanguard for the remaking of all things.'

'I shall oppose you,' Antyr said, the words coming unbidden.

'It is not within your power,' the voices replied, their words full of malevolence.

A memory rose in Antyr's mind. 'Adept you called me, and Adept I am,' he said. 'And Adepts of the White Way it was who bound you here, beyond the reach of all save for the gravest mischance.'

'You have not that skill, blunderer. They were great and powerful beyond your imagining. You are scarce an apprentice. You are a thing of clay and dross with the merest mote of past greatness trapped within you.'

For a timeless, fleeting instant, even as he stood in the Great Dream, Antyr was on the darkened battlefield again. He felt the fearful onslaught of Ivaroth's horde, and the furious courage of his defenders; and, deep inside him, the spirits of Tarrian and Grayle holding him firm, their quiet stillness belying utterly their slavering, wild-eyed stance about his body.

He spoke. 'I *am* indeed a weak vessel, but my making is beyond your knowledge by far, formed as I was in the world whose chance creation gave even MaraVestriss a measure of his wisdom. I am tainted by your works and the works of your kind, as are we all. But I *am* of the line of the Dream Warriors, and I see the taint, and I know it for what it is. And I will not allow it to turn me from the truth and the light.'

There was a terrible silence. It seemed to Antyr that the worlds about him waited.

Then, 'Mynedarion. Let him know our power,' the voices commanded.

Antyr turned and faced the blind man.

'You have followed many false paths, old man,' he said. 'And wrought great harm. But you are of my world. Know your frailty now, before it is too late.'

'You will obey me, slave,' the blind man hissed. 'Or you will know torment such as you could not have thought possible. And though you will cry for death, *yet you will live forever*. Obey, for this will be your last defiance no matter what your will.'

His long hands reached out towards Antyr.

Antyr met his gaze then reached out and took the menacing hands.

And he was the blind man. Saw through his sightless eyes. Knew his terrible secrets, his foul apprenticeship, the fearful loss that had taken his sight and his mind. The countless desires that held him thrall.

A great pity filled him.

But he could do no other than what he had to do.

For he knew, too, the power. Knew its heart. Knew that its use or misuse was, as ever, in the hands of the user.

And he was himself again.

The blind man staggered, bewildered by having found himself in the body of another, and staring at himself through sighted eyes. But unlike Antyr, he had not truly seen for that timeless moment whom he had become: had not learned.

He tore his hands free and, in his fury, unleashed the power that would bind Antyr forever.

Antyr opened his arms to receive it.

Pain and horror beyond description swept through his very soul, but at his centre he held his true self.

Then, with his new knowledge, he returned the blind man's power, cleansed of its malice and hatred, and all the other corruptions.

Darkness, swirling and turbulent, overwhelmed the

vantage, and a terrible cry of despair and rage rose from the blind man as he saw and knew his own, dark folly, and felt the impotence of his long garnered skill against this, his own onslaught.

And, too, a terrible cry rose from the long-bound spirits as their own malevolence returned upon them to reforge their ancient bonds.

Antyr reached again for the blind man, swaying frenziedly against the tortured darkness, his arms flailing, his mouth agape and raging. But he touched nothing.

And he was lying, wide-eyed, at the centre of the bloody circle before the farmhouse, his whole being ringing with the last cry of the Mynedarion as he had been swept into oblivion.

Then the sounds about him were the sounds of battle. Though now they were different.

Words more terrible than any Mantynnai's sword were cutting through the close-packed ranks of the invaders: 'The Mareth Hai is dead! The Mareth Hai is dead!'

And soon the defenders were motionless. Watching through battle-weary eyes, the ebbing of the great tide that had been Ivaroth's mighty army.

Chapter 42

On the other battlefield, the two great hosts were moving apart. The Serens moving from line to column and marching eastward back towards Whendrak, the Bethlarii dispersing and scattering to their various homes. The battle unfought.

As Menedrion had raised his lance to give the signal to advance, Feranc had laid a hand on his arm, untypically excited.

'No,' he had said. 'Not yet. Their line's going to break. If we attack they'll unite again, for sure.'

And even as he spoke, the Bethlarii line began to disintegrate.

Within the hour, ghalers, under flags of truce, had brought the news to Menedrion.

'There has been growing discontent at the increasing power of the priests,' was their gist. 'Few of us wanted this conflict, and fewer still applauded the manner of its making. Now we have received word that Navra, Endir, indeed the whole north-east, have been taken by a horde from across the mountains and that even now they may be moving against your own territories. It seems that the priests meddled in the affairs of the gods, and our whole land is now to pay for their folly.'

'I'd not have you linger further in superstition and ignorance,' Menedrion told them. 'No gods brought you that word, only my father's Dream Finders. It was they who discovered the reality of the deception that had been wrought on you and they visited you last night both to tell you the truth and to undermine your will to fight.'

It was a crucial admission.

'The dreams were but a test by Ar-Hyrdyn,' the priests had claimed in both bewilderment and desperation, as years of resentment at their oppression had begun to flicker into life amid the battle-ready Bethlarii following Antyr and Pandra's strange sending. Then, exhausted stragglers had arrived from Endir to confirm the news in graphic detail, and

589

all further priestly persuasions and threats had been swept aside.

Now Menedrion's revelation dispelled the last, lingering doubts in the minds of the Bethlarii that they had been both brought to the field and dismissed from it at the whim of some god.

The leader of the ghalers stepped forward and took Menedrion's hand. 'You and I would have fought a more honourable war than this, Duke to be, had true cause arisen. When all this is concluded, we shall debate an honourable peace.'

'You and I might well, soldier,' Menedrion replied. 'But you have your Hanestra and your Council of Five . . .'

The Bethlarii looked at him resolutely.

'When all this is concluded, we shall debate an honourable peace,' he said again slowly and deliberately.

Ibris, standing to one side, smiled as he felt a will the equal of his own and knew that the words needed no qualification.

The ghaler spoke again. 'But now we march for the north-east to relieve our cities and punish these invaders. That done, we shall send *proper* envoys to both Whendrak and Serenstad to discuss due reparation and the drawing up of a further treaty between us. The rule of the priests is over.'

'May the speed of your march ring down in legend, Bethlarii,' Menedrion replied. 'We go, too, though another way. Even now, I fear I may be losing my father's son and his finest warriors against this foe.'

When Menedrion and Feranc and the remainder of Ibris's regiment of bodyguards came to the farmhouse, however, it was to witness the stomach-turning horror of the cleansing of the battlefield.

The task had fallen to a reserve battalion from Viernce who had come in response to one of the many messengers that Ibris had sent following Antyr's revelation about Ivaroth.

The torn and mangled bodies of horses and men were being dragged across the churned earth to be thrown on to great bonfires. Birds and small animals were scurrying about the field and, despite the cold, clouds of flies were appearing. Those injured men, abandoned by their fleeing companions and whose injuries could be treated, were duly tended, but many could only be given ease by the physicians' long knives.

No count of Ivaroth's dead was made, though it numbered many hundreds. Of Arwain's force, some fifteen had died; six of the Mantynnai, nine Serens.

When the Bethlarii reached Navra and Endir, it was to find the cities abandoned by the tribesmen. They followed the trail of their reckless retreat for some way, but, exhausted from their own prodigious forced march across country, they made no attempt to pursue them into the mountains.

The tale of the return of the tribes to the plains is for another time.

Ivaroth's body was found on top of the hill, but there was no sign of the blind man.

'Where is he?' Ibris asked Antyr, concerned that this terrible individual might return in avenging fury, but the Dream Finder just shook his head and said, 'I don't know, sire. But he's gone from this world. And he's twice blinded now.'

Ciarll Feranc and the Mantynnai talked long to Haster and Jadric as they rode back from the battle, but that, too, is another tale.

In Ibris's dominions, much was changed and much remained the same.

The massacre of Larnss' reservists invoked shock and dismay throughout the land, while the stand of Arwain's force at Kirstfeorrd threatened to become legendary.

Antyr's role in the darker battle that had been fought that day was known only to a few, and even he laid no claim to understanding what he had truly done.

The Sened and the Gythrin-Dy talked and debated at endless length. The Guilds and the great trading houses protested at the disruption of the full voluntary mobilization, though none railed too loudly. The realization that their land could be threatened by powerful forces from beyond their borders did more to ease the more excessive internecine political squabbling and feuding than any amount of Ibris's urgings.

Even Nefron was strangely subdued, and erstwhile opponents of Ibris found they no longer had her covert support. Indeed, it was whispered that from the cold and bitter ashes of their long-spent passion, green shoots of friendship were appearing . . .

Arwain returned to his wife, while half-heartedly, Menedrion returned to his various conquests. Soon, however, he married a beautiful, sloe-eyed woman. A childhood companion who had been ever by him, watching, waiting, silently tending to his foolish needs until the time when he would more truly know both himself and her.

Ibris noted with some irony that it was his peace-loving son who had fought the terrible battles, and his warrior son who had sealed the peace. He noted too that they were both the wiser now, and he was well pleased.

His other son, Goran, returned to his painting and architectural studies, having been placed by his father, for want of anything more suitable, in charge of the building of temporary barracks for the many volunteers and reservists gathered in by the mobilization. 'You like studying buildings, don't you?' Ibris had told him.

Pandra returned to his retirement, though not for long. Within a month of his return he was proving to be a considerable thorn in the side of the Council of the Guild of Dream Finders. Several members resigned – in protest at his lack of respect, they said – as did their Companions: cats, for the most part.

Haster and Jadric made to leave the land as quietly as they had arrived, but Ibris, beginning to understand them, intercepted them personally.

'What of your duty to your king?' he said, appearing in front of them as they prepared to ride from the palace. 'Aren't you to take the Mantynnai back for an accounting and judgement?'

Haster smiled at the ambush. 'Our duty to our *queen*, and our people, lord, is to seek out our erstwhile countrymen and let them know that an accounting is required of them. We know what your Mantynnai have done since they came here and we shall carry their accounting for them.'

'You have that authority, soldier?' Ibris pressed.

Haster's smile widened. 'I shall account for it,' he replied.

Ibris nodded. 'As you wish,' he said. 'But, your intentions notwithstanding, I must tell you that you may not now leave here.'

Haster frowned slightly, but Ibris cast a glance upwards by way of explanation. Drifting lazily down from the dull grey sky were the black silhouettes of the first winter snowflakes.

'The mountains will be impassable, the seas bad. Stay with us until the spring,' Ibris said.

Haster cast a reproachful eye at the snow now beginning to fall more rapidly. 'We have some skill in such travelling, lord,' he said. 'And there are far worse who followed as the Mantynnai did. They were weak and foolish, and lured into evil as many of us could have been. They have long atoned. But there are others who did deeds for which they *must* be found and returned home for accounting and judgement, no matter where they hide, no matter how long it takes.'

Ibris in his turn frowned at the grim and fearful resolution in the man's voice, but he persisted. 'Nevertheless, stay with us until the spring,' he said again. 'Tell us about your people and their ways, and about your own terrible war that's cast its shadow this far. Bring your light to dispel it.'

Only Antyr seemed ill at ease. Politely declining the honours that Ibris would have thrust upon him, he returned to his own home and occupied himself with such matters as repairing the gutters and decorating, and oiling the screeching door. At Tarrian's urging – 'Don't be so blistering stupid, man!' – he did *not* decline Ibris's offer of a generous pension for life.

His new-found friends, however, visited him frequently and gossiped about palace affairs and occasionally tried to urge him to move into the greater comfort of the palace. But always he declined.

'I have to think,' he said. 'I have to understand what I saw, what I did. But I'm well,' he would conclude with a sad smile.

Then to Haster and Jadric one day, he said, 'I fear my ignorance, I feel I have a great . . . gift . . . but I've no measure of it. And struggle as I may, I become no wiser about it.' He was silent for some time. His two listeners waited. 'It burdens me fearfully. They said I was scarce an apprentice,' he said, eventually. 'I need to learn, but no one here can help me.'

Haster and Jadric looked at one another, and spoke briefly in their own language. Then they spoke to Antyr.

The city was alive with the Winterfest, the celebrations for the winter solstice. Snow covered the rooftops and piled up on sills and walls, and when swept aside by diligent householders left icy strips of treachery for the unwary. At

593

night, the Guild of Torchlighters, chilly-fingered, but diligent, ensured that the city glowed with a brilliance and beauty which, in all conscience, belied its true nature. Such is the way with snow.

Ibris, stepping briefly away from the grand feast of the solstice night, stood silently looking out over his glittering city. 'I'm glad you came tonight, Antyr,' he said to the unusually spruce figure at his side. 'It distresses me that I can do so little for you after all you've done.'

'Do as you've always done, sire,' Antyr replied. 'Build your great city and tend its people as they learn to tend themselves. I could ask you to do no more.'

Ibris nodded. 'It seems a little impersonal,' he said.

Antyr smiled. 'Very well then,' he said. 'If you wish to present me with a personal gift, tell Aaken to pay my pension on time in future. It'll stop Tarrian pestering me about it.'

Ibris laughed and gave his most solemn word.

Later, there was a soft knock on Antyr's door. He did not seem surprised, nor did either Tarrian or Grayle raise any alarm. Picking up his bag and pulling his cloak tightly about him, he opened it. It made no sound.

Silent in the cold, torchlit snow stood two horsemen. With them was a pack horse and a riderless horse with two large panniers.

As Antyr emerged, a figure appeared from the shadows. Both the riders started slightly.

'You've lost none of your old skill . . . Ciarll,' Haster said. He leaned forward and took Feranc's hand. 'It's been good to find you again. It still grieves me that we didn't look longer for you after the winter campaign. Will you return with us also, or are you come to take Antyr?'

Feranc shook his head. 'No, neither,' he replied. 'I smelt your plot and I've come to say my farewells. Grieve no more . . . Haster . . . No one could have found me in my flight, but your guidance carried me through the mountains and my madness as if you'd been by my side. My place is here now, like the Mantynnai. And while Ibris builds in the image of my birthland, I serve the king . . . the queen . . . still.'

Haster nodded and released his hand.

Feranc turned to Antyr and took his hand. 'Live well and light be with you, Dream Finder,' he said. 'I shall tell the Duke of your needs. And that you will return again one day.'

Then, silently, he was gone.

594

Antyr motioned his two Companions forward, and with a rather undignified, leg-scrabbling effort, hoisted them into the panniers.

'We will take you to a land that borders ours and which we must pass through on our way,' Haster had said. 'It's a land finer even than ours and there's a place there where you will find great knowledge. And a man of great wisdom; a healer. My heart tells me it is important that you meet him.'

'Are you comfortable?' Antyr asked his Companions. Tarrian's drowsy voice drifted back to him.

'Yes,' he said. 'This is really quite commodious.' He yawned noisily. As did Grayle; deep, silent, Grayle. 'It'll be nice to be home again. To hear the song. To see . . . the healer.'

'What?' Antyr said, his voice squeaking incongruously as he peered into the pannier. 'Where we're going is *your* land?'

'Yes,' came the sleepy reply.

'Why didn't you tell me?'

'You never asked.'

Antyr reached into the pannier and stroked Tarrian's head, then he walked round the horse and stroked Grayle's.

Gently lowering the lids of the panniers he looked up at the front of his house. The door stood open, and in the hallway a bent candle shone faithfully from its cracked earthenware holder.

He stepped inside and picked up the holder and the flint box beside it. Then he looked into his darkened house; his father's house; his childhood's house.

'Thank you,' he said softly, and a little hoarsely.

He closed the door slowly and quietly.

The snow crunched under his feet as he returned to his guides and his eyes were bright as he looked up at them.

Then he raised the candle to his face, and gently blew out the light.

ROGER TAYLOR

THE CALL OF THE SWORD

The Chronicles of Hawklan

Behind its Great Gate the castle of Anderras
Darion has stood abandoned and majestic for as
long as anyone can remember. Then from out of
the mountains comes the healer, Hawklan – a
man with no memory of anything that has gone
before – to take possession of the keep with his
sole companion, the raven Gavor.

Across the country, the great fortress of
Narsindalvak, commanding the inky wastes of
Lake Kedrieth, is a constant reminder of the
peace won by the hero Ethriss and the Guardians
in alliance with the three realms of Orthlund,
Riddin and Fyorlund against the Dark Lord,
Sumeral. But Rgoric, the ailing king of Fyorlund
and protector of the peace, has fallen under the
malign influence of the Lord Dan-Tor and from
the bleakness of Narsindal come ugly rumours.
It is whispered that Mandrocs are abroad again,
that the terrible mines of the northern mountains
have been re-opened, and that the Dark Lord
himself is stirring.

And in the remote fastness of Anderras Darion,
Hawklan feels deep within himself the echoes of
an ancient power and the unknown, yet strangely
familiar, call to arms . . .

FICTION/FANTASY   0 7472 3117 6

ROGER TAYLOR

THE WAKING OF ORTHLUND

The Chronicles of Hawklan

Fyorlund has fallen. The City of Vakloss has felt the terrifying Power that lies behind the evil Lord Dan-Tor; and King Rgoric lies dead, murdered by Dan-Tor who is now master of Fyorlund and ready to unleash the Dark Lord Sumeral's dread power over all the lands.

Yet Dan-Tor has been grievously wounded by Hawklan's arrow; and, against impossible odds, not all hope has been swallowed by the Darkness. Sylvriss, Rgoric's Queen, has escaped the blighted City to rally the Lords in Exile. In peaceful Orthlund the arts of war are painfully relearned. In the East, ancient foes of Sumeral are at last remembering their vows.

All look to the healer Hawklan for leadership. But he has lain in a coma since his confrontation with Dan-Tor, walking in a world from which none can call him back.

And in the mountains an ancient race stirs; but its allegiance is as yet unknown . . .

FICTION/FANTASY   0 7472 3440 3

A selection of bestsellers from Headline

FICTION

RINGS	Ruth Walker	£4.99 ☐
THERE IS A SEASON	Elizabeth Murphy	£4.99 ☐
THE COVENANT OF THE FLAME	David Morrell	£4.99 ☐
THE SUMMER OF THE DANES	Ellis Peters	£6.99 ☐
DIAMOND HARD	Andrew MacAllan	£4.99 ☐
FLOWERS IN THE BLOOD	Gay Courter	£4.99 ☐
A PRIDE OF SISTERS	Evelyn Hood	£4.99 ☐
A PROFESSIONAL WOMAN	Tessa Barclay	£4.99 ☐
ONE RAINY NIGHT	Richard Laymon	£4.99 ☐
SUMMER OF NIGHT	Dan Simmons	£4.99 ☐

NON-FICTION

MEMORIES OF GASCONY	Pierre Koffmann	£6.99 ☐
THE JOY OF SPORT		£4.99 ☐
THE UFO ENCYCLOPEDIA	John Spencer	£6.99 ☐

SCIENCE FICTION AND FANTASY

THE OTHER SINBAD	Craig Shaw Gardner	£4.50 ☐
OTHERSYDE	J Michael Straczynski	£4.99 ☐
THE BOY FROM THE BURREN	Sheila Gilluly	£4.99 ☐
FELIMID'S HOMECOMING: Bard V	Keith Taylor	£3.99 ☐

All Headline books are available at your local bookshop or newsagent, or can be ordered direct from the publisher. Just tick the titles you want and fill in the form below. Prices and availability subject to change without notice.

Headline Book Publishing PLC, Cash Sales Department, PO Box 11, Falmouth, Cornwall, TR10 9EN, England.

Please enclose a cheque or postal order to the value of the cover price and allow the following for postage and packing:
UK & BFPO: £1.00 for the first book, 50p for the second book and 30p for each additional book ordered up to a maximum charge of £3.00
OVERSEAS & EIRE: £2.00 for the first book, £1.00 for the second book and 50p for each additional book.

Name ....

Address ....

....

....